PENGUIN BOOKS

THE CAMPUS TRILOGY

David Lodge is the author of fourteen novels and a novella, including *Changing Places*, *Small World*, and *Nice Work* (the latter two of which were finalists for the Booker Prize); *Paradise News*; *Therapy*; *Thinks . . .* ; *Author, Author*; *Deaf Sentence*; and, most recently, *A Man of Parts*. He has also written many works of literary criticism. He lives in Birmingham, England.

DAVID LODGE

THE
CAMPUS TRILOGY

CHANGING PLACES

SMALL WORLD

NICE WORK

PENGUIN BOOKS

PENGUIN BOOKS

Published by the Penguin Group · Penguin Group (USA) Inc.,
375 Hudson Street, New York, New York 10014, U.S.A. · Penguin Group (Canada), 90 Eglinton Avenue
East, Suite 700, Toronto, Ontario, Canada M4P 2Y3 (a division of Pearson Penguin Canada Inc.) ·
Penguin Books Ltd, 80 Strand, London WC2R 0RL, England · Penguin Ireland, 25 St Stephen's Green,
Dublin 2, Ireland (a division of Penguin Books Ltd) · Penguin Group (Australia), 250 Camberwell Road,
Camberwell, Victoria 3124, Australia (a division of Pearson Australia Group Pty Ltd) · Penguin Books
India Pvt Ltd, 11 Community Centre, Panchsheel Park, New Delhi – 110 017, India · Penguin Group
(NZ), 67 Apollo Drive, Rosedale, Auckland 0632, New Zealand (a division of Pearson New Zealand Ltd) ·
Penguin Books (South Africa) (Pty) Ltd, 24 Sturdee Avenue, Rosebank, Johannesburg 2196, South Africa

Penguin Books Ltd, Registered Offices:
80 Strand, London WC2R 0RL, England

CHANGING PLACES
First published in Great Britain by Martin Secker & Warburg Limited 1975
Published in Penguin Books (UK) 1978; Published in Penguin Books (USA) 1979

SMALL WORLD
First published in Great Britain by Martin Secker & Warburg Limited 1984
First published in the United States of America by Macmillan Publishing Company 1985
Published in Penguin Books (UK) 1985; Published in Penguin Books (USA) 1995

NICE WORK
First published in Great Britain by Martin Secker & Warburg Limited 1988
First published in the United States of America by Viking Penguin, a division of
Penguin Books USA Inc., 1989; Published in Penguin Books (UK) 1989; Published in
Penguin Books (USA) 1990

This volume titled *The Campus Trilogy* published in Penguin Books (USA) 2011

1   3   5   7   9   10   8   6   4   2

CHANGING PLACES: Copyright © David Lodge, 1975
SMALL WORLD: Copyright © David Lodge, 1984
NICE WORK: Copyright © David Lodge, 1988
All rights reserved

NICE WORK
Grateful acknowledgment is made for permission to reprint the following lyrics:
"The Power of Love" (De Rouge, Mende, and Applegate). © 1985 SBK Songs Ltd.
"Come Give Me Your Hand" (De Rouge, Mende, and Rush). © 1983 SBK Songs Ltd.
"Surrender" (Rush and Klapperton). © 1985 SBK Songs Ltd.
By permission of SBK Songs Ltd., 3-5 Rathbone Place, London WIP IDA.

LIBRARY OF CONGRESS CATALOGING-IN-PUBLICATION DATA:
Lodge, David, 1935–
The campus trilogy / David Lodge
p. cm.
ISBN 978-0-14-312020-9 (pbk.)
1. College teachers—Fiction.   2. College stories.   I. Title.
PR6062.O36A6 2011
823'.914—dc23   2011025853
Printed in the United States of America
Designed by Elke Sigal

Contents

Introduction

The campus novel is a mainly Anglo-American literary phenomenon. The first classic example was American, Mary McCarthy's *The Groves of Academe* (1952), followed in England by Kingsley Amis's *Lucky Jim* in 1954, some years before the British had adopted the word "campus" to describe the enclosed territory of a university or college which makes it such an inviting location for a story. (One reason why there are very few European campus novels is that the typical Continental European university is less clearly demarcated, architecturally and socially, from its environment.) There had been novels about student life before the 1950s, of course, but what was distinctive about the campus novel was its focus on the lives of academic staff. It continued to evolve as higher education expanded in the postwar period and more and more novelists, or aspiring novelists, took jobs in universities, as I did myself. I don't think many of us set out to write a "campus novel" as one might set out to write a detective story or any other kind of fiction with formulaic components and conventions. We were trying to give literary form to ideas and experiences which had come to us in an academic milieu, and always seeking new variations on previous novels with similar settings. I certainly did not intend to write a "campus trilogy" linked by common characters and a fictional Midlands university—it just happened, as a consequence of three quite distinct sources of inspiration.

I. CHANGING PLACES

In January 1969 I took six months' leave of absence from my lectureship at Birmingham University to be a visiting Associate Professor at the University of California in Berkeley, taking my wife, Mary, and three young children with me. We had spent an idyllic summer in San Francisco, just across the Bay Bridge from Berkeley, in 1965, when I was on a Harkness Fellowship, but since then the ideological climate on campuses across Europe and America had changed dramatically. The student revolution, inspired by *les évenements* of May 1968 in Paris, was in full spate. Birmingham University experienced a relatively mild manifestation in the autumn term of that year, though the occupation of administration buildings by militant students traumatised many of my senior colleagues. In Berkeley I found something much more like a real revolution in progress, driven by opposition to the Vietnam War and the hippy counterculture of Flower Power, of which San Francisco was the fountainhead.

While I was there the struggle became focused on the effort to turn a piece of university property into a People's Park. The authorities responded with repressive law enforcement. There were violent confrontations between demonstrators and police, tear gas was sprayed onto the campus from helicopters, and the National Guard was called out. People were hurt, and sometimes jailed, but the analogies that were drawn with the contemporaneous occupation of Prague by Russian tanks were wide of the mark. Fundamental political liberties were not at stake, and there was a carnivalesque quality about much of the protest. It was a cultural and generational conflict, which I observed with keen but semidetached interest, like a war correspondent. At the same time, as I performed my teaching duties, I was intrigued and amused by the contrasts between American and British academic life—the competitiveness and professionalism of the former making the latter seem by comparison humane but amateurish. I promised myself that when I got home I would use all this experience to write a novel—a comic one, as campus novels tend to be, exploring the gap between the high ideals of academic institutions and the human flaws and follies of their members.

In recent years, however, several novels had been published by youngish British writers making use of their experience of visiting American universities, including *Stepping Westward*, by my friend and former Birmingham colleague, Malcolm Bradbury. I was conscious that my treatment of the subject would need some new, extra dimension. Pondering this problem, it occurred to me that as far as I knew, no novel had been written about an American academic spending time in a British university, though this was not uncommon in those days, and was usually brought about by some kind of exchange scheme between two institutions. Bingo! That was the moment when the cartoonist's lightbulb of inspiration lit up inside my head. Suppose I had not one academic central character but two, one British and one American, exchanging posts for six months, against the background of two campuses in revolt, and my narrative cut back and forth between them, following their fortunes, which would become increasingly entwined as they got to know each other's families. They might even come to exchange wives as well as jobs. . . .

This scenario required two protagonists who were typical of their respective national and professional environments. I had no difficulty in creating Philip Swallow, who, apart from his physical appearance and dearth of publications, has a good deal of myself in him. For Morris Zapp I drew on a great many Jewish academics I had encountered on my two visits to the United States, and one in particular, a friend who fortunately revels in the portrait and in fact rather exaggerates the resemblance to himself. The verbal energy and caustic wit of Morris and his wife Désirée also owe something to Jewish-American novelists and short-story writers I admired. One of the pleasures of writing *Changing Places* was the opportunity to extend my usual stylistic range in this way, savouring differences between two varieties of English by bringing them into conjunction, and sometimes collision. I am shamefully incompetent in foreign languages, but I believe I have a pretty good ear for American usage.

I needed to find names for my two geographical locations which would evoke the places that had inspired them, but were sufficiently playful to deter a literal-minded identification of the fictional institutions with real ones: "Esseph," "Euphoric State," "Rummidge," etc. With these locations established, and the characters in place, the story developed almost of its own accord, each event or scene in one country generating its counterpart in the other. The characteristic features of life (not just academic life, but social, sexual, and cultural life) in each country were made amusing by being observed through eyes unused to them—a device known in the lit.crit. trade as "defamiliarisation." When I was well into the novel I feared the symmetry of the plot might come to seem a little mechanical and predictable, so I loosened up the narrative method, writing the later chapters in different styles of discourse—letters, quotations from published documents, embedded retrospective narrative sequences, and finally a film script. Many of the documents were authentic press cuttings and fliers I collected while I was in Berkeley. I especially cherish the comment by a Californian eight-year-old: *"The police are just ruining their lives by being police, they're also keeping themselves from being a person."* As I approached the end of the novel I found that I didn't want to resolve the "long-distance wife-swapping" plot in a way that would favour any of the possible life choices it entailed. The conventions of film narrative provided a convenient solution.

The differences between Britain and America which generate much of the comedy are no longer as striking today as they were in 1969, or have disappeared altogether. In many ways British higher education has become more like the American model as it expanded: we have adopted the modular course system, small-group tutorial teaching has virtually disappeared, staff must publish or perish, and universities are run like businesses. The contrasts between everyday life on each side of the Atlantic have also become less marked. In Britain we have long taken for granted many of the material amenities, like central heating and big refrigerators, which were once enviously associated with American affluence; and the speed and cheapness of modern communications (air travel, TV, the Internet, etc.) have created an almost homogeneous transatlantic culture. *Changing Places*, in short, is now something of a period piece, but I hope still an entertaining one.

It was my fifth novel, and for me what publishers call the "breakthrough book," yet it did not have an easy progress to publication. It was turned down by the publisher who had an option on it and by two others, before Tom Rosenthal took it for Secker & Warburg on condition that I cut it by fifteen thousand words. (I agreed on considerably fewer with my sympathetic editor, but it was good advice.) Published in England in January 1975, some considerable time after I wrote it, the novel received unanimously good reviews, was awarded two prizes, and has never been out of print for more than a few weeks. Surprisingly, the novel struggled to find a publisher in America and was never issued in hardcover, having been turned down by umpteen publishers, including Viking, but when it was published as a paperback by Penguin in 1978, it soon became a kind of campus cult book, packed in the luggage of every college professor off to spend time in England, and it has never been out of print since.

Since its structure is based on the cinematic "cut" from one place to another, *Changing Places* was an obvious candidate for adaptation to that medium. The film rights were quickly sold to a British producer, who had had one success which unfortunately he was unable to replicate. With a script written by Peter Nichols, he tried for many years to put together a dream cast—John Cleese as Philip Swallow, Walter Matthau as Morris Zapp, Shirley MacLaine as Désirée—but he never managed to get them all together in the same frame; and as the rights were sold in perpetuity (which happened in those days) no one else has been able to make a movie. It is one of those might-have-beens that occur in most writers' lives, and recur occasionally in wistful retrospect. But overall I feel only gratitude for the good fortune of this novel.

2. SMALL WORLD

From 1970 onward, the educational needs of our children made it impracticable to live abroad for any length of time, but I continued to travel on academic business, at first within Europe, and then further afield. The occasion might be a lecture tour of universities in a foreign country organised by the British Council, or more often participation in an international conference on some aspect of literary studies in which I had an interest. It seemed a good way to see the world, with one's expenses paid and hospitality provided in return for giving a few lectures or delivering a paper. In the last days of 1978 I was invited to speak at the mother of all conferences, the annual convention of the Modern Language Association of America. The colossal scale and frantic pace of this event amazed and excited me: ten thousand academics crammed into two skyscraper hotels in mid-Manhattan for three days, listening to and participating in discussions of every conceivable subject from "Old English Riddles" to "Lesbian-Feminist Teaching and Learning" from 8:30 in the morning to 10:15 at night, with thirty sessions in progress simultaneously.

And that was only one level of conference activity. It was above all a place to meet people, old friends and old enemies, people whom you knew previously only from their publications, people you might hire or who might offer you a job. And it was clear that other, more intimate kinds of meeting were being arranged. A British colleague was accosted after his talk by an attractive woman who invited him to spend the night with her. "People only come to this circus to get laid," she assured him as he struggled politely to excuse himself. She was wrong, of course, but not entirely wrong. The combination of common professional interests and erotic opportunity makes the conference a likely place for academics off the domestic leash to form new, interesting relationships, and therefore a setting full of fictional possibilities. (My wife trusted me when I was away on these trips, but well-travelled colleagues sometimes complained that their wives regarded them suspiciously after reading *Small World*.)

The idea of writing a novel about international *conferenzlopers* (as the Dutch call them) didn't occur to me until the following June, when I attended the Seventh International James Joyce Symposium, held that year in Zurich, a city where Joyce himself lived for some years and wrote part of his novel *Ulysses*. I remember walking, soon after checking into my hotel, toward the conference venue and gradually becoming aware that all the other people moving on the broad, immaculately clean Swiss pavements were fellow academics and, as we clustered more closely together and squinted at each other's lapel badges, that I knew many of them by repute if not personally, and they knew me. Later, in the James Joyce Pub, an authentic Dublin bar dismantled and lovingly reconstructed on Pelikanstrasse, there were more greetings and introductions as draught Guinness was quaffed in the great writer's honour. From Zurich I flew directly to Israel to take part in another conference on "Poetics of Fiction and the Theory of Narrative," where the same experience was repeated—on a smaller scale, for it was a smaller, more select gathering of scholars—but in a setting that provided more piquant contrasts in the alternation of intense intellectual debate with episodes of hedonistic tourism. Several of the other participants had also been at the Zurich symposium. It dawned on me that jet travel had created a new academic community, a travelling caravan of professors with international contacts, lightweight luggage, and generous conference grants—a global campus to which, it seemed, I now belonged myself.

Two years, and several conferences, later, I prepared to write a novel about this phenomenon, set in 1979. I decided at an early stage that the characters would include Philip Swallow and Morris Zapp, and their wives, whose fortunes I had left conveniently indeterminate at the end of *Changing Places*, and several minor figures from that novel. There would be a young hero and heroine who would be novices in the glamorous world of academic travel, and a host of other characters of divers nationalities. But what could provide the structural principle of the novel, comparable to the exchange scheme in the earlier one?

Before I start writing a new work of fiction I dedicate a notebook to the project in which I jot down ideas, character sketches, draft synopses, possible situations, jokes, and memos to myself, and looking through my *Small World* notebook I find very early on this remark: "The main problem is to find some plot mechanism that will bring together a large number of varied academic types from different countries, and involve them in meeting each other frequently in different places and in different combinations, and have continuous narrative interest." It was a problem which I was unable to solve for some time. Thirty pages later in the notebook there is a somewhat desperate cry: "What could provide the basis for a *story*?" And just below that, "Could some myth serve, as in *Ulysses*?" (I was thinking of the way Joyce used the story of Homer's *Odyssey* as a template to give shape to the detailed rendering of a single day in the lives of several modern Dubliners.) And below that: "E.g., the Grail legend—involves a lot of different characters and long journeys."

The Grail legend—the quest for the cup which Jesus used at the Last Supper—is at the heart of the myth of King Arthur and the Knights of the Round Table. I thought of it at that moment because I had just seen *Excalibur*, John Boorman's slightly over-the-top but highly enjoyable movie treatment of this material, and been reminded what a wonderfully gripping narrative it is. I saw an analogy, comic and ironic, between modern academics jetting round the world to meet and compete with each other for fame and love in various exotic settings, and the knights of chivalric romance doing the same thing in a more elevated style, assisted, or hindered, by poetic licence and magic. The Grail sought by the modern knights might be a Chair of Literary Criticism endowed by UNESCO, with an enormous salary and negligible duties. The volatile state of contemporary literary studies, with various methodologies (structuralist, deconstructionist, Marxist, feminist, psychoanalytical, etc.) challenging traditional scholarship and each other, would generate rivalry and conflict. I also thought of T. S. Eliot's great poem, *The Waste Land*, and its use of the Grail legend as interpreted by the folklorist Jessie Weston, who saw it as a displaced and sublimated version of an older pagan myth of a Fisher King with a parched, infertile kingdom. I saw connections here with various kinds of sterility afflicting modern writers and literary intellectuals. There might be an elderly, immensely distinguished, unhappily impotent professor called Arthur Kingfisher somewhere in the story. . . .

Small World is packed with literary echoes and allusions: there is scarcely a character or event that does not have its analogue in medieval and Renaissance literature. But readers who haven't studied that subject on the graduate level should not be deterred, for essential information about it is integrated into the text. Miss Sybil Maiden, for instance, is on hand to comment on the Grail legend. The Heathrow check-in girl, Cheryl Summerbee, is eager to explain the difference between the Mills & Boon genre of "romance," from which she has weaned herself (Harlequin romances would be the equivalent in America), and the traditional kind: "Real romance is full of coincidence and surprises and marvels, and has lots of characters who are lost and enchanted or wandering about looking for each other, or for the Grail, or something like that. Of course, they're often in love too."

Explicitly invoking the model of traditional romance licenced me to contrive all kinds of improbable narrative twists and turns and coincidences which would be out of place in a realistic novel (see the second epigraph, from Nathaniel Hawthorne), but which were essential to contain my numerous characters and their movements around the globe in a unified narrative. The novel is, however, also rooted in modern reality. There really is, for instance, an underground Chapel of St. George, with a low curved roof like the upper cabin of a Boeing 747, at Heathrow Airport, and a noticeboard at the back with desperate prayers and pleas pinned to it—what a gift to my purposes that was! I had visited almost all the places described in the book, and in some cases had similar experiences there to those of my characters. Like my hero, Persse McGarrigle, I nearly sank with a boatload of middle-aged students of Irish literature when we were overtaken by a squall on our way to the Lake Isle of Innisfree. Like him I took shelter from the rain in a bar in Tokyo without ever having heard the word *karaoke* or knowing what it was (very few people in the West did, in 1982) and found myself, after much confused explanation and a few beers, singing "Hey Jude" to an appreciative audience of Japanese businessmen. Later, alone in my hotel bed, I laughed aloud at the memory and thought to myself: "this has to go into the novel."

Like most novels in progress, in my experience, *Small World* was hard work at first—I recall that getting all the minor characters established in their different milieux and time zones in Part Two was a lengthy process—but became progressively easier. I had a lot of fun writing it, and I hope that enjoyment transfers itself to the reading experience. It still makes *me* laugh, anyway, when I have occasion to dip into it.

3. NICE WORK

Small World was set explicitly in 1979, when I conceived the "global campus" as a subject for fiction. In Britain, it was also the year when the Conservative Party won a general election and Mrs. Thatcher became prime minister. By 1984, when my novel was published, her government's policies had made a decisive impact on British economic and social life, including higher education. Universities had their funding drastically cut, were obliged to freeze new appointments, and were exhorted to run themselves like businesses. Some of my colleagues, and a few reviewers with a foot in the academic world, thought it was an inopportune moment to publish a comic novel about academics swanning around the world on generous grants to attend conferences which seemed to involve as much partying as conferring: it didn't give a positive image of university life for the times. I was unrepentant: my novel was, I believed, faithful in its carnivalesque way to academic culture at the time when it was set; it was international, not parochially British in scope; and in any case novelists are not in the business of PR. However, I understood the reaction, and it may have had some influence on my next book, which, without renouncing comedy, took a more serious look at the state of the nation and the place of universities in it.

One effect of Thatcherite free-market economics, it seemed to me, was to put the concept of Work in a new light. The shakeout of uncompetitive British businesses created widespread unemployment, not least in the West Midlands, where Birmingham is situated, and university students could no longer count on getting jobs when they graduated. Our brightest ones, I observed, were not staying on to do research, since the prospects of an academic career were bleak, and many of them were going into financial services, which were booming. Fewer people were at work than before, but they were required to work harder than ever before. University teachers, at least in the humanities, had never seen their work as having any connection with commerce, but as a vocation, essential to their own self-fulfilment. They were unhappy with the new enterprise ethos, but ill-equipped to resist it.

I began to think of a novel about a businessman, the managing director of some manufacturing company, who had lived only for his work, but suddenly lost his job when the firm collapsed or was taken over, and was unable to find another equivalent one. Suddenly bereft of power and status, his occupation gone, he would fall into depression, then, through getting involved with a woman on the Arts side of his local university he would begin to re-evaluate the concept of work and its place in his life. Before I could develop this vague idea any further, I needed to know what kind of work he would have done before he was made redundant. Although I had lived in Birmingham for some twenty-five years, I knew very little of that side of its life, so I approached a friend, the husband of a student I had taught in the 1970s, who was managing director of an engineering firm, and asked if there was any way I could spend some time observing his working routine. "Of course," he said. "You could shadow me." Shadowing, i.e., following someone around as he worked, was, I gathered, a common practice in industry—used, for instance, to introduce potential recruits to the operations of a company. But what pretext could *I* use?

It so happened that the year which had just begun, 1986, had been designated "Industry Year" in the United Kingdom, with the aim of "bringing about a change of understanding and attitudes" to this sector of national life, and a number of documents were circulating at Birmingham University announcing various initiatives to strengthen its ties with local industry. I was by this point a half-time professor, and the spring term of 1986 was my term "off." My friend and I concocted a story that I was on sabbatical leave, doing my bit for Industry Year by learning about career opportunities for arts graduates in this area. I spent a couple of weeks, and occasional days after that, shadowing my friend in his professional activities, attending meetings, inspecting the workshops, visiting potential customers and other factories. Only once did someone identify me as a writer, and he kept a discreet silence; otherwise nobody raised an eyebrow at my presence.

I found the experience absolutely fascinating and highly educative. Literary studies do not encourage a sympathetic interest in commerce and industry, and much classic nineteenth- and twentieth-century literature is explicitly hostile to the Industrial Revolution and its social consequences. In some ways my experience as a shadow confirmed these prejudices. I was appalled by the soul-destroying, repetitive nature of much factory work and the squalid and sometimes dangerous conditions in which it is carried out. But I also recognized that many managers and skilled operatives had a commitment to achieving excellence in their occupations that was admirable. Furthermore, the whole experience of mixing with people constantly exercised with questions of cost and profit brought home to me a truth that academics and literary intellectuals tend to ignore: that high culture depends ultimately on the wealth created by trade.

Very quickly I realised that the cover story devised for my research was a marvellous foundation for a fictional plot, and it displaced the somewhat sentimental idea I had started with. It resembled the exchange scheme in *Changing Places*—my imagination seems drawn to binary structures which bring contrasting milieux, cultures, and characters into contact and conflict. Instead of a single central character and a single point of view, I would have two: a polytechnic-educated, down-to-earth MD struggling to keep a foundry and engineering company in the black, and an academic from the local university who was reluctantly obliged to shadow him for one day a week as an Industry Year exercise. It would raise the stakes, and increase the fun, of their forced collaboration if the shadow were a woman, and an intellectual of a kind with whom Vic Wilcox (as I called my MD) would have least sympathy. Accordingly I created Robyn Penrose, a young left-wing, feminist literary theorist and specialist in the Victorian "industrial novel," who has never been inside a factory in her life until she turns up in Vic Wilcox's office one day to his consternation and dismay (he has been expecting a man called "Robin"). They are two people who have absolutely nothing in common except a dedication to their work—work of two totally different kinds—and an underlying anxiety that they might soon be deprived of it.

The early Victorian "industrial novels," like Disraeli's *Sybil*, Elizabeth Gaskell's *North and South*, and Dickens's *Hard Times*, were sometimes called "Condition of England" novels in their own day, since they were responses to a period of great social and political tension, not unlike Britain in the 1980s. As Robyn Penrose explains in her lecture in Chapter 3 of my novel, in the 1840s there was widespread unemployment and poverty, especially in the industrial cities of the Midlands and the North, provoking strikes, lockouts, and violent demonstrations. Although Robyn is dismissive of the Victorian novelists' attempts to reconcile the conflicting class interests of their time, she does, as a result of the Shadow Scheme, to some extent re-enact the experience of their heroines, especially Mrs. Gaskell's Margaret Hale, and acquires a more informed and nuanced view of the relations between high culture and commerce—as does Vic, coming from the opposite direction ideologically. The typical Victorian narrative resolution of the initial antagonism between them—love and marriage—was for several reasons out of the question, but there is a romantic-sexual strand to the story which allowed me to reverse the basic plot device at a late stage and send Vic to shadow Robyn at the university. His participation in a tutorial on Tennyson's poetry is a scene which I particularly enjoyed writing.

"Rummidge" offered itself as the obvious setting for this novel, but not without attendant problems. As portrayed in *Changing Places* and *Small World*, it is a comic caricature of Birmingham, drawing, as the authorial note to the latter book admits, on popular prejudices about that city, but not corresponding exactly to it. *Nice Work* is a more realistic novel, which required a more truthful and fine-grained evocation of its setting. My colleagues at Birmingham, confident of the high reputation of the university and its English department, had mostly reacted to the two comic novels with good-humoured tolerance, but they would look more closely and critically at a realistic portrait of Rummidge University. Altogether I was beginning to feel that the distinction I had always tried to maintain between my novel-writing self and my professional academic persona was becoming increasingly difficult to preserve, and it was with considerable relief that I was able to take early retirement from my professorial post and become a full-time writer before *Nice Work* was published in 1988.

In the event the novel was well received by readers on both sides of the social and cultural divide it described, and I received no negative comments from my former colleagues. But when I adapted the novel as a TV drama serial for the BBC, and the producer arranged to film the relevant scenes on the Birmingham University campus, some voices were raised doubting the wisdom of inviting confusion of fiction with fact. The university administration, however, believed the TV drama would be good publicity for the institution (an opinion borne out by subsequent market research), and the filming went ahead. Thus I had the experience of seeing many scenes which I had created returned to the "real" locations which had inspired them. One Sunday morning in March 1989, for instance, I drove from my house to the main entrance of the university and there, like a dream or hallucination, was a traffic jam I had invented three years earlier, caused by placard-waving pickets of the Association of University Teachers protesting against higher education cuts.

As for my readers in commerce and industry, both locally and nationally, their reaction was wholly positive. They were, I think, delighted to read a literary novel that, for once, was about them and the kind of work they did, and they seemed to think I had portrayed their world accurately—so much so that for some years after publication I was frequently asked to give talks or take part in seminars on business management. I had to explain that everything I knew about business management was in my novel—indeed, rather more, since I had already forgotten some of what I once knew and was preoccupied with researching a quite different subject. Writing *Nice Work* had shown me what rewards there might be in deliberately exploring experience outside one's usual sphere, and henceforward my novels would become increasingly dependent on preliminary research.

Birmingham
November 2010

THE
CAMPUS TRILOGY

CHANGING PLACES

A Tale of Two Campuses

For Lenny and Priscilla, Stanley and Adrienne and
many other friends on the West Coast

1. Flying

High, high above the North Pole, on the first day of 1969, two professors of English Literature approached each other at a combined velocity of 1200 miles per hour. They were protected from the thin, cold air by the pressurized cabins of two Boeing 707s, and from the risk of collision by the prudent arrangement of the international air corridors. Although they had never met, the two men were known to each other by name. They were, in fact, in process of exchanging posts for the next six months, and in an age of more leisurely transportation the intersection of their respective routes might have been marked by some interesting human gesture: had they waved, for example, from the decks of two ocean liners crossing in mid-Atlantic, each man simultaneously focusing a telescope, by chance, on the other, with his free hand; or, more plausibly, a little mime of mutual appraisal might have been played out through the windows of two railway compartments halted side by side at the same station somewhere in Hampshire or the Mid-West, the more self-conscious party relieved to feel himself, at last, moving off, only to discover that it is the other man's train that is moving first . . . However, it was not to be. Since the two men were in airplanes, and one was bored and the other frightened of looking out of the window—since, in any case, the planes were too distant from each other to be mutually visible with the naked eye, the crossing of their paths at the still point of the turning world passed unremarked by anyone other than the narrator of this duplex chronicle.

"Duplex," as well as having the general meaning of "twofold," applies in the jargon of electrical telegraphy to "systems in which messages are sent simultaneously in opposite directions" (*OED*). Imagine, if you will, that each of these two professors of English Literature (both, as it happens, aged forty) is connected to his native land, place of employment and domestic hearth by an infinitely elastic umbilical cord of emotions, attitudes and values—a cord which stretches and stretches almost to the point of invisibility, but never quite to breaking-point, as he hurtles through the air at 600 miles per hour. Imagine further that, as they pass each other above the polar ice-cap, the pilots of their respective Boeings, in defiance of regulations and technical feasibility, begin to execute a series of playful aerobatics—criss-crossing, diving, soaring and looping, like a pair of mating bluebirds, so as thoroughly to entangle the aforesaid umbilical cords, before proceeding soberly on their way in the approved manner. It follows that when the two men alight in each other's territory, and go about their business and pleasure, whatever vibrations are passed back by one to his native habitat will be felt by the other, and vice versa, and thus return to the transmitter subtly modified by the response of the other party—may, indeed, return to him along the other party's cord of communication, which is, after all, anchored in the place where he has just arrived; so that before long the whole system is twanging with vibrations travelling backwards and forwards between Prof A and Prof B, now along this line, now along that, sometimes beginning on one line and terminating on another. It would not be surprising, in other words, if two men changing places for six months should exert a reciprocal influence on each other's destinies, and actually mirror each other's experience in certain respects, notwithstanding all the differences that exist between the two environments, and between the characters of the two men and their respective attitudes towards the whole enterprise.

One of these differences we can take in at a glance from our privileged narrative altitude (higher than that of any jet). It is obvious, from his stiff, upright posture, and fulsome gratitude to the stewardess serving him a glass of orange juice, that Philip Swallow, flying westward, is unaccustomed to air travel; while to Morris Zapp, slouched in the seat of his eastbound aircraft, chewing a dead cigar (a hostess has made him extinguish it) and glowering at the meagre portion of ice dissolving in his plastic tumbler of bourbon, the experience of long-distance air travel is tediously familiar.

. . .

Philip Swallow has, in fact, flown before; but so seldom, and at such long intervals, that on each occasion he suffers the same trauma, an alternating current of fear and reassurance that charges and relaxes his system in a persistent and exhausting rhythm. While he is on the ground, preparing for his journey, he thinks of flying with exhilaration—soaring up, up and away into the blue empyrean, cradled in aircraft that seem, from a distance, effortlessly at home in that element, as though sculpted from the sky itself. This confidence begins to fade a little when he arrives at the airport and winces at the shrill screaming of jet engines. In the sky the planes look very small. On the runways they look very big. Therefore close up they should look even bigger—

but in fact they don't. His own plane, for instance, just outside the window of the assembly lounge, doesn't look quite big enough for all the people who are going to get into it. This impression is confirmed when he passes through the tunnel into the cabin of the aircraft, a cramped tube full of writhing limbs. But when he, and the other passengers, are seated, well-being returns. The seats are so remarkably comfortable that one feels quite content to stay put, but it is reassuring that the aisle is free should one wish to walk up it. There is soothing music playing. The lighting is restful. A stewardess offers him the morning paper. His baggage is safely stowed away in the plane somewhere, or if it is not, that isn't his fault, which is the main thing. Flying is, after all, the only way to travel.

But as the plane taxis to the runway, he makes the mistake of looking out of the window at the wings bouncing gently up and down. The panels and rivets are almost painfully visible, the painted markings weathered, there are streaks of soot on the engine cowlings. It is borne in upon him that he is, after all, entrusting his life to a machine, the work of human hands, fallible and subject to decay. And so it goes on, even after the plane has climbed safely into the sky: periods of confidence and pleasure punctuated by spasms of panic and emptiness.

The sang-froid of his fellow passengers is a constant source of wonderment to him, and he observes their deportment carefully. Flying for Philip Swallow is essentially a dramatic performance, and he approaches it like a game amateur actor determined to hold his own in the company of word-perfect professionals. To speak the truth, he approaches most of life's challenges in the same spirit. He is a mimetic man: unconfident, eager to please, infinitely suggestible.

. . .

It would be natural, but incorrect, to assume that Morris Zapp has suffered no such qualms on his flight. A seasoned veteran of the domestic airways, having flown over most of the states in the Union in his time, bound for conferences, lecture dates and assignations, it has not escaped his notice that airplanes occasionally crash. Being innately mistrustful of the universe and its guiding spirit, which he sometimes refers to as Improvidence ("How can you attribute *that*," he will ask, gesturing at the star-spangled night sky over the Pacific, "to something called Providence? Just look at the *waste*!"), he seldom enters an aircraft without wondering with one part of his busy brain whether he is about to feature in Air Disaster of the Week on the nation's TV networks. Normally such morbid thoughts visit him only at the beginning and end of a flight, for he has read somewhere that eighty per cent of all aircraft accidents occur at either take-off or landing—a statistic that did not surprise him, having been stacked on many occasions for an hour or more over Esseph airport, fifty planes circling in the air, fifty more taking off at ninety-second intervals, the whole juggling act controlled by a computer, so that it only needed a fuse to blow and the sky would look like airline competition had finally broken out into open war, the companies hiring retired kamikaze pilots to destroy each other's hardware in the sky, TWA's Boeings ramming Pan Am's, American Airlines' DC8s busting United's right out of their Friendly Skies (hah!), rival shuttle services colliding head-on, the clouds raining down wings, fuselages, engines, passengers, chemical toilets, hostesses, menu cards and plastic cutlery (Morris Zapp had an apocalyptic imagination on occasion, as who has not in America these days?) in a definitive act of industrial pollution.

By taking the non-stop polar flight to London, in preference to the two-stage journey via New York, Zapp reckons that he has reduced his chances of being caught in such an Armageddon by fifty per cent. But weighing against this comforting thought is the fact that he is travelling on a charter flight, and chartered aircraft (he has also read) are several times more likely to crash than planes on scheduled flights, being, he infers, machines long past their prime, bought as scrap from the big airlines by cheapjack operators and sold again and again to even cheaper jacks (this plane, for instance, belonged to a company called Orbis; the phoney Latin name inspired no confidence and he wouldn't mind betting that an ultra-violet photograph would reveal a palimpsest of fourteen different airline insignia under its fresh paint) flown by pilots long gone over the hill, alcoholics and schizoids, shaky-fingered victims of emergency landings, ice-storms and hijackings by crazy Arabs and homesick Cubans wielding sticks of dynamite and dime-store pistols. Furthermore, this is his first flight over water (yes, Morris Zapp has never before left the protection of the North American landmass, a proud record unique among the faculty of his university) and he cannot swim. The unfamiliar ritual of instruction, at the commencement of the flight, in the use of inflatable life-jackets, unsettled him. That canvas and rubber contraption was a fetishist's dream, but he had as much chance of getting into it in an emergency as into the girdle of the hostess giving the demonstration. Furthermore, exploratory gropings failed to locate a life-jacket where it was supposed to be, under his seat. Only his reluctance to strike an undignified pose before a blonde with outsize spectacles in the next seat had dissuaded him from getting down on hands and knees to make a thorough check. He contented himself with allowing his long, gorilla-like arms to hang loosely over the edge of his seat, fingers brushing the underside unobtrusively in the style used for parking gum or nosepickings. Once, at full stretch, he found something that felt promising, but it proved to be one of his neighbour's legs, and was indignantly withdrawn. He turned towards her, not to apologize (Morris Zapp never apologized) but to give her the famous Zapp Stare, guaranteed to stop any human creature, from University Presidents to Black Panthers, dead in his tracks at a range of twenty yards, only to be confronted with an impenetrable curtain of blonde hair.

Eventually he abandons the quest for the lifejacket, reflecting that the sea under his ass at the moment is frozen solid anyway, not that that is a reassuring thought. No, this is not the happiest of flights for Morris J. Zapp ("Jehovah," he would murmur out of the side of his mouth to girls who inquired about his middle name, it never failed; all women longed to be screwed by a god, it was the source of all religion—"Just look at the myths, Leda and the Swan, Isis and Osiris, Mary and the Holy Ghost"—thus spake Zapp in his graduate seminar, pinning a brace of restive nuns to their seats with the Stare). There is something funny, he tells himself, about this plane—not just the implausible Latin name of the airline, the missing lifejacket, the billions of tons of ice underneath him and the minuscule cube melting in the bourbon before him—something else there is, something he hasn't figured out yet. While Morris Zapp is working on this problem, we shall take time out to explain something of the circumstances that have brought him and Philip Swallow into the polar skies at the same indeterminate (for everybody's watch is wrong by now) hour.

. . .

Between the State University of Euphoria (colloquially known as Euphoric State) and the University of Rummidge, there has long existed a scheme for the exchange of visiting teachers in the second half of each academic year. How two universities so different in character and so widely separated in space should be linked in this way is simply explained. It happened that the architects of both campuses independently hit upon the same idea for the chief feature of their designs, namely, a replica of the leaning Tower of Pisa, built of white stone and twice the original size at Euphoric State and of red brick and to scale at Rummidge, but restored to the perpendicular in both instances. The exchange scheme was set up to mark this coincidence.

Under the original agreement, each visitor drew the salary to which he was entitled by rank and seniority on the scale of the host institution, but as no American could survive for more than a few days on the monthly stipend paid by Rummidge, Euphoric State made up the difference for its own faculty, while paying its British visitors a salary beyond their wildest dreams and bestowing upon them indiscriminately the title of Visiting Professor. It was not only in these terms that the arrangement tended to favour the British participants. Euphoria, that small but populous state on the Western seaboard of America, situated between Northern and Southern California, with its mountains, lakes and rivers, its redwood forests, its blond beaches and its incomparable Bay, across which the State University at Plotinus faces the glittering, glamorous city of Esseph—Euphoria is considered by many cosmopolitan experts to be one of the most agreeable environments in the world. Not even its City Fathers would claim as much for Rummidge, a large, graceless industrial city sprawled over the English Midlands at the intersection of three motorways, twenty-six railway lines and half-a-dozen stagnant canals.

Then again, Euphoric State had, by a ruthless exploitation of its wealth, built itself up into one of America's major universities, buying the most distinguished scholars it could find and retaining their loyalty by the lavish provision of laboratories, libraries, research grants and handsome, long-legged secretaries. By this year of 1969, Euphoric State had perhaps reached its peak as a centre of learning, and was already in the process of decline—due partly to the accelerating tempo of disruption by student militants, and partly to the counter-pressures exerted by the right-wing Governor of the State, Ronald Duck, a former movie-actor. But such was the quality of the university's senior staff, and the magnitude of its accumulated resources, that it would be many years before its standing was seriously undermined. Euphoric State, in short, was still a name to conjure with in the senior common rooms of the world. Rummidge, on the other hand, had never been an institution of more than middling size and reputation, and it had lately suffered the mortifying fate of most English universities of its type (civic redbrick): having competed strenuously for fifty years with two universities chiefly valued for being old, it was, at the moment of drawing level, rudely overtaken in popularity and prestige by a batch of universities chiefly valued for being new. Its mood was therefore disgruntled and discouraged, rather as would be the mood of the middle class in a society that had never had a bourgeois revolution, but had passed directly from aristocratic to proletarian control.

For these and other reasons the most highly-qualified and senior members of staff competed eagerly for the honour of representing Rummidge at Euphoric State: while Euphoric State, if the truth were told, had sometimes encountered difficulty in persuading any of its faculty to go to Rummidge. The members of that élite body, the Euphoric State faculty, who picked up grants and fellowships as other men pick up hats, did not aim to teach when they came to Europe, and certainly not to teach at Rummidge, which few of them had even heard of. Hence the American visitors to Rummidge tended to be young and/or undistinguished, determined Anglophiles who could find no other way of getting to England or, very rarely, specialists in one of the esoteric disciplines in which Rummidge, through the support of local industry, had established an unchallenged supremacy: domestic appliance technology, tyre sciences and the biochemistry of the cocoa bean.

The exchange of Philip Swallow and Morris Zapp, however, constituted a reversal of the usual pattern. Zapp was distinguished, and Swallow was not. Zapp was the man who had published articles in *PMLA* while still in graduate school; who, enviably offered his first job by Euphoric State, had stuck out for twice the going salary, and got it; who had published five fiendishly clever books (four of them on Jane Austen) by the time he was thirty and achieved the rank of full professor at the same precocious age. Swallow was a man scarcely known outside his own Department, who had published nothing except a handful of essays and reviews, who had risen slowly up the salary scale of Lecturer by standard annual increments and was now halted at the top with slender prospects of promotion. Not that Philip Swallow was lacking in intelligence or ability; but he lacked will and ambition, the professional killer instinct which Zapp abundantly possessed.

In this respect both men were characteristic of the educational systems they had passed through. In America, it is not too difficult to obtain a bachelor's degree. The student is left very much to his own devices, he accumulates the necessary credits at his leisure, cheating is easy, and there is not much suspense or anxiety about the eventual outcome. He (or she) is therefore free to give full attention to the normal interests of late adolescence—sport, alcohol, entertainment and the opposite sex. It is at the postgraduate level that the pressure really begins, when the student is burnished and tempered in a series of gruelling courses and rigorous assessments until he is deemed worthy to receive the accolade of the PhD. By now he has invested so much time and money in the process that any career other than an academic one has become unthinkable, and anything less than success in it unbearable. He is well primed, in short, to enter a profession as steeped in the spirit of free enterprise as Wall Street, in which each scholar-teacher makes an individual contract with his employer, and is free to sell his services to the highest bidder.

Under the British system, competition begins and ends much earlier. Four times, under our educational rules, the human pack is shuffled and cut—at eleven-plus, sixteen-plus, eighteen-plus and twenty-plus—and happy is he who comes top of the deck on each occasion, but especially the last. This is called Finals, the very name of which implies that nothing of importance can happen after it. The British postgraduate student is a lonely, forlorn soul, uncertain of what he is doing or whom he is trying to please—you may recognize him in the tea-shops around the Bodleian and the British Museum by the glazed look in his eyes, the vacant stare of the shell-shocked veteran for whom nothing has been real since the Big Push. As long as he manages to land his first job, this is no great handicap in the short run, since tenure is virtually automatic in British universities, and everyone is paid on the same scale. But at a certain age, the age at which promotions and Chairs begin to occupy a man's thoughts, he may look back with wistful nostalgia to the days when his wits ran fresh and clear, directed to a single, positive goal.

Philip Swallow had been made and unmade by the system in precisely this way. He liked examinations, always did well in them. Finals had been, in many ways, the supreme moment of his life. He frequently dreamed that he was taking the examinations again, and these were happy dreams. Awake, he could without difficulty remember the questions he had elected to answer on every paper that hot, distant June. In the preceding months he had prepared himself with meticulous care, filling his mind with distilled knowledge, drop by drop, until, on the eve of the first paper (Old English Set Texts) it was almost brimming over. Each morning for the next ten days he bore this precious vessel to the examination halls and poured a measured quantity of the contents on to pages of ruled quarto. Day by day the level fell, until on the tenth day the vessel was empty, the cup was drained, the cupboard was bare. In the years that followed he set about replenishing his mind, but it was never quite the same. The sense of purpose was lacking—there was no great Reckoning against which he could hoard his knowledge, so that it tended to leak away as fast as he acquired it.

Philip Swallow was a man with a genuine love of literature in all its diverse forms. He was as happy with Beowulf as with Virginia Woolf, with *Waiting for Godot* as with *Gammer Gurton's Needle*, and in odd moments when nobler examples of the written word were not to hand he read attentively the backs of cornflakes packets, the small print on railway tickets and the advertising matter in books of stamps. This undiscriminating enthusiasm, however, prevented him from settling on a "field" to cultivate as his own. He had done his initial research on Jane Austen, but since then had turned his attention to topics as various as medieval sermons, Elizabethan sonnet sequences, Restoration heroic tragedy, eighteenth-century broadsides, the novels of William Godwin, the poetry of Elizabeth Barrett Browning and premonitions of the Theatre of the Absurd in the plays of George Bernard Shaw. None of these projects had been completed. Seldom, indeed, had he drawn up a preliminary bibliography before his attention was distracted by some new or revived interest in something entirely different. He ran hither and thither between the shelves of Eng. Lit. like a child in a toyshop—so reluctant to choose one item to the exclusion of others that he ended up empty-handed.

There was one respect alone in which Philip was recognized as a man of distinction, though only within the confines of his own Department. He was a superlative examiner of undergraduates: scrupulous, painstaking, stern yet just. No one could award a delicate mark like B+/B+?+ with such confident aim, or justify it with such cogency and conviction. In the Department meetings that discussed draft question papers he was much feared by his colleagues because of his keen eye for the ambiguous rubric, the repetition of questions from previous years' papers, the careless oversight that would allow candidates to duplicate material in two answers. His own papers were works of art on which he laboured with loving care for many hours, tinkering and polishing, weighing every word, deftly manipulating *eithers* and *ors*, judiciously balancing difficult questions on popular authors with easy questions on obscure ones, inviting candidates to consider, illustrate, comment on, analyse, respond to, make discriminating assessments of or (last resort) discuss brilliant epigrams of his own invention disguised as quotations from anonymous critics.

A colleague had once declared that Philip ought to publish his examination papers. The suggestion had been intended as a sneer, but Philip had been rather taken with the idea—seeing in it, for a few dizzy hours, a heaven-sent solution to his professional barrenness. He visualized a critical work of totally revolutionary form, a concise, comprehensive survey of English literature consisting entirely of questions, elegantly printed with acres of white paper between them, questions that would be miracles of condensation, eloquence and thoughtfulness, questions to read and re-read, questions to brood over, as pregnant and enigmatic as *haikus*, as memorable as proverbs; questions that would, so to speak, contain within themselves the ghostly, subtly suggested embryos of their own answers. *Collected Literary Questions*, by Philip Swallow. A book to be compared with Pascal's *Pensées* or Wittgenstein's *Philosophical Investigations* . . .

But the project had advanced no further than his more orthodox ones, and meanwhile Rummidge students had begun agitating for the abolition of conventional examinations, so that his one special skill was in danger of becoming redundant. There had been times, lately, when he had begun to wonder whether he was entirely suited to the career on which he had been launched some fifteen years earlier, not so much by personal choice as by the mere impetus of his remarkable First.

He had been awarded a postgraduate studentship automatically and had accepted his Professor's suggestion that he write an MA thesis on the juvenilia of Jane Austen. After nearly two years his work was still far from completion and, thinking that a change of scene might help, he applied in an idle moment for a Fellowship to America and for an Assistant Lectureship at the University of Rummidge. To his great surprise he was offered both (that First again) and Rummidge generously offered to defer his appointment for a year so that he would not have to choose between them. He didn't really want to go to America by this time because he had become sentimentally attached to a postgraduate student called Hilary Broome who was working on Augustan pastoral poetry, but he formed the impression that the Fellowship was not an opportunity that could be lightly refused.

So he went to Harvard and was extremely miserable for several months. Because he was working on his own, trying to finish his thesis, he made few friends; because he had no car, and couldn't drive anyway, he found it difficult to move around freely. Cowardice, and a dim, undefined loyalty to Hilary Broome, prevented him from dating the intimidating Radcliffe girls. He formed the habit of taking long solitary walks through the streets of Cambridge and environs, tailed by police cars whose occupants regarded gratuitous walking as inherently suspicious. The fillings he had prudently taken care to have put in his teeth before leaving the embrace of the National Health Service all fell out and he was informed by a contemptuous Boston dentist that he needed a thousand dollars' worth of dental work immediately. As this sum was nearly a third of his total stipend, Philip thought he had found the perfect excuse for throwing up his fellowship and returning to England with honour. The Fellowship Fund, however, promptly offered to meet the entire cost from its bottomless funds, so instead he wrote to Hilary Broome asking her to marry him. Hilary, who was growing bored with Augustan pastoral poetry, returned her books to the library, bought a wedding dress off the peg at C&A, and flew out to join him on the first available plane. They were married by an Episcopalian minister in Boston just three weeks after Philip had proposed.

One of the conditions of the Fellowship was that recipients should travel widely in the United States, and Fellows were generously provided with a rented car for the purpose. By way of a honeymoon, and to escape the severity of the New England winter, the young couple decided to start their tour immediately. With Hilary at the wheel of a gigantic brand-new Chevrolet Impala, they headed south to Florida, sometimes pulling off the highway to make fervent love on the amazingly wide back seat. From Florida they crossed the southern States in very easy stages until they reached Euphoria and settled for the summer in an attic apartment on the top of a hill in the city of Esseph. From their double bed they looked straight across the Bay at the verdant slopes of Plotinus, location of the Euphoric State campus.

This long honeymoon was the key that unlocked the American experience for Philip Swallow. He discovered in himself an unsuspected, long repressed appetite for sensual pleasure which he assuaged, not only in the double bed with Hilary, but also with simple amenities of the American way of life, such as showers and cold beer and supermarkets and heated open-air swimming pools and multi-flavoured ice-cream. The sun shone. Philip was relaxed, confident, happy. He learned to drive, and flung the majestic Impala up and down the roller-coaster hills of Esseph with native panache, the radio playing at full volume. He haunted the cellars and satirical night-clubs of South Strand, where the Beats, in those days, were giving their jazz-and-poetry recitals, and felt himself thrillingly connected to the *Zeitgeist*. He even finished his MA thesis, almost effortlessly. It was the last major project he ever finished.

Hilary was four months pregnant when they sailed back to England in

September. It was raining hard the morning they docked at Southampton, and Philip caught a cold which lasted for approximately a year. They rented a damp and draughty furnished flat in Rummidge for six months, and after the baby had arrived they moved to a small, damp and draughty terraced house, from which, three years later, with a second child and another on the way, they moved to a large, damp and draughty Victorian villa. The children made it impossible for Hilary to work, and Philip's salary was small. Life was riddled with petty privation. So were the lives of most people like the Swallows at this time, and he would not perhaps have repined had he not tasted a richer existence. Sometimes he came across snapshots of himself and Hilary in Euphoria, tanned and confident and gleeful, and, running a hand through his thinning hair, he would gaze at the figures in envious wonder, as if they were rich, distant relatives whom he had never seen in the flesh.

That is why there is a gleam in Philip Swallow's eye as he sits now in the BOAC Boeing, sipping his orange juice; why, despite the fact that the plane is shuddering and lurching in the most terrifying manner due to what the captain has just described soothingly over the public address system as "a spot of moderate turbulence," he would not be anywhere else for the world. Though he has followed the recent history of the United States in the newspapers, though he is well aware, cognitively, that it has become more than ever a violent and melodramatic land, riven by deep divisions of race and ideology, traumatized by political assassinations, the campuses in revolt, the cities seizing up, the countryside poisoned and devastated—emotionally it is still for him a kind of Paradise, the place where he was once happy and free and may be so once again. He looks forward with simple, childlike pleasure to the sunshine, ice in his drinks, *drinks*, parties, cheap tobacco and infinite varieties of ice-cream; to being called "Professor," to being complimented on his accent by anonymous telephonists, to being an object of interest simply by virtue of being British; and to exercising again his command of American idiom, grown a little rusty over the years from disuse.

On Philip's return from his Fellowship, newly acquired Americanisms had quickly withered on his lips under the uncomprehending or disapproving stares of Rummidge students and colleagues. A decade later, and a dash of American usage (both learned and vulgar) had become acceptable—indeed fashionable—in British academic circles, but (it was the story of his life) it was then too late for him to change his style, the style of a thoroughly conventional English don, keeping English up. American idiom still, however, retained for him a secret, subtle enchantment. Was it the legacy of a war-time boyhood—Hollywood films and tattered copies of the *Saturday Evening Post* having established in those crucial years a deep psychic link between American English and the goodies of which he was deprived by rationing? Perhaps, but there was also a purely aesthetic appeal, more difficult to analyse, a subtle music of displaced accents, cute contractions, quaint redundancies and vivid tropes, which he revives now as the shores of Britain recede and those of America rush to meet him. As a virgin spinster who, legatee of some large and unexpected bequest, heads immediately for Paris and points south and, leaning forward in a compartment of the Golden Arrow, eagerly practises the French phrases she can remember from school-lessons, restaurant menus and distant day-trips to Boulogne; so Philip Swallow, strapped (because of the turbulence) into the seat of his Boeing, lips perceptibly moving but all sound muffled by the hum of the jet engines, tries out on his tongue certain half-forgotten intonations and phrases: "*ci*garettes . . . prim*a*rily . . . Swiss on Rye to go . . . have it checked out . . . that's the way the cookie crumbles . . ."

No virgin spinster, Philip Swallow, a father of three and husband of one, but on this occasion he journeys alone. And a rare treat it is, this absence of dependents—one which, though he is ashamed to admit it, would make him lightsome were his destination Outer Mongolia. Now, for example, the stewardess lays before him a meal of ambiguous designation (could be lunch, could be dinner, who knows or cares four miles above the turning globe) but tempting: smoked salmon, chicken and rice, peach parfait, all neatly compartmentalized on a plastic tray, cheese and biscuits wrapped in cellophane, disposable cutlery, personal salt cellar and pepperpot in dolls'-house scale. He eats everything slowly and with appreciation, accepts a second cup of coffee and opens a pack of opulently long duty-free cigarettes. Nothing else happens. He is not required to cut up anyone else's chicken, or to guarantee the edibility of smoked salmon; no neighbouring trays spring suddenly into the air or slide resonantly to the floor; his coffee-cup is not dashed from his lips, to deposit its scalding contents in his crotch; his suit collects no souvenirs of the meal by way of buttered biscuit crumbs, smears of peach parfait and dribbles of mayonnaise. This, he reflects, must be what weightlessness is like in space, or the lowered gravity of moon-walks—an unwonted sensation of buoyancy and freedom, a sudden reduction of the effort customarily required by ordinary physical tasks. And it is not just for today, but for six whole months, that it will last. He hugs the thought to himself with guilty glee.

Guilty, because he cannot entirely absolve himself of the charge of having deserted Hilary, perhaps even at this moment presiding grimly over the rugged table-manners of the three young Swallows.

It is a consoling thought, in the circumstances, that the desertion was not of his own seeking.

Philip Swallow had never actually applied for the Rummidge-Euphoria exchange scheme, partly out of a well-founded modesty as to his claims, and partly because he had long come to think of himself as too trammelled and shackled by domestic responsibilities to contemplate such adventures. As he had said to Gordon Masters, the Head of his Department, when the latter asked him whether he'd ever thought of applying for the Euphoria Exchange:

"Not really, Gordon. It wouldn't be fair, you know, to disturb the children's education at this stage—Robert's taking the eleven-plus next year, and it won't be long before Amanda's in the thick of 'O' Levels."

"Mmmmmmner your own?" Masters replied. This habit of swallowing the first part of his sentences made communication with him a stressful proceeding, as did his way of closing one eye when he looked at you as though taking aim along the barrel of a gun. He was in fact a keen sportsman, and the walls of his room bore plentiful evidence of his marksmanship in the form of silently snarling stuffed animals. The strangled commencements of his sentences, Philip supposed, derived from his service in the Army, where in many utterances only the final word of command is significant. From long practise Philip was able to follow his drift pretty well, and therefore answered confidently:

"Oh, no, I couldn't leave Hilary behind to cope on her own. Not for six months."

"Mmmmmmmmmnerpose not," Masters muttered, conveying a certain disappointment or frustration by the way he shifted his weight restlessly from one foot to another. "Mmmmmmmmmmmmmmmmnnnnnertunity, though."

Straining every mental nerve, Philip gradually pieced together the information that the year's nominee for the Exchange scheme had withdrawn at the last moment because he had been offered a Chair in Australia. It appeared that the Committee concerned was looking rather urgently for a replacement and that Masters (who was Chairman) was prepared to work it for Philip if he was interested. "Mmmmmmmnnnerink about it," he concluded.

Philip did think about it. All day. With studied casualness he mentioned it to Hilary while they were washing up after dinner.

"You ought to take it," she said, after a moment's reflection. "You need a break, a change. You're getting stale here."

Philip couldn't deny it. "What about the children, though? What about Robert's eleven-plus?" he said, holding a dripping plate like hope in his hands.

Hilary took a longer pause for thought. "You go on your own," she said at last. "I'll stay here with the children."

"No, it wouldn't be fair," he protested. "I wouldn't dream of it."

"I'll manage," she said, taking the plate. "Anyway, it's quite out of the question for us all to go at such short notice. What would we do about the house, for one thing? You can't leave this place empty in the winter. And there's the fares . . ."

"I must admit," said Philip, freshening the washing-up water and stirring the suds with gusto, "that if I did go on my own I could probably save quite a lot of money. Enough to pay for the central heating, I should think."

The installation of central heating in their cold, damp, multi-roomed house had long been an impossible dream of the Swallows. "You go, darling," said Hilary, with a plucky smile. "You mustn't miss the opportunity. Gordon might not be Chairman of this committee again."

"Jolly decent of him to think of me, I must say."

"You always complain that he doesn't appreciate you."

"I know. I feel I've done him rather an injustice."

Actually, Gordon Masters had decided to back Philip for the Euphoria Exchange because he wanted to give a Senior Lectureship to a considerably younger member of the Department, a very prolific linguistician who was being tempted by offers from the new universities, and it would be less embarrassing to do so while Philip was absent. Philip was not to know this of course, though a less innocent politician might have suspected it.

"You're sure you don't mind?" he asked Hilary, and was to ask at least once a day until his departure. He was still at it when she saw him off at Rummidge station. "You're *quite* sure you don't mind?"

"Darling, how many more times? Of course we shall all miss you . . . And you'll miss us, I hope?" she teased him mildly.

"Oh, yes, of course."

But that was the source of his guilt. He didn't honestly think he *would* miss them. He bore his children no ill-will, but he thought he could manage quite nicely without them, thank you, for six months. And as for Hilary, well, he found it difficult after all these years to think of her as ontologically distinct from her offspring. She existed, in his field of vision, mainly as a transmitter of information, warnings, requests and obligations with regard to Amanda, Robert and Matthew. If *she* had been going to America, and himself left at home minding the children, he would have missed her all right. But if there were no children in the picture he couldn't readily put his finger on any reason why he should be in need of a wife.

There was sex, of course, but in recent years this had played a steadily diminishing role in the Swallow marriage. It had never been quite the same (had anything?) after their extended American honeymoon. In America, for instance, Hilary had tended to emit a high-pitched cry at the moment of climax which Philip found deeply exciting; but on their first night in Rummidge, as they were making up their bed in the flat they had rented in a clumsily converted old house, some unknown person had coughed lightly but very audibly in the adjoining room, and from that time onwards, though they moved in due course to better-insulated accommodation, Hilary's orgasms (if such they were) were marked by nothing more dramatic than a hissing sigh, rather like the sound of air escaping from a Lilo.

In the course of their married life in Rummidge, Hilary had never refused his advances, but she never positively invited them either. She accepted his embrace with the same calm, slightly preoccupied amiability with which she prepared his breakfasts and ironed his shirts. Gradually, over the years, Philip's own interest in the physical side of marriage declined, but he persuaded himself that this was only normal.

The sudden eruption of the Sexual Revolution in the mid-sixties had, it is true, unsettled him a little. The Sunday paper he had taken since first going up to the University, an earnest, closely printed journal bursting with book reviews and excerpts from statesmen's memoirs, broke out abruptly in a rash of nipples and coloured photographs of après-sex leisurewear; his girl tutees suddenly began to dress like prostitutes, with skirts so short that he was able to distinguish them, when their names escaped him, by the colour of their knickers; it became uncomfortable to read contemporary novels at home in case one of the children should glance over his shoulder. Films and television conveyed the same message: that other people were having sex more often and more variously than he was.

Or were they? There had always been, notoriously, more adulteries in fiction than in fact, and no doubt the same applied to orgasms. Looking around at the faces of his colleagues in the Senior Common Room he felt reassured: not a Lineament of Gratified Desire to be seen. There were, of course, the students—everyone knew they had lots of sex. As a tutor he saw mostly the disadvantages: it tired them out, distracted them from their work; they got pregnant and missed their examinations, or they went on the Pill and suffered side-effects. But he envied them the world of thrilling possibility in which they moved, a world of exposed limbs, sex manuals on railway bookstalls, erotic music and frontal nudity on stage and screen. His own adolescence seemed a poor cramped thing in comparison, limited, as far as satisfying curiosity and desire went, to the more risqué Penguin Classics and the last waltz at College Hops when they dimmed the lights and you might hold your partner, encased in yards of slippery taffeta, close enough to feel the bas-relief of her suspenders against your thighs.

That was something he *did* envy the young—their style of dancing, though he never betrayed the fact to a soul. Under the pretence of indulging his children, and with an expression carefully adjusted to express amused contempt, he watched *Top of the Pops* and similar TV programmes with a painful mingling of pleasure and regret. How enchanting, those flashing thighs and twitching buttocks, lolling heads and bouncing breasts; how deliciously mindless, liberating, it all was! And how infinitely sad the dancing of his own youth appeared in retrospect, those stiff-jointed, robot-like fox-trots and quicksteps, at which he had been so inept. This new dancing looked easy: no fear of making a mistake, of stepping on your partner's feet or steering her like a dodgem car into another robot-couple. It must be easy, he felt in his bones he could do it, but of course it was too late now, just as it was too late to comb his hair forward or wear Paisley shirts or persuade Hilary to experiment with new sexual postures.

In short, if Philip Swallow felt sensually underprivileged, it was in a strictly elegaic spirit. It never occurred to him that there was still time to rush into the Dionysian horde. It never occurred to him to be unfaithful to Hilary with one of the nubile young women who swarmed in the corridors of the Rummidge English Department. Such ideas, that is, never occurred to his conscious, English self. His unconscious may have been otherwise occupied; and perhaps, deep, deep down, there is, at the root of his present jubilation, the anticipation of sexual adventure. If this is the case, however, no rumour of it has reached Philip's ego. At this moment the most licentious project he has in mind is to spend his very next Sunday in bed, smoking, reading the newspapers and watching television.

Bliss! No need to get up for the family breakfast, wash the car, mow the lawn and perform the other duties of the secular British Sabbath. No need, above all, to go for a walk on Sunday afternoon. No need to rouse himself, heavy with Sunday lunch, from his armchair, to help Hilary collect and dress their querulous children, to try and find some new, pointless destination for a drive or to trudge out to one of the local parks, where other little knots of people wander listlessly, like lost souls in hell, blown by the gritty wind amid whirlpools of litter and dead leaves, past creaking swings and deserted football pitches, stagnant ponds and artificial lakes where rowing boats are chained up, by Sabbatarian decree, as if to emphasize the impossibility of escape. *La nausée*, Rummidge-style. Well, no more of that for six months.

Philip stubs out his cigarette, and lights another. Pipes are not permitted in the aircraft.

He checks his watch. Less than halfway to go now. There is a communal stirring in the cabin. He looks round attentively, anxious not to miss a cue. People are putting on the little plastic headphones that were lying, in transparent envelopes, on each seat when they boarded the plane. At the front of the tourist compartment a stewardess is fiddling with a piece of tubular apparatus. How delightful, they are going to have a film, or rather, *movie*. There is an extra charge: Philip pays it gladly. A withered old lady across the aisle shows him how to plug in his headphones which are, he discovers, already providing aural entertainment on three channels: Bartok, Muzak and some children's twaddle. Culturally conditioned to choose the Bartok, he switches, after a few minutes, to the Muzak, a cool, rippling rendition of, what is it, "These Foolish Things" . . . ?

· · ·

Meanwhile, back in the other Boeing, Morris Zapp has just discovered what it is that's bugging him about his flight. The realization is a delayed consequence of walking the length of the aircraft to the toilet, and strikes him, like a slow-burn gag in a movie-comedy, just as he is concluding his business there. On his way back he verifies his suspicion, covertly scrutinizing every row of seats until he reaches his own at the front of the aircraft. He sinks down heavily and, as is his wont when thinking hard, crosses his legs and plays a complex percussion solo with his fingernails on the sole of his right shoe.

Every passenger on the plane except himself is a woman.

What is he supposed to make of that? The odds against such a ratio turning up by chance must be astronomical. Improvidence at work again. What kind of a chance is he going to stand if there's an emergency, women and children first, himself a hundred and fifty-sixth in the line for the lifeboats?

"Pardon me."

It's the bespectacled blonde in the next seat. She holds a magazine open on her lap, index finger pressed to the page as if marking her place.

"May I ask your opinion on a question of etiquette?"

He grins, squinting at the magazine. "Don't tell me *Ramparts* is running an etiquette column?"

"If a lady sees a man with his fly open, should she tell him?"

"Definitely."

"Your fly's open, mister," says the girl, and recommences reading her copy of *Ramparts*, holding it up to screen her face as Morris hastily adjusts his dress.

"Say," he continues conversationally (for Morris Zapp does not believe in allowing socially disadvantageous situations to cool and set), "Say, have you noticed anything funny about this plane?"

"Funny?"

"About the passengers."

The magazine is lowered, the swollen spectacles turned slowly in his direction. "Only you, I guess."

"You figured it out too!" he exclaims. "It only just struck me. Right between the eyes. While I was in the john . . . That's why . . . Thanks for telling me, by the way." He gestures towards his crotch.

"Be my guest," says the girl. "How come you're on this charter anyway?"

"One of my students sold me her ticket."

"Now all is clear," says the girl. "I figured you couldn't be needing an abortion."

BOINNNNNNNNGGGGGGGGGG! The penny drops thunderously inside Morris Zapp's head. He steals a glance over the back of his seat. A hundred and fifty-five women ranked in various attitudes—some sleeping, some knitting, some staring out of the windows, all (it strikes him now) unnaturally silent, self-absorbed, depressed. Some eyes meet his, and he flinches from their murderous glint. He turns back queasily to the blonde, gestures weakly over his shoulder with his thumb, whispers hoarsely: "You mean all those women . . . ?"

She nods.

"Holy mackerel!" (Zapp, his stock of blasphemy and obscenity threadbare from everyday use, tends to fall back on such quaintly genteel oaths in moments of great stress.)

"Pardon my asking," says the blonde, "but I'm curious. Did you buy the whole package—round trip, surgeon's fee, five days' nursing with private room and excursion to Stratford-upon-Avon?"

"What has Stratford-upon-Avon got to do with it, for Chrissake?"

"It's supposed to give you a lift afterwards. You get to see a play."

"All's Well That Ends Well?" he snaps back, quick as a flash. But the jest conceals a deep unease. Of course he has heard of these package tours operating from States where legal abortions are difficult to obtain, and taking advantage of Britain's permissive new law. In casual conversation he would have shrugged it off as a simple instance of the law of supply and demand, perhaps with a quip about the limeys finally licking their balance of payments problem. No prude, no reactionary, Morris Zapp. He has gone down on many a poll as favouring the repeal of Euphoria's abortion laws (likewise its laws against fornication, masturbation, adultery, sodomy, fellatio, cunnilingus and sexual congress in which the female adopts the superior position: Euphoria had been first settled by a peculiarly narrow-minded Puritanical sect whose taboos retained a fossilized existence in the State legal code, one that rigorously enforced would have entailed the incarceration of ninety per cent of its present citizens). But it is a different matter to find oneself trapped in an airplane with a hundred and fifty-five women actually drawing the wages of sin. The thought of their one hundred and fifty-five doomed stowaways sends cold shivers roller-coasting down his curved spine, and a sudden vibration in the aircraft, as it runs into the turbulence recently experienced by Philip Swallow, leaves him quaking with fear.

For Morris Zapp is a twentieth-century counterpart of Swift's Nominal Christian—the Nominal Atheist. Underneath that tough exterior of the free-thinking Jew (exactly the kind T. S. Eliot thought an organic community could well do without) there is a core of old-fashioned Judaeo-Christian fear-of-the-Lord. If the Apollo astronauts had reported finding a message carved in gigantic letters on the backside of the moon, *"Reports of My death are greatly exaggerated,"* it would not have surprised Morris Zapp unduly, merely confirmed his deepest misgivings. At this moment he feels painfully vulnerable to divine retribution. He can't believe that Improvidence, old Nobodaddy, is going to sit placidly in the sky while abortion shuttle-services buzz right under his nose, polluting the stratosphere and giving the Recording Angel writer's cramp, no sir, one of these days he is going to swat one of those planes right out the sky, and why not this one?

Zapp succumbs to self-pity. Why should he suffer with all these careless callous women? He has knocked up a girl only once in his life, and he made an honest woman of her (she divorced him three years later, but that's another story, one indictment at a time, please). It's a frame-up. All the doing of the little bitch who had sold him her ticket, less than half-price, he couldn't resist the bargain but wondered at the time at her generosity since only a week before he'd refused to raise her course-grade from a C to a B. She must have missed her period, rushed to book a seat on the Abortion Express, had a negative pregnancy test and thought to herself, I know what I'll do, Professor Zapp is going to Europe, I'll sell him my ticket, then the plane might be struck by a thunderbolt. A fine reward for trying to preserve academic standards.

He becomes aware that the girl in the next seat is studying him with interest. "You're a college teacher?" she asks.

"Yeah, Euphoric State."

"Really! What d'you teach? I'm majoring in Anthropology at Euphoria College."

"Euphoria College? Isn't that the Catholic school in Esseph?"

"Right."

"Then what are you doing on this plane?" he hisses, all his roused moral indignation and superstitious fear focused on this kooky blonde. If even the Catholics are jumping on to the abortion bandwagon, what hope is there for the human race?

"I'm an Underground Catholic," she says seriously. "I'm not hung up on dogma. I'm very far out."

Her eyes, behind the huge spectacles, are clear and untroubled. Morris Zapp experiences a rush of missionary zeal to the head. He will do a good deed, instruct this innocent in the difference between good and evil, talk her out of her wicked intent. One brand plucked from the burning should be enough to assure him of a happy landing. He leans forward earnestly.

"Listen, kid, let me give some fatherly advice. Don't do it. You'll never forgive yourself. Have the baby. Get it adopted—no sweat, the adoption agencies are screaming for new stock. Maybe the father will want to marry you when he sees the kid—they often do, you know."

"He can't."

"Married already, huh?" Morris Zapp shakes his head over the depravity of his sex.

"No, he's a priest."

Zapp bows his head, buries his face in his hands.

"You feeling all right?"

"Just a twinge of morning-sickness," he mumbles through his fingers. He looks up. "This priest, is he paying for your trip out of parish funds? Did he take a special collection or something?"

"He doesn't know anything about it."

"You haven't told him you're pregnant?"

"I don't want him to have to choose between me and his vows."

"Has he any vows *left*?"

"Poverty, chastity and obedience," says the girl thoughtfully. "Well, I guess he's still poor."

"So who is paying for this trip?"

"I work nights on South Strand."

"One of those topless places?"

"No, record store. As a matter of fact I worked my first year through college as a topless dancer. But then I realized how exploitative it was, so I quit."

"They charge a lot in those joints, huh?"

"I mean exploiting *me*, not the customers," the girl replies, a shade contemptuously. "It was when I got interested in Women's Liberation."

"Women's Liberation? What's that?" says Morris Zapp, not liking the sound of it at all. "I never heard of it." (Few people have on this first day of 1969.)

"You will, Professor, you will," says the girl.

. . .

Meanwhile, Philip Swallow has also struck up conversation with a fellow passenger.

The movie over (it was a Western, the noisy sound track had given him a headache, and he watched the final gun-battle with his headphones tuned to Muzak), he finds that some of his *joie de vivre* has evaporated. He is beginning to weary of sitting still, he fidgets in his seat in an effort to find some untried disposition of his limbs, the muffled din of the jet engines is getting on his nerves, and looking out of the window still gives him vertigo. He tries to read a courtesy copy of *Time*, but can't concentrate. What he really needs is a nice cup of tea—it is mid-afternoon by his watch—but when he plucks up courage to ask a passing stewardess she replies curtly that they will be serving breakfast in an hour's time. He has had one breakfast already that day and doesn't particularly want another one, but of course it's a matter of the time change. In Euphoria now it's, what, seven or eight hours earlier than in London, or is it later? Do you add or subtract? Is it still the day he left on, or tomorrow already? Or yesterday? Let's see, the sun comes up in the east . . . He frowns with mental effort, but the sums won't make sense.

"Well, blow me down!"

Philip blinks up at the young man who has stopped in the aisle. His appearance is striking. He wears wide-bottomed suede trousers, and a kind of oversize homespun fringed jerkin hanging to his knees over a pink and yellow candy-striped shirt. His wavy, reddish hair falls to his shoulders and he has a bandit moustache of slightly darker hue. On his jerkin, arranged in three neat rows like military medals, are a dozen or more lapel buttons in psychedelic colours.

"You remember me, dontcha, Mr. Swallow?"

"Well . . ." Philip racks his brains. There is something vaguely familiar, but . . . Then the youth's left eye suddenly shoots disconcertingly sideways, as if catching sight of an engine falling off the wing, and Philip remembers.

"Boon! Good Lord, I didn't recognize . . . You've, er, changed."

Boon chuckles delightedly. "Fantastic! Don't tell me you're on your way to Euphoric State?"

"Well, yes, as a matter of fact I am."

"Great! Me too."

"You?"

"Dontcha remember writing a reference for me?"

"A great many references, Boon."

"Yeah, well, it's like a fruit machine, y'know, you got to keep pulling the old lever. Never say die. Then, Bingo! Anybody sitting next to you? No? I'll join you in a sec. Got to have a slash. Don't run away." He resumes his interrupted journey to the toilet, almost colliding with a stewardess coming in the opposite direction. Boon steadies her with a firm, two-handed gesture. "Sorry, darling," Philip hears him say, and she flashes him an indulgent smile. Still the same old Boon!

A chance reunion with Charles Boon would not, in normal circumstances, have gladdened Philip Swallow's heart. The young man had graduated a couple of years previously after a contentious and troublesome undergraduate career at Rummidge. He belonged to a category of students whom Philip referred to privately (showing his age) as "the Department's Teddy-Boys." These were clever young men of plebeian origin who, unlike the traditional scholarship boy (such as Philip himself), showed no deference to the social and cultural values of the institution to which they had been admitted, but maintained until the day they graduated a style of ostentatious uncouthness in dress, behaviour and speech. They came late to classes, unwashed, unshaven and wearing clothes they had evidently slept in; slouched in their seats, rolling their own cigarettes and stubbing them out on the furniture; sneered at the girlish, suburban enthusiasms of their fellow-students, answered questions addressed to them in dialect monosyllables, and handed in disconcertingly subtle, largely destructive essays written in the style of F. R. Leavis. Perhaps overcompensating for their own prejudices, the staff at Rummidge regularly admitted three or four such students every year. Invariably they caused disciplinary problems. In his memorable undergraduate career Charles Boon had involved the student newspaper *Rumble*, of which he was editor, in an expensive libel suit brought by the mayoress of Rummidge; caused the Lodgings warden to retire prematurely with a nervous disorder from which she still suffered; appeared on "University Challenge," drunk; campaigned (unsuccessfully) for the distribution of free contraceptives at the end of the Freshers' Ball, and defended himself (successfully) in a magistrate's court against a charge of shop-lifting from the University Bookshop.

As Boon's tutor in his third year, Philip had played a minor, but exhausting role in some of these dramas. After an examiners' meeting lasting ten hours, nine of which were spent in discussion of Boon's papers, he had been awarded a "low Upper Second"—a compromise grudgingly accepted by those who wanted to fail him and those who wanted to give him a First. Philip had shaken Boon's hand on Degree Day in joyful expectation of never having anything to do with him again, but the hope was premature. Though Boon had failed to qualify for a postgraduate grant, he continued to haunt the corridors of the Faculty of Arts for some months, giving other students to understand that he was employed as a Research Assistant, hoping in this way to embarrass the Department into actually making him one. When this gambit failed, Boon at last disappeared from Rummidge, but Philip, at least, was not allowed to forget his existence. Seldom did a week pass without a request for a confidential assessment of Mr. Charles Boon's character, intelligence and suitability for some position in the great world. At first these were usually teaching posts or postgraduate fellowships at home and abroad. Later, Boon's applications took on a random, reckless character, as of a man throwing dice compulsively, without bothering to note his score. Sometimes he aimed absurdly high, sometimes grotesquely low. At one moment he aspired to be Cultural Attaché in the Diplomatic Service, or Chief Programme Planning Executive for Ghana Television, at the next he was prepared to settle for Works Foreman, Walsall Screw Company, or Lavatory Attendant, Southport Corporation. If Boon was appointed to any of these posts he evidently failed to hold them for very long, for the stream of inquiries never ran dry. At first Philip had answered them honestly; after a while it dawned on him that he was in this way condemning himself to a lifetime's correspondence, and he began to suppress some of the less creditable features of his former student's character and record. He ended up answering every request for a reference with an unblushing all-purpose panegyric kept on permanent file in the Department Office, and this testimonial must have finally obtained Boon some kind of graduate fellowship at Euphoric State. Now Philip's perjury had caught up with him, as such sins always did. It was deuced awkward that they should both be going to Euphoric State at the same time—he fervently hoped that he would not be identified as Boon's original sponsor. And at all costs Boon must be prevented from enrolling in his own courses.

Despite these misgivings, Philip is not altogether displeased at finding himself on the same plane as Charles Boon. He awaits the latter's return, indeed, with something like eagerness. It is, he explains to himself, because he is bored with the journey, glad of company for the last, long hours of this interminable flight; but, truthfully, it is because he wants to show off. The glory of his adventure needs, after all, a reflector, someone capable of registering the transformation of the dim Rummidge lecturer into Visiting Professor Philip Swallow, member of the academic jet-set, ready to carry English culture to the far side of the globe at the drop of an airline ticket. And for once he will have the advantage of Boon, in his previous experience of America. Boon will be eager for advice and information: about looking left first when crossing the road, for example; about "public school" meaning the opposite of what it means in England, and "knock up" meaning something entirely different. He will also frighten Boon a little with the rigours of American graduate programmes. Yes, he has lots to say to Charles Boon.

"Now," says Boon, easing himself into the seat beside Philip's, "let me put you in the picture about the situation in Euphoria."

Philip gapes at him. "You mean you've been there already?"

Boon looks surprised. "Sure, this is my second year. I've just been home for Christmas."

"Oh," says Philip.

. . .

"I guess you must've visited England many times, Professor Zapp," says the blonde, whose name is Mary Makepeace.

"Never."

"Really? You must be all excited then. All those years of teaching English Literature, and now you finally get to see where it all happened."

"That's what I'm afraid of," says Morris Zapp.

"If I get the time I'm going to visit my great-grandmother's grave. It's in a village churchyard in County Durham. Don't you think that sounds idyllic?"

"You going to have the foetus buried there?"

Mary Makepeace turns her head away and looks out of the window. The word *"Sorry"* rises to Morris's lips, but he bites it back. "You don't want to face facts, do you? You want to pretend it's just like going to the dentist. Having a tooth extracted."

"I've never *had* a tooth extracted," she says, and he believes her. She continues to gaze out of the window, though there is nothing to see except cloud, stretching to the horizon like an endless roll of roof insulation.

"I'm sorry," he says, surprising himself.

Mary Makepeace turns her head back in his direction. "What's eating you, Professor Zapp? Don't you want to go to England?"

"You guessed it."

"Why not? Where are you going?"

"A dump called Rummidge. You don't have to pretend you've heard of it."

"Why are you going there?"

"It's a long story."

It was indeed, and the question put by Mary Makepeace had exercised many a group of gossiping faculty when it was announced that Morris Zapp was the year's nominee for the Rummidge-Euphoria exchange scheme. Why should Morris Zapp, who always claimed that he had made himself an authority on the literature of England not in spite of but *because* of never having set foot in the country, why should he of all people suddenly join the annual migration to Europe? And, still more pressingly, why did a man who could have gotten a Guggenheim by crooking his little finger, and spent a pleasant year reading in Oxford, or London, or on the Côte d'Azur if he chose, condemn himself to six months' hard labour at Rummidge? Rummidge. Where was it? What was it? Those who knew shuddered and grimaced. Those who did not went home to consult encyclopedias and atlases, returning baffled to confer with their colleagues. If it was a plot by Morris to further his career, no one could give a satisfactory account of how it would work. The most favoured explanation was that he was finally getting tired of the Student Revolution, its strikes, protests, issues, nonnegotiable demands, and was willing to go anywhere, even to Rummidge, for the sake of a bit of peace and quiet. Nobody dared actually to test this hypothesis on the man himself, since his resistance to student intimidation was as legendary as his sarcasm. Then at last the word got round that Morris was going to England on his own, and all was clear: the Zapps were breaking up. The gossip dwindled away; it was nothing unusual after all. Just another divorce.

Actually, it was more complicated than that. Désirée, Morris's second wife, wanted a divorce, but Morris didn't. It was not Désirée that he was loth to part from, but their children, Elizabeth and Darcy, the darlings of Morris Zapp's otherwise unsentimental heart. Désirée was sure to get custody of both children—no judge, however fairminded, was going to split up a pair of twins—and he would be restricted to taking them out to the park or a movie once a month. He had been all through that routine once before with his daughter by his first wife, and in consequence she had grown up with about as much respect for him as for the insurance salesman whom he must have resembled to her childish vision, turning up on her stoop at regular intervals with a shy, ingratiating smile, his pockets bulging with candy dividends; and this time it would cost him $300.00 per visit in fares since Désirée proposed moving to New York. Morris had been born and brought up in New York, but he had no intention of returning there, in fact he would not repine if he never saw the city again: on the evidence of his last visit it was only a matter of time before the garbage in the streets reached penthouse level and the whole population suffocated.

No, he didn't want to go through all that divorce hassle again. He pleaded with Désirée to give their marriage another chance, for the children's sake. She was unmoved. He was a bad influence on the children anyway, and as for herself she could never be a fulfilled person as long as she was married to him.

"What have I done?" he demanded rhetorically, throwing his arms about.

"You eat me."

"I thought you liked it!"

"I don't mean that, trust your dirty mind, I mean psychologically. Being married to you is like being slowly swallowed by a python. I'm just a half-digested bulge in your ego. I want out. I want to be free. I want to be a person again."

"Look," he said, "let's cut out all this encounter-group crap. It's that student you found me with last summer, isn't it?"

"No, but she'll do to get the divorce. Leaving me at the Dean's reception to go home and screw the baby-sitter, that should make an impression on the judge."

"I told you, she's gone back East, I don't even know her address."

"I'm not interested. Can't you get it into your head that I don't care where you keep your big, fat circumcised prick? You could be banging the entire women's field hockey team every night for all I care. We're past all that."

"Look, let's talk about this like two rational people," he said, making a gesture of serious concern by turning off the TV football game he had been watching with one eye throughout this argument.

After an hour's exhausting discussion, Désirée agreed to a compromise: she would delay starting divorce proceedings for six months on condition he moved out of the house.

"Where to?" he grumbled.

"You can find a room somewhere. Or shack up with one of your students, I'm sure you'll have plenty of offers."

Morris Zapp frowned, foreseeing what an ignominious figure he would cut in and around the University, a man turned out of his own home, washing his shirts in the campus launderette and eating lonely dinners at the Faculty Club.

"I'll go away," he said. "I'll take six months' leave at the end of the quarter. Give me till Christmas."

"Where will you go?"

"Somewhere." Inspiration came to him, and he added, "Europe maybe."

"Europe? You?"

Slyly he watched her out of the corner of his eye. For years Désirée had been pestering him to take her to Europe, and always he had refused. For Morris Zapp was that rarity among American Humanities Professors, a totally unalienated man. He liked America, Euphoria particularly. His needs were simple: a temperate climate, a good library, plenty of inviting ass around the place and enough money to keep him in cigars and liquor and to run a comfortable modern house and two cars. The first three items were, so to speak, natural resources of Euphoria, and the fourth, the money, he had obtained after some years of strenuous effort. He did not see how he could improve his lot by travelling, certainly not by trailing around Europe with Désirée and the kids. "Travel narrows," was one of the Zapp proverbs. Still, if it came to the crunch, he was prepared to sacrifice this principle in the interests of domestic harmony.

"Why don't we all go?" he said.

He watched the emotions working across her face, lust for Europe contending with disgust for himself. Disgust won by a knockout.

"Go fuck yourself," she said, and walked out of the room.

Morris fixed himself a stiff drink, put an Aretha Franklin LP on the hi-fi and sat down to think. He was in a spot. He had to go to Europe now, to save face. But it was going to be difficult to fix things at such short notice. He couldn't afford to go at his own expense: though his salary was considerable, so was the cost of running the house and supporting Désirée in the style to which she was accustomed, not to mention alimony payments to Martha. He couldn't apply for paid study-leave because he had just had two quarters off. It was too late to apply for a Guggie or a Fulbright and he had an idea that European universities didn't hire visitors as casually as they did in the States.

The next morning he called the Dean of Faculty.

"Bill? Look, I want to go to Europe for six months, as soon after Christmas as possible. I need some kind of a deal. What have you got?"

"Where in Europe, Morris?"

"Anywhere, Bill."

"England?"

"Even England."

"Gee, Morris, I wish you'd asked me earlier. There was a swell opening in Paris, with UNESCO, I fixed up Ed Waring in Sociology just a week ago."

"Spare me the narrow misses, Bill, what have you got?"

There was a rustling of papers. "Well, there is the Rummidge exchange, but you wouldn't be interested in that, Morris."

"Just give me the dope."

Bill gave it to him, concluding, "You see, it isn't your class, Morris."

"I'll take it."

Bill tried to argue him out of it for a while, then confessed that the Rummidge post had already been given to a young assistant professor in Metallurgy.

"Tell him he can't have it after all. Tell him you made a mistake."

"I can't do that, Morris. Be reasonable."

"Give him accelerated promotion to Associate Professor. He won't argue."

"Well . . ." Bill Moser hesitated, then sighed. "I'll see what I can do, Morris."

"Great, Bill, I won't forget it."

Bill's voice dropped to a lower, more confidential pitch. "Why the sudden yearning for Europe, Morris? Students getting you down?"

"You must be joking, Bill. No, I think I need a change. A new perspective. The challenge of a different culture."

Bill Moser roared with laughter.

Morris Zapp wasn't surprised that Bill Moser was incredulous. But there was a kind of truth in his answer that he wouldn't have dreamed of admitting except in the guise of a palpable lie.

For years Morris Zapp had, like a man exceptionally blessed with good health, taken his self-confidence for granted, and regarded the recurrent identity crises of his colleagues as symptoms of psychic hypochondria. But recently he had caught himself brooding about the meaning of his life, no less. This was partly the consequence of his own success. He was full professor at one of the most prestigious and desirably located universities in America, and had already served as the Chairman of his Department for three years under Euphoric State's rotating system; he was a highly respected scholar with a long and impressive list of publications to his name. He could only significantly increase his salary either by moving to some god-awful place in Texas or the Mid-West where no one in his right mind would go for a thousand dollars a day, or by switching to administration, looking for a college President's job somewhere, which in the present state of the nation's campuses was a through ticket to an early grave. At the age of forty, in short, Morris Zapp could think of nothing he wanted to achieve that he hadn't achieved already, and this depressed him.

There was always his research, of course, but some of the zest had gone out of that since it ceased to be a means to an end. He couldn't enhance his reputation, he could only damage it, by adding further items to his bibliography, and the realization slowed him down, made him cautious. Some years ago he had embarked with great enthusiasm on an ambitious critical project: a series of commentaries on Jane Austen which would work through the whole canon, one novel at a time, saying absolutely everything that could possibly be said about them. The idea was to be utterly exhaustive, to examine the novels from every conceivable angle, historical, biographical, rhetorical, mythical, Freudian, Jungian, existentialist, Marxist, structuralist, Christian-allegorical, ethical, exponential, linguistic, phenomenological, archetypal, you name it; so that when each commentary was written there would be simply *nothing further to say* about the novel in question. The object of the exercise, as he had often to explain with as much patience as he could muster, was not to enhance others' enjoyment and understanding of Jane Austen, still less to honour the novelist herself, but to put a definitive stop to the production of any further garbage on the subject. The commentaries would not be designed for the general reader but for the specialist, who, looking up Zapp, would find that the book, article or thesis he had been planning had already been anticipated and, more likely than not, invalidated. After Zapp, the rest would be silence. The thought gave him deep satisfaction. In Faustian moments he dreamed of going on, after fixing Jane Austen, to do the same job on the other major English novelists, then the poets and dramatists, perhaps using computers and teams of trained graduate students, inexorably reducing the area of English literature available for free comment, spreading dismay through the whole industry, rendering scores of his colleagues redundant: periodicals would fall silent, famous English Departments be left deserted like ghost towns . . .

As is perhaps obvious, Morris Zapp had no great esteem for his fellow-labourers in the vineyards of literature. They seemed to him vague, fickle, irresponsible creatures, who wallowed in relativism like hippopotami in mud, with their nostrils barely protruding into the air of common-sense. They happily tolerated the existence of opinions contrary to their own—they even, for God's sake, sometimes changed their minds. Their pathetic attempts at profundity were qualified out of existence and largely interrogative in mode. They liked to begin a paper with some formula like, "I want to raise some questions about so-and-so," and seemed to think they had done their intellectual duty by merely raising them. This manoeuvre drove Morris Zapp insane. Any damn fool, he maintained, could think of questions; it was *answers* that separated the men from the boys. If you couldn't answer your own questions it was either because you hadn't worked on them hard enough or because they weren't real questions. In either case you should keep your mouth shut. One couldn't move in English studies these days without falling over unanswered questions which some damn fool had carelessly left lying about—it was like trying to mend a leak in an attic full of dusty, broken furniture. Well, his commentary would put a stop to that, at least as far as Jane Austen was concerned.

But the work proceeded slowly; he was not yet halfway through *Sense and Sensibility* and already it was obvious that each commentary would run to several volumes. Apart from the occasional article, he hadn't published anything for several years now. Sometimes he would start work on a problem only to remember, after some hours' cogitation, that he had solved it very satisfactorily himself years before. Over the same period—whether as cause or effect he wasn't sure—he had begun to feel ill-at-ease in his own body. He was prone to indigestion after rich restaurant meals, he usually needed a sleeping-pill before retiring, he was developing a pot-belly, and he found it increasingly difficult to achieve more than one orgasm in a single session—or so he would complain to his buddies over a beer. The truth was that these days he couldn't count on making it even once, and Désirée had less cause for resentment than she knew over the baby-sitter last summer. Things weren't what they used to be in the Zapp loins, though it was a dark truth that he would scarcely admit to himself, let alone to anyone else. He would not publicly acknowledge, either, that he was finding it a strain to hold his students' attention as the climate on campus became increasingly hostile to traditional academic values. His style of teaching was designed to shock conventionally educated students out of a sloppily reverent attitude to literature and into an ice-cool, intellectually rigorous one. It could do little with students openly contemptuous of both the subject and his own qualifications. His barbed wisecracks sank harmlessly into the protective padding of the new gentle inarticulacy, which had become so fashionable that even his brightest graduate students, ruthless professionals at heart, felt obliged to conform to it, mumbling in seminars, "Well, it's like James, ah, well the guy *wants* to be a modern, I mean he has the symbolism bit and God is dead and all, but it's like he's still committed to intelligence, like he thinks it all *means* something for Chrissake—you dig?" Jane Austen was certainly not the writer to win the hearts of the new generation. Sometimes Morris woke sweating from nightmares in which students paraded round the campus carrying placards that declared KNIGHTLEY SUCKS and FANNY PRICE IS A FINK. Perhaps he *was* getting a little stale; perhaps, after all, he would profit from a change of scene.

In this fashion had Morris Zapp rationalized the decision forced upon him by Désirée's ultimatum. But, sitting in the airplane beside pregnant Mary Makepeace, all these reasons seemed unconvincing. If he needed a change, he was fairly sure it wasn't the kind that England would afford. He had neither affection nor respect for the British. The ones he had met— expatriates and visiting professors—mostly acted like fags and then turned out not to be, which he found unsettling. At parties they wolfed your canapés and gulped your gin as if they had just been released from prison, and talked all the time in high, twittering voices about the differences between the English and American university systems, making it clear that they regarded the latter as a huge, rather amusing racket from which they were personally determined to take the biggest possible cut in the shortest possible time. Their publications were vapid and amateurish, inadequately researched, slackly argued, and riddled with so many errors, misquotations, misattributions and incorrect dates that it was amazing they managed to get their own names right on the title page. They nevertheless had the nerve to treat American scholars, including even himself, with sneering condescension in their lousy journals.

He felt in his bones that he wasn't going to enjoy England: he would be lonely and bored, all the more so because he had taken a small provisional vow not to be unfaithful to Désirée, just to annoy her; and it was the worst possible place to carry on his research. Once he sank into the bottomless morass of English manners, he would never be able to keep the mythic archetypes, the patterns of iterative imagery, the psychological motifs, clear and radiant in his mind. Jane Austen might turn *realist* on him, as she had on so many other readers, with consequences all too evident in the literature about her.

In Morris Zapp's view, the root of all critical error was a naive confusion of literature with life. Life was transparent, literature opaque. Life was an open, literature a closed system. Life was composed of things, literature of words. Life was what it appeared to be about: if you were afraid your plane would crash it was about death, if you were trying to get a girl into bed it was about sex. Literature was never about what it appeared to be about, though in the case of the novel considerable ingenuity and perception were needed to crack the code of realistic illusion, which was why he had been professionally attracted to the genre (even the dumbest critic understood that *Hamlet* wasn't about how the guy could kill his uncle, or the *Ancient Mariner* about cruelty to animals, but it was surprising how many people thought that Jane Austen's novels were about finding Mr. Right). The failure to keep the categories of life and literature distinct led to all kinds of heresy and nonsense: to "liking" and "not liking" books for instance, preferring some authors to others and suchlike whimsicalities which, he had constantly to remind his students, were of no conceivable interest to anyone except themselves (sometimes he shocked them by declaring that, speaking personally on this low, subjective level, he found Jane Austen a pain in the ass). He felt a particularly pressing need to castigate naive theories of realism because they threatened his masterwork: obviously, if you applied an open-ended system (life) to a closed one (literature) the possible permutations were endless and the definitive commentary became an impossibility. Everything he knew about England warned him that the heresy flourished there with peculiar virulence, no doubt encouraged by the many concrete reminders of the actual historic existence of great authors that littered the country—baptismal registers, houses with plaques, second-best beds, reconstructed studies, engraved tombstones and suchlike trash. Well, one thing he was *not* going to do while he was in England was to visit Jane Austen's grave. But he must have spoken the thought aloud, because Mary Makepeace asks him if Jane Austen was the name of his great-grandmother. He says he thinks it unlikely.

. . .

Meanwhile, Philip Swallow is wondering more desperately than ever when this flight is going to end. Charles Boon has been talking at him for hours, it seems, permitting few interruptions. All about the political situation in Euphoria in general and on the Euphoric State campus in particular. The factions, the issues, the confrontations; Governor Duck, Chancellor Binde, Mayor Holmes, Sheriff O'Keene; the Third World, the Hippies, the Black Panthers, the Faculty Liberals; pot, Black Studies, sexual freedom, ecology, free speech, police violence, ghettoes, fair housing, school busing, Viet Nam; strikes, arson, marches, sit-ins, teach-ins, love-ins, happenings. Philip has long since given up trying to follow the details of Boon's argument, but the general drift seems to be concisely summed up by his lapel buttons:

LEGALIZE POT

NORMAN O. BROWN FOR PRESIDENT

SAVE THE BAY: MAKE WATER NOT WAR
KEEP THE DRAFT CARDS BURNING
THERE IS A FAULT IN REALITY—NORMAL
 SERVICE WILL RETURN SHORTLY
HAPPINESS IS (just IS)
KEEP GOD OUT OF AMERICA
BOYCOTT GRAPES
KEEP KROOP
SWINGING SAVES
BOYCOTT TRUFFLES
FUCK D*CK!

In spite of himself, Philip is amused by some of the slogans. Obviously it is a new literary medium, the lapel button, something between the classical epigram and the imagist lyric. Doubtless it will not be long before some postgraduate is writing a thesis on the genre. Doubtless Charles Boon is already doing so.

"What's your research topic, Boon?" he asks, firmly interrupting an involved legal disquisition on some persecuted group called the Euphoria Ninety-Nine.

"Uh?" Boon looks startled.

"Your PhD—or is it an MA?"

"Oh. Yeah, I'm still getting a Master's. That's mostly course work. Just a little baby dissertation."

"On what?"

"Well, uh, I haven't decided yet. To tell you the truth, Phil, I don't have too much time for work, academic work."

At some point in their conversation Boon has begun calling Philip by his first name, using moreover the contraction he has always detested. Philip resents the familiarity, but can think of no way of stopping him, though he has declined the invitation to address Boon as "Charles."

"What other kind of work are you doing?" he asks ironically.

"Well, you see, I have this radio show . . ."

"The Charles Boon Show?" Philip inquires, laughing heartily.

"That's right, you know about it?"

Boon is not laughing. The same old Boon, barefaced liar, weaver of fantasies. "No," says Philip. "Do tell me."

"Oh, it's just a late-night phone-in programme. You know, people call up and talk about what's on their mind and ask questions. Sometimes I have a guest. Hey, you must come on the programme one night!"

"Will I get paid?"

"'Fraid not. You get a free tape-recording of the programme and a coloured photograph of the two of us at the mike."

"Well . . ." Philip is unsettled by the particularity of the account. Could it conceivably be true? Some campus radio system perhaps? "How often have you done this programme?" he asks.

"Every night, that is morning, for the past year. Midnight till two."

"Every night! I'm not surprised your studies are suffering."

"To tell you the truth, Phil, I'm not too bothered about my studies. It suits me to be registered at Euphoric State—it allows me to stay in the country without getting drafted. But I don't really need any more degrees. I've decided my future's in the media."

"The Charles Boon Show?"

"That's just a beginning. I'm having discussions with a TV network right now about starting an experimental arts programme—'s'matter of fact, I'm flying at their expense, they sent me over to look at some European programmes. Then there's *Euphoric Times* . . ."

"What's that?"

"The underground newspaper. I do a weekly column for them, and now they want me to take over the editorship."

"The editorship."

"But I'm thinking of starting a rival paper instead."

Philip looks searchingly at Boon, whose left eye jumps abruptly to port. Philip relaxes: it is all a pack of lies after all. There is no radio programme, no TV show, no expense account, no newspaper column. It is all wish-fulfilment fantasy, like the Rummidge Research Assistantship and the career in the diplomatic service. Boon has certainly changed—not only in appearance and dress: his manner is more confident, more relaxed, his speech has lost some of its Cockney vowels and glottal stops, he sounds not unlike David Frost. Philip has always supposed he despised David Frost but now realizes that in a grudging kind of way he must respect David Frost quite a lot, so sickening has it been to entertain, even for a moment, the idea that Charles Boon is successfully launched upon a similar career. An extraordinarily plausible fibber, Boon, even after years of close acquaintance he could take you in, it was only the vagrant eye that gave him away. Well, it would make a good story for his first letter home. *Who should I meet on the plane but the incorrigible Charles Boon—you remember him, of course, the Parolles of the English Department, graduated a couple of years ago. He was all dolled up in the latest "gear," with hair down to his shoulders, but as full of tall stories as ever. Patronized me like mad, of course! But he's so transparent, you can't take offence.*

His train of thought, and Boon's continuing monologue, are interrupted by an announcement from the captain that they will be landing in approximately twenty minutes, and he hopes they have enjoyed the flight. The instruction to fasten safety belts is illuminated at the front of the cabin.

"Well, Phil, I'd better get back to my seat," says Boon.

"Yes, well, nice to have met you again."

"If there's anything I can do for you, Phil, just call me. My number's in the book."

"Yes, well, I have been to America before, you know. But thank you for the offer."

Boon waves his hand deprecatingly. "Any time, day or night. I have an answering service."

And to Philip's astonishment, Charles Boon gets up and walks, unchallenged, past a hovering stewardess, through the curtains that conceal the First Class cabin.

. . .

"I guess we must be over England, now," says Mary Makepeace, staring out of the window.

"Is it raining?" Zapp asks.

"No, it's very clear. You can see all the little fields, like a patchwork quilt."

"It can't be England if it's not raining. We must be off course."

"There's a great dark smudge over there. That must be a big city."

"It's probably Rummidge. A great dark smudge sounds like Rummidge."

. . .

And now, in the two Boeings, falls simultaneously the special silence that precedes an airliner's landing. The engines are all but cut off, and the conversation of the passengers is hushed as if in sympathy. The planes begin to lose height—clumsily, it seems, in a series of lurching, shuddering drops, as though bumping down an enormous staircase. The passengers swallow to relieve the pressure on their eardrums, close their eyes, finger their passports and vomit-bags. Time passes very slowly. Each person is alone, temporarily, with his own thoughts. But it is hard to think connectedly, swaying and lurching here between heaven and earth. Philip thinks of Hilary smiling bravely and the children waving forlornly on Rummidge station as his train drew away, of an essay that he has forgotten to return to a student, of the probable cost of a taxi from the airport to Plotinus. The future seems frighteningly blank and he has a sudden spasm of homesickness; then he wonders whether the plane will crash, and what it would be like to die and whether there is a God, and where did he put his luggage tickets. Morris Zapp debates whether to stay in London for a few days or go straight to Rummidge and know the worst at once. He thinks of his twins playing secretively in a corner of the yard and breaking off their game reluctantly to say goodbye to him and how Désirée had refused to make love the night before he left, it would have been the first time in months, and remembers the first girl he ever had, Rose Finkelpearl the fish-monger's daughter on the next block, and how puzzled he'd been when his second girl also reeked faintly of fish, and wonders how many people at the airport will know what this charter has come to England for.

The planes yaw and tilt. A wall of suburbs suddenly rears up behind Mary Makepeace's head, and falls away again. Cloud swirls round Philip Swallow's plane and the windows are slashed with rain. Then houses, hills, trees, hangars, trucks, skim by in recognizable scale, like old friends seen again after a long separation.

. . .

Bump!

. . .

Bump!

. . .

At exactly the same moment, but six thousand miles apart, the two planes touch down.

2. Settling

Philip Swallow rented an apartment in the top half of a two-storey house high up on Pythagoras Drive, one of many classically-named but romantically-contoured residential roads that corkscrewed their way up and around the verdant hills of Plotinus, Euph. The rent was low, by Euphoric standards, because the house stood on what was called a Slide Area. It had, in fact, already slid twelve feet towards the Bay of Esseph from its original position— a circumstance that had caused the owner hurriedly to vacate it, leasing the accommodation to tenants too indigent, or too careless of life, to complain. Philip fell into neither of these categories, but then he had not learned the full history of 1037 Pythagoras Drive until after signing the six months' lease. That history had been related to him on the first evening of his occupancy by Melanie Byrd, the prettiest and most wholesome-looking of the three girls who shared the ground-floor apartment, as she kindly explained to him the controls of the communal washing machine in the basement. At first he had felt exploited, but after a while he grew reconciled to the situation. If the apartment was not, after all, *surprisingly* cheap, it was still cheap; and as Melanie Byrd reminded him, there was no truly safe place to live in Euphoria, whose unique and picturesque landscape was the product of a huge geological fault running through the entire State. It had caused a major earthquake in the nineteenth century, and a repetition of this disaster before the end of the twentieth was confidently predicted by seismologists and local millennial sects: a rare and impressive instance of agreement between science and superstition.

When he drew back the curtains in his living-room each morning, the view filled the picture window like a visual *tour de force* at the beginning of a Cinerama film. In the foreground, and to his right and left, the houses and gardens of the more affluent Euphoric faculty clung picturesquely to the sides of the Plotinus hills. Beneath him, where the foothills flattened out to meet the Bay shore, was the campus, with its white buildings and bosky paths, its campanile and plaza, its lecture rooms, stadia and laboratories, bordered by the rectilinear streets of downtown Plotinus. The Bay filled the middle distance, stretching out of sight on both sides, and one's eye naturally travelled in a great sightseeing arc: skimming along the busy Shoreline Freeway, swerving out across the Bay via the long Esseph Bridge (ten miles from toll to toll) to the city's dramatic skyline, dark downtown skyscrapers posed against white residential hills, from which it leapt across the graceful curves of the Silver Span suspension bridge, gateway to the Pacific, to alight on the green slopes of Miranda County, celebrated for its redwood forests and spectacular sea coast.

This vast panorama was agitated, even early in the morning, by every known form of transportation—ships, yachts, cars, trucks, trains, planes, helicopters and hovercraft—all in simultaneous motion, reminding Philip of the brightly illustrated cover of a *Boy's Wonder Book of Modern Transport* he had received on his tenth birthday. It was indeed, he thought, a perfect marriage of Nature and Civilization, this view, where one might take in at a glance the consummation of man's technological skill and the finest splendours of the natural world. The harmony he perceived in the scene was, he knew, illusory. Just out of sight to his left a pall of smoke hung over the great military and industrial port of Ashland, and to his right the oil refineries of St. Gabriel fumed into the limpid air. The Bay, which winked so prettily in the morning sun, was, according to Charles Boon and other sources, poisoned by industrial waste and untreated effluent, and was being steadily contracted by unscrupulous dumping and filling.

For all that, Philip thought, almost guiltily, framed by his living-room window and seen at this distance, the view still looked very good indeed.

. . .

Morris Zapp was less enchanted with his view—a vista of dank back gardens, rotting sheds and dripping laundry, huge, ill-looking trees, grimy roofs, factory chimneys and church spires—but he had discarded this criterion at a very early stage of looking for furnished accommodation in Rummidge. You were lucky, he had quickly discovered, if you could find a place that could be kept at a temperature appropriate to human organisms, equipped with the more rudimentary amenities of civilized life and decorated in a combination of colours and patterns that didn't make you want to vomit on sight. He considered living in a hotel, but the hotels in the vicinity of the campus were, if anything, even worse than the private houses. Eventually he had taken an apartment on the top floor of a huge old house owned by an Irish doctor and his extensive family. Dr. O'Shea had converted the attic with his own hands for the use of an aged mother, and it was to the recent death of this relative, the doctor impressed upon him, that Morris owed the good fortune of finding such enviable accommodation vacant. Morris didn't see this as a selling point himself, but O'Shea seemed to think that the apartment's sentimental associations were worth at least an extra five dollars a week to an American torn from the bosom of his own family. He pointed out the armchair in which his mother had suffered her fatal seizure and, while bouncing on the mattress to demonstrate its resilience, contrived at the same time to reflect with a mournful sigh that it was scarcely a month since his beloved parent had passed to her reward from this very bed.

Morris took the flat because it was centrally heated—the first he had seen thus blessed. But the heating system turned out to be one of electric radiators perversely and unalterably programmed to come on at full blast when you were asleep and to turn themselves off as soon as you got up, from which time they leaked a diminishing current of lukewarm air into the frigid atmosphere until you were ready to go to bed again. This system, Dr. O'Shea explained, was extremely economical because it ran on half-price electricity, but it still seemed to Morris an expensive way to work up a sweat in bed. Fortunately the apartment was well provided with gas burners of antique design, and by keeping them on at full volume all day he was able to maintain a tolerable temperature in his rooms, though O'Shea evidently found it excessive, entering Morris's apartment with his arm held up to shield his face, like a man breaking into a burning house.

Simply keeping warm was Morris Zapp's main preoccupation in his first few days at Rummidge. On his first morning, in the tomb-like hotel room he had checked into after driving straight from London airport, he had woken to find steam coming out of his mouth. It had never happened to him indoors before and his first thought was that he was on fire. When he had moved his baggage into the O'Shea house, he filled the micro-refrigerator with TV dinners, locked his door, turned up all the fires and spent a couple of days thawing out. Only then did he feel ready to investigate the Rummidge campus and introduce himself to the English Department.

. . .

Philip Swallow was more impatient to inspect his place of work. On his very first morning he strolled out after a delicious breakfast of orange juice, bacon, hot cakes and maple syrup (maple syrup! how delightful it was to recover such forgotten sensations) to look for Dealer Hall, the location of the English Department. It was raining, as it had been the previous day. This had been a disappointment to Philip initially—in his memory Euphoria was bathed in perpetual sunlight, and he had forgotten—perhaps he had never known—that it had a rainy season in the winter months. It was, however, a fine, soft rain, and the air was warm and balmy. The grass was green, the trees and shrubs were in full leaf and, in some cases, flower and fruit. There was no real winter in Euphoria—autumn joined hands with spring and summer, and together they danced a three-handed jig all year long, to the merry confusion of the vegetable world. Philip felt his pulse beating to its exhilarating rhythm.

He had no difficulty in finding his way to Dealer Hall, a large, square building in the neoclassical style. He was prevented from entering it, however, by a ring of campus policemen. Quite a lot of students and staff were milling about, and a long-haired youth with a KEEP KROOP button in the lapel of his suede jacket informed Philip that the building was being checked out for a bomb allegedly planted during the night. The search, he understood, might take several hours; but as he was turning away it ended quite suddenly with a muffled explosion high up in the building and a tinkle of shattered glass.

. . .

As Morris Zapp learned much later, he made a bad impression on his first appearance in the Rummidge English Department. The Secretary, young Alice Slade, returning from her coffee break with her friend Miss Mackintosh of Egyptology, observed him doubled up in front of the Departmental noticeboard, coughing and wheezing and blowing cigar ash all over the floor. Miss Slade had wondered whether it was a mature student having a fit and asked Miss Mackintosh to run and fetch the porter, but Miss Mackintosh ventured the opinion that he was only laughing, which was indeed the case. The noticeboard distantly reminded Morris of the early work of Robert Rauschenberg: a thumb-tacked montage of variegated scraps of paper—letterheaded notepaper, memo sheets, compliment slips, pages torn clumsily from college notebooks, inverted envelopes, reversed invoices, even fragments of wrapping paper with tails of scotch tape still adhering to them—all bearing cryptic messages from faculty to students about courses, rendezvous, assignments and books, scribbled in a variety of scarcely decipherable hands with pencil, ink and coloured ball-point. The end of the Gutenberg era was evidently not an issue here: they were still living in a manuscript culture. Morris felt he understood more deeply, now, what McLuhan was getting at: it had tactile appeal, this noticeboard—you wanted to reach out and touch its rough, irregular surface. As a system for conveying information it was the funniest thing he'd seen in years.

Morris was still chuckling to himself as the mini-skirted secretary, looking, he thought, rather nervously over her shoulder from time to time, led him down the corridor to his office. Walking along the corridors of Dealer Hall was like passing through some Modern Language Association Hall of

Fame, but he recognized none of the nameplates here except the one on the door Miss Slade finally stopped at: MR. P. H. SWALLOW. That rang a distant bell—but, he recalled, as the girl fumbled with the key (she seemed very jumpy, this chick), it wasn't in print that he had encountered the name, merely in the correspondence about his trip. Swallow was the guy he was exchanging with. He recalled Luke Hogan, present Chairman of Euphoric's English Department, holding a letter from Swallow in his enormous fist (a handwritten letter, again, it came back to him) and complaining in his Montana cowboy's drawl, "Goddammit, Morris, what are we gonna do with this guy Swallow? He claims he ain't *got* a field." Morris had recommended putting Philip down to teach English 99, a routine introduction to the literary genres and critical method for English majors, and English 305, a course in novel-writing. As Euphoric State's resident novelist, Garth Robinson, was in fact very rarely resident, orbiting the University in an almost unbroken cycle of grants, fellowships, leaves of absence and alcoholic cures, the teaching of English 305 usually fell to some unwilling and unqualified member of the regular teaching staff. As Morris said, "If he makes a fuck-up of English 305, nobody's going to notice. And any clown with a PhD should be able to teach English 99."

"He doesn't have a PhD," Hogan said.

"What?"

"They have a different system in England, Morris. The PhD isn't so important."

"You mean the jobs are hereditary?"

Recollecting all this reminded Morris that he had not been able to prise any information about his own teaching programme from Rummidge before leaving Euphoria.

The girl finally got the door open and he went in. He was pleasantly surprised: it was a large, comfortable room, well-furnished with desk, table, chairs and bookshelves of matching polished wood, an armchair and a rather handsome rug. Above all, it was warm. Morris Zapp was to experience the same sense of surprise and paradox many times in his first weeks at Rummidge. Public affluence and private squalor, was how he formulated it. The domestic standard of living of the Rummidge faculty was far below that of the Euphoric faculty, but even the most junior teacher here had a large office to himself, and the Staff House was built like a Hilton, putting Euphoric State's Faculty Club quite in the shade. Even the building in which Morris's office was situated had its own spacious and comfortable lounge, restricted to faculty, where you could get fresh coffee and tea served in real china cups and saucers by two motherly women, whereas Dealer Hall boasted only a small room littered with paper cups and cigarette ends where you fixed yourself instant coffee that tasted like hot disinfectant. "Public affluence" was perhaps too flattering to Rummidge, and it couldn't be the socialism he'd heard so much about, either. It was more like a narrow band of privilege running through the general drabness and privation of life. If the British university teacher had nothing else, he had a room he could call his own, a decent place to sit and read his newspaper and the use of a john that was off-limits to students. That seemed to be the underlying principle. Such coherent thoughts were not yet forming in Morris Zapp's mind, however, as he first cast his eyes round Philip Swallow's room. He was still in a state of culture shock, and it gave him a giddy feeling when he looked out of the window and saw the familiar campanile of Euphoric State flushed an angry red and shrunk to half its normal size, like a detumescent penis.

"It's a bit stuffy in here, I'm afraid," said the secretary, making a move to open a window. Morris, already basking in the radiator's warmth, lurched with clumsy haste to prevent her, and she shrank back, quivering, as if he had been about to put his hand up her skirt—which, given its dimensions, wouldn't have been difficult, it could easily happen accidentally just shaking hands with her. He tried to soothe her by making conversation.

"Don't seem to be many people on campus today."

She looked at him as if he had just arrived from outer space. "It's the vacation," she said.

"Uhuh. Is Professor Masters around?"

"No, he's in Hungary. Won't be back till the beginning of term."

"At a conference?"

"Shooting wild pigs, I'm told."

Morris wondered if he had heard aright, but let it go. "What about the other professors?"

"There's only the one."

"I mean the other teachers."

"It's the vacation," she repeated, speaking with deliberation, as if to a slow-witted child.

"You do get them coming in from time to time, but I've not seen anybody this morning."

"Who should I see about my teaching programme?"

"Dr. Busby did say something about it the other day . . ."

"Yes?" Morris prompted, after a pause.

"I've forgotten, now," said the girl dejectedly. "I'm leaving in the summer to get married," she added, as if she had decided on this course as the only way out of a hopeless situation.

"Congratulations. Would there be a file on me somewhere?"

"Well, there might be. I could have a look," said the girl, obviously relieved to escape. She left Morris alone in his office.

He sat down at the desk and opened the drawers. In the top right-hand one was an envelope addressed to himself. It contained a long hand-written letter from Philip Swallow.

Dear Professor Zapp,

I gather you'll be using my room while you're here. I'm afraid I've lost the key to the filing cabinet, so if you have anything really confidential I should keep it under the carpet, at least I always do. Do feel free to use my books, though I'd be grateful if you wouldn't lend them to students, as they *will* write in them.

I gather from Busby that you'll probably be taking over my tutorial groups. The second-year groups are rather hard going, especially the Joint Honours, but the first-year group is quite lively, and I think you'll find the two final-year groups very interesting. There are a few points you might like to bear in mind. Brenda Archer suffers badly from pre-menstrual tension so don't be surprised if she bursts into tears every now and again. The other third-year group is tricky because Robin Kenworth used to be Alice Murphy's boyfriend but lately he's been going around with Miranda Watkins, and as they're all in the same group you may find the atmosphere rather tense . . .

The letter continued in this vein for several pages, describing the emotional, psychological and physiological peculiarities of the students concerned in intimate detail. Morris read through it in total bewilderment. What kind of a man was this, that seemed to know more about his students than their own mothers? And to care more, by the sound of it.

He opened the other drawers in the desk, hoping to find further clues to this eccentric character, but they were empty except for one containing a piece of chalk, an exhausted ball-point, two bent pipe-cleaners and a small, empty can that had once contained an ounce of pipe tobacco, Three Nuns Empire Blend. Sherlock Holmes might have made something of these clues . . . Morris moved on to examine the cupboards and bookshelves. The books did no more than confirm Swallow's confession that he had no particular scholarly field, being a miscellaneous collection of English literature, with a thin representation of modern criticism, Morris's own not included. He established that the cupboards were empty, except for one at the top of the bookshelves which was too high for him to reach. Its inaccessibility convinced Morris that it contained the revelation he was looking for—a dozen empty gin bottles, for instance, or a collection of women's underwear—and he clambered on to a chair to reach the catch of the sliding door. It was stuck, and the whole bookshelf began to sway dangerously as he tugged. The catch suddenly gave, however, and a hundred and fifty-seven empty tobacco cans, Three Nuns Empire Blend, fell on his head.

. . .

"You've been allocated room number 426," said Mabel Lee, the petite Asian secretary. "That's Professor Zapp's office."

"Yes," said Philip. "He'll be using my room at Rummidge."

Mabel Lee gave him an amiable, but non-attending smile, like that of an air-hostess—whom, indeed, she resembled, in her crisp white blouse and scarlet pinafore dress. The Departmental Office was full of people just admitted to the building, loudly discussing the bomb which had exploded in the fourth-floor men's room. Opinion seemed to be fairly evenly divided between those who blamed the Third World Students who were threatening to strike in the coming quarter, and those who suspected police provocateurs aiming to discredit the Third World Students and their strike. Though the conversation was excited, Philip missed the expected note of outrage and fear.

"Does, er, this sort of thing . . . happen often?" he asked.

"Hmm? Oh, yeah. Well, I guess it's the first *bomb* we've had in Dealer." With this ambiguous reassurance Mabel Lee proceeded to hand over the keys to his room, together with a wad of forms and leaflets which she briskly explained to him, dealing them out on the counter that divided the room: "Identity Card, don't forget to sign it, application for car parking, medical insurance brochures—choose any one plan, typewriter rental application— you can have electric or manual, course handbook, income tax immunity form, key to the elevator in this building, key to the Xerox room, just sign your name in the book each time you use the machine . . . I'll tell Professor Hogan you've arrived," she concluded. "He's busy with the Fire Chief right now. I know he'll call you."

Philip found his room on the fourth floor. A sallow youth with a mop of frizzy hair was squatting outside, smoking a cigarette. He was wearing some kind of army combat jacket with camouflage markings and he looked, Philip couldn't help thinking, just the sort of chap who might plant a bomb somewhere. As Philip fitted his key into the Yale lock, he scrambled to his feet. A fluorescent KEEP KROOP button glowed on his lapel.

"Professor Swallow?"

"Yes?"

"Could I see you?"

"What, now?"

"Now would be great."

"Well, I've only just arrived . . ."

"You have to run that key twice."

This was true. The door opened suddenly and Philip dropped some of his papers. The young man picked them up adroitly and made this an opportunity to follow him into the room. It was stuffy, and smelled of cigars. Philip threw up the window and observed with satisfaction that it opened on to a narrow balcony.

"Nice view," said the youth, who had stolen up silently behind him. Philip started.

"What can I do for you, Mr. er . . . ?"

"Smith. Wily Smith."

"Willy?"

"Wily."

Wily perched himself on the only part of the desk that was not covered with books. Philip's first thought was that it was rather careless of the Zapp fellow to leave his room so untidy. Then he registered that many of the books were still in unwrapped postal packaging and addressed to himself. "Good Lord," he said.

"What's the problem, Professor Swallow?"

"These books . . . Where have they come from?"

"Publishers. They want you to assign them for courses.

"And what if I don't?"

"You keep them anyway. Unless you want to sell them. I know a guy will give you fifty per cent of the list price . . ."

"No, no," Philip protested, greedily tearing the wrappers from huge, heavy anthologies and sleek, seductive paperbacks. A free book was a rare treat in England, and the sight of all this unsolicited booty made him slightly delirious. He rather wished Wily Smith would leave him to gloat in solitude.

"What is it you want to see me about, Mr. Smith?"

"You're teaching English 305 next quarter, right?"

"I really don't know what I'm teaching yet. What is English 305?"

"Novel-writing."

Philip laughed. "Well, it's certainly not me, then. I couldn't write a novel to save my life."

Wily Smith frowned and, plunging his hand inside his combat jacket, produced what Philip feared might be a bomb but which turned out to be a catalogue of courses. "English 305," he read out, "an advanced course in the writing of extended narrative. Selective enrolment. Winter Quarter: Professor Philip Swallow."

Philip took the catalogue from his hands and read for himself. "Good Lord," he said weakly. "I must stop this at once."

With Wily Smith's assistance he telephoned the Chairman of the Department.

"Professor Hogan, I'm sorry to bother you so soon, but—"

"Mr. Swallow!" Hogan's voice boomed out of the receiver. "Mighty glad to hear you arrived. Have a good flight?"

"Not at all bad, thank you. I—"

"Fine! Where are you staying, Mr. Swallow?"

"At the Faculty Club for the time being, while I look—"

"Fine, that's fine, Mr. Swallow. You and I must have lunch together real soon."

"Well, that would be very nice, but what I—"

"Fine. And while I think of it, Mrs. Hogan and I are having some folks round for drinks on Sunday, 'bout five, could you make it?"

"Well, yes, thank you very much. About my courses—"

"Fine. That's just fine. And how are you settling in, Mr. Swallow?"

"Oh, fine, thanks," said Philip mechanically. "I mean, no, that is—" But he was too late. With a last "Fine," Hogan had rung off.

"So do I get into the course?" said Wily Smith.

"I would strongly advise you against it," said Philip. "Why are you so keen, anyway?"

"I have this novel I want to write. It's about this black kid growing up in the ghetto . . ."

"Isn't that going to be rather difficult?" said Philip. "I mean, unless you actually *are* . . ."

Philip hesitated. He had been instructed by Charles Boon that "black" was the correct usage these days, but he found himself unable to pronounce a word associated in Rummidge with the crudest kind of racial prejudice. "Unless you've had the experience yourself," he amended his sentence.

"Sure. Like the story is autobiographical. All I need is technique."

"Autobiographical?" Philip scrutinized the young man, narrowing his eyes and cocking his head to one side. Wily Smith's complexion was about the shade of Philip's own a week after his summer holiday, when his tan would begin to fade and turn yellow. "Are you sure?"

"Sure I'm sure." Wily Smith looked hurt, not to say insulted.

Philip hastily changed the subject: "Tell me, that badge you're wearing—what *is* Kroop?"

Kroop turned out to be the name of an Assistant Professor in the English Department who had recently been refused tenure. "But there's a grass-roots movement to have him kept on here," Wily explained. "Like he's a real groovy teacher and his classes are very popular. The other professors make out he hasn't published enough, but really they're sick as hell because of the raves he gets in the *Course Bulletin*."

And what was that? It was apparently a kind of consumers' guide to teachers and courses based on questionnaires handed out to students in previous quarters. Wily produced the current issue from one of his capacious pockets.

"You won't be in there, Professor Swallow. But you will next quarter."

"Really?" Philip opened the book at random.

English 142. Augustan Pastoral Poetry. Asst. Professor Howard Ringbaum. Juniors and Seniors. Limited enrolment.

Ringbaum, according to most reports, does little to make his subject interesting to students. One commented: "He seems to know his material very well, but resents questions and discussion as they interrupt his train of thought." Another comment: "Dull, dull, dull." Ring-baum is a strict grader and, according to one report, "likes to set in-sidious little quizzes."

"Well," said Philip with a nervous smile. "They certainly don't mince their words, do they?" He leafed through other pages on English courses.

English 213. The Death of the Book? Communication and Crisis in Contemporary Culture. Asst. Professor Karl Kroop. Limited enrolment.

Rise early on Enrolment Day to sign on for this justly popular inter-disciplinary multi-media head-trip. "Makes McLuhan seem slow," was one comment, and another raved: "the most exciting course I have ever taken." Heavy reading assignments, but flexible assessment system. Kroop takes an interest in his students, is always available.

"Who compiles these reports?" Philip inquired.
"I do," said Wily Smith. "Do I get into your course?"
"I'll think about it," said Philip. He continued to browse.

English 350. Jane Austen and the Theory of Fiction. Professor Morris J. Zapp. Graduate Seminar. Limited enrolment.

Mostly good reports of this course. Zapp is described as vain, sarcastic and a mean grader, but brilliant and stimulating. "He makes Austen swing," was one comment. Only "A" students need apply.

. . .

Miss Slade was just about to knock on Morris Zapp's door to inform him that there was nothing in the files about his teaching programme, when she heard the noise of the hundred and fifty-seven tobacco cans falling out of the cup-board. He listened to the sound of her high heels fleeing down the corridor. She did not return. Neither did anyone else violate his privacy.

Morris came into the University most days to work on his *Sense and Sen-sibility* commentary and at first he appreciated the peace and quiet; but after a while he began to find these amenities oppressively absolute. In Euphoria he was constantly being pursued by students, colleagues, administrators, secretaries. He didn't expect to be so busy at Rummidge, at least not initially; but he had vaguely supposed the faculty would introduce themselves, show him around, offer the usual hospitality and advice. In all modesty Morris imagined he must be the biggest fish ever to swim into this academic backwater, and he was prepared for a reception of almost exaggerated (if that were possible) interest and excitement. When nobody showed, he didn't know what to do. He had lost the art, cultivated in youth, of making his existence known to people. He was used, by now, to letting the action come to him. But there was no action.

As the beginning of term approached, the Departmental corridor lost its tomb-like silence, its air of human desertion. The faculty began to trickle back to their posts. From behind his desk he heard them passing in the corridor, greeting each other, laughing and opening and shutting their doors. But when he ventured into the corridor himself they seemed to avoid him, bolting into their offices just as he emerged from his own, or else they looked straight through him as if he were the man who serviced the central heating. Just when he had decided that he would have to take the initiative by ambushing his British colleagues as they passed his door at coffee-time and dragging them into his office, they began to acknowledge his presence in a way which suggested long but not deep familiarity, tossing him a perfunctory smile as they passed, or nodding their heads, without breaking step or their own conversations. This new behaviour implied that they all knew perfectly well who he was, thus making any attempt at self-introduction on his part superfluous, while at the same time it offered no purchase for extending acquaintance. Morris began to think that he was going to pass through the Rummidge English Department without anyone actually speaking to him. They would fend him off for six months with their little smiles and nods and then the waters would close over him and it would be as if he had never disturbed their surface.

Morris felt himself cracking under this treatment. His vocal organs began to deteriorate from disuse—on the rare occasions when he spoke, his own voice sounded strange and hoarse to his ears. He paced his office like a prisoner in his cell, wondering what he had done to provoke this treatment. Did he have halitosis? Was he suspected of working for the CIA?

In his lonely isolation, Morris turned instinctively for solace to the media. He was at the best of times a radio and TV addict: he kept a radio in his office at Euphoric State tuned permanently to his favourite FM station, specializing in rock-soul ballads; and he had a colour TV in his study at home as well as in the living-room because he found it easier to work while watching sports broadcasts at the same time. (Baseball was most conducive to a ready flow of words, but football, hockey and basketball would also serve.) He rented a colour TV soon after moving into his apartment in Rummidge, but the programmes were disappointing, consisting mainly of dramatizations of books he had already read and canned American series he had already seen. There was, naturally, no baseball, football, hockey or basketball. There was soccer, which he thought he might get interested in, given time—he sniffed, there, the mixture of spite and skill, gall and grace, which characterized an authentic spectator sport—but the amount of screen time devoted to it was meagre. There was a four-hour programme of sport on Saturday afternoons which he had settled down to watch expectantly, but it seemed to be some kind of conspiracy to drive the population out to the soccer stadiums or to the supermarkets or anywhere rather than watch ladies' archery, county swimming championships, a fishing contest and a table-tennis tournament all in breathtaking succession. He switched on to the other channel and that seemed to be a cross-country race for wheel-chairs, as far as you could tell through the sleet.

He had a brief honeymoon with Radio One that turned into a kind of sadomasochistic marriage. Waking early in the Rummidge hotel on that morning when his breath turned to steam, he had flicked on his transistor and listened to what he took, at the time, to be a very funny parody of the worst kind of American AM radio, based on the simple but effective formula of having non-commercial commercials. Instead of advertising products, the disc-jockey advertised *himself*—pouring out a torrent of drivel generally designed to convey what a jolly, amusing and lovable guy he was—and also advertised his listeners, every one of whose names and addresses he seemed determined to read out over the air, plus, on occasion, their birthdays and car registration numbers. Now and again he played musical jingles in praise of himself or reported, in tones of unremitting jollity, a multiple accident on the freeway. There was almost no time left for playing records. It was a riot. Morris thought it was a little early in the morning for satire, but listened entranced. When the programme finished and was followed by one of exactly the same kind, he began to get restive. The British, he thought, must be gluttons for satire: even the weather forecast seemed to be some kind of spoof, predicting every possible combination of weather for the next twenty-four hours without actually committing itself to anything specific, not even the existing temperature. It was only after four successive programmes of almost exactly the same formula—DJ's narcissistic gabble, lists of names and addresses, meaningless anti-jingles—that the awful truth dawned on him: *Radio One was like this all the time.*

Morris's only human contact these lonely days was Doctor O'Shea, who came in to watch Morris's colour TV and to drink his whisky, and perhaps to escape the joys of family life for an hour or so, because he knocked softly on the door and tiptoed into the room, winking heavily and raising a cautionary finger as if to restrain Morris from speaking until the door was shut against the wails of Mrs. O'Shea and her babies rising up the staircase. O'Shea puzzled Morris. He didn't look like a doctor, not like the doctors Morris knew—sleek prosperous men who drove the biggest cars and owned the plushest houses in any neighbourhood he had ever lived in. O'Shea's suit was baggy and threadbare, his shirts were frayed, he drove a small car that had seen better days, he looked short of sleep, money, pleasures, everything except worries. By the same token Morris's possessions, few as they were, seemed to throw the doctor into fits of envious awe, as if his eyes had never beheld such opulence. He examined Morris's Japanese cassette recorder with the half-fearful, half-covetous curiosity of a nineteenth-century savage handling a missionary's tinder-box; he seemed astounded that a man might own so many shirts that he could send them to the laundry half-a-dozen at a time; and, invited to fix himself a drink, he was almost (but not quite) incapable of making a choice from three varieties of whisky, groaning and muttering under his breath as he handled the bottles and read the labels, "Mother of God, what is it we have here, Old Grandad Genuine Kentucky Bourbon and here's th'old josser himself looking none the worse for it, would you believe it . . ."

The installation of the colour TV had made Dr. O'Shea quite ill with excitement. He followed the delivery men up the stairs and skipped around the room getting in their way and sat enraptured before the tuning signal for hours after they left, getting up now and again to lay his hand reverently on the cabinet as if he expected to derive some special grace from the contact. "Sure, if I hadn't seen it with me own eyes I shouldn't have believed it," he said with a sigh. "You're a fortunate man, Mr. Zapp."

"But I just rented it," Morris protested in bewilderment. "Anybody can rent one. It only costs a few dollars a week."

"Well, now, that's easily said, Mr. Zapp, for a man in your position, that's easily said, but easier said than done, Mr. Zapp."

"Well, if there's anything you want to see, just drop by . . ."

"That's very kind of you, Mr. Zapp, very thoughtful. I'll take you up on that generous invitation." And so he did. Unfortunately, O'Shea's tastes in TV ran to situation comedy and sentimental serials, to which he reacted with naive, unqualified credulity, writhing and jumping up and down in his seat, pounding the arm of his chair and nudging Morris vigorously in the ribs, maintaining a stream of highly personal commentary on the action: "Ahah! Caught you there, laddie, you weren't expecting that . . . Oh! What's this, what's this, you little hussy? Ah, now, that's better, that's better . . . NO, DON'T DO IT! DON'T DO IT! Mother of God, that boy will be the death of me . . ." and so on. Fortunately, Dr. O'Shea usually fell asleep halfway through the programme, exhausted by the strains of audience participation and the rigours of the day's labours, and Morris would turn down the sound and get out a book. It wasn't exactly company.

. . .

To his considerable mortification, Philip Swallow's chief social asset at Euphoric State turned out to be his association with Charles Boon. He carelessly let this information slip in conversation with Wily Smith and, within hours it seemed, the news had been flashed to all points of the campus. His office began to fill up with people anxious to make his acquaintance for the sake of some anecdote of Charles Boon's early life, and before the end of the afternoon the Chairman's wife, Mrs. Hogan, had phoned to plead for Philip's assistance in persuading Boon to attend their cocktail party. It was hard to believe, but the Charles Boon Show was all the rage at Euphoric State. Philip listened to it at the first opportunity, and, by some kind of sadomasochistic compulsion, at most subsequent opportunities.

The basic formula of the programme—an open line on which listeners could call up to discuss various issues with the compère and with each other—was a familiar one. But the Charles Boon Show was different from the ordinary phone-in programme in several respects. To begin with, it was put out by the non-commercial network, QXYZ, which was supported by listeners' subscriptions and foundation grants, and was therefore free from business and political pressures. Where the compères of most American phone-in programmes were bland, evasive, middle-of-the-road men, giving a fair hearing to all sides of the question—endlessly patient, endlessly courteous, ultimately without convictions—Charles Boon was violently, wilfully opinionated. Where they provided the reassurance of a surrogate father or uncle, he offered the provocation of a delinquent-son-figure. He took an extreme radical position on all such issues as pot, sex, race, Viet Nam, and argued heatedly—often rudely—with callers who disagreed with him, sometimes abusing his control of the telephone line by cutting them off in mid-sentence. It was rumoured that he collected the phone numbers of likely-sounding girls and called them back after the programme to make dates. He would sometimes begin a programme by quoting a passage of Wittgenstein or Camus or by reading a poem of his own composition, and use this as a starting point for a dialogue with his listeners. And an extraordinary variety of listeners they were, those who faithfully tuned into QXYZ at midnight—students, professors, hippies, runaways, insomniacs, drug addicts and Hells Angels. Housewives sitting up for laggard husbands confided their marital problems to the Charles Boon Show; truck-drivers listening to the programme in their shuddering cabs, unable to suppress their rage at Boon, or Camus, any longer, swerved off the freeway to phone in their incoherent contributions from emergency call-boxes. Already a considerable folk-lore had accumulated about the Charles Boon Show, and Philip was regaled with the highlights of certain past programmes so often that he came to believe that he had heard them himself: the time, for instance, Boon had talked a panic-stricken pregnant mother through her first labour-pains, or when he argued a homosexual clergyman out of suicide, or when he invited—and obtained—postcoital reflections on the Sexual Revolution from bedside telephones around the Bay. There were, of course, no commercials on the progamme, but just to annoy the rival networks Boon would sometimes give an unsolicited and unpaid testimonial to some local restaurant or movie or shirt-sale that had taken his fancy. To Philip it seemed obvious that beneath all the culture and the eccentricity and the human concern there beat a heart of pure show-business, but to the local community the programme evidently appeared irresistibly novel, daring and authentic.

"Isn't Mr. Boon with you?" was his hostess's first question when he presented himself at the Hogans' palatial ranch-style house for their cocktail party. Her eyes raked him from head to foot as though she suspected that he had concealed Boon somewhere on his person. Philip assured her that he had passed on the invitation, as Hogan himself loomed up and crunched Philip's fingers in a huge, horny handclasp.

"Hi, there, Mr. Swallow, mighty glad to see you." He ushered Philip into the spacious living-room, where forty or more people were already assembled, and helped him to a gin and tonic of giant proportions. "Now, who would you like to meet? Nearly all English Department folk here, I guess."

Only one name would come into Philip's head. "I haven't met Mr. Kroop yet."

Hogan went slightly green about the jowls. "Kroop?"

"I've read so much about him, in buttonholes," Philip quipped, to cover what was evidently a *faux pas.*

"Yeah? Oh yeah. Ha, ha. I'm afraid you won't see Karl at many cocktail parties—Howard!" Hogan's enormous paw fell heavily on the shoulder of a sallow, bespectacled young man cruising past with a tumbler of Scotch held to pursed lips. He staggered slightly, but skilfully avoided spilling the drink. Philip was introduced to Howard Ringbaum. "I was telling Mr. Swallow," said Hogan, "that you don't often see Karl Kroop at faculty social gatherings."

"I hear," said Ringbaum, "that Karl has totally rethought his course on 'The Death of the Book?' He's removing the query mark this quarter."

Hogan guffawed and thumped Ringbaum between the shoulder blades before moving away. Ringbaum, swaying with the punch, kept his balance and his drink intact.

"What are you working on?" he asked Philip.

"Oh, I'm just trying to sort out my teaching at the moment."

Ringbaum nodded impatiently. "What's your field?"

"Yours is Augustan pastoral, I believe," Philip returned evasively.

Ringbaum looked pleased. "Right. How did you know? You've seen my article in *College English?*"

"I was looking through the Course Bulletin the other day . . ."

Ringbaum's countenance darkened. "You don't want to believe everything you read in that."

"Oh no, of course . . . What d'you think of this chap Kroop then?" Philip inquired.

"As little as possible. I'm coming up for tenure myself this quarter, and if I don't make it nobody around here is going to be wearing RETAIN RINGBAUM buttons."

"This tenure business seems to create a lot of tension."

"You must have the same thing in England?"

"Oh no. Probation is more or less a formality. In practise, once you're appointed they can never get rid of you—unless you seduce one of your students, or something equally scandalous." Philip laughed.

"You can screw as many students as you like here," said Ringbaum unsmilingly. "But if your publications are unsatisfactory . . ." He drew a finger expressively across his throat.

"Hey, Howard!"

A young man dressed in a black grained-silk shirt with a red kerchief knotted round his throat accosted Philip's companion. He towed behind him a delectable blonde in pink party pyjamas. "Hey, Howard, somebody just told me there's an English guy at this party who asked Hogan to introduce him to Karl Kroop. I'd love to have seen the old man's face."

"Ask him," said Ringbaum, nodding towards Philip.

Philip blushed and laughed uneasily.

"Oh my God, you aren't the English guy by any chance?"

"You goofed again, Sy, dear," said the woman.

"I'm terribly sorry," said the man. "Sy Gootblatt is the name. This is Bella. You might think by the way she's dressed that she's just got out of bed, and you wouldn't be far wrong."

"Take no notice of him, Mr. Swallow," said Bella. "How are you liking Euphoria?"

Of the two questions he was asked at the cocktail party by everyone he met, this was the one he preferred. The other was, "What are you working on?"

"What are you working on, Mr. Swallow?" Luke Hogan asked him when they bumped into each other again.

"Luke," said Mrs. Hogan, saving Philip from having to think of a reply, "I really think Charles Boon is here at last."

There was a flurry of activity in the hall, and heads turned all across the room. Boon had indeed arrived, dressed offensively in singlet and jeans, and escorting a handsome, haughty Black Pantheress who was to appear on his programme later that night. They sat in a corner of the room drinking Bloody Marys and giving audience to a neck-craning circle of entranced faculty and their wives. The Pantheress did little except look coolly around at the Hogans' opulent furnishings as if calculating how well they would burn, but Boon more than compensated for her taciturnity. Philip, who had rather counted on being himself the evening's chief focus of attention, found himself standing neglected on the fringes of this little court. Disgruntled, he wandered out of the living-room on to the terrace. A solitary woman was leaning against the balustrade, staring moodily at the Bay, where a spectacular sunset was in progress, the orange globe of the sun just balanced, it seemed, on the suspension cables of the Silver Span bridge. Philip took up his stand some four yards away from the woman. "Delightful evening," he said.

She looked at him sharply, then returned to the contemplation of the sunset. "Yeah," she said, at length.

Philip sipped his drink nervously. The silent, brooding presence of the woman made him uncomfortable, spoiled his enjoyment of the view. He decided to return to the living-room.

"If you're going back inside . . ." said the woman.

"Yes?"

"You might freshen my drink for me."

"Certainly," said Philip, taking her glass. "More ice?"

"More ice, more vodka. No more tonic. And look for the Smirnoff bottle under the bar. Ignore the gallon jar of cut-price stuff on the top."

Philip duly found the concealed Smirnoff bottle and refilled the woman's glass, rather underestimating the space required for ice, which (inexperienced in handling liquor) he added last. Boon was still talking away in the background, about his plans for a TV arts programme: "Something entirely different . . . art in action . . . train a camera on a sculptor at work for a month or two, then run the film through at about fifty thousand frames per second, see the sculpture taking shape . . . put an object in front of two painters, let them get on with it, use two cameras and a split screen . . . contrast . . . auction the pictures at the end of the programme . . ." Philip topped up his own gin and tonic and carried the two glasses out on to the terrace.

"Thanks," said the woman. "Is that little shit still shooting off his mouth in there?"

"Yes, he is, actually."

"You're not a fan?"

"Definitely not."

"Let's drink to that."

They drank to it.

"Wow," said the woman. "You mix a stiff drink."

"I just followed your instructions."

"To the brim," said the woman. "I don't think we've met, have we? Are you visiting here?"

"Yes, I'm Philip Swallow—exchanging with Professor Zapp."

"Did you say Zapp?"

"You know him?"

"Very well. He's my husband."

Philip choked on his drink. "You're Mrs. Zapp?"

"Is that so surprising? You think I look too old? Or too young?"

"Oh, no," said Philip.

"Oh no which?" Her small green eyes glinted with mockery. She was a red-head, striking but by no means pretty, and not particularly well-groomed. He guessed she was in her mid-thirties.

"I was just surprised," said Philip. "I suppose I assumed you had gone to Rummidge with your husband."

"Your wife with you?"

"No." She responded with a gesture which implied clearly enough that his assumption was therefore demonstrably unwarranted. "I would have liked to have brought her," he said. "But my visit was arranged at rather short notice. Also we have children, and there were problems about schooling and so on. And there was the house . . ." He heard himself going on like this for, it seemed, several hours, as if he were answering a formal accusation in court. He felt increasingly foolish, but Mrs. Zapp somehow kept him talking, involving himself deeper and deeper in implied guilt, by her silence and her mocking regard. "Do you have children yourself?" he concluded desperately.

"Two. Twins. Boy and girl. Aged nine."

"Ah, then you understand the problems."

"I doubt if we have the same problems, Mr. Sparrow."

"Swallow."

"Mr. Swallow. Sorry. A much nicer bird." She turned back to contemplate the sun, now sinking into the sea behind the Silver Span, and took a reflective draught from her glass. "Less promiscuous, for instance. How does your wife feel about it, Mr. Swallow, I mean is she with you about the kids and the schools and the house and all? She doesn't mind being left behind?"

"Well, we discussed it very thoroughly, of course . . . It was a difficult decision. I left it to her ultimately . . ." (He felt himself slipping into the groove of compulsive self-justification again.) "After all, she has the worst part of the bargain . . ."

"What bargain?" said the woman sharply.

"Just a figure of speech. I mean, for me, it's a great opportunity, a paid holiday if you like. But for her it's just life as usual, only lonelier. Well, you must know what it's like yourself."

"You mean, Morris being in England? It's great, just great."

Philip politely pretended not to have heard this remark.

"Just to be able to stretch out in my own bed"—she gestured appropriately, revealing a rusty stubble under her armpit—"without finding another human body in my way, breathing whisky fumes all over my face and pawing at my crotch . . ."

"I think I'd better be going back inside," said Philip.

"Do I embarrass you, Mr. Sparrow—Swallow? I'm sorry. Let's talk about something else. The view. Don't you think this is a great view? We have a view, too, you know. The same view. Everybody in Plotinus has the same view, except for the blacks and the poor whites on the flats down there. You've got to have a view if you live in Plotinus. That's the first thing people ask when you buy a house. Has it got a view? The same view, of course. There's only one view. Every time you go out to dinner or to a party, it's a different house, and different drapes on the windows, but the same fucking view. I could scream sometimes."

"I'm afraid I can't agree," said Philip stiffly. "I could never get tired of it."

"But you haven't lived with it for ten years. Wait a while. You can't rush nausea, you know."

"Well, I'm afraid that after Rummidge . . ."

"What's that?"

"Where I come from. Where your husband's gone."

"Oh yeah . . . What's it called, Rubbish?"

"Rummidge."

"I thought you said Rubbish." She laughed immoderately, and spilled some vodka on her frock. "Shit. What's it like, then, Rummidge? Morris tried to make out it was the greatest, but everybody else says it's the asshole of England."

"Both would be exaggerations," said Philip. "It's a large industrial city, with the usual advantages and disadvantages."

"What are the advantages?"

Philip racked his brains, but couldn't think of any. "I really ought to go back inside," he said. "I've scarcely met anyone . . ."

"Relax, Mr. Sparrow. You'll meet them all again. It's the same people at all the parties in this place. Tell me more about Rubbish. No, on second thoughts, tell me more about your family."

Philip preferred to answer the first question. "Well, it's not really as bad as people make out," he said.

"Your family?"

"Rummidge. I mean it has a decent art gallery, and a symphony orchestra and a Rep and that sort of thing. And you can get out into the country quite easily." Mrs. Zapp had lapsed into silence, and he began to listen to himself again, registering his own insincerity. He hated concerts, rarely visited the art gallery and patronized the local repertory theatre perhaps once a year. As for "getting out," what was that but the dire peregrinations of Sunday afternoons? And in any case, what kind of a recommendation for a place was it that you could get out of it easily? "The schools are pretty good," he said. "Well, one or two—"

"Schools? You seem really hung up on schools."

"Well, don't you think education is terribly important?"

"No. I think our culture's obsession with education is self-defeating."

"Oh?"

"Each generation is educating itself to earn enough money to educate the next generation, and nobody is actually *doing* anything with this education. You're knocking yourself out to educate your children so they can knock themselves out educating their children. What's the point?"

"Well, you could say the same thing about the whole business of getting married and raising a family."

"*Exactly!*" cried Mrs. Zapp. "I do, I do!" She looked at her watch suddenly, and said, "My God, I must go," somehow managing to imply that Philip had been detaining her.

Unwilling to make a Noël-Coward-type entrance through the French windows in the company of Mrs. Zapp, Philip bade her good evening and lingered alone on the terrace. When he had allowed her enough time to get off the premises, he would plunge back into the throng and try to find some congenial people who would offer him a lift home and perhaps invite him to share a meal. At that moment he became aware that the throng had fallen eerily silent. Alarmed, he hurried through the French windows and found that the living-room was quite deserted, except for a coloured, or rather black, woman emptying ashtrays. They stared at each other for a few moments.

"Er, where is everybody?" Philip stammered.

"Everybody gone home," said the woman.

"Oh dear. Is Professor Hogan somewhere? Or Mrs. Hogan?"

"Everybody gone home."

"But this *is* their home," Philip protested. "I just wanted to say goodbye."

"They gone somewhere to eat, I guess," said the woman with a shrug, and recommenced her leisurely tour of the ashtrays.

"Damn," said Philip. He heard the sound of a car starting outside the house, and hurried to the front door just in time to see Mrs. Zapp driving away in a big white station wagon.

. . .

Morris Zapp was standing at the window of his office at Rummidge, smoking a cigar (one of the last of the stock he had brought with him into the country) and listening to the sound of footsteps hurrying past his door. The hour for tea had arrived, and Morris debated whether to fetch a cup back to his office rather than drink it in the Senior Common Room, where the rest of the faculty would gather to gossip in the opposite corner or peer at him over their newspapers from his flanks. He gazed moodily down at the central quadrangle of the campus, a grassed area now thinly covered with snow. For some days, now, the temperature had wavered between freezing and thawing and it was difficult to tell whether the sediment thickening the atmosphere was rain or sleet or smog. Through the murk the dull red eye of a sun that had scarcely been able to drag itself above roof level all day was sinking blearily beneath the horizon, spreading a rusty stain across the snow-covered surfaces. Real pathetic fallacy weather, Morris thought. At which moment there was a knock on his door.

He swung round startled. *A knock on his door!* There must be some mistake. Or his ears were playing him tricks. The darkness of the room—for he had not yet switched on the lights—made this seem more plausible. But no—the knock was repeated. "Come in," he said in a thin, cracked voice, and cleared his throat. "Come in!" He moved eagerly towards the door to welcome his visitor, and to turn the lights on at the same time, but collided with a chair and dropped his cigar, which rolled under the table. He dived after it as the door opened. A segment of light from the corridor fell across the floor, but did not reveal the hiding-place of the cigar. A woman's voice said uncertainly, "Professor Zapp?"

"Yeah, come in. Would you switch the light on, please?"

The lights came on and he heard the woman gasp. "Where are you?"

"Under here." He found himself staring at a pair of thick fur-lined boots and the hemline of a shaggy fur coat. To these was added, a moment later, an inverted female face, scarved, red-nosed and apprehensive. "I'll be right with you," he said. "I dropped my cigar somewhere under here."

"Oh," said the woman, staring.

"It's not the cigar I'm worried about," Morris explained, crawling around under the table. "It's the rug . . . CHRIST!"

A searing pain bored into his hand and shot up his arm. He scrambled out from under the table, cracking his head on the underside in his haste. He stumbled round the room, cursing breathlessly, squeezing his right hand under his left armpit and clasping his right temple with his left hand. With one eye he was vaguely aware of the fur-coated woman backing away from him and asking what was the matter. He collapsed into his archchair, moaning faintly.

"I'll come back another time," said the woman.

"No, don't leave me," said Morris urgently. "I may need medical attention."

The fur coat loomed over him, and his hand was firmly removed from his forehead. "You'll have a bump there," she said. "But I can't see any skin broken. You should put some witch-hazel on it."

"You know a good witch?"

The woman tittered. "You can't be too bad," she said. "What's the matter with your hand?"

"I burned it on my cigar." He withdrew his injured hand from his armpit and tenderly unclasped it.

"I can't see anything," said the woman, peering.

"There!" He pointed to the fleshy cushion at the base of his thumb.

"Oh, well, I think those little burns are best left alone."

Morris looked at her reproachfully and rose to his feet. He went over to the desk to find a fresh cigar. Lighting it with trembling fingers, he prepared a little quip about getting your nerve back after a smoking accident, but when he turned round to deliver it the woman had disappeared. He shrugged and went to close the door, tripping, as he did so, over a pair of boots protruding from under the table.

"What are you doing?" he said.

"Looking for your cigar."

"Never mind the cigar."

"That's all very well," came the muffled reply. "But it isn't your carpet."

"Well, it isn't yours either, if it comes to that."

"It's my husband's."

"Your husband's?"

The woman, looking rather like a brown bear emerging from hibernation, backed slowly out from under the table and stood up. She held, between the thumb and forefinger of one gloved hand, a squashed and soggy cigar-end. "I didn't get a chance to introduce myself," she said. "I'm Hilary Swallow. Philip's wife."

"Oh! Morris Zapp." He smiled and extended his hand. Mrs. Swallow put the cigar butt into it.

"I don't think it did any damage," she said. "Only it's rather a good carpet. Indian. It belonged to Philip's grandmother. How do you do?" she added suddenly, stripping off a glove and holding out her hand. Morris disposed of the dead cigar just in time to grab it.

"Glad to meet you, Mrs. Swallow. Won't you take off your coat?"

"Thanks, but I can't stop. I'm sorry to barge in on you like this, but my husband wrote asking for one of his books. I've got to send it on to him. He said it was probably in here somewhere. Would you mind if I . . ." She gestured towards the bookshelves.

"Go ahead. Let me help you. What's the name of the book?"

She coloured slightly. "He said it's called *Let's Write a Novel.* I can't imagine what he wants it for."

Morris grinned, then frowned. "Perhaps he's going to write one," he said, while he thought to himself, "God help the students in English 305."

Mrs. Swallow, peering at the bookshelves, gave a sceptical grunt. Morris, drawing on his cigar, examined her with curiosity. It was difficult to tell what manner of woman was hidden beneath the woollen headscarf, the huge shapeless fur coat, the thick zippered boots. All that could be seen was a round, unremarkable face with rosy cheeks, a red-tipped nose and the hint of a double chin. The red nose was evidently the result of a cold, for she kept sniffing discreetly and dabbing at it with a Kleenex. He went over to the bookshelves. "So you didn't go to Euphoria with your husband?"

"No."

"Why was that?"

The look she gave him couldn't have been more hostile if he had inquired what brand of sanitary towels she used. "There were a number of personal reasons," she said.

"Yeah, and I bet you were one of them, honey," said Zapp, but only to himself. Aloud he said: "What's the name of the author?"

"He couldn't remember. It's a book he bought second-hand, years ago, off a sixpenny stall. He thinks it has a green cover."

"A green cover . . ." Morris ran his index finger over the rows of books. "Mrs. Swallow, may I ask you a personal question about your husband?"

She looked at him in alarm. "Well, I don't know. It depends . . ."

"You see that cupboard over your head? In that cupboard there are one hundred and fifty-seven tobacco cans. All the same brand. I know how many there are because I counted them. They fell on my head one day."

"They fell on your head? How?"

"I just opened the cupboard and they fell on my head."

A ghost of a smile hovered on Mrs. Swallow's lips. "I hope you weren't hurt?"

"No, they were empty. But I'm curious to know why your husband collects them."

"Oh, I don't suppose he collects them. I expect he just can't bear to throw them away. He's like that with things. Is that all you wanted to know?"

"Yeah, that's about all." He was puzzled why a man who used so much tobacco bought it in little tiny cans instead of the huge one-pound canisters like the ones Luke Hogan kept on his desk, but he thought this would be too personal for Mrs. Swallow.

"The book doesn't seem to be here," she said with a sigh. "And I must be going, anyway."

"I'll look out for it."

"Oh, please don't bother. I don't suppose it's all that important. I'm sorry to have been such a nuisance."

"You're welcome. I don't have too many visitors, to tell you the truth."

"Well, it's nice to have met you, Professor Zapp. I hope you'll enjoy your stay in Rummidge. If Philip were here I'd like to ask you round for dinner one evening, but as it is . . . You understand." She smiled regretfully.

"But if your husband was here, I wouldn't be," Morris pointed out.

Mrs. Swallow looked nonplussed. She opened her mouth a number of times, but no words came out. At last she said, "Well, I mustn't keep you any longer," and abruptly departed, closing the door behind her.

"Uptight bitch," Morris muttered. Little as he coveted her company, he hungered for a home-cooked meal. He was tiring rapidly of TV dinners and Asian restaurants, which was all Rummidge seemed to offer the single man.

He found *Let's Write a Novel* five minutes later. The cover had come away from the spine, which was why they hadn't spotted it earlier. It had been published in 1927, as part of a series that included *Let's Weave a Rug, Let's Go*

Fishing and *Let's Have Fun With Photography.* "Every novel must tell a story," it began. "Oh, dear, yes," Morris commented sardonically.

> And there are three types of story, the story that ends happily, the story that ends unhappily, and the story that ends neither happily nor unhappily, or, in other words, doesn't really end at all.

Aristotle lives! Morris was intrigued in spite of himself. He turned back to the title page to check out the author. "A. J. Beamish, author of *A Fair But Frozen Maid, Wild Mystery, Glynis of the Glen*, etc., etc." He read on.

> The best kind of story is the one with a happy ending; the next best is the one with an unhappy ending, and the worst kind is the story that has no ending at all. The novice is advised to begin with the first kind of story. Indeed, unless you have Genius, you should never attempt any other kind.

"You've got something there, Beamish," Morris murmured. Maybe such straight talking wouldn't hurt the students in English 305 after all, lazy, pretentious bastards, most of them, who thought they could write the Great American Novel by just typing out their confessions and changing the names. He put the book aside for further reading. Then he would take it round to Mrs. Swallow one suppertime and stand on her stoop, salivating ostentatiously. Morris had a hunch she was a good cook, and he prided himself he could pick out a good cook in a crowd as fast as he could spot an easy lay (they were seldom the same person). Good plain food, he would predict; nothing fancy, but the portions would be lavish.

There was a knock at his door. "Come in," he called, expectantly, hoping that Mrs. Swallow had repented and returned to invite him to share a chicken dinner. But it was a man who bustled in, a small, energetic, elderly man with a heavy moustache and bright beady eyes. He wore a tweed jacket, curiously stained, and advanced into the room with both hands extended. "Mmmmmmmmmner, mmmmmmmmmmmmmmmner, mmmmmmmmmmmmmmmmmner," he bleated. "Mmmmmmmmmmmmmmner mmmmmmmmmmmmmmmmmmmner Masters." He pumped Morris's hands up and down in a double handshake. "Mmmmmmmmmmner Zapp? Mmmmmmmmmmmmmmmmner all right? Mmmmmmmmmmmmmmmner cup of tea? Mmmmmmmmmmmner jolly good."

He stopped bleating, cocked his head to one side and closed one eye. Morris deduced that he was in the presence of the Head of the Rummidge English Department, home from his Hungarian pig-shoot, and was being invited to partake of refreshment in the Senior Common Room.

Evidently the return of Professor Masters was the signal for which the rest of the faculty had been waiting. It was as if some obscure taboo had restrained them from introducing themselves before their chief had formally received him into the tribe. Now, in the Senior Common Room, they hurried forward and clustered around Morris's chair, smiling and chattering, pressing upon him cups of tea and chocolate cookies, asking him about his journey, his health, his work in progress, offering him belated advice about accommodation and discreetly interpreting the strangled utterances of Gordon Masters for his benefit.

"How d'you know what the old guy is saying?" Morris asked Bob Busby, a brisk, bearded man in a double-breasted blazer with whom he found himself walking to the car park—or rather running, for Busby maintained a cracking pace that Morris's short legs could hardly match.

"I suppose we've got used to it."

"Has he got a cleft palate or something? Or is it that moustache getting between his teeth when he talks?"

Busby stepped out faster. "He's a great man, really, you know," he said, with faint reproach.

"He is?" Morris panted.

"Well, he was. So I'm told. A brilliant young scholar before the war. Captured at Dunkirk, you know. One has to make allowances . . ."

"What has he published?"

"Nothing."

"Nothing?"

"Nothing anybody's been able to discover. We had a student once, name of Boon, organized a bibliographical competition to find something Gordon had published. Had students crawling all over the Library, but they drew a complete blank. Boon kept the prize." He gave a short, barking laugh. "Terrific cheek he had, that chap Boon. I wonder what became of him."

Morris was pooped, but curiosity kept him moving along beside Busby. "How come," he gasped, "Masters is Head of your Department?"

"That was before the war. Gordon was extraordinarily young, of course, to get the Chair. But the Vice-Chancellor in those days was a huntin,' shootin', fishin' type. Took all the candidates down to his place in Yorkshire for a spot of grouse-shooting. Naturally Gordon made a great impression. Story goes the most highly qualified candidate had a fatal accident with a gun. Or that Gordon shot him. Don't believe it myself."

Morris could keep up the pace no longer. "You'll have to tell me more another time," he called after the figure of Busby as it receded into the gloom of the ill-lit car park.

"Yes, good night, good night." To judge by the sound of his feet on the gravel, Busby had broken into a trot. Morris was left alone in the darkness. The flame of sociability lit by Masters' return seemed to have gone out as abruptly as it had flared up.

But the excitements of the day were not over. The very same evening he made the acquaintance of a member of the O'Shea ménage hitherto concealed from his view. At the customary hour the doctor knocked on his door and pushed into the room a teenage girl of sluttish but not unsexy appearance, raven-haired and hollow of cheek, who stood meekly in the middle of the floor, twisting her hands and peeping at Morris through long dark eyelashes.

"This is Bernadette, Mr. Zapp," said O'Shea gloomily. "You've no doubt seen her about the house."

"No. Hi, Bernadette," said Morris.

"Say good evening to the gentleman, Bernadette," said O'Shea, giving the girl a nudge which sent her staggering across the room.

"Good evening, sir," said Bernadette, making a clumsy little bob.

"Manners a little lacking in polish, Mr. Zapp," said O'Shea in a loud whisper. "But we must make allowances. A month ago she was milking cows in Sligo. My wife's people, you know. They have a farm there."

Morris gathered that Bernadette had come to live with the O'Sheas as domestic slave labour, or "Oh pear" as O'Shea preferred to phrase it. As a special treat the doctor had brought her along this evening to watch the colour TV. "If that's not inconveniencing you, Mr. Zapp?"

"Sure. What is it you want to watch, Bernadette, 'Top of the Pops'?"

"Er, no, not exactly, Mr. Zapp," said O'Shea. "The BBC 2 has a documentary on the Little Sisters of Misery, and Bernadette has an aunt in the Order. We can't get BBC 2 on the set downstairs, you see."

This was not Morris's idea of an evening's entertainment, so having switched on the TV he retired to his bedroom with a copy of *Playboy* that had caught up with him in the mail. Stretched out on the penultimate resting place of Mrs. O'Shea Sr. he ran an expert eye over Miss January's boobs and settled down to read a photo-feature on the latest sports cars, including the Lotus Europa which he had just ordered. One of the few satisfactions Morris had promised himself from his visit to England was the purchase of a new sports car to replace the Chevrolet Corvair which he had bought in 1965 just three days before Ralph Nader published *Unsafe at Any Speed*, thus reducing its value by approximately fifteen hundred dollars overnight and depriving Morris of any further pleasure in owning it. He had left Désirée with instructions to sell the Corvair for what she could get for it: that wouldn't be much, but he would save a considerable amount on the Lotus by taking delivery in England and shipping it back to Euphoria himself. *Playboy*, he was glad to note, approved of the Lotus.

Returning to the living-room to fetch a cigar, he found O'Shea asleep and Bernadette looking sullenly bored. On the screen a lot of nuns, photographed from behind, were singing a hymn.

"Seen your aunt yet?" he inquired.

Bernadette shook her head. There was a knock on the door and one of the O'Shea children stuck his head round the door.

"Please sir, will you tell me Dad Mr. Reilly phoned and Mrs. Reilly is having one of her turns."

Such summonses were a common occurrence in the life of Dr. O'Shea, who seemed to spend a fantastic amount of time on the road—compared, anyway, to American doctors, who in Morris's experience would only visit you at home if you were actually dead. Roused from his slumbers, O'Shea departed, groaning and muttering under his breath. He offered to remove Bernadette, but Morris said she could stay to watch out the programme. He returned to his bedroom and after a few minutes heard the sound of plainsong change abruptly into the driving beat of a current hit by the Jackson Five. There was still hope for Ireland, then.

A few moments later he heard footsteps thundering up the stairs, and the sound of the TV reverted to sacred music. Morris went into the living-room just as O'Shea burst in through the opposite door. Bernadette cowered in her seat, looking between the two men as if calculating which one was going to beat her first.

"Mr. Zapp," O'Shea panted, "the devil take me if I can get my car to start. Would you be so good as to give me a push down the road? Mrs. O'Shea would do it, but she's feeding the baby at this minute."

"You want to use my car?" said Morris, producing the keys.

O'Shea's jaw sagged. "God bless you, Mr. Zapp, you're a generous man, but I'd hate to take the responsibility."

"Go ahead. It's only a rented car."

"Aye, but what about the insurance?" O'Shea went into the matter of insurance at such length that Morris began to fear for the life of Mrs. Reilly, so he cut the discussion short by offering to drive O'Shea himself. The doctor thanked him effusively and galloped down the stairs, shouting over his shoulder to Bernadette that she was to leave Morris's room. "Take your time," said Morris to the girl, and followed him out.

Between giving Morris directions through the badly-lit back streets, O'Shea complimented Morris extravagantly on his car, a perfectly ordinary, rather underpowered Austin that he had rented at London Airport. Morris tried with some difficulty to imagine the likely reaction of O'Shea when he drove up in the burnt-orange Lotus, with its black leather bucket seats, remote-control spot lamp, visored headlights, streamlined wing-mirrors and eight-track stereo. Mother of God, he'd have a coronary on the spot.

"Down there, down there to your left," said Dr. O'Shea. "There's Mr. Reilly at the door, looking out for us. God bless you, Mr. Zapp. It's terribly good of you to turn out on a night like this."

"You're welcome," said Morris, drawing up in front of the house, and fending off the attempts of the distracted Mr. Reilly, evidently under the impression that Morris was the doctor, to drag him from behind the wheel.

But it *was* good of him, uncharacteristically good of Morris Zapp. The truth of the sentiment struck him more and more forcibly as he sat in the cold and cheerless parlour of the Reilly house waiting for O'Shea to finish his ministrations, and as he drove him back through the shadowy streets, listening with half an ear to lurid descriptions of Mrs. Reilly's symptoms. He cast his mind back over the day—helping Mrs. Swallow look for her husband's book, letting the Irish kid watch his TV, driving O'Shea around to his patients—and wondered what had come over him. Some creeping English disease of being nice, was it? He would have to watch himself.

. . .

Philip decided it was not too far to walk home from the Hogans' party, but wished he had phoned for a cab when it began to rain. He would really have to set about getting himself a car, a business he had postponed from fear of tangling with American second-hand car dealers, no doubt even more intimidating, venal and treacherous than their British counterparts. When he arrived at the house on Pythagoras Drive he discovered that he had forgotten his latchkey—the final aggravation of an evening already thoroughly spoiled by Charles Boon and Mrs. Zapp. Fortunately someone was in the house, because he could hear music playing faintly; but he had to ring the bell several times before the door, retained by a chain, opened a few inches and the face of Melanie Byrd peered apprehensively through the aperture. Her face brightened.

"Oh, hi! It's you."

"Terribly sorry—forgot my key."

She opened the door, calling over her shoulder, "It's OK, only Professor Swallow." She explained with a giggle: "We thought you were the fuzz. We were smoking."

"Smoking?" Then his nostrils registered a sweetish, acrid odour on the air and the penny dropped. "Oh, yes, of course." The "of course" was an attempt to sound urbane, but succeeded only in sounding embarrassed, which indeed he was.

"Like to join us?"

"Thank you, but I don't smoke. Not, that is . . ."

Philip floundered. Melanie laughed. "Have some coffee, then. Pot is optional."

"Thanks awfully, but I'd better get myself something to eat." Melanie, he couldn't help observing, looked remarkably fetching this evening in a white peasant-style dress that reached to her bare feet, her long brown hair loose about her shoulders, her eyes bright and dilated. "First," he added.

"There's some pizza left from dinner. If you like pizza."

Oh, yes, he assured her, he loved pizza. He followed Melanie down the hall to the ground-floor living-room, luridly lit by a large orange paper globe suspended about two feet from the floor, and furnished with low tables, mattresses, cushions, an inflatable armchair, brick-and-plank bookshelves and an expensive-looking complex of stereo equipment emitting plaintive Indian music. The walls were covered with psychedelic posters and the floor was littered with ashtrays, plates, cups, glasses, magazines and record sleeves. There were three young men in the room and two young women. The latter, Melanie's flat-mates Carol and Deirdre, Philip had already met. Melanie introduced him casually to the three young men, whose names he promptly forgot, identifying them by the various kinds of fancy dress they wore—one in

Confederate Civil War uniform, one in cowboy boots and a tattered ankle-length suede topcoat and the third in loose black judo garb—he was also black himself and wore sunglasses with black frames, just in case there was any doubt about where he stood on the racial issue.

Philip sat down on one of the mattresses, feeling the shoulders of his English suit ride up to nuzzle his ears as he did so. He took off the jacket and loosened his tie in a feeble effort to fit in with the general sartorial style of the company. Melanie brought him a plate of pizza and Carol poured him a glass of harsh red wine from a gallon bottle in a wicker basket. While he ate, the others passed from hand to hand what he knew must be a "joint." When he had finished the pizza he hastily lit his pipe, thus excusing himself from partaking of the drug. Puffing clouds of smoke into the air, he gave a humorous account, which went down quite well, of how he had found himself left alone in the Hogans' house.

"You were trying to make out with this woman?" asked the black wrestler.

"No, no, I got trapped. As a matter of fact, she's the wife of the man I'm replacing here. Professor Zapp."

Melanie looked startled. "I didn't know that."

"D'you know him?" Philip asked.

"Slightly."

"He's a fascist," said the Confederate Soldier. "He's a well-known campus fascist. Everybody knows Zapp."

"I took a course with Zapp once," said the Cowboy. "Gave me a lousy 'C' for a paper that got an 'A' the last time I used it. I told him, too."

"What did he say."

"Told me to fuck off."

"Man!" The black wrestler dissolved into giggles.

"How about Kroop?" said the Confederate Soldier. "Kroop lets his students grade themselves."

"You're putting us on," said Deirdre.

"It's true, I swear."

"Don't everybody give themselves 'A's?" asked the black wrestler.

"It's funny, but no. As a matter of fact there was a chick who flunked herself."

"Come on!"

"No bullshit. Kroop tried to talk her out of it, said her paper was worth at least a 'C,' but no, she insisted on flunking."

Philip asked Melanie if she was a student at Euphoric State.

"I was. I sort of dropped out."

"Permanently?"

"No. I don't know. Maybe."

All of them, it appeared, either were or had been students at the University, but like Melanie they were vague and evasive about their backgrounds and plans. They seemed to live entirely in the present tense. To Philip, who was always squinting anxiously into his putative future and casting worried glances over his shoulder at the past, they were scarcely comprehensible. But intriguing. And friendly.

He taught them a game he had invented as a postgraduate student, in which each person had to think of a well-known book he hadn't read, and scored a point for every person present who *had* read it. The Confederate Soldier and Carol were joint winners, scoring four points out of a possible five with *Steppenwolf* and *The Story of O* respectively, Philip in each case accounting for the odd point. His own nomination, *Oliver Twist*—usually a certain winner—was nowhere.

"What d'you call that game?" Melanie asked Philip.

"Humiliation."

"That's a great name. *Humiliation . . .*"

"You have to humiliate yourself to win, you see. Or to stop others from winning. It's rather like Mr. Kroop's grading system."

Another joint was circulating, and this time Philip took a drag or two. Nothing special seemed to happen, but he had been drinking the red wine steadily enough to keep up with the developing and enveloping mood of the party—for a party was what it appeared to be, or perhaps encounter group. This was a term new to Philip, which the young people did their best to explain to him.

"It's like, to get rid of your inhibitions."

"Overcome loneliness. Overcome the fear of loving."

"Recover your own body."

"Understand what's really bugging you."

They exchanged anecdotes.

"The worst is the beginning," said Carol. "When you're feeling all cold and uptight and wishing you hadn't come."

"And the one I went to," said the Confederate Soldier, "we didn't know who was the group leader, and he didn't identify himself, like deliberately, and we all sat there for an hour, a solid hour, in total silence."

"Sounds like one of my seminars," said Philip. But they were too engrossed in the subject to respond to his little jokes.

Carol said: "Our leader had a neat idea to break the ice. Everybody had to empty their purses and wallets on to the table. The idea was total self-exposure, you know, turning yourself inside out, letting everybody see what you usually keep hidden. Like rubbers and tampax and old love letters and holy medals and dirty pictures and all. It was a revelation, you've no idea. Like one guy had this picture of this man on a beach, completely naked except for a gun in a holster. Turned out to be the guy's father. How about that?"

"Groovy," said the Confederate Soldier.

"Let's do it now," said Philip, tossing his wallet into the ring.

Carol spread the contents on the floor. "This is no good," she said. "Just what you'd expect to find. All very boring and moral."

"That's me," sighed Philip. "Who's next?" But no one else had a wallet or a purse to hand.

"That's a lot of crap anyway," said the Cowboy. "In *my* group we're trying to learn body-language . . ."

"Are these your children?" Melanie asked, going through his photographs. "They're cute, but they look kind of sad."

"That's because I'm so uptight with them," said Philip.

"And is this your wife?"

"She's uptight, too," he said. He found the new word expressive. "We're a very uptight family."

"She's lovely."

"That was taken a long time ago," said Philip. "Even I was lovely then."

"I think you're lovely now," said Melanie. She leaned over and kissed him on the mouth.

Philip felt a physical sensation he hadn't felt for more than twenty years: a warm, melting sensation that began in some deep vital centre of his body and spread outwards, gently fading, till it reached his extremities. He recaptured, in that one kiss, all the helpless rapture of adolescent eroticism—and all its embarrassment too. He couldn't bring himself to look at Melanie, but stared sheepishly at his shoes, dumb, his ears burning. Fool! Coward!

"Look, I'll show you," said the Cowboy, stripping off his suede coat. He stood up and shoved aside with his foot some of the dirty crockery littering the floor. Melanie stacked up the plates and carried them out to the kitchen.

Philip trotted ahead of her, opening doors, happy at the prospect of a tête-à-tête at the sink. Washing up was more his scene than body language.

"Shall I wash or wipe?" he asked, and then, as she looked blank: "Can I help you with the dishes?"

"Oh, I'll just leave them to soak."

"I don't mind washing up, you know," he wheedled. "I quite like it, really."

Melanie laughed, showing two rows of white teeth. One of the upper incisors was crooked: it was the only flaw he could detect in her at this moment. She was pretty as a poster in her long white dress gathered under the bosom and falling straight to her bare feet.

"Let's just leave them here."

He followed her back to the living-room. The Cowboy was standing back to back with Carol in the middle of the room. "What you have to do is communicate by rubbing against each other," he explained, suiting actions to words. "Through your spine, your shoulder-blades—"

"Your ass . . ."

"Right, your ass. Most people's backs are dead, just *dead*, from not being used for anything, you dig?" The Cowboy made way for the Confederate Soldier, and began to supervise Deirdre and the black wrestler.

"You want to try?" Melanie said.

"All right."

Her back felt straight and supple against his scholar's stoop, her bottom was pressed firmly and blissfully against his thin shanks, her hair was thrown back and cascaded down his chest. He was transported. She was giggling.

"Hey, Philip, what are you trying to tell me with the shoulder-blades?"

Someone dimmed the lights and turned up the sitar music. They swayed and pressed and wriggled against each other in the twanging, orange, smoky twilight, it was a kind of dance, they were all dancing, he was dancing—at last: the free, improvised, Dionysian dancing he'd hankered after. He was doing it.

Melanie's eyes were fixed on his, but vacantly. Her body was listening to the music. Her eyelids listened, her nipples listened, her little toes listened. The music had gone very quiet, but they didn't lose it. She swayed, he swayed, they all swayed, swayed and nodded, very slightly, keeping time, responsive to the sudden accelerations and slowings of the plucking fingers, the light patter of the drum, the swerves and undulations of tone and timbre. Then the tempo became faster, the twanging notes louder, faster and louder, and they moved more violently in response to the music, they writhed and twitched, stamped and lifted their arms and snapped their fingers and clapped their hands. Melanie's hair swept the floor and soared towards the ceiling, catching the orange light in its million fine filaments, as she bent and straightened from the waist. Eyes rolled, sweat glistened, breasts bounced, flesh smacked flesh; cries, shrill and ecstatic, pierced the smoke. Then abruptly the music stopped. They collapsed on to cushions, panting, perspiring, grinning.

Next, the Cowboy had them do foot massage. Philip lay face down on the floor while Melanie walked up and down his back in her bare feet. The experience was an exquisite mixture of pleasure and pain. Though his face was pressed to the hard floor, his neck twisted, the breath squeezed out of his lungs, his shoulder-blades pushed nearly through his chest and his spine was creaking like a rusty hinge, he could have had an orgasm without difficulty— hardly surprising when you thought about it, some men paid good money in brothels for this kind of thing. He groaned softly as Melanie balanced on his buttocks. She jumped off.

"Did I hurt you?"

"No, no, it's all right. Carry on."

"It's my turn."

No, he protested, he was too heavy, too clumsy, he would break her back. But she insisted, prostrated herself before him in her white dress like a virgin sacrifice. Talk about brothels . . . Out of the corner of his eye he saw Carol jumping up and down on the mountainous figure of the black wrestler, "Stomp me baby, stomp me," he moaned; and in a dark corner the Cowboy and the Confederate soldier were doing something extraordinary and complicated with Deirdre that involved much grunting and deep breathing.

"Come on, Philip," Melanie urged.

He took off his shoes and socks and climbed gingerly on to Melanie's back, balancing himself with outstretched arms as the flesh and bone yielded under his weight. Oh God, there was a terrible kind of pleasure in kneading the soft girl's body under his calloused feet, treading grapes must be rather like it. He felt a dark Lawrentian joy in his domination over the supine girl even as he felt concern for her lovely bosom crushed flat against the hard floor, unprotected, unless he was much mistaken, by any undergarment.

"I'm hurting you?"

"No, no, it's great, it's doing my vertebrae a whole lot of good, I can feel it."

He balanced himself on one foot planted firmly in the small of her back and with the other gently rotated the cheek of each buttock in turn. The foot, he decided, was a much underestimated erogenous zone. Then he overbalanced and stepped backwards on to a coffee cup and saucer, which broke into several pieces.

"Oh dear," said Melanie, sitting up. "You haven't cut your foot?"

"No, but I'd better get rid of these pieces." He slipped on his shoes and shuffled out to the kitchen with the broken fragments. As he was disposing of these in the trash can, the Cowboy rushed into the kitchen and began opening cupboards and drawers. He was wearing only jockey shorts.

"Seen the salad oil anywhere, Philip?"

"People getting hungry again?"

"No, no. We're all gonna strip and rub each other with oil. Ever tried it? It's terrific. Ah!" He pulled out of a cupboard a large can of corn-oil and tossed it triumphantly in the air.

"Do you need pepper and salt?" Philip jested weakly, but the Cowboy was already on his way out. "C'mon!" he threw over his shoulder. "The party's beginning to swing."

Philip laced up his shoes slowly, deferring decision. Then he went into the hall. Laughter, exclamations and more sitar music were coming from the darkened living-room. The door was ajar. He hesitated at the threshold, then moved on, out of the apartment, up the staircase to his own empty rooms, one part of himself saying ruefully, "You're too old for that sort of thing, Swallow, you'd only feel embarrassed and make a fool of yourself and what about Hilary?" and another part of himself saying, "Shit!" (a word he was surprised to hear himself using, even mentally) "Shit, Swallow, when were you ever *young* enough for that sort of thing? You're just scared, scared of yourself and scared of your wife and think of what you've missed, rubbing salad oil into Melanie Byrd, just think of that!" Thinking of it, he actually turned round outside his door, debating whether to go back, but was surprised to find Melanie herself rustling up the stairs behind him to whisper, "Mind if I crash in your place tonight? I happen to know one of those guys had clap not too long ago."

"Not at all," he murmured faintly, and let her in to the apartment, suddenly sober, his heart thumping and his bowels melting, wondering, was this it?—after twelve years' monogamy, was he going to make love to another woman? Just like that? Without preliminaries, without *negotiations*? He switched on the light inside the apartment, and they both blinked in the sudden dazzle. Even Melanie looked a little shy.

"Where d'you suggest I sleep?" she said.

"I don't know, where would you like to sleep?" He led her down the hall, throwing open doors like a hotel porter. "This is the main bedroom," he said, switching on the light and exhibiting the king-size bed that felt as big as a playing field when he stretched out in it at night. "Or there's this other room which I use as a study, but it has a bed in it." He went into the study and swept some books and papers off the couch. "It's really quite comfortable," he said, pressing the mattress with splayed fingers. "Take your choice."

"Well, I guess it depends on whether you want to fuck or not."

Philip winced. "Well, how do you feel about it?"

"I'd just as soon not, to tell you the truth, Philip. Nothing personal, but I'm tired as hell." She yawned like a cat.

"In that case, you take my bed, and I'll sleep in here."

"Oh no, I'll take the couch." She sat down on it emphatically. "This is fine, really."

"Well, if you insist . . . the bathroom is at the end of the hall."

"Thanks. This is really kind of you . . ."

"Don't mention it," Philip said, bowing himself out of the room. He didn't know whether to feel glad or sorry at his dismissal, and the indecision kept him awake, rolling fretfully about in his king-size bed. He turned the clock-radio on low, hoping it would send him to sleep. It was tuned where he had left it the previous night, to the Charles Boon Show. The Black Pantheress was explaining to a caller the application of Marxist-Leninist revolutionary theory to the situation of oppressed racial minorities in a late stage of industrial capitalism. Philip switched off. After a while he went to the bathroom to get an aspirin. The door of his study was ajar, and without premeditation he turned into it. Melanie was sleeping peacefully: he could hear her deep, regular breathing. He sat down at his desk and turned on the reading lamp. Its hooded light threw a faint radiance on the sleeping girl; her long hair spread romantically over the pillow, one bare arm hanging to the floor. He sat in his pyjamas and looked at her until one of his feet went to sleep. As he tried to rub life back into it, Melanie opened her eyes, staring at him blankly, then fearfully, then with drowsy recognition.

"I was looking for a book," he said, still rubbing his foot. "Can't seem to get to sleep." He laughed nervously. "Too excited . . . at the thought of you in here."

Melanie raised the corner of the coverlet in a silent gesture of invitation.

"Very kind of you, you're sure you don't mind?" he murmured, like someone for whom room has been made in a crowded railway compartment. The bed was indeed crowded when he got into it, and he had to cling to Melanie to avoid falling out. She was warm and naked and lovely to cling to. "Oh," he said, and, "Ah." But it wasn't altogether satisfactory. She was still half-asleep and he was half-distracted by the novelty of the situation. He came too soon and gave her little pleasure. Afterwards, in her sleep, tightening her arms round his neck, she whimpered, "Daddy." He stealthily disengaged himself from her embrace and crept back to his king-size bed. He did not lie down on it: he knelt at it, as though it were a catafalque bearing the murdered body of Hilary, and buried his face in his hands. Oh God, the guilt, the guilt!

And Morris Zapp felt some pangs of guilt as he listened, cowering behind his door, to the wails of Bernadette and the imprecations of Dr. O'Shea, as the latter chastised the former with the end of his belt, having caught her in the act of reading a filthy book, and not merely reading it but abusing herself at the same time—an indulgence that was (O'Shea thundered) not only a mortal sin which would whisk her soul straight to hell should she chance to expire before reaching the confessional (as seemed, from her screams, all too possible) but was also a certain cause of physical and mental degeneration, leading to blindness, sterility, cancer of the cervix, schizophrenia, nymphomania and general paralysis of the insane . . . Morris felt guilty because the filthy book in question was the copy of *Playboy* he had been perusing earlier that evening, and which he himself had given to Bernadette an hour before, having discovered her reading it by the flickering light of the TV on his return from ferrying O'Shea to and from Mrs. Reilly, so engrossed that she was a microsecond too late in closing the magazine and pushing it under the chair. Blushing and cringing, she stammered some apology as she sidled towards the door.

"You like *Playboy*?" Morris said soothingly. She shook her head suspiciously. "Here, borrow it," he said, and tossed her the magazine. It fell on the floor at her feet, opening, as it happened, on the centrefold of Miss January, tilting her ass invitingly at the camera. Bernadette flashed him a disconcertingly gap-toothed grin.

"T'anks mister," she said; and snatching up the magazine, she disappeared.

Now her screams had subsided to a muffled sobbing and, hearing the footsteps of the outraged *paterfamilias* approaching, Zapp scuttled back to his chair and turned on the TV.

"Mr. Zapp!" said O'Shea, bursting into the room and taking up his stand between Morris and the TV.

"Come in," said Morris.

"Mr. Zapp, it's no business of mine what you choose to read—"

"Would you mind raising your right arm just a little?" said Morris. "You're cutting out part of the screen."

O'Shea obligingly lifted his arm, thus resembling a man taking the oath in court. A luridly coloured advertisement for Strawberry Whip swelled like an obscene blister under his armpit. "But I must ask you not to bring pornography into the house."

"Pornography? Me? I haven't even got a pornograph," Morris quipped, confident that the gag would be new to O'Shea.

"I'm referring to a disgusting magazine which Bernadette took from your room. Without your knowledge, I trust."

Morris evaded this probe, which indicated that plucky Bernadette hadn't squealed. "You don't mean my copy of *Playboy*, by any chance? But that's ridiculous, *Playboy* isn't *pornography*, for heaven's sake! Why, clergymen read it. Clergymen *write* for it!"

"Protestant clergymen, perhaps," O'Shea sniffed.

"Can I have it back, please," said Morris. "The magazine."

"I have destroyed it, Mr. Zapp," O'Shea declared severely. Morris didn't believe him. Inside thirty minutes he would be holed up somewhere, jerking himself off and drooling over the *Playboy* pix. Not the girls, of course, but the full-colour ads for whisky and hi-fi equipment . . .

The commercials on the TV ended and the credits for one of O'Shea's favourite series appeared on the screen accompanied by its unmistakable theme tune. The doctor began to watch out of the corner of his eye, while his body maintained a stiff pose of umbrage.

"Why don't you siddown and watch?" said Morris.

O'Shea subsided slowly into his customary chair.

"It's nothing personal you understand, Mr. Zapp," he muttered sheepishly. "But Mrs. O'Shea would never let me hear the last of it if she found the girl reading that sort of stuff. Bernadette being her niece, she feels responsible for the girl's moral welfare."

"That's natural," Morris said soothingly. "Scotch or Bourbon?"

"A little drop of Scotch would be very welcome, Mr. Zapp. I apologize for my outburst just now."

"Forget it."

"We're men of the world, of course. But a young girl straight from Sligo . . . I think it would put our minds at rest if you would keep any inflammatory reading matter under lock and key."

"You think she may break in here?"

"Well she does come in to clean the rooms, in the daytime . . ."

"You don't say?"

Morris paid an extra thirty shillings a week for this service, and doubted whether much, if any, of the money found its way to Bernadette. Passing her on the stairs the next morning, Morris slipped her a pound note. "I understand you've been cleaning my rooms," he said. "You've done a real nice job." She flashed him her toothless grin and looked yearningly into his eyes.

"Shall I come to ye tonight?"

"No, no." He shook his head in alarm. "You misunderstand me." But she had heard the heavy tread of Mrs. O'Shea on the landing, and passed on. There was a time when Morris would have snapped up a chance like this, teeth or no teeth, but now—whether it was his age, or the climate, he didn't know—but he didn't feel up to it, he couldn't make the effort, or face the possible complications. He could picture all too easily the consequences of being found by the O'Sheas in bed with Bernadette, or even behind a door at which she was suing for admittance. Nothing was worth the price of looking for new accommodation in Rummidge in mid-winter. To avoid any accidents, and to give himself a well-deserved break, Morris decided to take a trip to London and stay overnight.

. . .

Philip woke sweating from a dream in which he was washing up in the kitchen at home. Plate after plate dropped from his nerveless fingers and smashed on the tiles underneath the sink. Melanie, who seemed to be helping him, was staring with dismay at the growing pile of shards. He groaned and rubbed his eyes. At first he was conscious only of physical discomfort: indigestion, headache and a sulphurous taste in his mouth. On his way to the bathroom his bleary gaze was drawn, through the open door of his study, to the tousled sheets on the couch, and he remembered. He croaked her name: "Melanie?" There was no answer. The bathroom was empty. So was the kitchen. He drew the curtains in the living-room and cringed as daylight flooded the room. Empty. She had gone.

Now what?

His soul, like his stomach, was in turmoil. Melanie's casual compliance with his tired, clumsy lust seemed, in retrospect, shocking, moving, exciting, baffling. He couldn't guess what significance she might attach to the event; and didn't know, therefore, how to behave when they next met. But, he reminded himself, holding his throbbing head in both hands, problems of etiquette were secondary to problems of ethics. The basic question was: did he want to do it again? Or rather (since that was a silly question, who wouldn't want to do it again) *was* he going to do it again, if the opportunity presented itself? Not for nothing had he taken up residence in a Slide Area, he thought sombrely, gazing out of the window at the view.

He did a lot of looking out of the window that day, unwilling to venture out of his apartment until he had decided what to do about Melanie— whether to cultivate the connection, or pretend that nothing had happened. He thought of putting through a long-distance call to Hilary to see whether the sound of her voice would act like some kind of electro-shock therapy on his muddled mind, but at the last minute his courage failed him and he asked the operator for Interflora instead. The sun set on his indecision. He retired early and woke in the middle of the night after a wet dream. Clearly he was reverting rapidly to adolescence. He turned on the radio and the first word he heard was "pollution." Charles Boon was talking about the end of the world. Apparently the U.S. Army had buried some canisters of nerve gas, enough to kill the entire population of the globe, deep in underground caves and encased in solid concrete, but unfortunately the U.S. Army had overlooked the fact that the caves were on the line of the same geological fault that ran through the state of Euphoria.

The thing to do, Philip decided, was to see Melanie and have a heart-to-heart talk with her. If he explained his feelings, perhaps she could sort them out for him. What he had vaguely in mind was a mature, relaxed, friendly relationship which wouldn't entail their sleeping together again, but wouldn't entirely rule out such a possibility either. Yes, tomorrow he would see Melanie. He fell asleep again and dreamed, this time, that he was the last man out of Esseph at the time of its second and final earthquake. He was alone in an airplane taking off from Esseph airport, and as it hurtled down the runway he looked out of the window and saw cracks spreading like crazy paving in the tarmac. The plane lifted off just as the ground seemed to open to swallow it. It climbed steeply, and banked, and he stared out of the window at the unbelievable sight of the city of Esseph, its palaces and domes, its cloud-capped skyscrapers, burning and collapsing and sliding into the sea.

Next morning the Bay and the city were still there, smiling in the sunshine, awaiting the rabbit punch of the earthquake; but Melanie was not to be found—not that day, nor the next day, nor the day after that. Philip went in and out of the house at all hours, found pretexts for lingering in the hall and whistled loudly on the stairs, all to no avail. He saw Carol and Deirdre often enough and eventually summoned up the courage to ask them if Melanie was around. No, they said, she had gone away for a few days. Was there anything they could do for him? He thanked them: no.

That afternoon he fell over a pair of boots in a corridor of Dealer Hall which proved to belong to the Cowboy, squatting on the floor outside Howard Ringbaum's door, waiting for a consultation.

"Hi!" said the Cowboy, with a leer. "How's Melanie?"

"I don't know," said Philip. "I haven't seen her lately. Have you?"

The Cowboy shook his head.

Ringbaum's thin, nasal voice floated out into the corridor: "You seem to confuse the words *satire* and *satyr* in your paper, Miss Lennox. A satire is a species of poem; a satyr is a lecherous creature, half man, half goat, who spends his time chasing nymphs."

"I have to be going," said Philip.

"Ciao," said the Cowboy. "Hang loose."

That was easier said than done. He felt himself sliding into obsession. That night he was sure it was Melanie's voice that he heard talking to Charles Boon on the radio. Tantalizingly, it was only the tail-end of the conversation that he caught when he switched on. "Don't you think," Melanie was saying, "that we have to aim towards a whole new concept of interpersonal relationships based on sharing rather than owning? I mean, like a socialism of the emotions . . ."

"Right on!"

"And a socialism of sensations, and . . ."

"Yeah?"

"Well, that's all, I guess."

"Well, thanks anyway, that was great."

"Well, that's what I think, Charles. Good night."

"Good night, and call again. Anytime," Boon added meaningfully. The girl—was it Melanie?—laughed and rang off.

"Queue Ex Why Zee Underground Radio," Charles Boon intoned. "This is the Charles Boon Show, the one Governor Duck tried to get banned. Call 024-9898 and let's hear what's on your mind."

Philip jumped out of bed, pulled on his dressing gown, and ran downstairs to the ground-floor apartment. He rang the bell. After a longish pause, Deirdre came to the door and called through it.

"Who are you?"

"It's me, Philip Swallow. I want to speak to Melanie."

Deirdre opened the door. "She's not here."

"I just heard her speaking on the radio. She phoned in to the Charles Boon show."

"Well, she didn't call from here."

"Are you sure?"

Deirdre opened the door wide. "You want to search the apartment?" she inquired ironically.

"I'm terribly sorry," said Philip.

I must snap out of this, he said to himself as he climbed the stairs. I need a break, some distraction. On his next free day he took a bus across the long, double-decker bridge into downtown Esseph. He alighted at exactly the same moment (though seven hours earlier by the clock) that Morris Zapp, seated in the grill-room of the London Hilton, sank his teeth luxuriously into the first respectable-looking steak he had seen since arriving in England.

. . .

The Hilton was a damned expensive hotel, but Morris reckoned that he owed himself some indulgence after three weeks in Rummidge and in any case he was making sure that he got full value out of his occupation of the warm, sound-proofed and sleekly furnished room on the sixteenth floor. He had already showered twice since checking in, and walked about naked on the fitted carpet, bathed in fluent waves of heated air, had climbed back into bed to watch TV and ordered his lunch from Room Service—a club sandwich with french fries on the side preceded by a large Manhattan and followed by apple pie *à la mode*. All simple everyday amenities of the American way of life—but what rare pleasures they seemed in exile.

However, perhaps it was time he put his nose outside the revolving doors and took a look at Swinging London, he conceded, as he waddled from the dining-room with a comfortably full belly and selected an expensive Pana-tella from the cigar store in the lobby. He donned overcoat and gloves and a Khrushchev hat in black nylon fur he had bought from a Rummidge chain store, and sallied out into the raw London night. He walked along Pic-cadilly to the Circus, and then, via Shaftesbury Avenue, he found himself in Soho. Touts shivering in the doorways of strip-clubs accosted him every few yards.

Now Morris Zapp, who had lived for years on the doorstep of one of the world's great centres of the strip industry, namely South Strand in Esseph, had never actually sampled this form of entertainment. Blue movies, yes. Dirty books, of course. Pornography was an accepted diversion of the Euphoric intelligentsia. But strip-tease, and all the specialized variations on it indigenous to Esseph . . .

. . .

Which at this very moment Philip Swallow is observing for the first time: having walked to the South Strand district to look up old haunts he now stands gawping incredulously at the strip-joints that jostle each other all along Cortez Avenue—topless and bottomless ping-pong, roulette, shoe-shine, barbecue, all-in wrestling and go-go dancing—where once stood sober saloons and cafés and handicraft shops and art galleries and satirical night-clubs and poetry cellars, now GIRLS! GIRLS! GIRLS! and STRIP-STRIP-STRIP-STRIP in giant neon letters strain against the sun (for it is still only afternoon in Euphoria) and seek to lure the idle male into the smoky-coloured darkness behind the velvet curtains where rock music twangs and thuds and the girls pictured outside with huge polished breasts like the nose-cones of missiles "DANCE BEFORE YOU ENTIRELY NAKED THEY HIDE ABSOLUTELY NOTHING . . ."

. . .

. . . that was strictly for hicks, tourists and businessmen. Morris Zapp's repu-tation as a sophisticate would have been destroyed the moment he was seen by a colleague or student patronizing one of the South Strand strip-bars. "What, Morris Zapp? going to *topless* shows? Morris Zapp *paying* to see bare tits? What is this, Morris, not getting enough of it these days?" And so on and thus would have been the badinage. So Morris had never crossed the thresh-old of any strip-club on South Strand, though he had often felt a stab of low curiosity, passing on his way to a restaurant or movie-house; and now, standing amid the alien porn of Soho, six thousand miles from home, only strangers around to observe him, and not many of those (for it is a cold, raw night) he thinks, "Why not?" and ducks into the very next strip-joint he comes to, under the nose of a disconsolate-looking Indian at the door.

. . .

And "Why not?" thought Philip Swallow. "It's something I've never seen and always wanted to and what's the harm and who's to know and anyway it's a phenomenon of cultural and sociological interest. I wonder how much it would cost." He walked up and down the length of the Avenue assessing the establishments that were open this early in the day and eventually selected a small bar calling itself the Pussycat Go-go, which promised topless and bottomless dancers with no cover charge or other extras. He took a deep breath and plunged into the darkness.

. . .

"Good evening, sir," said the Indian, smiling brilliantly. "One pound, please sir. The performance is about to begin, sir."

Morris paid his pound and pushed through a baize curtain and a swing door. He found himself in a small, dimly-lit room, with three rows of bentwood chairs drawn up before a small, low stage. A spotlight threw a pool of violet light on to the stage, and an ancient amplifier wheezed laboured pop music. The room was very cold and, except for Morris, entirely empty. He sat down in the middle of the front row of chairs and waited. After a few minutes, he went back to the entrance.

"Hey," he said to the Indian.

"You like a drink, sir? Beer, sir?"

"I'd like to see some strip-tease."

"Certainly, sir. One moment sir. If you would be a little patient. The girl arrives very soon, sir."

"Is there only one?"

"One at a time, sir."

"And it's cold as hell in there."

"I bring heat, sir."

Morris returned to his place and the Indian followed, trailing a small electric heater on a long cord—but not quite long enough to reach Morris. The heater glowed feebly in the violet murk some yards from his seat. Morris put on his hat and gloves, buttoned up his topcoat, and grimly lit a fresh cigar, determined to stick it out. He had made a terrible mistake, but he wasn't going to admit it. So he sat and smoked and stared at the empty stage, chafing his chilled limbs from time to time to keep the circulation going.

. . .

While Philip Swallow, having been prepared to be disappointed, cheated, frustrated and finally bored (for was that not the conventional wisdom concerning commercialized sex, that it was a fake and a bore?) found that on the contrary he was not at all bored, but quite entranced and delighted, sitting over a gin and tonic (dear at $1.50, but it was true there was no cover charge) while one of three beautiful young girls danced quite naked not three yards from his nose. And not only were they beautiful, but also unexpectedly wholesome and intelligent-looking, not at all the blowsy, blasé hoydens he had anticipated, so that one might almost suppose that they did it for love rather than money—as though liking, in any case, to shuffle their feet and wiggle their hips to the sound of pop music they thought they might as well take off their clothes while they were about it and give a little harmless pleasure to others at the same time. Three of them there were, and while one danced, another served drinks and the third rested. They wore briefs and little shifts like children's vests and they slipped in and out of these simple garments modestly but quite unselfconsciously in full view of the bar's clientele, for there was no changing-room in the cramped premises, striptease was quite the wrong term, there was no tease about it at all, and they gave each other little friendly pats on the shoulder as they changed over, with all the considerate camaraderie of a convent school relay team. Nothing could have been less sordid.

. . .

Morris's cigar was about half smoked when he heard the voice of a girl raised—apologetically or protestingly, he couldn't be sure, for she was suffering from a head cold—on the other side of the baize curtain. At length the Indian escorted her behind a rough-and-ready screen in one corner of the room. As she scuffed past in boots like Mrs. Swallow's, wearing a headscarf and carrying a little plastic zipper-bag, she looked about as sexy as a Siberian Miss Five Year Plan. The Indian, however, plainly thought his reputation was saved. He was all smiles. Picking up a hand mike and fixing his gaze on Morris, who was still the only customer, he boomed out:

"GOOD EVENING LADIES AND GENTLEMEN! Our first performer this evening is Fifi the French Maid. Thank you."

The music swelled as the Indian manipulated the knobs on his tape recorder, and a blonde wearing a minuscule lace apron over black underwear and stockings stepped into the spotlight and posed with a feather duster.

"Well I'm damned," said Morris aloud.

Mary Makepeace (for that was who it was) took a step forward, shielding her eyes against the light. "Who's that? I know that voice."

"How was Stratford-upon-Avon?"

"Hey, Professor Zapp! What are you doing here?"

"I was going to ask you the same question."

The Indian hurried forward. "Please! please! Customers are not permitted to converse with the artistes. Kindly continue the performance, Fifi."

"Yeah, continue, Fifi," said Morris.

"Listen, this is no customer, this is someone I know," said Mary Makepeace. "I'm darned if I'm going to strip for *him*. With nobody else in the audience, too. It's indecent."

"It's supposed to be indecent. That's what strip-tease is for," said Morris.

"Please Fifi!" the Indian pleaded. "If you begin, maybe other customers will come."

"No," said Mary.

"You're fired," said the Indian.

"OK," said Mary.

"Come and have a drink," said Morris.

"Where?"

"At the Hilton?"

"You talked me into it," said Mary. "I'll fetch my coat."

Morris hurried off eagerly to get a cab. The evening had been suddenly redeemed. He looked forward to getting better acquainted with Mary Makepeace in his cosy room at the Hilton. As the cab drew away from the kerb, he put his arm round her shoulders.

"What's a nice girl like you doing in a joint like that?" he said. "To coin a phrase."

"I hope it's understood I'm just having a drink with you, Professor Zapp?"

"Of course," he said blandly. "What else?"

"For one thing, I'm still pregnant. I didn't go through with the abortion."

"I'm very glad to hear it," Morris said flatly, removing his arm.

"I thought you would be. But there was nothing ethical about my decision, you understand? I still believe in a woman's right to determine her own biological destiny."

"You do?"

"But I chickened out at the last moment. It was the nursing home. Girls wandering about in bedsocks with tears streaming down their cheeks. Toilet bowls full of blood . . ."

Morris shuddered. "Spare me the details," he begged. "But what about the stripping bit? Isn't that exploitation?"

"Sure, but I desperately need the bread. This is one job you can do without a work permit."

"What d'you want to stay in this lousy country for?"

"To have the baby here. I want him to have dual nationality, so he can avoid the draft when he grows up."

"How d'you know it's going to be a boy?"

"Either way, I can't lose. Having babies is free in this country."

"But how much longer can you do this type of work? Or are you changing your act to Fifi the pregnant maid?"

"I see your sense of humour hasn't changed, Professor Zapp."

"I do my best," he said.

. . .

While Philip, now nursing his fourth gin and tonic, and having studied the anatomies of the three Pussycat Go-go girls for some two hours, had reached, he felt, a profound insight into the nature of the generation gap: it was a difference of age. The young were younger. Hence more beautiful. Their skin had a bloom, they still had their back teeth, their bellies were flat, their breasts (ah!) were firm, their thighs (ah! ah!) were not veined like Danish Blue cheese. And how was the gap to be bridged? By love, of course. By girls like Melanie generously giving their firm young flesh to withered old sticks like himself, restoring the circulation of the sap. Melanie! How simple and good her gesture seemed in the clear light of his new understanding. How needlessly he had complicated it with emotions and ethics.

He stood up to leave at last. His foot had gone to sleep again, but his heart was full of goodwill to all men. It seemed entirely natural that, coming out of the Pussycat Go-go, dazzled by the sunbeams slanting low over Cortez Avenue, and a trifle unsteady on his feet because of the liquor and the pins and needles, he should collide with Melanie Byrd herself, as if she had materialized on the pavement in obedience to his wishes.

"Why, Professor Swallow!"

"Melanie! My dear girl!" He grasped her fondly with both hands. "Where have you been? Why did you run away from me?"

"I didn't run away from anybody, Professor Swallow."

"'Philip,' please."

"I've just been staying here in the city, with a friend."

"A boy friend?" he asked anxiously.

"A girl friend. Her husband's in jail—he's one of the Euphoria Ninety-Nine, you know? She gets kind of lonely . . ."

"I'm lonely too. Come back to Plotinus with me, Melanie," he said, the words sounding thrillingly passionate and poetic to his own ears.

"Well, I'm kind of tied up right now, Philip."

"Come live with me and be my love. And we will all the pleasures prove." He leered at her.

"Take it easy, Philip." Melanie smiled apprehensively, and attempted to disengage her arms from his grip. "Those go-go girls have gotten you all excited. Tell me, I've always wondered, are they really quite naked?"

"Quite. But not as beautiful as you, Melanie."

"That's very sweet of you, Philip." She managed to free herself. "I guess I must be going now. See you." She began walking briskly towards the junction of Cortez Avenue and Main Street. Philip limped along beside her. The Avenue was getting busy. Cars honked and hummed in the road, pedestrians jostled them on the pavement.

"Melanie! You can't disappear again. Have you forgotten what happened the other night?"

"Do you have to tell everybody in the street?"

Philip lowered his voice: "It was the first time it ever happened to me."

She stopped and stared "You mean—you were a *virgin*?"

"I mean apart from my wife, of course."

She put her hand sympathetically on his arm. "I'm sorry Philip. If I'd realized what a big deal it was for you, I wouldn't have gotten involved."

"I suppose it meant absolutely nothing to you?" he said bitterly, hanging his head. The sun had dropped behind the rooftops and he shivered in a sudden gust of chill wind off the Bay. The glory had gone from the afternoon.

"It was one of those things that happen when you get a little high. It was nice, but . . . you know." She shrugged.

"I know it wasn't very successful," he mumbled. "But give me another chance."

"Philip, please."

"At least have dinner with me here. I must talk . . ."

She shook her head. "Sorry, Philip. I just can't. I have a date."

"A date? Who with?"

"Just a guy. I don't know him all that well, actually, so I don't want to keep him waiting."

"What are you going to do with him?"

Melanie sighed. "If you must know, I'm going to help him look for an apartment. Seems his roommate freaked out on LSD and burned their place down last night. See you, Philip."

"He can sleep in my spare room, if you like," Philip bid desperately, clutching at her arm.

Melanie frowned, hesitated. "Your spare room?"

"Just for a few days, while he's looking round. Phone him up and tell him. Then come and have dinner with me."

"You can tell him yourself," said Melanie. "He's over there outside Modern Times."

Philip stared across the gleaming, throbbing river of cars to the Modern Times Bookshop, once famous as the headquarters of the Beat Generation. Outside, hunched slightly against the wind, hands thrust deep into the pockets of his jeans, making a bulge like a codpiece, was Charles Boon.

3. Corresponding

Hilary to Philip

Dearest,

Many thanks for your airletter. We were all glad to hear that you had arrived safely, especially Matthew, who saw pictures of an aircrash in America on television and was convinced that it was your plane. Now he's worried by your joke about living in a house that's going to slide into the sea at any moment, so will you please put that right in your next letter.

I expect the girls underneath you will take pity on your wifeless state and offer to wash your shirts and sew buttons etc. I can't see you coping with that washing-machine in the basement. Incidentally I'm afraid our own washing-machine is making a terrible grinding noise and the service man says the main bearing is going and it will cost £21 to repair. Is it worth it, or shall I trade it in for a new one while it's still working?

Yes, the view, I do remember it so well, though from the other side of the Bay of course—you remember that funny little attic apartment we had in Esseph. When we were young and foolish . . . Ah well, no point in getting sentimental, with you 6000 miles away, and me with the washing up still to do.

Oh—before I forget—I've not been able to find *Let's Write a Novel*, either here or at the University. Though I couldn't make a really thorough search at the University because Mr. Zapp is already occupying your room. I can't say I took to him. I asked Bob Busby how he was settling in, and he said that very few people had seen much of him—he seems to be a rather silent and standoffish person, who spends most of his time in his room.

Fancy your meeting that rogue Charles Boon on the plane, and his being such a success out there. Americans *are* rather gullible, aren't they?

Love from all of us here,
Hilary

Désirée to Morris

Dear Morris,

Thank you for your letter. Really. I enjoyed it. Especially the bits about Dr. O'Shea and about the four different kinds of electric sockets in your rooms and the Department noticeboard. The kids enjoyed those bits too.

I guess it's the first real letter I've ever received from you—I mean apart from scrawls on hotel notepaper about meeting you at the airport or sending on your lecture notes. Reading it made you seem almost human, somehow. Of course, I could see you were trying like hell to be witty and charming, but that's all right, as long as I'm not taken in. And I'm not. Are you receiving me, Morris? I AM NOT TAKEN IN.

I'm not going to change my mind about the divorce, so please don't waste typewriter ribbon trying to make me. And for that matter, don't abstain from sexual intercourse on my account, either. There was a hint to that effect in your letter, and I'd hate you to feel, when you return, that you'd thrown away six months' good screwing for nothing.

Apropos of that, isn't the Lotus Europa you've ordered a somewhat *young* car for you? I saw one in downtown Esseph yesterday and, well, frankly it's just a penis on wheels, isn't it? As regards the Corvair, I didn't forget to put a card in the Co-op last week, but there's been only one inquiry so far and unfortunately I was out. Darcy took the call and God knows what he told the guy.

The Winter quarter begins this week and, surprise, surprise, there are signs of trouble on campus. A bomb exploded in the men's john on the fourth floor of Dealer last week, presumably intended to go off while one of your colleagues was taking a crap, but the building was evacuated as the result of a tip-off. The Hogans invited me to a lousy cocktail party, but I didn't talk to anyone much, it was the usual crowd of schmucks plus a new one, Charles Boon of the ditto radio show. Oh yes, I nearly forgot, and I met your opposite number, Philip Swallow. I was somewhat slewed by this time and kept calling him Sparrow, but he took it straight on the stiff upper lip. Jesus, if all the British are like him I don't know how you're going to survive. He hadn't even

. . .

Coincidence: just as I was writing that last sentence, I looked out of the window and who should be walking up the drive but Mr. Swallow himself. Not so much walking, actually, as crawling up on his hands and knees. He'd climbed all the way up here on foot from the campus—said it didn't look so far on the street map and he hadn't realized that the road was practically vertical. Turned out he was the guy who had called about the Corvair and he'd come to look at it. So it was too bad I'd met him at the Hogans' because of course I had to tell him all about Nader etc. And naturally enough he decided against it. Actually, I felt kind of sorry for him. Apparently he's already been conned into renting a house built on a slide area so if he'd bought the Corvair he'd have been a pretty lousy actuarial risk whether he went out or stayed at home.

It is very quiet and pleasant here without you, Morris. I have turned the TV to the wall, and spend a lot of time reading and listening to classical music on the hi-fi—Tchaikovsky and Rimsky-Korsakov and Sibelius, all that Slav romanticism you made me feel ashamed of liking when we first met.

The twins are fine. They spend a lot of time holed up together somewhere and I expect they are experimenting sexually but figure there's nothing I can do about it. Biology is their great passion at the moment. They have even developed an interest in gardening, which I have encouraged, naturally, by donating a sunny corner of our precipitous yard. They send you their love. It would be hypocritical of me to do the same.

 Désirée

PS. No, I haven't seen Melanie around. Why don't you write to her yourself?

Hilary to Philip

Dearest,

 A man from Johnson's came round this morning with a huge bunch of red roses which he said you had sent by Interflora. I said there must be some mistake because it wasn't my birthday or anything, but he wouldn't take them back to the shop. I phoned Johnson's and they said, yes, you had ordered them. Philip, is anything the matter? It's not like you. Roses in January must have cost the earth. They were hothouse, naturally, and are dying already.

 Did you get my last letter about not being able to find *Let's Write a Novel*? It seems a long time since we heard from you. Have you started teaching yet?

 I met Janet Dempsey at the supermarket and she said that Robin was determined to move if he doesn't get promotion this session. But surely they can't give him a senior lectureship before you, can they? He's so much younger.

 Write soon, love from
 Hilary

PS. The noise from the washing-machine is getting worse.

Philip to Hilary

Darling,

I was stricken with guilt as soon as I saw your second airletter this morning. *Mea culpa*, but it has been a rather hectic week, with the term, or quarter as they call it, beginning; and I'd hoped that the roses would have been some assurance that I was alive and kicking and thinking of you. Instead of which they seem to have had the opposite effect. I confess I'd put back a fair amount of gin the night before, and perhaps the roses were a morning-after act of atonement. The cocktail party was given by Luke Hogan, the Chairman of the Department, whose wife enlisted my help in coaxing Charles Boon to come and be lionized, an irony I could have done without. Among the other guests was Mrs. Zapp, extremely tight, and in a highly aggressive mood. I didn't take to her at all, but since then, through an odd coincidence, I've had to revise my estimate somewhat in her favour. I followed up an advertisement for a second-hand Chevrolet Corvair, which turned out to be the Zapps' second car. But when Mrs. Zapp recognized me she told me that the Corvair is considered an unsafe model, and very honestly advised me not to buy it.

The Zapps live in a luxurious house, in some disarray when I called, at the top of an incredibly steep hill. There are two young Zapps, twins, called rather preposterously Elizabeth and Darcy (Zapp is a Jane Austen man, of course—indeed *the* Jane Austen man in the opinion of many). The gossip here is that their marriage is breaking up, and Mrs. Zapp intimated as much to me, so I suppose that might account for her rather off-putting manner, and his too, by the sound of it. The divorce rate is fantastically high here. It's rather disturbing when one is used to a more stable social environment. So is the way everybody, including Mrs. Zapp, uses four-letter words all the time, even in front of their own children. It's a bit of a shock at first, hearing faculty wives and nice young girls saying "shit" and "fuck," as one might say "Gee whizz," or "darn it." Rather like one's first week in the army.

I confess I had something of the raw-recruit feeling when I went to meet my classes for the first time this week. The system is so different, and the students are so much more heterogeneous than they are at home. They've read the most outlandish things and not read the most obvious ones.

I had a student in my room the other day, obviously very bright, who appeared to have read only two authors, Gurdjieff (is that how you spell him?) and somebody called Asimov, and had never even heard of E. M. Forster.

I'm teaching two courses, which means I meet two groups of students three times a week for ninety minutes, or would do if it weren't for the Third World Students' strike. There's a student called Wily (*sic*) Smith, who claims he's black, though in fact he looks scarcely darker than me, and he pestered me from the day I arrived to let him enrol in my creative writing course. Well, I finally agreed, and then on the first occasion the class met, what d'you think happened? Wily Smith harangued his fellow students and persuaded them that they must support the strike by boycotting my class. There's nothing personal in it, of course, as he was kind enough to explain, but it did seem rather a nerve.

Well, darling, I hope the length of this letter will make up for my remissness of late. Please assure Matthew that my house is not about to slide into the sea. As to Robin Dempsey, I think it's unlikely that he'll get a senior lectureship this year, promotion prospects being what they are at Rummidge, but not through any competition with me, I'm afraid. He has published quite a lot of articles.

All my love,
     Philip

Morris to Désirée

All right, so you're determined to divorce me, Désirée. OK, so you hate my guts, but don't break my heart. I mean, punish me if you must, but there's no need to be downright sadistic about it. Unless you're joking. You're joking, yes? You didn't really throw away the chance to sell the Corvair to Swallow? You didn't actually *advise* him NOT to buy it? Swallow—very probably the only prospective purchaser of a used Corvair in the State of Euphoria. If by any chance Mr. Swallow is still thinking it over, get on the phone at once, please, and offer to come down a couple of hundred dollars. Offer green stamps and a tankful of gas, too, if that will help.

Désirée, your letter did nothing to lighten a heavy week. It isn't true after all that there are no students at British universities: this week they returned from their prolonged Christmas vacation. Too bad, I was just beginning to get the hang of things. Now the teaching has thrown me back to square one. I swear the system here will be the death of me. Did I say system? A slip of the tongue. There is no system. They have something called tutorials, instead. Three students and me, for an hour at a time. We're supposed to discuss some text I've assigned. This, apparently, can be anything that comes into my head, except that the campus bookshop doesn't have anything that comes into my head. But supposing we manage to agree, me and the students, on some book of which four copies can be scratched together, one of them writes a paper and reads it out to the rest of us. After about three minutes the eyes of the other two glaze over and they begin to sag in their chairs. It's clear they have stopped listening. I'm listening like hell but can't understand a word because of the guy's limey accent. All too soon, he stops. "Thank you," I say, flashing him an appreciative smile. He looks at me reproachfully as he blows his nose, then carries on from where he paused, in mid-sentence. The other two students wake up briefly, exchange glances and snigger. That's the most animation they ever show. When the guy reading the paper finally winds it up, I ask for comments. Silence. They avoid my eye. I volunteer a comment myself. Silence falls again. It's so quiet you can hear the guy's beard growing. Desperately I ask one of them a direct question. "And what did *you* think of the text, Miss Archer?" Miss Archer falls off her chair in a swoon.

Well, to be fair, it only happened once, and it had something to do with the kid's period that she fainted, but somehow it seemed symbolic.

Believe it or not, I'm feeling quite homesick for Euphoric State politics. What this place needs is a few bomb outrages. They could begin by blowing up the Chairman of the English Department, one Gordon Masters, whose main interest is murdering wildlife and hanging the corpses on the walls of his office. He was captured at Dunkirk and spent the war in a POW camp. I can't imagine how the Germans stood him. He runs the Department very much in the spirit of Dunkirk, as a strategic withdrawal against overwhelming odds, the odds being students, administrators, the Government, long hair on boys, short skirts on girls, promiscuity, Casebooks, ball-point pens—just about the whole modern world, in short. I knew he was mad the first time I saw him, or half-mad, because it only shows in one eye and he's cunning enough to keep it closed most of the time, while he hypnotizes the faculty with the other one. They don't seem to mind. The tolerance of people here is enough to turn your stomach.

If you notice a certain acidity in my prose today, and hypothesize some wound inflicted on that tender plant, my pride, you wouldn't be far wrong, Désirée, my dear. I was in the Library today, looking through the files of *The Times Literary Supplement* for something, when quite by chance I turned up a long review of that Festschrift for Jackson Milestone that I contributed to in '64, remember? No, of course, you make a point of forgetting anything I have written. Anyway, take my word for it, I wrote a dashing piece on "Apollonian-Dionysian Dialectic in the novels of Jane Austen" for this collection, but for some reason I had never seen this particular review before. Naturally I skimmed through the columns to see whether there was any comment on my contribution, and sure enough there it is: "Turning to Professor Zapp's essay . . ." and I can see at a glance that my piece is honoured with extensive discussion.

Imagine receiving a poison-pen letter, or an obscene telephone call, or discovering that a hired assassin has been following you about the streets all day with a gun aimed at the middle of your back. I mean, the shock of finding some source of anonymous malice in the world directed specifically at you, without being able to identify it or account for it. Because this guy really wanted to hurt. I mean, he wasn't content merely to pour scorn on my arguments and my evidence and my accuracy and my style, to make my article out to be some kind of monument to imbecility and perversity in scholarship, no, he wanted my blood and my balls too, he wanted to beat my ego to a pulp.

Of course I need hardly say that the author was completely out of his mind, that his account of my essay was a travesty, and his own arguments riddled with false assumptions and errors of fact that a child could have seen through. But, but—this is the turn of the screw—there's nothing I can do about it. I mean I can't write to the *TLS* saying, in the usual style, "My attention has been drawn to a review published in your journal four years ago . . ." I should just look ridiculous. That's what bugs me about the whole business—the time-slip. It's only just happened to *me*, but to everybody else it's history. All these years I've been walking around with a wound I never knew had been inflicted. All my friends must have known—they must have seen the knife sticking out between my shoulder-blades—but not one sonofabitch had the decency to tell me. Afraid I'd bite their fucking heads off, I suppose, and so I would have done, but what are friends for anyway? And my enemy, who is he? Some PhD student I flunked? Some limey scholar whose book I chewed up in a footnote? Some guy whose mother I ran over in my car without noticing? Do you remember, Désirée, any exceptionally heavy bump in the road, driving somewhere four or five years ago?

Désirée, your concern that I should have a full sex-life while I am over here is touching, but you should think twice before you put such generous thoughts in writing: it could louse up your divorce petition, though I continue to hope that our marital problem is not terminal. In any case, I haven't felt inclined to avail myself of your kind dispensation. They have winter here, you see, Désirée—the old seasonal bit, and the sap is sunk low at the moment.

Tell me more about the twins. Or, better, ask them to write a line to their old Dad, if the Euphoric public school system is still teaching such outdated skills as writing. But that is great about the gardening. O'Shea is what you might call an avant-gardener. He believes in randomness. His yard is a wilderness of weeds and heaps of coal and broken play equipment and wheelless prams and cabbages, silted-up bird baths and great gloomy trees slowly dying of some unspecified disease. I know how they must feel.

Love,

Morris

ps. I did write to M. but it was sent back marked Not Known Here. Try to get me her new address, will you, from the Dean of Students' Office?

Hilary to Philip

Dearest,

Many thanks for your long and interesting letter. What a pity, though, that you had to write those words in it. Because I couldn't of course let Amanda read it, though she pestered me for days. Rather thoughtless of you, dear, wasn't it, because naturally the children are interested in your letters. And I must say it seemed to me quite uncalled for.

You didn't tell me, by the way, that there was a bomb explosion in your building shortly after you arrived, but I suppose you didn't want to worry us. Were you in any danger? If things get any worse you'll just have to come home, and bother the money.

By the way, as you didn't answer my question about the washing-machine I have bought a new one. Fully automatic and rather expensive, but it's super.

I heard about the bomb from Mr. Zapp. A very curious encounter, which I must tell you about. He came round the other evening with *Let's Write a Novel*, which he'd found in your room after all. It was the most awkward time, about 6, just as I was about to serve up the dinner, but I felt I had to invite him in since he'd taken the trouble to bring your book round and he looked rather pathetic standing in the slush outside the front door wearing galoshes and an absurd kind of cossack's hat. He didn't need any persuading—practically knocked me over in his eagerness to get in the house. I took him into the front room for a quick sherry, but it was like an iceberg—I don't bother to light a fire in there now you're away—so I had to take him into the dining-room, where the children were just beginning a fight because they were hungry for their dinner. I asked him if he would mind finishing his drink while I served the children their meal, hoping this would be a hint to him to leave promptly, but he said no, he didn't mind and I should eat too, and he took off his hat and coat and sat down to watch us. And I mean watch us. His eyes followed every movement from dish to plate to mouth. It was acutely embarrassing. The children fell eerily silent, and I could see that Amanda and Robert were looking at each other and going red in the face with suppressed giggles. In the end I had to ask him if he wouldn't like to join us at the table.

I don't think I've ever seen anyone so heavily built move quite so fast. It was lucky that I'd cooked a biggish joint because there wasn't much left on the bone by the time Mr. Zapp had had his third helping. Though his table manners left something to be desired, I didn't really begrudge him the food, since he was obviously starved of decent home cooking. He also did his best to entertain the children, and made quite a hit with Amanda because he seemed to know all about her favourite pop songs—the names of the singers and the titles of the records and how high they had got in the Top Twenty and so on, which seemed to me quite extraordinary in a man of his age and profession, but impressed the children hugely, especially Amanda as I say. But I presumed he'd have the tact to scoot off fairly soon after dinner, and served coffee straight away to give him the hint. No such luck. He sat on and on, telling stories—admittedly rather funny ones—about the extraordinary household he is living in (a doctor called O'Shea—have you heard of him?) until eventually I just had to send Matthew off to bed and Robert and Amanda to do their homework. When I started ostentatiously clearing the table he insisted on helping me wash up. He obviously had no idea how to do it and broke two plates and a glass before I could stop him. By this time I was beginning to panic a bit, wondering if I was ever going to get him out of the house.

Then suddenly he completely changed. He asked me where the lavatory was and when he came back he was fully dressed in his outdoor clothes and scowling all over his face. He growled out a goodbye and a curt thank you and rushed out of the house into a whirling snowstorm. He started his car and let out the clutch far too quickly and as a result got stuck in the gutter. I listened to his wheels spinning and his engine howling until I couldn't stand it any longer. So I put on my fur coat and boots and went out to give him a push. I got him out all right, but overbalanced in the process and fell sprawling.

As I picked myself off the ground I saw him disappear round the corner, skidding wildly, for he didn't stop or even call out thank you. If Mrs. Zapp wants to divorce him she has my sympathy.

I saw Janet Dempsey again this morning (we seem to have fixed on the same day for supermarket shopping) and she said Robin knows that he's definitely on Gordon's list of nominations for senior lectureships. Are you on it? I think what gets me is the way Janet implies that I'm naturally going to be as fascinated by her husband's career as she is. Also the pointed way she never refers to or asks about yours, as if it were a dead issue. Professor Zapp says you have to push yourself to get on in the academic world, that nobody ever gets anything unless they ask for it, and I'm inclined to think he's right.

Do you still want me to send on *Let's Write a Novel*? What a funny little book it is. There's a whole chapter on how to write an epistolary novel, but surely nobody's done that since the eighteenth century?

Love from all of us here,
Hilary

Philip to Hilary

Darling,

Many thanks for your letter. What an extraordinary fellow Zapp seems to be. I hope he won't bother you any more. Frankly, the more I hear about him, the less I like him. In particular, I shouldn't like Amanda to see more of him than is absolutely unavoidable. The fact is that the man is entirely unprincipled where women are concerned, and while he's not, as far as I know, another Humbert Humbert, I feel he might have an insidiously corrupting influence on an impressionable girl of Amanda's age. So, at least, I infer from Mrs. Zapp, who recited a catalogue of her husband's sins to me in the course of an extremely drunken and disorderly party to which we were both invited last Saturday. Our hosts were Sy and Bella Gootblatt. He's a young associate professor here—very brilliant, I believe, has written the definitive study of Hooker. The Hogans were there, and three other couples all from the English Department, which may sound rather inbred, but you must remember that the English Department here is nearly as big as the entire Arts Faculty at Rummidge.

The tempo of a Plotinus dinner party takes some getting used to. To begin with, the invitation for eight really means eight-thirty to nine, as I realized from the consternation on my host's face when I appeared on his doorstep one minute after the appointed hour; and even when all the guests are assembled there are several hours' hard drinking to be got through before you actually sit down to eat. During this time the hostess (Bella Gootblatt in see-through blouse and flared crushed velvet trousers) brings from the kitchen delicious snacks—sausages rolled in crisp bacon, cheese fondue, sour-cream dips, tender hearts of artichokes, smoked fish and suchlike tangy delicacies, thus increasing one's thirst for the lavish whisky-sours and daiquiris being prepared by the host. The consequence is that when you finally sit down to dine, at about eleven pm, everyone is totally sloshed and not very hungry. The food is half-spoiled anyway by being kept warm so long. Everybody drinks a great deal of wine to try and wash down a respectable amount of food and so they all get drunker than ever. Everybody is shouting at the tops of their voices and cracking jokes frenziedly and screaming with laughter and then someone will say something just a bit too outrageous and suddenly there's murder in the air.

Mrs. Zapp was seated next to me at dinner. As we were sitting over the coffee and the ruins of some intolerably sweet chocolate gateau, I tried to stem her flow of intimate reminiscence by teaching the company how to play "Humiliation." Do you remember that old game? You've no idea how difficult it was to get across the basic idea. On the first round they kept naming books they *had* read and thought everyone else hadn't. But when they finally got the hang of it, they began to play with almost frightening intensity, especially a young chap called Ringbaum who ended up having a tremendous row with our host and left the house in a huff. The rest of us stayed on for an hour or so, mainly (as far as I was concerned anyway, for I was quite exhausted) to smooth over the awkwardness of this contretemps with Ringbaum.

The bomb, yes, I didn't think there was any point in worrying you by mentioning it. There's been no repetition of the incident, though there's still a good deal of disruption on campus due to the strike. As I write this, sitting in my "office" as they call it, I can hear the chanting of the pickets rising up from Mather gate just below my window, "ON STRIKE, SHUT IT DOWN, ON STRIKE, SHUT IT DOWN!" A very strange sound in an academic environment. Every now and then there is a confrontation at the Gate between the pickets and people trying to get through and then the campus police intervene and occasionally the Plotinus police force too and there's usually a scuffle and a few arrests. Yesterday the police made a sweep through the campus and students were running in all directions. I was sitting at my desk reading *Lycidas* when Wily Smith burst into my room and shut the door behind him, leaning against it with closed eyes, just like a film. He was wearing a motor-cycle helmet as protection against the police truncheons (nightsticks as they rather sinisterly call them) and his face was glistening with Vaseline which is supposed to protect your skin against MACE. I asked him what he wanted and he said he wanted a consultation. I had my doubts but dutifully plied him with questions about his ghetto novel. He answered distractedly, his ears cocked for sounds of police activity in the building. Then he asked me if he could use my window. I said, certainly. He threw his leg over the sash and climbed out on to the balcony. After a few minutes I put my head out, but he had disappeared. I suppose he must have found a window open further along the balcony and left that way. The noise gradually faded. I went on reading *Lycidas* . . .

I've no idea whether I've been nominated for a Senior Lectureship and I'd rather keep it that way, since I shan't then have the mortification of knowing that I was definitely turned down. If Dempsey wants to poke his nose into such matters, let him. I think myself that there's a lot to be said for the English system of clandestine patronage. Here, for instance, it's a jungle in which the weakest go to the wall. There's been the most tremendous row going on all this week about a question of tenure—involving the Ringbaum chap, as it happens—and I'm glad to be well out of it.

You'll be surprised to learn that Charles Boon is living with me at the moment! He had to leave his previous quarters at short notice due to a fire and I offered to put him up temporarily at the request of his girlfriend, who lives downstairs. I can't say he's applied himself very energetically to looking for a new apartment, but he's not much trouble to me as he sleeps most of the day and is out most of the night.

All my love,

Philip

Morris to Désirée

What does he look like, Désirée, for Christ's sake? What manner of man is he? Swallow, I mean. Do his canines hang out over his lower lip? Is his handshake cold and clammy? Do his eyes have a murderous glint?

He wrote it, Désirée, he wrote that review, out of pure impersonal spite, one sunny day five years ago he dipped his pen in gall and plunged it into the heart of my lovely article.

I can't prove it—yet. But the circumstantial evidence is overwhelming.

When I think that you dissuaded him from buying the Corvair . . . the perfect revenge! Désirée, how could you?

I found a copy of that Festschrift, you see, in his house. In the john, to be exact. A very strange john it is, too, a large room obviously designed originally for some other purpose, perhaps ballroom dancing, in which the WC has been placed on a plinth in one corner. A tiled floor and a small oil lamp burning to prevent the water pipes from freezing give the whole place a slightly spooky ecclesiastical atmosphere. There are books there too, not specially selected reading for the can, but overspill from the rest of the house, which is practically lined with crappy old books stinking of wet-rot and bookworm droppings. The Milestone book has been festering in my subconscious ever since I read that review in the *TLS*, so I identified its binding and gilt lettering right away. A curious coincidence, I thought to myself, picking the volume off the shelf—for after all it wasn't exactly a world best-seller—and leafed through it as I sat on the can. Imagine my feelings when I turned to my article and found that *the passages which had been marked exactly corresponded to those cited by the TLS reviewer.* Imagine the effect on my bowels.

Why don't you write to me any more, Désirée? I am lonely here these long English nights. Just to give you an idea how lonely I am, this evening I'm going to the English Department's Staff Seminar to listen to a paper on linguistics and literary criticism.

Love,
Morris

Désirée to Morris

Dear Morris,

If you really want to know, Philip Swallow is about six feet tall and weighs I should say about 140 pounds—that is, he's tall and skinny and stooped. He holds his head forward as if he's hit it too often on low doorways. His hair is the texture of Brillo pads before they've been used and is deeply receding at the temples. He has dandruff, but who hasn't? He has nice eyes. I couldn't say anything positively in favour of his teeth, but they don't protrude like fangs. His handshake is normal in temperature, if a little on the limp side. He smokes one of those patent air-cooled pipes which leaks tobacco juice all over his fingers.

I had an opportunity to observe all this because I was seated next to him at dinner last Saturday. The Gootblatts invited me. There seems to be a general conspiracy here to pretend that I am lonely in your absence and must be invited out. It turned out to be a fairly sensational evening, with our friend Swallow right in the centre of the action.

Doing his British best to redeem what was looking to be a draggy dinner, he taught us a game he claims to have invented, called "Humiliation." I assured him I was married to the World Champion, but no, he said, this was a game you won by humiliating *yourself*. The essence of the matter is that each person names a book which he hasn't read but assumes the others have read, and scores a point for every person who has read it. Get it? Well, Howard Ringbaum didn't. You know Howard, he has a pathological urge to succeed and a pathological fear of being thought uncultured, and this game set his two obsessions at war with each other, because he could succeed in the game only by exposing a gap in his culture. At first his psyche just couldn't absorb the paradox and he named some eighteenth-century book so obscure I can't even remember the name of it. Of course, he came last in the final score, and sulked. It was a stupid game, he said, and refused to play the next round. "I pass, I pass," he said sneeringly, like Mrs. Elton on Box Hill (I may not read your books, Zapp, but I remember my Jane Austen pretty good). But I could see he was following the play attentively, knitting his brows and twisting his napkin in his fingers as the point of the game began to dawn on him. It's quite a groovy game, actually, a kind of intellectual strip poker. For instance, it came out that Luke Hogan has never read *Paradise Regained*. I mean, I know it isn't his field, but to think you can get to be Chairman of the English Department at Euphoric State without ever having read *Paradise Regained* makes you think, right? I could see Howard taking this in, going a bit pale when he realized that Luke was telling the truth. Well, on the third round, Sy was leading the field with *Hiawatha*, Mr. Swallow being the only other person who hadn't read it, when suddenly Howard slammed his fist on the table, jutted his jaw about six feet over the table and said:

"*Hamlet!*"

Well, of course, we all laughed, not very much because it didn't seem much of a joke. In fact it wasn't a joke at all. Howard admitted to having seen the Lawrence Olivier movie, but insisted that he had never read the text of *Hamlet*. Nobody believed him of course, and this made him sore as hell. He said did we think he was lying and Sy more or less implied that we did. Upon which Howard flew into a great rage and insisted on swearing a solemn oath that he had never read the play. Sy apologized through tight lips for having doubted his word. By this time, of course, we were all cold sober with embarrassment. Howard left, and the rest of us stood around for a while trying to pretend nothing had happened.

A piquant incident, you must admit—but wait till I tell you the sequel. Howard Ringbaum unexpectedly flunked his review three days later and it's generally supposed that this was because the English Department dared not give tenure to a man who publicly admitted to not having read *Hamlet*. The story had been buzzed all round the campus, of course, and there was even a paragraph alluding to it in the *Euphoric State Daily*. Furthermore, as this created an unexpected vacancy in the Department, they've reconsidered the case of Kroop and offered him tenure after all. I don't suppose he's read *Hamlet* either, but nobody was asking. The students are wild with joy. Ringbaum is convinced Swallow conspired to discredit him in front of Hogan. Mr. Swallow himself is blissfully ignorant of his responsibility for the whole drama.

I'm sorry to have to report that the twins' sudden craze for gardening turned out to be an attempt to cultivate marijuana. I had to root up all the plants and burn them before the cops got wise.

I'm told Melanie hasn't enrolled this term, so I couldn't get her address from the University.

Désirée

Hilary to Philip

Dearest,

I had the most frightful shock this morning. Bob Busby rang me up to ask how you were. I said you were fine as far as I knew, and he said, "Jolly good, so he's out of hospital, then?" and poured out a horrifying story he'd got from some student about how you had been taken hostage by a gang of desperate Black Panthers and held out of a fourth-floor window by your ankles and finally shot in the arm when the police burst into the building blazing away with their guns. It was only about halfway through this lurid tale that I recognized it as a wildly distorted and embroidered version of an anecdote in your last letter which I presumably put into circulation in the first place. I think I must have mentioned it to Janet Dempsey.

Incidentally, Bob told me that Robin took rather a pasting from Morris Zapp at the last Staff Seminar. It seems that Mr. Zapp, despite his somewhat Neanderthal appearance and loutish manners, is really quite clever and knows all about these fashionable people like Chomsky and Saussure and Lévi-Strauss that Robin has been browbeating the rest of you with, or at least enough about them to make Robin look fairly silly. I gather all present derived a certain quiet satisfaction from the proceedings. Anyway, I began to think more kindly of Mr. Zapp, which was rather fortunate for him, as he turned up again yesterday evening to beg a rather odd favour.

It took him some time to get to the point. He kept looking round the room, and asking me about the house and how many bedrooms it had, and wasn't I lonely living on my own, until I began to fear that he wanted to move in with me. But no, it appeared he was looking for accommodation for a friend, a young lady, and he wondered whether I would consider, as a special favour, letting her rent a room. I told him that we'd had students living in the house once and found it such hell that we'd vowed never to have lodgers again. He looked rather crestfallen at that, so I asked him if he'd looked in the Rummidge papers. He shook his head dolefully and said it was no good, they'd already tried several addresses and nobody would have the girl. People were prejudiced against her, he said. Was she coloured, I asked compassionately. No, he said, she was pregnant.

Well, after what you'd said in your last letter about Mr. Zapp's reputation, I drew my own conclusions, which must have been pretty clearly written on my face, for he hastily assured me that he was not responsible. He'd met her on the plane coming over, he said, and he was the only person she knew in England, so she'd turned to him for help. She's an American girl who came to England to get an abortion, but decided at the last moment that she didn't want to go through with it. She wants to have the baby in England because it would then have dual nationality and if it was a boy he would be able to avoid the draft, should the Viet Nam War still be going on in twenty years' time. She'd worked illegally for a while in Soho as a waitress, but had to give it up because her pregnancy was beginning to show. And then she had some money stolen.

Well, this story sounded so implausible that I wondered whether he could possibly have invented it. I didn't know what to think. Where was this girl now, I asked? Outside in his car, he replied, to my astonishment. Well, it was a freezing night, so I told him to bring her inside at once. He was off like a shot and I followed him to the front door. It was like some scene from a Victorian novel, the snow, the fallen woman, etc., but in reverse, because she was coming in instead of going out, if you see what I mean. And I admit to feeling a mite sentimental as she crossed the threshold, with snowflakes melting in her long blonde hair. She was turning blue with cold, poor thing, and practically speechless either from that or shyness. Mary Makepeace is her name. There didn't seem to be anything else to do but ask her to stay the night, so I made some soup (Professor Zapp wolfed three bowls) and packed her off to bed with a hot water bottle. I told Mr. Zapp I would have her to stay for a few days while they worked out something but that I couldn't commit myself to having her indefinitely. However, I'm seriously thinking of letting her stay on. She seems to be a very nice girl, and would be company in the evenings. You know I still get frightened in the night sometimes—silly, I know, but there it is. I'll have to see how we get on on closer acquaintance, of course, and I haven't made any promises. But if I should be inclined to let Mary stay, I presume you wouldn't have any objections? She'd pay for her board and lodging, of course—apparently she didn't lose all her money, and Mr. Zapp was very insistent that he would help financially. I imagine he can afford it. He was driving some incredibly low-slung and expensive-looking orange sports car yesterday, which is to replace the one you didn't buy.

I hope, by the way, that Charles Boon is making a contribution to *your* rent. A hint to that effect might be one way of getting rid of him.

All love,
Hilary

PS. Mr. Zapp asked particularly that if I wrote to you about Mary you should regard all information about her as confidential.

Philip to Hilary

Darling,

Just a note in haste to say that I should think very carefully before you take this girl of Zapp's into the house. And she surely *is* Zapp's girl. Whether he's the father of her child, or not, is another question, but doesn't affect the likely nature of their relationship. I can understand how you would naturally feel sorry for the girl and want to help, but I think you've got to consider yourself in this, and the children, especially Amanda. She's at a very sensitive and impressionable age now—have you thought of the consequences of having an unmarried mother on the premises? The same goes for Robert, for that matter. I can't believe that it would be a good thing for the children. Then Zapp would no doubt be in and out of the house all day—and possibly all night too. Have you thought of *that*? I'm a reasonably tolerant person but I draw the line at providing a room in my house for Mr. Zapp to have it off with his pregnant girlfriend, and I wonder whether you would be able to cope with such a situation, should it arise. Then one has to face the fact, whether one likes it or not, that "people will talk"—and I don't mean just the neighbours, but the people at the University, too.

All in all, I'm not in favour. But of course you must do what you think best.

The situation is getting uglier here. Some windows have been smashed, and catalogue cards in one of the small specialist libraries scattered over the floor. Every lunch hour there is a ritual confrontation which I watch from the balcony outside my room. A large crowd of students, hostile to the police if not positively sympathetic to the strikers, gathers to watch the pickets parading. Eventually someone is jostled, the police intervene, the crowd howls and screams, rocks are thrown, and out of the scrimmage the police come running, dragging some unfortunate student behind them and take him to a temporary lockup under the Administration building, pursued by the hooting mob. Perched up on my safe balcony I feel rather despicable, like those ancient kings who used to watch their set battles from specially built towers. Afterwards one goes home and watches it all over again on the local TV news. And the next morning there are reports and photos in the *Euphoric State Daily*—that's the campus paper, produced with incredible speed and professionalism by the students; makes our own once-a-week *Rumble* seem a rather amateurish effort.

All my love,
Philip

ps. I hope you realize that Mary Makepeace is almost certainly an *illegal immigrant* in the eyes of the law, and that you could get into trouble for harbouring her?

Hilary to Philip

Dear Philip,

I may as well come straight to the point. I've had what I believe is called a poison-pen letter from Euphoria, an anonymous letter. It says you are having an affair with Morris Zapp's daughter. I know it's not true but please write at once and tell me that it isn't. I keep bursting into tears and can't tell anybody why.

Love,
Hilary

XY42 Ab 151 INTL PLOTINUS EUPH 60 9
WESTERN UNION

MRS. HILARY SWALLOW
49 ST JOHNS RD
RUMMIDGE
ENGLAND

POTTY UPPERCOOK COCK COCK COCK
UTTER POPPYCOCK OF COURSE STOP ZAPPS
DAUGHTER ONLY NINE YEARS OLD STOP
LETTER FOLLOWS LOVE PHILIP

PHILIP SWALLOW
1037 PYTHAGORAS DR
PLOTINUS EUPH

Morris to Désirée

Will you do me a favour, Désirée, and move your ass over to 1037 Pythagoras Drive and find out what the hell is going on there? I had a letter this morning, no signature, saying that Philip Swallow is shacked up with Melanie at that address. You may laugh, but just check it out for me, will you? There is a kind of outrageous logic in the notion that makes me think it may just be true. It would fit my idea of Swallow and the role he seems destined to play in my life. Having assassinated my academic character in the *TLS*, he proceeds to screw my daughter. That figures. I tremble, Désirée, I tremble.

    Morris

  PS. The envelope is franked by the University, so it must be someone on the faculty or a secretary who sent the letter. Who?

Philip to Hilary

Darling Hilary,
  This is the most difficult letter I have ever had to write.
  Morris Zapp *has* got a daughter—apart from the nine-year-old. Her name is Melanie and I *did* sleep with her once. Just once. So the wire I sent you was not quite true. But it wasn't a lie, either. I have only just discovered that Zapp is Melanie's father and it's been as much of a shock to me as it will have been to you. Let me try and explain.

Melanie is Zapp's daughter by his first marriage. She calls herself Melanie Byrd, which is her mother's maiden name, because she doesn't want to be associated with her father at Euphoric State, for several good reasons. She came here as a student because as the child of a tenured faculty member she is entitled to free tuition, but she has stayed away from Zapp as much as possible and kept their relationship strictly secret. I got all this information from Mrs. Zapp and Melanie this afternoon. They were in the house together when I got home. I should explain that Melanie is one of the girls on the ground floor. Early on in my time here I quite by chance got drawn into a kind of impromptu party downstairs. I'd just come from cocktails at the Hogans' and was a bit squiffy already. What with one thing and another I suppose I got quite "high," but when they started making preparations for an orgy, I retired gracefully. So, however, did Melanie. She took it for granted that we should sleep together. So I'm afraid we did.

I'm not going to try and justify or excuse myself. I was wretched afterwards, thinking what I'd done to you. It wasn't even particularly enjoyable at the time, because I was fuddled with drink and Melanie was half-asleep. I'm quite sure it meant absolutely nothing to her, and you must believe that it only happened on that one occasion. In fact since then—this would be funny in a less anguished context—she's become Charles Boon's steady girlfriend. In the circumstances, there seemed to be no point in upsetting you by saying anything about the episode, and it began to sink into oblivion. When I got your letter it revived my guilty conscience, though I didn't connect Melanie with Morris Zapp for a moment. I presumed someone was playing a rather sick joke—who and for what reason I couldn't, and still can't—imagine. But it put me in a difficult moral dilemma.

Well, as you know, I took the easier way out, one which I persuaded myself would also be easier on you. But when I discovered the true state of affairs, I immediately sat down to put the record straight. It's now about midnight, so you'll realize how difficult I've found it. I'm sorry, very sorry, Hilary. Please forgive me.

All my love,
    Philip

Désirés to Morris

Dear Morris,

Much as I hate to do you a favour, my curiosity got the better of me, so I hied me over to 1037 Pythagoras in accordance with your brusque instructions. I had to take a detour through the downtown area as the traffic was snarled up due to riots on the Campus at the Cable Street entrance. I could hear gas grenades popping and a lot of yelling and a police helicopter circling overhead all the time: I tell you, it gets more like Viet Nam here every day.

1037 Pythagoras is a house that has been converted into two apartments. Nobody answered the bell on the first floor so I went upstairs and tried the second-floor apartment. Eventually Melanie answered the door, looking flushed and rumpled. Before you start grinding your teeth and fingering your horsewhip, let me finish. We were both surprised, Melanie more so, naturally. "Désirée! What are you doing here?" she exclaimed. "I might ask you the same question," I snapped back in my best Perry Mason manner. "I thought Philip Swallow lived here." "He does but he's out." "Who is it, Mel, the Gestapo?" said a voice from within. I looked over Melanie's shoulder and there was Charles Boon, propped up against the wall dressed in a towelling bathrobe and smoking a cigarette. "Somebody for Philip," she called back. "Philip's out," he said. "He's at the University." "Do you mind if I wait?" I asked. Melanie shrugged: "Please yourself."

I eased myself over the threshold and penetrated into the apartment. Melanie closed the door and followed me. "This is Désirée, my father's second wife," she said to the gaping Boon. "And this is—" "I recognize Mr. Boon, dear," I interrupted. "We were at the same party a few weeks ago. I didn't have the opportunity, Mr. Boon," I prattled on, "to tell you how much I hate your show." He smiled and blew smoke through his teeth while he thought up a riposte; one of his eyes was levelled on me while the other one was shooting about the room as if in search of inspiration. "If someone your age liked the show," he said at last, "I'd know I'd failed." We fenced like this for a while, weighing each other up. It was apparent that Boon was living in Swallow's apartment, which I must say surprised me because I always understood from Swallow that he couldn't stand the guy. However, it certainly looked as though Boon and Melanie had been in the sack together that afternoon, and as neither of them showed any sign of panic when Swallow's latchkey turned in the hall door I assumed that this was not a possibility they were anxious to conceal from him. He was startled of course to see me there, fussed around getting us all tea, but didn't seem particularly defensive. I had just decided that his relationship to Melanie was purely avuncular when it came out that you were her father. He went white, Morris. I mean, if he'd just discovered that he'd screwed his *own* daughter, he couldn't have looked more shocked. I suppose, on reflection, there is something kind of incestuous about sleeping with the daughter of the guy you've exchanged jobs with. Though if he's having sex with Melanie presently, it must be something very kinky because Charles Boon is right in there too, for sure.

As to the author of the poison-pen letter, I will hazard a guess that the author is Howard Ringbaum, who has a motive and is cheap enough to use university mail facilities for the purpose—he's the kind of guy who would make a heavy-breathing call collect if he could get away with it.

Désirée

Morris to Désirée

Many thanks for your quick reply, but why didn't you ask Swallow straight out for Chrissake? I enclose a Xerox of the anonymous letter so that you can confront him with it. What a louse. Mrs. Swallow has been looking so miserable lately that I have a shrewd suspicion she's had one of those letters too. She's a kind-hearted person, I've found, and I feel sorry for her. She told me, by the way, that Boon was once a student of Swallow's. Yes, they're old buddies, so it's all too probable they've got some very corrupt scene going there with Melanie. Poor little Melanie. I feel really bad about her. I mean I didn't suppose she was still a virgin or anything, but that is no life for a young girl, being passed from one guy to another. Maybe if you and I could make a fresh start, Désirée, she would come and live with us.

Morris

Désirée to Morris

Dear Morris,

Will you stop putting on this concerned parent act before I die laughing? It's a little late in the day to start talking about giving a stable home life to "little Melanie." You should have thought about that before you walked out on her and her mother. Little Melanie, in case you've forgotten, hasn't forgiven you for that; and since it was me you walked out on her for (leaving her a five-dollar bill to buy candy, if I remember rightly, the most sordid transaction in the history of conscience-money) she isn't exactly spilling over with love for me either.

I've no intention of confronting Philip Swallow with your dirty little piece of paper. Neither he nor Melanie owe *me* any explanation. Write and ask them yourself if you must. But before you work up too much righteous indignation, and as long as explanations are the order of the day, you might come clean about that blonde cookie you've parked on big-hearted Mrs. Swallow. Rumour has it that she's pregnant. Don't tell me that you're going to pollute the planet with another little Zapp, Zapp? I've heard about the hypocrisy of the English, but I didn't know it was contagious.

Désirée

Philip to Hilary

Darling Hilary,

It's two weeks now since I wrote to you, and I am finding it a strain waiting for your reply. If you haven't already written, please don't keep me waiting any longer. I had hoped that by making a clean breast of everything I should make it possible for you to forgive and forget, and that we could put the whole thing behind us.

I hope you aren't thinking of divorce, or anything silly like that?

It's very difficult to discuss these things by letter. How can you make up a misunderstanding when you're 6000 miles apart? We need to see each other, talk, kiss and make up. I've been thinking, why don't you come out here at Easter on a 17-day excursion? I know the fare is expensive, but what the hell. I expect your mother would take the children in the holiday, wouldn't she? Or perhaps you could even leave them with this Mary Makepeace girl. It would be a real holiday for both of us, away from the kids and everything. What is called a "second honeymoon," I believe—a rather horribly coy phrase but not such a bad idea. D'you remember what fun we had in that scruffy little apartment in Esseph?

Do think about it seriously, darling, and don't be put off by the student troubles. The signs are that with the end of the winter quarter things will quieten down and some kind of compromise will be worked out between the students and the Administration. Today there were no arrests for the first time in weeks. Perhaps the weather has something to do with it. Spring has really arrived, the hills are green, the sky is blue, and it's eighty degrees in the shade. The bay is winking in the sun, and the cables of the Silver Span are shimmering like harpstrings on the horizon. I walked through the campus today at lunchtime and you could sense the change of mood. Girls in summer dresses and people playing guitars. You would enjoy it.

All my love,
    Philip

Morris to Désirée

Désirée,

You're not going to believe this, I know, but Mary Makepeace and I are just good friends. I have never made love to her. I admit the thought has crossed my mind, but she was pregnant when I first met her and I'm squeamish about laying girls who are already pregnant by other guys. Something not quite kosher about it, if you know what I mean. Especially in this case, since the father is a Catholic priest. Did I tell you the plane I flew over in was full of women going to England for abortions? Mary was one of them—she was sitting next to me and we got talking. A few weeks ago I came back from the University one afternoon to be ambushed by O'Shea in the lobby. He leaped out at me from behind the grandfather clock and dragged me into the front parlour, which at this time of year is like the North Pole, huge upholstered armchairs looming out of the fog like icebergs. O'Shea was very agitated. He said that a young woman who was obviously in "a certain condition," but not wearing a ring, had called asking for me and had insisted on waiting in my rooms. It was Mary, of course—she'd decided to stay in England and have the baby, but she'd just lost her job and had some money stolen and turned for help to the only person in the country she knew—me. I tried to calm O'Shea down, but he had the fear of God and Mrs. O'Shea in him. It was obvious that nothing was going to persuade him I wasn't responsible for Mary's "condition." He gave me an ultimatum: either Mary had to leave or me. I couldn't very well abandon the girl, so I tried to find her a place to stay. But there was nothing doing in Rummidge that night. The landladies we talked to obviously regarded Mary as a whore and me as a small-time gangster. I couldn't even find a hotel that admitted to having a vacant room. Then we happened to pass Mrs. Swallow's house, and I thought, why not try her? Which we did, successfully. In fact the two of them have become great buddies and it looks like Mary is going to stay there until she has the baby. I didn't see the point of boring you with all this, and I didn't think Swallow would be so cheap as to run to you with the story.

Morris

Hilary to Philip

Dear Philip,

Many thanks for your last letter. I'm sorry I didn't reply immediately to the previous one, but as it took you six or seven weeks to get round to telling me about Melanie Zapp (or Byrd) it seemed to me that I was entitled to take as many days thinking about my reply.

That doesn't mean to say that I'm considering a divorce—a remarkably panicky reaction on your part, I thought. I take it that you've been quite candid with me, and that you're no longer involved with the girl. I must say it was unfortunate that of all the girls in Euphoria, you had to pick on Mr. Zapp's daughter. Also somewhat ironic, not to say hypocritical, that you should have been so exercised about *his* bad influence on *your* daughter. I showed Mary your letters and she says your obsessive concern to protect Amanda's innocence indicates that you are really in love with her yourself, and that your affair with Melanie was a substitute gratification for the incestuous desire. An interesting theory, you must admit. Does Melanie look anything like Amanda?

As to your suggestion that I fly out to Euphoria for a holiday, it's not on, I'm afraid. First of all I wouldn't dream of asking either Mary or my mother to take on the responsibility of the children, and I don't think we could afford to fly them out to Euphoria—or me on my own for that matter. You see, Philip, I decided not to wait any longer for the central heating, but to have it put in immediately on the HP. It was the first thing I did after receiving your letter about Melanie: I got out the telephone book and began ringing round to heating contractors for estimates. I suppose that sounds funny, but it was quite logical. I thought to myself, here I am, slaving away, running a house and family single-handed for the sake of my husband's career and my children's education, and I'm not even warm while I'm doing it. If he can't wait for sex till he gets home, why should I wait for central heating? I suppose a more sensual woman would have taken a lover in revenge.

Mr. Zapp kindly helped me with the estimates, and managed to knock £100 off the lowest—wasn't that clever of him? But of course the repayments are pretty heavy and the deposit has put our current account in the red, so please send some more money home soon.

But quite apart from the expense and the problem of the children, Philip, I don't think I would want to fly out anyway. I've read through your letter very carefully and I'm afraid I can't avoid the conclusion that you desire my presence mainly for the purpose of lawful sexual intercourse. I suppose you've been frightened off attempting any more extra-marital adventures, but the Euphoric spring has heated your blood to the extent that you're prepared to fly me six thousand miles to obtain relief. I'm afraid I'd find it a strain coming over in that kind of context, Philip. Even the 17-day excursion fare costs £165–15–6, and nothing I can do in bed could possibly be worth that money.

Does this sound cutting? It's not meant to be. Mary says that men always try to end a dispute with a woman by raping her, either literally or symbolically, so you're only conforming to type. Mary is full of fascinating theories about men and women. She says there is a movement for the liberation of women starting in America. Have you come across any signs of it?

I was glad to hear that things are quietening down on the Euphoric campus at last. Believe it or not, we may be in for some student trouble here. There is talk of a sit-in next term. Apparently it's thrown the older members of staff into a flat spin. According to Morris,

Gordon Masters is quite unhinged—has taken to coming into the Department wearing his old Territorial Army uniform.

Love,

Hilary

Désirée to Morris

Dear Morris,

Oddly enough I do believe you about this Mary Makepeace, though the kosher reference was despicable as only you know how to be. But don't blame Philip Swallow for the leak. It was your Irish colleen, the toothless Bernadette, if orthography is any clue, who betrayed you and your "yaller-hared whoor" in a smudged, greasy and tear-stained epistle which I received the other day, unsigned.

Have you ever heard of Women's Liberation, Morris? I've just discovered it. I mean I read about the way they busted up the Miss America competition last November, but I thought they were just a bunch of screwballs. Not at all. They've just started up a discussion group in Plotinus, and I went along the other night. I was fascinated. Boy, have they got *your* number!

Désirée

4. Reading

COUPLE, mid-thirties, fat wife, would like to meet discreet couple.

NESTLING earth couple would like to find water brothers to grock with in peace.

NATURE is where it's at. Big Sur Dylan Hesse Bach baby racoons grass seashores sensitivity creativity sex and love. I want to groove with girl who likes same.

LOOKING for two or more bi girls for joyous 3 or more-somes with attractive man in early thirties. Shapely wife may also join in. Also, if desired, wife's young very feminine attractive transvestite cousin. Inquiries welcomed from gals in pairs or even singly. Especially urge novice inquiries from young singles or jaded housewives who'd like to try on the joys of group sex. Discretion assured. Photo optional but appreciated. If not sure, write anyway.

—small ads., *Euphoric Times*

PLOTINUS WOMEN ON MARCH
The Plotinus Women's Liberation Movement hit the streets Saturday in its first public appearance, to celebrate International Women's Day. Among the banners they carried: "Is it smart to play Dumb?" "You Earn More as a *Real* Whore" and "Free Child Care Centers 24 Hours a Day." The last of these slogans moved a Puerto Rican housewife to hold up the procession: where, please, could she find one of the Centers? The marchers explained regretfully that they didn't exist yet.

—*Plotinus Gazette*

PEOPLE'S GARDEN FOR PLOTINUS
Students and street people moved on to a vacant lot on Poplar Ave, between Clifton and King Streets, at the weekend, to construct what they declared a People's Garden. The land was acquired by the University two years ago, but has been used as an unofficial parking lot since then.

A spokesman for the gardeners said: "This land does not belong to the University. If it belongs to anyone, it's the Costanoan Indians, from whom it was stolen by force two hundred years ago. If any Costanoans show, we'll gladly move out. Meanwhile, we're providing an open space for the people of Plotinus. The University has shown itself indifferent to the needs of the community."

The gardeners worked through the weekend, digging and leveling the ground and laying turf. "I never thought to see a hippie working," said an elderly resident of nearby Pole St.

—*Plotinus Gazette*

EXTRAORDINARY MEETING OF
RUMMIDGE STUDENTS UNION COUNCIL
The following resolutions will be moved under Agendum 4 (*b*): That Union Council:

1. *Urges* the Union Executive to initiate direct action if the University Court of Governors, at its meeting of next Wednesday, does not agree to the following demands:

(*a*) acceptance *in toto* of the document *Student Participation* submitted by the Union to the Senate and Court last November.

(*b*) immediate action to set up a Commission to investigate the structure and function of the University.

(*c*) suspension of classes in all Departments for a two-day teach-in on the constitution and scope of the proposed commission.

HOUSE SLIDE
A small landslip on Pythagoras Avenue has made a house unsafe for habitation, public health officials decided today. Occupants of 1037 Pythagoras were woken at 1:30 am last Saturday night when their house slewed through a 45° turn due to subsidence after a freak rainstorm. No one was hurt.

—*Plotinus Gazette*

CONCERNING THE SITE ON POPLAR AVENUE
BETWEEN CLIFTON AND KING STREETS
This property was purchased and cleared by the University approximately 18 months ago. The University was unable to proceed promptly with the construction of a playing field on the site because of financial difficulties. Funds are now available, and plans for the playing field are moving ahead.

In fairness to those who have worked on the land in recent weeks—many of them motivated by a genuine spirit—the disutility of any additional labour there should be pointed out. The area will be cleared soon in preparation for work on the recreational field.

—Information Office, State University of Euphoria

PARADISE REGAINED
A new Eden is being created in the People's Garden in Plotinus—the most spontaneous and encouraging event so far in the continuing

struggle between the University-Industrial-Military complex and the Alternative Society of Love and Peace. Not just street people and students are working and playing together in the Garden, but ordinary men and women, housewives and children—even professors!

—Euphoric Times

RUMMIDGE GRAND PRIX PROPOSED

A newly formed consortium of Rummidge businessmen and motor-racing enthusiasts put forward plans yesterday to hold Formula 1 motor races on the city's new Inner Ringway system. "The new Ringway is just perfect for motor racing," said the group's spokesman, Jack "Gasket" Scott. "You might have thought this was what the designers had in mind all along."

—Rummidge Evening Mail

EUPHORIC PROF AND STUDENTS ARRESTED
FOR BRICK THEFT

Sixteen persons, including a visiting professor from England and several students, were arrested on Saturday for stealing used bricks from the demolition site of the Lutheran Church on Buchanan Street. The bricks, valued at $7.50, were apparently destined for the People's Garden, where a People's Fishpond is under construction.

—Plotinus Gazette

MILITANT STUDENTS OCCUPY
RUMMIDGE UNIVERSITY ASSEMBLY HALL

Members of Rummidge University's Court of Governors had to push their way through student pickets to attend their meeting yesterday afternoon. The students were demanding that the meeting—called to discuss their Union's document *Student Participation*—should be open to all-comers. Eventually the President of the Union and two other students were allowed to address the Court, but the governors declined to give an immediate answer to the students' demands.

As soon as this was known, about 150 students, already prepared with sleeping bags and blankets, moved into the Assembly Hall of the University. After a discussion on the ideal structure of a reorganized University, an improvised discotheque was set up. About 85 students were still in the hall at 2 am. Later this morning an Extraordinary

General Meeting of the Union will debate a proposal that the occupation of University buildings be endorsed and extended.

—*Rummidge Morning Post*

VISITING PROF AND STUDENTS DISCHARGED

Professor Philip Swallow, British visitor to the English Department, was among sixteen people arrested on Saturday for allegedly stealing bricks from the demolition site on Buchanan St. Charges against the sixteen, mostly Euphoric students, were dismissed at Plotinus Municipal Court yesterday because the owner of the bricks, Mr. Joe Mattiessen, refused to sign the complaint. Some of Professor Swallow's students gathered outside the Court and cheered as he emerged, smiling.

"I've never been busted before," he said. "It was a memorable experience, but I shouldn't care to repeat it."

—*Euphoric State Daily*

STATEMENT BY CHANCELLOR BINDE

We have been presented with a Garden we hadn't planned or even asked for, and no one is entirely happy about it. The people who have been working on the Garden are anxious about the future of their gift. The residents of the area are unhappy about the crowds, the noise and the behaviour of some users of the Garden. The city officers are worried about the crime and control problems presented by the Garden. Many taxpayers are indignant at what they regard as an illegal seizure of university—and therefore State—property. The organizers of intramural sport are unhappy about the prospective loss of playing fields. Most people are worried about the possibility of a confrontation, although others are afraid there might not be one. As for me, I feel the burden of these worries and several I haven't mentioned.

So what happens next? First, we shall have to put up a fence to re-establish the conveniently forgotten fact that the field is indeed the University's property and to exclude unauthorized persons from the site. That's a hard way to make the point, but that's the way it has to be.

—Release from the Chancellor's Office, State University of Euphoria

DEFEND THE GARDEN!
We have taken a solemn oath to defend the Garden, and wage a war
of retaliation against the University if it moves against the Garden. If
we fight the same way as we have worked together on the Garden—
together in teams, with determination, in brotherhood—we shall win.

NO FENCES AGAINST THE PEOPLE

NO BULLDOZERS

**BE MASTERS OF SILENCE, MASTERS OF THE NIGHT
WITH SHOVELS AND GUNS**

POWER TO THE PEOPLE AND THEIR GUNS
                                          The Gardeners
              —Manifesto distributed on the streets of Plotinus

SUPPORT THE OCCUPATION
Students of Rummidge! Support the Occupation at today's Meeting,
then join us in the Assembly Hall. Show the Administration that this
is *your* University, not theirs.
              —Flysheet issued by the Occupation Steering Committee

**POLICE HOLD GARDEN, SHOOT 35. MARCH TRIGGERS
CABLE AV. GASSING. BYSTANDERS, STUDENTS WOUNDED.
EMERGENCY, CURFEW ENFORCED.**
A noon rally and march yesterday to protest the University's seizure of
the People's Garden erupted into a brutal battle between police and
demonstrators lasting all afternoon. Sixty people were hospitalized
and by dusk tear gas had spread through the south campus and adjoining residential districts. Police, openly wielding shotguns, fired
birdshot into surging crowds of demonstrators, many of whom fled
with blood streaming down their faces. One policeman was stabbed
and three others received minor injuries from rocks and shattered
glass. The National Guard has been called out by Governor Duck, and
a curfew has been enforced between the hours of 10 pm and 6 am.

At 6 am yesterday, after police had evicted students and others sleeping out in the People's Garden, the Esseph Fence Company arrived to erect a 10-foot high steel-link

(Contd. back page)
—*Euphoric State Daily*

RUMMIDGE SIT-IN CONTINUES

An extraordinary meeting of the Rummidge University Students' Union, attended by over 1000 students, voted today to endorse and continue the "sit-in" already initiated by 150 left-wing extremists yesterday evening. At the end of their meeting the students went in a body to the Assembly Hall and a number of them forced their way into the office of the Vice-Chancellor's secretary and demanded that the Vice-Chancellor Mr. Stewart Stroud appear to hear their grievances.

"It was a waste of time," one of the students present commented afterwards. "He showed no understanding of the legitimate demands of students for democratic participation in university decision-making."

The students occupied several offices in the Administration Block, causing "considerable alarm" among the secretarial staff, according to a senior official.

—*Rummidge Evening Mail*

GARDENERS AND COPS, GUARDSMEN
CLASH IN DOWNTOWN PLOTINUS

Supporters of the fenced-off People's Garden played cat-and-mouse with police and National Guardsmen over the weekend. On Saturday they invaded the shopping area of downtown Plotinus. Milling over a three block area on Shamrock Ave, they were confronted by a line of guardsmen who herded them back at bayonet point.

At approximately 1 pm, Miranda County Sheriff's Deputies jumped and clubbed a young man spraying WELCOME TO PRAGUE on a window of Cooper's Department Store with an aerosol paint container. He was dragged off to the police station bleeding profusely, and was later identified as Wily Smith, 21, a black student at Euphoric State.

On Sunday a huge procession of Garden supporters coiled its way through the streets of Plotinus, planting miniature "People's Gardens" on every vacant lot they passed. Asked why he had instructed his men to remove the grass and flowers, Sheriff O'Keene said, "They're a violation of property."

—Esseph Chronicle

UNIVERSITY AT WAR, RUMMIDGE PROFESSOR WARNS
Gordon Masters, Professor of English Literature at the University of Rummidge, has condemned the present sit-in by students in strong terms.

"The situation closely resembles that of Europe in 1940," he said yesterday. "The unacceptable ultimatum, followed by a *Blitzkrieg* and occupation of neighbouring territory, was Hitler's basic strategy. But we did not yield then and we shall not yield now."

On the wall of his office, Professor Masters has a large map showing the plan of the University's central heating system. "The heating pipes are conveyed through a maze of tunnels," he explained, "which would make an excellent base for resistance activity should Senate and the Administration have to go underground. I don't doubt that the Vice-Chancellor has a secret bunker to which he can retreat at short notice."

The Vice-Chancellor's Office declined to comment.

—Rummidge Morning Post

RIOT VICTIM ROBERTS DIES
STUDENT REFERENDUM TO BE HELD
ACADEMIC SENATE SETS MEETING ON GARDEN

—Headlines, Euphoric State Daily

WE ACCUSE! WE SHALL OVERCOME!
The People of Plotinus know who was responsible for the death of John Roberts.

Chancellor Binde, who declared war on the people over a piece of land.

Sheriff O'Keene, who armed his blue meanies with shotguns and let them loose on the streets.

The nameless pig who pumped two rounds of buckshot into the back of a defenceless young man at point-blank range.

Our land is desecrated, but the spirit of the Garden is alive on Shamrock Avenue and Howle Plaza. The people of Plotinus are united against the pigs and tyrants. The bullshit barriers are coming down, the barricades of love are going up against the pigs. Street freaks, politicos, frat rats, sallys and jocks and mommas for peace are pulling off their masks of isolation and touching each other's hearts.

—Euphoric Times

PROFESSOR RESIGNS

Professor Gordon H. Masters, Professor of English at Rummidge University, yesterday tendered his resignation to the Vice-Chancellor, who has accepted it "with regret."

It is well known that Professor Masters, who was due to retire in a few years' time, has not enjoyed good health lately, and friends close to him say that the current student troubles at the University have been a source of severe strain for him.

Professor Masters' resignation takes effect from next October, but he has already left Rummidge for a period of rest and recuperation.

—Rummidge Morning Post

CHOPPER SPRAYS DEMONSTRATORS—TEAR GAS BLANKETS CAMPUS

A National Guard helicopter clattered over the Euphoric State campus yesterday, spraying white tear gas over some 700 students and faculty trapped in Howle Plaza by a tight ring of guardsmen.

The gas attack was authorized by Miranda County Sheriff Hank O'Keene, to disperse the remnants of a procession of 3000 mourners marching in memory of John Roberts. Wind blew the gas and carried it hundreds of yards away. It blanketed residential houses, entered university classrooms and offices, seeped into the wards of the University Hospital. Faculty wives and children in the Blueberry Creek swimming pool 3/4 mile away were affected by the gas. A group of faculty have lodged a strong protest with Chancellor

Binde against the indiscriminate use of gas by the law enforcement agencies.

—*Esseph Chronicle*

AN EIGHT-YEAR-OLD'S VIEW OF THE CRISIS

I didn't get to see the People's Garden really, but I could feel that it was beautiful. In the Garden it was made of people's feelings, not just their hands, they made it with their heart, who knew if they made it to stay, there are hundreds of people that built that garden, and so we'll never know if they meant it to stay.

The police are just ruining their lives by being police, they're also keeping themselves from being a person. They act like they are some kind of nervous creatures.

—Submitted by Plotinus schoolteacher
to *Euphoric State Daily*

ASSEMBLY HALL TEACH-IN

This weekend the organizers of the sit-in have arranged a teach-in on the subject of THE UNIVERSITY AND THE COMMUNITY.

What is the role of the University in modern society?

What is the social justification of University Education?

What do ordinary people really think about Universities and Students?

These are some of the questions we shall be discussing.

—Handout, Rummidge University

RUMMIDGE SCHOOLKIDS ON STUDENTS

most students don,t like the way colleges and universitys are run tats why they have protested and sit-in. When students are older they will find it was ran in a good way. Students waste people and police-mens time, i think just for a laff. Most of them are hippeys and act like big fools and waste thier brain when someone else would be proud to be brainy.

I think students are stupid they throw stink bombs at people on purpose ony because they want to be noticed. They are a load of old tramps with their long dirty hair. They look like they haven't had a wash. Their clothes are disgraceful and they don,t have any money. They go on the television and smoke drugs in front of the viewers.

They cause riots in the streets fighting and destroying everything that comes their way. Some students are sensable they wear nice clothes and got nice hair, they have a nice home and are not stupid.

if a student came to me and said something i would walk on. Lets say you are a cat and the students pick you up and you think he is kind. but they cut you up and experiment on you. Some students are all right but they are stuck up noses.

I don't like students cos they all follow each other in what they do they all wear the same clothes and they all talk like americans, and they smoke drugs and have injections to make themselves happy and they talk about love and peace when their unhappy.

if i was the police i would hang them.

—submitted to *Rumble* by Education student

RUMMIDGE DONS PROPOSE MEDIATOR

The non-professorial staff association at Rummidge University has proposed that a mediator be nominated to chair negotiations between the University Administration and the Students' Union Executive, to try and bring the sit-in to an end. Earlier today, the students voted to continue the sit-in.

Professor Morris J. Zapp, a visiting professor from the State University of Euphoria, U.S.A., has been suggested as a possible candidate for the job of mediator.

—*Rummidge Evening Mail*

EARTHQUAKE CURE

Earthquakes, said a speaker at yesterday's Euphoric State teach-in on Ecology and Politics, were nature's way of protesting all the concrete that had been laid on top of the good earth. By planting things, one was liberating the ground, and therefore preventing earthquakes.

—*Plotinus Gazette*

CHANCELLOR PROPOSES LEASE OF GARDEN.
MAYOR HAS DOUBTS. GIANT MARCH PLANNED
FOR MEMORIAL DAY

Chancellor Harold Binde told a press conference yesterday that he thought the vexed problem of the People's Garden could be solved if the University leased part of the land to the City of Plotinus for development as a park, incorporating the present arrangements as far as possible.

Plotinus City Council will probably consider the proposal at its next meeting, but Mayor Holmes is known not to favour it. There is doubt, too, whether Governor Duck, an *ex officio* member of the University Council, would allow the lease to be approved, as he is bitterly opposed to any concession to the Gardeners.

Meanwhile the latter are making plans for an enormous march through the streets of Plotinus on Memorial Day. It is to be a peaceful, non-violent protest, organizers insist; but local citizens, hearing estimates that 50,000 may converge on Plotinus for the occasion, from places as far away as Madison and New York, are apprehensive.

"A permit for a march has been applied for," a spokesman confirmed at the City Hall today, "and is being studied by the appropriate officials."

—*Esseph Chronicle*

ICE CUBE DAMAGES ROOF
A block of green ice one cubic foot in size fell through the roof of a house in south Rummidge last night, damaging a room on the top floor. The room was unoccupied and no one was hurt.

Scientists called in to examine the ice, at first thought to be a freak hailstone, quickly established that it was frozen urine. It is thought to have been illegally discharged from an airliner flying at high altitude.

The owner of the house, Dr. Brendan O'Shea, said this morning, "I'm flabbergasted. I don't even know if I'm insured against this kind of thing. Some people might say it was an act of God."

—*Rummidge Evening Mail*

5. Changing

"You don't think it's on the small side?"

"It looks fine to me."

"I've been thinking lately it was rather small."

"A recent survey showed that ninety per cent of American men think their penises are less than average size."

"I suppose it's only natural to want to be in the top ten per cent . . ."

"They aren't the *top* ten per cent, stupid, they're the ten per cent who aren't worried about it. The point is you can't have ninety per cent who are less than average."

"Ah. I never was any good at statistics."

"I'm disappointed in you, Philip, really I am. I thought you didn't have a virility hangup. That's what I like about you."

"My small penis?"

"Your not demanding applause for your potency all the time. Like with Morris it had to be a four-star fuck every time. If I didn't groan and roll my eyes and foam at the mouth at climax he would accuse me of going frigid on him."

"Was he one of the ninety per cent too?"

"Well, no."

"Ah."

"Anyway, it looks smaller to you, because you're always looking down on it. It gets foreshortened."

"That's a thought."

"Go take a look in the mirror."

"No, I'll take your word for it."

But the next morning, drying off after his shower, Philip stood on a chair to examine his torso in the mirror above the handbasin. It was true that one's normal angle of vision entailed a certain foreshortening effect, though not as much as one might have wished. Forty was admittedly a rather advanced age at which to begin worrying on this score, but it was only recently that he had acquired any standards of comparison. Not since he was at school, probably, had he taken a good look at another male organ until he came to Euphoria. Since then penises had been flaunted at him from all sides. First there was Charles Boon, who scorned pyjamas and was often to be encountered walking about the apartment on Pythagoras Drive in a state of nature. Then the record stores along Cable Avenue began displaying the John Lennon/Yoko Ono album with the full-frontal nude photo of the famous couple on the sleeve. There was the hero of *I am Curious Yellow*, which they had gone to see in Esseph, queuing two hours with what Désirée had described as a couple of hundred other middle-aged voyeurs hoping it would turn them on (which, one had to admit, it did); and the young man in the audience of an *avant-garde* theatre group who upstaged the actors by taking off his clothes before they did. These displays had impressed Philip with a sense of his own inferiority. Désirée was unsympathetic. "Now you know what it was like growing up flat-chested in a big-tit culture," she said.

"I think your chest is very nice."

"What about your wife?"

"Hilary?"

"Is she well-stacked?"

"A good figure, yes. Mind you . . ."

"What?"

"She couldn't do without a bra, like you."

"Why not?"

"Well, you know, it would be flopping about all over the place."

"It? Don't you mean them?"

"Well, all right, them."

"Who says they shouldn't flop? Who says they have to stick out like cantilevered terraces? I'll tell you who, the brassiere industry."

"I expect you're right."

"How would you like it if you had to wear a codpiece all the time?"

"I'd hate it, but I bet you could sell them if you advertised in *Euphoric Times.*"

"Morris was always a big-tit man. I don't know why he married me. I don't know why I married him. Why do people marry people? Why did you marry Hilary?"

"I don't know. I was lonely at the time."

"Yes. That's about it. If you ask me, loneliness has a lot to answer for."

Philip climbed down from the chair and finished drying off. He rubbed talcum into his skin, feeling with a certain narcissistic pleasure the new cushions of tissue that had appeared on his hips and chest. Since giving up smoking he had begun to put on weight, and he thought it rather suited him. His rib-cage was now covered by a smooth sheath of flesh, and his collar-bone no longer stood out with a frightening starkness that suggested he had swallowed a coat-hanger.

He shrugged on the cotton happi-coat that Désirée had loaned him. His own bathrobe had been left behind at Pythagoras Drive and Charles Boon had borrowed it so often that Philip no longer cared to recover it. If Boon wasn't walking about the apartment ostentatiously naked, he was forever pinching your clothes. How much nicer life was on Socrates Avenue. How providential, in retrospect, the landslip that had pitched him out of one address and into the other. The happi-coat was patterned in marine shades of blue and green, lined with white towelling and was immensely comfortable. It made him look, and even feel, vaguely athletic and masterful, like an oriental wrestler. He frowned at his reflection in the mirror, narrowing his eyes and dilating his nostrils. He did a lot of looking into mirrors lately. Hoping to surprise himself, perhaps, in some revealing, explanatory attitude or expression.

He padded into his bedroom, pulled back the covers on his bed and dented the pillow a little. It was his one, vestigial gesture towards the conventions: when he slept with Désirée, to rise early and come into his room to rumple the bedclothes. Whom he was supposed to be fooling, he couldn't imagine. Not the twins, surely, because Désirée, in the terrifying way of progressive American parents, believed in treating children like adults and had undoubtedly explained to them the precise nature of her relationship with himself. I wish she would explain it to me, he thought wryly, gazing into another mirror, I'm damned if I can make head or tail of it.

Though not one of Nature's early risers, Philip found it no hardship to be up betimes these sunny mornings in 3462 Socrates. He liked showering in jets of hot water sharp as laser beams, walking about the quiet carpeted house in his bare feet, taking possession of the kitchen that was like the flight deck of some computer-guided spaceship, all gleaming white and stainless steel, with its dials, gadgets and immense humming fridge. Philip laid breakfast places for himself and the twins, mixed a jug of frozen orange juice, put bacon rashers in the electric Grillerette, turned it on low, and poured boiling water on to a teabag. Shuffling into a pair of abandoned mules, he took his tea through the patio into the garden and squatted against a sunny wall to absorb the unfailing view. It was a very still, clear morning. The waters of the Bay were stretched taut and you could almost count the cables on the Silver Span. Down on the ever-moving Shoreline Freeway, the cars and trucks raced along like Dinky toys, but their noise and fumes did not carry this far. Here the air was cool and sweet, perfumed with the sub-tropical vegetation that grew luxuriantly in the gardens of affluent Plotinus.

A silver jet, with engines cut back, planed in from the north almost at his eye level, and he followed its lazy progress across the cinemascope of the sky. This was a good hour to arrive in Euphoria. It was almost possible to imagine what it must have been like for the first mariners who sailed, probably quite by chance, through the narrow strait now bridged by the Silver Span, and found this stupendous bay in the state God left it at the creation. What was that passage in *The Great Gatsby*? "A fresh, green breast of the new world . . . for a transitory enchanted moment man must have held his breath in the presence of this continent . . ." As Philip hunted the quotation through his mind the tranquillity of the morning was shattered by a hideous noise as of a gigantic lawn-mower passing overhead, and a dark spidery shadow flashed across the gardens on the hillside. The first helicopter of the day swooped down upon the Euphoric State campus.

Philip returned to the house. Elizabeth and Darcy were up. They came into the kitchen in their pyjamas, yawning and rubbing their eyes and pushing back their long matted hair. Not only were they identical twins, but to make things more difficult Darcy had the more feminine good looks, so that it was on Elizabeth's dental brace that Philip relied to tell them apart. They were an enigmatic pair. Communicating telepathically with each other, they were uncommonly sparing in their own use of ordinary language. Philip found this restful after his own precociously articulate and tirelessly inquisitive children, but disconcerting too. He often wondered what the twins thought of him, but they gave nothing away.

"Good morning!" he greeted them brightly. "I think it's going to be hot."

"Hi," they murmured politely. "Hi, Philip." They sat down at the breakfast bar and began to munch large quantities of some patent sugar-coated cereal.

"Would you like some bacon?"

They shook their heads, mouths full of cereal. He extracted the crisp, uniform strips of bacon from the Grillerette and made himself a bacon sandwich and another cup of tea. "What d'you want for your lunch today?" he inquired. The twins looked at each other.

"Peanut butter and jelly," Darcy said.

"All right. What about you, Elizabeth?" As if he needed to ask.

"The same, please."

He made the sandwiches with the ready-sliced, vitamin-enriched, totally tasteless white bread they seemed to like, and packed them with an apple each in their lunch-boxes. The twins took second helpings of cereal. *Euphoric*

Times had recently reported an experiment in which rats fed on cornflake packets had proved healthier than rats fed on the cornflakes. He told them about it. They smiled politely.

"Have you washed?" he inquired.

While they were washing, he put the kettle on to boil for Désirée's coffee and picked up yesterday's *Chronicle*. "It is to be a peaceful, non-violent protest, the organizers insist," he read. "But local citizens, hearing estimates that 50,000 may converge on Plotinus for the occasion, from places as far away as Madison and New York, are apprehensive." He looked out of the window, down to where the helicopter darted and hovered like a dragonfly over downtown Plotinus. Over two thousand troops were in the city, some bivouacked in the Garden itself. It was said that they were secretly watering the flowers. Certainly the soldiers often looked as if they would like to throw down their arms and join the protesting students, especially when the girl supporters of the Garden taunted them by stripping to the waist and opposing bare breasts to their bayonets, a juxtaposition of hardware and software that the photographers of *Euphoric Times* found irresistible. Most of the troopers were young men who had only joined the National Guard to get out of the Viet Nam War anyway, and they looked now just like the GIs that one saw in Viet Nam on the television newsreels, bewildered and unhappy and, if they were bold enough, making peace signs to the cameras. In fact the whole episode of the Garden was much like the Viet Nam War in miniature, with the University as the Thieu regime, the National Guard as the U.S. Army, the students and hippies as Viet Cong . . . escalation, overkill, helicopters, defoliation, guerilla warfare: it all fitted together perfectly. It would be something to say on the Charles Boon Show. He couldn't imagine what else he was going to say.

The twins reappeared in the kitchen to collect their lunch-boxes, looking marginally cleaner and tidier in blue jeans, sneakers and faded T-shirts.

"Have you said goodbye to your mother?"

They called perfunctorily, "'Bye, Désirée," as they left the house, and received a muffled shout in reply. Philip put coffee, orange juice, toasted muffins and honey on a tray and took it into Désirée's bedroom.

"Hi!" she said. "Your timing is terrific."

"It's a beautiful day," he said, setting down the tray and going to the window. He adjusted the louvres of the Venetian blinds so that the sunshine fell across the room in long strips. Désirée's red plaits flamed against the saffron pillows of the huge bed.

"Was that a helicopter nearly took the roof off the house?" she asked, tucking zestfully into her breakfast.

"Yes, I was in the garden."

"The sonofabitch. Kids get off to school OK?"

"Yes, I made them peanut butter sandwiches. I used up the last of the jar."

"Yeah, I must go marketing today. You got anything planned?"

"I've got to go into the University this morning. The English faculty are holding a vigil on the steps of Dealer."

"A what?"

"I'm sure it's the wrong word, but that's what they're calling it. A vigil is an all-night thing, isn't it? I think we're just going to stand on the steps for an hour or two. In silent protest."

"You think Duck is gonna call off the National Guard just because the English faculty quit talking for a couple of hours? I admit it would be quite an achievement, but—"

"I gather the protest is aimed at Binde. He's got to be pressured into standing up to Duck and O'Keene."

"Binde?" Désirée snorted derisively. "Chancellor Facing-both-ways."

"Well, you must admit he's in a difficult position. What would you do in his position?"

"I couldn't be in his position. The State University of Euphoria has never had a woman chancellor in its history. Are you going to be in tonight, by the way, because we'll need a baby-sitter if you're not. It's my Karate class."

"I shall be out late. I've got to do this wretched broadcast with Charles Boon."

"Oh, yeah. What are you talking about?"

"I think I'm supposed to give my impressions of the Euphoric scene, from a British point of view."

"Sounds like a pushover."

"But I don't feel British any more. Not as much as I used to, anyway. Nor American, for that matter. 'Wandering between two worlds, one lost, the other powerless to be born.'"

"You'll have plenty of questions about the Garden, anyway. As one of its most celebrated supporters."

"That was a complete accident, as you very well know."

"Nothing is completely accidental."

"I never felt more than mildly sympathetic to the Garden. I've never even set foot in the place. Now people, complete strangers, come up to me and shake my hand, congratulate me on my commitment. It's most embarrassing."

"There is a tide in the affairs of men, Philip. You've gotten caught up in the historical process."

"I feel a complete fraud."

"Why are you going on this vigil, then?"

"If I don't, it will look as if I've joined the other side, and that certainly isn't true. Anyway, I do feel strongly about getting the troops off campus."

"Well, take care not to get arrested. It may not be so easy to bail you out next time."

Désirée finished her muffin, licked her fingers and settled back into the pillows with a cup of coffee held to her lips. "You know," she said, "you look really good in that happi-coat."

"Where can I get one like it?"

"Keep it. Morris never wore the damn thing. I bought it for a Christmas present two years ago. Have you written to Hilary, by the way? Or are you hoping another poison-pen letter will do the job for you?"

"I don't know what to say." He paced the room, trying, for no reason at all, to avoid treading on the strips of sunlight. Three images of himself converged in the triptych of mirrors over Désirée's dressing-table, and cold-shouldered him as he turned to retrace his steps.

"Tell her what's happened and what you plan to do about it."

"But I don't know what I'm going to do about it. I haven't got any plans."

"Isn't your time running out?"

"I know, I know," he said despairingly, running fingers through his hair. "But I'm not used to this sort of thing. I've no experience in adultery. I don't know what would be best for Hilary, the children, for me, for you—"

"Don't worry about me," said Désirée. "Forget about me."

"How can I?"

"I'll just say one thing. I've no intention of marrying again. Just in case it had crossed your mind."

"You're going to get a divorce, aren't you?"

"Sure. But from now on I'm a free woman. I stand on my own two feet and without a pair of balls round my neck." Perhaps he looked hurt, for she continued: "Nothing personal, Philip, you know I like you a lot. We get on fine together. The kids like you too."

"Do they? I often wonder."

"Sure, you take them out to the park and suchlike. Morris never did that."

"Funny, that's one of the things I thought I was getting away from when I came out here. It must be compulsive."

"You're welcome to stay here as long as you like. Or go. Feel entirely free to do what you think best."

"I have felt very free these last few weeks," he said. "Freer than I've ever felt in my life."

Désirée flashed him one of her rare smiles. "That's nice." She got out of bed and scratched herself through her cotton nightdress.

"I just wish we could go on like this indefinitely. You and me and the twins here. And Hilary and the children quite happy and not knowing."

"How much longer d'you have?"

"Well, the exchange ends officially in a month's time."

"Could you stay on at Euphoric State if you wanted to? I mean, would they give you a job?"

"Not a hope."

"Somebody told me you got a terrific write-up in the last *Course Bulletin*."

"That was just Wily Smith."

"You're too modest, Philip." Pulling the nightdress over her head, Désirée walked into the adjoining bathroom. Philip followed her appreciatively, and sat on the toilet cover while she showered.

"Couldn't you get a job in one of the smaller colleges around here?" she called through the hiss of hot water.

"Perhaps. But there would be problems about visas. Of course, if I married an American citizen, there'd be no problem."

"That sounds like blackmail."

"It wasn't meant to be." He stood up, and his reflection rose to face him in the mirror over the handbasin. "I must shave. This conversation is getting more and more unreal. I'll go back in a month's time, of course. Back to Hilary and the children. Back to Rummidge. Back to England."

"Do you want to?"

"Not in the least."

"You could work for me if you like."

"For you?"

"As a housekeeper. You do it very well. Much better than me. I want to go back to work."

He laughed. "How much would you pay me?"

"Not much. But there'd be no visa problems. Would you get me a towel from the closet, honey?"

He held the towel open as she stepped glistening from the shower, and began rubbing her down briskly.

"Mmm, that's nice." After a while she said: "You really ought to write home, you know."

"Have you told Morris?"

"I don't owe Morris any explanations. Besides, he'd be round to your wife like a shot."

"I hadn't thought of that. Of course, they both know I've been staying here . . ."

"But they think Melanie is here too, as chaperone. Or is it me who's supposed to be keeping an eye on you and Melanie? I've lost track."

"I lost track weeks ago," said Philip, rubbing less briskly. He was on his knees now, drying her legs. "You know this is rather exciting."

"Cool it, baby," said Désirée. "You have a vigil to keep, remember?"

Darling,

Many thanks for your last letter. I'm glad to hear you have got over your cold. I haven't started my hay fever yet and am hoping that I won't be allergic to Euphoric pollen. By the way, I'm having an affair with Mrs. Zapp. I should have mentioned it before but it slipped my . . .

Dear Hilary,

Not "Darling" because I've forfeited the right to that term of endearment. Only a few months after the Melanie affair . . .

Dearest Hilary,

You were very perceptive when you said I seemed more relaxed and cheerful in my last few letters. Not to put too fine a point on it, I have been getting laid by Désirée Zapp three or four times a week lately, and it's done me the world of good . . .

He composed letters to Hilary in his head all the way to the campus, tearing them up, mentally, almost as soon as he had started them. His thoughts seemed to spin out of control, into absurdity, sentimentality, obscenity, as soon as he tried to bring into a single frame of reference images of home, Rummidge, Hilary and the children, and the image of his present existence. It was difficult to believe that by boarding an aeroplane he could be back, within hours, in that grey, damp, sedate environment from which he had come. As easy to believe that he could step through Désirée's dressing-table mirror and find himself back in his own bedroom. If only he could send home, when the time came, some zombie replica of himself, a robot Swallow programmed to wash dishes, take tutorials, make mortgage repayments on the 3rd of every month, while he himself lay low in Euphoria, let his hair grow and grooved quietly with Désirée . . . No one would notice in Rummidge. Whereas if he went back in person, in his present state of mind, they would say he was an impostor. *Will the real Philip Swallow please stand up?* I should be interested to meet him myself, Philip thought, steering the Corvair round the tight bends of Socrates Avenue, tyres squealing softly on the smooth tarmac, houses and gardens rotating dizzily in the rear-view mirror. He had ended up driving Morris Zapp's car after all. "You might as well keep the battery charged," Désirée had said, a few days after he moved into the house. "I can't watch you going off to catch the bus every morning with that car idle in the garage."

It all started, you see, on the night of the landslide. Mrs. Zapp and I had been invited to the same party again, and she offered me a lift home, because there was a kind of tropical storm . . . Pythagoras Drive was like a river in flood. The rain swept in great folds across the beam of the headlights, drummed on the roof and almost overpowered the windscreen wipers. The streetlamps were out, shorted probably. It was like driving on the bottom of the sea. "Jesus Christ," Désirée muttered, peering through the flooded windshield. "I think I'll sit this out, when I've dropped you."

For politeness' sake he invited her in for a cup of coffee, and to his surprise she accepted. "You're going to get awfully wet, I'm afraid," he said.

"I've got an umbrella. We can run for it."

They ran for it—straight into the side of the house.

"I can't understand it," he said. "The front door should be here."

"You must be drunk," said Désirée unsympathetically. Despite her umbrella, she was getting very wet. Philip was totally saturated. Furthermore they appeared to be standing in several inches of mud, instead of the garden path.

"I'm perfectly sober," he said, groping in the dark for the porch steps.

"Somebody must have moved the house," she said sarcastically.

Which, in a manner of speaking, was quite true. Rounding a corner of the building in search of the front door, they came upon three terrified girls in mud-stained nightwear—Melanie, Carol and Deirdre—who had just been jolted out of their beds as the house slewed round in a great arc (lucky Charles Boon was warm and dry in his snug studio). "We thought it was the earth-quake," they said. "We thought it was the end of the world."

"You'd better all come home with me," Désirée said.

It was, you see, purely an act of charity, and meant to be a very temporary arrangement. Just to give us a roof over our heads until we could return to Py-thagoras Drive, or make other arrangements . . . Carol and Deirdre soon moved on. Melanie set up with Charles Boon in the South Campus area—they had thrown themselves wholeheartedly into the cause of the Garden, and wanted to be near the scene of the action. Eventually, of the refugees from the land-slip, only Philip was left in the Zapps' house. He hung on, waiting to see if the house on Pythagoras Drive would be made safe: Désirée told him not to worry. He began to look desultorily for another apartment: Désirée told him to take his time. He didn't feel too bad about imposing on her because she was often out in the evenings at meetings and he saved her the trouble of get-ting baby-sitters. Also she was a slow riser and appreciated his willingness to make breakfast for the twins and see them off to school. Imperceptibly they settled into a routine. It was almost like being married. On Sundays he would drive the twins into the State Park on the other side of the Plotinus hills and take them for rambles through the pine-woods. He felt himself reverting to a more comfortable, loose-fitting version of his life in England. The interreg-num of Pythagoras Drive seemed like a drugged dream as it receded into the past. There had been something unnatural, unhealthy about it, after all, something ignoble and ridiculous about the role he had played there, a middle-aged parasite on the alternative society, hanging around the young folk with a doggy, ingratiating look, anxious to please, anxious not to offend, hoping for a game that never materialized: the game he had seen developing that first evening in the girls' downstairs apartment, with the Cowboy and the Confederate Soldier and the black wrestler. They never seemed to play it again, or else they took care to play it when he was out. He never sniffed the hint of an orgy from that night onwards, though he kept his senses alert for a sign. The nearest he got to group sex was reading the swingers' small ads in *Euphoric Times.* Perhaps he should have put one in himself. *British Professor, not especially well hung, likes Jane Austen, Top of the Pops, gin and tonic, seeks orgy, suitable beginner.* Or a personal message. *Melanie. Give me a second chance. I need you but can't speak. I am awake in my room and waiting for you.* Awake and sweating into the darkness, listening to the muffled sounds of her and Charles Boon making love in the next room. It had been sick, really. The landslip had swept away a whole Sodom and Gomorrah of private fantasies and unacted desires. He felt a new man in the calm, initially sexless atmosphere of Désirée Zapp's luxurious eyrie high up on the peak of Socrates Avenue. He began to eat better, sleep better. Together he and Désirée gave up smoking. "If you'll throw away that stinking pipe, I'll throw away my stinking cigarettes, is that a deal?" It was the karate that determined her to quit, she said, she felt humiliated gasping for breath after ten minutes' exercise. Philip found it surprisingly easy and decided that he'd never really liked the pipe anyway. He was glad to be free of the paraphernalia of smoking. Now the days were warm and he could wear lightweight trousers and slimline shirts without displaying unsightly bulges like cysts all over his torso. Admittedly he drank more these days: usually a couple of gin and tonics before dinner, and wine or beer with the meal, and perhaps a Scotch afterwards as they watched the day's rioting on television. One evening when they were doing this he said, "I found quite a nice apartment today. On Pole Street."

"Why don't you stay on here?" Désirée said, without taking her eyes from the screen. "There's plenty of room."

"I can't go on imposing on you."

"You can pay me rent if you like."

"All right," he said. "How much?"

"How about fifteen dollars a week for the room plus twenty dollars a week for food and liquor plus three dollars heating and lighting that makes thirty-eight dollars a week or one hundred and sixty dollars per calendar month?"

"Goodness me," said Philip. "You're very quick off the mark."

"I've been thinking about it. It seems like a very convenient arrangement to me. Are you in tomorrow night, by the way? I have a consciousness-raising workshop."

Philip stopped at a red light and wound down his window. The buzz of a helicopter told him he was now in the militarized zone, though you wouldn't otherwise have guessed that there was any trouble at the University on this side of the campus, he thought, as he steered the car through the broad entrance on the West perimeter, past lawns and shrubberies where the spume of rotating water sprinklers rainbowed in the sun and a solitary security man in his shelter lifted a lazy hand in salute. But as he approached Dealer, the signs of conflict became more evident: windows smashed and boarded up, leaflets and gas canisters littering the paths, Guardsmen and campus police watchfully patrolling the paths, guarding buildings, muttering into walkie-talkies.

He found a vacant space in the car park behind Dealer, driving in beside Luke Hogan, just arrived in his big green Thunderbird.

"Nice car you've got there, Phil," said the Chairman. "Morris Zapp used to have one just like it."

Philip shifted the subject of conversation slightly. "One thing to be said for the troubles on campus," he observed, "it makes parking easier."

Hogan nodded dolefully. The crisis was no fun at all for him, sandwiched between his radical and conservative colleagues. "I'm real sorry, Phil, that you had to visit us at a time like this."

"Oh, it's quite interesting really. Perhaps more interesting than it ought to be."

"You'll have to come back another year."

"Supposing I asked you for a permanent job?" Philip asked, half-seriously, recalling his conversation with Désirée.

Hogan's response was entirely serious. An expression of great pain passed over his big, brown face, parched and eroded like a Western landscape. "Gee, Phil, I wish I could . . ."

"I was only joking."

"Well, that was a mighty fine review you had in the *Course Bulletin* . . . And these days, teaching counts, really counts."

"I haven't got the publications behind me, I know that."

"Well, I have to admit Phil . . ." Luke Hogan sighed. "To make you an offer appropriate to your age and experience, we should expect a book or two. Now if you were *black*, of course, it would be different. Or better still, Indian. What I wouldn't give for an indigenous Indian with a PhD," he murmured wistfully, like a man on a desert island dreaming of steak and chips. Part of the settlement of the previous quarter's strike had been an undertaking by the University to employ more Third World faculty, but most other universities in the country were pursuing the same quarry, so the supply was running short.

"That's another thing, I haven't got a PhD," Philip observed.

This was a fact known to Hogan but he evidently considered it bad taste on Philip's part to draw attention to it, for he made no reply. They entered

Dealer, and waited for the lift, in silence. A roughly painted notice on the wall said, "ENGLISH FACULTY VIGIL, DEALER STEPS 11 A.M." As the lift door slid open and they entered, Karl Kroop hurried in beside them. He was a short, bespectacled man with thinning hair—a disappointingly unheroic figure, Philip had thought when he first identified him. He still wore a KEEP KROOP button in his lapel, as a veteran might wear a combat medal. Or perhaps he wore it merely to embarrass Hogan, who had presided over his firing and rehiring.

"Hi, Luke, hi, Philip," he greeted them jauntily. "See you guys on the steps later?"

Hogan responded with a sickly smile. "'Fraid I'm going to be tied up in a committee this morning, Karl." He leapt out of the lift as soon as it opened, and disappeared into his office.

"Motherfucking liberal," Kroop muttered.

"Well, I'm a liberal," Philip demurred.

"Then I wish," said Kroop, patting Philip on the back, "that there were more liberals like you, Philip, prepared to lay their liberalism on the line, to go to jail for their liberalism. You're coming to the vigil?"

"Oh yes," said Philip, blushing.

As he entered the Department Office to check his mailbox, Mabel Lee greeted him. "Oh, Professor Swallow, Mr. Boon left a note in your mailbox." She simpered. "Hear you're going to be on his show tonight. I'll be sure to listen."

"Oh dear, I wouldn't recommend it."

He took a copy of the *Euphoric State Daily* from the pile on the counter and scanned the front page: RESTRAINING ORDER ISSUED AGAINST SHERIFF O'KEENE . . . OTHER CAMPUSES PLEDGE SUPPORT . . . PHYSICIANS, SCIENTISTS PROBE ALLEGED BLISTER GAS . . . WOMEN AND CHILDREN IN PROTEST MARCH TO GARDEN. There was a photograph of the Garden, now rapidly reverting to a dusty waste lot, with a few pieces of play equipment and some withered shrubs in one corner, surrounded by the familiar wire fence. A few stolid soldiers inside, a crowd of women and children outside, like some surrealistic inversion of a concentration camp. Something for the Charles Boon Show? "Who, one wonders, are the real prisoners here? Who is inside, and who is outside the fence?" Etc., etc. He lifted the flap on what he still called, to the immense amusement of his American colleagues, his pigeonhole. A small, queerly shaped package addressed in Hilary's handwriting gave him a moment of queasiness until he saw that it had come by surface mail and had been posted months ago. Mail from outside Euphoria disturbed him these days, reminding him of his connections and responsibilities beyond its borders; especially did he shrink from Hilary's airletters, pale blue, wafer-thin missives, the very profile of the Queen in the right-hand corner transmitting, to his guilty eye, a pained disapproval of his conduct. Not that the actual text of Hilary's recent letters had expressed any sense of grievance or suspicion. She chatted amiably enough about the children, Mary Makepeace, and Morris Zapp, who seemed to be taking quite a leading part in affairs at Rummidge these days, having successfully sorted out a spot of student bother they seemed to be having there . . . really, he had scarcely taken in her news, skimming the lines of neat, round script as quickly as he could to reassure himself that no rumour of his infidelity had been wafted to Rummidge to rebound in a cry of outrage and anger. It was no secret around Plotinus that he was living in the Zapps' house, but people seemed too preoccupied with the Garden troubles to inquire further. Either that or, as Désirée maintained, they thought Philip was gay because he had taken Charles Boon into his apartment and that she was a lesbian because of the Women's Liberation bit, so didn't imagine that the two of them might be having an affair. Also, Howard Ringbaum, prime suspect as author of the poison-pen letter about Melanie (the Cowboy, being one of his students, could have been his source of information) had left Euphoria, having been offered a job in Canada and released at short notice by a relieved Hogan.

Philip read Charles Boon's note reminding him of the time and place of the broadcast. He recalled their meeting on the plane, it seemed years ago. "Hey, you must come on the programme one night . . ." Many things had changed since then, including his attitude to Charles Boon, which had swung through a whole spectrum of feelings—amusement, annoyance, envy, anger, raging sexual jealousy and now, all that passion spent, a kind of grudging respect. You saw Boon everywhere these days, on the streets and on television, wherever there was a march, or a demonstration, conspicuous by a white plaster cast on one arm, as though he were daring the police to break the other. His nerve, his cheek, his self-confidence, knew no bounds; it turned into a kind of courage. Melanie's infatuation, which showed no signs of slackening, had become a little more explicable.

He crumpled the note and tossed it into the wastepaper basket. The package from England he would open in the privacy of his office. On his way there he visited the men's room on the fourth floor that had been bombed on his first day—now repaired and repainted. It was said that the view through the open window above the urinal, straight across the Bay to the Silver Span, was the finest obtainable from such a position anywhere in the world, but today Philip kept his eyes down. Foreshortened, yes, definitely.

You must believe me, Hilary, that there was absolutely nothing sexual in the arrangement at all. On the few occasions we'd met up to that time we hadn't particularly taken to each other, and in any case Désirée was in the first flush of her conversion to this Women's Liberation business and extremely hostile to men in general. In fact, that was what appealed to her about our arrangement . . .

"Oh, dear!" Désirée sighed after they made love for the first time.

"What's the matter?"

"It was nice while it lasted."

"It was tremendous," he said. "Did I come too soon?"

"I don't mean that, stupid. I mean our chastity was nice while it lasted."

"Chastity?"

"I've always wanted to be chaste. It's been so nice these last few weeks, don't you think, living like brother and sister? Now we're having an affair, like everybody else. How banal."

"You don't have to go on with it if you don't want to," he said.

"You can't go back, once you've started. You can only go forwards."

"Good," he said, and to make quite sure of the principle, woke her up early the next morning to make love again. It took a long time to rouse her, but she came in the end in a series of backarching undulations that lifted him clean off the bed.

"If I didn't know the vaginal orgasm was a myth," she said afterwards, "you could have fooled me. It was never so good with Morris."

"I find that hard to believe," he said. "But nice of you to say so."

"It's true. His technique was terrific, in the old days anyway, but I always felt like an engine on a test-bed. Being, what do they call it, tested to destruction?"

He went into his office, opened the window and sat down at the desk. The package from Hilary evidently contained a book, and was marked DAMAGED BY SEA WATER which explained its strange, almost sinister shape. He peeled the wrapping paper off to reveal a warped, faded, wrinkled volume which he could not immediately identify. The spine was missing and the pages were stuck together. He managed to prise it open in the middle, however, and read:

"Flashbacks should be used sparingly, if at all. They slow down the progress of the story and confuse the reader. Life, after all, goes forwards, not backwards."

. . .

They assembled self-consciously on the steps of Dealer Hall, the professors, instructors and teaching assistants of the English Department. Karl Kroop bustled round handing out black armbands. There were a few home-made placards in evidence, which declared TROOPS OFF CAMPUS and END THE OC-CUPATION NOW. Philip nodded and smiled to friends and acquaintances in the shirtsleeved, summerfrocked throng. It was a nice day for a demonstration. Indeed, the atmosphere was more like a picnic than a vigil. Karl Kroop seemed to think so, too, for he called the company to order with a clap of his hands.

"This is supposed to be a *silent* demonstration, folks," he said. "And I think it would add dignity to our protest if you didn't smoke during the vigil."

"Or drink or have sex," a wag in the back row added. Sy Gootblatt, standing beside Philip, groaned and threw down his cigarette. "It's all right for you," he said, "you've quit. How d'ya do it?"

"I compensate with more drink and sex," Philip replied, smiling. Telling the truth with a jesting air was, he had discovered, the safest way of protecting your secrets in Euphoria.

"Yeah, but what about the post-coital cigarette? Doncha miss it?"

"I smoked a pipe myself."

"And remember," said Karl Kroop gravely, "if the cops, or the troopers try to break this up, just go limp, but don't resist. Any pig roughs you up, make sure you get his number, not that the motherfuckers wear their numbers these days. Any questions?"

"Suppose they use gas?" someone asked.

"Then we're screwed. Just retreat with as much dignity as you can. Walk, don't run."

Sobriety at last settled on the group. The English Faculty contained very few genuine radicals, and no would-be martyrs. Karl Kroop's words had reminded them that, in the present volatile atmosphere, they were all, just the tiniest bit, sticking their necks out. Technically they were in violation of Governor Duck's ban on public assemblies on campus.

It all started with my arrest. If it hadn't been for that, I think nothing would have happened. It was Désirée, you see, who bailed me out . . .

"Hallo, is that you Désirée?"

"About time! Have you forgotten I'm supposed to be going out tonight?"

"No, I haven't forgotten."

"Where in hell are you?"

"I'm in prison, actually."

"In prison?"

"I've been arrested for stealing bricks."

"Jesus. *Did* you steal them?"

"No, of course not. I mean, I had them in the car, but I didn't steal them . . . It's a long story."

"Better cut it short, Professor," said the police officer who was standing guard over him.

"Look Désirée, can you come down here and try and bail me out? They say it will cost about a hundred and fifty dollars."

"Cash," said the policeman.

"Cash," he repeated.

"I don't have that much, and the banks are shut. Will they accept an American Express credit card?"

"Do you accept credit cards?" Philip asked the policeman.

"No."

"No, they don't."

"I'll get the money somehow," said Désirée. "Don't worry."

"Oh, I'm not worried," said Philip miserably. He heard Désirée hang up, and put his own receiver down.

"You're allowed one other phone call," said the policeman.

"I'll save it up," he said.

"You got to make it now or not at all. And you better not count on getting bailed out, leastways not till Monday. You're an alien, see? That can complicate things."

"Oh dear. What happens now?"

"What happens now is that I lock you up. Too bad the misdemeanour cell is full right up with other folk been taking bricks that don't belong to them. I'm gonna have to put you in the felons' cell."

"Felons?" The word had a dread sound to his ears, and his misgivings were not allayed by the two powerfully built Negroes who sprang to their feet with feral agility as the cell door was opened.

"This here's a Professor, boys," said the policeman, propelling Philip firmly inside and locking the door. "So mind you speak nice to him."

The felons prowled around him.

"What you busted for, Professor?"

"Stealing bricks."

"Hear that, Al?"

"I heard it, Lou."

"Like how many bricks, Professor?"

"Oh, about twenty-five."

The felons looked wonderingly at each other. "Perhaps they was gold bricks," said one. The other gave a high-pitched, wailing laugh.

"Any cigarettes, Professor?"

"I'm sorry, no." It was the only time he ever regretted having given up smoking.

"That's a sharp pair of pants the Professor is wearing, Al."

"Sure is, Lou."

"I like a pair of pants that fits nice and snug around the ass, Al."

"Me too, Lou."

Philip sat down quickly on the wooden bench that ran round the wall, and didn't move until Désirée bailed him out. "You came just in time," he told her as they drove away from police headquarters. "I should have been raped if I'd stayed the night."

It was funny in retrospect, but he had no wish to repeat the experience. If a posse of cops were to come rushing through Mather Gate right now to arrest them, he thought he would probably be among the first to break ranks and flee to the sanctuary of his office. Fortunately it was a quiet day on campus and the vigil seemed unlikely to provoke a breach of the peace. Passers-by just stared and smiled. A few made peace signs or Black Power salutes and shouted "Right on!" and "Power to the People!" A television team, a reporter and his cameraman, toting the heavy equipment on his back like a bazooka, filmed them for a few minutes, the lens of the camera slowly traversing along the length of the steps, irresistibly recalling the annual school photograph. Sy Gootblatt held a copy of the *Euphoric State Daily* in front of his face. "How do we know they aren't working for the FBI?" he explained.

To begin at the beginning: I was driving through Plotinus one Saturday afternoon—I'd been shopping downtown—and on the way back I passed the site of a church that was being demolished and noticed that lots of people, mostly students, were carrying away the old bricks in wheelbarrows and supermarket trolleys. I overtook a group labouring along with a load of bricks in paper sacks and shopping baskets, and recognized one of my own students . . . Wily Smith. With two black friends from the Ashland ghetto and a white girl in a kaftan and bare feet. They accepted his offer of a lift to the Garden with alacrity, loaded the bricks into the boot of the Corvair and jumped into the passenger seats. As Philip drew up at an intersection near the Garden, Wily Smith suddenly yelled "Pigs!" Three of the car's doors flew open simultaneously and Philip's passengers fled in four different directions. The two policemen in the car that drew up behind him did not bother to pursue them. They homed in on Philip, sitting at the wheel, paralysed with fright. "Did I go through a red light or something?" he quavered.

"Open up your trunk, please."

"It's only got some old bricks in it."

"Just open up the trunk."

He was so flustered he forgot the Corvair was a rear-engined car and opened the engine cowling by mistake.

"Don't play games with me, Mac, I haven't the time."

"Terribly sorry!" Philip opened up the luggage compartment.

"Where'd those bricks come from?"

"The, er, there's a building, a church, being demolished down the road, you must have seen it. Lots of people are taking the old bricks away."

"You have written permission to take those bricks?"

"Look, officer, *I* didn't take the bricks. Those students who were in the car had them. I was just giving them a lift."

"What are their names and addresses?"

Philip hesitated. He knew Wily Smith's address, and it was his habit to tell the truth, especially to policemen.

"I don't know," he said. "I assumed they had permission."

"Nobody had permission. Those bricks are stolen goods."

"Really? They can't be worth very much, can they? But I'll take them back to the church right away."

"Nobody's going to church. You got identification?"

Philip produced his Faculty Identity Card and British driver's licence. The former provoked a curt homily against professors encouraging their students to violate property, the latter provoked deep but silent suspicion. Both documents were confiscated. A second police car drew up beside them and the occupants began to unload the bricks from Philip's car and to transfer them into the police cars. Then they all went to police headquarters.

The room they put him in first was small, windowless and airless. He was strongly cautioned against damaging it or defacing the walls with obscenities, frisked for weapons, and left alone for half an hour to meditate on his sins. Then they brought him out and booked him. His faculty identity card and British driver's licence were scrutinized again. The contents of his pockets were itemized and confiscated—a discomfiting experience, which reminded him of a game played long ago on Pythagoras Drive. There was much amusement around the duty-sergeant's desk at the appearance of a marble, belonging to Darcy, in his jacket pocket ("Ho, ho, you're sure losing your marbles now, hey Professor?"), turning into moral disapproval mingled with prurient envy when it became evident that the car he was driving and the house he was living in belonged to a woman other than the wife whose portrait was in his wallet. He was photographed, and his fingerprints taken. After that he was allowed his phone call to Désirée and then he was locked up with the felons. Désirée succeeded in bailing him out at seven in the evening, just when he had given up hope of being out before Monday. She was waiting for him in the lobby of the Hall of Justice, cool, crisp and confident in a cream-coloured trouser-suit, her red hair drawn back in a bun. He fell on her neck.

"Désirée . . . Thank God you came."

"Hey, you look strung out. They been beating you up or something?"

"No, no, but it was . . . upsetting."

Désirée was gentle, even tender, for the first time in their acquaintance. She stood on her toes to kiss him on the lips, linked arms and drew him towards the exit. "Tell me all about it," she said.

He told her in rambling, disconnected sentences. It wasn't just the shock of relief: as once before, the unexpected kiss had melted some glacier within him—unsuspected emotions and forgotten sensations were suddenly in full flood. He wasn't thinking about the arrest any more. He was thinking that it was the first time they had touched one another. And it almost seemed as if Désirée was thinking the same thing. To his disconnected remarks, she gave disconnected answers; driving home, she took her eyes off the road for dangerously long periods to look at him, she laughed and swore a little hysterically. Observing and interpreting these signs he felt still more excited and bewildered. His limbs trembled uncontrollably as he got out of the car, and went into the house. "Where are the twins?" he asked. "Next door," said Désirée, looking at him strangely. She shut the front door, and took off her jacket. And her shoes. And her trousers. And her shirt. And her panties. She didn't wear a bra.

"Excuse me, Phil," Sy Gootblatt whispered. "But I think you're having an erection and it doesn't look nice at a vigil."

. . .

At about 12:30, the vigil came to an uneventful end, and the demonstrators dispersed, chattering, for lunch. Philip had a shrimp salad sandwich with Sy Gootblatt in the Silver Steer restaurant on campus. Afterwards, Sy went back to his office to pound out another Hooker article on his electric typewriter. Philip, too restless to work (he hadn't read a book, not a real book, right through, for weeks), took the air. He strolled across Howie Plaza, soaking up the sunshine, past the booths and stalls of student political groups—a kind of ideological fair, this, at which you could join SDS, buy the literature of the Black Panthers, contribute to the Garden Bail Fund, pledge yourself to Save the Bay, give blood to the Viet Cong, obtain leaflets on first-aid in gas attacks, sign a petition to legalize pot, and express yourself in a hundred other interesting ways. On the street side of the plaza, a fundamentalist preacher and a group of chanting Buddhist monks vied with each other for the souls of those less committed to the things of this world. It was a relatively quiet day in Plotinus. Although there were State Troopers stationed on every intersection along Cable Avenue, directing the traffic, keeping the pavements clear, preventing people from congregating, there was little tension in the air, and the crowds were patient and good-humoured. It was a kind of hiatus between the violence, gassing and bloodshed of the recent past and the unpredictable future of the Great March. The Gardeners were busy with their preparations for that event; and the police, having had some bad publicity for their role in the Garden riots, were keeping a low profile. It was business as usual along Cable Avenue, though several windows were shattered and boarded up, and there was a strong, peppery smell of gas in the Beta Bookshop, a favourite gathering place for radicals into which the police had lobbed so many gas grenades it was said you could tell which students in your class had bought their books there by the tears streaming down their faces. The more wholesome and appetizing fumes of hamburger, toasted cheese and pastrami, coffee and cigars, seeped into the street from crowded bars and cafés, the record shops were playing the latest rock-gospel hit *Oh Happy Day* through their external speakers, the bead curtains rattled in the breeze outside Indian novelty shops reeking of joss-sticks, and the strains of taped sitar music mingled with the sounds of radios tuned to twenty-five possible stations in the Bay area coming from the open windows of cars jammed nose to tail in the narrow roadway.

Philip snapped up a tiny vacant table at the open window of Pierre's café, ordered himself an ice-cream and Irish coffee, and sat back to observe the passing parade: the young bearded Jesuses and their barefoot Magdalenes in cotton maxis, Negroes with Afro haircuts like mushroom clouds and metallic-lensed sunglasses flashing heliographed messages of revolution to their brothers across the street, junkies and potheads stoned out of their minds groping their way along the kerb or sitting on the pavement with their backs to a sunny wall, ghetto kids and huckleberry runaways hustling the parking meters, begging dimes from drivers who paid up for fear of getting their fenders scratched, priests and policemen, bill-posters and garbage collectors, a young man distributing, without conviction, leaflets about courses in Scientology, hippies in scarred and tattered leather jackets toting guitars, and girls, girls of every shape and size and description, girls with long straight hair to their waists, girls in plaits, girls in curls, girls in short skirts, girls in long skirts, girls in jeans, girls in flared trousers, girls in Bermuda shorts, girls without bras, girls very probably without panties, girls white, brown, yellow, black, girls in kaftans, saris, skinny sweaters, bloomers, shifts, muu-muus, granny-gowns, combat jackets, sandals, sneakers, boots, Persian slippers, bare feet, girls with beads, flowers, slave bangles, ankle bracelets, earrings, straw boaters, coolie hats, sombreros, Castro caps, girls fat and thin, short and tall, clean and dirty, girls with big breasts and girls with flat chests, girls with tight, supple, arrogant buttocks and girls with loose globes of pendant flesh wobbling at every step and one girl who particularly caught Philip's attention as she waited at the kerb to cross the street, dressed in a crotch-high mini with long bare white legs and high up one thigh a perfect, mouth-shaped bruise.

Sitting there, taking it all in with the same leisurely relish as he sucked the fortified black coffee through its filter of whipped cream, Philip felt himself finally converted to expatriation; and he saw himself, too, as part of a great historical process—a reversal of that cultural Gulf Stream which had in the past swept so many Americans to Europe in search of Experience. Now it was not Europe but the West Coast of America that was the furthest rim of experiment in life and art, to which one made one's pilgrimage in search of liberation and enlightenment; and so it was to American literature that the European now looked for a mirror-image of his quest. He thought of James's *The Ambassadors* and Strether's injunction to Little Bilham, in the Paris garden, to "Live . . . live all you can; it's a mistake not to," feeling himself to partake of both characters, the speaker who had discovered this insight too late, and the young man who might still profit by it. He thought of Henry Miller sitting over a beer in some scruffy Parisian café with his notebook on his knee and the smell of cunt still lingering on his fingers and he felt some distant kinship with that coarse, uneven, priapic imagination. He understood American Literature for the first time in his life that afternoon, sitting in Pierre's on Cable Avenue as the river of Plotinus life flowed past, understood its prodigality and indecorum, its yea-saying heterogeneity, understood Walt Whitman who laid end to end words never seen in each other's company before outside of a dictionary, and Herman Melville who split the atom of the traditional novel in the effort to make whaling a universal metaphor and smuggled into a book addressed to the most puritanical reading public the world has ever known a chapter on the whale's foreskin and got away with it; understood why Mark Twain nearly wrote a sequel to *Huckleberry Finn* in which Tom Sawyer was to sell Huck into slavery, and why Stephen Crane wrote his great war-novel first and experienced war afterwards, and what Gertrude Stein meant when she said that "anything one is remembering is a repetition, but existing as a human being, that is being, listening and hearing is never repetition;" understood all that, though he couldn't have explained it to his students, some thoughts do often lie too deep for seminars, and understood, too, at last, what it was that he wanted to tell Hilary.

. . .

Because I've changed, Hilary, changed more than I should have thought possible. I've not only, as you know, been lodging with Désirée Zapp since the night of the landslip, I've also been sleeping with her quite regularly since the day of my arrest, and to be honest I can't seem to work up any guilt or regret about it. I should be very sorry, naturally, to cause you any pain, but when I ask myself what injury have I done to you, what have I taken away from you that you had before, I come up with the answer: nothing. It's not my relationship with Désirée that has been wrong, it seems to me, but our marriage. We have possessed each other totally, but without joy. I suppose, in the thirteen years of our married life, this trip of mine to America has been the only occasion on which we have been separated for more than a day or two. In all that time I don't suppose there was one hour when you didn't know, or couldn't guess, what I was doing, and when I didn't know, or couldn't guess what you were doing. I think we even knew, each of us, what the other was thinking, so that it was scarcely necessary for us even to talk to each other. Every day was pretty much like the last one, and the next one was sure to be like this one. We knew what we both believed in: industry, thrift, education,

*moderation. Our marriage—the home, the children—was like a machine which
we served, and serviced, with the silent economy of two technicians who have
worked together for so long that they never have to ask for the appropriate tool,
never bump into each other, never make an error or have a disagreement and are
bored out of their minds by the job.*

*I see I've slipped unconsciously into the past tense, I suppose because I can't
conceive of returning to that kind of relationship. Which is not to say that I want
a divorce or separation, but simply that if we are going to go on together it will
have to be on a new basis. Life, after all, should go forwards, not backwards. I'm
sure it would be a good idea if you could come out here for a couple of weeks so that
you could understand what I'm trying to say in context, so to speak, and make
your own mind up about it all. I'm not sure I could explain myself in Rummidge.*

*Incidentally, as regards Désirée: she has no claims on me, nor I on her. I'll
always regard her with affection and gratitude, and nothing could make me regret our relationship, but of course I'm not asking you to come out and join a
ménage à trois. I'll be moving into my own apartment soon . . .*

Yes, that should do it, Philip thought, as he paid his bill. I won't send it
off just yet, but when the time comes, that should do very nicely.

. . .

"I think one has to accept," Philip said earnestly into the QXYZ microphone,
"that those who originally conceived the Garden were radicals looking for an
issue on which to confront the Establishment. It was an essentially political
act by the radical Left, designed to provoke an extreme display of force by the
law-and-order agencies, thus demonstrating the revolutionary thesis that this
allegedly democratic society is in fact totalitarian, repressive and intolerant."

"If I understand you correctly, Professor Swallow," said the nasal-voiced
caller, "you're saying that the people who started the Garden were ultimately
responsible for all the violence that followed."

"Is that what you're saying, Phil?" Boon cut in.

"In a sense, yes. But there's another sense, perhaps a more important
one, in which the thesis has been proved right. I mean, when you have two
thousand troops camped in this small community, helicopters buzzing overhead all day, a curfew at night, people shot in the streets, gassed, arrested indiscriminately, and all to suppress a little public garden, then you have to
admit that there does seem to be something wrong with the system. In the
same way, the idea of the Garden may have been a political stratagem to
those who conceived it, but perhaps it's become an authentic and valuable

idea in the process of being realized. I hope you don't think I've evaded your question."

"No," said the voice in his earphones. "No. That's very interesting. Tell me, Professor Swallow, has anything like this ever happened at your own University in England?"

"No," said Philip.

"Thanks for calling," said Boon.

"Thank you," said the caller.

Boon flicked the switch that controlled the open line and intoned his station identification into the mike. His left arm was in plaster and bore the legend, "Broken by Arcadia County Sheriff's Deputies, Saturday May 17th, at Shamrock and Addison. Witnesses needed." "Uh, we have time for just one or two more calls," he said. The red light flashed. "Hallo and good evening. This is Charles Boon, and my guest, Professor Philip Swallow. What's on your mind?"

This time it was an old lady, evidently a regular caller, for Boon rolled one eye in despair at the sound of her slow, quavering voice.

"Don't you think, Professor," she said, "that what young folks need today is some college courses in self-control and self-denial?"

"Well—"

"Now, when I was a girl—that was a while ago, I can tell you, heh heh . . . Would you like to guess how old I am, Professor?"

Charles Boon cut in ruthlessly: "OK Grandma, what is it you're trying to tell us? A girl's best friend is N-O spells NO?"

After a brief silence, the voice quavered, "Why, bless my soul Mr. Boon, that's exactly what I was going to say."

"What about that, Phil?" said Charles Boon. "You got any views on N-O spells NO as a panacea for our times?" He took a swig from the Coke bottle in front of him, and gave a practised silent burp. Through the glass panel to Boon's left Philip could see the sound engineer yawning over his knobs and dials. The engineer looked, ungratefully, rather bored. Philip wasn't in the least bored. He had enjoyed the broadcast enormously. For nearly two hours he had been dispensing liberal wisdom to the audience of the Charles Boon Show on every conceivable subject—the Garden, drugs, law and order, academic standards, Viet Nam, the environment, nuclear testing, abortion, encounter groups, the Underground press, the death of the novel, and even now he had enough energy and enthusiasm left to find a word on the Sexual Revolution for the old lady.

"Well," he said, "sexual morality has, of course, always been a bone of contention between the generations. But there's more honesty, less hypocrisy about these matters than there used to be, and I think that must be a good thing."

Charles Boon couldn't stand any more of this. He cut off the old lady and started to wind up the show. The red light flashed again, and he said OK, they would take one last call. The voice sounded distant, but quite clear.

"Is that you Philip?"

"Hilary!"

"At last!"

"Good God! Where are you?"

"At home, of course. You can't imagine the trouble I've had getting through."

"You can't speak to me now."

"It's now or never, Philip."

Charles Boon was sitting up tensely in his seat, clutching his earphones with his free hand as if he had just picked up a conversation from outer space. The engineer behind the glass screen had stopped yawning and was making frantic signals.

"This is a private call that's been put through by mistake," Philip said. "Please disconnect it."

"Don't you dare, Philip," said Hilary. "I've been trying for a whole hour to get through to you."

"How in God's name did you get the number?"

"Mrs. Zapp gave it to me."

"Did she happen to mention that it was the number of a phone-in programme?"

"Eh? She said you were anxious to get in touch with me. Was it about my birthday?"

"My God, I forgot all about that."

"It doesn't matter in the least."

"Look, Hilary, you must get off this line." He leaned across the green baize table to reach the control switch, but Boon, grinning demonically, fended him off with his plaster cast and made signals to the engineer to turn up the volume. His vagrant eye was shooting in all directions with excitement. "What is it you want, Hilary?" Philip asked anguishedly.

"You've got to come home at once, Philip, if you want to save our marriage."

Philip laughed, briefly and hysterically.

"Why do you laugh?"

"I was writing to tell you more or less the same thing."

"I'm not joking, Philip."

"Neither am I. By the way, have you any idea how many people are listening to this conversation?"

"I don't know what you're talking about."

"Exactly, so will you kindly get off the bloody phone."

"If that's the way you feel about it . . . I just hope you understand that I'm very probably going to have an affair."

"I'm having one already!" he cried. "But I don't want to tell the whole world about it."

That finally stopped Hilary. There was a gasp, a silence and a click.

"Terrific," Charles Boon said, when the red and green lights went out and the mike was dead at last. "Terrific. Sensational. Fantastic radio."

. . .

The weather forecast had predicted sunny spells, and the first of them woke Morris early, shining straight on to his face through the thin cotton drapes. Sunny spells. "Who is casting these sunny spells?" he used to ask his Rummidge acquaintances. "What kind of a witch wastes her time casting *sunny* spells?" Nobody else seemed to think it was funny, however, and now even he was getting used to the quaint meteorological idiom. "Temperature about the seasonal average." "Rather cool." "Scattered showers and bright periods." The imprecision of these terms no longer bothered him. He accepted that, like so much British usage, it was a language of evasion and compromise, designed to take the drama out of the weather. No talk of "lows" or "highs" here: all was moderate, qualified, temperate.

He lay on his back for a while, eyes closed against the sunlight, and against the almost equally blinding floral wallpaper adorning the walls of the Swallows' guest room, listening to the house rousing itself for a new day, the whole structure stretching and groaning like a flophouse full of old men. The floorboards creaked, the plumbing whined and throbbed, doorhinges squeaked and windows rattled in their frames. The noise was deafening. Morris added his quota with a prolonged fart that nearly lifted him off the mattress. It was his customary salute to the dawn; something about Rummidge, the water probably, gave him terrible wind.

His ears twitched at the sound of a footfall on the landing. Hilary? He leapt out of bed, rushed to the window, flung it open and furiously flapped the bedclothes.

All wasted effort. The feet belonged to Mary Makepeace: he recognized her heavy pregnant tread. For a moment he'd thought Hilary had relented and was going to slip into his room for a quick roll in the hay before reveille. He slammed the window shut and hopped shivering back to bed. How close, actually, he'd come to getting into the sack with Hilary last night.

She'd been blue because it was her birthday and Swallow hadn't sent her a gift, not even a goddam card. "When I don't want them he sends me roses by Interflora, then he goes and forgets my birthday," she complained with a crooked smile. "He's hopeless about things like that. Usually the children remind him." To cheer her up, Morris invited her out for a meal. She demurred. He pressed. Mary supported him, also Amanda. Hilary allowed herself to be persuaded. Took a shower, washed her hair, and changed into a fetching black maxi that he hadn't seen before, with a low-cut neckline that showed off the smooth creamy texture of her shoulders and bosom. "Hey, you look terrific," he said sincerely, and she blushed right down to her cleavage. She kept fiddling with her shoulder straps and hitching a shawl round her shoulders until she'd had a second dry martini, after which she leaned negligently forward across the restaurant table and didn't seem to mind his taking long appreciative looks down inside her dress.

He took her to the one tolerable trattoria in Rummidge, and afterwards to Petronella's, a small club in a basement near the station where they usually had decent music and the clientele were not too oppressively adolescent. This evening the entertainment was provided by a so-so folk-blues group called Morte D'Arthur with a wistful girl singer who sang pastiches of recordings by Joan Baez and other vocalists of that ilk; but it could have been worse, a heavy rock band for instance which Hilary wouldn't have liked at all. She seemed to enjoy herself, anyway, looking round at the Tudor-adobe decor wonderingly, and applauding enthusiastically after each song, saying, "I never knew there were places like this in Rummidge, however did you discover it?" He didn't like to point out that Petronella's and a dozen places like it were advertised every evening in the local paper, it would have seemed like a put-down, but it was a fact that Hilary and her peer group simply didn't see most of what was happening in the city around them. There was, believe it or not, a Rummidge scene of sorts, though you had to search quite hard for parts of it—the gay clubs, for instance, or the West Indian dives in the Arbury ghetto—but there were other parts, almost as interesting, that were accessible enough. For instance, the cocktail bar of the Ritz, Rummidge's best hotel, on a Saturday night, when the car-workers gathered with their wives and girlfriends for the conspicuous consumption of alcohol. However high the hotel pegged its prices in an effort to maintain a classy atmosphere, the car-workers could match them. They gathered round the tables or perched at the bar, the women balancing their huge beehive wigs, towering like cumulus cloud above their stocky, broad-shouldered escorts who sat stiffly, calloused horny hands sticking out of their sharp new suits, ordering round after round of daiquiris, whisky-sours, White Ladies, Orange Blossoms, and special inventions of Harold, the prize-winning barman—Mushroom Cloud, Supercharger, Fireball and Rummidge Dew . . . "I'll take you there some time," he promised Hilary.

"Goodness, you do seem terribly *au fait* with everything, Morris. Anyone would think you'd lived in Rummidge for years."

"Sometimes it feels like that," he joked mildly.

"You must be looking forward to going back to Euphoria."

"Well, I don't know. I'll be sorry to miss the first Rummidge Grand Prix."

"Surely the climate . . . and your family?"

"I'll be glad to see the twins again. But it may be the last time. You know Désirée wants a divorce."

Hilary's eyes filled with ginny tears. "I'm sorry," she said.

He shrugged and put on his stoical, weary, Humphrey Bogart expression. There was a rose-tinted mirror behind Hilary's head in which he was able to make small, unobtrusive adjustments to his face when he wasn't occupied in looking down Hilary's neckline.

"Isn't there a chance of a reconciliation?" she asked.

"I was hoping this trip of mine would swing it. But by the way she's been writing, her mind's made up."

"I'm sorry," she said again.

The girl in Morte D'Arthur was singing "Who Knows Where The Time Goes?" in a very passable imitation of Judy Collins. "You and Philip ever have any . . . problems?" he risked asking.

"Oh, no, never. Well, I say never—" She stopped, embarrassed.

He reached across the table and covered her hand with his. "I know about Melanie, you know."

"I know." She stared at his big, brown hand, hair luxuriant on the knuckles.

It looked like a bear's paw, Désirée used to say, but Hilary didn't flinch. "That was the first time," she said.

"How do you know?"

"Oh, I know." She looked up at him. "I'm sorry it had to be your daughter."

If there was a correct formula for accepting this kind of apology, Morris couldn't think of it. He shrugged again. "And you've forgiven him for that?" he said.

"Oh yes. Well, I think so."

"I wish Désirée was as understanding as you," he sighed.

"Perhaps she has more to forgive?" she said timidly.

He grinned rakishly. "Perhaps."

The girl vocalist had been joined by the lead and bass guitars and they were singing "Puff the Magic Dragon" in imitation of Peter, Paul and Mary. The lead guitar was the weak link in the ensemble, Morris decided. Perhaps he was Arthur. In which case the group's name was a consummation devoutly to be wished. "Shall we move on to some other place?" he said. Now that the pubs were shut, Petronella's was filling up with less refined customers, heavy drinkers and the odd hooker. Any minute now Morte D'Arthur would finish their set, and a rowdy disco would begin. There was a roadhouse Morris knew that had a juke box loaded exclusively with forties swing records.

"I think we should be going home," Hilary said.

He glanced at his watch. "What's the hurry? Mary is baby-sitting."

"Even so. I'm getting drowsier and drowsier. I'm not used to drinking this much in an evening."

In the Lotus, she let her head fall back against the head-restraint and closed her eyes. "It's been a lovely evening, Morris. Thank you so much."

"It's my pleasure." He leaned across and kissed her experimentally on the lips. She put her arms round his neck and responded with relaxed enjoyment. Morris decided to take her home after all.

The household was asleep when they got back, and they tiptoed around without speaking. While Hilary was laying the breakfast table ready for the next morning, Morris went to the bathroom, briskly washed his private parts and brushed his teeth, changed into clean pyjamas and silk kimono, and waited expectantly in his room until she mounted the stairs. He gave her a few minutes, then quietly crossed the landing and entered the bedroom. Hilary was sitting at the dressing-table in her slip, brushing her hair. She turned round, startled.

"What is it, Morris?"

"I thought maybe I would sleep in here tonight. Isn't that what you had in mind?"

She shook her head, aghast. "Oh no, I couldn't."

"Why not?"

"Not here. Not with all the children in the house. And Mary."

"Where else? When else? Tomorrow I go back to O'Shea's. The roof is fixed."

"I know. I'm sorry Morris."

"Come on, Hilary, let yourself go. Relax. You're all tensed up. Let me give you a little massage." He moved up behind her, and placed his hands on the back of her neck. He began to work his fingers into Hilary's shoulder muscle. But she did not relax, held her head rigid and averted, so that in the mirror they resembled a tableau of a strangler and his victim. "I'm sorry, Morris, I just couldn't," she murmured.

"OK," he said coldly, and left her, immobile before the mirror.

A few minutes later they met again on the landing, coming and going between their bedrooms and the bathroom. Hilary was in nightdress and dressing-gown, her face shiny with face-cream. He must have looked grim and resentful, because she put a hand on his arm as he passed.

"Morris, I'm sorry," she whispered.

"Forget it."

"I wish I could . . . I wish . . . You've been so kind." She swayed against him. He caught and kissed her, slipped his hand under her gown and was going great when a floorboard creaked somewhere nearby and she tore herself away from him and rushed back into her room. Nobody was around, of course. It was just the goddam house talking to itself as usual. Hilary said it was the central heating that caused the ancient wood to shrink and expand. Could be. There were huge gaps between the floorboards in the guestroom, through which a delicious aroma of bacon and coffee now began to percolate from the kitchen below. Morris decided it was time to get up.

He found Mary Makepeace cooking breakfast for the three children in one of Hilary's button-through overalls that scarcely met across her bulging stomach.

"What did you do to Hilary last night?" she greeted him.

"What d'you mean?"

"No sign of her this morning. You fill her up with liquor?"

"Just a couple of martinis."

"Eggs with your bacon?"

"Uh, I'll have two, scrambled."

"What d'you think this is, Howard Johnson's?"

"Yeah, and let me have a side order of golden-crisp ranch-fried potatoes." He winked at Matthew, openmouthed over his bowl of cornflakes. The young Swallows were not used to adult repartee over the breakfast table.

"Morris, could you possibly take me to the railroad station on your way to work this morning?"

"Sure. Taking a trip somewhere?"

"You remember I told you I was going to visit my family's grave in County Durham?"

"Isn't that a long way from here?"

"I'll stay overnight in Durham. Be back tomorrow."

Morris sighed. "I shan't be here. O'Shea has fixed his roof, so I'll be going back to the apartment. I'm going to miss the cooking here."

"Aren't you scared to go back to that place?"

"Oh, well, you know what they say: a lump of frozen urine never strikes in the same place twice."

"Hey kids, hurry up, or you'll be late for school." Mary put a plate of scrambled eggs and bacon in front of Morris and he tucked in appreciatively.

"You know, Mary," he said when the children had left the room, "your talents are wasted as an unmarried mother. Why don't you persuade that priest of yours to become a Protestant? Then you could make an honest man of him."

"Funny you should say that," she replied, taking an airmail envelope from her pocket and wagging it in the air. "He just wrote to say he's been laicized."

"Great! He wants to marry you?"

"He wants to shack up with me anyway."

"What are you going to do?"

"I'm thinking about it. I wonder what's the matter with Hilary? There are some things I have to tell her before I leave."

Amanda appeared at the door, arrayed in her school uniform—dark maroon blazer, white shirt and tie, grey skirt. The students of Rummidge High School for Girls wore their skirts very, very short indeed, so that they resembled mythical biform creatures like mermaids or centaurs, all prim austerity above the waist, all bare forked animal below. The bus stops in the neighbourhood were a nympholept's paradise at this time of the morning. Amanda blushed under Morris's scrutiny. "I'm off, Mary," she said.

"Just run upstairs first, Mandy, and ask your mother if she'd like a cup of tea or something, would you?"

"Mummy's not upstairs. She's in Daddy's study."

"Really? I must tell her about the meal tonight." Mary bustled out.

"I see the Bee Gees are giving a concert in town the week after next," Morris said to Amanda. "Shall I get tickets?"

Amanda's eyes gleamed. "Oh, yes please!"

"Perhaps Mary will come with us, or even your mother. D'you dig the Bee Gees?" he asked Mary, who had returned.

"Can't stand them. Amanda, you'd better be on your way. Your mother's tied up on the telephone."

Hilary was still on the phone when it was time for Mary to leave. She scribbled a note for Hilary while Morris backed the Lotus into the road, its exhaust booming in a deep baritone that rattled the house windows in their frames.

"What time is your train?" he asked as Mary, manoeuvering her belly with care, lowered herself into the passenger seat.

"Eight-fifty. Will we make it?"

"Sure."

"This car wasn't built for pregnant women, was it?"

"The seat reclines. How's that?"

"That's great. Mind if I practise my relaxation?"

"Go ahead."

Almost at once they hit a tailback of rush-hour traffic in the Midland Road. A line of people waiting at a bus stop gazed curiously at Mary Makepeace practising shallow breathing in the bucket seat of the Lotus.

"What's that all about?" Morris inquired.

"Psychoprophylaxis. Painless childbirth to you. Hilary's teaching me."

"You believe in it?"

"Of course. The Russians have been using it for years."

"Only because they can't afford anaesthetics, I'll bet."

"Who wants anaesthetics at the most important moment of a woman's life?"

"Désirée wanted the hospital to put her out for the whole goddam nine months."

"She was brainwashed, if you'll pardon the expression. The medical profession has succeeded in persuading women that pregnancy is a kind of illness that only doctors know how to cure."

"What does O'Shea think about it all?"

"He just believes in old-fashioned pain."

"That figures. You know, Mary, I can't understand why you put yourself in that guy's hands. He looks like the kind of doctor who used to take bullets out of gangsters in old 'B' pictures."

"It's the system here. You have to register with a local doctor to get referred to the hospital. O'Shea was the only doctor I knew."

"I don't like to think of him examining you . . . I mean, he has dirt under his fingernails!"

"Oh, he leaves that kind of thing to the hospital. He only gave me a prenatal once and it seemed to embarrass hell out of him. He fixed his eyes on this hideous picture of the Sacred Heart on the wall and kept muttering under his breath like he was praying."

Morris laughed. "That's O'Shea."

"It was a kind of spooky occasion all round. There was this nurse of his—"

"Nurse?"

"A black-haired girl with no teeth—"

"That's no nurse, that's Bernadette, the Irish slavey."

"Well, she was wearing a nurse's uniform."

"A con trick. O'Shea is just saving money."

"Anyway, she kept glowering at me from out of the corner of the room like a wild animal. I don't know, perhaps she was smiling at me and it just looked like a snarl."

"She wasn't smiling, Mary. I should keep out of Bernadette's way if I were you. She's jealous."

"Jealous of me?"

"She thinks I knocked you up."

"Good Lord!"

"Don't sound so surprised. I'm perfectly capable of it. What time did you say your train was? Eight-fifty?"

"That's right."

"We're going to have to break the law a little bit."

"Take it easy, Morris. It's not that important."

The traffic appeared to be backed up for nearly a mile from the intersection with the Inner Ring. Mcrris pulled out and varoomed down the wrong side of the road, scandalized drivers honking protest in his wake. Just before he reached the Inner Ring an invalid carriage, as they were called (more like euthanasia on wheels, he would have said, a frontwheel blowout in one of those crazy boxed-in tricycles and you were a goner) handily stalled and gave him space to get the Lotus back into line.

"How about that?" he said elatedly. But unfortunately a cop on traffic duty had observed the manner of Morris's arrival. He came across, unbuttoning his tunic pocket.

"Oh dear," said Mary Makepeace. "Now you're going to get a ticket."

"Would you mind going back into that quick-breathing routine?"

The policeman had to bend almost double to peer into the car. Morris gestured with his thumb at Mary Makepeace panting for all she was worth, her eyes closed and her tongue hanging out like a dog's, hands clasping her belly. "Emergency, officer. This young lady's going to have a baby."

"Oh," said the cop. "Well, all right, but drive more carefully or you'll both end up in hospital." Smiling at his own joke, he held up the traffic for them to proceed against the lights. Morris waved his thanks. He got Mary Makepeace to the station with five minutes to spare.

. . .

Driving back to the University, Morris took the newly opened section of the Inner Ring, an exhilarating complex of tunnels and flyovers that was part of the proposed Grand Prix circuit. He leaned back in the bucket seat and drove with straight, extended arms in the style of a professional racing driver. In the longest tunnel, safe from police observation, he put his foot down and heard with satisfaction the din of the Lotus's exhaust reverberating from the walls. He came out of the tunnel like a bullet, into a long canted curve elevated above roof level. From here you got a panorama of the whole city and the sun came out at that moment, shining like floodlighting on the pale concrete façades of the recent construction work, tower blocks and freeways, throwing them into relief against the sombre mass of nineteenth-century slums and decayed factories. Seen from this perspective, it looked as though the seeds of a whole twentieth-century city had been planted under the ground a long time ago and were now beginning to shoot up into the light, bursting through the caked, exhausted topsoil of Victorian architecture. Morris found it an oddly stirring sight, for the city that was springing up was unmistakably American in style—indeed that was what the local blimps were always beefing about—and he had the strange feeling of having stumbled upon a new American frontier in the most unexpected place.

But one thing was for sure, they had a long way to catch up in music on radio. The clock in the campanile was striking nine and one godawful disc jockey was handing over to another on Radio One as he swept through the main gates of the University. The security man saluted smartly: since his success in ending the sit-in Morris had become a well-known and respected man-about-campus, and the orange Lotus made him instantly identifiable. There was, naturally, no difficulty in finding parking space this early in the morning. The Rummidge faculty liked to complain about timetable clashes, but the real problem was their reluctance to teach before ten o'clock in the morning or after four in the afternoon or in the lunch period or on Wednesday afternoons or any time at weekends. That scarcely left them time to open their mail, let alone teach. Unaware of this gentlemanly tradition, Morris had fixed one of his tutorials at nine am, much to the disgust of the students concerned, and it was to meet this group that he now stepped out to his office—not with excessive haste, for they were invariably late.

The English Department had changed its quarters since his arrival at Rummidge. It was now situated on the eighth floor of a newly built hexagonal block, one of those he had surveyed from the Inner Ring. The changeover had taken place in the Easter vacation amid much wailing and gnashing of teeth. Oy, oy, Exodus was nothing in comparison. With a characteristically whacky, yet somehow endearing tenderness for individual liberty over logic and efficiency, the Administration had allowed each faculty member to decide which items of furniture he would like transferred from his old accommodation to the new, and which he would like replaced. The resulting permutations were totally confusing to the men carrying out the work and innumerable errors were made. For days two caravans of porters could be seen tottering from one building to the other, carrying almost as many tables, chairs and filing cabinets out of the new one as they carried into it. For a new building, the Hexagon had already acquired quite a mythology. It was built on a prefabricated principle and confidence in the soundness of the structure had been undermined by hastily issued restrictions on the weight of books each faculty member was allowed on his bookshelves. The more conscientious members of staff were to be observed in the first weeks of their occupation resentfully weighing their books on kitchen or bathroom scales and adding up long columns of figures on pieces of paper. There were also restrictions on the number of persons allowed into each office and classroom, and it was alleged that the windows on the West side were sealed up because if all the occupants of those rooms were to lean out at the same time the building would fall over. The exterior had been faced with glazed ceramic tiles guaranteed to resist the corrosion of the Rummidge atmosphere for five hundred years, but they had been attached with an inferior adhesive material and were already beginning to fall off here and there. Notices bearing the motto "Beware of Falling Tiles" decorated the approach to the new building. These warnings were not superfluous: a tile fell in fragments at Morris's feet just as he mounted the steps at the entrance.

All in all, it was hardly surprising that the move was the subject of bitter complaint by members of the English Department; but there was one feature of the new building that entirely redeemed it in Morris's eyes at least. This was a type of elevator which he had never seen before, quaintly named a paternoster, that consisted of an endless belt of open compartments moving up and down two shafts. The movement was slower, naturally, than that of a normal elevator, since the belt never stopped and one had to step into it while it was moving, but the system eliminated all tedious waiting. It also imparted to the ordinary, quotidian action of taking an elevator a certain existential edge of drama, for one had to time one's leap into and out of the moving compartment with finesse and positive commitment. Indeed for the elderly and infirm the paternoster constituted a formidable challenge, and most of them preferred to labour up and down the staircase. Admittedly the notice pasted beside the red-painted Emergency device on every floor did not inspire confidence: "In case of emergency, pull the red lever downwards. Do not attempt to free persons trapped in the paternoster or its machinery. The maintenance staff will attend to malfunctions at the earliest possible opportunity." One day there would be a conventional elevator as well, but as yet it wasn't in operation. Morris didn't complain: he loved the paternoster. Perhaps it was a throwback to his childhood delight in fairground carousels and suchlike; but he also found it a profoundly poetic machine, especially if one stayed on for the round trip, disappearing into darkness at the top and bottom and rising or dropping into the light again, perpetual motion readily symbolizing all systems and cosmologies based on the principle of eternal recurrence, vegetation myths, death and rebirth archetypes, cyclic theories of history, metempsychosis and Northrop Frye's theory of literary modes.

This morning, however, he contented himself with a direct journey to the eighth floor. His tutorial students were already waiting, slumped against the wall beside the door of his office, yawning and scratching themselves. He greeted them and unlocked the door, which bore his name on a slip of paper pasted over the nameplate of Gordon Masters. As soon as he got inside, the communicating door opposite opened and Alice Slade inched her way apologetically into the room, clutching a large stack of files.

"Oh," she said, "are you teaching, Professor Zapp? I wanted to ask you about these postgraduate applications."

"Yeah, teaching till ten, Alice, OK? Why don't you ask Rupert Sutcliffe about it?"

"Oh, all right. Sorry I disturbed you." She backed out.

"Siddown," he said to the students, thinking to himself that he would have to move back into Swallow's room. On accepting the job of mediator between the Administration and the students he'd asked for secretarial assistance and an outside telephone line—requests which had been promptly and economically satisfied by moving him into the office made vacant by the abrupt departure of Gordon Masters. You could still tell from the marks on the walls where the hunting trophies had hung. Although his work as mediator was virtually finished, it hardly seemed worthwhile moving back into Swallow's room, but in the meantime the Departmental Secretary, conditioned to refer all problems, inquiries and decisions to Masters, had begun to bring them, as though compelled by a deep-seated homing instinct, to him, Morris Zapp, although Rupert Sutcliffe was supposed to be the Acting Head of the Department. In fact Sutcliffe himself was inclined to come to Morris with oblique appeals for advice and approval, and other members of staff too.

Suddenly freed from Masters' despotic rule after thirty years, the Rummidge English Department was stunned and frightened by its own liberty, it was going round and round in circles like a rudderless ship, no, more like a ship whose tyrannical captain had unexpectedly fallen overboard one dark night, taking with him sealed instructions about the ship's ultimate destination. The crew kept coming out of habit to the bridge for orders, and were only too glad to take them from anyone who happened to be occupying the captain's seat.

Admittedly it was a comfortable seat—a padded, tip-back, executive's swivel chair—and for that reason alone Morris was reluctant to move back into Philip Swallow's room. He leaned back into it, put his feet on the desk and lit a cigar. "Well now," he said to the three dejected-looking students. "What are you bursting to discuss this morning?"

"Jane Austen," mumbled the boy with the beard, shuffling some sheets of foolscap covered with evil-looking handwriting.

"Oh yeah. What was the topic?"

"I've done it on Jane Austen's moral awareness."

"That doesn't sound like my style."

"I couldn't understand the title you gave me, Professor Zapp."

"Eros and Agape in the later novels, wasn't it? What was the problem?"

The student hung his head. Morris felt in the mood for a little display of high-powered exposition. Agape, he explained, was a feast through which the early Christians expressed their love for one another, it symbolized non-sexual, non-individualized love, it was represented in Jane Austen's novels by social events that confirmed the solidarity of middle-class agrarian capitalist communities or welcomed new members into those communities—balls and dinner parties and sightseeing expeditions and so on. Eros was of course sexual love and was represented in Jane Austen by courtship scenes, tête-à-têtes, walking in pairs—any encounter between the heroine and the man she loved, or thought she loved. Readers of Jane Austen, he emphasized, gesturing freely with his cigar, should not be misled by the absence of overt reference to physical sexuality in her fiction into supposing that she was indifferent or hostile to it. On the contrary, she invariably came down on the side of Eros against Agape—on the side, that is, of the private communion of lovers over against the public communion of social events and gatherings which invariably caused pain and distress (think for instance of the disastrous nature of group expeditions, to Sotherton in *Mansfield Park*, to Box Hill in *Emma*, to Lyme Regis in *Persuasion*). Getting into his stride, Morris demonstrated that Mr. Elton was obviously implied to be impotent because there was no lead in the pencil that Harriet Smith took from him; and the moment in *Persuasion* when Captain Wentworth lifted the little brat Walter off Anne Elliot's shoulders . . . He snatched up the text and read with feeling:

"*. . . she found herself in the state of being released from him . . . Before she realized that Captain Wentworth had done it . . . he was resolutely borne away . . . Her sensations on the discovery made her perfectly speechless. She could not even thank him. She could only hang over little Charles with the most disordered feelings.*' How about that?" he concluded reverently. "If that isn't an *orgasm*, what is it?" He looked up into three flabbergasted faces. The internal telephone rang.

It was the Vice-Chancellor's secretary, asking if Morris would be free to see the VC some time that morning. Was the President of the Student Council quibbling about representation on the Promotions and Appointments Committee, Morris inquired. The secretary didn't know, but Morris was willing to take a bet he was right. He'd always been surprised by the readiness with which the Student President had waived representation on Promotions and Appointments: no doubt his militant henchmen had been leaning on him to raise the issue again. Morris smiled knowingly to himself as he scribbled an appointment for 10:30 in his desk diary. Mediating between the two sides in this dispute at Rummidge he often felt like a grandmaster of chess overlooking a match between two novices—able to predict the entire pattern of the game while they sweated over every move. To the Rummidge faculty his prescience seemed uncanny, his expertise in chairing negotiations amazing. They didn't realize that he had seen so many campus disturbances in Euphoria that he knew the basic scenario by heart.

"Where were we?" he said.

"Persuasion . . ."

"Oh, yeah."

The telephone rang again. "An outside call for you," said Alice Slade.

"Alice," Morris sighed. "Please don't put any calls through until this class is over."

"Sorry. Shall I ask her to call back?"

"Who is it?"

"Mrs. Swallow."

"Put her on."

"Morris?" Hilary's voice sounded trembly.

"Hi."

"Are you teaching or something?"

"No, no, not really." He covered the mouthpiece with one hand and said to the students, "Just read through that scene in *Persuasion* will you and try to analyse how it builds up to a climax. In every sense of the word." He leered at them encouragingly, and resumed his conversation with Hilary. "What's new?"

"I just wanted to apologize for last night."

"Honey, it's me that should apologize," said Morris, taken by surprise.

"No, I behaved like a silly young girl. Leading you on and then backing away in a panic. After all, it's nothing to make a fuss about, is it?"

"No, no." Morris swung round in his chair to turn his back on the students, and spoke in a low voice. "What isn't?"

"Anyway, I haven't had such a nice evening for years."

"Let's do it again. Soon."

"Could you bear it?"

"Sure. Delighted."

"Lovely."

There was a pause, in which he could hear Hilary breathing.

"Is that OK, then?" he asked.

"Yes. Morris . . ."

"Yeah?"

"Are you going back to your flat today?"

"Yeah. I'll come round to pick up my bag this evening."

"I was going to say, you could stay another night if you wanted to."

"Well . . ."

"Mary's away tonight. Sometimes I get scared in the night, in the house on my own."

"Sure. I'll stay."

"You're sure it's no trouble?"

"No, no. That's fine."

"All right. See you this evening, then." She hung up abruptly. Morris swung round in his chair to replace the receiver and rubbed his chin thoughtfully.

"Shall I read my paper or not?" said the bearded student, with a trace of impatience.

"What? Oh, yeah. Read it. Read it."

While the boy drawled on about Jane Austen's moral awareness, Morris pondered the implications of Hilary's surprising call. Could she possibly mean what he thought she meant? He found it difficult to concentrate on the paper, and was relieved when the clock in the campanile struck ten. As the students shuffled out through the door, Rupert Sutcliffe shuffled in, a tall, stooped, melancholy figure, with ill-fitting glasses that kept slipping to the end of his nose. Sutcliffe was the Department Romantics man, but he was short on joy, and being made Acting Head on Masters' departure hadn't apparently raised his spirits.

"Oh, Zapp. Could you spare a minute?"

"Can we discuss it over a cup of coffee?"

"I'm afraid not. Not in the Senior Common Room. It's a rather delicate matter." He closed the door conspiratorially behind him and tip-toed towards

Morris. "These postgraduate applications—" He placed a stack of files (the same that Alice Slade had brought in earlier) on to Morris's desk. "We've got to decide which ones to put forward for approval by the Faculty Committee."

"Yeah?"

"Well, one of them is from Hilary Swallow. Swallow's wife, you know."

"Yes, I know. I'm one of her referees."

"God bless my soul, are you really? I hadn't noticed. You know all about it then?"

"Well, something. What's the problem? She was halfway through a Master's course when she got married and quit. Now her kids are growing up and she'd like to get back into research."

"That's all very well, but it puts us in a rather awkward position. I mean, the wife of a colleague . . ."

He was a bachelor, Sutcliffe, a genuine old-fashioned bachelor, as distinct from being gay or hip—and women scared him to death. The two on the Department staff he treated as honorary men. If his colleagues had to have wives, he intimated, the least they could do was to keep them at home in decent obscurity. "I think Swallow might at least have discussed the matter with us before letting his wife make a formal application," he sighed.

"I don't think he knows anything about it," said Morris carelessly.

Sutcliffe's glasses nearly jumped off his nose. "You mean—she's *deceiving* him?"

"No, no. She wants to be considered on her own merits, without any favouritism."

Sutcliffe looked doubtful. "That's all very well," he grumbled. "But who's to supervise her, if she does come?"

"I think she was rather hoping you would, Rupert," Morris said mischievously.

"God forbid!" Sutcliffe picked up the files and made for the door, as if fearing that Hilary might jump out of a cupboard at him and demand a supervision. He paused with his hand on the doorknob. "By the way, will you be coming to the Departmental Meeting this morning?"

"Can't be sure, Rupert," said Morris, rising from his executive's chair and shrugging on his jacket. "I have an appointment with the VC at ten thirty."

"That's unfortunate. I was hoping you would chair the meeting. We've got to discuss next session's lecture programme, and there's bound to be a lot of disagreement. They will argue so, since Masters left . . ."

He drifted out. Morris followed him and was locking the door of his office when Bob Busby came running down the corridor, money and keys jingling in his pockets.

"Morris!" he panted. "Glad I caught you. You're coming to the meeting?"

Morris explained that he probably wouldn't be able to make it. Busby looked glum. "That's too bad. Sutcliffe will take the chair, and he's hopeless. I'm afraid Dempsey is going to try and force through some proposal about compulsory linguistics."

"Is that bad?"

Busby stared. "Well, of course it's bad. I thought from the way you tore into Dempsey's paper at the staff seminar . . ."

"I was attacking his paper, not his discipline. I have nothing against linguistics as such."

"Well, for practical purposes Dempsey *is* linguistics around here," said Busby. "Compulsory linguistics means compulsory Dempsey for the students and I don't think even they deserve that."

"You may have something there, Bob," said Morris. He had ambivalent feelings about Robin Dempsey. In one sense he was the nearest thing the Department had to a recognizable professional academic. He was industrious, ambitious and hard-headed. He had no quirks or crotchets. He was, apart from being necessarily less brilliant, very much what Morris himself had been at the same age, and indeed had made some overtures of friendship, or at least collusion, with Morris in the course of his visit. Morris, however, had found these advances surprisingly resistible. He did not feel inclined to join Dempsey in patronizing the rest of the Rummidge faculty. Even if they were in many respects a bunch of freaks, he found them easy to get along with. Never in his academic career had he felt less threatened than in the last five months. "Look, Bob," he said. "I've got an appointment with the VC."

"Yes, I must be on my way, too," said Busby. He jog-trotted off in the direction of the Senior Common Room. "Get to the meeting if you can!" he shouted over his shoulder. Morris had no intention of attending the meeting if he could possibly avoid it. Staff meetings at Rummidge had been bad enough under Masters' whimsically despotic regime. Since his departure they made the Mad Hatter's Tea Party seem like a paradigm of positive decision-making.

He stepped with a lithe, well-timed movement into the paternoster and subsided gently to the ground floor. As he emerged into the bright air (another sunny spell was in progress) the clock in the campanile struck the half hour and he accelerated his pace. It was as well he did so, for another tile sprang from the wall above his head with a resounding crack like a bullet ricocheting and scattered in fragments just behind him. This isn't even funny any more, he thought looking up at the façade of the building, now beginning to look like a gigantic crossword puzzle. Before long somebody was going to get seriously killed and sue the University for a million dollars. He made a mental note to mention it to the Vice-Chancellor.

. . .

"Ah, Zapp! Awfully good of you to drop in," the Vice-Chancellor murmured, half-rising from his desk as Morris was ushered in. Morris waded through the deep-pile carpeting and shook the hand limply extended to him. Stewart Stroud was a tall, powerfully built man who affected a manner of extreme languor and debility. He seldom spoke above a whisper, and moved about with the caution of an elderly invalid. Now he sank back into his chair as if the effort of rising and shaking hands had exhausted him. "Do pull up a chair, old man," he said.

"Cigarette?" He made a feeble attempt to push a wooden cigarette box across his desk in Morris's direction.

"I'll have a cigar, if you don't mind. Will you join me?"

"No, no, no." The VC smiled and shook his head wearily. "I want to ask your advice concerning one or two little problems." He propped his elbows on the arms of his chair and, by interlacing his fingers, formed a shelf on which to rest his chin.

"Promotions and Appointments?" Morris queried.

The shelf collapsed, and the VC's jaw sagged momentarily. "How did you know?"

"I guessed the students wouldn't let you get away with excluding them from that committee."

Stroud's face cleared. "Oh, it's nothing to do with the *students*, dear fellow." He permitted himself an almost vigorous gesture of dismissal. "All that unpleasantness is over and done with, thanks to you. No, this is something exclusively concerning academic staff, and absolutely confidential. I have here"—he nodded at a manilla file reposing on his otherwise immaculate desk—"a list of nominations from the various Faculties for Senior Lecture-ships, due to come before the Promotions and Appointments Committee this afternoon. There are two names from the English Department. Robin

Dempsey, whom you probably know, and your opposite number, now in Euphoria."

"Philip Swallow?"

"Precisely. The problem is that we have fewer Senior Lectureships to play with than we thought, and one of these men will have to be unlucky. The question is, which one? Who is the more deserving? I'd like to have your opinion, Zapp. I'd really value your opinion on this ticklish question." Stroud slumped back in his seat and closed his eyes in fatigue after this uncharacteristically long speech. "Do have a look at the file, old chap, if that would help," he murmured.

The file merely confirmed what Morris knew already: that Dempsey was much the stronger candidate on grounds of research and publication, while Swallow's claim was based on seniority and general service to the University. As teachers there was no evidence on which to discriminate between them. Normally, Morris wouldn't have hesitated to back brains and recommend Dempsey. Service, after all, was cheap. The laws of academic *Realpolitik* indicated that if Dempsey didn't get quick promotion, he might leave, whereas Swallow would stay on, doing his job in the same dull, conscientious way whether he got promoted or not. Furthermore, if Morris had no great personal warmth for Dempsey, he had several good reasons for positively disliking Philip Swallow, who had screwed his daughter, butchered his work in the *TLS* and, for all he knew, filled that cupboard with empty cans as a booby trap. It was a strange and should have been a satisfying twist of circumstance that had placed the fate of this man in his hands. Yet Morris, mentally fingering the executioner's axe and studying the bared neck of Philip Swallow held out on the block before him, hesitated. It wasn't, after all, only Swallow's happiness and prosperity that were at stake here. Hilary and the children were also involved, and for their welfare he felt a warm concern. A rise for Swallow meant more bread for the whole family. And, he couldn't help thinking, whatever it was that Hilary had meant to imply by the invitation to stay an extra night, her welcome could only be made warmer by the news that Philip was to get a promotion partly through his (Morris's) influence, right? Right.

"I'd say, promote Swallow," Morris said, handing back the file.

"Really?" Stroud drawled. "I thought you'd favour the other man. He seems the better scholar."

"Dempsey's publications are OK, but they've more show than substance. He's never gonna really make it in linguistics. The senior class at MIT could run rings round him."

"Is that so?"

"Also, he's not popular in the Department. If he gets promoted over so many older people, all hell will break out. The Department is already drifting into collective paranoia. No point in making things worse."

"Very true, I'm sure," Stroud murmured, making a tiny, fatal stroke on the list of names with his gold fountain pen. "I'm much obliged to you, my dear fellow."

"You're welcome," said Morris, getting to his feet.

"Don't go yet, old chap. There's something else I wanted to—"

The VC broke off and stared indignantly at the door which connected with his secretary's office and had suddenly opened. The secretary hovered timidly at the threshold. "Yes? What is it, Helen? I said I was not to be disturbed." Irritation made his manner almost brisk.

"I'm sorry Vice-Chancellor. But there are two gentlemen . . . and Mr. Biggs of Security. It's very important, they say."

"If you would just ask them to wait until Professor Zapp has left—"

"But it's Professor Zapp they want to see. A matter of life and death, they said."

Stroud lifted an eyebrow in Morris's direction. Morris shrugged his incomprehension, but felt a twinge of apprehension. Had Mary Makepeace given birth on the 8:50 to Durham?

"Oh, very well, you'd better let them come in," said the Vice-Chancellor.

Three men entered the room. One was the superintendent of the campus security force. The other two introduced themselves as a doctor and a male nurse from a private psychiatric clinic somewhere in the sticks. They came quickly to the point of their intrusion. Professor Masters had escaped from their care the night before and it was thought that he would probably make for the University. Unfortunately, there was reason to believe that he might be intending violence to certain parties, in particular Professor Zapp.

"Me?" Morris exclaimed. "Why me? What have I ever done to the old guy?"

"It appears from notes made by one of our staff," said the doctor, looking curiously at Morris, "that he associated you with certain recent disturbances at the University. He feels that you conspired with the students to weaken the authority of the senior staff."

"You was a Quisling, was how he put it, sir," said the male nurse, with a friendly grin. "Said you plotted to get him removed."

"That's ridiculous! He resigned of his own free will," Morris exclaimed, looking appealingly to Stroud, who coughed and lowered his eyes.

"Well, we did have to use a little persuasion," he murmured.

"Professor Masters is of course a sick man," said the doctor. "Subject to delusions. But I noticed, Professor Zapp—we looked for you in the English Department first—that you're occupying Professor Masters' old room—"

"That's just chance!"

"Quite so. But just the sort of thing to confirm Professor Masters in his delusion, should he discover it."

"I'll move back into my old room directly."

"I think, Professor Zapp, for your own safety, you should stay away from the University altogether until Professor Masters is traced and safely returned to the clinic. You see, we're afraid he may have obtained a weapon . . ."

"Oh, come now, doctor," said the Vice-Chancellor. "Don't let's be too alarmist."

"Well, it is alarming, sir," said the Superintendent of Security, speaking for the first time. "After all, Professor Masters is an old soldier, and a sports-man. A crack shot, I was always given to understand."

"Jesus," said Morris, trembling with backdated fear. "Those tiles."

"What tiles?" said the VC.

"Twice today I've been shot at and I didn't realize. I thought it was just your lousy new building shedding tiles. Jesus, I might have been killed. That crazy old man's been sniping at me, you dig? I'll bet he's been up on the clock tower with telescopic sights. I thought this was supposed to be a peaceful country! I've lived forty years in the States and never once heard a shot fired in anger. I come over here and what happens?" He became aware that he was shouting.

"Steady on, Zapp," the VC murmured.

"Sorry," Morris mumbled. "It's just the shock of discovering that you've been near death without knowing it."

"Quite natural I'm sure," said Stroud. "Why don't you go straight home and stay safely indoors until this little problem is solved?"

"I think that's the wisest thing you could do," said the doctor.

"You talked me into it," said Morris, making for the door. He slowed down when he realized that he was not being accompanied, and turned. The four men, grouped around the desk, smiled encouragingly at him. Too proud to ask for an escort, Morris made a gesture of farewell, stalked purposefully out through the secretary's office, and only as he descended the stairs of the Administration Block remembered that he had left his car keys in his office and would have to return to the Hexagon before leaving the University. He made a complicated detour which kept cover between himself and the campanile, and entered the Hexagon from the rear at the lower ground floor. He boarded the paternoster, here at its lowest accessible point, and was borne silently aloft to the eighth floor. As he stepped out on to the landing, the first thing he saw was Gordon Masters ripping from his office door the temporary paper slip bearing Morris's name. Morris froze. Masters looked up from grinding the paper under his heel and stared at Morris with puzzled half-recognition: both his eyes were bright with lunacy. He took a pace forward, gnawing and tugging at his unkempt moustache. Morris retreated rapidly into the paternoster and was borne upwards. He could hear Masters galloping up the staircase that spiralled round the shaft of the paternoster. Each time Masters arrived on a landing, Morris was just moving out of sight. On the eleventh floor Morris, thinking to trick his pursuer, jumped out of the elevator and boarded a downward-moving compartment, but not before Masters glimpsed the manoeuvre. Morris heard a heavy thump above his head as Masters leapt into the next compartment. On the fifth floor Morris hopped out and boarded a rising compartment. He was preparing to get out at the eighth floor again when he saw Masters' feet coming into view, upon which he quickly turned to face the rear wall and continued his upwards journey. Numb with fright he passed the ninth, tenth, eleventh and twelfth floors and then entered the limbo of grinding machinery and flashing lights that was at the top of the shaft. The cabin he was in lurched sideways and then began its descent. Morris hopped out at the twelfth floor to meditate his next move. As he stood pondering on the landing Masters appeared before him moving slowly downwards, standing on his head. They gazed at each other in mutual puzzlement until Masters sank from Morris's sight. It was only much later that Morris deduced that Masters, having been carried upwards beyond the top floor of the paternoster's circuit, and being under the impression that the compartment turned over to make its descent, had performed a handstand in the belief that he would drop harmlessly from ceiling to floor when his compartment was inverted.

Now Morris could hear him running indefatigably up the stairs towards the twelfth floor. Morris jumped into the paternoster on the down side. As he passed the tenth floor, Masters whizzed past on foot, glimpsed him out of the corner of his eyes, skidded to a halt, and jumped into the compartment above Morris. Morris went down to the sixth floor, crossed the landing and travelled up to the ninth, walked across, went down past the eighth checking that the coast was clear, decided that it was, and got out on the seventh floor to re-ascend. Leaping across the landing to board the paternoster going up, he brushed against Masters agilely transferring himself in the opposite direction.

Morris went up to the ninth floor, across and down to the sixth, up to the tenth, down to the ninth, up to the eleventh, down to the eighth, up to the eleventh, down to the tenth, up and over the top, and got out on the twelfth, going down.

Masters was standing there, with his back to Morris, looking into the shaft of the upward-moving side of the paternoster. With a hard, well-aimed thrust, Morris bundled him into the paternoster and he was borne aloft into limbo. As Masters' feet disappeared from view, Morris broke the seal on the safety device embedded in the wall and pulled the red lever. The moving chain of compartments suddenly jerked to a halt, and a bell began to ring shrilly. Very faintly, muffled shouts and the hammering of fists could be heard coming from the top of the shaft.

. . .

Hilary wore a preoccupied frown as she opened the door. When she recognized Morris she went pale, then blushed. "Oh," she said faintly. "It's you. I was just going to phone you."

"Again?"

She let him in and closed the door. "What have you come for?"

"I don't know, what are you offering?" He waggled his eyebrows like Groucho Marx.

Hilary looked distressed. "Aren't you teaching today?"

"It's a long story. D'you want to hear it in the lobby or shall we sit down?" Hilary was still lingering by the front door.

"I was going to say that after all I don't think it would be a good idea for you to stay the night." She spoke very quickly, averting her eyes from his.

"Oh? Why's that?"

"I just don't think it would be a good idea."

"OK. If that's the way you want it. I'll take my bag round to O'Shea's now." He moved towards the stairs.

"I'm sorry."

"Hilary," Morris said, in a tone of fatigue, stopping on the first stair, but not turning round. "If you don't want to sleep with me, that's your privilege, but for Christ's sake don't keep saying you're sorry."

"I'm—" She choked back the word. "Have you had lunch?"

"No."

"There's nothing in the house, I'm afraid. I should have gone shopping this morning. I could open a tin of soup."

"Don't bother."

"It's no bother."

He went up to the guest room to get his suitcase. When he came downstairs, Hilary was in the kitchen, stirring cream of asparagus soup in a saucepan and frying croutons. They ate at the kitchen table. Morris recounted his adventures with Masters, to which Hilary reacted with a surprising lack of excitement—indeed she scarcely seemed to be listening, politely murmuring, "Really?" "Goodness me," and "How terrifying," just a little late on cue.

"Do you believe what I'm telling you?" he said at last. "Or d'you think I'm making it all up?"

"*Are* you making it up?"

"No."

"Then of course I believe you, Morris. What happened next?"

"You seem to be taking it pretty coolly. Anyone would think this kind of thing happened every week. I don't know what happened next. I phoned security to tell them Masters was trapped in the top of the paternoster and got the hell out of the place . . . Hey, this is good." He slurped the soup greedily. "By the way," he said, "your husband is going to get promoted."

"What?" Hilary laid down her soup spoon.

"Your husband is going to get a Senior Lectureship."

"Philip?"

"That's right."

"But why? He doesn't deserve it."

"I'm inclined to agree with you, but I thought you'd be pleased."

"How do you know?"

Morris explained.

"So really," said Hilary slowly, "you fiddled this for Philip."

"Well, I wouldn't say it was entirely my doing," said Morris modestly. "I just gave Stroud a nudge in the right direction."

"I think it's perfectly foul."

"What?"

"It's corrupt. To think that people's careers can be made or marred like that."

Morris dropped his spoon with a deliberate clatter, and appealed to the kitchen walls. "Well, that's gratitude—"

"Gratitude? Am I supposed to feel grateful, then? It's like the films, what do they call it, the casting couch. Do you have a promotions couch in your office in America?" Hilary was on the verge of tears.

"What's gotten into you, Hilary?" Morris expostulated. "How many times have you said that Philip would have done better in his career if only he'd pushed, like Robin Dempsey? Well, I pushed for him."

"Bully for you. I just hope it's not wasted effort."

"What d'you mean?"

"Suppose he doesn't come back to Rummidge?"

"What are you talking about? He's got to come back, hasn't he?"

"I don't know." Hilary was crying now, great big tears that plopped into her soup like raindrops into a puddle.

Morris got up and went round to the other side of the table. He put a hand on each of her shoulders and shook her gently. "What is this all about, for Chrissake?"

"I phoned Philip this morning. After last night . . . I wanted him to come home. Straight away. He was horrible. He said he was having an affair—"

"With Melanie?"

"I don't know. I don't care who it is. I felt such a fool. There I was, tortured with guilt because I kissed you last night, because I wanted to sleep with you—"

"Did you, Hilary?"

"Of course I did."

"Then what are we waiting for?" Morris tried to pull her to her feet, but she shook her head and clung to the chair.

"No, I don't feel like it now."

"Why not? What did you ask me to stay over for anyway?"

Hilary blew her nose on a Kleenex. "I changed my mind."

"Change it again. Seize the moment. We have the house to ourselves. Come on, Hilary, we both need some loving."

He was standing behind her now, gently kneading the muscles of her neck and shoulders, as he had offered to do the night before. This time she did not resist, but leaned back against him and closed her eyes. He unfastened the buttons of her blouse and slid his hands down over her breasts.

"All right," said Hilary. "Let's go upstairs."

"Morris," said Hilary, shaking him by the shoulder. "Wake up."

Morris opened his eyes. Hilary, rosy-complexioned and demure in a pink dressing-gown, was sitting on the edge of the bed. Two cups steamed on the bedside table. He detached a wiry pubic hair from his lower lip. "What time is it?" he said.

"Gone three. I've made a cup of tea."

Morris sat up and sipped the scalding tea. He met Hilary's eyes over the rim of the cup and she blushed. "Hey," he said softly. "That was terrific. I feel great. How about you?"

"It was lovely."

"You're lovely."

Hilary smiled. "Don't overdo it, Morris."

"I'm serious. You are one lovely piece of ass, you know that?"

"I'm fat and forty."

"Nothing wrong with that. So am I."

"I'm sorry I hit you about the head when you started, you know, that kissing stuff. Not very sophisticated, you see."

"I like that. Now Désirée—"

Hilary lost a little of her radiance. "Could we not talk about your wife, please? Or Philip. Not just now."

"OK," said Morris. "Let's neck instead." He pulled her down on to the bed.

"No, Morris!" she protested, struggling feebly. "The children will be home soon."

"There's plenty of time," he replied, delighted to find himself capable of making love again. The telephone began to ring downstairs in the hall.

"Telephone," Hilary moaned.

"Let it ring."

But Hilary wrenched herself free. "If something had happened to the children, I'd never forgive myself," she said.

"Be quick."

Hilary soon returned, her eyes wide with surprise.

"It's for you," she said. "It's the Vice-Chancellor."

Morris took the call standing in the hall in his underpants.

"Ah, Zapp. Terribly sorry to bother you," the VC murmured. "How are you feeling after your adventures?"

"I'm feeling terrific right now. What happened to Masters?"

"Professor Masters, I'm glad to say, is back in the care of his doctors."

"I'm glad to hear that."

"Remarkably quick thinking on your part, old man, to trap him in the lift. Very neat. Allow me to congratulate you."

"Thanks."

"Reverting to our conversation of this morning: I've just come from the Promotions and Appointments Committee. Swallow's Senior Lectureship went through without a hitch, you'll be glad to know."

"Uhuh."

"And you may remember that I was on the point of asking you something else when we were interrupted by Doctor Smithers."

"Yeah?"

"You haven't guessed what it is?"

"No."

"Quite simply, I've been wondering whether you've given any thought to applying for the Chair of English."

"You mean the Chair here?"

"Precisely."

"Well, no. It never crossed my mind. You wouldn't want an American as Head of the Department. The staff wouldn't stand for it—"

"On the contrary, my dear fellow, all the members of the English Department who have been sounded out on the subject suggested your name. I don't say there may not be something of the better-the-devil-you-know attitude behind it, but obviously you've impressed them as someone capable of running the Department efficiently. I need hardly say that, after your part in resolving the crisis over the sit-in, you would be highly acceptable to the University community at large, staff and students alike. And personally I should be delighted. Not to put too fine a point on it, old friend, if you want the job, it's yours."

"Thank you very much," said Morris. "I'm very honoured. But I'd never sleep easy. Supposing Masters escaped again? He might well think his suspicions of me had been justified."

"I shouldn't let that worry you, old man," Stroud murmured soothingly. "I think you must have imagined that Masters was shooting at you today. There was no evidence that he'd been armed, or that he was intending any violence to you personally."

"What was he chasing me all over the Hexagon for, then?" Morris demanded. "To kiss me on both cheeks?"

"He wanted to talk to you."

"*Talk* to me?"

"It appears that a long time ago he reviewed one of your books very unfavourably in *The Times Literary Supplement*, and he thought you might have found out about it and be bearing a grudge. Does that make any kind of sense?"

"I guess it does, yes. Look, Vice-Chancellor, I'll think about the Chair."

"Yes, do, my dear fellow. Take your time."

"What would the salary be?"

"Well, that is open to negotiation. The University has funds at its disposal for discretionary supplementary awards in special cases. I'm sure this would be regarded as a very special case."

Morris tracked Hilary down in the bathroom. She was lying in the huge, claw-footed Victorian tub and, as he burst in, covered her breasts and pubis with washcloth and loofah.

"Come, come!" he said. "This is no time for prudery. Move up and I'll get in behind you."

"Don't be absurd, Morris. What did the VC want?"

"I'll scrub your back." He slipped off his underpants and climbed into the tub. The water rose dangerously high and began to run out of the overflow outlet.

"Morris! You're mad. I'm getting out."

But she didn't get out. She leaned forward and wriggled her shoulders ecstatically as he scrubbed.

"Did Philip ever borrow books from Gordon Masters?" he asked.

"All the time. Why?"

"It doesn't matter."

He pulled her back between his knees and began to soap her big melon-shaped breasts.

"Oh, Lord," she moaned. "How are we ever going to get out of this before the children come home?"

"Relax. There's plenty of time."

"What did the VC want?"

"He offered me the Chair of English."

Trying to turn round to look at him, Hilary skidded on the bottom of the bath and nearly went under the water. "What—Gordon Masters' Chair?"

"That's right."

"And what did you say?"

"I said I'd think about it."

Hilary rinsed herself and climbed out of the tub. "What an extraordinary thing. Could you face settling in England?"

"Right now, the idea has great attractions," he said meaningfully.

"Don't be silly, Morris." She covered herself modestly with a bath towel. "You know very well this is just an episode."

"What makes you say that?"

She shot him a shrewd glance. "How many women have there been in your life?"

He stirred uncomfortably in the tepid water, and ran some more into the tub. "That's an unfair question. At a certain age a man can find satisfaction in one woman alone. He needs stability."

"Besides, Philip will be coming back soon."

"I thought you said he wasn't?"

"Oh, that won't last. He'll be back, with his tail between his legs. Now *there's* someone who really does need stability."

"Maybe we could fix him up with Désirée," Morris joked.

"Poor Désirée. Hasn't she suffered enough?" The telephone began to ring. "Please hurry up and get dressed, Morris." She pulled on her dressing-gown and went out.

Morris lay half-floating in the deep tub, fondling his genitals and pondering Hilary's question. *Could* he face settling in England? Six months ago, the question would have been absurd, the answer instantaneous. But now he wasn't so sure . . . It would be a solution, of sorts, to the problem of what to do with his career. Rummidge wasn't the greatest university in the world, agreed, but the set-up was wide open to a man with energy and ideas. Few American professors wielded the absolute power of a Head of Department at Rummidge. Once in the driver's seat, you could do whatever you liked. With his expertise, energy and international contacts, he could really put Rummidge on the map, and that would be kind of fun . . . Morris began to project a Napoleonic future for himself at Rummidge: sweeping away the English Department's ramshackle Gothic syllabus and substituting an immaculately logical course system that took some account of developments in the subject since 1900; setting up a postgraduate Centre for Jane Austen Studies; making the use of typewriters by students obligatory; hiring bright American academic refugees from student revolutions at home; staging conferences, starting a new journal . . .

He heard a tinkle as Hilary replaced the telephone receiver, and pulled the plug out by its chain with his big toe. The waters gradually receded, making islands, archipelagos and then continents of his knees, belly, cock, chest and shoulders. As regards his domestic life, he had nothing to lose by staying in England. If Désirée insisted on leaving him and taking the twins with her, Rummidge, after all, was no further from New York than Euphoria. Possibly she might even be coaxed into giving their marriage another chance in Europe. Not that Rummidge was exactly what Désirée had in mind when she thought of Europe, but still, you could fly to Paris in fifty minutes from Rummidge airport if you wanted to . . .

The last water gurgled away, tugging at the hairs on his legs and buttocks, and he lay on the bottom of the tub, damp and naked, like a stranded castaway. Gulliver. Crusoe. A new life?

Hilary came in.

"OK, OK," he said. "I'm getting out." Then he noticed she was looking at him strangely. "What's the matter?"

"That phone call . . ."

"Yeah, who was it? The VC had second thoughts?"

"It was Désirée."

"*Désirée!* Why didn't you fetch me?" He leaped out of the bath and grabbed a towel.

"She didn't want to speak to you," said Hilary. "She wanted to speak to me."

"You? What did she say, then?"

"The woman Philip has been having an affair with . . ."

"Yeah?"

"Is her. Désirée."

"You're kidding."

"No."

"I don't believe it."

"Why not?"

"Why not? I know Désirée. She hates men. Especially weak-kneed men like your husband."

"How do you know he's weak-kneed?" Hilary demanded, with some irritation.

"I just know. Désirée is a ball-breaker. She eats men like your husband for breakfast."

"Philip can be very gentle, and tender. Perhaps Désirée likes that for a change," Hilary said stiffly.

"The bitch!" Morris exclaimed, slapping the side of the tub with his towel. "The double-crossing bitch."

"I thought she was being remarkably straightforward, myself. She said she heard my conversation with Philip this morning—I don't know quite how, because when I phoned your house she gave me a different number . . . But anyway, she knew all about it, and she thought it only fair to put me in the picture, since Philip hasn't had the courage to tell me what's been going on. Naturally I felt I had to be equally honest."

"You mean you told her about . . . this afternoon?"

"Of course. I particularly wanted Philip to know."

"What did Désirée say?" he asked almost fearfully.

"She said," Hilary replied, "that perhaps we ought to meet somewhere to talk the situation over."

"You and Désirée?"

"All of us. Philip too. A sort of summit conference, she said."

6. Ending

Exterior: BOAC VC 10 flying from left to right across screen—afternoon, clear sky. Sound: jet engines.

    Cut to:

Interior: VC 10—afternoon.

Angle on MORRIS *and* HILARY *seated halfway down cabin.*

Sound: muted noise of jet engines.

HILARY *is turning pages of* Harper's, *nervously and inattentively.* MORRIS yawns, looks out of window.

Zoom through window. Shot: eastern seaboard of America.

Long Island, Manhattan.

    Cut to:

Exterior: TWA Boeing 707 flying from right to left across screen—afternoon, clear sky. Sound: noise of jet engines.

    Cut to:

Interior: TWA Boeing 707—afternoon. Sound: cool instrumental version of "These Foolish Things."

Close-up: PHILIP, asleep, wearing headphones, his mouth slightly open. Draw back to reveal DÉSIRÉE sitting next to him, reading Simone de Beauvoir's *The Second Sex.* DÉSIRÉE looks out of the window, then at her wristwatch, then at PHILIP. She twists the knob above his head which controls the in-flight entertainment. *Sound changes abruptly to narration of "The Three Bears."*

RECORDED VOICE: And the Daddy Bear said, "Who's been sleeping in MY bed?" and the Mummy Bear said, "Who's been—"

PHILIP wakes with a guilty start, tears off his earphones.

Sound: muted noise of jet engines.

DÉSIRÉE: (*smiles*) Wake up, we're nearly there.

PHILIP: New York? Already?

DÉSIRÉE: Of course, you never know how long you're going to be stacked at this time of the year.

> *Cut to:*

Interior: VC 10—afternoon.

MORRIS: (*To* HILARY) I hope to hell we aren't stacked for hours over Kennedy.

> *Cut to:*

Exterior: VC 10—afternoon. We see the plane head-on. It begins to lose height. Sound: jet engines changing note.

> *Cut to:*

Exterior: Boeing 707—afternoon. We see the plane head-on. It begins to bank to the right. Sound: jet engines changing note.

> *Cut to:*

Interior: Flight deck, VC 10—afternoon. BRITISH CAPTAIN, scanning the sky, looks to his right. *Close-up:* BRITISH CAPTAIN registers alarm.

> *Cut to:*

Interior: Flight deck, Boeing 707—afternoon. Close-up: AMERICAN CAPTAIN registers horror.

> *Cut to:*

Interior: Flight deck, VC 10—afternoon. Looking over the BRITISH CAPTAIN's shoulder we see the Boeing 707, terrifyingly near, cross the path of the VC 10, banking in an effort to avoid collision. The BRITISH CAPTAIN manipulates the controls to bank in the opposite direction.

Cut to:

Interior: Boeing 707, passengers' cabin—afternoon. Alarm and confusion among passengers as the plane tilts violently. *Sound: screams, cries etc.*

Cut to:

Interior: VC 10 passengers' cabin—afternoon. Alarm and confusion among passengers as the plane tilts violently. *Sound: screams, cries etc.*

Cut to:

Interior: Flight deck, VC 10—afternoon.

BRITISH CAPTAIN: (*coolly into microphone*) Hello Kennedy Flight Control. This is BOAC Whisky Sugar Eight. I have to report an air miss.

Cut to:

Interior: Flight deck, Boeing 707—afternoon.

AMERICAN CAPTAIN: (*enraged, into microphone*) What the fuck do you think you guys are doing down there?

Cut to:

Interior: VC 10 passengers' cabin—afternoon. Sound: babble of conversation—"Did you see that?" "Must have missed us by inches," "Sure was a near thing" etc.

MORRIS: (*mopping his brow*) I always said, if God had meant us to fly he'd have given me guts.

HILARY: I feel sick.

Cut to:

Interior: Boeing 707 passengers' cabin—afternoon. Sound: babble of conversation.

DÉSIRÉE: (*shakily, to* PHILIP) What was that?

PHILIP: I think we nearly collided with another plane.

DÉSIRÉE: Jesus Christ!

Fade out.

Fade in on interior: hotel room in mid-town Manhattan, blue decor—late afternoon. Sound: TV commentary on baseball game, turned low. There are two suitcases open, but not unpacked. HILARY is lying, fully dressed but without her shoes, on one of the twin beds, her eyes closed. MORRIS, in shirt sleeves, is crouched in front of the TV, watching a ball game, drinking Scotch on the rocks which he has fixed from a tray with bottle, ice, glasses etc. on the dressing table. There is a knock on the door. *Shot:* HILARY's eyes flick open.

MORRIS: Yeah? Come in.

DÉSIRÉE: (*entering, followed by* PHILIP) Morris?

HILARY sits up quickly, swings her feet to the floor.

MORRIS: Désirée! (*sets down his drink, comes to door with open arms*) Honey!

DÉSIRÉE catches MORRIS's wrists deftly and brings him to a dead stop. She
  kisses him demurely on the cheek, then releases him.

DÉSIRÉE: Hallo, Morris.

MORRIS: (*rubbing his wrists*) Hey, you've gotten awfully strong.

DÉSIRÉE: I've been taking karate lessons.

MORRIS: Very good! You should go into the Park tonight and practise on the
  rapists. (*He extends hand to* PHILIP) You must be Philip.

  Shot: PHILIP staring, speechless, across the room at HILARY. Zoom in on
  HILARY, sitting bolt upright on the bed, staring across at PHILIP.

MORRIS: Well, if you're *not* Philip, things are even more complicated than I
  thought they were. (*He takes* PHILIP's *hand and shakes it*)

PHILIP: Sorry! How do you do. (PHILIP *looks back at* HILARY)

HILARY: (*faintly*) Hello, Philip.

PHILIP: Hello, Hilary.

DÉSIRÉE: (*walks across to* HILARY) Hilary—I'm Désirée. (HILARY *rises*) Don't
  get up.

HILARY: (*apologetically, putting on her shoes*) I was just lying down . . .

HILARY and DÉSIRÉE shake hands.

DÉSIRÉE: How was your flight?

MORRIS: Great! We nearly collided with another plane.

DÉSIRÉE: (*wheels round*) So did we!

MORRIS: (*gapes*) You nearly collided . . . ?

PHILIP: Yes, just coming into New York. One wonders how often it
  happens.

MORRIS: (*soberly*) I think it can only have happened once this afternoon.

PHILIP: You mean . . . ?

MORRIS: (*nods*) We were nearly introduced in mid-air.

PHILIP: Phew!

HILARY: (*sits down quickly on the bed*) How frightful!

DÉSIRÉE: It would have solved a lot of problems, of course. A spectacular
  finale to our little drama.

HILARY: Oh don't!

MORRIS: But we escaped. Perhaps God isn't angry with us after all.

PHILIP: Who says he is?

MORRIS: Well, Hilary . . .

PHILIP: (*To* HILARY) Do you?

HILARY: (*defensive*) Of course not. It's Morris who's afraid of God, only he won't admit it. I just want to get things sorted out.

DÉSIRÉE: Sure. That's what we're here for.

PHILIP: (*To* HILARY) How are the children?

HILARY: They're all right. Mary is looking after them. You've put on weight, Philip.

PHILIP: Yes, a little.

HILARY: It suits you.

MORRIS: (*To* DÉSIRÉE) I like the pants suit. How are the twins?

DÉSIRÉE: They're fine. How about a drink for the rest of us?

MORRIS: Sure. (*hastens to pour drinks*) Hilary? Philip? Scotch?

HILARY: No thanks, Morris.

MORRIS: About rooms. Shall Désirée and I take this one?

DÉSIRÉE: Who says I'm sharing with you?

MORRIS: (*shrugs*) OK, honey. You and Philip have the other room. We'll stay here.

HILARY: Either way, isn't it rather prejudging the issue?

MORRIS: (*spreads hands*) OK. What do you suggest?

   Cut to:

Interior: blue hotel room—night.

   PHILIP and MORRIS are in the twin beds. PHILIP, wearing pyjamas, is apparently asleep. MORRIS, bare-chested, is awake, one hand behind his head, the other under his sheet.

MORRIS: We shouldn't have let them get away with it.

   (*pause*)

It's ridiculous.

   (*pause*)

I get so goddam horny in hotel rooms.

   (*pause*)

Philip.

PHILIP: Mmm?

MORRIS: How d'ya make out with Désirée?

PHILIP: Very nice.

MORRIS: I mean, in the sack.

PHILIP: Very nice.

MORRIS: Hard work, though, isn't it?

PHILIP: I wouldn't have said so.

    (*pause*)

MORRIS: Uh, ever get her to, uh, blow you?

PHILIP: No.

MORRIS: (*sighs*) Neither did I.

    (*pause*)

PHILIP: I never thought of asking.

    (*pause*)

PHILIP sits up suddenly, wide awake.

PHILIP: Did you ever ask Hilary?

MORRIS: Sure.

PHILIP: What happened?

MORRIS: Nothing.

    PHILIP relaxes, sinks back on to the bed, closes eyes.

    (*pause*)

MORRIS: She didn't know what I was talking about.

    Cut to:

Interior: hotel room, pink decor—night.

DÉSIRÉE and HILARY asleep in the twin beds. Telephone on bedside table between them. Telephone rings. DÉSIRÉE gropes, picks up receiver.

DÉSIRÉE: (*half asleep*) Hallo.

    Intercut close-ups of MORRIS *and* DÉSIRÉE.

MORRIS: Hallo, sweetheart.

DÉSIRÉE: (*annoyed*) What do you want? I was asleep.

MORRIS: Uh . . . Philip and I were wondering (*looks across at* PHILIP) if we couldn't come to some more comfortable arrangement . . .

DÉSIRÉE: Like what?

MORRIS: Like if one of you girls would like to change places with one of us . . .

DÉSIRÉE: You mean *either* of us? With either of you? You don't have any preference?

MORRIS: (*laughs uneasily*) We leave it to you.

DÉSIRÉE: You're despicable. (*Puts down receiver*)

MORRIS: Désirée!

    MORRIS rattles the receiver.

    (*gloomily*) Bitch!

    Cut to:

Interior: pink hotel room—night.

HILARY: Who was that?

DÉSIRÉE: Morris.

HILARY: What did he want?

DÉSIRÉE: Either of us. He wasn't fussy.

HILARY: What?

DÉSIRÉE: Philip too. I'm afraid Morris is a bad influence.

HILARY: (*sits up*) I'd like to talk to Philip.

DÉSIRÉE: *Now?*

HILARY: I'm wide awake.

DÉSIRÉE: Please yourself. (*turns over*)

HILARY: Don't you want to talk to Morris on your own?

DÉSIRÉE: No!

> Cut to:

Interior: hotel corridor—night.

HILARY, in dressing-gown, emerges from door on left, leaving it ajar, crosses corridor and knocks on door to right. It opens. HILARY goes in, door shuts. After a short interval, door on right opens and MORRIS, in dressing-gown, comes out, closes door behind him, crosses corridor, enters door left, closes it behind him.

> Cut to:

Interior: blue hotel room—night.

HILARY: (*nervously*) I only came in here to talk, Philip.

> Cut to:

Interior: pink hotel room—night. Sound: door clicks shut.

DÉSIRÉE: (*levelly*) You lay a finger on me, Zapp, and you'll regret it.

Blackout

> Cut to:

Interior: blue room—early morning.

PHILIP and HILARY asleep in each other's arms in one of the beds.

> Cut to:

Interior: pink room—early morning.

Pan slowly round room, which is in a mess—chairs overturned, lamps knocked over, bedclothes ripped from beds etc. There is no sign of MORRIS and DÉSIRÉE until they are discovered on the floor between the two twin beds, naked, tangled together in a heap of pillows and bedclothes. They are fast asleep.

> Cut to:

Interior: coffee-shop in hotel—morning.

MORRIS, DÉSIRÉE, PHILIP and HILARY are finishing breakfast. They are sitting in a booth, men on one side of the table, women on the other.

MORRIS: Well, what are we going to do this morning? Shall we show these two hicks the town, Désirée?

DÉSIRÉE: It's gonna be hot. In the nineties, the radio said.

HILARY: Shouldn't we have a serious talk? I mean, that's what we've come all this way for. What are we going to do? About the future.

MORRIS: Let's consider the options. Coolly. (*prepares to light cigar*) First: we could return to our respective homes with our respective spouses.

MORRIS lights cigar, and examines the tip. HILARY looks at PHILIP, PHILIP looks at DÉSIRÉE, DÉSIRÉE looks at MORRIS.

DÉSIRÉE: Next option.

MORRIS: We could all get divorced and remarry each other. If you follow me.

PHILIP: Where would we live?

MORRIS: I could take the Chair at Rummidge, settle down there. I guess you could get a job in Euphoria . . .

PHILIP: I'm not so sure.

MORRIS: Or you could take Désirée to Rummidge, and I'd go back to Euphoria with Hilary.

HILARY rises to her feet.

Where are you going?

HILARY: I don't wish to listen to this childish conversation.

PHILIP: What's wrong? You started it.

HILARY: This is not what I meant by a serious talk. You sound like a couple of scriptwriters discussing how to wind up a play.

MORRIS: Hilary, honey! There are choices to be made. We must be aware of all the possibilities.

HILARY: (*sitting down*) All right, then. Have you considered the possibility that Désirée and I might divorce you two and *not* remarry?

DÉSIRÉE: Right on!

MORRIS: (*thoughtfully*) True. Another possibility is group marriage. You know? Two couples live together in one house and pool their resources. Everything is common property.

PHILIP: Including, er . . .

MORRIS: Including that, naturally.

HILARY: What about the children?

MORRIS: It's great for children. They amuse each other, while the parents . . .

DÉSIRÉE: Screw each other.

HILARY: I never heard of anything so immoral in my life.

MORRIS: Oh, come on Hilary! The four of us already hold the world record for long-distance wife-swapping. Why not do it under one roof? That way you get domestic stability plus sexual variety. Isn't that what all of us want? I don't know how you two made out last night, but Désirée and I really had a—

DÉSIRÉE: OK, OK, that's enough of that.

PHILIP: I must say it's an intriguing idea.

DÉSIRÉE: In theory I'm sympathetic—I mean as a first step towards getting rid of the nuclear family, it has possibilities. But if Morris is in favour there must be a twist in it somewhere.

HILARY: (*sardonically, to* MORRIS) As a matter of academic interest: in this so-called group marriage, what happens if the two men both fancy the same woman at the same time?

DÉSIRÉE: Or the two women want to sleep with the same man?

(*Pause*) MORRIS rubs his chin thoughtfully.

PHILIP: (*grins*) I know. The one who's left out watches the other three.

MORRIS and DÉSIRÉE crack up laughing. HILARY joins in despite herself.

HILARY: But can't we be serious for a moment? Where is this all going to *end?*

    Cut to:

Interior: blue hotel room—afternoon.

The door opens and in come MORRIS, DÉSIRÉE, HILARY and PHILIP. They carry packages and carrier bags with Manhattan store names on them. They look hot and sweaty, but relaxed. They flop down on chairs, beds.

MORRIS: We made it.

DÉSIRÉE: Jesus, I'd forgotten what a New York heatwave was like.

PHILIP: Thank God for air conditioning.

MORRIS: I'll go get some ice.

MORRIS goes out. PHILIP sits up suddenly.

PHILIP: Désirée.

DÉSIRÉE: What?

PHILIP: D'you realize what day this is . . . The day of the March!

DÉSIRÉE: The march? Oh, yeah, the March.

HILARY: What's that?

PHILIP: (*excitedly*) The educational network is carrying it.

PHILIP goes over to TV, turns it on.

DÉSIRÉE: It was this morning, wasn't it? It's all over by now.

PHILIP: It's still morning in Euphoria. Pacific time.

DÉSIRÉE: That's right! (*to* HILARY) Have you heard about the trouble at Plotinus? Over the People's Garden?

HILARY: Oh that. You missed a lot of excitement at Rummidge this term, you know, Philip. The sit-in and everything.

PHILIP: Somehow I can't think of anything seriously revolutionary happening at Rummidge.

HILARY: I hope you're not going to turn into one of these violence snobs, who think that nothing's important unless people are getting killed.

DÉSIRÉE: "Violence snobs," I like that . . .

PHILIP: Well, as a matter of fact people *could* be killed today in Plotinus, quite easily.

DÉSIRÉE: You have to make allowances, Hilary. Philip got very involved with the Garden and all that. He even went to jail.

HILARY: Good God! You never told me, Philip.

PHILIP: (*crouching over set as it begins to warm up*) It was only for a few hours. I was going to write to you about it but . . . it was connected with other things.

HILARY: Oh.

A Western film comes up on the TV screen. PHILIP switches channels until he hits the transmission of the Plotinus March.

PHILIP: Ah! (*tunes TV. Sound: chanting, cheers, bands etc.*)

MORRIS enters with ice and soft drinks.

MORRIS: What's that?

DÉSIRÉE: The big March at Plotinus.

MORRIS: No kidding?

VOICE OF COMMENTATOR: And it certainly looks as though the great March is going to pass off peacefully after all . . .

MORRIS watches with interest as he prepares the drinks. *Close-up* of TV screen. We see the column of marchers passing the fenced-in Garden. It is a warm sunny morning in Plotinus. The crowd is festive, good-humoured. The marchers carry banners, flags, flowers and sod. Inside the fence, National Guardsmen stand at ease. The camera zooms in on various sections of the crowd. We see trucks with rock bands and topless dancers performing on them, people dancing in the spray from hosepipes, marching arm-in-arm etc. We can recognize various familiar

faces among the marchers. Over these pictures, the voice of the
COMMENTATOR and the comments of MORRIS, PHILIP, HILARY and DÉSIRÉE.

VOICE OF COMMENTATOR: A lot of people feared blood would run in the streets
of Plotinus today, but so far the vibrations are good . . . The marchers are
throwing flowers instead of rocks . . . they're weaving flowers into the mesh
of the hurricane fence . . . they're planting sod on the sidewalk outside the
Garden . . . that's how they're making their point . . .

PHILIP: I say, there's Charles Boon. And Melanie!

MORRIS: Melanie? Where?

DÉSIRÉE: Next to that guy with his arm in plaster.

HILARY: She's very pretty.

VOICE OF COMMENTATOR: So far, nobody has tried to scale the fence. The
guardsmen, as you can see, are standing at ease. Some of them have
been waving to the marchers . . .

PHILIP: And there's Wily Smith! D'you remember, Hilary, I told you about
him. In the corner of the picture in the baseball cap. He was in my
writing class. Never wrote me a single word.

VOICE OF COMMENTATOR: Sheriff O'Keene and his men, the blue meanies as
the students call them, are well out of sight . . .

DÉSIRÉE: Hey, look at the topless dancers!

PHILIP: That's Carol and Deirdre, surely?

DÉSIRÉE: I think you're right.

VOICE OF COMMENTATOR: The column has been going past for about thirty
minutes now, and I still can't see the end of it.

PHILIP: And there's the Cowboy and the Confederate Soldier! Everybody in
Plotinus must be on this march.

VOICE OF COMMENTATOR: I think these pictures say it all.

HILARY: (*a little wistfully*) You sound as if you wish you were there yourself,
Philip.

DÉSIRÉE: You bet he does.

PHILIP: No, not really.

PHILIP turns down the volume of the TV but leaves the vision on. *Draw
back* to reveal the four of them gathered round the TV, drinks in hand.

PHILIP: "That is no country for old men . . ."

MORRIS: Come now, Philip, let's have no defeatism.

PHILIP: I'd be an impostor there.

DÉSIRÉE: Explain yourself.

PHILIP: Those young people (*gestures at TV screen*) really care about the Garden. It's like a love affair for them. Take Charles Boon and Melanie. I could never feel like that about any public issue. Sometimes I wish I could. For me, if I'm honest, politics is background, news, almost entertainment. Something you switch on and off, like the TV. What I really worry about, what I can't switch off at will is, oh, sex, or dying or losing my hair. Private things. We're private people, aren't we, our generation? We make a clear distinction between private and public life; and the important things, the things that make us happy or unhappy are private. Love is private. Property is private. Parts are private. That's why the young radicals call for fucking in the streets. It's not just a cheap shock-tactic. It's a serious revolutionary proposition. You know that Beatles' song, "Let's Do It In The Road" . . . ?

DÉSIRÉE: Bullshit.

PHILIP: Eh?

DÉSIRÉE: Absolute bullshit, Philip. You've been brainwashed by the Plotinus Underground. You've been reading too many copies of *Euphoric Times*. Who's going to get fucked in the streets when the revolution comes, tell me that?

PHILIP: Who?

DÉSIRÉE: Women, that's who, whether they like it or not. Listen, there are girls getting raped every night down at the Garden, only *Euphoric Times* doesn't recognize the word rape, so you'd never know it. Any girl who goes down to help with the Garden is caught in a sexual trap. If she won't put out the men will accuse her of being bourgeois and uptight and if she complains to the cops they'll tell her she deserves everything she gets by simply being there. And if the girls aren't being screwed against their will, they're slaving over the stewpot or washing dishes or looking after kids, while the men sit around rapping about politics. Call that a revolution? Don't make me laugh.

HILARY: Hear, hear!

PHILIP: Well, you may be right, Désirée. All I'm saying is that there is a generation gap, and I think it revolves around this public/private thing. Our generation—we subscribe to the old liberal doctrine of the inviolate self. It's the great tradition of realistic fiction, it's what novels are all about. The private life in the foreground, history a distant rumble of gunfire, somewhere offstage. In Jane Austen not even a rumble. Well, the novel is dying, and us with it. No wonder I could never get anything out of my novel-writing class at Euphoric State. It's an unnatural medium for their experience. Those kids (*gestures at screen*) are living a film, not a novel.

MORRIS: Oh, come on, Philip! You've been listening to Karl Kroop.

PHILIP: Well, he makes a lot of sense.

MORRIS: It's a very crude kind of historicism he's peddling, surely? And bad aesthetics.

HILARY: This is all very fascinating, I'm sure, but could we discuss something a little more practical? Like what the four of us are going to do in the immediate future?

DÉSIRÉE: It's no use, Hilary. Don't you recognize the sound of men talking?

MORRIS: (*To* PHILIP) The paradigms of fiction are essentially the same whatever the medium. Words or images, it makes no difference at the structural level.

DÉSIRÉE: "The structural level," "paradigms." How they love those abstract words. "Historicism"!

PHILIP: (*To* MORRIS) I don't think that's entirely true. I mean, take the question of endings.

DÉSIRÉE: Yeah, let's take it!

PHILIP: You remember that passage in *Northanger Abbey* where Jane Austen says she's afraid that her readers will have guessed that a happy ending is coming up at any moment.

MORRIS: (*nods*) Quote, "Seeing in the tell-tale compression of the pages before them that we are all hastening together to perfect felicity." Unquote.

PHILIP: That's it. Well, that's something the novelist can't help giving away, isn't it, that his book is shortly coming to an end? It may not be a happy ending, nowadays, but he can't disguise the tell-tale compression of the pages.

HILARY and DÉSIRÉE begin to listen to what PHILIP is saying, and he becomes the focal point of attention.

I mean, mentally you brace yourself for the ending of a novel. As you're reading, you're aware of the fact that there's only a page or two left in the book, and you get ready to close it. But with a film there's no way of telling, especially nowadays, when films are much more loosely structured, much more ambivalent, than they used to be. There's no way of telling which frame is going to be the last. The film is going along, just as life goes along, people are behaving, doing things, drinking, talking, and we're watching them, and at any point the director chooses, without warning, without anything being resolved, or explained, or wound up, it can just . . . end.

PHILIP shrugs. The camera stops, freezing him in mid-gesture.

THE END

SMALL WORLD

AN ACADEMIC ROMANCE

To Mary
With all my love

AUTHOR'S NOTE

Like *Changing Places*, to which it is a kind of sequel, *Small World* resembles what is sometimes called the real world, without corresponding exactly to it, and is peopled by figments of the imagination (the name of one of the minor characters has been changed in later editions to avoid misunderstanding on this score). Rummidge is not Birmingham, though it owes something to popular prejudices about that city. There really is an underground chapel at Heathrow and a James Joyce Pub in Zürich, but no universities in Limerick or Darlington; nor, as far as I know, was there ever a British Council representative resident in Genoa. The MLA Convention of 1979 did not take place in New York, though I have drawn on the programme for the 1978 one, which did. And so on.

Special thanks for information received (not to mention many other favours) are due to Donald and Margot Fanger and Susumu Takagi. Most of the books from which I have derived hints, ideas and inspiration for this one are mentioned in the text, but I should acknowledge a debt to two which are not: *Inescapable Romance: Studies in the Poetics of a Mode* by Patricia A. Parker (Princeton University Press, 1979) and *Airport International* by Brian Moynahan (Pan Books, 1978).

Caelum, non animum mutant, qui trans mare currunt.

HORACE

When a writer calls his work a Romance, it need hardly be observed that he wishes to claim a certain latitude, both as to its fashion and material, which he would not have felt himself entitled to assume had he professed to be writing a Novel.

NATHANIEL HAWTHORNE

Hush! Caution! Echoland!

JAMES JOYCE

Prologue

When April with its sweet showers has pierced the drought of March to the root, and bathed every vein of earth with that liquid by whose power the flowers are engendered; when the zephyr, too, with its dulcet breath, has breathed life into the tender new shoots in every copse and on every heath, and the young sun has run half his course in the sign of the Ram, and the little birds that sleep all night with their eyes open give song (so Nature prompts them in their hearts), then, as the poet Geoffrey Chaucer observed many years ago, folk long to go on pilgrimages. Only, these days, professional people call them conferences.

The modern conference resembles the pilgrimage of medieval Christendom in that it allows the participants to indulge themselves in all the pleasures and diversions of travel while appearing to be austerely bent on self-improvement. To be sure, there are certain penitential exercises to be performed—the presentation of a paper, perhaps, and certainly listening to the papers of others. But with this excuse you journey to new and interesting places, meet new and interesting people, and form new and interesting relationships with them; exchange gossip and confidences (for your well-worn stories are fresh to them, and vice versa); eat, drink and make merry in their company every evening; and yet, at the end of it all, return home with an enhanced reputation for seriousness of mind. Today's conferees have an additional advantage over the pilgrims of old in that their expenses are usually paid, or at least subsidised, by the institution to which they belong, be it a government department, a commercial firm, or, most commonly perhaps, a university.

There are conferences on almost everything these days, including the works of Geoffrey Chaucer. If, like his hero Troilus at the end of *Troilus and Criseyde*, he looks down from the eighth sphere of heaven on

> *This litle spot of erthe, that with the se Embraced is*

and observes all the frantic traffic around the globe that he and other great writers have set in motion—the jet trails that criss-cross the oceans, marking the passage of scholars from one continent to another, their paths converging and intersecting and passing, as they hasten to hotel, country house or ancient seat of learning, there to confer and carouse, so that English and other academic subjects may be kept up—what does Geoffrey Chaucer think?

Probably, like the spirit of Troilus, that chivalrous knight and disillusioned lover, he laughs heartily at the spectacle, and considers himself well out of it. For not all conferences are happy, hedonistic occasions; not all conference venues are luxurious and picturesque; not all Aprils, for that matter, are marked by sweet showers and dulcet breezes.

PART I

1

"April is the cruellest month," Persse McGarrigle quoted silently to himself, gazing through grimy windowpanes at the unseasonable snow crusting the lawns and flowerbeds of the Rummidge campus. He had recently completed a Master's dissertation on the poetry of T. S. Eliot, but the opening words of *The Waste Land* might, with equal probability, have been passing through the heads of any one of the fifty-odd men and women, of varying ages, who sat or slumped in the raked rows of seats in the same lecture-room. For they were all well acquainted with that poem, being University Teachers of English Language and Literature, gathered together here, in the English Midlands, for their annual conference, and few of them were enjoying themselves.

Dismay had been already plainly written on many faces when they assembled the previous evening for the traditional sherry reception. The conferees had, by that time, acquainted themselves with the accommodation provided in one of the University's halls of residence, a building hastily erected in 1969, at the height of the boom in higher education, and now, only ten years later, looking much the worse for wear. They had glumly unpacked their suitcases in study-bedrooms whose cracked and pitted walls retained, in a pattern of rectangular fade marks, the traces of posters hurriedly removed (sometimes with portions of plaster adhering to them) by their youthful owners at the commencement of the Easter vacation. They had appraised the stained and broken furniture, explored the dusty interiors of cupboards in vain for coat-hangers, and tested the narrow beds, whose springs sagged dejectedly in the middle, deprived of all resilience by the battering of a decade's horseplay and copulation. Each room had a washbasin, though not every washbasin had a plug, or every plug a chain. Some taps could not be turned on, and some could not be turned off. For more elaborate ablutions, or to answer a call of nature, it was necessary to venture out into the draughty and labyrinthine corridors in search of one of the communal washrooms, where baths, showers and toilets were to be found—but little privacy, and unreliable supplies of hot water.

To veterans of conferences held in British provincial universities, these were familiar discomforts and, up to a point, stoically accepted; as was the rather inferior sherry served at the reception (a little-known brand that seemed to protest too much its Spanish origins by the lurid depiction of a bullfight *and* a flamenco dancer on the label); as was the dinner which awaited them afterwards—tomato soup, roast beef and two vegetables, jam tart with custard—from every item of which all trace of flavour had been conscientiously removed by prolonged cooking at high temperatures. More than customary aggravation was generated by the discovery that the conference would be sleeping in one building, eating in another, and meeting for lectures and discussions on the main campus, thus ensuring for all concerned a great deal of tiresome walking to and fro on paths and pavements made dangerous and unpleasant by the snow. But the real source of depression, as the conferees gathered for the sherry, and squinted at the little white cardboard lapel badges on which each person's name, and university, were neatly printed, was the paucity and, it must be said, the generally undistinguished quality of their numbers. Within a very short time they had established that none of the stars of the profession was in residence—no one, indeed, whom it would be worth travelling ten miles to meet, let alone the hundreds that many had covered. But they were stuck with each other for three days: three meals a day, three bar sessions a day, a coach outing and a theatre visit—long hours of compulsory sociability; not to mention the seven papers that would be delivered, followed by questions and discussion. Long before it was all over they would have sickened of each other's company, exhausted all topics of conversation, used up all congenial seating arrangements at table, and succumbed to the familiar conference syndrome of bad breath, coated tongue and persistent headache, that came from smoking, drinking and talking five times as much as normal. The foreknowledge of the boredom and distemper to which they had condemned themselves lay like a cold, oppressive weight on their bowels (which would also be out of order before long) even as they sought to disguise it with bright chatter and hearty bonhomie, shaking hands and clapping backs, gulping down their sherry like medicine. Here and there people could be seen furtively totting up the names on the conference list. Fifty-seven, including the non-resident home team, was a very disappointing turn-out.

So Persse McGarrigle was assured, at the sherry party, by a melancholy-looking elderly man sipping a glass of orange juice into which his spectacles threatened to slide at any moment. The name on his lapel badge was "Dr. Rupert Sutcliffe," and the colour of the badge was yellow, indicating that he was a member of the host Department.

"Is that right?" Persse said. "I didn't know what to expect. It's the very first conference I've ever been to."

"UTE conferences vary a lot. It all depends on where it's held. At Oxford or Cambridge you would expect at least a hundred and fifty. I told Swallow nobody would come to Rummidge, but he wouldn't listen."

"Swallow?"

"Our Head of Department." Dr. Sutcliffe seemed to have some difficulty in forcing these words between his teeth. "He claimed it would put Rummidge on the map if we offered to host the conference. Delusions of grandeur, I'm afraid."

"Was it Professor Swallow who was giving out the little badges?"

"No, that's Bob Busby, he's just as bad. Worse, if anything. Been beside himself with excitement for weeks, organizing outings and so forth. I should think we'll lose a pretty penny on this affair," Dr. Sutcliffe concluded, with evident satisfaction, looking over his glasses at the half-filled room.

"Hallo, Rupert, old man! A bit thin on the ground, aren't we?"

A man of about forty, dressed in a bright blue suit, hit Sutcliffe vigorously between the shoulder blades as he pronounced these words, causing the latter's spectacles to fly off the end of his nose. Persse caught them neatly and returned them to their owner.

"Oh, it's you, Dempsey," said Sutcliffe, turning to face his assailant.

"Only fifty-seven on the list, and a lot of *them* haven't turned up, by the look of it," said the newcomer, whose lapel badge identified him as Professor Robin Dempsey, from one of the new universities in the north of England. He was a broad-shouldered, thickset man, with a heavy jaw that jutted aggressively, but his eyes, small and set too close together, seemed to belong to some other person, more anxious and vulnerable, trapped inside the masterful physique. Rupert Sutcliffe did not seem overjoyed to see Professor Dempsey, or disposed to share with him his own pessimism about the conference.

"I dare say a lot of people have been held up by the snow," he said coldly. "Shocking weather for April. Excuse me, I see Busby waving urgently. I expect the potato crisps have run out, or some such crisis." He shuffled off.

"God!" said Dempsey, looking round the room. "What a shower! Why did I come?" The question sounded rhetorical, but Dempsey proceeded to answer it at some length, and without apparently pausing for breath. "I'll tell you why, I came because I have family here, it seemed a good excuse to see them. My children, actually. I'm divorced, you see. I used to work here, in this Department, believe it or not. Christ, what a retarded lot they were, still are by the look of it. The same old faces. Nobody ever seems to move. Old Sutcliffe, for instance, been here forty years, man and boy. Naturally I got out as soon as I could. No place for an ambitious man. The last straw was when they gave a senior lectureship to Philip Swallow instead of me, though I had three books out by then, and he'd published practically nothing. Now—you wouldn't credit it—they've gone and given him the Chair here, and he's still published practically nothing. There's supposed to be a book about Hazlitt—*Hazlitt*, I ask you—it was announced last year, but I've never seen a single review of it. Can't be much good. Well, anyway, as soon as they gave Swallow the senior lectureship, I said to Janet, right, that's it, we're off, put the house up for sale, we're going to Darlington—they'd been wooing me for some time. A Readership straight away, and a free hand to develop my special interests—linguistics and stylistics—they always hated that sort of thing here, blocked me at every turn, talked to students behind my back, persuaded them to drop my courses, I was glad to shake the dust of Rummidge off my feet, I can tell you. That was ten years ago, Darlington was small in those days, still is, I suppose, but it was a challenge, and the students are quite good, you'd be surprised. Anyway, I was happy enough, but unfortunately Janet didn't like it, took against the place as soon as she saw it. Well, the campus is a bit bleak in winter, outside the town, you know, on the edge of the moors, and mostly prefabricated huts in those days, it's better now, we've got rid of the sheep and our Metallurgy building won a prize recently, but at the time, well, anyway, we couldn't sell the house here, there was a freeze on mortgages, so Janet decided to stay on in Rummidge for a while, we thought it would be better for the kids anyway, Desmond was in his last year at junior school, so I commuted, came home every weekend, well, nearly every weekend, it was a bit hard on Janet, hard on me, too, of course, and then I met this girl, a postgraduate student of mine, well, you can appreciate that I was pretty lonely up there, it was inevitable when you come to think of it, I said to Janet, it was inevitable—she found out about the girl, you see . . ."

He broke off, frowning into his sherry glass. "I don't know why I'm telling you all this," he said, shooting a slightly resentful look at Persse, who had been puzzled on the same score for several minutes. "I don't even know who you are." He bent forward to read Persse's lapel badge. "University College, Limerick, eh?" he said, with a leer. "*There was a young lecturer from Limerick . . .* I suppose everyone says that to you."

"Nearly everyone," Persse admitted. "But, you know, they very seldom get further than the first line. There aren't many rhymes to 'Limerick.'"

"What about '*dip his wick*'?" said Dempsey, after a moment's reflection. "That should have possibilities."

"What does it mean?"

Dempsey looked surprised. "Well, it means, you know, having it off. Screwing."

Persse blushed. "The metre's all wrong," he said. "'Limerick' is a dactyl."

"Oh? What's 'dip his wick,' then?"

"I'd say it was a catalectic trochee."

"Would you, indeed? Interested in prosody, are you?"

"Yes, I suppose I am."

"I bet you write poetry yourself, don't you?"

"Well, yes, I do."

"I thought so. You have that look about you. There's no money in it, you know."

"So I've discovered," said Persse. "Did you marry the girl, then?"

"What?"

"The postgraduate student. Did you marry her?"

"Oh. No. No, she went her way. Like they all do, eventually." Dempsey swilled the dregs of his sherry at the bottom of his glass.

"And your wife won't have you back?"

"Can't, can she? She's got another bloke now."

"I'm very sorry," said Persse.

"Oh, I don't let it get me down," said Dempsey unconvincingly. "I don't regret the move. It's a good place, Darlington. They've just bought a new computer especially for me."

"And you're a professor, now," said Persse respectfully.

"Yes, I'm a professor now," Dempsey agreed. His face darkened as he added, "So is Swallow, of course."

"Which one *is* Professor Swallow?" Persse enquired, looking round the room.

"He's here somewhere." Dempsey rather unwillingly scanned the sherry drinkers in search of Philip Swallow.

At that moment the knots of chatting conferees seemed to loosen and part, as if by some magical impulsion, opening up an avenue between Persse and the doorway. There, hesitating on the threshold, was the most beautiful girl he had ever seen in his life. She was tall and graceful, with a full, womanly figure, and a dark, creamy complexion. Black hair fell in shining waves to her shoulders, and black was the colour of her simple woollen dress, scooped out low across her bosom. She took a few paces forward into the room and accepted a glass of sherry from the tray offered to her by a passing waitress. She did not drink at once, but held the glass up to her face as if it were a flower. Her right hand held the stem of the glass between index finger and thumb. Her left, passed horizontally across her waist, supported her right elbow. Over the rim of the glass she looked with eyes dark as peat pools straight into Persse's own, and seemed to smile faintly in greeting. She raised the glass to her lips, which were red and moist, the underlip slightly swollen in appearance, as though it had been stung. She drank, and he saw the muscles in her throat move and slide under the skin as she swallowed. "Heavenly God!" Persse breathed, quoting again, this time from *A Portrait of the Artist as a Young Man*.

Then, to his extreme annoyance, a tall, slim, distinguished-looking man of middle age, with a rather dashing silver-grey beard, and a good deal of wavy hair of the same hue around the back and sides of his head, but not much on top, darted forward to greet the girl, blocking Persse's view of her.

"There's Swallow," said Dempsey.

"What?" said Persse, coming slowly out of his trance.

"Swallow is the man chatting up that rather dishy girl who just came in, the one in the black dress, or should I say half out of it? Swallow seems to be getting an eyeful, doesn't he?"

Persse flushed and stiffened with a chivalrous urge to protect the girl from insult. Professor Swallow, leaning forward to scrutinize her lapel badge, did indeed seem to be peering rudely down her décolletage.

"Fine pair of knockers there, wouldn't you say?" Dempsey remarked.

Persse turned on him fiercely. "Knockers? *Knockers?* Why in the name of God call them that?"

Dempsey backed away slightly. "Steady on. What would you call them, then?"

"I would call them . . . I would call them . . . twin domes of her body's temple," said Persse.

"Christ, you really are a poet, aren't you? Look, excuse me, I think I'll grab another sherry while there's still time." And Dempsey shouldered his way to the nearest waitress, leaving Persse alone.

But not alone! Miraculously, the girl had materialized at his elbow.

"Hallo, what's your name?" she said, peering at his lapel. "I can't read these little badges without my glasses." Her voice was strong but melodious, slightly American in accent, but with a trace of something else he could not identify.

"Persse McGarrigle—from Limerick," he eagerly replied.

"Perce? Is that short for Percival?"

"It could be," said Persse, "if you like."

The girl laughed, revealing teeth that were perfectly even and perfectly white. "What do you mean, if I like?"

"It's a variant of 'Pearce.'" He spelled it out for her.

"Oh, like in *Finnegans Wake*! The Ballad of Persse O'Reilley."

"Exactly so. Persse, Pearce, Pierce—I wouldn't be surprised if they were not all related to Percival. Percival, *per se*, as Joyce might have said," he added, and was rewarded with another dazzling smile.

"What about McGarrigle?"

"It's an old Irish name that means 'Son of Super-valour.'"

"That must take a lot of living up to."

"I do my best," said Persse. "And your own name . . . ?" He inclined his head towards the magnificent bosom, appreciating, now, why Professor Swallow had appeared to be almost nuzzling it in his attempt to read the badge pinned there, for the name was not boldly printed, like everyone else's, but written in a minute italic script. "*A. L. Pabst*," it austerely stated. There was no indication of which university she belonged to.

"Angelica," she volunteered.

"Angelica!" Persse exhaled rather than pronounced the syllables. "That's a beautiful name!"

"Pabst is a bit of a let-down, though, isn't it? Not in the same class as 'Son of Super-valour.'"

"Would it be a German name?"

"I suppose it was originally, though Daddy is Dutch."

"You don't look German or Dutch."

"No?" she smiled. "What do I look then?"

"You look Irish. You remind me of the women in the south-west of Ireland whose ancestors intermarried with the sailors of the Spanish Armada that was shipwrecked on the coast of Munster in the great storm of 1588. They have just your kind of looks."

"What a romantic idea! It could be true, too. I have no idea where I came from originally."

"How's that?"

"I'm an adopted child."

"What does the 'L' stand for?"

"A rather silly name. I'd rather not tell you."

"Then why draw attention to it?"

"If you use initials in the academic world, people think you're a man and take you more seriously."

"No one could mistake you for a man, Angelica," Persse said sincerely.

"I mean in correspondence. Or publications."

"Have you published much?"

"No, not a lot. Well, nothing, yet, actually. I'm still working on my PhD. Did you say you teach at Limerick? Is it a big Department?"

"Not very big," said Persse. "As a matter of fact, there's only the three of us. It's basically an agricultural college. We've only recently started offering a general arts degree. Do you mean to say that you don't know who your real parents were?"

"No idea at all. I was a foundling."

"And where were you found, if that isn't an impertinent question?"

"It *is* a little intimate, considering we've only just met," said Angelica. "But never mind. I was found in the toilet of a KLM Stratocruiser flying from New York to Amsterdam. I was six weeks old. Nobody knows how I got there."

"Did Mr. Pabst find you?"

"No, Daddy was an executive of KLM at the time. He and Mummy adopted me, as they had no children of their own. Have you really only three members of staff in your Department?"

"Yes. There's Professor McCreedy—he's Old English. And Dr. Quinlan—Middle English. I'm Modern English."

"What? All of it? From Shakespeare to . . . ?"

"T. S. Eliot. I did my MA thesis on Shakespeare's influence on T. S. Eliot."

"You must be worked to death."

"Well, we don't have a great number of students, to tell you the truth. Not many people know we exist. Professor McCreedy believes in keeping a low profile . . . And yourself, Angelica, where do you teach?"

"I haven't got a proper job at the moment." Angelica frowned, and began to look about her a trifle distractedly, as if in search of employment, so that Persse missed the crucial word in her next sentence. "I did some part-time teaching at . . ." she said. "But now I'm trying to finish my doctoral dissertation."

"What is it on?" Persse asked.

Angelica turned her peat-dark eyes upon him. "Romance," she said.

At that moment a gong sounded to announce dinner, and there was a general surge towards the exit in the course of which Persse got separated from Angelica. To his chagrin, he found himself obliged to sit between two medievalists, one from Oxford and one from Aberystwyth, who, leaning back at dangerous angles on their chairs, conducted an animated discussion about Chaucerian metrics behind his back, while he bent forward over his roast shoe-leather and cast longing looks up to the other end of the table, where Philip Swallow and Robin Dempsey were vying to entertain Angelica Pabst.

"If you are looking for the gravy, young man, it's right under your nose."

This observation came from an elderly lady sitting opposite Persse. Though her tone was sharp, her face was friendly, and she allowed herself a smile of complicity when Persse expressed his opinion that the beef was beyond the help of gravy. She wore a black silk dress of antique design and her white hair was neatly retained in a snood decorated with tiny beads of jet. Her name badge identified her as Miss Sybil Maiden, of Girton College, Cambridge. "Retired many years ago," she explained. "But I still attend these conferences whenever I can. It helps to keep me young."

Persse enquired about her scholarly interests.

"I suppose you would call me a folklorist," she said. "I was a pupil of Jessie Weston's. What is your own line of research?"

"I did my Master's thesis on Shakespeare and T. S. Eliot."

"Then you are no doubt familiar with Miss Weston's book, *From Ritual to Romance*, on which Mr. Eliot drew for much of the imagery and allusion in *The Waste Land*?"

"Indeed I am," said Persse.

"She argued," Miss Maiden continued, not at all deterred by this answer, "that the quest for the Holy Grail, associated with the Arthurian knights, was only superficially a Christian legend, and that its true meaning was to be sought in pagan fertility ritual. If Mr. Eliot had taken her discoveries to heart, we might have been spared the maudlin religiosity of his later poetry."

"Well," said Persse placatingly, "I suppose everyone is looking for his own Grail. For Eliot it was religious faith, but for another it might be fame, or the love of a good woman."

"Would you mind passing the gravy?" said the Oxford medievalist. Persse obliged.

"It all comes down to sex, in the end," Miss Maiden declared firmly. "The life force endlessly renewing itself." She fixed the gravy boat in the Oxford medievalist's hand with a beady eye. "The Grail cup, for instance, is a female symbol of great antiquity and universal occurrence." (The Oxford medievalist seemed to have second thoughts about helping himself to gravy.) "And the Grail spear, supposed to be the one that pierced the side of Christ, is obviously phallic. *The Waste Land* is really all about Eliot's fears of impotence and sterility."

"I've heard that theory before," said Persse, "but I feel it's too simple."

"I quite agree," said the Oxford medievalist. "This business of phallic symbolism is a lot of rot." He stabbed the air with his knife to emphasize the point.

Preoccupied with this discussion, Persse failed to observe when Angelica left the dining-room. He looked for her in the bar, but she was not to be found there, or anywhere else that evening. Persse went to bed early, and tossed restlessly on his narrow, lumpy mattress, listening to the plumbing whining in the walls, footfalls in the corridor outside his room, and the sounds of doors slamming and engines starting in the car park beneath his window. Once he thought he heard the voice of Angelica calling "Goodnight," but by the time he got to the window there was nothing to be seen except the fading embers of a departing car's rear lights. Before he got back into bed he switched on the lamp above his sink, and stared critically at his reflection in the mirror. He saw a white, round, freckled face, snub nose, pale blue eyes, and a mop of red curly hair. "I wouldn't say you were handsome, exactly," he murmured. "But I've seen uglier mugs."

. . .

Angelica was not present at the first formal session of the conference the next morning, which was one reason why Persse muttered "April is the cruellest month" under his breath as he sat in the lecture-room. Other reasons included the continuing cold, damp weather, which had not been anticipated by the Rummidge heating engineers, the inedibility of the bacon and tomatoes served at breakfast that morning, and the tedium of the paper to which he was listening. It was being given by the Oxford medievalist and was on the subject of Chaucerian metrics. He had heard the substance of it already, last night at dinner, and it did not improve on reacquaintance.

Persse yawned and shifted his weight from one buttock to another in his seat at the back of the lecture-room. He could not see the faces of many of his colleagues, but as far as could be judged from their postures, most of them were as disengaged from the discourse as himself. Some were leaning back as far as their seats allowed, staring vacantly at the ceiling, others were slumped forwards onto the desks that separated each row, resting their chins on folded arms, and others again were sprawled sideways over two or three seats, with their legs crossed and arms dangling limply to the floor. In the third row a man was surreptitiously doing *The Times* crossword, and at least three people appeared to be asleep. Someone, a student presumably, had carved into the surface of the desk at which Persse sat, cutting deep into the wood with the force of a man driven to the limits of endurance, the word "BORING." Another had scratched the message, "*Swallow is a wanker.*" Persse saw no reason to dissent from either of these judgments.

Suddenly, though, there were signs of animation in the audience. The speaker was commencing his peroration, and had made reference to something called "structuralism."

"Of course, to our friends across the Channel," he said, with a slight curl of his lip, "everything I have been saying will seem vanity and illusion. To the structuralists, metre, like language itself, is merely a system of differences. The idea that there might be anything inherently expressive or mimetic in patterns of stress would be anathema . . ."

Some, probably the majority, of the audience, smiled and nodded and nudged each other. Others frowned, bit their lips and began making rapid notes. The question session, chaired by the Aberystwyth medievalist, was lively.

There followed a break for coffee, which was served in a small common-room not far away. Persse was delighted to find Angelica already ensconced here, fetchingly dressed in a roll-neck jumper, tweed skirt and high leather boots. Her cheeks had a healthy glow. She had been for a walk. "I slept through breakfast," she explained, "and I was too late for the lecture."

"You didn't miss much," said Persse. "Both were indigestible. What happened to you last night? I looked all over for you."

"Oh, Professor Swallow asked some people back to his house for a drink."

"You're a friend of his, then, are you?"

"No. Well, not really. I've never met him before, if that's what you mean. But he *is* very friendly."

"Hmmph," said Persse.

"What was the paper about, this morning?" Angelica asked.

"It was supposed to be about Chaucer's metre, but the discussion was mostly about structuralism."

Angelica looked annoyed. "Oh, what a nuisance that I missed it. I'm very interested in structuralism."

"What is it, exactly?"

Angelica laughed.

"No, I'm serious," said Persse. "What is structuralism? Is it a good thing or a bad thing?"

Angelica looked puzzled, and wary of having her leg pulled. "But you must know something about it, Persse. You must have *heard of it*, even in . . . Where did you do your graduate work?"

"University College Dublin. But I wasn't there much of the time. I had TB, you see. They were very decent about it, let me work on my dissertation in the sanatorium. I had a visit from my supervisor occasionally, but mostly I worked on my own. Then before that, I did my BA at Galway. We never heard anything about structuralism there. Then after I got my Master's degree, I went home to work on the farm for two years. My people are farmers, in county Mayo."

"Did you mean to be a farmer yourself?"

"No, it was to get my strength back, after the TB. The doctors said an open-air life was the thing."

"And did you—get your strength back?"

"Oh yes, I'm sound as a bell, now." He struck himself vigorously on the chest. "Then I got the job at Limerick."

"You were lucky. Jobs are hard to find these days."

"I *was* lucky," Persse agreed. "Indeed I was. I found out afterwards that I was called to the interview by mistake. They really meant to interview another fellow called McGarrigle—some highflying prize scholar from Trinity. But the letter was addressed to me—someone slipped up in the Registry— and they were too embarrassed to retract the invitation."

"Well, you made the most of the lucky break," said Angelica. "They could have appointed one of the other candidates."

"Well, that was another piece of luck," said Persse. "There *were* no other candidates—not called for interview anyway. They were quite sure they wanted to appoint this McGarrigle fellow, and they were after saving train fares. Anyway, what I'm trying to say is that I've never been in what you might call the swim, intellectually speaking. That's why I've come to this conference. To improve myself. To find out what's going on in the great world of ideas. Who's in, who's out, and all that. So tell me about structuralism."

Angelica took a deep breath, then expelled it abruptly. "It's hard to know where to start," she said. A bell sounded to summon them back to the lecture room. "Saved by the bell!" she laughed.

"Later, then," Persse urged.

"I'll see what I can do," said Angelica.

As the conferees shuffled back towards the lecture-room for the second paper of the morning, they cast wistful glances over their shoulders at the figure of the Oxford medievalist shaking hands with Philip Swallow. He had his overcoat on and his briefcase in his hand. "That's the trouble with these conferences," Persse heard someone say, "the chief speakers tend to bugger off as soon as they've done their party piece. Makes you feel like a besieged army when the general flies out in a helicopter."

"Are you coming, Persse?" Angelica enquired.

Persse looked at his programme. "'Animal Imagery in Dryden's Heroic Tragedies,'" he read aloud.

"It could be interesting," Angelica said earnestly.

"I think I'll sit this one out," said Persse. "I think I'll write a poem instead."

"Oh, do you write poetry? What kind?"

"Short poems," said Persse. "Very short poems."

"Like *haikus?*"

"Shorter than that, sometimes."

"Goodness! What are you going to write about?"

"You can read it when it's finished."

"All right. I'll look forward to that. I'd better go." A vaguely smiling Philip Swallow hovered nearby, like a sheepdog rounding up strays.

"I'll see you in the bar before lunch, then," said Persse. He made a show of hurrying to the Gents, intending to loiter there until the lecture on Dryden had begun. To his consternation, however, Philip Swallow, accompanied by Bob Busby, followed him. Persse locked himself in a closet and sat down on the toilet seat. The two men seemed to be talking about a missing speaker as they stood at the urinal. "When did he phone?" Philip Swallow was saying, and Busby replied, "About two hours ago. He said he would do his best to get here by this afternoon. I told him to spare no expense." "Did you?" said Swallow. "I'm not sure that was entirely wise, Bob."

Persse heard the spurt of tapwater at the sinks, the rattle of the towel dispenser, and the banging of the door as the two men left. After a minute or two, he emerged from hiding and quietly approached the lecture-room. He peered through the little observation window in the door. He could see Angelica in profile, sitting alone in the front row, gracefully alert, a stainless-steel ballpen poised in one hand, ready to take notes. She was wearing spectacles with heavy black frames, which made her look formidably efficient, like a high-powered secretary. The rest of the audience was performing the same tableau of petrified boredom as before. Persse tiptoed away, and out into the open air. He crossed the campus and took the road that led to the site of the halls of residence.

The melting snow dripped from the trees, and ran down the back of his neck as he walked, but he was oblivious to the discomfort. He was trying to compose a poem about Angelica Pabst. Unfortunately some lines of W. B. Yeats kept interposing themselves between him and his muse, and the best he could do was to adapt them to his own case.

> How can I, that girl standing there,
> My attention fix
> On Chaucer or on Dryden
> Or structuralist poetics?

As he recited the words to himself, it occurred to Persse McGarrigle that perhaps he was in love. "I am in love," he said aloud, to the dripping trees, to a white-bonneted pillar-box, to a sodden mongrel lifting its hind leg against the gatepost of the halls of residence site. "I am in love!" he exclaimed, to a long line of depressed-looking sparrows perched on the railings that ran alongside the slushy drive. "I AM IN LOVE!" he cried, startling a gaggle of geese beside the artificial lake, as he ran up and down, round and round, in the virgin snow, leaving a trail of deep footprints behind him.

Panting from this exercise, he came up to the entrance of Lucas Hall, the tall tower block in which sleeping accommodation had been provided for the conferees. (Martineau Hall, in which they ate and drank, was in contrast, a low cylindrical building, confirming Miss Maiden's views on the universality of sexual symbolism.) A taxi was drawn up outside Lucas Hall, its engine churning, and a thickset man with a fat cigar in his mouth, and a deerstalker, with the flaps down, on his head, was getting out. Seeing Persse, he called "Hi" and beckoned. "Say, is this where the conference is being held?" he asked, in an American accent. "The University Teachers of English Conference? It's the right name, but it doesn't look right."

"This is where we're sleeping," said Persse. "The meetings are held on the main campus, up the road."

"Ah, that figures," said the man. "OK, driver, we made it. How much?"

"Forty-six pounds eighty, guv'nor," the man appeared to say, looking at his meter.

"OK, there you go," said the newcomer, stripping ten crisp new five-pound notes from a thick wad, and pushing them through the cab window. The driver, catching sight of Persse, leaned out and addressed him. "You don't wanner cab to London by any chance?"

"No thank you," said Persse.

"I'll be on my way, then. Thanks guv'nor."

Awed by this display of wealth, Persse picked up the new arrival's suitcase, a handsome leather affair with the vestiges of many labels on it, and carried it into the lobby of Lucas Hall. "Have you really and truly come all the way from London by taxi?" he said.

"I had no choice. When I landed at Heathrow this morning they tell me that my connecting flight is cancelled, Rummidge airport is socked in by snow. They give me a railroad ticket instead. So I take a cab to the railroad station in London and they tell me the power lines for the trains to Rummidge are down. Great drama, the country paralysed, Rummidge cut off from the capital, everybody enjoying every minute of it, the porters can hardly contain their joy. When I said I'd take a cab all the way, they said I was crazy, tried to talk me out of it. '*You'll never get through,*' they said, '*the motorways are covered in snowdrifts, there are people who have been trapped in their cars all night.*' So I go along the cab rank till I find a driver with the guts to give it a whirl, and what do we find when we get here? Two inches of melting snow. What a country!" He took off his deerstalker and held it at arm's length. It was made from a hairy tweed, with a bold red check on a yellowy-brown background. "I bought this hat at Heathrow this morning," he said. "The first thing I always seem to have to do when I arrive in England is buy myself a hat."

"It's a fine hat," said Persse.

"You like it? Remind me to give it to you when I leave. I'm travelling on to warmer climes."

"That's very kind of you."

"You're welcome. Now, where do I check in?"

"There's a list of rooms over here," said Persse. "What's your name?"

"Morris Zapp."

"I'm sure I've heard that name before."

"I should hope so. What's yours?"

"Persse McGarrigle, from Limerick. Aren't you giving a paper this afternoon?" he said. "'Title to be announced'?"

"Right, Percy. That's why I strained every nerve to get here. Look at the bottom of the list. There are never many zees."

Persse looked. "It says here that you're a non-resident."

"Ah, yeah, Philip Swallow said something about staying with him. How's it going, the Conference?"

"I can't really say. I've never been to a conference before, so I've no standards of comparison."

"Is that right?" Morris Zapp regarded him with curiosity. "A conference virgin, huh? Where is everybody, by the way?"

"They're at a lecture."

"Which you cut? Well, you've learned the first rule of conferences, kid. Never go to lectures. Unless you're giving one yourself, of course. Or *I'm* giving one," he added reflectively. "I wouldn't want to discourage you from hearing my paper this afternoon. I went over it last night in the plane, while the movie was showing, and I was pretty pleased with it. The movie was OK, too. What size of audience am I likely to get?"

"Well, there are fifty-seven people at the conference, altogether," Persse said.

Professor Zapp nearly swallowed his cigar. "*Fifty-seven*? You must be joking. No? You're not joking? You mean I've travelled six thousand miles to talk to fifty-seven people?"

"Of course, not everybody goes to every lecture," said Persse. "As you can see."

"Listen, do you know how many attend the American equivalent of this conference? *Ten thousand.* There were ten thousand people at the MLA in New York last December."

"I don't think we have that many lecturers over here," said Persse apologetically.

"There must be more than fifty-seven," growled Morris Zapp. "Where are they? I'll tell you where. Most of them are holed up at home, decorating their living-rooms or weeding their gardens, and the few with two original ideas to rub together are off somewhere at conferences in warmer, more attractive places than this." He looked around the lobby of Lucas Hall, at its cracked and dusty floor tiles, its walls of grimy untreated concrete, with disfavour. "Is there anywhere you can get a drink in this place?"

"The bar will be opening soon in Martineau Hall," said Persse.

"Lead me to it."

"Have you really flown all the way from America for this conference, Professor Zapp?" Persse enquired, as they picked their way through the slush.

"Not exactly. I was coming to Europe anyway—I'm on sabbatical this quarter. Philip Swallow heard I was coming over and asked me to take in his conference. So, to oblige an old friend, I said I would."

The bar in Martineau Hall was empty except for the barman, who watched their approach through a kind of chrome-plated portcullis that stretched from counter to ceiling.

"Is this to keep you in, or us out?" quipped Morris Zapp, tapping the metal. "What's yours, Percy? Guinness? A pint of Guinness, barman, and a large scotch on the rocks."

"We're not open yet," said the man. "Not till twelve-thirty."

"And have something yourself."

"Yes, sir, thank you sir," said the barman, cranking the portcullis with alacrity. "I wouldn't say no to a pint of bitter."

While he was drawing the draught Guinness, the other conferees, released from the second lecture of the morning, began to straggle in, Philip Swallow in the van. He strode up to Morris Zapp and wrung his hand.

"Morris! It's marvellous to see you after—how many years?"

"Ten, Philip, ten years, though I hate to admit it. But you're looking good. The beard is terrific. Was your hair always that colour?"

Philip Swallow blushed. "I think it was starting to go grey in '69. How did you get here in the end?"

"That'll be one pound fifty, sir," said the barman.

"By taxi," said Morris Zapp. "Which reminds me: you owe me fifty pounds for the cab fare. Hey, what's the matter, Philip? You've gone white."

"And the Conference has just gone into the red," said Rupert Sutcliffe, with doleful satisfaction. "Hello, Zapp, I don't suppose you remember me."

"Rupert! How could I ever forget that happy face? And here comes Bob Busby, right on cue," said Morris Zapp, as a man with a less impressive beard than Philip Swallow's cantered into the bar, a clipboard under his arm, keys and coins jingling in his pockets. Philip Swallow took him aside and urgent whispers were exchanged.

"I'm afraid you're landed with me as your chairman this afternoon, Zapp," said Rupert Sutcliffe.

"I'm honoured, Rupert."

"Have you, er, decided on a title?"

"Yep. It's called, 'Textuality as Striptease.'"

"Oh," said Rupert Sutcliffe.

"Does everybody know this young man, who kindly looked after me when I arrived?" said Morris Zapp. "Percy McGarrigle from Limerick."

Philip Swallow nodded perfunctorily at Persse and turned his attention back to the American. "Morris, we must get you a lapel badge so that everybody will know who you are."

"Don't worry, if they don't know already, I'll tell them."

"When I said 'Take a cab,'" said Bob Busby reproachfully to Morris Zapp, "I meant from Heathrow to Euston, not from London to Rummidge."

"Never mind that now," said Philip Swallow impatiently. "It's no use crying over spilt milk. Morris, where is your luggage? I thought you'd be more comfortable staying with us than in Hall."

"I think so too, now I've seen the hall," said Morris Zapp.

"Hilary is dying to see you," said Swallow, leading him away.

"Hmm. That should be an interesting reunion," murmured Rupert Sutcliffe, peering at the departing pair over his glasses.

"What?" Persse responded absently. He was looking out for Angelica.

"Well, you see, about ten years ago those two were nominated for our exchange scheme with Euphoria—in America, you know. Zapp came here for six months, and Swallow went to Euphoric State. Rumour has it that Zapp had an affair with Hilary Swallow, and Swallow with Mrs. Zapp."

"You don't say so?" Persse was intrigued by this story, in spite of the distraction of seeing Angelica come into the bar with Robin Dempsey. He was talking to her with great animation, while she wore the slightly fixed smile of someone who is being sung at in a musical comedy.

"Quite. 'What a set,' as Matthew Arnold said of the Shelley circle . . . Anyway, at the same time, Gordon Masters, our Head of Department, retired prematurely after a nervous breakdown—it was 1969, the year of the student revolution, a trying time for everybody—and Zapp was being mooted by some as his successor. One day, however, just when things were coming to a head, he and Hilary Swallow suddenly flew off to America together, and we really didn't know which couple to expect back: Zapp and Hilary, Philip and Hilary, Philip and Mrs. Zapp, or both Zapps."

"What was Mrs. Zapp's name?" said Persse.

"I've forgotten," said Rupert Sutcliffe. "Does it matter?"

"I like to know names," said Persse. "I can't follow a story without them."

"Anyway, we never saw her. The Swallows returned together. We gathered they were going to give the marriage another chance."

"It seems to have worked."

"Mmm. Though in my opinion," Sutcliffe said darkly, "the whole episode had a deplorable effect on Swallow's character."

"Oh?"

Sutcliffe nodded, but seemed disinclined to elaborate.

"So then they gave Philip Swallow the chair?" said Persse.

"Not *then*, oh goodness me, no. No, then we had Dalton, he came from Oxford, until three years ago. He was killed in a car accident. Then they appointed Swallow. Some people would have preferred me, I believe, but I'm getting too old for that sort of thing."

"Oh, surely not," said Persse, because Rupert Sutcliffe seemed to hope he would.

"I'll say one thing," Sutcliffe volunteered. "If they'd appointed me, they'd have had a Head of Department who stuck to his last, and wasn't flying off here there and everywhere all the time."

"Travels a lot, does he—Professor Swallow?"

"Lately he seems to be absent more often than he's present."

Persse excused himself and pushed his way through the crowd at the bar to where Angelica was waiting for Dempsey to bring her a drink. "Hallo, how was the lecture?" he greeted her.

"Boring. But there was an interesting discussion of structuralism afterwards."

"Again? You've really got to tell me what structuralism is all about. It's a matter of urgency."

"Structuralism?" said Dempsey, coming up with a sherry for Angelica just in time to hear Persse's plea, and all too eager to show off his expertise. "It all goes back to Saussure's linguistics. The arbitrariness of the signifier. Language as a system of differences with no positive terms."

"Give me an example," said Persse. "I can't follow an argument without an example."

"Well, take the words *dog* and *cat*. There's no absolute reason why the combined phonemes *d-o-g* should signify a quadruped that goes 'woof woof' rather one that goes 'miaou.' It's a purely arbitrary relationship, and there's no reason why English speakers shouldn't decide that from tomorrow, *d-o-g* would signify 'cat' and *c-a-t*, 'dog.'"

"Wouldn't it confuse the animals?" said Persse.

"The animals would adjust in time, like everyone else," said Dempsey. "We know this because the same animal is signified by different acoustic images in different natural languages. For instance, 'dog' is *chien* in French, *Hund* in German, *cane* in Italian, and so on. 'Cat' is *chat, Katze, gatto*, according to what part of the Common Market you happen to be in. And if we are to believe language rather than our ears, English dogs go *'woof woof,'* French dogs go *'wouah wouah,'* German dogs go *'wau wau'* and Italian ones *'baau baau.'*"

"Hallo, this sounds like a game of Animal Snap. Can anyone play?" said Philip Swallow. He had returned to the bar with Morris Zapp, now provided with a lapel badge. "Dempsey—you remember Morris of course?"

"I was just explaining structuralism to this young man," said Dempsey, when greetings had been exchanged. "But you never did have much time for linguistics, did you Swallow?"

"Can't say I did, no. I never could remember which came first, the morphemes or the phonemes. And one look at a tree-diagram makes my mind go blank."

"Or blanker," said Dempsey with a sneer.

An embarrassed silence ensued. It was broken by Angelica. "Actually," she said meekly, "Jakobson cites the gradation of positive, comparative and superlative forms of the adjective as evidence that language is not a totally arbitrary system. For instance: *blank, blanker, blankest*. The more phonemes, the more emphasis. The same is true of other Indo-European languages, for instance Latin: *vacuus, vacuior, vacuissimus*. There does seem to be some iconic correlation between sound and sense across the boundaries of natural languages."

The four men gaped at her.

"Who is this prodigy?" said Morris Zapp. "Won't somebody introduce me?"

"Oh, I'm sorry," said Philip Swallow. "Miss Pabst—Professor Zapp."

"Morris, please," said the American professor, extending his hand, and peering at Angelica's lapel badge. "Glad to meet you Al."

"That was marvellous," said Persse to Angelica, later, at lunch. "The way you put that Dempsey fellow in his place."

"I hope I wasn't rude," said Angelica. "Basically he's right of course. Different languages divide up the world differently. For instance, this mutton we're eating. In French there's only one word for 'sheep' and 'mutton'—*mouton*. So you can't say 'dead as mutton' in French, you'd be saying 'dead as a sheep,' which would be absurd."

"I don't know, this tastes more like dead sheep than mutton to me," said Persse, pushing his plate aside. An overalled lady with bright yellow curls pushing a trolley piled high with plates of half-eaten food took it from the table. "Finished, love?" she said. "I don't blame you. Not very nice, is it?"

"Did you write your poem?" said Angelica.

"I'll let you read it tonight. You have to come to the top floor of Lucas Hall."

"Is that where your room is?"

"No."

"Why then?"

"You'll see."

"A mystery." Angelica smiled, wrinkling her nose. "I like a mystery."

"Ten o'clock on the top floor. The moon will be up by then."

"Are you sure this isn't just an excuse for a romantic tryst?"

"Well, you said your research topic was romance . . ."

"And you thought you'd give me some more material? Alas, I've got too much already. I've read hundreds of romances. Classical romances and medieval romances, renaissance romances and modern romances. Heliodorus and Apuleius, Chrétien de Troyes and Malory, Ariosto and Spenser, Keats and Barbara Cartland. I don't need any more data. What I need is a theory to explain it all."

"Theory?" Philip Swallow's ears quivered under their silvery thatch, a few places further up the table. "That word brings out the Goering in me. When I hear it I reach for my revolver."

"Then you're not going to like my lecture, Philip," said Morris Zapp.

. . .

In the event, not many people did like Morris Zapp's lecture, and several members of the audience walked out before he had finished. Rupert Sutcliffe, obliged as chairman to sit facing the audience, assumed an aspect of glazed impassivity, but by imperceptible degrees the corners of his mouth turned down at more and more acute angles and his spectacles slid further and further down his nose as the discourse proceeded. Morris Zapp delivered it striding up and down the platform with his notes in one hand and a fat cigar in the other. "You see before you," he began, "a man who once believed in the possibility of interpretation. That is, I thought that the goal of reading was to establish the meaning of texts. I used to be a Jane Austen man. I think I can say in all modesty I was *the* Jane Austen man. I wrote five books on Jane Austen, every one of which was trying to establish what her novels meant— and, naturally, to prove that no one had properly understood what they meant before. Then I began a commentary on the works of Jane Austen, the aim of which was to be utterly exhaustive, to examine the novels from every conceivable angle—historical, biographical, rhetorical, mythical, structural, Freudian, Jungian, Marxist, existentialist, Christian, allegorical, ethical, phenomenological, archetypal, you name it. So that when each commentary was written, there would be *nothing further to say* about the novel in question.

"Of course, I never finished it. The project was not so much Utopian as self-defeating. By that I don't just mean that if successful it would have eventually put us all out of business. I mean that it couldn't succeed because it isn't possible, and it isn't possible because of the nature of language itself, in which meaning is constantly being transferred from one signifier to another and can never be absolutely possessed.

"To understand a message is to decode it. Language is a code. *But every decoding is another encoding.* If you say something to me I check that I have understood your message by saying it back to you in my own words, that is, different words from the ones you used, for if I repeat your own words exactly you will doubt whether I have really understood you. But if I use *my* words it follows that I have changed *your* meaning, however slightly; and even if I were, deviantly, to indicate my comprehension by repeating back to you your own unaltered words, that is no guarantee that I have duplicated your meaning in my head, because I bring a different experience of language, literature, and non-verbal reality to those words, therefore they mean something different to me from what they mean to you. And if you think I have not understood the meaning of your message, you do not simply repeat it in the same words, you try to explain it in different words, different from the ones you used originally; but then the *it* is no longer the *it* that you started with. And for that matter, you are not the *you* that you started with. Time has moved on since you opened your mouth to speak, the molecules in your body have changed, what you intended to say has been superseded by what you did say, and that has already become part of your personal history, imperfectly remembered. Conversation is like playing tennis with a ball made of Krazy Putty that keeps coming back over the net in a different shape.

"Reading, of course, is different from conversation: It is more passive in the sense that we can't interact with the text, we can't affect the development of the text by our own words, since the text's words are already given. That is what perhaps encourages the quest for interpretation. If the words are fixed once and for all, on the page, may not their meaning be fixed also? Not so, because the same axiom, *every decoding is another encoding*, applies to literary criticism even more stringently than it does to ordinary spoken discourse. In ordinary spoken discourse, the endless cycle of encoding-decoding-encoding may be terminated by an action, as when for instance I say, 'The door is open,' and you say, 'Do you mean you would like me to shut it?' and I say, 'If you don't mind,' and you shut the door—we may be satisfied that at a certain level my meaning has been understood. But if the literary text says, 'The door was open,' I cannot ask the text what it means by saying that the door was open, I can only speculate about the significance of that door—opened by what agency, leading to what discovery, mystery, goal? The tennis analogy will not do for the activity of reading—it is not a to-and-fro process, but an endless, tantalising leading on, a flirtation without consummation, or if there is consummation, it is solitary, masturbatory. [Here the audience grew restive.] The reader plays with himself as the text plays upon him, plays upon his curiosity, desire, as a striptease dancer plays upon her audience's curiosity and desire.

"Now, as some of you know, I come from a city notorious for its bars and nightclubs featuring topless and bottomless dancers. I am told—I have not personally patronized these places, but I am told on the authority of no less a person than your host at this conference, my old friend Philip Swallow, who *has* patronized them, [here several members of the audience turned in their seats to stare and grin at Philip Swallow, who blushed to the roots of his silver-grey hair] that the girls take off all their clothes before they commence dancing in front of the customers. This is not striptease, it is all strip and no tease, it is the terpsichorean equivalent of the hermeneutic fallacy of a recuperable meaning, which claims that if we remove the clothing of its rhetoric from a literary text we discover the bare facts it is trying to communicate. The classical tradition of striptease, however, which goes back to Salome's dance of the seven veils and beyond, and which survives in a debased form in the dives of your Soho, offers a valid metaphor for the activity of reading. The dancer teases the audience, as the text teases its readers, with the promise of an ultimate revelation that is infinitely postponed. Veil after veil, garment after garment, is removed, but it is the *delay* in the stripping that makes it exciting, not the stripping itself; because no sooner has one secret been revealed than we lose interest in it and crave another. When we have seen the girl's underwear we want to see her body, when we have seen her breasts we want to see her buttocks, and when we have seen her buttocks we want to see her pubis, and when we see her pubis, the dance ends—but is our curiosity and desire satisfied? Of course not. The vagina remains hidden within the girl's body, shaded by her pubic hair, and even if she were to spread her legs before us [at this point several ladies in the audience noisily departed] it would still not satisfy the curiosity and desire set in motion by the stripping. Staring into that orifice we find that we have somehow overshot the goal of our quest, gone beyond pleasure in contemplated beauty; gazing into the womb we are returned to the mystery of our own origins. Just so in reading. The attempt to peer into the very core of a text, to possess once and for all its meaning, is vain—it is only ourselves that we find there, not the work itself. Freud said that obsessive reading (and I suppose that most of us in this room must be regarded as compulsive readers)—that obsessive reading is the displaced expression of a desire to see the mother's genitals [here a young man in the audience fainted and was carried out] but the point of the remark, which may not have been entirely appreciated by Freud himself, lies precisely in the concept of displacement. To read is to surrender oneself to an endless displacement of curiosity and desire from one sentence to another, from one action to another, from one level of the text to another. The text unveils itself before us, but never allows itself to be possessed; and instead of striving to possess it we should take pleasure in its teasing."

Morris Zapp went on to illustrate his thesis with a number of passages from classic English and American literature. When he sat down, there was scattered and uneven applause.

"The floor is now open for discussion," said Rupert Sutcliffe, surveying the audience apprehensively over the rims of his glasses. "Are there any questions or comments?"

There was a long silence. Then Philip Swallow stood up. "I have listened to your paper with great interest, Morris," he said. "Great interest. Your mind has lost none of its sharpness since we first met. But I am sorry to see that in the intervening years you have succumbed to the virus of structuralism."

"I wouldn't call myself a structuralist," Morris Zapp interrupted, "A poststructuralist, perhaps."

Philip Swallow made a gesture implying impatience with such subtle distinctions. "I refer to that fundamental scepticism about the possibility of achieving certainty about anything, which I associate with the mischievous influence of Continental theorizing. There was a time when reading was a comparatively simple matter, something you learned to do in primary school. Now it seems to be some kind of arcane mystery, into which only a small élite have been initiated. I have been reading books for their meaning all my life— or at least that is what I have always thought I was doing. Apparently I was mistaken."

"You weren't mistaken about what you were trying to do," said Morris Zapp, relighting his cigar, "you were mistaken in trying to do it."

"I have just one question," said Philip Swallow. "It is this: what, with the greatest respect, is the point of our discussing your paper if, according to your own theory, we should not be discussing what you actually *said* at all, but discussing some imperfect memory or subjective interpretation of what you said?"

"There is no point," said Morris Zapp blithely. "If by point you mean the hope of arriving at some certain truth. But when did you ever discover *that* in a question-and-discussion session? Be honest, have you ever been to a lecture or seminar at the end of which you could have found two people present who could agree on the simplest précis of what had been said?"

"Then what in God's name *is* the point of it all?" cried Philip Swallow, throwing his hands into the air.

"The point, of course, is to uphold the institution of academic literary studies. We maintain our position in society by publicly performing a certain ritual, just like any other group of workers in the realm of discourse—lawyers, politicians, journalists. And as it looks as if we have done our duty for today, shall we all adjourn for a drink?"

"Tea, I'm afraid it will have to be," said Rupert Sutcliffe, clutching with relief this invitation to bring the proceedings to a speedy close. "Thank you *very* much for a most, er, stimulating and, ah, suggestive lecture."

"'Suggestive and stimulating'—the old fellow hit the nail on the head," said Persse to Angelica as they filed out of the lecture room. "Does your mother know you're away out listening to that sort of language?"

"I thought it was interesting," said Angelica. "Of course, it all goes back to Peirce."

"Me?"

"Peirce. Another variant spelling of your name. He was an American philosopher. He wrote somewhere about the impossibility of stripping the veils of representation from meaning. And that was before the First World War."

"Was it, indeed? You're a remarkably well-read young woman, Angelica, do you know that? Where were you educated at all?"

"Oh, various places," she said vaguely. "Mainly England and America."

They passed Rupert Sutcliffe and Philip Swallow in the corridor, in urgent consultation with Bob Busby, apparently about theatre tickets. "Are you going to the Repertory Theatre tonight?" said Angelica.

"I didn't put down to go. It didn't say on the form what the play was."

"I believe it's *Lear*."

"Are you going, then?" Persse asked anxiously. "What about my poem?"

"Your poem? Oh dear, I forgot. Ten o'clock on the top floor, wasn't it? I'll try and get back promptly. Professor Dempsey is taking me in his car, so that will save time."

"Dempsey? You want to be careful of that fellow, you know. He preys on young women like yourself. He told me so."

Angelica laughed. "I can take care of myself."

They found Morris Zapp drinking tea alone in the common room, the other conferees having left a kind of *cordon sanitaire* around him. Angelica went boldly up to the American.

"Professor Zapp, I did so enjoy your lecture," she said, with a greater degree of enthusiasm than Persse had expected or could, indeed, bring himself to approve.

"Well, thank you, Al," said Morris Zapp. "I certainly enjoyed giving it. I seem to have offended the natives, though."

"I'm working on the subject of romance for my doctorate," said Angelica, "and it seemed to me that a lot of what you were saying applied very well to romance."

"Naturally," said Morris Zapp. "It applies to everything."

"I mean, the idea of romance as narrative striptease, the endless leading on of the reader, a repeated postponement of an ultimate revelation which never comes—or, when it does, terminates the pleasure of the text . . ."

"Exactly," said Morris Zapp.

"And there's even a good deal of actual striptease in the romances."

"There is?" said Morris Zapp. "Yes, I guess there is."

"Ariosto's heroines for instance, are always losing their clothes and being gloated over by the heroes who rescue them."

"It's a long time since I read Ariosto," said Morris Zapp.

"And of course, *The Faerie Queene*—the two girls in the fountain in the Bower of Blisse . . ."

"I must look at that again," said Morris Zapp.

"Then there's Madeline undressing under the gaze of Porphyro in 'St. Agnes' Eve.'"

"Right, 'St. Agnes' Eve.'"

"Geraldine in 'Christabel.'"

"—'Christabel'—"

At this point Philip Swallow came bustling up. "Morris, I hope you didn't mind my having a go at you just now—"

"Of course not, Philip. *Vive le sport.*"

"Only nobody else seemed inclined to speak, and I *am* very concerned about these matters, I really think the subject is in a state of crisis—" He broke off, as Angelica politely backed away. "Oh, I'm sorry, have I interrupted something?"

"It's quite all right, we've finished," said Angelica. "Thank you very much, Professor Zapp, you've been most helpful."

"Any time, Al."

"Actually, you know, my name is Angelica," she smiled.

"Well, I thought Al must be short for something," said Morris Zapp. "Let me know if I can give you any more help."

"He didn't give you any help at all," said Persse indignantly, as they helped themselves to tea and biscuits. "You provided the ideas *and* the examples."

"Well, his lecture provided the stimulus."

"You told me he cribbed it all from the other fellow, my namesake."

"I didn't say he cribbed it, silly. Just that Peirce had the same idea."

"Why didn't you tell Zapp that?"

"You have to treat these professors carefully, Persse," said Angelica, with a sly smile. "You have to flatter them a bit."

"Ah, Angelica!" A bright blue suit interposed itself between them. "I'd like to discuss that very interesting idea of Jakobson's you mentioned this morning," said Robin Dempsey. "We can't allow McGarrigle to monopolize you for the duration of the conference."

"I need to see Dr. Busby, anyway," said Persse, retiring with dignity.

He found Bob Busby in the conference office. A young man from London University, whom Persse had overheard making the remark about generals deserting their armies at the coffee break that morning, was waving a theatre ticket under Busby's nose.

"Are you trying to tell me that this ticket isn't for *Lear* after all?" he was saying.

"Well, unfortunately, the Rep has postponed the opening of *King Lear*," said Busby apologetically. "And extended the run of the Christmas pantomime."

"Pantomime? *Pantomime?*"

"It's the only production in the whole year that makes a profit, you can't really blame them," said Busby. "*Puss in Boots.* I believe it's very good."

"Jesus wept," said the young man. "Is there any chance of getting my money back on the ticket?"

"I'm afraid it's too late now," said Busby.

"I'll buy it," said Persse.

"I say, will you really?" said the young man turning round. "It costs two pounds fifty. You can have it for two quid."

"Thanks," said Persse, handing over the money.

"Don't go telling everybody it's *Puss in Boots*," Busby pleaded. "I'm making out it's a sort of mystery trip."

"It's a mystery to me," said the young man, "why any of us came to this Godforsaken hole in the first place."

"Oh, it's not as bad as all that," said Busby. "It's very central."

"Central to what?"

Bob Busby frowned reflectively. "Well, since they opened the M50 I can get to Tintern Abbey, door to door, in ninety-five minutes."

"Go there often, do you?" said the young man. He fingered Persse's pound notes speculatively. "Is there a good fish-and-chip shop near here? I'm starving. Haven't been able to eat a thing since I arrived."

"There's a Chinese takeaway at the second traffic lights on the London Road," said Bob Busby. "I'm sorry that you're not enjoying the food. Still, there's always tomorrow night to look forward to."

"What happens tomorrow night?"

"A medieval banquet!" said Busby, beaming with pride.

"I can hardly wait," said the young man, as he left.

"I thought it would make a rather nice climax to the conference," said Bob Busby to Persse. "We're having an outside firm in to supervise the catering and provide the entertainment. There'll be mead, and minstrels and"—he rubbed his hands together in anticipatory glee—"wenches."

"My word," said Persse. "Life runs very high in Rummidge, surely. By the way, do you have a streetplan of the city? There's an aunty of mine living here, and I ought to call on her. The address is Gittings Road."

"Why, that's not far from here!" Busby exclaimed. "Walking distance. I'll draw you a map."

. . .

Following Busby's directions, Persse left the campus, walked through some quiet residential streets lined with large, handsome houses, their snowy drives scored by the tyre tracks of Rovers and Jaguars; crossed a busy thoroughfare, where buses and lorries had churned the snow into furrows of black slush; and penetrated a region of older and less well-groomed property. After a few minutes he became aware of a figure slipping and sliding on the pavement ahead of him, crowned by a familiar deerstalker.

"Hallo, Professor Zapp," he said, drawing level. "Are you taking a stroll?"

"Oh, hi, Percy. No, I'm on my way to visit my old landlord. I spent six months in this place, you know, ten years ago. I even thought of staying here once. I must have been out of my mind. Do you know it well?"

"I've never been here before, but I have an aunty living here. Not a real aunty, but related through cousins. My mother said to be sure to look her up. I'm on my way now."

"A duty call, huh? I take a right here."

Persse consulted his map. "So do I."

"How d'you like Rummidge, then?"

"There are too many streetlights."

"Come again?"

"You can't see the stars properly at night, because of all the streetlights," said Persse.

"Yeah, and there are a few other disadvantages I could tell you about," said Morris Zapp. "Like not a single restaurant you would take your worst enemy to, four different kinds of electric socket in every room, hotel bedrooms that freeze your eyebrows to the pillows, and disc jockeys that deserve to have their windpipes slit. I can't say that the absence of stars bugged me all that much."

"Even the moon seems dimmer than at home," said Persse.

"You're a romantic, Percy, you know that? You ought to write poetry. This is the street: Gittings Road."

"My aunty's street," said Persse.

Morris Zapp stopped in the middle of the pavement. "That's a remarkable coincidence," he said. "What's your aunty's name?"

"Mrs. O'Shea, Mrs. Nuala O'Shea," said Persse. "Her husband is Dr. Milo O'Shea."

Morris Zapp performed a little jig of excitement. "It's him, it's him!" he cried, in a rough imitation of an Irish brogue. "It's himself, my old landlord! Mother of God, won't he be surprised to see the pair of us."

"Mother of God!" said Dr. O'Shea, when he opened the front door of his large and gloomy-looking house. "If it isn't Professor Zapp!"

"And here's your nephew from the Emerald Isle, Percy McGarrigle, come to see his aunty," said Morris Zapp.

Dr. O'Shea's face fell. "Ah, yes, your mammy wrote, Persse. But I'm afraid you've missed Mrs. O'Shea—she left for Ireland yesterday. But come in, come in. I've nothing to offer you, and surgery starts in twenty minutes, but come in." He ushered them into a chilly parlour, smelling faintly of mildew and mothballs, and switched on an electric fire in the hearth. Simulated coals lighted up, though not the element. "Cheerful, I always think—makes you feel warm just to look at it," said the doctor.

"I've brought you a little duty-free hooch," said Morris Zapp, taking a half-bottle of scotch from his raincoat pocket.

"God love you, it's just like old times," groaned Dr. O'Shea. He got down on his knees and groped in a sideboard for glasses. "The whisky flowed like water," he confided in Persse, "when Professor Zapp lived here."

"Don't get the wrong idea, Percy," said Morris Zapp. "It's just Milo's way of saying I usually had a bottle or two of Old Grandad in the cupboard. Here's looking at you, Milo."

"So where's Aunty Nuala?" Persse enquired, when they had sunk the whisky, and O'Shea was refilling their glasses.

"Back in Sligo. Family troubles." Dr. O'Shea shook his head gravely. "Her sister is very bad, very bad. All on account of that daughter of hers, Bernadette."

"Bernadette?" Morris Zapp cut in. "You mean that black-haired kid who was living with you when I had the apartment upstairs?"

"The same. Do you know your cousin Bernadette, Persse?"

"I haven't seen her since we were children. But I did hear rumours of a scandal."

"Aye, there was a scandal, all right. After she left us, she went to work in a hotel in Sligo Town, as a chambermaid in a hotel there, and one of the guests took advantage of her. To cut a long story short, she became pregnant and was dismissed."

"Who was the guy?" said Morris Zapp.

"Nobody knows. Bernadette refused to say. Of course, when she came home, her parents were very shocked, very angry."

"Told her never to darken their doorstep again?" said Morris Zapp.

"Not in so many words, but the result was the same," said Dr. O'Shea. "Bernadette packed her bags and left the house in the middle of the night." He paused impressively, drained his glass, and drew the back of his hand across his mouth, making a rasping sound on his five-o'clock shadow. "And niver a word has been heard of her since. Her mother's gone into a decline with the worry of it. Of course, what we all dread is that Bernadette went to London to get rid of the baby in one of them abortion clinics. Who knows, she may have died that way, in a state of mortal sin." Jumping rather hastily to this sad conclusion, Dr. O'Shea crossed himself and sighed. "Let us hope that the good Lord gave her the grace to repent at the last."

In the hall a telephone began to ring.

"That'll be the surgery, wanting to know what's become of me," said Dr. O'Shea. He stood up, and stooped to switch off the illumination of the electric fire.

"We'll be on our way," said Morris Zapp. "Nice to see you, Milo." Outside the house, he turned and surveyed the top storey of the house with a sigh. "I had the apartment up there—Bernadette used to clean it. Poor kid, she was kind of cute, even if she had lost all her teeth. It makes me mad to hear of girls getting knocked up in this day and age. You'd think that the guy, whoever he was, would have taken precautions."

"You can't obtain contraceptives in Ireland," said Persse. "It's against the law to sell them."

"Is that right? I guess you'll be filling your suitcase with, what do they call condoms here, Durex, right?"

"No," said Persse. "I believe in premarital chastity for both sexes."

"Well, it's a nice idea, Percy, but if you want my opinion, I don't think it will catch on."

They separated at the corner of Gittings Road, since Morris Zapp was going to the Swallows' house, not far away, and Persse was returning to the halls of residence. "Will you be going to the theatre tonight?" Persse asked.

"No, Philip Swallow warned me against it. I guess I'll have an early night, catch up on my jet-lag. Take care."

Persse hurried back to Martineau Hall, but found that he was too late for dinner, which had been brought forward because of the theatre outing. "Never mind, love, it wasn't very nice," said the lady with yellow curls, laying out breakfast things in the empty dining-room. "Shepherd's Pie, made from lunchtime's leftovers. There's some biscuits and cheese left if that's any use to you."

Gratefully cramming cream crackers and cheddar cheese into his mouth, Persse hurried to the foyer of Lucas Hall. Dempsey, spruce and expectant in a dark brown blazer and grey flannels, was standing near the door.

"Are you going to the theatre?" Persse asked. "I need a lift."

"Sorry, old man, my car's full. There's a coach leaving from the bottom of the drive. If you run, you'll probably catch it."

Persse ran, but did not catch it. As he stood at the gates of the hall site, wondering what to do, Dempsey swept by at the wheel of a Volkswagen Golf, spattering Persse with slush. Angelica was in the front passenger seat. She smiled and waved. There was nobody in the back seat.

It was cold, and growing dark. Persse turned up the collar of his anorak, thrust his hands into his pockets, and set off in the direction of the city centre. By the time he found the Repertory Theatre, a large futuristic concrete structure near the Town Hall, the performance of *Puss in Boots* was well under way, and he was ushered to his seat while a man, dressed apparently as Robin Hood, was coaching the audience in hissing whenever they saw the wicked Baron Blunderbuss appear. There followed a duet for the Miller's son and the princess with whom he was in love; a slapstick comic interlude in which two incompetent decorators, who were supposed to be papering the

King's parlour, covered each other with paste and dropped their implements repeatedly on the King's gouty foot; and, as a finale to the first act, a spectacular song and dance number for the whole company, entitled "Caturday Night Fever," in which Puss in Boots triumphed in a Royal Disco Dancing competition at the Palace.

The lights went up for the Interval, revealing to Persse the bemused countenances of his fellow conferees. Some declared their intention of leaving immediately and looking for a good film. Others tried to make the best of it—"After all it *is* the only *genuinely popular* form of theatre in Britain today, I think one has a *duty* to experience it oneself"—and some had obviously been enjoying themselves immensely, hissing and clapping and joining in the singsongs, but didn't want to admit it. Of Angelica and Dempsey, however, there was no sign.

Searching for them in the crowded foyer, Persse encountered Miss Maiden, who presented a striking figure among the drab provincial throng, wearing a fox-fur stole over a full-length evening dress, and wielding opera glasses mounted on a stick. It struck Persse that she must have been a very handsome woman in her prime. "Hallo, young man," she said. "How are you enjoying the play?"

"I'm finding it very hard to follow," he said. "What is Robin Hood doing in it? I thought *Puss in Boots* was a French fairy tale."

"Pooh, pooh, you mustn't be so literal-minded," said Miss Maiden, tapping him reprovingly with her rolled-up programme. "Jessie Weston describes a mumming play performed near Rugby in Warwickshire, of which the *dramatis personae* are Father Christmas, St. George, a Turkish Knight, the Knight's mother Moll Finney, a Doctor, Humpty Jack, Beelzebub and Big-Head-and-Little-Wit. What would you make of that?"

"Nothing very much, I'm afraid."

"It's easy!" Miss Maiden cried triumphantly. "St. George kills the knight, the mother grieves, the Doctor brings him back to life. It symbolizes the death and rebirth of the crops in winter and summer. It all comes back to the same thing in the end: the life-force endlessly renewing itself. Robin Hood, you know, is connected to the Green Man of medieval legend, who was originally a tree-god or nature spirit."

"But what about this show?"

"Well, the gouty King is obviously the Fisher King ruling over a sterile land, and the miller's son is the hero who restores its fertility through the magic agency of Puss in Boots, and is rewarded with the hand of the King's daughter."

"So Puss in Boots is equivalent to the Grail?" Persse said facetiously.

Miss Maiden was not discomposed. "Certainly. Boots are phallic, and you are no doubt familiar with the vulgar expression 'pussy'?"

"Yes, I have heard it occasionally," said Persse weakly.

"It is a very ancient and widely distributed metaphor, I assure you. So you see the character of Puss in Boots represents the same combination of male and female principles as the cup and spear in the Grail legend."

"Amazing," said Persse. "It makes you wonder that they allow children to see these pantomimes. By the way, Miss Maiden, have you seen Angelica Pabst and Professor Dempsey this evening?"

"Yes, I saw them leaving the theatre just before the performance started," said Miss Maiden. "They'll be sorry when they hear what they've missed. Ah, there's the bell. We must get back to our seats."

Persse did not return to his seat, but left the theatre and made his way back to Lucas Hall. He took the lift to the top floor, which was dark and deserted, since it had not been necessary to accommodate anyone so far from the ground. The building consisted of twin tower blocks, connected at alternate floors by glassed-in walkways. The walkway on the top floor, as Persse had already ascertained, gave a fine aerial view of the grounds of the two halls, the artificial lake between them, and the south-western suburbs of Rummidge. He stared at the sky: there were wisps of cloud about, but generally it was clear, and the moon was rising.

After nearly an hour had passed, Persse heard the whine of a lift climbing the shaft. He ran to the doors of the lift and stood there, smiling expectantly. The doors opened to reveal the frowning figure of Dempsey. Persse rearranged his features.

"What are you doing here?" Dempsey demanded.

"Thinking," said Persse.

Dempsey stepped out of the lift. "I'm looking for Angelica," he said.

"She isn't here."

The doors of the lift closed automatically behind Dempsey. "Are you sure?" he said. "It's very dark up here. Why haven't you got the lights on?"

"I think better in the dark," said Persse.

Dempsey switched on the landing lights and looked around him suspiciously. "What are you thinking about?"

"A poem."

Dempsey's frown momentarily dissolved into a leer. "I've been working on that limerick," he said. "What about this for a start:

> *There was a young fellow from Limerick*
> *Who tried to have sex with a candlestick . . .*"

"It scans better than your last effort," said Persse. "That's about all I can say in its favour."

Dempsey pressed the button to open the lift doors. "If you see Angelica, tell her I'm in the bar."

As the lift descended, the door of the emergency exit opened and Angelica stepped out on to the landing. Her beauty looked a little tousled, and she was out of breath—indeed her bosom was swelling and sinking in the most amazing fashion under the high-necked white silk blouse she was wearing. It looked to Persse as if a button was missing from the blouse.

"Has that fellow been annoying you?" he said fiercely.

"Who?"

"That Dempsey. Big-Head-and-Little-Wit."

Angelica grinned. "I told you, I can look after myself," she panted. She put a hand to her bosom. "I'm out of breath from the stairs."

"Why didn't you make Dempsey stop his car when you passed me in the drive?" he said accusingly.

"You told me you weren't going to the theatre."

"I changed my mind. So did you, apparently. I couldn't find you there."

"No, when we discovered it was *Puss in Boots* instead of *King Lear*, we went to a pub instead. Robin wanted to go on to a discothèque, but I explained that I had an appointment back here. So here I am. Where's the poem?"

"It's a one-word poem," said Persse, somewhat mollified by this account. "The most beautiful word in the world, actually. And you can only read it in the dark." He turned off the landing lights. "Here, take my hand." He led Angelica out on to the glassed-in walkway, and showed her the view. "Down there," he said. "By the lake."

The snow-covered landscape brilliantly reflected the light of the nearly full moon, now high in the sky. The lawn that sloped gently upwards from the margin of the artificial lake was an expanse of dazzling whiteness, except where a trail of footprints, that had melted in the day's slow thaw, spelled out in huge, wavering script, a name:

"Oh, Persse," she whispered. "What a lovely idea. An earth poem."

"Why do you call it that? I would have said a snow poem."

"I was thinking of earth art—you know, those designs miles long that you can only appreciate from an aeroplane."

"Well, it's also a sun poem and a moon poem, because the sun melted the snow in my footprints, and the moon lit them up for you to see."

"How bright the moon is tonight," Angelica murmured. She had not withdrawn her hand from his.

"Have you ever thought, Angelica," said Persse, "what a remarkable thing it is that the moon and the sun look to our eyes approximately the same size?"

"No," said Angelica, "I've never thought about it."

"So much mythology and symbolism depends on the equivalence of those two round disc-shapes in our sky, one presiding over the day and the other over the night, as if they were twins. Yet it's just a trick of perspective, the product of the relative size of the moon and the sun, and their distance from us and from each other. The odds against its happening like that by chance must be billions to one."

"You don't think it was chance?"

"I think it's one of the great proofs of a divine creator," said Persse. "I think He had an eye for symmetry."

"Like Blake," Angelica smiled. "Have you read Frye's *Fearful Symmetry*, by the way? An excellent book, I think."

"I don't want to talk about literary criticism," said Persse, squeezing her hand, and drawing closer. "Not alone with you, up here, in the moonlight. I want to talk about us."

"Us?"

"Will you marry me, Angelica?"

"Of course not!" she exclaimed, snatching her hand away and laughing incredulously.

"Why not?"

"Well, for a hundred reasons. I've only just met you, and I don't want to get married anyway."

"Never?"

"I don't say never, but first I want a career of my own, and that means I must be free to go anywhere."

"I wouldn't mind," said Persse. "I'd go with you."

"What, and give up your own job?"

"If necessary," he said.

Angelica shook her head. "You're a hopeless romantic, Persse," she said. "Why do you want to marry me, anyway?"

"Because I love you," he said, "and I believe in premarital chastity."

"Perhaps I don't," she said archly.

"Oh, Angelica, don't torment me! If you've had other lovers, I don't want to hear about them."

"That's not what I meant," said Angelica.

"I don't mind if you're not a virgin," said Persse. He added, "Of course, I'd prefer it if you were."

"Ah, virginity," mused Angelica. "What is it? A presence or an absence? The presence of a hymen, or the absence of a penis?"

"God forbid it's either," said Persse, blushing, "for I'm a virgin myself."

"Are you?" Angelica looked at him with interest. "But nowadays people usually sleep together before they get married. Or so I understand."

"It's against my principles," said Persse. "But if you promised to marry me eventually, I might stretch a point."

Angelica tittered. "Don't forget that this is entirely *your* idea." She suddenly prodded the glass. "Oh, look, there's a little creature in the snow down there—can it be a rabbit, or a hare?"

"'*The hare limped trembling through the frozen grass,*'" he quoted.

"What's that? Oh yes, 'The Eve of St. Agnes.'"

And silent was the flock in woolly fold.

I love that phrase, 'woolly fold,' don't you? It makes one think of being snuggled up in a blanket, but it could also be a metaphor for a snowdrift, so that it sort of epitomizes the forcing together of the extremes of heat and cold, sensuousness and austerity, life and death, that runs through the whole poem."

"Oh, Angelica!" Persse exclaimed. "Never mind the verbal texture. Remember how the poem ends:

> *And they are gone: ay, ages long ago*
> *Those lovers fled away into the storm.*

Be my Madeline, and let me be your Porphyro!"

"What, and miss the rest of the conference?"

"I can wait till tomorrow night.

> *Awake! Arise! my love, and fearless be,*
> *For o'er the southern moors I have a home for thee."*

Angelica giggled. "It *would* be kind of fun to re-enact the poem tomorrow night. There's actually going to be a medieval banquet."

"I know."

"You could hide in my room and watch me go to bed. Then I might dream of you as my future husband."

"Suppose you didn't?"

"That's a risk you'd have to take. Porphyro found a way to make sure of it, I seem to remember," Angelica said dreamily, gazing out across the moonlit snowfields.

Persse looked doubtfully at her exquisite profile—the perfectly straight nose, the slight, unmanning droop of the underlip, the firm but gently rounded chin. "Angelica—" he began. But at that moment they heard the sound of the lift approaching the top floor. "If that's Dempsey again," Persse exclaimed, "I'll push him down the liftshaft." He hurried back to the landing and adopted a challenging posture, facing the doors of the lift. They opened to reveal the figure of Philip Swallow.

"Oh, hallo McGarrigle," he said. "I'm looking for Miss Pabst. Robin Dempsey said she might be up here."

"No, she's not," said Persse.

"Oh, I see," said Philip Swallow. He seemed to be considering whether to push past Persse and investigate for himself, but to decide against it. "Do you want to go down?" he said.

"No, thank you."

"Oh, well, goodnight then." Philip Swallow took his finger off the "Hold" button, and the doors closed.

Persse hurried back to the walkway. "That was Philip Swallow," he said. "What the blazes do all these old men want with you?"

But there was no reply. Only moonlight filled the glassy space. Angelica had gone.

. . .

So, by the next morning, had Persse's inscription of her name upon the landscape. The wind had changed direction during the night, bringing a warm rain which had melted and washed away the snow. Drawing back the curtains of his bedroom window, Persse saw damp green lawns and muddy flowerbeds under low, scudding rainclouds. And there, splashing through the puddles in the carpark, was the surprising figure of Morris Zapp, clad in a bright red track suit and training shoes, a dead cigar clenched between his teeth. Quickly pulling on a sweater, jeans, and the tennis shoes that served him for slippers, Persse ran out into the mild morning air and soon overtook the American, whose pace was in fact rather slower than normal walking.

"Good morning, Professor Zapp!"

"Oh, hi, Percy," Morris Zapp mumbled. He took the cigar butt from between his teeth, inspected it with faint surprise, and tossed it into a laurel bush. "You jogging too? Look, don't let me hold you back."

"I would never have guessed that you were a runner."

"This is jogging, Percy, not running. Running is sport. Jogging is punishment."

"You mean you don't enjoy it?"

"Enjoy it? Are you kidding? I only do this for my health. It makes me feel so terrible, I figure it must be doing me good. Also it's very fashionable these days in American academic circles. Success is not just a matter of how many articles you published last year, but how many miles you covered this morning."

"It seems to be catching on over here, too," said Persse. "I can see another runner in front of us. But surely, Professor Zapp, you don't have to worry about success? You're famous already."

"It's not just a question of making it, Percy, there's also keeping it. You have to remember the young men in a hurry."

"Who are they?"

"Have you never read Cornford's *Microcosmographia Academica*? I have whole chunks of it by heart. *'From far below you will mount the roar of a ruthless multitude of young men in a hurry. You may perhaps grow to be aware of what they are in a hurry to do. They are in a hurry to get you out of the way.'"*

"Who was Cornford?"

"A Cambridge classicist at the turn of the century, under the spell of Freud and Frazer. You know Freud's idea of primitive society as a tribe in which the sons kill the father when he gets old and impotent, and take away his women? In modern academic society they take away your research grants. And your women, too, of course."

"That's very interesting," said Persse. "It reminds me of Jessie Weston's *Ritual and Romance.*"

"Yep, it's the same basic idea. Except that in the Grail legend the hero cures the king's sterility. In the Freudian version the old guy gets wasted by his kids. Which seems to me more true to life."

"So that's why you keep jogging?"

"That's why I keep jogging. To show I'm not on the heap yet. Anyway, my ambitions are not yet satisfied. Before I retire, I want to be the highest paid Professor of English in the world."

"How high is that?"

"I don't know, that's what keeps me on my toes. The top people in this profession are pretty tight-lipped about their salaries. Maybe I already *am* the highest paid professor of English in the world, without knowing it. Every time I threaten to leave Euphoric State, they jack up my salary by five thousand dollars."

"Do you want to move, then, Professor Zapp?"

"Not at all, I just have to stop them from taking me for granted. There's no point in moving from one university to another these days. There was a time when that was how you got on. There was a very obvious pecking order among the various schools and you measured your success by your position on that ladder. The assumption was that all the most interesting people were concentrated into a few institutions, like Harvard, Yale, Princeton and such-like, and in order to get into the action you had to be at one of those places yourself. That isn't true any more."

"It isn't?"

"No. The day of the individual campus has passed. It belongs to an obsolete technology—railways and the printing press. I mean, just look at *this* campus—it epitomizes the whole thing: the heavy industry of the mind."

They had reached a summit which offered a panoramic view of Rummidge University, dominated by its campanile (a blown-up replica in red brick of the Leaning Tower of Pisa), flanked on one side by the tree-filled residential streets that Persse had walked through the previous evening, and on the other by factories and cramped, grey terraced houses. A railway and a canal bisected the site, which was covered by an assemblage of large buildings of heterogeneous design in brick and concrete. Morris Zapp seemed glad of an excuse to stop for a moment while they viewed the scene. "See what I mean?" he panted, with an all-embracing, yet dismissive sweep of his arm. "It's huge, heavy, monolithic. It weighs about a billion tons. You can *feel* the weight of those buildings, pressing down the earth. Look at the Library—built like a huge warehouse. The whole place says, '*We have learning stored here; if you want it, you've got to come inside and get it.*' Well, that doesn't apply any more."

"Why not?" Persse set off again at a gentle trot.

"Because," said Morris Zapp, reluctantly following, "information is much more portable in the modern world than it used to be. So are people. *Ergo*, it's no longer necessary to hoard your information in one building, or keep your top scholars corralled in one campus. There are three things which have revolutionized academic life in the last twenty years, though very few people have woken up to the fact: jet travel, direct-dialling telephones and the Xerox machine. Scholars don't have to work in the same institution to interact, nowadays: they call each other up, or they meet at international conferences. And they don't have to grub about in library stacks for data: any book or article that sounds interesting they have Xeroxed and read it at home. Or on the plane going to the next conference. I work mostly at home or on planes these days. I seldom go into the university except to teach my courses."

"That's a very interesting theory," said Persse. "And rather reassuring, because my own university has very few buildings and hardly any books."

"Right. As long as you have access to a telephone, a Xerox machine, and a conference grant fund, you're OK, you're plugged into the only university that really matters—the global campus. A young man in a hurry can see the world by conference-hopping."

"Oh, I'm not in a hurry," said Persse.

"You must have some ambitions."

"I would like to get my poems published," said Persse. "And I have another ambition too personal to be divulged."

"Al Papps!" Morris Zapp exclaimed.

"How did you guess?" Persse asked, astonished.

"Guess what? I just said that's Al Papps running ahead of us."

"So it is!" The figure Persse had glimpsed earlier was indeed Angelica: she must have taken some detour, and had now reappeared on the path ahead of them, scarcely a hundred yards distant.

"That sure is some girl! She looks like a million dollars, has read everything you can name, and she can really run, can't she?"

"Like Atalanta," Persse murmured. "Let's catch her up."

"You catch her up, Percy, I'm pooped."

Morris Zapp soon fell behind as Persse accelerated, but the distance between himself and Angelica remained constant. Then she gave a quick glance over her shoulder, and he realized that she was aware of his pursuit. They were descending a long sloping path that led to the halls of residence. Faster and faster grew the pace, until both were sprinting. Persse narrowed the gap. Angelica's head went back, and her black hair streamed out behind her. Her supple haunches, bewitchingly sheathed in a tight-fitting orange track suit, thrust the tarmac away from under her flying feet. They reached the entrance to Lucas Hall shoulder to shoulder, and leaned against the outside wall, panting and laughing. The driver of a taxi that was waiting by the entrance grinned and applauded.

"What happened to you last night?" Persse gasped.

"I went to bed, of course," said Angelica. "In my room. Room 231."

Morris Zapp laboured up, wheezing stertorously. "Who won?"

"It was a dead heat," said the cab driver, leaning out of his window.

"Very diplomatic, driver. Now you can take me back to St. John's Road," said Morris Zapp, climbing into the taxi. "See you around, kids."

"Do you usually jog by taxi, Professor Zapp?" Persse inquired.

"Well, I'm staying with the Swallows, as you know, and I didn't fancy running through the streets of Rummidge inhaling the rush hour. *Ciao!*" Morris Zapp sank back into the seat of the taxi, and took from a pocket in his track suit a fat cigar, a cigar clipper and a lighter. He was busying himself with this apparatus as the taxi drew away.

Persse turned to address Angelica, but she had disappeared. "Was there ever such a girl for disappearing?" he muttered to himself in vexation. "It's as if she had a magic ring for making herself invisible."

. . .

Somehow, Angelica eluded Persse for the rest of the morning. When, after showering and dressing, he went to the Martineau Hall refectory for breakfast, he found her already seated at a fully occupied table, next to Dempsey. She was not a member of the little caravan of conferees who, with a conspicu-

ous lack of enthusiasm, and buffeted by occasional squalls of rain, made their
way down the hill from the halls of residence to the main campus for the first
lecture of the morning. Persse, having watched them depart, and waited in
vain for a few extra minutes, finally hurried after them, only to be overtaken
by Dempsey's car, with Angelica in the front passenger seat. The pair contrived, however, to be late for the lecture, tip-toeing in after the proceedings
had begun. Persse paid little attention to the lecture, which was about the
problem of identifying the authentically Shakespearian portions of the text of
Pericles, being preoccupied himself with the problem of exactly what Angelica
had meant by her proposal, the night before, that they should re-enact "The
Eve of St. Agnes." By pointedly telling him the number of her room that
morning, she seemed to have confirmed the arrangement. What he was not
sure of was how she read the poem. Failing to spot her in the crush at the coffee break, Persse hurried over to the University Library to consult the text.

He skimmed quickly through the early stanzas about the coldness of the
weather, the tradition that maidens who went fasting to bed on St. Agnes'
Eve would see their future husbands in their sleep, the abstractedness of Madeline, with this intention in mind, amid the feasting and merrymaking in the
hall, the secret arrival of Porphyro, risking his life in the hostile castle for a
glimpse of his beloved, his persuading of the old woman, Angela, to hide him
in Madeline's bedroom, Madeline's arrival and preparations for bed. Persse
lingered for a moment over stanza XXVI—

> *Of all its wreathed pearls her hair she frees,*
> *Unclasps her warmed jewels one by one;*
> *Loosens her fragrant bodice: by degrees*
> *Her rich attire creeps rustling to her knees*

—and, with flushed cheeks, read on through the description of the delicacies
Porphyro laid out for Madeline, his attempts to wake her with lute music,
hovering over her sleeping figure; Madeline's eyes opening on the vision of
her dream, and her half-conscious address to Porphyro. Then came the crucial stanza:

> *Beyond a mortal man impassioned far*
> *At these voluptuous accents, he arose,*
> *Ethereal, flushed, and like a throbbing star*

Seen 'mid the sapphire heaven's deep repose;
Into her dream he melted, as the rose
Blendeth its odour with the violet—
Solution sweet.

It was all very well for Morris Zapp to insist upon the indeterminacy of literary texts: Persse McGarrigle needed to know whether or not sexual intercourse was taking place here—a question all the more difficult for him to decide because he had no personal experience to draw upon. On the whole he was inclined to think that the correct answer was in the affirmative, and Porphyro's later reference to Madeline as his "bride" seemed to clinch the matter.

This conclusion, however, only pitchforked Persse into another dilemma. Angelica might be inviting him to become her lover, but she would not allow him to make her his bride, not in the immediate future anyway, so a contingency had to be thought of, distasteful and unromantic as it was. Probably it would never have occurred to Persse McGarrigle if the sad story of his cousin Bernadette had not been fresh in his mind, together with the censorious comment of Morris Zapp: "It makes me mad to hear of girls getting knocked up in this day and age." Accordingly, though he shrank inwardly from the task, he set his features grimly and set off in search of a chemist's shop.

He walked a long way, to be sure of not being observed by any stray members of the conference, and eventually found, or rather lost, himself in the city centre, a bewildering labyrinth of dirty, malodorous stairs, subways and walkways that funnelled the local peasantry up and down, over and under the huge concrete highways, vibrating with the thunder of passing juggernauts. He passed many chemist's shops. Some were too empty, some too full, for his comfort. Eventually, impatient with his own pusillanimity, he chose one at random and plunged recklessly inside.

The shop appeared to be deserted, and he looked rapidly around for the object of his quest, hoping that, when the chemist appeared, he would be able merely to point. He could not see what he was looking for, however, and to his dismay a young girl in white overalls appeared from behind a barricade of shelves.

"Yis?" she said listlessly.

Persse felt throttled by his embarrassment. He wanted to run and flee through the door, but his limbs refused to move.

"Kinoielpyew?" said the girl impatiently.

Persse stared at his boots. "I'm after wanting some Durex, please," he managed to mutter, in strangled accents.

"Small meedyum or large?" said the girl coolly.

This was a turn of the screw Persse had not anticipated. "I thought they were all the one size," he whispered hoarsely.

"Nah. Small meedyum or large," drawled the girl, inspecting her fingernails.

"Well, medium, then," said Persse.

The girl vanished momentarily, and reappeared with a surprisingly big box wrapped in a paper bag, for which she demanded 75p. Persse snatched the package—it was also surprisingly heavy—from her, thrust a pound note across the counter, and fled from the shop without waiting for his change.

In a dark and noisome subway, decorated with football graffiti and reeking of urine and onions, he paused beneath a lightbulb to inspect his purchase. He withdrew from the paper bag a cardboard box which bore on its wrapper the picture of a plump, pleased-looking baby in a nappy, being fed something that looked like porridge. The brand-name of this product, displayed in large letters, was "Farex."

Persse walked broodingly back towards the University. He had no inclination to return to the shop to explain the mistake, or to make a second attempt at another chemist's shop. He took the frustration of his design to be providential, an expression of divine displeasure at his sinful intentions. On a broad thoroughfare lined with motorcar showrooms, he passed a Catholic church, and hesitated for a moment before a noticeboard which declared, "Confessions at any time." It was a heaven-sent opportunity to shrive himself. But he decided that he could not in good faith promise to break his appointment with Angelica that night. He crossed the road—carefully, for he was undoubtedly in a state of sin now—and walked on, allowing his imagination to dwell voluptuously on images of Angelica coming to her bedroom in which he was hidden, Angelica undressing under his very eyes, Angelica naked in his arms. But what then? He feared that his inexperience would destroy the rapture of that moment, his knowledge of sexual intercourse being entirely literary and rather vague as to the mechanics.

As if the devil had planted it there, another notice, printed in bold black lettering on flame-coloured fluorescent paper, caught his eye:

THIS CINEMA IS A CLUB SHOWING ADULT FILMS
WHICH INCLUDE THE EXPLICIT AND UNCENSORED

DEPICTION OF SEXUAL ACTS. IMMEDIATE MEMBERSHIP
AVAILABLE. REDUCED RATES FOR OLD AGE PENSIONERS.

Persse swerved in through the doors, quickly, before his conscience had time to react. He found himself in a discreetly dim, carpeted foyer. A man behind a desk welcomed him suavely. "Membership form, sir? That will be three pounds altogether."

Persse put down the name of Philip Swallow.

"That's a coincidence, sir," said the man, with a svelte smile, "We already have a Mr. Philip Swallow on the books. Through the door over there."

Persse pushed through padded doors into almost total darkness. He stumbled against a wall, and remained pressed to it for a moment while his sight accommodated to the gloom. The air was full of strange noises, an amplified mélange of heavy breathing, throttled cries, panting, moaning and groaning, as of souls in torment. A dim luminescence guided him forward, through a curtain, round a corner, and he found himself at the back of a small auditorium. The noise was louder than ever, and it was still very dark, impossible to see anything except the flickering images on the screen. It took Persse some moments to realize that what he was looking at was a hugely magnified penis going in and out of a hugely magnified vagina. The blood rushed to his face, and to another part of his anatomy. Bent forward, he shuffled down the sloping aisle, peering vainly to each side of him for an empty seat. The images on the screen shifted, close-up gave way to a wider, deeper perspective, and it became apparent that the owner of the vagina had another penis in her mouth, and the owner of the first penis had his tongue in another vagina, whose owner in turn had a finger in someone else's anus, whose penis was in *her* vagina; and all were in frantic motion, like the pistons of some infernal machine. Keats it was not. It was a far cry from the violet blending its odour with the rose. "Siddown, can't you?" someone hissed in the circumambient darkness. Persse groped for a seat, but his hand fell on a padded shoulder, and was shaken off with a curse. The moans and groans rose to a crescendo, the pistons jerked faster and faster, and Persse registered with shame that he had polluted himself. Perspiration poured from his brow and dimmed his sight. When what seemed, for one hallucinatory moment, to be the face of Angelica loomed between two massive hairy thighs, Persse turned and fled from the place as if from the pit of hell.

The man behind the reception desk looked up, startled, as Persse catapulted into the foyer. "Too tame for you?" he said. "You can't have a refund, I'm afraid. Try next week, we've got some new Danish stuff coming in."

Persse grabbed the man by his lapels and hauled him halfway across the desk. "You have made me defile the image of the woman I love," he hissed. The man paled, and lifted his hands in a gesture of surrender. Persse pushed him back into his seat, ran out of the cinema, across the road, and into the Catholic church.

A light was burning above a confessional bearing the name of "Fr. Finbar O'Malley," and within a few minutes Persse had unburdened his conscience and received absolution. "God bless you, my son," said the priest in conclusion.

"Thank you, Father."

"By the way, do you come from Mayo?"

"I do."

"Ah. I thought I recognized the sound of Mayo speech. I'm from the West myself." He sighed behind the wire grille. "This is a terrible sinful city for a young Irish lad like yourself to be cast adrift in. How would you like to be repatriated?"

"Repatriated?" Persse repeated blankly.

"Aye. I administer a fund for helping Irish youngsters who have come over here looking for work and think better of it, and want to go back home. It's called the Our Lady of Knock Fund for Reverse Emigration."

"Oh, I'm only visiting, Father. I'm going back to Ireland tomorrow."

"You have your ticket?"

"Yes, Father."

"Then good luck to you, and God speed. You're going to a better place than this, I can tell you."

. . .

By the time Persse got back to the University it was afternoon, and the Conference had departed on a coach tour of literary landmarks in the region. Persse took a bath and slept for a few hours. He awoke feeling serene and purified. It was time to go to the bar for a drink before dinner.

The conferees were back from the sightseeing trip, which had not been a success: the owners of George Eliot's childhood home had not been warned in advance, and would not let them inside the house, so they had had to content themselves with milling about in the garden and pressing their faces to the windows. Then Ann Hathaway's cottage proved to be closed for maintenance; and finally the coach had broken down just outside Kenilworth, on the way to the Castle, and a relief vehicle had taken an hour to arrive.

"Never mind," said Bob Busby, moving among the disgruntled conferees in the bar, "there's still the medieval banquet to look forward to."

"I hope to God Busby knows what he's doing," Persse heard Philip Swallow saying. "We can't afford another cockup." He was speaking to a man in a rather greasy charcoal grey suit whom Persse had not seen before.

"What's it all about, then?" said this man, who had a Gauloise smouldering in one hand and a large gin and tonic in the other.

"Well, there's a place in town called 'Ye Merrie Olde Round Table,' where they put on these mock medieval banquets," said Philip Swallow. "I've never been myself, but Busby assured us it's good fun. Anyway, he's booked their team to lay it on here tonight.

They have minstrels, I understand, and mead, and . . ."

"And wenches," Persse volunteered.

"I say," said the man in the charcoal grey suit, turning smoke-bleared eyes upon Persse and treating him to a yellow-fanged smile. "It sounds rather fun."

"Oh, hello McGarrigle," said Philip Swallow, without enthusiasm. "Have you met Felix Skinner, of Lecky, Windrush and Bernstein? My publishers. Not that our professional association has been particularly profitable to either party," he concluded with a forced attempt at jocularity.

"Well, it has been a teeny bit disappointing," Skinner admitted with a sigh.

"Only a hundred and sixty-five copies sold a year after publication," said Philip Swallow accusingly. "And not a single review."

"You know we all thought it was an absolutely *super* book, Philip," said Skinner. "It's just that there's not much of an educational market for Hazlitt these days. And I'm sure the reviews will come eventually, in the scholarly journals. I'm afraid the Sundays and weeklies don't pay as much attention to lit. crit. as they used to."

"That's because so much of it is unreadable," said Philip Swallow. "*I* can't understand it, so how can you expect ordinary people to? I mean, that's what my book is *saying*. That's why I *wrote it*."

"I know, Philip, it's awfully unfair," said Skinner. "What's your own field, Mr. McGarrigle?"

"Well, I did my research on Shakespeare and T. S. Eliot," said Persse.

"I could have helped you with that," Dempsey butted in. He had just come into the bar with Angelica, who was looking heart-stoppingly beautiful in a kaftan of heavy wine-coloured cotton, in whose weave a dark, muted pattern of other rich colours dimly gleamed. "It would just lend itself nicely to computerization," Dempsey continued. "All you'd have to do would be to put the texts on to tape and you could get the computer to list every word, phrase and syntactical construction that the two writers had in common. You could precisely quantify the influence of Shakespeare on T. S. Eliot."

"But my thesis isn't about that," said Persse. "It's about the influence of T. S. Eliot on Shakespeare."

"That sounds rather Irish, if I may say so," said Dempsey, with a loud guffaw. His little eyes looked anxiously around for support.

"Well, what I try to show," said Persse, "is that we can't avoid reading Shakespeare through the lens of T. S. Eliot's poetry. I mean, who can read *Hamlet* today without thinking of 'Prufrock'? Who can hear the speeches of Ferdinand in *The Tempest* without being reminded of 'The Fire Sermon' section of *The Waste Land*?"

"I say, that sounds rather interesting," said Skinner. "Philip, old chap, do you think I might possibly have another one of these?" Depositing his empty glass in Philip Swallow's hand, Felix Skinner took Persse aside. "If you haven't already made arrangements to publish your thesis, I'd be very interested to see it," he said.

"It's only an MA," said Persse, his eyes watering from the smoke of Skinner's cigarette.

"Never mind, the libraries will buy almost anything on either Shakespeare or T. S. Eliot. Having them both in the same title would be more or less irresistible. Here's my card. Ah, thank you Philip, your very good health . . . Look, I'm sorry about *Hazlitt*, but I think the best thing would be to put it down to experience, and try again with a more fashionable subject."

"But it took me eight years to write that book," Philip Swallow said plaintively, as Skinner patted him consolingly on the shoulder, sending a cascade of grey ash down the back of his suit.

The bar was now crowded with conferees drinking as fast as they could to get themselves into an appropriate mood for the banquet. Persse squeezed his way through the crush to Angelica.

"You told *me* your thesis was about the influence of Shakespeare on T. S. Eliot," she said.

"So it is," he replied. "I turned it round on the spur of the moment, just to take that Dempsey down a peg or two."

"Well, it's a more interesting idea, actually."

"I seem to have let myself in for the job of writing it up, now," said Persse. "I like your dress, Angelica."

"I thought it was the most medieval thing I had with me," she said, a gleam in her dark eyes. "Though I can't guarantee that it will actually rustle to my knees."

The allusion pierced him with a thrill of desire, instantly shattering his "firm purpose of amendment." He knew that nothing could prevent him from keeping watch in Angelica's room that evening.

Persse did not intend to sit next to Angelica at dinner, for he thought it would be more in the spirit of her romantic scenario that he should view her from afar. But he didn't want Robin Dempsey sitting next to her either, and detained him in the bar with earnest questions about structuralist linguistics while the others went off to the refectory.

"It's quite simple, really," said Dempsey impatiently. "According to Saussure, it's not the relation of words to things that allows them to signify, but their relations with each other, in short, the differences between them. *Cat* signifies cat because it sounds different from *cot* or *fat*."

"And the same goes for *Durex* and *Farex* and *Exlax*?" Persse enquired.

"It's not the first example that springs to mind," said Dempsey, a certain suspicion in his close-set little eyes, "but yes."

"I think you reckon without the variation in regional accents," said Persse.

"Look, I haven't got time to explain it now," said Dempsey irritably, moving towards the door. "The bell has gone for dinner."

Persse found himself an inconspicuous place in the dining-hall, half-hidden from Angelica's view by a pillar. It was no great sacrifice to be on the margins of this particular feast. The mead tasted like tepid sugar-water, the medieval fare consisted of fried chicken and jacket potatoes eaten without the convenience of knives and forks, and the wenches were the usual Martineau Hall waitresses who had been bribed or bullied into wearing long dresses with plunging necklines. "Don't look at me, sir," the yellow-haired lady begged Persse as she served him his drumsticks. "If this is 'ow they dressed in the middle ages, well, all I can say is, they must 'ave got some very nasty chest colds." Presiding over the festivities from a platform at one end of the dining-room were a pair of entertainers from Ye Merrie Olde Round Table, one dressed up as a king, the other as a jester. The king had a piano accordion and the jester a set of drums, both provided with microphone and amplifier. While the meal was being served, they entertained the diners with jokes about chambers and thrones, sang bawdy ballads, and encouraged the diners to pelt each other with bread rolls. It was a rule of the court that anyone wishing to leave the room was required to bow or curtsey to the king, and when anyone did so the jester blew into an instrument that made a loud farting noise. Persse slipped out of the room while the medievalist from Aberystwyth was being humiliated in this fashion. Angelica, sitting between Felix Skinner and Philip Swallow on the far side of the room, flashed him a quick smile, and fluttered her fingers. She had not touched the food on her plate.

Persse stole away from Martineau Hall, towards Lucas Hall, drawing in deep breaths of the cool night air, and gazing at the ruffled reflection of the moon in the artificial lake. The strains of a new song which the king and jester had just started, their hoarse and strident voices powerfully amplified, pursued him:

> *King Arthur was a foolish knight,*
> *A foolish knight was he,*
> *He locked his wife in a chastity belt,*
> *And then he lost the key!*

Lucas Hall was deserted. Persse trod lightly on the stairs, and along the corridors, as he searched for room 231. Its door was unlocked, and he stepped inside. He did not turn on the light, as the room was sufficiently illuminated through a fanlight over the door, and by the moon shining in through the open casement. Snatches of song still carried on the night breeze:

> *Sir Lancelot, he told the Queen,*
> *"I soon will set you free."*
> *But when he tried with a pair of pliers*
> *She said, "Stop, you're tickling me!"*

Persse looked round the small, narrow room for somewhere to conceal himself. The only possible place was the built-in wardrobe. The packet of Farex was heavy in the pocket of his anorak. He took it out and placed it on the bedside table, reflecting that it was a rather poor substitute for jellies soother than the creamy curd, and lucent syrops, tinct with cinnamon, even if those did sound like baby-food.

He heard in the distance the thud and whine of the lift in operation, and stepped hastily into the dark interior of the wardrobe, pushing clothing to one side as he did so. He pulled the door to behind him, leaving it open an inch, through which he could breathe and see.

He heard the lift doors open at the end of the corridor, and footsteps approaching. The door handle turned, the door opened, and into the room came Robin Dempsey. He switched on the light, closed the door, and went across to the window to draw the curtains. As he took off his blazer, and draped it over the back of a chair, his eye was caught by the box of Farex, which he inspected with evident puzzlement. He eased off his shoes, and removed his trousers, revealing striped boxer shorts and sock suspenders. He took off one garment after another, folding and draping them neatly over the chair, until he was quite naked. It was not the spectacle Persse had been looking forward to. Dempsey sniffed himself under both armpits, then pushed a finger down into his crotch and sniffed that too. He disappeared from Persse's line of vision for a few moments, during which he could be heard splashing about at the sink, cleaning his teeth and gargling. Then he reappeared, still naked, shivering slightly, and got into bed. He turned off the light from a bedside switch, but enough illumination came through the fanlight above the door to reveal that he was lying on his back with his eyes open, staring at the ceiling, and glancing occasionally at a small digital clock whose figures glowed green on the bedside table. A profound silence settled in the room.

Persse coughed.

Robin Dempsey sat up in bed with the force of a released spring, his torso seeming to quiver for some seconds after achieving the perpendicular. "Who's there?" he quavered, fumbling for the light switch. As the light came on, an archly fond smile suffused his features. "Angelica," he said. "Have you been hiding in the wardrobe all the time? You minx!"

Persse pushed open the door of the wardrobe and stepped out.

"McGarrigle! What the fuck are you doing here?"

"I might ask you the same question," said Persse.

"Why shouldn't I be here? It's my room."

"*Your* room?" Persse looked around. Now that the light was on, he could see some signs of masculine occupation: an electric razor and a flask of Old Spice aftershave on the shelf over the sink, a pair of large leather slippers under the bed. He looked back at the wardrobe he had occupied and saw a bright blue suit on the solitary hanger inside. "Oh," he said weakly; then, with more resolution, "Why did you think Angelica was hiding in the wardrobe?"

"It's none of your business, but it so happens that I have an appointment with Angelica. I'm expecting her here at any moment, as a matter of fact, so

I'd be obliged if you would kindly piss off. What were you doing in my wardrobe, anyway?"

"I had an appointment with Angelica too. She told me this was her room. I was to hide in it and watch her going to bed. Like in 'The Eve of St. Agnes.'" It sounded rather silly to his own ears when he said it.

"I was to go to bed and wait for her to come to me," said Dempsey, "Like Ruggiero and Alcina, she said. Couple of characters in one of those long Eyetie poems, apparently. She told me the story—it sounded pretty sexy."

They were both silent for a moment.

"It looks as if she was having a bit of a joke," said Persse at last.

"Yes, it does," said Dempsey flatly. He got out of bed and took a pair of pyjamas from under his pillow. When he had put them on he got back into bed and pulled the blankets over his head. "Don't forget to turn off the light when you leave," he said in muffled tones.

"Oh, yes. Goodnight, then."

Persse ran downstairs to the lobby, to look at the noticeboard which he had consulted for Morris Zapp. Angelica's name did not appear anywhere on the list of residents. He hurried back to Martineau Hall. In the bar the conferees, who earlier had been drinking heavily to get themselves into the mood for the medieval banquet, were now drinking even more heavily in an effort to erase it from their memories. Bob Busby was nursing a glass of whisky alone in a corner, smiling fixedly in a brave effort to pretend that it was by his own choice that nobody was speaking to him. "Oh, hallo," he said gratefully, as Persse sat down beside him.

"Can you tell me what is Angelica Pabst's room number?" Persse asked him.

"It's funny you should ask me that," said Busby. "Somebody just mentioned that they saw her going off in a taxi, with her suitcase."

"What?" exclaimed Persse, jumping to his feet. "When? How long ago?"

"Oh, at least half an hour," said Bob Busby. "But, you know, as far as I know she never had a room. I certainly never allocated her one, and she doesn't seem to have paid for one. I don't really know how she got on this conference at all. She doesn't seem to belong to any university."

Persse ran down the drive to the gates of the hall site, not because he entertained any hopes of catching up with Angelica's taxi, but just to relieve his frustration and despair. He stood at the gates, looking up and down the empty road. The moon had disappeared behind a cloud. In the distance a train rattled along an embankment. He ran back up the drive, and went on running, past the two halls of residence, around the artificial lake, following the route he had taken with Morris Zapp that morning, until he reached the top of the hill that afforded a panoramic view over the city and the University. A yellowish glow from a million streetlamps lit up the sky and dimmed the light of the stars. A faint hum of traffic, the traffic that never ceased, night and day, to roll along the concrete thoroughfares, vibrated on the night air. "Angelica!" he cried desolately, to the indifferent city, "Angelica! Where are you?"

2

Meanwhile, Morris Zapp had been having a quiet evening, tête à tête with Hilary Swallow. Philip was at Martineau Hall, doing his medieval bit. The two eldest Swallow children were away from home, at college, and the youngest, Matthew, was out playing rhythm guitar in a school band. "Do you know," Hilary sighed, as the front door slammed behind him, "his sixth form has *four* rock groups, and no debating society? I don't know what education is coming to. But I expect you approve, Morris, I remember that you used to like that frightful music."

"Not punk, Hilary, which seems to be what your son is into."

"It all sounds the same to me," she said.

They ate dinner in the kitchen, which had been extended and expensively refitted since he had last been in the house, with teak veneer cabinets, a split-level cooker and cork tiling on the floor. Hilary cooked them a tasty steak *au poivre* with baby squash and new potatoes, followed by one of her delicious fruit puddings, in which a viscous fruit compôte lurked beneath and partly, but only partly, permeated a thick stratum of light-textured, slightly waxy spongecake, glazed, fissured and golden brown on top.

"Hilary, you're an even better cook than you were ten years ago, and that's saying something," Morris declared sincerely, as he finished his second helping of the pudding.

She pushed a ripe Brie across the table. "Food is one of my few remaining pleasures, I'm afraid," she said. "With the dire consequences for my figure that you can see. Do help yourself to wine." It was their second bottle.

"You're in great shape, Hilary." Morris said, but in truth she wasn't. Her heavy bosom looked in need of the support of a good old-fashioned bra, and there were thick rolls of flesh at her waist and over her hips. Her hair, a dull brown, flecked with grey, was dragged back into a bun which did nothing to hide or soften the lines, wrinkles and broken blood vessels in her facial skin. "You should take up jogging," he said.

Hilary snorted derisively. "Matthew says that when I run I look like a blancmange in a panic."

"Matthew should be ashamed of himself."

"That's the trouble with living with two men. They gang up on you. I was better off when Amanda was at home. What about *your* family, Morris? What are they doing these days?"

"Well, the twins will be going to college in the fall. Of course *I* shall have to pay for their tuition, even though Désirée is rich as Croesus from her royalties. It makes me mad, but her lawyers have me over a barrel, which is where she always wanted me."

"What's Désirée doing?"

"Trying to finish her second book, I guess. It's been five years since the first one, so I figure she must be badly blocked. Serves her right for trying to screw every last cent out of me."

"I read her novel, what was it called?"

"*Difficult Days*. Nice title, huh? Marriage as one long period pain. Sold a million and a half in paperback. What did you think of it?"

"What did *you* think of it, Morris?"

"You mean because the husband is such a monster? I kind of liked it. You wouldn't believe the number of women who propositioned me after that book came out. I guess they wanted to experience a real male chauvinist pig before the species became extinct."

"Did you oblige?"

"Nuh, I gave up screwing around a long time ago. I came to the conclusion that sex is a sublimation of the work instinct." Hilary tittered. Thus encouraged, Morris elaborated: "The nineteenth century had its priorities right. What we really lust for is power, which we achieve by work. When I look around at my colleagues these days, what do I see? They're all screwing their students, or each other, like crazy, marriages are breaking up faster than you can count, and yet nobody seems to be happy. Obviously they would rather be working, but they're ashamed to admit it."

"Maybe that's Philip's problem," said Hilary, "but somehow I don't think so."

"Philip? You don't mean to tell me that he's been cheating on you?"

"Nothing serious—or not that I know of. But he has a weakness for pretty students. For some reason they seem to have a weakness for him. I can't think why."

"Power, Hilary. They wet their pants at the thought of his power. I bet this started when he got the chairmanship, right?"

"I suppose it did," she admitted.

"How did you find out?"

"A girl tried to blackmail the Department over it. I'll show you."

She unlocked a leather writing case, and took from it what appeared to be the Xerox copy of an examination script. She passed it to Morris, who began to read.

Question 5. By what means did Milton try to "justify the ways of God to man" in "Paradise Lost"?

"You can always tell a weak examinee," Morris observed. "First they waste time copying out the question. Then they take out their little rulers and rule *lines* under it."

I think Milton succeeded very well in justifying the ways of God to man by making Satan such a horrible person, though Shelley said that Milton was of the Devil's party without knowing it. On the other hand it is probably impossible to justify the ways of God to man because if you believe in God then he can do anything he likes anyway, and if you don't there's no point trying to justify Him. "Paradise Lost" is an epic poem in blank verse, which is another clever way of justifying the ways of God to man because if it rhymed it would seem too pat. My tutor Professor Swallow seduced me in his office last February, if I don't pass this exam I will tell everybody. John Milton was the greatest English poet after Shakespeare. He knew many languages and nearly wrote "Paradise Lost" in Latin in which case nobody would be able to read it today. He locked the door and made me lie on the floor so nobody could see us through the window. I banged my head on the wastepaper bin. He also considered writing his epic poem about King Arthur and the knights of the Round Table, which is a pity he didn't as it would have made a more exciting story.

"How did you get hold of this?" Morris asked, as he skimmed through the script.

"Someone in the Department sent it to me, anonymously. I suspect it was Rupert Sutcliffe. He was first marker on the paper. It was a resit, in September, a couple of years ago. The girl had failed in June. Sutcliffe and some of the other senior members of staff confronted Philip with it."

"And?"

"Oh, he admitted he'd had the girl, on his office carpet, like she said— that rather nice Indian you burned a hole in with your cigar, do you remember?" Hilary's tone was casual, even flippant, but it seemed to Morris that it concealed a deep hurt. "*He* claimed that she seduced him—started unbuttoning her blouse in the middle of a consultation. As if he couldn't have just told her to do it up again. The girl didn't take it any further, fortunately. She left shortly afterwards—her family went abroad."

"Is that all?"

"What do you mean?"

"I mean, is that the only time Philip has cheated on you?"

"How do I know? It's the only time he's been caught. But nobody I discussed it with seemed particularly surprised. And when I go to Department do's I get a look that I can only describe as pitying."

They were both silent for a few moments. Then Morris said: "Hilary, are you trying to tell me that you're unhappy?"

"I suppose I am."

After another pause, Morris said: "If Désirée were sitting here now, she'd tell you to forget Philip, make your own life. Get yourself a job, find another guy."

"It's too late."

"It's never too late."

"I took a postgraduate certificate of education course a few years ago," said Hilary, "and as soon as I finished it, they started closing down schools in the city because of the falling birthrate. So there are no jobs. I do a little tutoring for the Open University, but it's not a career. As to lovers, it's definitely too late. You were my first and last, Morris."

"Hey," he said softly.

"Don't be nervous, I'm not going to drag you upstairs for a trip down memory lane . . ."

"Too bad," said Morris gallantly, but with a certain relief.

"For one thing, Philip will be back soon . . . No, I made my bed ten years ago, and I must lie in it, cold and lumpy as it often seems."

"How d'you mean?"

"Well, you know, when the four of us were . . . carrying on. Philip wanted a separation, but I begged him to come back home, give our marriage another chance, go back to being where we were before, a reasonably contented married couple. I was weak. If I'd said, to hell with you, do what you like, I daresay he would have come crawling back with his tail between his legs inside a year. But because I *asked* him to come back, with no conditions, he, well, has me over a barrel, as you would say."

"Do you still, ah, make it together?"

"Occasionally. But presumably he's not satisfied. There was a story in the paper the other day, about a man who'd had a heart attack and asked his doctor if it was safe to have sexual intercourse, and the doctor said, 'Yes, it's good exercise, but nothing too exciting, just with your wife.'"

Morris laughed.

"I thought it was funny, too," said Hilary. "But when I read it out to Philip he scarcely cracked a smile. He obviously thought it was a deeply poignant story."

Morris shook his head, and cut himself another slice of Brie. "I'm amazed, Hilary. Frankly, I always thought of you as the dominant partner in this marriage. Now Philip seems to be calling all the shots."

"Yes, well, things have gone rather well for him lately. He's started to make a bit of name for himself at last. He's even started to look more handsome than he ever did before in his life."

"I noticed," said Morris. "The beard is a knockout."

"It conceals his weak chin."

"That silver-grey effect is very distinguished."

"He has it touched up at the barber's," said Hilary. "But middle age becomes him. It's often the way with men. Whereas women find themselves hit simultaneously by the menopause and the long-term effects of childbearing. It doesn't seem quite fair . . . Anyway, Philip managed to get his Hazlitt book finished at last."

"I never knew about that," Morris said.

"It's had very little attention—rather a sore point with Philip. But it *was* a book, and he had it accepted by Lecky, Windrush and Bernstein just when the chair here became vacant, which was a bit of luck. He'd been effectively running the Department for years, anyway, so they appointed him. His horizons began to expand immediately. You've no idea of the *mana* the title of Professor carries in this country."

"Oh, I have, I have!" said Morris Zapp.

"He started to get invited to conferences, to be external examiner at other universities, he got himself on the British Council's list for overseas lecture tours. He's always off travelling somewhere these days. He's going to Turkey in a few weeks time. Last month it was Norway."

"That's how it is in the academic world these days," said Morris Zapp. "I was telling a young guy at the conference just this morning. The day of the single, static campus is over."

"And the single, static campus novel with it, I suppose?"

"Exactly! Even two campuses wouldn't be enough. Scholars these days are like the errant knights of old, wandering the ways of the world in search of adventure and glory."

"Leaving their wives locked up at home?"

"Well, a lot of the knights are women, these days. There's positive discrimination at the Round Table."

"Bully for them," said Hilary gloomily. "I belong to the generation that sacrificed their careers for their husbands. I never did finish my MA, so now I sit at home growing fat while my silver-haired spouse zooms round the world, no doubt pursued by academic groupies like that Angelica Thingummy he brought here the other night."

"Al Pabst? She's a nice girl. Smart, too."

"But she needs a job, and Philip might be in a position to give her one some day. I could see that in her eyes as she hung on his every word."

"Most of the conference she's been going around with our old friend Dempsey."

"Robin Dempsey? That's a laugh. No wonder Philip was making snide comments about him at breakfast, he's probably jealous. Perhaps Dempsey has a job to fill at Darlington. Shall I make some coffee?"

Morris helped her stack the dishwasher, and then they took their coffee into the lounge. While they were drinking it, Philip returned.

"How was the banquet?" Morris asked.

"Awful, awful," Philip groaned. He sank into a chair and covered his face with his hands. "I don't want to talk about it. Busby deserves to be taken out and shot. Or hung in chains from the walls of Martineau Hall—that would be more appropriate."

"I could have told you it would be awful," said Hilary.

"Why didn't you, then?" said Philip irritably.

"I didn't want to interfere. It's your conference."

"*Was* my conference. Thank God it's over. It's been a total disaster from start to finish."

"Don't say that, Philip," said Morris. "After all, there was my paper."

"It's all very well for you, Morris. You've had a nice quiet evening at home. I've been listening to two degenerate oafs shrieking obscene songs into a microphone for the last two hours, and trying to look as if I was enjoying myself. Then they put me in some stocks and encouraged the others to throw bread rolls at me, and I had to look as if I was enjoying that too."

Hilary crowed with laughter, and clapped her hands. "Oh, now I wish I'd gone," she said. "Did they really throw rolls at you?"

"Yes, and I thought one or two of them did it in a distinctly vindictive fashion," said Philip sulkily. "But I don't want to talk about it any more. Let's have a drink."

He produced a bottle of whisky and three glasses, but Hilary yawned and announced her intention of retiring. Morris said he would have to leave early the next morning to catch his plane to London, and perhaps he had better say goodbye to her now.

"Where are you off to, then?" Hilary asked.

"The Rockefeller villa at Bellagio," he said. "It's a kind of scholar's retreat. But I also have a number of conferences lined up for the summer: Zürich, Vienna, maybe Amsterdam. Jerusalem."

"Goodness," said Hilary. "I see what you mean about errant knights."

"Some are more errant than others," said Morris.

"I know," said Hilary meaningfully.

They shook hands and Morris pecked her awkwardly on the cheek. "Take care," he said.

"Why should I?" she said. "*I'm* not doing anything adventurous. Incidentally, I thought you were against foreign travel, Morris. You used to say that travel narrows the mind."

"There comes a moment when the individual has to yield to the *Zeitgeist* or drop out of the ball game," said Morris. "For me it came in '75, when I kept getting invitations to Jane Austen centenary conferences in the most improbable places—Poznan, Delhi, Lagos, Honolulu—and half the speakers turned out to be guys I knew in graduate school. The world is a global campus, Hilary, you'd better believe it. The American Express card has replaced the library pass."

"I expect Philip would agree with you," said Hilary; but Philip, pouring out the whisky, ignored the cue. "Goodnight, then," she said.

"Goodnight, dear," said Philip, without looking up from the glasses. "We'll just have a nightcap." When Hilary had closed the door behind her, Philip handed Morris his drink. "What are all these conferences you're going to this summer?" he asked, with a certain covetousness.

"Zürich is Joyce. Amsterdam is Semiotics. Vienna is Narrative. Or is it Narrative in Amsterdam and Semiotics in Vienna . . . ? Anyway. Jerusalem I *do* know is about the Future of Criticism, because I'm one of the organizers. It's sponsored by a journal called *Metacriticism*, I'm on the editorial board."

"Why Jerusalem?"

"Why not? It's a draw, a novelty. It's a place people want to see, but it's not on the regular tourist circuit. Also the Jerusalem Hilton offers very competitive rates in the summer because it's so goddam hot."

"The Hilton, eh? A bit different from Lucas Hall and Martineau Hall," Philip mused ruefully.

"Right. Look, Philip, I know you were disappointed by the turnout for your conference, but frankly, what can you expect if you're asking people to live in those tacky dormitories and eat canteen meals? Food and accommodation are the most important things about any conference. If the people are happy with *those*, they'll generate intellectual excitement. If they're not, they'll sulk, and sneer, and cut lectures."

Philip shrugged. "I see your point, but people here just can't afford that sort of luxury. Or their universities won't pay for it."

"Not in the UK, they won't. But when I worked here I discovered an interesting anomaly. You could only have up to fifty pounds a year or some such paltry sum to attend conferences in this country, but there was no limit on grants to attend conferences overseas. The solution is obvious: you should hold your next conference abroad. Somewhere nice and warm, like Monte Carlo, maybe. Meanwhile, why don't you come to Jerusalem this summer?"

"Who, me? To your conference?"

"Sure. You could knock off a paper on the future of criticism, couldn't you?"

"I don't think it *has* much of a future," said Philip.

"Great! It will be controversial. Bring Hilary along for the ride."

"Hilary?" Philip looked disconcerted. "Oh, no, I don't think she could stand the heat. Besides, I doubt if we could afford her fare. Two children at university is a bit of a drain, you know."

"Don't tell me, I'm bracing myself for it next fall."

"Did Hilary put you up to suggesting this, Morris?" said Philip, looking slightly ashamed of his own question.

"Certainly not. What makes you think so?"

Philip squirmed uncomfortably in his seat. "It's just that she's been complaining lately that I'm away too much, neglecting the family, neglecting her."

"And are you?"

"I suppose I am, yes. It's the only thing that keeps me going these days, travelling. Changes of scene, changes of faces. It would defeat the whole object to take Hilary along with me on my academic trips."

"What *is* the object?"

Philip sighed. "Who knows? It's hard to put it into words. What are we all looking for? Happiness? One knows that doesn't last. Distraction, perhaps—distraction from the ugly facts: that there is death, there is disease, there is impotence and senility ahead."

"Jesus," said Morris, "are you always like this after a medieval banquet?"

Philip smiled wanly and refilled their glasses. "Intensity," he said. "Intensity of experience is what we're looking for, I think. We know we won't find it at home any more, but there's always the hope that we'll find it abroad. I found it in America in '69."

"With Désirée?"

"Not just Désirée, though she was an important part of it. It was the excitement, the richness of the whole experience, the mixture of pleasure and danger and freedom—and the sun. You know, when we came back here, for a long while I still went on living in Euphoria inside my head. Outwardly I returned to my old routine. I got up in the morning, put on a tweed suit, read the *Guardian* over breakfast, walked into the University, gave the same old tutorials on the same old texts . . . and all the while I was leading a completely different life inside my head. Inside my head, I had decided not to come back to England, so I was waking up in Plotinus, sitting in the sun in my happi-coat, looking out over the Bay, putting on Levis and a sports shirt, reading the *Euphoric Times* over breakfast, and wondering what would happen today, would there be a protest, a demonstration, would my class have to fight their way through teargas and picket lines or should we meet off-campus in somebody's apartment, sitting on the floor surrounded by posters and leaflets and paperbacks about encounter groups and avant garde theatre and Viet Nam."

"That's all over now," said Morris. "You wouldn't recognize the place. The kids are all into fraternities and preppy clothes and working hard to get into law school."

"So I've heard," said Philip. "How depressing."

"But this intensity of experience, did you never find it again since you were in America?"

Philip stared into the bottom of his glass. "Once I did," he said. "Shall I tell you the story?"

"Just let me get myself a cigar. Is this a cigarillo story or a panatella story?"

"I don't know, I've never told it to anyone before."

"I'm honoured," said Morris. "This calls for something special."

. . .

Morris left the room to fetch one of his favourite Romeo y Julietas. When he returned, he was conscious that the furniture and lighting had been rearranged in his absence. Two highbacked armchairs were inclined towards each other across the width of the hearth, where a gas fire burned low. The only other light in the room came from a standard lamp behind the chair in which Philip sat, his face in shadow. Between the two chairs was a long, low coffee table bearing the whisky bottle, water jug, glasses and an ashtray. Morris's glass had been refilled with a generous measure.

"Is this where the narratee sits?" he enquired, taking the vacant chair. Philip, gazing absently into the fire, smiled vaguely, but made no reply. Morris rolled the cigar next to his ear and listened approvingly to the crackle of the leaves. He pierced one end of the cigar, clipped the other, and lit it, puffing vigorously. "OK," he said, examining the tip to see that it was burning evenly. "I'm listening."

"It happened some years ago, in Italy," Philip began. "It was the very first lecture tour I did for the British Council. I flew out to Naples, and then worked my way up the country by train: Rome, Florence, Bologna, Padua, ending up at Genoa. It was a bit of a rush on the last day. I gave my lecture in the afternoon, and I was booked to fly home the same evening. The Council chap in Genoa, who'd been shepherding me about the place, gave me an early dinner in a restaurant, and then drove me out to the airport. There was a delay in the flight departure—a technical problem, they said, so I told him not to wait. I knew he had to get up early the next morning to drive to Milan for a meeting. That comes into the story."

"I should hope so," said Morris. "There should be nothing irrelevant in a good story."

"Anyway, the British Council man, J. K. Simpson, I can't remember his first name, a nice young chap, very friendly, enthusiastic about his job, he said, "OK, I'll leave you then, but if the flight's cancelled, give me a ring and I'll get you into a hotel for the night.""

"Well, the delay went on and on, but eventually we took off, at about midnight. It was a British plane. I was sitting next to an English businessman, a salesman in woollen textiles I think he was . . ."

"Is that relevant?"

"Not really."

"Never mind. Solidity of specification," said Morris with a tolerant wave of his cigar. "It contributes to the reality effect."

"We were sitting towards the rear of the aircraft, just behind the wing. He had the window seat, and I was next to him. About ten minutes out of Genoa, they were just getting ready to serve drinks, you could hear the clink of bottles from the back of the plane, when this salesman chap turned away from the window, and tapped me on the arm and said, 'Excuse me, but would you mind having a look out there. Is it my imagination or is that engine on fire?' So I leaned across him and looked out of the window. It was dark of course, but I could see flames sort of licking round the engine. Well, I'd never looked closely at a jet engine at night before, for all I knew that was always the effect they gave. I mean you might expect to see a kind of fiery glow coming out of the engine at night. On the other hand, these were definitely flames, and they weren't just coming out of the hole at the back. 'I don't know what to think,' I said. 'It certainly doesn't look quite right.' 'Do you think we should tell somebody?' he said. 'Well, they must have seen it for themselves, mustn't they?' I said. The fact was, neither of us wanted to look a fool by suggesting that something was wrong, and then being told that it wasn't. Fortunately a chap on the other side of the aisle noticed that we were exercised about something, and came across to have a look for himself. 'Christ!' he said, and pushed the button to call the stewardess. I think he was probably some sort of engineer. The stewardess came by with the drinks trolley at that moment.

'If it's a drink you want, you'll have to wait your turn,' she said. The cabin staff were a bit snappish because of the long delay. 'Does the captain know that his starboard engine is on fire?' said the engineer. She gaped at him, squinted out of the window, then ran up the aisle, pushing her trolley in front of her, like a nursemaid running with a pram. A minute later and a man in uniform, the second pilot I suppose, came down the aisle, looking worried and carrying a big torch, which he shone out of the window at the engine. It was on fire all right. He ran back to the cockpit. Very soon the plane banked and headed back to Genoa. The Captain came on the PA to say that we would be making an emergency landing because of a technical problem, and that we should be prepared to leave the aircraft by the emergency exits. Then somebody else told us exactly what to do. I must say he sounded remarkably cool, calm and collected."

"It was a cassette," said Morris. "They have these prerecorded cassettes for all contingencies. I was in a Jumbo, once, going over the Rockies, and a stewardess put on the emergency ditching tape by mistake. We were having lunch at the time, I remember, a perfect sunny day at 30,000 feet, when this voice suddenly said, *'We are obliged to make an emergency landing on water. Do not panic if you are unable to swim. The rescue services have been advised of our intentions.'* People froze with their forks halfway to their mouths. Then all hell let loose until they sorted it out."

"There was a fair amount of wailing and gnashing of teeth in our plane—quite a lot of the passengers were Italian, and you know what they're like—they don't hide their feelings. Then the pilot put the plane into a terrifying dive to put the fire out."

"Jesus!" said Morris Zapp.

"He was thoughtful enough to explain first what he was going to do, but only in English, so all the Italians thought we were going to crash into the sea and started to scream and weep and cross themselves. But the dive worked—it put the fire out. Then we had to circle over the sea for about twenty minutes, jettisoning fuel, before we tried to land back at Genoa. It was a very long twenty minutes."

"I'll bet."

"Frankly, I thought they were going to be my last twenty minutes."

"What did you think about?"

"I thought, how stupid. I thought, how unfair. I suppose I prayed. I imagined Hilary and the children hearing about the crash on the radio when they woke up the next morning, and I felt bad about that. I thought about surviving but being terribly crippled. I tried to remember the terms of the British Council's insurance policy for lecturers on Specialist Tours—so much for an arm, so much for a leg below the knee, so much for a leg above the knee. I tried not to think about being burned to death.

"Landing at Genoa is a pretty hairy experience at the best of times. I don't know if you know it, but there's this great high promontory that sticks out into the sea. Planes approaching from the north have to make a U-turn round it, and then come in between it and the mountains, over the city and the docks. And we were doing it at night with one engine kaput. The airport was on full emergency alert, of course, but being a small airport, in Italy, that didn't amount to much. As we hit the ground, I could see the fire trucks with their lights flashing, racing towards us. As soon as the plane stopped, the cabin crew opened the emergency exits and we all slid out down those inflatable chute things. The trouble was they couldn't open the emergency exit nearest to us, me and the wool man, because it gave on to the wing with the duff engine. So we were the last out of the plane. I remember thinking it was rather unfair, because if it hadn't been for us the whole thing might have blown up in mid-air.

"Anyway, we got out all right, ran like hell to a bus they had waiting, and were taken to the terminal. The fire engines smothered the plane in foam. While they were getting our baggage out of the plane I telephoned the British Council chap. I suppose I wanted to express my relief at having survived by telling somebody. It was queer to think that Hilary and the children were asleep in England, not knowing that I'd had a narrow escape from death. I didn't want to wake Hilary up with a call and give her a pointless retrospective fright. But I felt I had to tell *someone*. Also, I wanted to get out of the airport. A lot of the Italian passengers were in hysterics, kissing the ground and weeping and crossing themselves and so on. It was obvious that we shouldn't be flying out till the next morning and that it was going to take hours to sort out our accommodation for the night. And Simpson had told me to phone him if there was any problem, so although it was by now well past one o'clock, I did. As soon as he grasped what had happened, he said he'd come straight out to the airport. So about half an hour later, he picked me up and drove me into the city to find a hotel. We tried a few, but no luck—either they were shut up for the night or they were full, there was a trade fair on in Genoa that week. So he said, look, why don't you come home with me, we haven't got a guest bedroom, I'm afraid, but there's a kind of put-u-up in the living-room. So he took me home to his apartment, in a modern block, half-way up the mountain that overlooks the city and the sea. I felt extraordinarily calm and wide-awake, I was rather impressed by my own sangfroid, as a matter of fact. But when he offered me some brandy I didn't say no. I looked around the living-room, and felt a sudden pang of homesickness. I'd been living in hotel rooms for the past twelve days, and eating meals in restaurants. I rather enjoy that nowadays, but then I was still a bit of a novice at the foreign lecture tour, and I'd found it quite a strain. And here was a little oasis of English domesticity, where I could relax and feel completely at home. There were toys scattered about the living-room, and English newspapers, and in the bathroom St. Michael's underwear hanging up to dry. While we were drinking the brandy, and I was telling Simpson the whole story of the plane, his wife came into the room, in her dressing-gown, yawning and rubbing the sleep out of her eyes. I hadn't met her before. Her name was Joy."

"Ah," murmured Morris. "You remember *her* first name."

"I apologized for disturbing her. She said it didn't matter, but she didn't look particularly pleased. She asked me if I would like something to eat, and I suddenly realized that I was ravenously hungry. So she brought some Parma ham from the kitchen, and some cake, and a pot of tea, and we ended up having a sort of impromptu meal. I was sitting opposite Joy. She was wearing a soft blue velour dressing-gown, with a hood, and a zip that went from hem to throat. Hilary had one just like it once, and looking at Joy out of the corner of my eye was like looking at some younger, prettier version of Hilary— I mean, Hilary when she was young and pretty herself, when we were first married. Joy was, I guessed, in her early thirties, with fair wavy hair and blue eyes. A rather heavy chin, but with a wide, generous mouth, full lips. She had a trace of a northern accent, Yorkshire I thought. She did a little English teaching, conversation classes at the university, but basically saw her rôle as supporting her husband's career. I daresay she made the effort to get up and be hospitable to me for his sake. Well, as we talked, and ate, and drank, I suddenly felt myself overcome with the most powerful desire for Joy."

"I knew it," said Morris.

"It was as if, having passed through the shadow of death, I had suddenly recovered an appetite for life that I thought I had lost for ever, since returning from America to England. In a way it was keener than anything I had ever known before. The food pierced me with its exquisite flavours, the tea was fragrant as ambrosia, and the woman sitting opposite to me seemed unbearably beautiful, all the more because she was totally unconscious of her attractions for me. Her hair was tousled and her face was pale and puffy from sleep, and she had no make-up or lipstick on, of course. She sat quietly, cradling her mug of tea in both hands, not saying much, smiling faintly at her husband's jokes, as if she'd heard them before. I honestly think that I would have felt just the same about any woman, in that situation, at that moment, who wasn't downright ugly. Joy just represented woman for me then. She was like Milton's Eve, Adam's dream—he woke and found it true, as Keats says. I suddenly thought how nice women were. How soft and kind. How lovely it would be, how *natural*, to go across and put my arms round her, to bury my head in her lap. All this while Simpson was telling me about the appalling standards of English-language teaching in Italian secondary schools. Eventually he glanced at his watch and said that it had gone four, and instead of going back to bed he thought he would drive to Milan while he was wide awake and rest when he got there. He was taking the Council car, he told me, so Joy would run me to the airport in theirs."

"I know what's coming," said Morris, "yet I can hardly believe it."

"He had his bag already packed, so it was only a few minutes before he was gone. We shook hands, and he wished me better luck with my flight the next day. Joy went with him to the front door of the apartment, and I heard them kiss goodbye. She came back into the living-room, looking a little shy. The blue dressing-gown was a couple of inches too long for her, and she had to hold up the skirt in front of her—it gave her a courtly, vaguely medieval air as she came back into the room. I noticed that her feet were bare. 'I'm sure you'd like to get some sleep now,' she said. 'There is a second bed in Gerard's room, but if I put you in there he might be scared when he wakes up in the morning.' I said the sofa would be fine. 'But Gerard gets up frightfully early, I'm afraid he'll disturb you,' she said. 'If you don't mind taking our bed, I could quite easily go into his room myself.' I said no, no; she pressed me, and said would I just give her a few moments to change the sheets, and I said I wouldn't dream of putting her to such trouble. The thought of that bed, still warm from her body, was too much for me. I started to shake all over with the effort to stop myself from taking an irrevocable leap into moral space, pulling on the zip-tab at her throat like a parachute ripcord, and falling with her to the floor."

"That's a very fancy metaphor, Philip," said Morris. "I can hardly believe you've never told this story before."

"Well, actually, I did write it down," said Philip, "for my own satisfaction. But I've never shown it to anybody." He refilled their glasses. "Anyway, there we were, looking at each other. We heard a car accelerate away outside, down the hill, Simpson presumably. 'What's the matter?' she said, 'You're trembling all over.' She was trembling herself a little. I said I supposed it was shock. Delayed reaction. She gave me some more brandy, and swallowed some herself. I could tell that she knew it wasn't really shock that was making me tremble, that it was herself, her proximity, but she couldn't quite credit her own intuition. 'You'd better lie down,' she said, 'I'll show you the bedroom.'

"I followed her into the main bedroom. It was lit by a single bedside lamp with a purple shade. There was a large double bed, with a duvet half thrown back. She straightened it out, and plumped the pillows. I was still shaking all over. She asked me if I would like a hot water bottle. I said: 'There's only one thing that would stop me shaking like this. If you would put your arms round me . . .'

"Although it was a dim light in the room, I could see that she went very red. 'I can't do that,' she said. 'You shouldn't ask me.' 'Please,' I said, and took a step towards her.

"Ninety-nine women out of a hundred would have walked straight out of the room, perhaps slapped my face. But Joy just stood there. I stepped up close to her and put my arms round her. God, it was wonderful. I could feel the warmth of her breasts coming through the velour dressing-gown, and my shirt. She put her arms round me and gently clasped my back. I stopped shaking as if by magic. I had my chin on her shoulder and I was moaning and raving into her ear about how wonderful and generous and beautiful she was, and what ecstasy it was to hold her in my arms, and how I felt reconnected to the earth and the life force and all kinds of romantic nonsense. And all the time I was looking at myself reflected in the dressing-table mirror, in this weird purple light, my chin on her shoulder, my hands moving over her back, as if I were watching a film, or looking into a crystal ball. It didn't seem possible that it was really happening. I saw my hands slide down the small of her back and cup her buttocks, bunching the skirt of her dressing-gown, and I said to the man in the mirror, silently, in my head, you're crazy, now she'll break away, slap your face, scream for help. But she didn't. I saw her back arch and felt her press against me. I swayed, and staggered slightly, and as I recovered my balance I altered my position a little, and now in the mirror I could see her face, reflected in another mirror on the other side of the room, and, my God, there was an expression of total abandonment on it, her eyes were half shut and her lips were parted and she was smiling. Smiling! So I pulled back my head and kissed her, full on the lips. Her tongue went straight into my mouth like a warm eel. I pulled gently at the zip on the front of her dressing-gown and slid my hand inside. She was naked underneath it."

Philip paused and stared into the fire. Morris discovered that he was sitting forward on the edge of his seat and that his cigar had gone out. "Yeah?" he said, fumbling for his lighter. "Then what happened?"

"I slipped the dressing-gown from her shoulders, and it crackled with static electricity as it slid off and settled at her feet. I fell on my knees and buried my face in her belly. She ran her fingers through my hair, and dug her nails into my shoulders. I lay her down on the bed and began to tear off my clothes with one hand while I kept stroking her with the other, afraid that if I once let go of her I would lose her. I had just enough presence of mind to ask if she was protected, and she nodded, without opening her eyes. Then we made love. There was nothing particularly subtle or prolonged about it, but I've never had an orgasm like it, before or since. I felt I was defying death, fucking my way out of the grave. She had to put her hand over my mouth, to stop me from shouting her name aloud: Joy, Joy, Joy.

"Then, almost instantly, I fell asleep. When I woke up I was alone in the bed, naked, covered with the duvet. Sunlight was coming through the cracks in the window shutters, and I could hear a vacuum cleaner going in another room. I looked at my watch. It was 10:30. I wondered if I had just dreamed of making love to Joy, but the physical memory was too keen and specific, and my clothes were scattered round the floor where I had thrown them off the night before. I put on my shirt and trousers and went out of the bedroom, into the living-room. A little Italian woman with a scarf round her head was hoovering the carpet. She grinned at me, turned off the Hoover and said something unintelligible. Joy came into the room from the kitchen, with a little boy at her side, holding a Dinky car, who stared at me. Joy looked quite different from the night before—smarter and more poised. She seemed to have cut her hand and was wearing an Elastoplast, but otherwise she was immaculately turned out, in some kind of linen dress, and her hair was smooth and bouncy as if she had just washed it. She gave me a bright, slightly artificial smile, but avoided eye contact. 'Oh, hallo,' she said, 'I was just going to wake you.' She had phoned the airport and my plane left at 12:30. She would run me down there as soon as I was ready. Would I like some breakfast, or would I like to take a shower first? She was the complete British Council hostess—polite, patient, detached. She actually asked me if I'd slept well. I wondered again whether the episode with her the night before had been a wet dream, but when I saw the blue dressing-gown hanging on the back of the bathroom door, it brought the whole thing back with a sensuous detail that just couldn't have been imaginary. The exact shape of her nipples, blunt and cylindrical, was imprinted on the nerve-endings of my finger-tips. I remembered the unusual luxuriance of her pubic hair, and its pale gold colour, tinged with purple from the bedside lamp, and the line across her belly where her sun-tan stopped. I couldn't have dreamed all that. But it was impossible to have any kind of intimate conversation with her, what with the cleaning woman hoovering away, and the little boy round her feet all the time. And it was obvious that she didn't want to anyway. She bustled about the flat and chattered to the cleaning woman and the boy. Even when she drove me to the airport she brought the kid along with her, and he was a sharp little bugger, who didn't miss much. Although he was sitting in the back, he kept leaning forward and poking his head between the two of us, as if to stop us getting intimate. It began to look as if we would part without a single reference to what had happened the night before. It was absurd. I just couldn't make her out. I felt I had to discover what had prompted her extraordinary action. Was she some kind of nymphomaniac, who would give herself to any man who was available—was I the most recent of a long succession of British Council lecturers who had passed through that purple-lit bedroom? It even crossed my mind that Simpson was in collusion with her, that I had been a pawn in some kinky erotic game between them, that perhaps he had returned silently to the flat and hidden himself behind one of those mirrors in the bedroom. A glance at her profile at the wheel of the car was enough to make such speculations seem fantastic—she looked so normal, so wholesome, so English. What had motivated her, then? I was desperate to know.

"When we got to the airport, she said, 'You won't mind if I just drop you, will you?' But she had to get out of the car to open the boot for me, and I realized that this was my only chance to say anything to her privately. 'Aren't we going to talk about last night?' I said, as I lifted my bag out of the boot. 'Oh,' she said, with her bright hostess's smile, 'you mustn't worry about disturbing our sleep. We're used to it in this job, people arriving at all sorts of odd hours. Not usually, of course, in burning aeroplanes. I do hope you have a less eventful flight today. Goodbye, Mr. Swallow.'

"'Mr. Swallow!' This was the woman who just a few hours before had had her legs wrapped somewhere round the back of my neck! Well, it was very clear that, whatever her motives, she wanted to pretend that nothing had happened between us the night before—that she wanted to excise the whole episode from history, cancel it, unweave it. And that the best way I could convey my own gratitude was to play along with her. So, with great reluctance, I didn't press for an inquest. I just allowed myself one indulgence. She'd extended her hand, and, instead of just shaking it, I pressed it to my lips. I reckoned it wouldn't seem a particularly showy gesture in an Italian airport. She blushed, as deeply as she had blushed the night before when I asked her to put her arms round me, and the whole unbelievable tenderness of that embrace flooded back into my consciousness, and hers too, I could see. Then she went back to the front of the car, got into the driver's seat, gave me one last look through the window, and drove away. I never saw her again."

"Maybe you will one day," said Morris.

Philip shook his head. "No, she's dead."

"Dead?"

"All three of them were killed in an air-crash the following year, in India. I saw their names in the list of passengers. There were no survivors. 'Simpson, J. K., wife Joy and son Gerard.'"

Morris expelled his breath in a low whistle. "Hey, that's really sad! I didn't think this story was going to have an unhappy ending."

"Ironic, too, isn't it, when you think of how we met? At first I felt horribly guilty, as if I had somehow passed on to her a death which I had narrowly escaped myself. I convinced myself that it was just superstition. But I shall always keep a little shrine to Joy in my heart."

"A little what?"

"A shrine," Philip said solemnly. Morris coughed cigar smoke and let it pass. "She gave me back an appetite for life I thought I had lost for ever. It was the total unexpectedness, the gratuitousness of that giving of herself. It convinced me that life was still worth living, that I should make the most of what I had left."

"And have you had any more adventures like that one?" Morris enquired, feeling slightly piqued at the extent to which he had been affected, first by the eroticism of Philip's tale, then by its sad epilogue.

Philip blushed slightly. "One thing I learned from it, was never to say no to someone who asks for your body, never reject someone who freely offers you theirs."

"I see," said Morris drily. "Have you agreed this code with Hilary?"

"Hilary and I don't see eye to eye on a lot of things. Some more whisky?"

"Positively the last one. I have to get up at five tomorrow."

"And what about you, Morris?" said Philip, pouring out the whisky. "How's your sex life these days?"

"Well, after Désirée and I split up I tried to get married again. I had various women living in, graduate students mostly, but none of them would marry me—girls these days have no principles—and I gradually lost interest in the idea. I'm living on my own right now. I jog. I watch TV. I write my books. Sometimes I go to a massage parlour in Esseph."

"A massage parlour?" Philip looked shocked.

"They have a very nice class of girl in those places, you know. They're not hookers. College-educated. Clean, well-groomed, articulate. When I was a teenager I spent many exhausting hours trying to persuade girls like that to jerk me off in the back seat of my old man's Chevvy. Now it's as easy as going to the supermarket. It saves a lot of time and nervous energy."

"But there's no relationship!"

"Relationships kill sex, haven't you learned that yet? The longer a relationship goes on, the less sexual excitement there is. Don't kid yourself, Philip—do you think it would have been as great with Joy the second time, if there'd been one?"

"Yes," said Philip. "Yes."

"And the twenty-second time? The two hundredth time?"

"I suppose not," Philip admitted. "Habit ruins everything in the end, doesn't it? Perhaps *that's* what we're all looking for—desire undiluted by habit."

"The Russian Formalists had a word for it," said Morris.

"I'm sure they did," said Philip. "But it's no use telling me what it was, because I'm sure to forget it."

"*Ostranenie*," said Morris. "Defamiliarization. It was what they thought literature was all about. '*Habit devours objects, clothes, furniture, one's wife and the fear of war . . . Art exists to help us recover the sensation of life.*' Viktor Shklovsky."

"Books used to satisfy me," said Philip. "But as I get older I find they aren't enough."

"But you're hitting the trail again soon, eh? Hilary tells me Turkey. What are you doing there?"

"Another British Council tour. I'm lecturing on Hazlitt."

"Are they very interested in Hazlitt in Turkey?"

"I shouldn't think so, but it's the bicentenary of his birth. Or rather, it was, last year, when this trip was first mooted. It's taken rather a long time to get off the ground . . . By the way, did you receive a copy of my Hazlitt book?"

"No—I was just saying to Hilary, I hadn't even heard about it."

Philip uttered an exclamation of annoyance. "Isn't that typical of publishers? I specifically asked them to send you a complimentary copy. Let me give you one now." He took from the bookcase a volume in a pale blue wrapper, scribbled a dedication inside, and handed it to Morris. It was entitled *Hazlitt and the Amateur Reader*. "I don't expect you to agree with it, Morris, but if you think it has any merit at all, I'd be very grateful if you could do anything to get it reviewed somewhere. It hasn't had a single notice, so far."

"It doesn't look like the sort of thing *Metacriticism* is interested in," said Morris. "But I'll see what I can do." He riffled through the pages. "Hazlitt is kind of an unfashionable subject, isn't he?"

"Unjustly neglected, in my view," said Philip. "A very interesting man. Have you read *Liber Amoris*?"

"I don't think so."

"It's a lightly fictionalized account of his obsession with his landlady's daughter. He was estranged from his wife at the time, hoping rather vainly to get a divorce. She was the archetypal pricktease. Would sit on his knee and let him feel her up, but not sleep with him or promise to marry him when he was free. It nearly drove him insane. He was totally obsessed. Then one day he saw her out with another man. End of illusion. Hazlitt shattered. I can feel for him. That girl must have—"

Philip's voice faltered, and Morris saw him turn pale, staring at the living-room door. Following the direction of his gaze, Morris saw Hilary standing at the threshold, wearing a faded blue velour dressing-gown, with a hood and a zip that ran from throat to hem.

"I couldn't sleep," she said. "Then I realized I'd forgotten to tell you not to lock the front door. Matthew isn't in yet. Are you feeling all right, Philip? You look as if you'd seen a ghost."

"That dressing-gown . . ."

"What about it? I dug it out because my other one's at the cleaners."

"Oh, nothing, I thought you'd got rid of it years ago," said Philip. He drained his glass. "Time for bed, I think."

PART II

1

At 5 a.m., precisely, Morris Zapp is woken by the bleeping of his digital wristwatch, a sophisticated piece of miniaturized technology which can inform him, at the touch of a button, of the exact time anywhere in the world. In Cooktown, Queensland, Australia, for instance, it is 3 p.m., a fact of no interest to Morris Zapp, as he yawns and gropes for the bedside lamp switch—though as it happens, at this very moment in Cooktown, Queensland, Rodney Wainwright, of the University of North Queensland, is labouring over a paper for Morris Zapp's Jerusalem conference on the Future of Criticism.

It is hot, very hot, this afternoon, in North Queensland; sweat makes the ballpen in Rodney Wainwright's fingers slippery to hold, and dampens the page where the cushion of his palm rests upon it. From his desk in the study of his one-storey house here on the steamy outskirts of Cooktown, Rodney Wainwright can hear the sounds of the waves breaking on the nearby beach. There, he knows, are most of his students in English 351, "Theories of Literature from Coleridge to Barthes," cleaving the blue and white water or lying prone on the dazzling sand, the girls with their bikini bra straps trailing, untied for an even tan. Rodney Wainwright knows they are there because this morning, after the class broke up, they invited him to join them, grinning and nudging each other, a friendly but challenging gesture which, being decoded, meant: *"OK, we've played your cultural game this morning—are you willing to play ours this afternoon?"* "Sorry," he had said, "There's nothing I'd like more, but I have this paper to write." Now they are on the beach and he is at his desk. Later, as the sun sinks behind their backs, they will break out cans of beer and light a barbecue fire and someone will pick out a tune on a guitar. When it is quite dark there may be a proposal to go swimming in the nude—Rodney Wainwright has heard rumours that this is the usual climax to a beach party. He imagines the participation in such exercise of Sandra Dix, the buxom blonde from England who always sits in the front row of English 351 with her mouth and blouse-front perpetually agape. Then, with a sigh, he focuses his vision on the ruled foolscap before him, and re-reads what he wrote ten minutes ago.

> *The question is, therefore, how can literary criticism maintain its Arnoldian function of identifying the best which has been thought and said, when literary discourse itself has been decentred by deconstructing the traditional concept of the author, of authority?*

Rodney Wainwright inserts a pair of inverted commas around *"authority"* and wills his mind to think of the next sentence. The paper must be finished soon, for Morris Zapp has asked to see a draft before accepting it for the conference, and on acceptance depends the travel grant which will enable Rodney Wainwright to fly to Europe this summer (or rather winter), to refresh his mind at the fountainhead of modern critical thought, making useful and influential contacts, adding to the little pile of scholarly honours, distinctions, achievements, that may eventually earn him a chair at Sydney or Melbourne. He does not want to grow old in Cooktown, Queensland. It is no country for old men. Even now, at thirty-eight, he stands no chance with the likes of Sandra Dix beside the bronzed and bulging heroes of the beach. The effects of twenty years' dedication to the life of the mind are all too evident when he puts on a pair of swimming trunks, however loosely cut: beneath the large, balding, bespectacled head is a pale, pear-shaped torso, with skinny limbs attached like afterthoughts in a child's drawing. And even if by some miracle Sandra Dix should be inclined to overlook these imperfections of the flesh in the dazzled contemplation of his mind, his wife Beverley would soon put a stop to any attempt at friendship beyond the call of tutorial duty.

As if to reinforce his thought, Bev's broad bum, inadequately disguised by an ethnic print frock, now intrudes into the frame of Rodney Wainwright's abstracted vision. Bent nearly double, and sweating profusely under her floppy sunhat, she is shuffling backwards across the rank lawn, dragging something—what? A hosepipe? A rope? Some animal on a lead? Eventually it proves to be a child's toy, some brightly coloured wheeled object that wags and oscillates obscenely as it moves along, followed by a gurgling toddler, child of some visiting neighbour. A strong-minded woman, Bev. Rodney Wainwright regards her bottom with respect, but without desire. He imagines Sandra Dix executing the same movement in her blue jeans, and sighs. He forces his eyes back on to the ruled foolscap before him.

"*One possible solution,*" he writes, and then pauses, gnawing the end of his ballpen.

One possible solution would be to run to the beach, seize Sandra Dix by the hand, drag her behind a sand dune, pull down her bikini pants and

"Cuppa tea, Rod? I'm just going to make one for Meg and me."

Bev's red perspiring face peers in at the open window. Rodney stops writing and guiltily covers his pad. After she has gone, he rips out the page, tears it up into small pieces, and tosses it into the wastepaper basket, where it joins several other torn and screwed-up pieces of paper. He starts again on a clean sheet.

The question is, therefore, how can literary criticism . . .

Morris Zapp, who has nodded off these last few minutes, suddenly wakes again in a flurry of panic, but, examining the illuminated face of his digital watch, is relieved to discover that it is only 5:15. He gets out of bed, scratching himself and shivering slightly (the Swallows, with typical British parsimony, switch off the central heating at night), pulls on a bathrobe and pads softly across the landing to the bathroom. He tugs at the lightcord just inside the door and flinches as blinding fluorescent light pings and ricochets off white and yellow tiles. He micturates, washes his hands, and puts out his tongue at the mirror above the handbasin. It resembles, this tongue, the dried-out bed of a badly polluted river. Too much alcohol and too many cigars last night. And every night.

This is a low point in the day of the globe-trotting academic, when he must wrench himself from sleep, and rise alone in the dark to catch his early plane; staring at his coated tongue in the mirror, rubbing red-rimmed eyes, fingering the stubble on his jowls, he wonders momentarily why he is doing it, whether the game is worth the candle. To shake off these depressing thoughts, Morris Zapp decides to take a quick shower, and too bad if the whining and shuddering of the water pipes wakes his hosts. He whines and shudders himself in some degree, since the water is barely tepid, but the effect of the shower is invigorating. His world-wide traveller's razor, designed to operate on all known electric currents, and if need be on its own batteries, hums, and Morris Zapp's brain begins to hum too. He glances at his watch again: 5:30. The taxi has been ordered for six, time enough for him to fix himself a cup of coffee in the kitchen downstairs. He will breakfast at Heathrow while he waits for his connection to Milan.

. . .

Three thousand miles to the west, at Helicon, New Hampshire, a writers' colony hidden deep in a pine forest, Morris Zapp's ex-wife, Désirée, tosses restlessly in bed. It is 12:30, and she has been awake since retiring an hour earlier. This is, she knows, because she is anxious about the previous day's work. A thousand words she managed to write in one of the little cabins in the woods to which, each morning, the resident writers repair with their lunch pails and thermos flasks, to lock themselves away with their respective muses; and she came back to the main house in the late afternoon exhilarated by this exceptional achievement. But as she chatted with the other writers and artists in the course of the evening, over dinner, in front of the TV, across the ping-pong table, tiny doubts began to assail her about those thousand words. Were they the right, the only possible words? She resisted the urge to rush upstairs to her room to read them through again. The routine at Helicon is strict, almost monastic: the days are for silent, solitary wrestling with the creative act; the evenings for sociability, conversation, relaxation. Désirée promised herself she would not look at her manuscript before she went to bed, but let it lie till morning, let the first minutes of the next day be reserved for the purpose—the longer she left it the more likely she was to forget what she had written, the more likely therefore that she would be able to read *herself* with something like an objective eye, to feel, without anticipating it, the shock of recognition she hoped to evoke in her readers.

She went to bed at 11:30, with her eyes consciously averted from the orange folder, lying on top of the pine chest, which contained the precious thousand words. But it seemed to glow in the dark—even now, with her eyes closed, she can feel its presence, like a pulsing source of radioactivity. It is part of a book that Désirée has been trying to write for the past four years, a book combining fiction and nonfiction—fantasy, criticism, confession and speculation; a book entitled, simply, *Men*. Each section has at its head a well-known proverb or aphorism about women in which the key-word has been replaced by "man" or "men." She has already written, "Frailty Thy Name Is Man," "No

Fury Like A Man Scorned" and "Wicked Men Bother One. Good Men Bore One. That Is The Only Difference Between Them." Presently she is working on the inversion of Freud's celebrated cry of bafflement: "What Does A Man Want?" The answer, according to Désirée is, "Everything—and then some."

Désirée turns on to her stomach and kicks impatiently at the skirt of her nightdress, which has gotten entangled round her legs with all her twisting and turning. She wonders whether to try and relax with the help of her vibrator, but it is an instrument she uses, as a nun her discipline, more out of principle than real enthusiasm, and besides, the battery is nearly flat, it might run out of juice before she reached her climax, just like a man—hey, that's quite good! She switches on the lamp on the night-table and scrawls in the little notebook she keeps always within reach: "*Vibrator with flat battery just like a man.*" Out of the corner of her eye she can see the orange folder burning into the varnished wood of the chest. She turns out the light, but now she is wide awake, it is hopeless, there is nothing to be done but to take a sleeping pill, though it will make her sluggish for the first couple of hours in the morning. She turns on the night-table lamp again. Now where are the pills? Oh yes, on the chest, next to the manuscript. Perhaps if she allows herself one tiny peep, just one sentence to go to sleep on . . .

Standing at the chest in her bare feet, with a sleeping tablet in one hand, arrested halfway to her mouth, Désirée opens the folder and begins to read. Before she knows it, she has come to the end of the three typed pages, swallowed them in three greedy gulps. She can hardly believe that the words which it cost her so many hours and so much effort to find and weld together could be consumed so quickly; or that they could seem so vague, so tentative, so uncertain of themselves. It will all have to be rewritten tomorrow. She swallows a pill, then a second, wanting only oblivion now. Waiting for the pills to do their work, she stands at the window and looks out at the tree-covered hills which surround the writers' colony, a monotonous, monochrome landscape in the cold light of the moon. Trees as far as the eye can see. Enough trees to make a million and a half paperback copies of *Men*. Two million. "Grow, trees, grow!" Désirée whispers. She refuses to admit the possibility of defeat. She returns to the bed and lies stiffly on her back, her eyes closed, her arms at her side, waiting for sleep.

. . .

Morris Zapp returns to the guest bedroom, dresses himself comfortably for travelling—corduroy pants, white cotton polo-neck, sports jacket—closes and locks the suitcase he had packed the night before, checks the closet and drawers for any stray belongings, pats various pockets to confirm the presence of his life-support system: billfold, passport, tickets, pens, spectacles, cigars. He tiptoes, as far as it is possible for a man carrying a heavy suitcase to tiptoe, across the landing, and carefully descends the stairs, each tread of which creaks under his weight. He puts the case down beside the front door and glances at his watch again. 5:45.

. . .

Far out above the cold North Atlantic ocean, aboard TWA Flight 072 from Chicago to London, time suddenly jumps from 2:45 to 3:45, as the Lockheed Tristar slips through the invisible interface between two time-zones. Few of the three hundred and twenty-three souls aboard are aware of the change. Most of them still have their watches adjusted to Chicago local time, where it is 11:45 p.m. on the previous day, and anyway most of them are asleep or trying to sleep. Aperitifs and dinner have been served, the movie has been shown, duty-free liquor and cigarettes dispensed to those desirous of purchasing them. The cabin crew, weary from the performance of these tasks, are clustered round the galleys, quietly gossiping as they check their stocks and takings. The refrigerated cabinets, the microwave ovens and electric urns, which were full when the aircraft took off from O'Hare airport, are now empty. Most of the food and drink they contained is now in the passengers' bellies, and before they land at Heathrow much of it will be in the septic tanks in the aircraft's belly.

The main lights in the passenger section, doused for the showing of the film, have not been switched on again. The passengers, replete, and in many cases sozzled, sleep uneasily. They slump and twist in their seats, trying vainly to arrange their bodies in a horizontal position, their heads loll on their shoulders as if they have been garrotted, their mouths gape in foolish smiles or ugly sneers. A few passengers, unable to sleep, are listening to recorded music on stereophonic headphones, or even reading, in the narrow beams of the tiny spotlights artfully angled in the cabin ceiling for that purpose; reading books about sex and adventure by Jacqueline Susann and Harold Robbins and Jack Higgins, thick paperbacks with gaudy covers bought from the bookstalls at O'Hare. Only one reader has a hardback book on her lap, and actually seems to be making notes as she reads. She sits erect, alert, in a window seat in row 16 in the Ambassador class. Her face is in shadow, but looks handsome, aristocratic, in profile, like a face on an old medallion, with a high, noble brow, a haughty Roman nose, and a determined mouth and chin. In the pool of light shed onto her lap, an exquisitely manicured hand guides a slender gold-plated propelling pencil across the lines of print, occasionally pausing to underline a sentence or make a marginal note. The long, spear-shaped fingernails on the hand are lacquered with terracotta varnish. The hand itself, long and white and slender, looks almost weighed down with three antique rings in which are set ruby, sapphire and emerald stones. At the wrist there is a chunky gold bracelet and the hint of a cream silk shirt-cuff nestling inside the sleeve of a brown velvet jacket. The reader's legs are clothed in generously cut knickerbockers of the same soft material, terminating just below the knee. Her calves are sheathed in cream-coloured textured hose and her feet in kidskin slippers which have replaced, for the duration of the flight, a pair of high-heeled fashion boots made of cream leather, engraved, under the instep, with the name of an exclusive Milanese maker of custom footwear. The lacquered nails flash in the beam of the reading lamp as a page is crisply turned, flattened and smoothed, and the slender gold pencil continues its steady traversing of the page. The heading at the top of the page is "Ideology and Ideological State Apparatuses" and the title on the spine is *Lenin and Philosophy and Other Essays*, an English translation of a book by the French political philosopher, Louis Althusser. The marginal notes are in Italian. Fulvia Morgana, Professor of Cultural Studies at the University of Padua, is at work. She cannot sleep in airplanes, and does not believe in wasting time.

· · ·

In the same airplane, some forty metres to the rear of Fulvia Morgana, Howard Ringbaum is trying to persuade his wife Thelma to have sexual intercourse with him, there and then, in the back row of the economy section. The circumstances are ideal, he points out in an urgent whisper: the lights are dim, everybody within sight is asleep, and there is an empty seat on either side of them. By pushing back the arm-rests dividing these four places they could create enough room to stretch out horizontally and screw.

"Ssh, someone will hear you," says Thelma, who does not realize that her spouse is perfectly serious.

Howard presses the call-button for cabin service, and when a stewardess appears, requests two blankets and two pillows. Nobody, he assures Thelma, will know what they are doing under the blankets.

"All I'm going to do under mine is sleep," Thelma says. "As soon as I've finished this chapter." She is reading a novel entitled *Could Try Harder*, by a

British author, Ronald Frobisher. She yawns and turns a page. The book is rather dull. She bought it years ago on their last visit to England, took it home to Canada unopened, packed it again when they moved back to the States; then, looking yesterday for something to read on the plane, plucked it down from a high shelf and blew the dust off it, thinking this would be a good way to re-attune herself to English speech and manners. But the novel is set in the Industrial Midlands, and the dialogue is thick with a dialect that they are unlikely to encounter in the vicinity of Bloomsbury. Howard has a grant from the National Endowment for the Humanities, to work at the British Museum for six months. They have arranged to rent a small apartment over a shop just off Russell Square. Thelma is going to enrol in a lot of those wonderfully cheap adult education classes they have in England on everything from foreign languages to flower arranging, and really *do* all the museums and galleries in the capital.

The stewardess brings blankets and pillows in polythene bags. Howard spreads the blankets over their knees and puts his hand up Thelma's skirt. She pushes it away.

"Howard! *Stop* it! What's gotten into you anyway?" Though flustered, she is not altogether displeased by this unwonted display of ardour.

What has gotten into Howard Ringbaum is, in fact, the Mile High club, an exclusive confraternity of men who have achieved sexual congress while airborne. Howard read about this club in a magazine, while waiting his turn in a barbershop about a year ago, and ever since has been consumed with an ambition to belong. A colleague at Southern Illinois, where Howard now teaches English pastoral poetry, to whom Howard confessed this unfulfilled ambition one night, revealed himself to be a member of the club, and offered to put Howard's name forward if he fulfilled the single condition of membership. Howard asked if wives counted. The colleague said that it wasn't customary, but he thought the membership committee might stretch a point. Howard asked what proof was required, and the colleague said a semen-stained paper napkin bearing the logo of a recognized commercial airline and countersigned by the partner in congress. It is a measure of Howard Ringbaum's humourless determination to succeed in every form of human competition that he succumbed to this crude hoax without a moment's hesitation. The same characteristic trait, displayed in a party game called Humiliation devised by Philip Swallow many years before, cost Howard Ringbaum dear—cost him his job, in fact, led to his exile to Canada, from which he has only recently been able to return by dint of writing a long succession of boring articles on English pastoral poetry amid the windswept prairies of Alberta—but he has not learned from the experience. "What about the toilet?" he whispers. "We could do it in the toilet."

"Are you crazy?" Thelma hisses. "There's hardly room to pee in there, let alone . . . For heaven's sake, honey, control yourself. Wait till we get to our little apartment in London." She smiles at him indulgently.

"Take off your panties and sit on my prick," says Howard Ringbaum unsmilingly.

Thelma hits Howard in the crotch with her book and he doubles up in pain. "Howard?" she says anxiously. "Are you all right, honey? I didn't mean to hurt you."

. . .

Morris Zapp goes into the Swallows' kitchen, boils a kettle, and fixes himself a cup of strong, black, instant coffee. Outside the sky is growing lighter, and a few birds are chirping hesitantly in the trees. It is 6 a.m. by the kitchen clock. Morris drains his cup and stations himself in the front hall to forestall the cab-driver's ring on the doorbell, which might waken the household.

But someone is already awake. There is a creak on the stairs, and Philip comes into view in the order of: leather slippers, bare bony ankles, striped pyjama trousers, mud-coloured dressing-gown, and silver beard.

"Just off, then?" he says, stifling a yawn.

"I hope I didn't waken you," says Morris.

"Oh, no. Anyway, can't let you go off without a word of goodbye."

An awkward silence ensues. Both men are perhaps a little embarrassed by the memory of confidences exchanged the night before under the influence of whisky.

"You might let me know what you think about my book, some time," says Philip.

"Wilco. I have it with me to read on the plane. By the way, I have a new book coming out soon myself."

"Another one?"

"It's called *Beyond Criticism*. Neat huh? I'll send you a copy."

Both men jump at the shrill noise of the doorbell.

"Ah, there's your taxi!" says Philip. "Plenty of time, it only takes half an hour to get to the airport at this time of day. Well, goodbye then, old man. Thanks for coming."

"Thanks for everything, Philip," says Morris, grasping the other's hand. "See you in the new Jerusalem."

"Pardon?"

"The conference. The Jerusalem Hilton is in the new part of the city."

"Oh, I'm with you. Well, we'll see. I'll think about it."

The cab driver picks up Morris's suitcase and carries it to the car, a courtesy that never ceases to amaze Morris Zapp, coming as he does from a country where cab drivers are locked into their driving seats and snarl at their customers through bars, like caged animals. As the taxi turns the corner, Morris looks back to see Philip waving from the front porch, clutching the flaps of his dressing-gown together with his other hand. Above his head a curtain is drawn back from a bedroom window and a face—Hilary's?— hovers palely behind the glass.

. . .

In Chicago it is midnight; yesterday hesitates for a second before turning into today. A cold wind blows off the lake, sends litter bowling across the pavement like tumbleweed, chills the bums and whores and drug addicts who huddle for shelter beneath the arches of the elevated railway. Inside the city's newest and most luxurious hotel, however, it is almost tropically warm. The distinctive feature of this building is that everything you would expect to find outside it is inside, and vice versa, except for the weather. The rooms are stacked around a central enclosed space, and their balconies project inwards, into a warm, air-conditioned atmosphere, overlooking a fountain and a lily pond filled with multi-coloured fish. There are palm-trees growing in here, and flowering vines that climb up the walls and cling to the balconies. Outside, transparent elevators like tiny glass bubbles creep up and down the sheer curtain walling of the building, giving the occupants vertigo. It is the architecture of inside-out.

In a penthouse suite from whose exterior windows the bums and whores and drug addicts are quite invisible, and even the biggest automobiles on the Loop look like crawling bugs, a man lies, naked, on his back, at the centre of a large circular bed. His arms and legs are stretched out in the form of an X, so that he resembles a famous drawing by Leonardo, except that his body is thin and scraggy, an old man's body, tanned but blotchy, the chest hair grizzled, the legs bony and slightly bowed, the feet calloused and horny. The man's head, however, is still handsome: long and narrow, with a hooked nose and a mane of white hair. The eyes, if they were open, would be seen to be dark brown, almost black. On the bedside table is a pile of magazines, academic quarterlies, some of which have fallen, or been thrown, to the floor. They have titles like *Diacritics, Critical Inquiry, New Literary History, Poetics and Theory of Literature, Metacriticism*. They are packed with articles set in close lines of small print, with many footnotes in even smaller print, and long lists of references. They contain no pictures. But who needs pictures when he has a living breathing centrefold all his own?

Kneeling on the bed beside the man, in the space between his left arm and his left leg, is a shapely young Oriental woman, with long, straight, shining black hair falling down over her golden-hued body. Her only garment is a tiny *cache-sexe* of black silk. She is massaging the man's scrawny limbs and torso with a lightly perfumed mineral oil, paying particular attention to his long, thin, circumcised penis. It does not respond to this treatment, flopping about in the young woman's nimble fingers like an uncooked chippolata.

This is Arthur Kingfisher, doyen of the international community of literary theorists, Emeritus Professor of Columbia and Zürich Universities, the only man in academic history to have occupied two chairs simultaneously in different continents (commuting by jet twice a week to spend Mondays to Wednesdays in Switzerland and Thursdays to Sundays in New York), now retired but still active in the world of scholarship, as attender of conferences, advisory editor to academic journals, consultant to university presses. A man whose life is a concise history of modern criticism: born (as Arthur Klingelfischer) into the intellectual ferment of Vienna at the turn of the century, he studied with Shklovsky in Moscow in the Revolutionary period, and with I. A. Richards in Cambridge in the late twenties, collaborated with Jakobson in Prague in the thirties, and emigrated to the United States in 1939 to become a leading figure in the New Criticism in the forties and fifties, then had his early work translated from the German by the Parisian critics of the sixties, and was hailed as a pioneer of structuralism. A man who has received more honorary degrees than he can remember, and who has at home, at his house on Long Island, a whole room full of the (largely unread) books and offprints sent to him by disciples and admirers in the world of scholarship. And this is Song-Mi Lee, who came ten years ago from Korea on a Ford Foundation fellowship to sit at Arthur Kingfisher's feet as a research student, and stayed to become his secretary, companion, amenuensis, masseuse and bedfellow, her life wholly dedicated to protecting the great man against the importunities of the academic world and soothing his despair at no longer being able to achieve an erection or an original thought. Most men of his age would have resigned themselves to at least the first of these impotencies, but Arthur Kingfisher had always led a very active sex life and regarded it as vitally connected, in some deep and mysterious way, with his intellectual creativity.

The telephone beside the bed emits a discreet electronic cheep. Song-Mi Lee wipes her oily fingers on a tissue and stretches across the prone body of Arthur Kingfisher, her rosy nipples just grazing his grizzled chest, to pick up the receiver. She squats back on her heels, listens, and says into the instrument, "One moment please, I will see if he is available." Then, holding her hand over the mouthpiece, she says to Arthur Kingfisher: "A call from Berlin—will you take it?"

"Why not? It's not as though it's interrupting anything," says Arthur Kingfisher gloomily. "Who do I know in Berlin?"

. . .

The taxi jolts and rumbles through the outer suburbs of Rummidge, throwing Morris Zapp from side to side on the back seat, as the driver negotiates the many twists and turns in the route to the airport. An endless ribbon of nearly identical three-bedroomed semi-detached houses unwinds beside the moving cab. The curtains are still drawn across the windows of most of these houses. Behind them people dream and doze, fart and snore, as dawn creeps over the roofs and chimneys and television aerials. For most of these people, today will be much like yesterday or tomorrow: the same office, the same factory, the same shopping precinct. Their lives are closed and circular, they tread a wheel of habit, their horizons are near and unchanging. To Morris Zapp such lives are unimaginable, he does not even try to imagine them; but their stasis gives zest to his mobility—it creates, as his cab speeds through the maze of streets and crescents and dual carriageways and roundabouts, a kind of psychic friction that warms him in some deep core of himself, makes him feel envied and enviable, a man for whom the curvature of the earth beckons invitingly to ever new experiences just over the horizon.

. . .

Back in the master bedroom of the Victorian villa in St. John's Road, Philip and Hilary Swallow are copulating as quietly, and almost as furtively, as if they were stretched out on the rear seats of a jumbo jet.

Returning to bed after seeing off Morris Zapp, Philip, slightly chilled from standing at the front door in his dressing gown and pyjamas, found the warmth of Hilary's ample body irresistible. He snuggled up to it spoonwise, curving himself around the soft cushion of her buttocks, passing his arm round her waist and cupping one heavy breast in his hand. Unable to sleep, he became sexually excited, lifted Hilary's nightdress and began to caress her belly and crotch. She seemed moist and compliant, though he was not sure if she was fully awake. He entered her slowly, from behind, holding his breath like a thief, in case she should suddenly come to her senses and push him away (it had happened before).

Hilary is, in fact, fully awake, though her eyes are closed. Philip's eyes are also shut. He is thinking of Joy, a purple-lit bedroom on a warm Italian night. She is thinking of Morris Zapp, in this same bed, in this same room, curtains drawn against the afternoon sun, ten years ago. The bed creaks rhythmically; the headboard bangs once, twice, against the wall; there is a grunt, a sigh, then silence. Philip falls asleep. Hilary opens her eyes. Neither has seen the other's face. No word has passed between them.

. . .

Meanwhile the telephone conversation between Berlin and Chicago is coming to its conclusion. A voice whose English is impeccable, and only slightly tinged with a German accent, is speaking.

"So, Arthur, we cannot tempt you to speak at our conference in Heidelberg? I am most disappointed, your thoughts on *Rezeptionsästhetik* would have been deeply appreciated, I am sure."

"I'm sorry Siegfried, I just have nothing to say."

"You are excessively modest, as usual, Arthur."

"Believe me, it's not false modesty. I wish it was."

"But I quite understand. You have many demands upon your time . . . By the way, what do you think of this new UNESCO chair of literary criticism?"

After a prolonged pause, Arthur Kingfisher says: "News travels fast. It's not even official yet."

"But it is true?"

Choosing his words with evident care, Arthur Kingfisher says, "I have reason to think so."

"I understand you will be one of the chief assessors for the chair, Arthur, is that so?"

"Is this what you really called me about, Siegfried?"

Hearty, mirthless laughter from Berlin. "How could you imagine such a thing, my dear fellow? I assure you that our desire for your presence at Heidelberg is perfectly sincere."

"I thought you had the chair at Baden-Baden?"

"I do, but we are collaborating with Heidelberg for the conference."

"And what are you doing in Berlin?"

"The same as you are doing in Chicago, I presume. Attending another conference—what else? 'Postmodernism and the Ontological Quest.' Some interesting papers. But our Heidelberg conference will be better organized . . . Arthur, since you raise the question of the UNESCO chair—"

"I didn't raise it, Siegfried. You did."

"It would be hypocritical of me to pretend that I would not be interested."

"I'm not surprised, Siegfried."

"We have always been good friends, Arthur, have we not? Ever since I reviewed the fourth volume of your *Collected Papers* in the *New York Review of Books*."

"Yes, Siegfried, it was a nice review. And nice talking to you."

· · ·

The hand that replaces the telephone receiver in its cradle in a sleekly functional hotel room on the Kurfürstendamm is sheathed in a black kid glove, in spite of the fact that its owner is sitting up in bed, wearing silk pyjamas and eating a Continental breakfast from a tray. Siegfried von Turpitz has never been known to remove this glove in the presence of another person. No one knows what hideous injury or deformity it conceals, though there have been many speculations: a repulsive birthmark, a suppurating wound, some *unheimlich* mutation such as talons instead of fingers, or an artificial hand made of stainless steel and plastic—the original, it is alleged by those who favour this theory, having been crushed and mangled in the machinery of the Panzer tank which Siegfried von Turpitz commanded in the later stages of World War II. He allows the black hand to rest for a moment on the telephone receiver, as if to seal the instrument against any leakage of information left in the cable that connected him, a few moments before, to Chicago, while with his ungloved hand he meditatively crumbles a croissant. Then he removes the receiver and with a black leathern index finger dials the operator. Consulting a black leather-bound notebook, he places a long-distance call to Paris. His face is pale and expressionless beneath a skullcap of flat blond hair.

· · ·

Morris Zapp's taxi throbs impatiently at red traffic-lights on a broad shopping street, deserted at this hour except for a milk float and a newspaper delivery van. A large billboard advertising British Airways Poundstretcher fares suggests that the airport is not far away. Another, smaller advertisement urging the passer-by to "*Have a Fling with Faggots Tonight*" is not, Morris knows from his previous sojourn in the region, a manifesto issued by Rummidge Gay Liberation, but an allusion to some local delicacy based on offal. With any luck he himself will be tucking in, tonight, to a steaming dish of tender, fragrant *tagliatelli*, before passing on to, say, *costoletta alla milanese*, and perhaps a slice or two of *panettone* for dessert. Morris's mouth floods with saliva. The taxi lurches forward. A clock above a jeweller's shop says that the time is 6:30.

. . .

In Paris, as in Berlin, it is 7:30, because of the different arrangements on the Continent for daylight saving. In the high-ceilinged bedroom of an elegant apartment on the Boulevard Huysmans, the telephone rings beside the double bed. Without opening his eyes, hooded like a lizard's in the brown, leathery face, Michel Tardieu, Professor of Narratology at the Sorbonne, extends a bare arm from beneath his duvet to lift the telephone from its cradle. "*Oui?*" he murmurs, without opening his eyes.

"Jacques?" inquires a Germanic voice.

"*Non.* Michel."

"Michel *qui?*"

"Michel Tardieu."

There is a Germanic grunt of annoyance. "Please accept my profound apologies," says the caller in correct but heavily accented French. "I dialled the wrong number."

"But don't I know you?" says Michel Tardieu, yawning. "I seem to recognize your voice."

"Siegfried von Turpitz. We were on the same panel at Ann Arbor last autumn."

"Oh yes, I remember. 'Author-Reader Relations in Narrative.'"

"I was trying to call a friend called Textel. His name is next to yours in my little book, and both are Paris numbers, so I mixed them up. It was excessively stupid of me. I hope I did not disturb you too much."

"Not too much," says Michel, yawning again. "*Au revoir.*" He turns back to embrace the naked body beside him in the bed, curving himself spoonwise around the soft cushion of the buttocks, brushing with his fingers the suave, silky skin of belly and inner thigh, nuzzling the slender nape beneath the perfumed locks of golden hair. "*Chéri,*" he whispers soothingly, as the other stirs in his sleep.

. . .

In his oak-panelled bedroom at All Saints' College, Oxford, the Regius Professor of Belles-Lettres sleeps chastely alone. No other person, man or woman, has shared that high, old-fashioned single bed—or, indeed, any other bed—with Rudyard Parkinson. He is a bachelor, a celibate, a virgin. Not that you would guess that from the evidence of his innumerable books, articles and reviews, which are full of knowing and sometimes risqué references to the variations and vagaries of human sexual behaviour. But it is all sex in the head—or on the page. Rudyard Parkinson was never in love, nor wished to be, observing with amused disdain the disastrous effects of that condition on the work-rate of his peers and rivals. When he was thirty-five, already secure and successful in his academic career, he considered the desirability of marrying—coolly, in the abstract, weighing the conveniences and drawbacks of the married state—and decided against it. Occasionally he would respond to the beauty of a young undergraduate to the extent of laying a timid hand on the young man's shoulder, but no further.

From an early age, reading and writing have entirely occupied Rudyard Parkinson's waking life, including those parts allocated by normal people to love and sex. Indeed, it could be said that reading is his love and writing his sex. He is in love with literature, with the English poets in particular—Spenser, Milton, Wordsworth, and the rest. Reading their verse is pure, selfless pleasure, a privileged communion with great minds, a rapt enjoyment of truth and beauty. Writing, his own writing, is more like sex: an assertion of will, an exercise of power, a release of tension. If he doesn't write something at least once a day he becomes irritable and depressed—and it has to be for publication, for to Rudyard Parkinson unpublished writing is like masturbation or *coitus interruptus*, something shameful and unsatisfying.

The highest form of writing is of course a book of one's own, something that has to be prepared with tact, subtlety, and cunning, and sustained over many months, like an affair. But one cannot always be writing books, and even while thus engaged there are pauses and lulls when one is merely reading secondary sources, and the need for some release of pent-up ego on to the printed page, however trivial and ephemeral the occasion, becomes urgent. Hence Rudyard Parkinson never refuses an invitation to write a book review; and as he is a witty, elegant reviewer, he receives many such invitations. The literary editors of London's daily and weekly newspapers are constantly on the telephone to him, parcels of books arrive at the porter's lodge by every post, and he always has at least three assignments going at the same time—one in proof, one in draft and one at the note-taking stage. The book on which he is taking notes at this time lies, spreadeagled, open and face-down, on the bedside cabinet, next to his alarm clock, his spectacles and his dental plate. It is a work of literary theory by Morris Zapp, entitled *Beyond Criticism*, which Rudyard Parkinson is reviewing for the *Times Literary Supplement*. His denture seems to menace the volume with a fiendish grin, as though daring it to move while Rudyard Parkinson takes his rest.

The alarm rings. It is 6:45. Rudyard Parkinson stretches out a hand to silence the clock, blinks and yawns. He opens the door of his bedside cabinet and pulls out a heavy ceramic chamber pot emblazoned with the College arms. Sitting on the edge of the bed with his legs apart, he empties his bladder of the vestiges of last night's sherry, claret and port. There is a bathroom with toilet in his suite of rooms, but Rudyard Parkinson, a South African who came to Oxford at the age of twenty-one and perfected an impersonation of Englishness that is now indistinguishable from authentic specimens, believes in keeping up old traditions. He replaces the chamber pot in its cupboard, and closes the door. Later a college servant, handsomely tipped for the service, will empty it. Rudyard Parkinson gets back into bed, turns on the bedside lamp, puts on his spectacles, inserts his teeth, and begins to read Morris Zapp's book at the page where he abandoned it last night.

From time to time he underlines a phrase or makes a marginal note. A faint sneer plays over his lips, which are hedged by grey muttonchop whiskers. It is not going to be a favourable review. Rudyard Parkinson does not care for American scholars on the whole. His own work is sometimes treated by them with less respect than is its due. Or, as in the case of Morris Zapp, not treated at all, but totally ignored (he had of course checked the Index under P for his own name—always the first action to be taken with a new book). Besides, Rudyard Parkinson has written three favourable reviews in succession in the last ten days—for the *Sunday Times*, the *Listener*, and the *New York Review of Books*, and he is feeling a little bored with praise. A touch of venom would not come amiss this time, and what better target than a brash, braggart American Jew, pathetically anxious to demonstrate his familiarity with the latest pretentious critical jargon?

. . .

In Central Turkey it is 8:45. Dr. Akbil Borak, BA (Ankara) PhD (Hull), is having breakfast in his little house on a new estate just outside the capital. He sips black tea from a glass, for there is no coffee to be found in Turkey these days. He warms his hands on the glass because the air is cool inside the house, there being no oil for the central heating either. His plump, pretty wife, Oya, puts before him bread, goat cheese and rose-hip jam. He eats abstractedly, reading a book propped up on the dining-room table. It is *The Collected Works of William Hazlitt*, Vol. XIV. At the other side of the table his three-year-old son knocks over a glass of milk. Akbil Borak turns a page obliviously.

"I do not think you should read at breakfast," Oya complains, as she mops up the milk. "It is a bad example for Ahmed, and it is not nice for me. All day I am on my own here with no one to talk to. The least you can do is be sociable before you leave for work."

Akbil grunts, wipes his moustache, closes the book, and rises from the table. "It will not be for much longer. There are only seven more volumes, and Professor Swallow arrives next week."

The news, abruptly announced a few weeks earlier, of Philip Swallow's imminent arrival in Turkey to lecture on William Hazlitt has struck dismay into the English faculty at Ankara, since the only member of the teaching staff who knows anything about the Romantic essayists (the man, in fact, who had originally mooted, two years earlier, the idea of marking Hazlitt's bicentenary with a visiting lecturer from Britain, but, hearing no more about the proposal gradually forgot all about it) is absent on sabbatical leave in the United States; and nobody else in the Department, at the time of receiving the message, had knowingly read a single word of Hazlitt's writings. Akbil, who was delegated, because of the acknowledged excellence of his spoken English, to meet Philip Swallow at the airport and escort him around Ankara, felt obliged to make good this deficiency and defend the honour of the Department. He has, accordingly, withdrawn the *Complete Works* of William Hazlitt in twenty-one volumes from the University Library, and is working his way through them at the rate of one volume every two or three days, his own research on Elizabethan sonnet sequences being temporarily sacrificed to this end.

Volume XIV is *The Spirit of the Age*. Akbil pops it into his briefcase, buttons up his topcoat, kisses the still pouting Oya, pinches Ahmed's cheek, and leaves the house. It is the end unit of a row of new terraced houses, built of grey breeze-blocks. Each house has a small garden of identical size and shape, their boundaries neatly demarcated by low breeze-block walls. These gardens have a rather forlorn aspect. Nothing appears to grow inside the walls except the same coarse grass and spiky weeds that grow outside. They seem purely symbolic gardens, weak gestures towards some cosy suburban life-style glimpsed by an itinerant Turkish town-planner on a quick tour of Coventry or Cologne; or perhaps feeble attempts to ward off the psychic terror of the wilderness. For beyond the boundary walls at the bottom of each garden the central Anatolian plain abruptly begins. There is nothing for thousands of miles but barren, dusty, windswept steppes. Akbil shivers in a blast of air that comes straight out of central Asia, and climbs into his battered Citroën Deux Chevaux. He wonders, not for the first time, whether they did right to move out of the city, to this bleak and desolate spot, for the sake of a house of their own, a garden, and clean air for Ahmed to breathe. It had reminded him and Oya, when they first saw pictures of the estate in the brochure, of the little terraced house in which they had lived during his three years' doctoral research as a British Council scholar. But in Hull there had been a pub and a fish-and-chip shop on the corner, a little park two streets away with swings and a see-saw, cranes and ships' masts visible over the roofs, a general sense of nature well under the thumb of culture. This past winter—it had been a harsh one, made all the worse by the shortages of oil, food and electricity—he and Oya had huddled together round a small wood-burning stove and warmed themselves with the shared memories of Hull, murmuring the enchanted names of streets and shops, "George Street," "Hedden Road," "Marks and Spencer's," "British Home Stores." It never seemed odd to Akbil and Oya Borak that the city's main railway terminus was called Hull Paragon.

. . .

Inside the Rummidge Airport terminal, in contrast to the sleepy suburb beyond the perimeter fence, the day has already well and truly begun. Morris Zapp is not, after all, the only man in Rummidge who is on the move. Beefy businessmen in striped suits, striped shirts and striped ties, carrying sleek executive briefcases and ingenious overnight wardrobe bags, all zips, buttons, straps and pouches, are checking in for their flights to London, Glasgow, Belfast, and Brussels. A group of early vacationers, bound for a package tour in Majorca, and dressed in garish holiday gear, wait patiently for a delayed plane: fat, comfortable folk, who sit in the departure lounge with their legs apart and their hands on their knees, yawning and smoking and eating sweets. A small line of people standing by for seats on the flight to Heathrow looks anxiously at Morris Zapp as he marches up to the British Midland desk and dumps his suitcase on the scales. He checks it through to Milan, and is directed to Gate Five. He goes to the newstand and buys a copy of *The Times*. He joins a long line of people shuffling through the security checkpoint. His handbaggage is opened and searched. Practised fingers turn over the jumble of toiletries, medicines, cigars, spare socks, and a copy of *Hazlitt and the*

Amateur Reader by Philip Swallow. The lady making the search opens a cardboard box, and small, hard, cylindrical objects, wrapped in silver foil, roll into the palm of her hand. *"Bullets?"* her eyes seem to enquire. "Suppositories," Morris Zapp volunteers. Few privacies are vouchsafed to the modern traveller. Strangers rifling through your luggage can tell at a glance the state of your digestive system, what method of contraception you favour, whether you have a denture that requires a fixative, whether you suffer from haemorrhoids, corns, headaches, eye fatigue, flatulence, dry lips, allergic rhinitis and premenstrual tension. Morris Zapp travels with remedies for all these ailments except the last.

He passes through the electronic metal detector, first handing over his spectacle case, which he knows from experience will activate the device, collects his shoulderbag and proceeds to the waiting lounge by Gate 5. After a few minutes the flight to Heathrow is called, and Morris follows the ground hostess and the other passengers out on to the tarmac apron. He frowns at the sight of the plane they are to board. It is a long time since he has flown in a plane with *propellers*.

· · ·

In Tokyo, it is already late afternoon. Akira Sakazaki has come home from his day's work at the University, where he teaches English, just in time to miss the worst of the rush hour, and avoid the indignity of being manhandled into the carriages of the subway trains by burly officials specially employed for this purpose so that the automatic doors may close. A bachelor, whose family home is in a small resort far away in the mountains, he lives alone in a tall modern apartment block. He is able to afford this accommodation because, though well appointed, it is extremely restricted in space. In fact he cannot actually stand up in it, and on unlocking the door, and having taken off his shoes, is obliged to crawl, rather than step, inside.

The apartment, or living unit, is like a very luxurious padded cell. About four metres long, three metres wide and one and a half metres high, its walls, floor and ceiling are lined with a seamless carpet of soft, synthetic fibre. A low recessed shelf along one wall acts as a sofa by day, a bed by night. Shelves and cupboards are mounted above it. Recessed or fitted flush into the opposite wall are a stainless steel sink, refrigerator, microwave oven, electric kettle, colour television, hi-fi system and telephone. A low table sits on the floor before the window, a large, double-glazed porthole which looks out on to a blank, hazy sky; though if one goes up close and squints downwards one can see people and cars streaming along the street below, converging, meeting and dividing, like symbols on a video game. The window cannot be opened. The room is air-conditioned, temperature-controlled and soundproof. Four hundred identical cells are stacked and interlocked in this building, like a tower of eggboxes. It is a new development, an upmarket version of the "capsule" hotels situated near the main railway termini that have proved so popular with Japanese workers in recent years.

There is a small hatch in one wall that gives access to a tiny windowless bathroom, with a small chair-shaped tub just big enough to sit in, and a toilet that can be used only in a squatting position, which is customary for Japanese men in any case. In the basement of the building there is a traditional Japanese bathhouse with showers and big communal baths, but Akira Sakazaki rarely makes use of it. He is well satisfied with his accommodation, which provides all modern amenities in a compact and convenient form, and leaves him the maximum amount of time free for his work. How much time people waste in walking from one room to another—especially in the West! Space is time. Akira was particularly shocked by the waste of both in Californian homes he visited during his graduate studies in the United States: separate rooms not just for sleeping, eating and excreting, but also for cooking, studying, entertaining, watching television, playing games, washing clothes and practising hobbies—all spread out profligately over acres of land, so that it could take a whole minute to walk from say, one's bedroom to one's study.

Akira now takes off his suit and shirt, and stows them carefully away in the fitted cupboard above the sofa/bed. He crawls through the hatch into his tiny bathroom, soaps and rinses himself all over, then fills the armchair-shaped tub with very hot water. Silent fans extract the steam from the bathroom as he simmers gently, opening his pores to cleanse them of the city's pollution. He splashes himself with clean, lukewarm water, and crawls back into the main room. He dons a cotton *yukata* and sits cross-legged on the floor before the low table, on which there is a portable electric typewriter. To one side of the typewriter there is a neat stack of sheets of paper whose surface is divided into two hundred ruled squares, in each of which a Japanese character has been carefully inscribed by hand; on the other side of the typewriter is a neat pile of blank sheets of the same squared paper, and a hardcover edition of a novel, with a well-thumbed dustjacket: *Could Try Harder*, by Ronald Frobisher. Akira inserts a blue aerogramme, carbon paper and flimsy into the typewriter, and begins a letter in English.

Dear Mr. Frobisher,

I am now nearly halfway through my translating of "Could Try Harder." I am sorry to bother you so soon with further questions, but I would be very grateful if you would help me with the following points. Page references are to the second impression of 1970, as before.

Akira Sakazaki takes up the book to find the page reference to his first query, and pauses to scrutinize the photograph of the author on the back flap of the jacket. He often pauses thus, as if by contemplating the author's countenance he may be able to enter more sympathetically into the mind behind it, and intuitively solve the problems of tone and stylistic nuance which are giving him so much trouble. The photograph, however, dark and grainy, gives away few secrets. Ronald Frobisher is pictured against a door with frosted glass on which is engraved in florid lettering the word "PUBLIC." This itself is a puzzle to Akira. Is it a public lavatory, or a public library? The symbolism would be quite different in each case. The face of the author is round, fleshy, pock-marked, and peppered with tiny black specks, like grains of gunpowder. The hair is thin, dishevelled. Frobisher wears thick, horn-rimmed spectacles and a grubby raincoat. He glares somewhat truculently at the camera. The note under the photograph reads:

> Ronald Frobisher was born and brought up in the Black Country. He was educated at a local grammar school, and at All Saints' College, Oxford. After graduating, he returned to his old school as a teacher of English until 1957, when the publication of his first novel, *Any Road*, immediately established him as a leading figure in the new generation of "Angry Young Men." Since 1958 he has been a full-time writer, and now lives with his wife and two children in Greenwich, London. *Could Try Harder* is his fifth novel.

And still his most recent, though it was published nine years ago. Akira has often wondered why Ronald Frobisher published no new novel in the last decade, but it does not seem polite to enquire.

Akira finds the page he is looking for, and lays the book open on the table. He touchtypes:

p. 107, 3 down. "Bugger me, but I feel like some faggots tonight."

Does Ernie mean that he feels a sudden desire for homosexual intercourse?
If so, why does he mention this to his wife?

Morris Zapp should have been in Heathrow by now, but there has been a delay in leaving Rummidge. The plane is still parked on the apron outside the terminal building.

"What do you think they're doing—winding up the elastic?" he quips to the man sitting in the aisle seat next to him.

The man stiffens and pales. "Is there something wrong?" he says in the accents of the American Deep South.

"It could be visibility. Looks kinda foggy out there in the middle of the airfield. You from the South?"

"Fog?" says the man in alarm, peering across Morris out of the window. He is wearing faintly tinted rimless glasses.

At that moment the four engines of the plane cough into life, one by one, just like an old war movie, and the propellers carve circles in the damp morning air. The plane taxis to the end of the runway, and goes on taxiing, wheels bumping over the cracks in the concrete, with no perceptible increase in speed. Morris cannot see much beyond the plane's wingtip. The man in the tinted spectacles has his eyes closed, and grips the arms of his seat with white knuckles. Morris has never seen anyone look so frightened. The plane turns again and carries on taxiing.

"Have we taken off yet?" says the man, after some minutes have passed in this fashion.

"No, I think the pilot is lost in the fog," says Morris.

The man hurriedly undoes his safety belt, muttering, "I'm getting out of this crazy plane." He shouts towards the pilot's cabin, "Stop the plane, I'm getting off."

A hostess hurries down the aisle towards him. "You can't do that, sir, please sit down and fasten your safety belt."

Protesting, the man is persuaded back into his seat. "I have one of these extended travel tickets," he remarks to Morris, "so I thought I would go from London to Stratford-on-Avon by air. Never again."

At that moment the captain comes on the intercom to explain that he has been taxiing up and down the runway to try and disperse the ground mist with his propellers.

"I don't believe it," says Morris.

The manoeuvre is, however, evidently successful. They are given permission to take off. The plane halts at the end of the runway, and the engine note rises to a higher pitch. The cabin shudders and rattles. The Southerner's teeth are chattering, whether from fear or vibration it is impossible to tell. Then the plane lurches forward, gathers speed and, surprisingly quickly, rises into the air. Soon they are through the cloud cover, and bright sunlight floods the cabin. The Southerner's spectacles are the photosensitive sort and turn into two opaque black discs, so it is difficult to tell whether his fear has abated. Morris wonders whether to strike up a conversation with the man, but there is so much noise from the engines that he shrinks from the effort, and there is something slightly spooky about the opaque glasses that does not inspire friendly overtures. Instead, Morris takes out his newspaper and pricks his ears at the welcome sound of the coffee trolley coming up the aisle.

Morris Zapp basks in the sun, a cup of coffee steaming on the tray before him, and reads in his copy of *The Times* of clashes between police and protesters against the National Front in Southall; of earthquakes in Yugoslavia, fighting in Lebanon, political murders in Turkey, meat shortages in Poland, car bombs in Belfast, and of many other tragedies, afflictions, outrages, at various points of the globe. But up here, in the sun, above the clouds, all is calm, if not quiet. The plane is not as smooth and fast as a jet, but there is more legroom than usual, and the coffee is good and hot. As the newspaper informs him, there are many worse places to be.

. . .

"Bugger me," grunts Ronald Frobisher, stooping to pick up the morning's mail from the doormat. "If there isn't another letter from that Jap translator of mine."

It is eight thirty-five a.m. in Greenwich—Greenwich Mean Time, indeed, the zero point from which all the world's time zones are calculated. The blue aerogramme that Ronald Frobisher turns over in his fingers is not, of course, the one that Akira Sakazaki typed a few minutes ago, but one he mailed last week. Another is at this moment in the cargo section of a jumbo jet somewhere over the Persian Gulf, *en route* to London, and yet another is hurtling through the computerized machinery of the Tokyo Central Post Office, racing along the conveyor belts, veering left, veering right, submerging and resurfacing like a kayak shooting rapids.

"That must be at least the fifth or sixth one in the last month," Ronald Frobisher grumbles, as he returns to the breakfast-room.

"Eh?" says his wife, Irma, without looking up from the *Guardian*.

"That bloke who's translating *Could Try Harder* into Japanese. I must have answered about two hundred questions already."

"I don't know why you bother," says Irma.

"Because it's interesting, to tell you the truth," says Ronald Frobisher, sitting down at the table and slitting open the aerogramme with a knife.

"An excuse to postpone work, you mean," says Irma. "Don't forget that script for Granada is due next Friday." She has not taken her eyes off the *Guardian*'s Woman's page. Conversations with Ronald are predictable enough for her to read and talk to him simultaneously. She can even pour herself a cup of tea at the same time, and does so now.

"No, really, it's fascinating. Listen. *Page 86, 7 up. 'And a bit of spare on the back seat.' Is it a spare tyre that Enoch keeps on the back seat of his car?*"

Irma sniggers, not at his query from Akira Sakazaki, but at something on the *Guardian*'s Woman's page.

"I mean, you can see the problem," says Ronald. "It's a perfectly natural mistake. I mean, why *does* 'a bit of spare' mean sex?"

"I don't know," says Irma, turning a page. "You tell me. You're the writer."

"*Page 93, 2 down. 'Enoch, 'e went spare.' Does this mean Enoch went to get a spare part for his car?* You've got to feel sorry for the bloke. He's never been to England, which makes it all the more difficult."

"Why does he bother? I can't see the Japanese being interested in reading about sex life in the back streets of Dudley."

"Because I'm an important figure in postwar British fiction, that's why. You never did grasp that fact, did you? You never could believe that I could be considered *literature*. You just think I'm a hack that turns out TV scripts."

Irma, used to Ronald Frobisher's little tantrums, reads blithely on. Frobisher crunches angrily on toast and marmalade and opens another letter. "Listen to this," he says. "'*Dear Mr. Frobisher, We are holding a conference in Heidelberg in September on the subject of the Reception of the Literary Text, and we are anxious to have the participation of some distinguished contemporary writers such as yourself . . .*' You see what I mean? It could be quite interesting, actually. I've never been to Heidelberg. Some kraut called von Turpitz."

"Aren't you going to rather a lot of these conferences?"

"It's all experience. You could come as well, if you like."

"No thanks, I've had enough of traipsing around churches and museums while you chew the fat with the local sycophants. Why are all your fans foreigners, these days? Don't they know that the Angry Young Man thing is all over?"

"It's got nothing to do with the Angry Young Man thing!" says Ronald Frobisher, angrily. He opens another envelope. "D'you want to come to the Royal Academy of Literature do? It's on a boat this year. I'm supposed to be giving away one of the prizes."

"No, thanks." Irma turns another page of the *Guardian*. A jet drones overhead, on the flightpath to Heathrow.

· · ·

Fog at Heathrow, which caused TWA Flight 072 from Chicago to be diverted to Stanstead, has suddenly cleared, so the plane has turned back and is making its approach to Heathrow from the east. Three thousand feet above the heads of Ronald and Irma Frobisher, Fulvia Morgana snaps shut her copy of *Lenin and Philosophy* and puts it away, along with her kidskin slippers, in her capacious burnt-orange suede shoulder-bag by Fendi. She eases her feet into the cream-coloured Armani boots, and fastens them snugly round her calves, taking care not to snag her tights in the zips. She gazes haughtily down at the winding Thames, St. Paul's, the Tower of London, Tower Bridge. She picks out the dome of the British Museum, beneath which Marx forged the concepts that would enable man not only to interpret the world, but also to change it: dialectical materialism, the surplus theory of value, the dictatorship of the proletariat. But the pseudo-gothic fantasy of the Houses of Parliament, propping up the top-heavy bulk of Big Ben, reminds the airborne Marxist how slow the rate of change has been. The Mother of Parliaments, and therefore the Mother of Repression. All parliaments must be abolished.

"Ooh, look, Howard! Big Ben!" exclaims Thelma Ringbaum, nudging her husband in the back row of the economy class.

"I've seen it before," he says sulkily.

"We'll be landing in a minute. Don't forget the duty-free liquor."

Howard gropes under his seat for the plastic bag in which there are two fifths of scotch, purchased at O'Hare airport, which have travelled approximately eight thousand miles since they were distilled, and are now within a few hundred of their place of origin. A muffled thud announces that the undercarriage has been lowered. The Tristar begins its descent to Heathrow.

· · ·

Morris has already landed at Heathrow, and is gobbling ham and eggs and toast, sitting on a high stool at the counter of the Terminal One Restaurant, with Philip Swallow's *Hazlitt and the Amateur Reader* propped up against the sugar bowl. It is greed, not urgency, that makes him eat so fast, for he has two hours to wait before his flight to Milan is due to depart. Licking the butter from his fingers, he opens the book, which has, unsurprisingly, an epigraph from William Hazlitt:

> *I stand merely upon the defensive. I have no positive inferences to make, nor any novelties to bring forward, and I have only to defend a common sense feeling against the refinement of a false philosophy.*

Morris Zapp sighs, shakes his head, and butters another slice of toast.

. . .

In Cooktown, Queensland, Rodney Wainwright is chewing his dinner with more deliberation, partly because he has a loose molar and the chops are overdone, partly because he has no appetite. "Jesus Christ, it's hot," he mutters, dabbing at his forehead with his serviette. "Language, Rod," Bev murmurs reprovingly, glancing at their two children, Kevin aged fourteen, Cindy aged twelve, who are gnawing their bones zestfully out of greasy fingers. Rodney Wainwright's paper on the future of criticism has not gone well in the past three or four hours. He covered two sheets of foolscap, then tore them up. The argument remains blocked at, "The question is therefore, how can criticism . . ." Shadows are long on the rank lawn. The boom of the waves carries through the open casement. On the beach, no doubt, at this very moment Sandra Dix, her wet bikini exchanged for faded sawn-off jeans and clinging tee-shirt, is turning over freshly caught fish on a hot gridiron.

. . .

In Helicon, New Hampshire, Désirée Zapp sleeps, breathing heavily, and dreams of flying—swooping and soaring in her nightgown in a clear blue sky above the multitudinous pine trees.

. . .

Philip Swallow wakes for the second time this morning, and touches his genitals lightly, swiftly, a gesture of self-reassurance performed every morning since he was five years old and his mother told him that if he didn't stop playing with his willie it would drop off. He stretches out beneath the sheets. Where Hilary was, there is a cooling hollow in the mattress. He looks at the clock on the bedside table, rubs his eyes, stares, blasphemes and jumps out of bed. Hurrying downstairs, he passes his son, Matthew, on his way up. "'Ullo, our Dad," says Matthew, whose current humour it is to pretend to be a working-class youth from the North of England. "Shouldn't you be at school?" Philip coldly enquires. "Trooble at t'pit," says Matthew. "Industrial action by the Association of Schoolmasters." "Disgraceful," says Philip, over his shoulder, "University teachers would never strike." "Only because no one would notice," Matthew calls down the stairs.

. . .

Arthur Kingfisher sleeps, curled spoonwise around the shapely back and buttocks of Song-Mi Lee, who, before they retired, prepared for him a pipe of opium. So his dreams are psychedelic: deserts of purple sand with dunes that move like an oily sea, a forest of trees with little golden fingers instead of leaves that caress the wayfarer as he brushes against them, a vast pyramid with a tiny glass elevator that goes up one side, down the other, a chapel at the bottom of a lake, and on the altar, where the crucifix should be, a black hand, cut off at the wrist, its fingers splayed.

. . .

Siegfried von Turpitz now has black gloves on both of his hands. They grip the steering wheel of his black BMW 635CSi coupé, with 3453 cc Bosch L-jetronic fuel-injection engine and five speed Getrag all-synchromesh gearbox. He holds the car to a steady one hundred and eighty kilometres per hour in the fast lane of the autobahn between Berlin and Hanover, compelling slower vehicles to move over not by flashing his headlights (which is forbidden by law) but by moving up behind them swiftly, silently and very close; so that when a driver glances into a rear-view mirror which only moments ago was empty save for a small black dot on the horizon, he finds it, to his astonishment and terror, entirely filled by the dark mass of the BMW's bonnet and tinted windscreen, behind which, under a skullcap of flat, colourless hair, floats the pale impassive visage of Siegfried von Turpitz—and, as fast as the shock to his nerves permits, such a driver swerves aside to let the BMW pass.

. . .

In the rather old-fashioned kitchen of the high-ceilinged apartment on the Boulevard Huysmans, Michel Tardieu grinds coffee beans by hand (for he cannot bear the shriek of a Moulinex) and wonders idly why Siegfried von Turpitz should have wanted so urgently to speak to Jacques Textel that he tried to phone him at 7:30 in the morning. Michel Tardieu is himself acquainted with Textel, a Swiss anthropologist who once occupied the chair at Berne, but moved into international cultural administration and is now somebody quite important in UNESCO. It is time, Michel reflects, that he and Textel had lunch together.

As he finishes the grinding, he hears the front door of the apartment slam. Albert, ravishing in dark blue woollen blouson and the tight white Levis that Michel brought him back after his last visit to the States, comes in and dumps on the kitchen table, with a distinctly sulky air, a paper bag of croissants and rolls, and a copy of *Le Matin*. Albert resents this regular early morning errand, and complains about it frequently. He complains now. Michel urges him to look upon the chore in the light of modern narrative theory. "It is a quest, *chéri*, a story of departure and return: you venture out, and you come back, loaded with treasure. You are a hero." Albert's response is brief and obscene. Michel smiles good-humouredly, pouring boiling water into the coffee-filter. He intends to keep Albert to this matutinal duty, just to remind him who pays for the coffee and croissants, not to mention the clothes and shoes and coiffures and records and ice-skating lessons.

. . .

In Ankara, Akbil Borak has at last arrived at the precincts of the University, some ninety minutes after leaving home, thirty of which were spent queuing for petrol. Crowds are converging on the campus, walking indifferently in the roadway and on the pavements. Sounding his horn at frequent intervals, Akbil nudges his way through this stream of humanity that parts in front of the Deux Chevaux and meets again behind. He spots a vacant space on the pavement and mounts the kerb to park. The stream of pedestrians breaks and scatters momentarily, then swirls again around the stationary vehicle. Akbil locks his car and walks briskly across the central square. Two rival political groups of students, one of the left, the other of the right, are engaged in heated argument. Voices are raised, there is pushing and scuffling, someone falls to the ground and a girl screams. Suddenly two armed soldiers come running in their heavy boots, firearms levelled at the trouble-makers, shouting at them orders to disperse, which they do, some retreating backwards with their arms raised in surrender or supplication. It was not like this at Hull, Akbil reflects, as he takes cover behind a massive statue of black iron representing Kemal Ataturk inviting the youth of Turkey to partake of the benefits of learning.

. . .

Akira Sakazaki has typed his last question, for the time being, to Ronald Frobisher (a tricky one concerning the literal and metaphorical meanings of *crumpet* and its relation to *pikelet*), addressed, sealed and stamped the letter ready for mailing tomorrow morning, popped a TV dinner into the microwave oven, and, while waiting for it to cook, reads his airmail edition of the *Times Literary Supplement* and listens to Mendelssohn's Violin Concerto on his stereo headphones.

. . .

Big Ben strikes nine o'clock. Other clocks, in other parts of the world, strike ten, eleven, four, seven, two.

. . .

Morris Zapp belches, Rodney Wainwright sighs, Désirée Zapp snores. Fulvia Morgana yawns—a quick, surprisingly wide yawn, like a cat's—and resumes her customary repose. Arthur Kingfisher mutters German in his sleep. Siegfried von Turpitz, caught in a traffic jam on the autobahn, drums on the steering-wheel impatiently with the fingers of one hand. Howard Ringbaum chews gum to ease the pressure on his eardrums and Thelma Ringbaum struggles to squeeze her swollen feet back into her shoes. Michel Tardieu sits at his desk and resumes work on a complex equation representing in algebraic terms the plot of *War and Peace*. Rudyard Parkinson helps himself to kedgeree from the hotplate on the sideboard in the Fellows' breakfast-room and takes his place at the table in a silence broken only by the rustle of newspapers and the clinking and scraping of crockery and cutlery. Akbil Borak sips black tea from a glass in a small office which he shares with six others and grimly concentrates on *The Spirit of the Age*. Akira Sakazaki strips the foil from his TV dinner and tunes his radio to receive the BBC World Service. Ronald Frobisher looks up "*spare*" in the *Oxford English Dictionary*. Philip Swallow bustles into the kitchen of his house in St. John's Road, Rummidge, avoiding the eye of his wife. And Joy Simpson, who Philip thinks is dead, but who is alive, somewhere on this spinning globe, stands at an open window, and draws the air deep into her lungs, and shades her eyes against the sun, and smiles.

2

The job of check-in clerk at Heathrow, or any other airport, is not a glamorous or particularly satisfying one. The work is mechanical and repetitive:

inspect the ticket, check it against the passenger list on the computer terminal, tear out the ticket from its folder, check the baggage weight, tag the baggage, ask Smoking or Non-smoking, allocate a seat, issue a boarding pass. The only variation in this routine occurs when things go wrong—when flights are delayed or cancelled because of bad weather or strikes or technical hitches. Then the checker bears the full brunt of the customers' fury without being able to do anything to alleviate it. For the most part the job is a dull and monotonous one, processing people who are impatient to conclude their brief business with you, and whom you will probably never see again.

Cheryl Summerbee, a checker for British Airways in Terminal One at Heathrow, did not, however, complain of boredom. Though the passengers who passed through her hands took little notice of her, she took a lot of notice of them. She injected interest into her job by making quick assessments of their characters and treating them accordingly. Those who were rude or arrogant or otherwise unpleasant she put in uncomfortable or inconvenient seats, next to the toilets, or beside mothers with crying babies. Those who made a favourable impression she rewarded with the best seats, and whenever possible placed them next to some attractive member of the opposite sex. In Cheryl Summerbee's hands, seat allocation was a fine art, as delicate and complex an operation as arranging blind dates between clients of a lonely-hearts agency. It gave her a glow of satisfaction, a pleasant sense of doing good by stealth, to reflect on how many love affairs, and even marriages, she must have instigated between people who imagined they had met by pure chance.

Cheryl Summerbee was very much in favour of love. She firmly believed that it made the world go round, and did her bit to keep the globe spinning on its axis by her discreet management of the seating on British Airways Tridents. On the shelf under her counter she kept a Bills and Moon romance to read in those slack periods when there were no passengers to deal with. The one she was reading at the moment was called *Love Scene*. It was about a girl called Sandra who went to work as a nanny for a film director whose wife had died tragically in a car accident, leaving him with two young children to look after. Of course Sandra fell in love with the film director, though unfortunately he was in love with the actress taking the leading role in the film he was making—or was he just pretending to be in love with her to keep her sweet? Of course he was! Cheryl Summerbee had read enough Bills and Moon romances to know that—indeed she hardly needed to read any further to predict exactly how the story would end. With half her mind she despised these love-stories, but she devoured them with greedy haste, like cheap sweets. Her own life was, so far, devoid of romance—not for lack of propositions, but because she was a girl of old-fashioned moral principle, who intended to go to the altar a virgin. She had met several men who were very eager to relieve her of her virginity, but not to marry her first. So she was still waiting for Mr. Right to appear. She had no very clear image of what he would look like except that he would have a hard chest and firm thighs. All the heroes of Bills and Moon romances seemed to have hard chests and firm thighs.

The man wearing the tweed deerstalker didn't look as if he had these attributes—quite the contrary—but Cheryl took an instant liking to him. He was a little larger than life, every line in his figure slightly exaggerated, like a cartoon character; but he seemed to know it himself, and not to give a damn. It made you smile just to look at him, swaggering across the floor of the crowded terminal, with his absurd hat tilted forward, and a fat cigar clenched in his teeth, his double-breasted trench-coat flapping open on a loud check sports jacket. Cheryl smiled at him as he hesitated in front of the two desks servicing the Milan flight, and, catching this smile, he joined the line in front of her.

"Hi," he said when his turn came to be attended to. "Have we met before?"

"I don't think so, sir," said Cheryl. "I was just admiring your hat." She took his ticket and read the name on it: *Zapp M., Prof.*

Professor Zapp took off his deerstalker and held it at arm's length. "I bought it right here in Heathrow just a few days ago," he said. "I don't suppose I'll need it in Italy." Then his expression changed from complacency to annoyance. "Goddammit, I promised to give it to young McGarrigle before I left." He slapped the hat against his thigh, confirming this limb's lack of firmness. "Is there anywhere I can mail a parcel from here?"

"Our Post Office is closed for alterations, but there's another one in Terminal Two," said Cheryl. "I presume you would like a seat in the smoking section, Professor Zapp? Window or aisle?"

"I'm easy. The question is, how am I going to wrap this hat in a parcel?"

"Leave it with me. I'll post it for you."

"Really? That's very sweet of you, Cheryl."

"All part of the service, Professor Zapp," she smiled. He was one of those rare passengers who noticed the name badge pinned to her uniform, or, having noticed it, used it. "Just write your friend's name and address on this label, and I'll see to it when I go off duty." While he was occupied with this task, she scanned the seating plan in front of her, and ran through on the computer display the list of passengers who had already checked in. About a quarter of an hour ago she had dealt with an extremely elegant Italian lady professor, of about the right age—younger, but not too young—and who spoke very good English, apart from a little trouble with her aspirates. Ah yes, here she was: MORGANA F. PROF. She had been very particular, requesting a window-seat in the smoking section as far forward as possible on the left-hand side of the plane. Cheryl didn't mind this; she respected people who knew what they wanted, as long as they didn't kick up a fuss if it wasn't available. Professor Morgana had looked as if she was capable of kicking up a royal fuss, but the occasion had not arisen. Cheryl had been able to accommodate her exactly as requested, in row 10, window seat A. She now removed the sticker from seat 10B on the seat-plan in front of her, and affixed it to Professor Zapp's boarding pass. He gave her his hat, with the label and two pound notes tucked into one of the flaps.

"I don't think it will cost that much to send," she said, reading the label: "*Percy McGarrigle, Department of English, University College, LIMERICK, Ireland.*"

"Well, if there's any change, have a drink on me."

As he spoke they both heard a small, muffled explosion—the sound, distinctive and unmistakable, of a bottle of duty-free liquor hitting the stone composition floor of an airport concourse and shattering inside its plastic carrier bag; also a cry of "Shit!" and a dismayed, antiphonal "Oh, *Howard*!" A few yards away, a man and a woman were glaring accusingly at each other across a loaded baggage trolley from which the plastic carrier bag had evidently fallen. Professor Zapp, who had turned his head to locate the origin of the fatal sound, now turned back to face Cheryl, hunching his shoulders and turning up the collar of his raincoat.

"Don't do anything to attract that man's attention," he hissed.

"Why? Who is he?"

"His name is Howard Ringbaum and he is a well-known fink. Also, although he doesn't know it yet, I have rejected a paper he submitted for a conference I'm organizing."

"What is a fink?"

"A fink is a generally despicable person, like Howard Ringbaum."

"What's so awful about him? He doesn't look so bad."

"He's very self-centred. He's very mean. He's very calculating. Like, for instance, when Thelma Ringbaum says it's time they gave a party, Howard doesn't just send out invitations—he calls you up and asks you whether, if he were to give a party, you would come."

"That must be his wife with him now," said Cheryl.

"Thelma's all right, she's just fink-blind," said Professor Zapp. "No one can figure out how she can stand being married to Howard."

Over Professor Zapp's shoulder, Cheryl watched Howard Ringbaum gingerly pick up the plastic carrier bag by its handles. It bulged ominously at the bottom with the weight of spilled liquor. "Maybe I could filter it," Howard Ringbaum said to his wife. As he spoke, a piece of jagged glass pierced the plastic and a spout of neat scotch poured on to his suede shoe. "Shit!" he said again.

"Oh, *Howard!*"

"What are we doing in this place, anyway?" he snarled. "You said it was the way out."

"No, Howard, *you* said it was the way out, I just agreed."

"Have they gone yet?" Professor Zapp muttered.

"They're going," said Cheryl. Observing that the passengers waiting in line behind Professor Zapp were getting restive, she brought their business to a rapid conclusion. "Here's your boarding card, Professor Zapp. Be in the Departure Lounge half an hour before your flight time. Your baggage has been checked through to Milan. Have a pleasant journey."

· · ·

Thus it was that about one hour later Morris Zapp found himself sitting next to Fulvia Morgana in a British Airways Trident bound for Milan. It didn't take them long to discover that they were both academics. While the plane was still taxiing to the runway, Morris had Philip Swallow's book on Hazlitt out on his lap, and Fulvia Morgana her copy of Althusser's essays. Each glanced surreptitiously at the other's reading matter. It was as good as a masonic handshake. They met each other's eyes.

"Morris Zapp, Euphoric State." He extended his hand.

"Ah, yes, I 'ave 'eard you spick. Last December, in New York."

"At the MLA? You're not a philosopher, then?" He nodded at *Lenin and Philosophy*.

"No, cultural studies is my field. Fulvia Morgana, Padua. In Europe critics are much interested in Marxism. In America not so much."

"I guess in America we've always been more attracted by Freud than

Marx, Fulvia." Fulvia Morgana. Morris flicked rapidly through his mental card index. It was a name he vaguely remembered having seen on the title-pages of various prestigious journals of literary theory.

"And now Derrida," said Fulvia Morgana. "Everybody in Chicago—I 'ave just been to Chicago—was reading Derrida. America is crazy about deconstruction. Why is that?"

"Well, I'm a bit of a deconstructionist myself. It's kind of exciting—the last intellectual thrill left. Like sawing through the branch you're sitting on."

"Exactly! It is so narcissistic. So 'opeless."

"What was your conference about?"

"It was called, 'The Crisis of the Sign.'"

"Oh, yeah. I was invited but I couldn't make it. How was it?"

Fulvia Morgana shrugged her shoulders inside her brown velvet jacket. "As usual. Many boring papers. Some interesting parties."

"Who was there?"

"Oh, everyone you would expect. The Yale hermeneutic gang. The Johns Hopkins reader-response people. The local Chicago Aristotelians, naturally. And Arthur Kingfisher was there."

"Really? He must be pretty old now."

"He gave the—what do you call it—keynote address. On the first evening."

"Any good?"

"Terrible. Everybody was waiting to see what line he would take on deconstruction. Would 'e be for it or against it? Would 'e follow the premises of 'is own early structuralist work to its logical conclusion, or would 'e recoil into a defence of traditional humanist scholarship?" Fulvia Morgana spoke as though she were quoting from some report of the conference that she had already drafted.

"Let me try and guess," said Morris.

"You would be wasting your time," said Fulvia Morgana, unfastening her seat belt and smoothing her velvet knickerbockers over her knees. The plane had taken off in the course of this conversation, though Morris had hardly noticed. "'E said, on the one hand this, on the other hand that. 'E talked all around the subject. 'E waffled and wandered. 'E repeated things 'e said twenty, thirty years ago, and said better. It was embarrassing, I am telling you. In spite of all, they gave 'im a standing ovation."

"Well, he's a great man. *Was* a great man, anyway. A king among literary theorists. I think that to many people he kind of personifies the whole profession of academic literary studies."

"Then I must say that the profession is in a very un'ealthy condition," said Fulvia. "What are you reading—a book on 'Azlitt?"

"It's by a British friend of mine," said Morris. "He gave it to me just yesterday. It's not the sort of thing I usually go for." He felt anxious to dissociate himself from Philip's quaintly old-fashioned subject, and equally archaic approach to it.

Fulvia Morgana leaned over and peered at the name on the dust jacket. "Philip Swallow. I know 'im. 'E came to Padua to give a lecture some years before."

"Right! He was telling me about his trip to Italy last night. It was very eventful."

"'Ow was that?"

"Oh, his plane caught fire on the way home—had to turn back and make an emergency landing. But he was OK."

"'Is lecture was not very eventful, I must say. It was very boring."

"Yeah, well, that doesn't surprise me. He's a nice guy, Philip, but he doesn't exactly set your pulse racing with intellectual excitement."

"What is the book like?"

"Well, listen to this, it will give you the flavour." Morris read aloud a passage he had marked in Philip's book: "'*He is the most learned man who knows the most of what is farthest removed from common life and actual observation, that is of the least practical utility, and least liable to be brought to the test of experience, and that, having been handed down through the greatest number of intermediate stages, is the most full of uncertainty, difficulties and contradictions.*'"

"Very interesting," said Fulvia Morgana. "Is that Philip Swallow?"

"No, that's Hazlitt."

"You surprise me. It sounds very modern. 'Uncertainties, difficulties, contradictions.' 'Azlitt was obviously a man ahead of his time. That is a remarkable attack on bourgeois empiricism."

"I think it was meant to be ironic," said Morris gently. "It comes from an essay called 'The Ignorance of the Learned.'"

Fulvia Morgana pouted. "Ooh, the English and their ironies! You never know where you are with them."

The arrival of the drinks trolley at this point was a happy distraction.

Morris requested scotch on the rocks and Fulvia a Bloody Mary. Their conversation turned back to the topic of the Chicago conference.

"Everybody was talking about this UNESCO chair," said Fulvia. "Be'ind their 'ands, naturally."

"What chair is that?" Morris felt a sudden stab of anxiety, cutting through the warm glow imparted by the whisky and the agreeable happenstance of striking up acquaintance with this glamorous colleague. "I haven't heard anything about a UNESCO chair."

"Don't worry, it's not been advertised yet," said Fulvia, with a smile. Morris attempted a light dismissive laugh, but it sounded forced to his own ears. "It's supposed to be a chair of Literary Criticism, endowed by UNESCO. It's just a rumour, actually. I expect Arthur Kingfisher started it. They say 'e is the chief assessor."

"And what else," said Morris, with studied casualness, "do they say about this chair?"

He did not really have to wait for her reply to know that here, at last, was a prize worthy of his ambition. The UNESCO Chair of Literary Criticism! That *had* to carry the highest salary in the profession. Fulvia confirmed his intuition: $100,000 a year was being talked about. "Tax-free, of course, like all UNESCO salaries." Duties? Virtually non-existent. The chair was not to be connected with any particular institution, to avoid favouring any particular country. It was a purely conceptual chair (except for the stipend) to be occupied wherever the successful candidate wished to reside. He would have an office and secretarial staff at the Paris headquarters, but no obligation to use it. He would be encouraged to fly around the world at UNESCO's expense, attending conferences and meeting the international community of scholars, but entirely at his own discretion. He would have no students to teach, no papers to grade, no committees to chair. He would be paid simply to think— to think and, if the mood took him, to write. A roomful of secretaries at the Place Fontenoy would wait patiently beside their word-processors, ready to type, duplicate, collate, staple and distribute to every point of the compass his latest reflections on the ontology of the literary text, the therapeutic value of poetry, the nature of metaphor, or the relationship between synchronic and diachronic literary studies. Morris Zapp felt dizzy at the thought, not merely of the wealth and privilege the chair would confer on the man who occupied it, but also of the envy it would arouse in the breasts of those who did not.

"Will he have the job for life, or for a limited tenure?" Morris asked.

"I think she will be appointed for three years, on secondment from 'er own university."

"She?" Morris repeated, alarmed. Had Julia Kristeva or Christine Brooke-Rose already been lined up for the job? "Why do you say, 'she'?"

"Why do you say 'e'?"

Morris relaxed and raised his hands in a gesture of surrender. "*Touché!* Someone who was once married to a best-selling feminist novelist shouldn't walk into that kind of trap."

"'Oo is that?"

"She writes under the name of Désirée Byrd."

"Oh yes, *Giorni Difficili.* I 'ave read it." She looked at Morris with new interest. "It is autobiographical?"

"In part," said Morris. "This UNESCO chair—would you be tempted by it yourself?"

"No," said Fulvia emphatically.

Morris didn't believe her.

. . .

As Morris Zapp and Fulvia Morgana addressed themselves to a light lunch served 30,000 feet above south-eastern France, Persse McGarrigle arrived at Heathrow by the Underground railway. With Angelica gone, there had been nothing to detain him at Rummidge, so he had skipped the Business Meeting which constituted the last formal session of the Conference and taken the train to London. He was hoping to get a cheap standby seat on the afternoon flight to Shannon, since his conference grant had been based on rail/sea travel and would not cover the normal economy air fare. The Aer Lingus desk in Terminal Two took his name and asked him to come back at 2:30. While he was hesitating about what to do in the intervening couple of hours, the concourse was temporarily immobilized by a hundred or more Muslim pilgrims, with "Saracen Tours" on their luggage, who turned to face Mecca and prostrated themselves in prayer. Two cleaners leaning on their brooms within earshot of Persse viewed this spectacle with disgust.

"Bloody Pakis," said one. "If they *must* say their bloody prayers, why don't they go and do it in the bloody chapel?"

"No use to them, is it?" said his companion, who seemed a shade less bigotted. "Need a mosque, don't they?"

"Oh *yerse!*" said the first man sarcastically. "That's all we need in 'Eathrow, a bloody mosque."

"I'm not sayin'" we ought to 'ave one," said the second man patiently, "I'm just sayin'" that a Christian chapel wouldn't be no use to 'em. Them bein' in-fid-els." He seemed to derive great satisfaction from the pronunciation of this word.

"I s'pose you think we ought to 'ave a synagogue an' a 'Indoo temple too, an' a totem pole for Red Indians to dance around? What they doin' 'ere, anyway? They should be in Terminal Free if they're goin' to bloody Mecca."

"Did I hear you say there was a chapel in this airport?" Persse cut in.

"Well, I know there *is* one," said the more indignant of the two men. "Near Lorst Property, innit, Fred?"

"Nah, near the Control Tower," said Fred. "Go dahn the subway towards Terminal Free, then follow the signs to the Bus Station. Go right to the end of the bus station and then sorter bear left, then right. Yer can't miss it."

Persse did, however, miss it, more than once. He traipsed up and down stairs and escalators, along moving walkways, through tunnels, over bridges. Like the city centre of Rummidge, Heathrow discouraged direct, horizontal movement. Pedestrians about and about must go, by devious and labyrinthine ways. Once he saw a sign "To St. George's Chapel," and eagerly followed its direction, but it led him to the airport laundry. He asked several officials the way, and received confusing and contradictory advice. He was tempted to give up the quest, for his feet were aching, and his grip dragged ever more heavily on his arm, but he persevered. The spectacle of the Muslim pilgrims at prayer had reminded him of the sorry state of his own soul, and though he did not expect to find a Catholic priest in attendance at the chapel to hear his confession, he felt an urge to make an act of contrition in some consecrated place before entrusting himself to the air.

When he found himself outside Terminal Two for the third time he almost despaired, but seeing a young woman in the livery of British Airways ground staff approaching, he accosted her, promising himself that this would be his last attempt.

"St. George's Chapel? It's near the Control Tower," she said.

"That's what they all tell me, but I've been searching high and low this last half hour, and the devil take me if I can find it."

"I'll show you, if you like," said the young woman cheerfully. A small plastic badge on her lapel identified her as "Cheryl Summerbee."

"That's wonderfully kind of you," said Persse. "If you're quite sure I'm not interfering with your work."

"It's my lunch break," said Cheryl, who walked with a curious high-stepping gait, lifting her knees high and planting her feet down daintily and deliberately, like a circus pony. She gave an impression of energetic movement without actually covering much ground, but her style of walking made her shoulder-length blonde hair and other parts of her anatomy bounce about in a pleasing manner. She had a slight squint which gave her blue eyes a starry, unfocused look that was attractive rather than otherwise. She was carrying a shopping bag of bright plastic-coated canvas, from the top of which protruded a romantic novelette entitled *Love Scene*, and a deerstalker of yellowish brown tweed with a bold red check which looked familiar to Persse. "It's not my hat," Cheryl explained, when he remarked upon it. "A passenger left it with me this morning, to mail to a friend of his."

"It wasn't a Professor Zapp, by any chance?"

Cheryl stopped in mid-stride, one foot poised above the pavement. "How did you know?" she said wonderingly.

"He's a friend of mine. Who were you to send the hat to?"

"Percy McGarrigle, Limerick."

"Then I can save you the trouble," said Persse. "For I'm the very man." He took from his jacket pocket the white cardboard identification disc issued to him at the Rummidge Conference, and presented it for Cheryl's inspection.

"Well," she said. "There's a coincidence." She took the hat from her bag and, holding it by the flaps, placed it with a certain ceremony on his head. "A perfect fit," she smiled. "Like Cinderella's slipper." She tucked the label addressed in Morris Zapp's hand in Persse's breast pocket, and it seemed to him, inexplicably, that she gave a quick poulterer's pinch to his pectoral muscles as she did so. She held up two pound notes. "Your American professor friend told me to buy a drink with the change. Now there's enough for two drinks and a couple of sandwiches."

Persse hesitated. "I'd love to join you, Cheryl," he said, "but I must find that chapel." This was only part of the reason. A sense of loyalty to Angelica, in spite of the trick she had played on him the night before, also restrained him from accepting Cheryl's invitation.

"Oh, yes," said Cheryl, "I was forgetting the chapel." She conducted him another fifty yards, then pointed out the shape of a large wooden crucifix in the middle distance. "There you are."

"Thanks a million," he said, and watched with admiration and regret as she pranced away.

Apart from the plain wooden cross, the chapel resembled, from outside, an air raid shelter rather than a place of worship. Behind a low wall of liver-coloured brick, all that was visible was a domed roof built of the same material, and an entrance with steps leading underground. At the bottom of the stairs there was a small vestibule with a table displaying devotional literature, and an office door leading off. On the wall was a small green baize noticeboard on which visitors to the chapel had pinned various prayers and petitions written on scraps of paper. *"May our son have a safe journey and return home soon." "God save the Russian Orthodox Church." "Lord, look with favour on Thy servants Mark and Marianne, as they go to sow Thy seed in the mission fields." "Lord, please let me get my luggage back (lost in Nairobi)."* The chapel itself had been scooped out of the earth in a fan-shape, with the altar at the narrowest point, and a low ceiling, studded with recessed lights, that curved to meet the floor; so that to sit in one of the front pews was rather like taking one's place in the forward passenger cabin of a wide-bodied jet, and one would not have been surprised to see a *No Smoking—Fasten Safety Belts* sign light up above the altar, and a stewardess rather than an usher patrolling the aisle.

There was a small side chapel, where, much to Persse's surprise and pleasure, a red sanctuary lamp was flickering beside a tabernacle fixed to the wall, indicating that the Blessed Sacrament was reserved. Here he said a simple but sincere prayer, for the recovery of Angelica and of his own purity of heart (for he interpreted her flight as a punishment for his lust). Feeling calmed and fortified, he rose to his feet. It occurred to him that he might leave a written petition of his own on the noticeboard. He wrote, on a page torn from a small notebook, *"Dear God, let me find Angelica."* He wrote her name on a separate line, in the trailing continuous script he had used to inscribe it in the snow at Rummidge. If it was God's will, she might pass this way, recognize his hand, relent, and get in touch with him.

Persse did not immediately approach the noticeboard with his petition, since a young woman was standing before it in the act of pinning one of her own to the green baize. Even with her back to him she presented an incongruous figure in this setting: jet-black hair elaborately curled and coiffed, a short white imitation-fur jacket, the tightest of tight red needlecord trousers, and high-heeled gold sandals. Having fixed her prayer to the noticeboard, she stood immobile before it for a moment, then took from her handbag a silk scarf decorated with dice and roulette wheels, which she threw over her head. As she turned and tottered past him on her high heels into the chapel, Persse glimpsed a pale, pretty face which he vaguely felt he had seen before, perhaps in the course of his peregrinations around Heathrow that morning. As he pinned his petition to the noticeboard, he could not resist glancing at the rectangle of pink card he had seen the girl place there:

> *Please God, don't let my father or my mother worry themselves to death*
> *about me and don't let them find out what I am doing now or any of the*
> *workpeople on the farm or the other girls at the hotel God please.*

Persse levered the card from the noticeboard with his thumbnail, turned it over and read what was printed on the other side:

GIRLS UNLIMITED
Hostesses Escorts Masseuses Artistes
An International Agency. Headquarters: Soho Sq.,
LONDON, W.I. Tel: 012 4268 Telegrams CLIMAX London.

Persse replaced the card on the noticeboard as he had found it, and went back into the chapel. The girl was kneeling in the back row, her face bowed, her heavily mascaraed eyelids lowered. Persse sat down in the corresponding pew on the other side of the central aisle, and studied her profile. After a few minutes the girl crossed herself, stood up and stepped into the aisle. Persse followed suit and accosted her:

"Is it Bernadette McGarrigle?"

He caught her in his arms as she fainted away.

. . .

As Morris Zapp and Fulvia Morgana flew over the Alps, dissecting the later work of Roland Barthes and enjoying a second cup of coffee, the municipal employees of Milan called a lightning strike in support of two clerks in the tax department dismissed for alleged corruption (according to the senior management they had been exempting their families from property taxes, according to the union they were being victimized for not exempting the senior management from property taxes). The British Airways Trident landed, therefore, in the midst of civic chaos. Most of the airport staff were refusing to work, and the passengers had to recover their baggage from a heap underneath the aircraft's belly, and carry it themselves across the tarmac to the terminal building. The queues for customs and passport control were long and unruly.

"'Ow are you travelling to Bellagio?" Fulvia asked Morris, as they stood in line.

"The villa said they would send a car to meet me. Is it far?"

"Not so far. You must visit us in Milano during your stay."

"That would be very nice, Fulvia. Is your husband an academic too?"

"Yes, 'e is Professor of Italian Renaissance Literature at Rome."

Morris pondered this for a moment or two. "He works in Rome. You work in Padua. Yet you live in Milan?"

"The communications are good. You can fly several times a day between Milan and Rome, and there is an *autostrada* to Padua. Besides, Milan is the true capital of Italy. Rome is sleepy, lazy, provincial."

"What about Padua?"

Fulvia Morgana looked at him as if suspecting irony. "Nobody lives in Padua," she said simply.

They got through customs with surprising speed. Something about Fulvia's elegant, authoritative mien, or maybe her velvet knickerbockers, attracted an official as though by magnetism, and soon they were free of the sweating, milling, impatient throng. On the other side of passport control, however, was another sweating, milling impatient throng, of meeters and greeters. Some held up cards with names printed on them, but none of the names was Zapp.

"Don't let me keep you, Fulvia," said Morris, unhappily. "If nobody shows I guess I can take a bus."

"The buses will be on strike," said Fulvia. "Do you have a phone number for the villa?"

Morris gave her the letter confirming that he would be met. "But this says you are arriving last Saturday, at Malpensa—the other airport," she observed.

"Yeah, well I changed my plans, to take in Rummidge. I wrote them about it."

"I don't suppose they received your letter," she said. "The postal service here is a national disgrace. If I have a really urgent letter for the States I drive to Switzerland to mail it. Look after the bags." She had spied an empty phone booth, and swooped down on it, snatching the prize from under the nose of an infuriated businessman. Moments later she returned to confirm her guess. "As I thought, they 'ave not received your letter."

"Oh, shit," said Morris. "What shall I do?"

"It is all arranged," said Fulvia. "You will spend tonight with us, and tomorrow the villa will send a car to our 'ouse."

"Well, that's very kind of you," said Morris.

"Wait outside the doors with the luggage," said Fulvia, "and I will bring the car."

Morris stood guard over their bags, basking in the warm spring sunshine, and casting a connoisseur's eye over the more interesting automobiles that drew up outside the terminal to collect or deposit passengers. A bronze-coloured Maserati coupé which until now he had seen only in magazines, priced at something over $50,000, drew his attention, but it was some moments before he realized that Fulvia was seated at the wheel behind its tinted glass and beckoning him urgently to get in. As they swept through the airport gates, she appeared to shake her fist at the pickets, but when they smiled broadly and responded with the same gesture, Morris realized that it was one of solidarity with the workers' cause.

"There's something I must ask you, Fulvia," said Morris Zapp, as he sipped Scotch on the rocks poured from a crystal decanter brought on a silver tray by a black-uniformed, white-aproned maid to the first-floor drawing-room of the magnificent eighteenth-century house just off the Villa Napoleone, which they had reached after a drive so terrifyingly fast that the streets and boulevards of Milan were just a pale grey blur in his memory. "It may sound naive, and even rude, but I can't suppress it any longer."

Fulvia arched her eyebrows above her formidable nose. They had both rested, showered, and changed, she into a long, loose flowing robe of fine white wool, which made her look more than ever like a Roman empress. They faced each other, sunk deep in soft, yielding, hide-covered armchairs, across a Persian rug laid on the honey-coloured waxed wooden floor. Morris looked around the spacious room, in which a few choice items of antique furniture had been tastfully integrated with the finest specimens of modern Italian design, and whose off-white walls bore, he had ascertained by close-range inspection, original paintings by Chagall, Mark Rothko and Francis Bacon. "I just want to know," said Morris Zapp, "how you manage to reconcile living like a millionaire with being a Marxist."

Fulvia, who was smoking a cigarette in an ivory holder, waved it dismissively in the air. "A very American question, if I may say so, Morris. Of course I recognize the contradictions in our way of life, but those are the very contradictions characteristic of the last phase of bourgeois capitalism, which will eventually cause it to collapse. By renouncing our own little bit of privilege"—here Fulvia spread her hands in a modest proprietorial gesture which implied that she and her husband enjoyed a standard of living only a notch or two higher than that of, say, a Puerto Rican family living on welfare in the Bowery—"we should not accelerate by one minute the consummation of that process, which has its own inexorable rhythm and momentum, and is determined by the pressure of mass movements, not by the puny actions of individuals. Since in terms of dialectical materialism it makes no difference to the 'istorical process whether Ernesto and I, as individuals, are rich or poor, we might as well be rich, because it is a role that we know 'ow to perform with a certain dignity. Whereas to be poor with dignity, poor as our Italian peasants are poor, is something not easily learned, something bred in the bone, through generations." Fulvia spoke rapidly and fluently, as though quoting something she and her husband had had occasion to say more than once. "Besides," she added, "by being rich we are able to 'elp those 'oo are taking more positive action."

"Who are they?"

"Oh, various groups," Fulvia said vaguely, as the telephone began to ring. She swept across the room, her white robe billowing out behind her, to answer it; and conducted a conversation in rapid Italian of which Morris understood nothing except an occasional *caro* and, once, the mention of his own name. Fulvia replaced the receiver and returned more deliberately to her seat. "My 'usband," she said, "'E is delayed in Rome because of the strike. Milan airport is closed. 'E will not return tonight."

"Oh, I'm sorry," said Morris.

"Why?" said Fulvia Morgana, with a smile as faint and enigmatic as the Mona Lisa's.

. . .

"Won't you go back home, Bernadette? Your Mammy is destroyed with worrying about you, and your Daddy too."

Bernadette shook her head vigorously, and lit a cigarette, fumbling nervously with the lighter and chipping her scarlet nail polish in the process. "I cannot go home," she said in a voice which, though hoarse from too many cigarettes and, no doubt, strong drinks, still retained the lilting accent of County Sligo. "I can never go home again." She did not raise her eyes, under their long, mascara-clogged lashes, to meet Persse's, but shaped the tip of her cigarette in the green moulded plastic ashtray on the white moulded plastic table in the Terminal Two snackbar. A ham salad, of which she had eaten barely two mouthfuls, was on a plate before her. Cutting up his own food, Persse studied her face and figure, and wondered that he had traced in them, as she passed him in the chapel, the lineaments of Bernadette as he had last seen her: on a family outing to the strand at Ross's Point, one summer when they were both thirteen or fourteen, shy and tongue-tied with each other. He remembered her as a slim, wild tomboy, with tangled black hair and a gap-toothed smile, running into the surf with her best frock tucked up, and being scolded by her mother for getting it soaked with spray. "Why can you not?" he gently pressed her.

"Because I have a child and no husband, is why."

"Ah," said Persse. He knew the mores of the West of Ireland well enough not to discount the gravity of this obstacle. "So you did have the baby?"

"Is that what they think, then?" Bernadette flashed at him, looking up to meet his eye. "That I had it brought off?"

Persse blushed. "Well, your uncle Milo . . ."

"Uncle Milo? That auld scheymer!" The memory of Dr. O'Shea seemed to bring the brogue flooding back into her speech, like saliva into the mouth or adrenalin into the bloodstream. "What the divil does he have to do with it?"

"Well, it was through him that I found out about your trouble, just the day before yesterday. In Rummidge."

"Been up there, have you? I haven't been near the place in years. God, but that was a terrible gloomy old house in, what was it, Gittings Road, that you had to lug the vacuum up three flights of stairs and you could break your neck it was so dark on the landings because himself was too mean to put proper bulbs into the lights . . ." Bernadette shook her head and snorted cigarette smoke through her nostrils. "A slave I was there—working in the hotel in Sligo was a rest cure in comparison. The only mortal creature who was kind to me was a lodger they had on the top floor, an American professor. He used to let me watch his colour telly and read his dirty books." Bernadette chuckled reminiscently, displaying teeth that were white, even, and presumably false. "*Playboy* and *Penthouse* and that sort of stuff. Pictures of girls naked as God made them, bold as brass and letting their names be printed underneath. It was a real eyeopener to an innocent young girl from County Sligo, I can tell you." Bernadette glanced slyly at Persse to see if she was embarrassing him. "One day my Uncle Milo caught me lookin' at them, and beat the livin' daylights out of me."

"Where is your child now?" Persse asked.

"He's with foster parents," said Bernadette. "In London."

"Then you could go back home on your own?"

"And abandon Fergus?"

"Well, for a short visit."

"No thank you. I know too well what it would be like. The looks from behind the curtains in the windows. The starin' and whisperin' after mass on a Sunday morning."

"So what are your plans for the future?"

"To save enough money to retire, buy a little business—a boutique maybe—and have Fergus back to bring him up myself."

"Retire from what, Bernadette?"

"I'm in the entertainment business," she said vaguely. She glanced at her wristwatch. "I must go soon."

"First, give me your address."

She shook her head. "I don't have one. I travel about a lot in my work."

"I suppose Girls Unlimited would forward a letter?"

She paled under her makeup. "How do you know about that?" Then the penny dropped. "You shouldn't read other people's private prayers," she said indignantly. "Or what's written on the other side of them."

"You're right, Bernadette, I shouldn't have. But then I'd never have recognized you. Now I'll be able to tell your Mammy and Daddy that you're safe and well."

"Don't tell them about Girls Unlimited, whatever you do," she begged.

"What is it that you do, then, Bernadette? You're not one of those hostesses, are you?"

"I certainly am not!" she said indignantly. "There's no money in that unless you sleep with the customers afterwards, and I've had enough of sleepin' with." She lit another cigarette and looked at Persse appraisingly through the smoke. "I'm a stripper, if you must know," she said at length.

"Bernadette! You're not!"

"I am, so," she said, brazening it out. "I do a little dance, and I take off my belongings one by one. My best act is called The Chambermaid. Marlene the Chambermaid—that's my professional name, Marlene. I'm better rewarded for takin' that uniform off than I ever was for puttin' it on, I can tell you."

"But how can you bear to . . ."

"The first time was hard, but you get used to it quick enough."

"Used to those men staring at you?"

"You needn't act so superior, Persse McGarrigle," said Bernadette, tossing her head. "What about that day in the cowshed at your people's farm, when you begged me to let down my drawers and show you all my secrets?"

Persse blushed furiously. "We must have been mere children then. I can hardly remember it."

"I remember you wouldn't show me your own little gadget, anyhow," said Bernadette drily. "Wasn't that just typical? Honest to God, when I see the men starin' at me in the clubs, when I'm doin' my act, and I'm down to my G-string, they look just like a bunch of dirty-minded little boys. What do they keep comin' for, I ask myself. Are they expectin' to see somethin' different one day? Sure, every woman is made much the same in that portion of her anatomy. What's the fascination?"

Persse evaded the question by asking one of his own. "What about the father of your child?" he said. "Shouldn't he be helping you with money?"

"I don't know where he is."

"Wasn't he a guest at your hotel? It should be possible to trace him from the register."

"I wrote him a letter once. It came back with 'Not Known At This Address' on it."

"Who was he? What was his name?"

"I'm not telling," said Bernadette. "I've no wish to get involved with him again. He might try and get Fergus off me. He was a queer gloomy sort of fellow." She looked again at her watch. "I really must go now. Thanks for the salad." She looked at it apologetically. "Sorry I had no appetite."

"Never mind that," said Persse. "Look, Bernadette, if you ever change your mind about going back to Ireland, there's a priest in Rummidge who will help you. He has a fund for repatriating young Irish people. The Our Lady of Knock Fund."

"Our Lady of the Knocked-Up would be more like it," said Bernadette, sardonically.

"Knocked-up?"

"Haven't you heard that expression before?"

"Indeed I have. Anyway, this priest is called Father Finbar O'Malley—"

"O'Malley, is it? Sure his people have the farm three miles up the road from ours," said Bernadette. "His mother is the biggest gossip in the parish. He's the last person in the world I'd go to. Remember now—don't tell Mammy and Daddy what I'm doing. You can give them my love."

"I will," he said.

She leaned across the table and brushed his cheek with her lips. He inhaled a heady waft of perfume. "You're a good fellow, Persse."

"And you're a better girl than you pretend," he said.

"Goodbye," she said huskily, and hobbled away without a backward glance, unsteady on her gold high heels.

Soon she was lost to his sight in the restless ebb and flow of humanity on the concourse floor. Persse meditatively consumed her uneaten ham salad. Then he went to the Aer Lingus desk, where they told him apologetically that the flight to Shannon was full. There was, however, a British Airways flight to Dublin leaving shortly, with plenty of spare seats, if that was any use to him. Persse decided to fly to Dublin and hitch from there to Limerick. He accordingly hurried to Terminal One, and presented himself at the check-in desk for the Dublin flight.

"Hallo again," said Cheryl Summerbee. "Did you find the chapel all right?"

"Yes thank you."

"Do you know, I've never been inside, all the time I've been working here. What's it like?"

"Rather like an airplane," said Persse, glancing anxiously at his watch.

"Nice and quiet, I expect," said Cheryl, leaning forward on her elbows and bringing her blue, slightly askew eyes quite close to his.

"Yes, it is very peaceful," said Persse. "Er, excuse me, Cheryl, but doesn't the plane leave quite soon?"

"Don't worry, you'll catch it," said Cheryl. "Now let's find you a really nice seat. Smoking or non-smoking?"

"Non-smoking."

Cheryl tapped on her computer keyboard, and frowned at the screen. Then her brow cleared. "16B," she said. "A lovely seat."

Persse was the last to board the plane. He couldn't see anything special about seat 16B, which was the middle one in a row of three. The window and aisle seats were both occupied by nuns.

. . .

The dinner—*gazpacho*, roast guinea fowl and stuffed peppers, fresh sliced oranges in a caramel sauce, and a *dolcelatte* cheese—was superb, as was the wine, made and bottled, Fulvia informed Morris, on the estate of her father-in-law, the Count. They ate by candlelight in a panelled dining-room, shadows and highlights flickering over the dark wooden surfaces of walls and table, discreetly waited on by a maid and a manservant. At the conclusion of the meal, Fulvia regally dismissed this pair to their own quarters, and informed Morris that coffee and liqueurs awaited them in the drawing-room.

"This lavish hospitality overwhelms me, Fulvia," said Morris, leaning up against the white marble mantelpiece and sipping his coffee, a thimbleful of sweet, scalding liquid the colour and consistency of pitch, with a caffeine kick like a thousand volts. "I don't know how to thank you."

Fulvia Morgana looked up at him from the sofa where she was half-reclined, the slit skirt of her white robe falling away from one shapely leg. Her red lips curled back over two rows of sharp, white, even teeth. "Soon I show you 'ow," she said; and the possibility, which Morris Zapp had been mentally assessing all evening with a mixture of alarm and incredulity, that Fulvia Morgana meant to seduce him, now became a certainty. "Sit 'ere," she said, patting the sofa cushions, as though addressing a pet dog.

"I'm OK here for a minute," said Morris, setting down his cup and saucer on the mantelpiece with a nervous rattle, and busying himself with the lighting of a cigar. "Tell me, Fulvia, who d'you think will be in the running for this UNESCO chair?"

She shrugged. "I don't know. Tardieu, perhaps."

"The narratologist? Hasn't his moment passed? I mean, ten years ago everybody was into that stuff, actants and functions and mythymes and all that jazz. But now . . ."

"Only ten years! Does fashion in scholarship 'ave such a short life?"

"It's getting shorter all the time. There are people coming back into fashion who never even knew they were out of it. Who else?"

"Oh, I don't know. Von Turpitz is surely to apply."

"That Nazi?"

"'E was not a Nazi, I believe, just a conscripted soldier."

"Well, he looks like a Nazi. Like all the ones I've seen, anyway, which is admittedly only in movies."

Fulvia abandoned her pose on the sofa and went to the drinks trolley. "Cognac or liqueur?"

"Cognac would be great. What about Turpitz's last book—did you read it? It's just a rehash of Iser and Jauss."

"Don't let us talk any more about books," she said, floating across the dimly lit room with a brandy glass like a huge bubble in her hand. "Or about chairs and conferences." She stood very close to him and rubbed the back of her free hand over his crotch. "Is it really twenty-five centimetres?" she murmured.

"What gives you that idea?" he said hoarsely.

"Your wife's book . . ."

"You don't want to believe everything you read in books, Fulvia," said Morris, grabbing the glass of cognac and draining it in a single gulp. He coughed and his eyes filled with tears. "A professional critic like you should know better than that. Novelists exaggerate."

"But 'ow much do they exaggerate, Morris?" she said. "I would like to see for myself."

"Like, practical criticism?" he quipped.

Fulvia did not laugh. "Didn't you make your wife measure it with her tape measure?" she persisted.

"Of course I didn't! That's just feminist propaganda. Like the whole book."

He lurched towards one of the deep armchairs, puffing clouds of cigar smoke like a retreating battleship, but Fulvia steered him firmly towards the sofa, and sat down beside him, pressing her thigh against his. She undid a button of his shirt and slid a cool hand inside. He flinched as the gems on one of her rings snagged in his chest hair.

"Lots of 'air," Fulvia purred. "*That* is in the book."

"I'm not saying the book is entirely fictitious," said Morris. "Some of the minor details are taken from life—"

"'Airy as a beast . . . You were a beast to your wife, I think."

"Ow!" exclaimed Morris, for Fulvia had dug her long lacquered nails into his flesh for emphasis.

"'Ow? Well, for example, tying 'er up with leather straps and doing all those degrading things to 'er."

"Lies, all lies!" said Morris desperately.

"You can do those things to me, if you like, *caro*," Fulvia whispered into his ear, pinching his nipple painfully at the same time.

"I don't want to do anything to anybody, I never did," Morris groaned. "The only time we ever fooled around with that S/M stuff, it was Désirée's idea, not mine."

"I don't believe you, Morris."

"It's true. Novelists are terrible liars. They make things up. They change things around. Black becomes white, white black. They are totally unethical beings. Ouch!" Fulvia had nibbled his earlobe hard enough to draw blood.

"Come," she said, rising abruptly to her feet.

"Where are we going?"

"To bed."

"Already?" Morris consulted his digital watch. "It's only ten after ten. Can't I finish my cigar?"

"No, there isn't time."

"What's the hurry?"

Fulvia sat down beside him again. "Don't you find me desirable, Morris?"

she said. She pressed herself seductively against him, but there was a faintly menacing glint in her eyes which suggested that her patience was running out.

"Of course I do, Fulvia, you're one of the most attractive women I've ever met," he hastened to assure her. "That's the trouble. You're bound to be disappointed, especially after Désirée's write-up. I mean, I retired from this sort of thing years ago."

Fulvia drew away and stared at him, dismayed. "You mean, you're . . ."

"No, not impotent. But out of practise. I live on my own. I jog. I write my books. I watch TV."

"No love affairs?"

"Not in a long while."

Fulvia looked at him with compassion. "You poor man."

"You know, I don't miss it as much as I thought I would. It's a relief to be free of all the hassle."

"'Assle?"

"Yeah, you know—all the undressing and dressing again in the middle of the day, and showering before and after, and making sure your undershorts are clean and brushing your teeth all the time and gargling with mouthwash."

Fulvia threw back her head and laughed loud and long. "You funny man," she gasped.

Morris Zapp grinned uncertainly, for he had not intended to be *that* funny.

Fulvia stood up again, tugging Morris to his feet. "Come on, you funny man, I will remind you of what you are missing."

"Well, if you insist," he sighed, stubbing out his cigar. In this more relaxed mood Fulvia seemed less intimidating. "Give me a kiss," he said.

"A kiss?"

"Yeah, you remember kissing. It used to come between saying '*Hi*' and fucking. I'm an old-fashioned guy."

Fulvia smiled and pressed the length of her body against him. Pulling his face down to meet her own, she kissed him long and fiercely. Morris ran his hands down her back and over her hips. She appeared to be wearing nothing underneath the white robe. He felt desire stirring in him like dull roots after spring rain.

Fulvia's bedroom was a deeply carpeted octagon, lined, walls and ceiling, with rose-tinted mirrors that multiplied every gesture like a kaleidoscope.

A bevy of Fulvias stepped, naked as Botticelli's Venus, from the white foam of their discarded dresses and converged upon him with a hundred outstretched arms. A whole football team of Morris Zapps stripped to their undershorts with clumsy haste and clamped hairy paws on ranks of peach-shaped buttocks receding into infinity.

"How do you like it?" murmured Fulvia, as they stroked and grappled on the crimson sheets of the huge circular bed.

"Amazing!" Morris said. "It's like being at an orgy choreographed by Busby Berkeley."

"No more jokes, Morris," said Fulvia. "It isn't erotic."

"Sorry. What would you like me to do?"

Fulvia had her answer ready. "Tie me up, gag me, then do whatever you desire." She pulled from a bedside cabinet a pair of handcuffs, leather thongs, sticky tape and bandages.

"How do these work?" said Morris, fumbling with the handcuffs.

"Like so." Fulvia slipped the cuffs over his wrists and fastened them with a snap. "Ha, ha! Now you are my prisoner." She pushed him down on to the bed.

"Hey, what are you doing?"

What she was doing was pulling off his undershorts. "I think your wife exaggerated just a *leetle*, Morris," she said, kneeling over him, her long cool fingers busy.

"*Ars longa*, in life shorter," Morris murmured. But it was like the last despairing witticism of a drowning man. He closed his eyes and surrendered himself to sensation.

Then Morris heard a thud from below stairs, as of a door closing, and a male voice called out Fulvia's name. Morris opened his eyes, his body rigid with apprehension, apart from one zone which was limp with it. "Who's that?" he hissed.

"My 'usband," said Fulvia.

"*What?*" A score of naked, handcuffed Morris Zapps leapt from the bed and exchanged looks of alarm and consternation. "I thought you said he was stuck in Rome?"

"'E must 'ave decided to drive," said Fulvia calmly. She raised her head, and her voice, to call out something in Italian.

"What are you doing? What did you say?" demanded Morris, struggling with his undershorts. It wasn't easy, he discovered, to put them on while wearing handcuffs.

"I told 'im to come up."

"Are you crazy? How am I supposed to get out of here?" He hopped around the room with his undershorts half on and half off, opening closet doors, looking for a second exit or somewhere to hide, and tripped over his own shoes. Fulvia laughed. He shook the handcuffs an inch from her Roman nose. "Will you kindly take these fucking things off my wrists," he said, in a whisper that was like a suppressed scream. Fulvia searched lackadaisically for the key in a drawer of the bedside cabinet. "Quick, quick!" Morris urged frantically. He could hear someone mounting the stairs, humming a popular song.

"Relax, Morris, Ernesto is a man of the world," said Fulvia. She inserted a key into the handcuffs and with a click he was free. But with another click the bedroom door opened, and a man in a pale, elegant suit, grey-haired and deeply tanned, came in. "Ernesto, this is Morris," said Fulvia, kissing her husband on both cheeks and leading him across the room to where Morris was hastily pulling up his undershorts.

"Felice di conoscerla, signore," Ernesto's face crinkled in a broad smile and he extended a hand which Morris shook limply.

"Ernesto does not speak English," said Fulvia. "But 'e understands."

"I wish I did," said Morris.

Ernesto opened one of the mirrored closet doors, hung up his suit, kicked off his shoes, and walked towards the *en suite* bathroom, pulling his shirt over his head. A stream of muffled Italian came from inside the shirt.

"What did he say?" Morris gaped, as the bathroom door closed behind Ernesto.

"'E is going to take a shower," said Fulvia, plumping the pillows on the bed. "Then 'e will join us."

"Join us? Where?"

"'Ere, of course," said Fulvia, getting into the bed, and arranging herself in the centre of it.

Morris stared. "Hey!" he accused her. "I believe you planned this all along!" Fulvia smiled her Mona Lisa smile.

. . .

In the tiny bathroom of their apartment in Fitzroy Square, Thelma Ringbaum was preparing for bed with more than usual care. It had been a long and tiring day: the agency through which they were renting the apartment had lost the key and kept them waiting several hours while a duplicate was obtained. Then, when they finally got into it they found that the water had been turned off in some inscrutable fashion and they had to phone the agency to send a man to turn it on—and to do *that* they had to go out and search the neighbourhood for an unvandalized phone booth because the telephone in the apartment had been disconnected. The kitchen stove was so filthy that Thelma decided she would have to clean it before they even made themselves a cup of coffee, and the inside of the icebox was like a small working model of a glacier and had to be defrosted before they could use it. Having had no proper sleep the previous night, Thelma was, by the time she had completed these tasks, and gone marketing for basic foods at the local stores, and fixed their supper (because Howard wouldn't go out to a restaurant), ready to drop. But there was a tryst pending between herself and Howard, and Thelma's life was not so full of romance that she could afford to break it. Also, Howard needed cheering up after finding that disappointing letter from Morris Zapp on the doormat.

In spite of her weariness, and the discouraging décor of the bathroom, all cobwebs and peeling paint, Thelma felt a quickening of erotic excitement as she prepared herself for Howard's pleasure. She softened her bathwater with fragrant foam, massaged herself afterwards with scented skin cream, dabbed perfume behind her ears and in other intimate hollows and crevices of her anatomy, and put on her sexiest nightgown, a frivolous garment of sheer black nylon. She brushed her hair for one hundred strokes, and bit her lips to make them red. Then she tip-toed to the living-room, threw open the door and posed on the threshold. "Howard!" she cooed.

Howard was crouched in front of the ancient black-and-white TV, fiddling with the controls while the picture buzzed and flickered. "Yes?" he said, without turning round.

Thelma giggled. "*Now* you can have me, honey."

Howard Ringbaum turned round in his seat and looked at her stonily. "Now I don't want you," he said, and resumed his fiddling with the controls of the television.

At that moment, Thelma Ringbaum determined that she would be unfaithful to her husband at the earliest possible opportunity.

. . .

All around the world people are in different states of dress and undress, alone or in couples, waking or sleeping, working or resting. As Persse McGarrigle walks along an Irish country road in the middle of the night, with Morris Zapp's deerstalker tipped back on his head, the same sunbeam that, reflected off the moon, now illuminates his way, and shows him the shapes of darkened farms and cottages where men and beasts slumber and snore, has just a few seconds ago woken up the pavement dwellers of Bombay and the factory workers of Omsk, shining directly into their wincing faces or stealing through the gaps in tattered curtains and broken blinds.

Further east, it is already midmorning. In Cooktown, Queensland, in his office at the University of North Queensland, Rodney Wainwright is working at his paper on the Future of Criticism. To try and recover the impetus of his argument, he is copying out what he has already written, from the beginning, as a pole vaulter lengthens his run-up to achieve a particularly daunting jump. His hope is that the sheer momentum of discourse will carry him over that stubborn obstacle which has delayed him for so long. So far it is going well. His hand is moving fluently across the foolscap. He is introducing many new gracenotes and making various subtle revisions of his original text as he proceeds. He tries to suppress his own knowledge of what comes next, tries not to see the crucial passage looming ahead. He is trying to trick his own brain. Don't look, don't look! Keep going, keep going! Gather all your strength up into one ball, ready to spring, NOW!

The question is, therefore, how can literary criticism maintain its Arnoldian function of identifying the best which has been thought and said, when literary discourse itself has been decentred by deconstructing the traditional concept of the author, of "authority." Clearly

Yes, clearly . . . ?

Clearly

Clearly what?

The vaulter hangs suspended in the air for a moment, his face red with effort, eyes bulging, tendons knotted, the pole bent almost to breaking point under his weight, the crossbar only inches from his nose. Then it all collapses: the pole breaks, the bar is dislodged, the athlete falls back to earth, limbs flailing. Rodney Wainwright slumps forward onto his desk and buries his face in his hands. Beaten again.

There is a timid knock on the door. "Come in," Rodney Wainwright moans, looking up through latticed fingers. A blonde, girlish head peers round the door, eyes wide.

"Are you all right, Dr. Wainwright?" says Sandra Dix. "I came to see you about my assignment."

. . .

On a different latitude, but much the same longtitude, Akira Sakazaki, seated crosslegged in his carpeted cubicle in the sky, is grading papers—English-language exercises by his first year students at the University. "*Having rescued girl drowning, lifeguard raped in blanket her*," he reads. Sighing, shaking his head, Akira inserts articles, rearranges word order, and corrects the spelling of "*wrapped*." Such work is small beer to the translator of Ronald Frobisher. "Small beer," says Akira aloud, and smiles toothily to himself. It is an English phrase whose meaning he has learned only this morning, from one of the novelist's letters.

Akira is dressed in his Arnold Palmer sports shirt this morning, and his Jack Nicklaus golf shoes stand beside the door ready to be slipped on when it is time to leave for the University. For today is his day for golf. This evening he will break his journey home to play for an hour at one of Tokyo's many driving ranges. Already his fingers itch to curl themselves round the shaft of his club. Standing on the upper gallery of the floodlit, netted range, erected like a gigantic birdcage in the isosceles triangle made by three criss-crossing railway lines, he will lash a hundred yellow-painted golfballs into space, see them rise, soar above the million roofs and TV aerials, only to hit the net and fall anticlimatically to earth, like stricken birds.

In this sport, Akira sees an allegory of the elations and frustrations of his work as translator. Language is the net that holds thought trapped within a particular culture. But if one could only strike the ball with sufficient force, with perfect timing, it would perhaps break through the netting, continue on its course, never fall to earth, but go into orbit around the world.

. . .

In London, Ronald Frobisher is asleep in his study, wearing dressing-gown and pyjamas, slumped in front of the television set on which he was watching, some hours earlier, the repeat of an episode from a police thriller series for which he wrote the script. Bored by his own dialogue, he dropped off to sleep in his chair; and the late news, weather forecast, and an epilogue by an earnest Evangelical clergyman on the reality of sin, have all washed over him unheeded. Now the television set emits only a high-pitched whine and a faint bluish light which imparts to the novelist's stubbly, pock-marked jowls a deathlike hue. Neglected at his feet lies a blue aerogramme with questions neatly typed: "*p. 152, 'jam-butty.' What is it? p. 182, 'Y-fronts.' What are they? p. 191 'sweet fanny adams.' Who is she?*"

. . .

Arthur Kingfisher is also seated in front of a television set, though he is not asleep, since it is still early evening in Chicago (where he is staying on for a few days after the conclusion of the conference on "The Crisis of the Sign" in order to repeat his keynote address in the form of a lecture at Northwestern University for a one-thousand-dollar fee). He is watching, intermittently, a pornographic movie ordered by telephone and piped to his room on one of the hotel's video channels—intermittently, because he is at the same time reading a book on hermeneutics which he has agreed to review for a learned journal, an assignment which is now long overdue, and he glances up from the page only when the aridity of the discourse becomes too much for even his dry old brain to bear, or when the film's sound track, shifting from banal dialogue to panting and moaning, warns him that its feeble pretence of telling a story has been abandoned in favour of its real point and purpose. At the same time, Song-Mi Lee, stooping over his shoulder in a charming silk kimono, is excavating the wax from Arthur Kingfisher's ear, using a small carved bamboo implement specially designed for the purpose and widely used in Korean bathhouses.

Suddenly, Arthur Kingfisher becomes excited—whether it is the images of copulation on the small screen, or the subtle stimulation of his inner ear, or the mental glimpse of some new horizon of conceptual thought prompted by the writer on hermeneutics, it would be difficult to say; but he feels a distinct sensation of life between his legs, drops the book, and hurries Song-Mi Lee towards the bed, pulling off his bathrobe and urging her to do likewise.

She obeys; but the kimono is delicate and valuable, its sash is wound around Song-Mi Lee's tiny waist in a complex knot, and it is at least half a minute before she has disrobed, by which time Arthur Kingfisher's excitement has subsided—or perhaps it was always an illusion, a phantom, wishful thinking. He returns despondently to his book and his seat in front of the TV. But he has forgotten what new theoretical leap he had begun to see the possibilities of a few moments ago, and the naked bodies writhing and clutching and quivering on the screen now seem merely to mock his impotence. He slaps the book shut, snaps off the TV and closes his eyes in despair. Song-Mi Lee silently recommences the removal of wax from his ear.

. . .

In Helicon, New Hampshire, it is evening, dinner is over, and Désirée Zapp is crouched conspiratorially over the payphone in the lobby of the writers' colony, talking to her agent in New York in an urgent whisper, anxious not to be overhead by any of the other residents. For what she is confessing to her agent is that she is "blocked," and this word, like "cancer" in a surgical ward, is never under any circumstances to be uttered aloud, though it is in the minds of all. "It's not working out for me, this place, Alice," she whispers into the telephone.

"What? I can't hear you, this must be a bad line," says Alice Kauffman, from her apartment on 48th Street.

"I'm no further forward than when I came here six weeks ago," says Désirée, risking a slight increase of volume. "The first thing I do every morning is to tear up what I wrote the day before. It's driving me crazy."

A great sigh, like a bellows emptying, comes down the line from New York to New Hampshire. Alice Kauffman weighs two hundred and thirty pounds and runs her agency from her apartment because she is too heavy to travel comfortably even by taxi to another part of Manhattan. If Désirée knows her, and she does know Alice very well, her agent will at this moment be sprawled on a divan with a pile of manuscripts on one side of her massive hips and an open box of Swiss cherry-liqueur chocolates on the other. "Then quit, honey," says Alice. "Check out tomorrow. Run."

Désirée looks nervously over her shoulders, fearful that this heretical advice might be overhead. "Where to?"

"Give yourself a treat, a change of scene," says Alice. "Take a trip someplace. Go to Europe."

"Hmm," says Désirée thoughtfully. "I did get an invitation to a conference in Germany, just this morning."

"Accept," says Alice. "Your expenses will be tax-deductible."

"They were offering to pay my expenses."

"There'll be extras," said Alice. "There always are. Did I tell you by the way, that *Difficult Days* is going to be translated into Portuguese? That's the seventeenth language, not counting Korea which pirated it."

. . .

Far away in Germany, Siegfried von Turpitz, who sent the conference invitation to Désirée, is asleep in the bedroom of his house on the edge of the Black Forest. Tired from his long drive, he lies to attention, on his back, his black hand outside the sheets. His wife, Bertha, asleep in the other twin bed, has never seen her husband without the glove. When he is taking a bath, his right hand dangles over the side of the tub to keep dry; when he takes a shower it projects horizontally from between the curtains like a traffic policeman's signal. When he comes to her bed she is not always sure, in the dark, whether it is a penis or a leather-sheathed finger that probes the folds and orifices of her body. On their wedding night she begged him to remove the glove, but he refused. "But if the lights are out, Siegfried?" she pleaded. "My first wife asked me to do that once," said Siegfried von Turpitz cryptically, "but I forgot to put the glove back on before I fell asleep." Von Turpitz's first wife was known to have died of a heart attack, found one morning by her husband lying dead in the bed beside him. Bertha never asked Siegfried again to remove his glove.

. . .

Most people in Europe are asleep now, though Michel Tardieu is awake behind his reptilian eyelids, troubled by a faint aroma of perfume emanating from the body of Albert, asleep beside him, which is not the familiar fragrance of his own favourite toilet water, *Tristes Tropiques*, which Albert customarily borrows in liberal quantities, but something sickly and cloying, vulgarly synthetic, something (his nose twitches as he strives to translate olfactory sensations into verbal concepts) such as (his lizard eyelids flick open in horror at the thought) a *woman* might use! Akbil Borak, however, is not awake, having fallen asleep sitting up in bed, fifty pages from the end of *The Spirit of the Age*, and is bowed forward as if poleaxed, his nose flattened against the open book reposing on his knees, while Oya, her head turned away from the light of the reading lamp, slumbers obliviously beside him. And Philip and Hilary Swallow are asleep back to back in their double bed which, being as old as their marriage, sags in the middle like a shallow trench, so that they tend to roll towards each other in their sleep; but whenever Philip's bony haunches touch Hilary's fleshy ones, their bodies spring apart like opposed magnets and, without waking, each shifts back to the margins of the mattress.

. . .

Persse McGarrigle stops in the middle of the road to transfer his bag from one aching arm to another. The hitching had gone well enough as far as Mullingar, but there he was picked up by a man on his way home from a wedding and far gone in his cups, who drove past the same signpost three times, finally confessed that he was lost, and fell abruptly asleep over the wheel of his car. Persse rather regrets, now, that he didn't doss down himself in the back seat of the car, for his chances of getting another lift this night seem remote.

He stops again, and looks speculatively about him. It is warm and dry enough to sleep out. Spying a haystack in a field to his right, Persse climbs over the gate and makes towards it. A startled donkey rises to its feet and canters away. He throws down his grip, kicks off his shoes and stretches out in the fragrant hay, staring up at the immense sky arching above his head, studded with a million stars. They pulse with a brilliance that city-dwellers could never imagine. One of them seems to be moving across the sky in relation to other stars, and at first Persse thinks he has discovered a new comet. Then he realizes from its slow and steady progress that it is a communications satellite in geostable orbit, a tiny artificial moon that faithfully keeps its station above the Atlantic, moving in pace with the earth's rotation, receiving and sending back messages, images and secrets, to and from countless human beings far below. "Bright satellite!" he murmurs, "Would I were steadfast as thou art." And he recites the whole sonnet aloud, willing it to rebound from space into Angelica's thoughts, or dreams, wherever she is, that she might feel the strength of his longing to be with her.

> *Pillowed upon my fair love's ripening breast*
> *To feel for ever its soft fall and swell*
> *Awake for ever in a sweet unrest,*
> *Still, still to hear her tender taken breath*
> *And so live ever—or else swoon to death.*

But no, cancel that last bit about dying. Poor old Keats was at his last gasp when he wrote that—he knew he had no chance of getting his head down on Fanny Brawne's ripening breast, having hardly any lungs left in his own. But he, Persse McGarrigle, has no intention of dying yet awhile. Living for ever is more the ticket, especially if he can find Angelica.

So musing, Persse fell peacefully asleep.

PART III

1

When Persse finally got back to his Department at University College Limerick, there were two letters from London waiting for him. He could tell at a glance that neither was from Angelica—the envelopes were too official-looking, the typing of his name and address too professional—but their contents were not without interest. One was from Felix Skinner, reminding him that Lecky, Windrush and Bernstein would be very interested to see Persse's thesis on the influence of T. S. Eliot on Shakespeare. The other was from the Royal Academy of Literature, informing him that he had been awarded a prize of £1000 under the Maud Fitzsimmons Bequest for the Encouragement of Anglo-Irish Poetry. Persse had sent in a sheaf of manuscript poems for this prize six months before, and had forgotten all about it. He whooped and threw the letter into the air. Catching it as it floated to the ground, he read the second paragraph, which stated that the prize, together with a number of other awards administered by the Academy, would be presented at a reception, which it was hoped Mr. McGarrigle would be able to attend, to be held in three weeks' time on the *Annabel Lee*, Charing Cross Embankment.

Persse went to see his Head of Department, Professor Liam McCreedy, and asked if he could take a sabbatical in the coming term.

"A sabbatical? This is a rather sudden request, Persse," said McCreedy, peering at him from behind his usual battlements of books. Instead of using a desk, the Professor sat at an immense table, almost entirely covered with tottering piles of scholarly tomes—dictionaries, concordances and Old English texts—with just a small area in front of him cleared for writing. The visitor seated on the other side of these fortifications was placed at a considerable disadvantage in any discussion by not always being able to see his interlocutor. "I don't think you've been here long enough to qualify for a sabbatical," McCreedy said doubtfully.

"Well, leave of absence, then. I don't need any pay. I've just won a thousand-pound prize for my poetry," said Persse, in the general direction of a variorum edition of *The Battle of Maldon*; but Professor McCreedy's head bobbed up at the other end of the table, above Skeat's *Dialect Dictionary.*

"Have you, now?" he exclaimed. "Well, hearty congratulations. That puts a rather different complexion on the matter. Er, what would you be wanting to be doing during this leave, exactly?"

"I want to study structuralism, sir," said Persse.

This announcement sent the Professor diving for cover again, into some slit trench deep in the publications of the Early English Text Society, from which his voice emerged muffled and plaintive. "Well, I don't know that we can manage the modern literature course without you, Mr. McGarrigle."

"There are no lectures in the summer term," Persse pointed out, "because all the students are swotting for their examinations."

"Ah, but that's just it!" said McCreedy triumphantly, taking aim from behind Kloeber's *Beowulf.* "Who will mark the Modern Literature papers?"

"I'll come back and do that for you," Persse offered. It was not a very onerous commitment, since there were only five students in the course.

"Well, all right, I'll see what I can do," sighed McCreedy.

Persse went back to his digs near the Limerick gasworks and drafted a two-thousand-word outline of a book about the influence of T. S. Eliot on modern readings of Shakespeare and other Elizabethan writers, which he typed up and sent off to Felix Skinner with a covering note saying that he would prefer not to submit the original thesis at this stage, since it needed a lot of revision before it would be suitable for publication.

. . .

Morris Zapp took his departure from Milan as soon as he decently could, if "decent" was a word that could be applied to the Morgana ménage, which he ventured to doubt. The troilism party had not been a success. As soon as it became evident that he was expected to fool around with Ernesto as well as Fulvia, Morris had made his excuses and left the mirrored bedchamber. He also took the precaution of locking the door of the guest bedroom behind him. When he rose the next morning, Ernesto, evidently an *autostrada* addict, had already left to drive back to Rome, and Fulvia, coolly polite across the coffee and croissants, made no allusion to the events of the previous night, so that Morris began to wonder whether he had dreamed the whole episode; but the sting of the various superficial flesh wounds Fulvia's long nails had inflicted on his chest and shoulders convinced him otherwise.

A uniformed driver from the Villa Serbelloni called soon after breakfast, and Morris exhaled a sigh of relief as the big Mercedes pulled away from Fulvia's front porch: he couldn't help thinking of her as a kind of sorceress within whose sphere of influence it would be dangerous to linger. Milan was socked in by cloud, but as the car approached its destination the sun came out and Alpine peaks became visible on the horizon. They skirted a lake for some miles, driving in and out of tunnels that had windows cut at intervals in the rock to give lantern-slide glimpses of blue water and green shoreline. The Villa Serbelloni proved to be a noble and luxurious house built on the sheltered slope of a promontory that divided two lakes, Como and Lecco, with magnificent views to east, south and west from its balconies and extensive gardens.

Morris was shown into a well-appointed suite on the second floor, and stepped out on to his balcony to inhale the air, scented with the perfume of various spring blossoms, and to enjoy the prospect. Down on the terrace, the other resident scholars were gathering for the pre-lunch aperitif—he had glimpsed the table laid for lunch in the dining-room on his way up: starched white napery, crystal glass, menu cards. He surveyed the scene with complacency. He felt sure he was going to enjoy his stay here. Not the least of its attractions was that it was entirely free. All you had to do, to come and stay in this idyllic retreat, pampered by servants and lavishly provided with food and drink, given every facility for reflection and creation, was to apply.

Of course, you had to be distinguished—by, for instance, having applied successfully for other, similar handouts, grants, fellowships and so on, in the past. That was the beauty of the academic life, as Morris saw it. To them that had had, more would be given. All you needed to do to get started was to write one really damned good book—which admittedly wasn't easy when you were a young college teacher just beginning your career, struggling with a heavy teaching load on unfamiliar material, and probably with the demands of a wife and young growing family as well. But on the strength of that one damned good book you could get a grant to write a second book in more favourable circumstances; with two books you got promotion, a lighter teaching load, and courses of your own devising; you could then use your teaching as a way of doing research for your next book, which you were thus able to produce all the more quickly. This productivity made you eligible for tenure, further promotion, more generous and prestigious research grants, more relief from routine teaching and administration. In theory, it was possible to wind up being full professor while doing nothing except to be permanently absent on some kind of sabbatical grant or fellowship. Morris hadn't quite reached that omega point, but he was working on it.

He stepped back into the cool, restful shade of his spacious room, and discovered an adjoining study. On the broad, leather-topped desk was a neat stack of mail that had been forwarded to Bellagio by arrangement. It included a cable from someone called Rodney Wainwright in Australia, whom Morris had forgotten all about, apologizing for the delay in submitting his paper for the Jerusalem conference, an enquiry from Howard Ringbaum about the same conference which had crossed with Morris's rejection of Ringbaum's paper, and a letter from Désirée's lawyers about college tuition fees for the twins. Morris dropped these communications in the waste basket and, taking a sheet of the villa's crested notepaper from the desk drawer, typed, on the electric typewriter provided, a letter to Arthur Kingfisher, reminding him that they had been co-participants in an English Institute seminar on Symbolism some years before; saying that he had heard that he, Arthur Kingfisher, had given a brilliant keynote address to the recent Chicago conference on "The Crisis of the Sign," and begging him, in the most flattering of terms, for the favour of an offprint or Xerox of the text of this address. Morris read through the letter. Was it a shade too fulsome? No, that was another law of academic life: *it is impossible to be excessive in flattery of one's peers.* Should he mention his interest in the UNESCO Chair? No, that would be premature. The time would come for the hard sell. This was just a gentle, preliminary nudge of the great man's memory. Morris Zapp licked the envelope and sealed it with a thump of his hairy-knuckled fist. On his way to the terrace for aperitifs he dropped it into the mail box thoughtfully provided in the hall.

. . .

Robin Dempsey went back to Darlington in a thoroughly demoralized state of mind. After the humiliation of Angelica's practical joke (his cheeks still burned, all four of them, whenever he thought of that Irish bumpkin observing his preparations for bed from inside the wardrobe) another day of frustration and aggravation had followed. The conference business meeting, chaired by Philip Swallow, somewhat flustered and breathless from a late arrival, had rejected his own offer to hold next year's conference at Darlington, and voted in favour of Cambridge instead. Then, when he called later in the morning at his former home to take his two younger children out for the day, he overheard them complaining that they didn't want to go. Janet had ensured that they accompanied him in the end, but only, she made clear to Robin, so that she and her boyfriend, Scott, an ageing flowerchild who still affected denim and long hair at the age of thirty-five, could go to bed together in the afternoon. Scott was a freelance photographer, seldom in employment, and one of Robin Dempsey's many grudges against his ex-wife was that she was spending part of the maintenance money he paid her on keeping this good-for-nothing layabout in cigarettes and lenses.

Jennifer, sixteen, and Alex, fourteen, sulkily escorted him to the City Centre, where they declined the offer of a visit to the Art Gallery or Science Museum in favour of looking through endless racks of records and clothing in the Shopping Centre boutiques. They cheered up somewhat when Robin bought them a pair of jeans and an LP each, and even condescended to talk to him over the hamburgers and chips which they demanded for lunch. This conversation did not, however, improve his spirits, consisting as it did mainly of allusions to musicians he had never heard of, and enthusiastic tributes to Scott, who evidently had.

So the day wore on. The hamburgers, coming on top of the medieval banquet, made him flatulent, and the drive back to Darlington uncomfortable. He arrived home at dusk. His small modern town house, newspapers and junk mail drifted up behind the front door, seemed chilly and unwelcoming. He walked from room to room, turning on radio, TV, electric fires, to try and dispel his loneliness and depression, but to no avail. Instead of unpacking, he got back into his Golf and drove down to the University's Computer Centre.

As he had expected, Josh Collins, the Senior Lecturer in Computing, was still there, alone in the brightly-lit prefabricated building, working on a program. Some people claimed that Josh Collins never went home, that he had no home, but dossed down at night on the floor between his humming, blinking, clicking machines.

"Hallo, Josh, what's new?" said Robin with forced joviality.

Josh looked up from a long scroll of data printout. "Eliza's arrived," he said.

"Really? That's great!" said Robin Dempsey. It was just the diversion he needed.

ELIZA, so named after the heroine of *Pygmalion*, was a program designed to enable computers to talk, that is, to conduct coherent conversations in standard English with human users, by means of a visual display. The conversations had to be of a contextually specific type, with well-defined rules and goals, in which the computer could take an essentially prompting and questioning role, programmed with a repertoire of possible responses to cues likely to appear in the context. The psychiatrist-patient interview was considered ideal for this purpose, being one of the most regulated discourse situations, and had accordingly been adopted as the model for ELIZA. The experiment was of considerable interest to linguisticians researching into the systematic aspects of verbal interaction.

"Let me try it out," said Robin.

"OK," said Josh. "Use that terminal in the corner. When I give you the nod, write in 'Hallo.'"

Robin Dempsey seated himself at a console consisting of a typewriter keyboard and visual display screen. Josh took a large spool of tape into the glass-partitioned section of the room where the mainframe computer was situated, and soon nodded to Robin to indicate that ELIZA was on line.

"HALLO," Robin typed on the keyboard.

"HALLO, HOW ARE YOU FEELING?" replied ELIZA, the printed words appearing instantly on the VDU.

"I'M FEELING TERRIBLE," Robin replied.

"WHAT DO YOU MEAN BY THAT PRECISELY?"

"I'M FEELING DEPRESSED."

"WHY DO YOU THINK YOU ARE DEPRESSED?"

"BECAUSE I'M LONELY."

"DO YOU LIVE WITH YOUR FAMILY?"

"NO."

"DO YOU HAVE ANY FRIENDS?"

"NOT REALLY."

"WHY IS THAT?"

Robin Dempsey paused for some considerable time before he typed in his reply: "I DON'T KNOW."

"DO YOU REALLY NOT KNOW OR ARE YOU JUST AVOIDING THE QUESTION?"

Robin Dempsey flushed and typed rapidly: "I USED TO HAVE FRIENDS ONCE."

"WHEN WAS THAT?"

"BEFORE I WAS MARRIED."

"YOU DIDN'T TELL ME YOU WERE MARRIED."

"I'M DIVORCED."

"TELL ME ABOUT YOUR DIVORCE."

Robin Dempsey typed rapidly for fifteen minutes without stopping, until he became *aware* of Josh Collins, hovering at his shoulder. "Yes?" he said coldly, screening the VDU from Josh's view.

"You OK, Robin?"

"Yes, thank you."

"Interesting?"

"Very."

"Can I read the printout?"

"No," said Robin Dempsey, "you can't."

. . .

Felix Skinner skimmed through Persse's outline and thought it distinctly promising. "But before we give him a contract, we need a reader's report," he said. "Who shall we send it to?"

"I don't know, Mr. Skinner, I'm sure," said Gloria, his secretary, crossing her legs and patting her wavy, honey-coloured hair. She waited patiently with her pencil poised above her notepad. She had only been Felix Skinner's personal secretary for a couple of months, but already she was used to her boss's habit of thinking aloud by asking her questions that she hadn't a clue how to answer.

Felix Skinner bared his yellow fangs, noting, not for the first time, what a very shapely pair of legs Gloria possessed. "What about Philip Swallow?" he proposed.

"All right," said Gloria. "Is his address on file?"

"On second thoughts," said Felix, holding up a cautionary finger, "perhaps not. I have a feeling he was a teeny weeny bit jealous of my interest in young McGarrigle, the other day. He might be prejudiced."

Gloria yawned daintily, and picked a speck of fluff from the front of her jumper. Felix lit a fresh Gauloise from the stub smouldering between his fingers and admired the contours of the jumper. "I tell you what!" he exclaimed triumphantly, "Rudyard Parkinson."

"I know the name," said Gloria gamely. "Isn't he at Cambridge?"

"Oxford. My old tutor, actually. Shall we phone him first?"

"Well, perhaps you'd better, Mr. Skinner."

"Wise counsel," said Felix Skinner, reaching for the telephone. When he had dialled he leaned back in his swivel chair and treated Gloria to another canine grin. "You know, Gloria, I think it's time you called me Felix."

"Oh, Mr. Skinner . . ." Gloria blushed with pleasure. "Thank you."

Felix got through to Rudyard Parkinson quite quickly. (He was supervising a postgraduate, but the porter at All Saints had instructions to put all long-distance calls straight through to the Professor's room even if he was engaged. Long-distance calls usually meant books to review.) Parkinson declined, however, to take on the assessment of Persse McGarrigle's proposal. "Sorry, old man, got rather a lot on my plate at the moment," he said. "They're giving me an honorary degree in Vancouver next week. It didn't really sink in, when I accepted, that I'd actually have to *go* there to collect it."

"I say, what a bore," said Felix Skinner sympathetically. "Could you suggest anyone else? It's sort of about the modern reception of Shakespeare and Co. being influenced by T. S. Eliot."

"Reception? That rings a bell. Oh yes, I had a letter yesterday about a conference on something like that. A hun called von Turpitz. Know him?"

"Yes, we published a translation of his last book, actually."

"I should try him."

"Good idea," said Felix Skinner. "I should have thought of him myself."

He rang off and dictated a letter to Siegfried von Turpitz asking for his opinion of Persse McGarrigle's outline and offering him a fee of £25 or £50 worth of books from Lecky, Windrush and Bernstein's current list. "Enclose a copy of our catalogue with that, will you Gloria, and of course a Xerox of McGarrigle's typescript." He stubbed out his cigarette and glanced at his watch. "I feel quite fagged after all that effort. Am I having lunch with anybody today?"

"I don't think so," said Gloria, consulting his diary. "No."

"Then would you care to join me for a little Italian nosh and a glass or two of *vino* at a *trattoria* I know in Covent Garden?"

"That would be very nice . . . Felix," said Gloria complacently.

. . .

"Cheek!" Rudyard Parkinson exclaimed, putting down the telephone receiver. The postgraduate he was supervising, not sure whether he was being addressed or not, made no comment. "Why should he think I would want to read some totally unknown bog-Irishman's ramblings? Some of one's former students do rather presume on the relationship." The postgraduate, who had taken his first degree at Newcastle and whose initial awe of Parkinson was rapidly turning into disillusionment, tried to arrange his features in some appropriate expression of sympathy and concern. "Now, where were we?" said Rudyard Parkinson. "Yeats's death wish . . ."

"Keats's death wish."

"Ah, yes, I beg your pardon," Rudyard Parkinson stroked his muttonchop whiskers and gazed out of his window at the cupola on top of the Sheldonian and, further off, the spire of St. Mary's Church. "Tell me, if you were flying to Vancouver would you go by British Airways or Air Canada?"

"I'm not much of an expert on air travel," said the young man. "A charter flight to Majorca is about the limit of my experience."

"Majorca? Ah yes, I remember visiting Robert Graves there once. Did you happen to meet him?"

"No," said the postgraduate. "It was a package holiday. Robert Graves wasn't included."

Rudyard Parkinson glanced at the young man with momentary suspicion. Was it possible that callow Newcastle could be capable of irony—and at *his* expense? The youth's impassive countenance reassured him. Parkinson turned back to face the window. "I thought I'd be patriotic and go British Airways," he said. "I hope I've done the wise thing."

. . .

Oxford was still in vacation as far as the undergraduates were concerned, but at Rummidge it was the first day of the summer term, and a fine one. The sun blazed down from a cloudless sky on the Library steps and the grass quadrangle. Philip Swallow stood at the window of his office and surveyed the scene with a mixture of pleasure, envy and unfocused lust. A warm afternoon always brought out the girls in their summer dresses, like bulbs forcing their way through the turf and abruptly flowering in a blaze of colour. All over the lawns they were strewn, in attitudes of abandonment, straps down and skirts hitched up to tan their winter-pale limbs. The boys lounged in clusters, eyeing the girls, or pranced between them, stripped to their jeans, skimming frisbees with an ostentatious display of muscle and skill. Here and there pair-bonding had already occurred, and youthful couples sunned themselves clasped in each other's arms, or wrestled playfully in a thinly disguised mime of copulation. Books and ringbinders lay neglected on the greensward. The compulsion of spring had laid its irresistible spell upon these young bodies. The musk of their mutual attraction was almost visible, like pollen, in the atmosphere.

Right under Philip's window, a girl of great beauty, dressed simply but ravishingly in a sleeveless cotton shift, clasped the hands of a tall, athletic young man in tee-shirt and jeans. They held hands at arm's length and gazed raptly into each other's eyes, unable, it seemed, to tear themselves apart to attend whatever lecture or lab session called. Philip couldn't blame them. They made a handsome couple, glowing with health and the consciousness of their own good looks, trembling on the threshold of erotic bliss. "More happy love," Philip murmured behind his dusty windowpane.

> "More happy, happy love!
> For ever warm and still to be enjoyed,
> For ever panting and for ever young."

Unlike the lovers on the Grecian Urn, however, these ones did eventually kiss: a long and passionate embrace that lifted the girl on to the tips of her toes, and that Philip felt vicariously down to the very roots of his being.

He turned away from the window, disturbed and slightly ashamed. There was no point in getting all worked up by the Rummidge rites of spring. He had forsworn sexual interest in students ever since the unfortunate affair of Sandra Dix—Rummidge students, anyway. He had to rely on his trips abroad for amorous adventure. He didn't know quite what to expect of Turkey, straddling the line between Europe and Asia. Would the women be liberated and available, or locked up in purdah? The telephone rang.

"Digby Soames here, British Council. It's about your lectures in Turkey."

"Oh yes. Didn't I give you the titles? There's 'The Legacy of Hazlitt' and 'Jane Austen's Little Bit of Ivory'—that's a quotation from—"

"Yes, I know," Soames interrupted. "The trouble is, the Turks don't want it."

"Don't want it?" Philip felt slightly winded.

"I've just had a telex from Ankara. It says, 'No mileage in Jane Austen here, can Swallow lecture on Literature and History and Society and Philosophy and Psychology instead.'"

"That's a tall order," said Philip.

"Yes, it is, rather."

"I mean, there isn't much time for preparation."

"I could telex back 'No,' if you like."

"No, don't do that," said Philip. He was always cravenly eager to please his hosts on these trips abroad; eager to please the British Council, too, in case they stopped inviting him to go on them. "I expect I can cobble something together."

"Jolly good, I'll telex to that effect, then," said Soames. "Everything else all right?"

"I think so," said Philip. "I don't know quite what to expect of Turkey. I mean, is it a reasonably . . . modern country?"

"The Turks like to think it is. But they've had a hard time lately. A lot of terrorism, political murders and so on, from both left and right."

"Yes, I've read about it in the papers," said Philip.

"Rather plucky of you to go, really," said Soames, with a jovial laugh. "The country is on the rocks, no imports allowed, so there's no coffee, no sugar. No bumpaper, either, I understand, so I should take some with you. Petrol shortages won't affect you, but power cuts might."

"Doesn't sound too cheerful," said Philip.

"Oh, you'll find the Turks very hospitable. If you don't get shot by accident and you take your tea without sugar you should have a very enjoyable trip," said Soames with another merry chuckle, and rang off.

Philip Swallow resisted the temptation to return to the window and resume his covert observation of student mating behaviour. Instead, he ran his eyes along his bookshelves in search of inspiration for a lecture on Literature and History and Society and Philosophy and Psychology. What, as always, caught his attention was a row of mint copies of *Hazlitt and the Amateur Reader* in their pale blue wrappers, which he had bought from Lecky, Windrush and Bernstein at trade discount to give away to visitors, having despaired of commercial distribution of the book. A little spasm of resentment against his publishers prompted him to pick up the phone and make a call to Felix Skinner.

"Sorry," said the girl who answered, "Mr. Skinner's at a meeting."

"I suppose you mean lunch," said Philip sarcastically, glancing at his watch. It was a quarter to three.

"Well, yes."

"Can I speak to his secretary?"

"She's at lunch too. Can I take a message?"

Philip sighed. "Just tell Mr. Skinner that Professor Zapp never received the complimentary copy of my book, which I specifically requested should be sent to him on publication."

"OK, Professor Zapp."

"No, no, my name's Swallow, Philip Swallow."

"OK, Mr. Swallow. I'll tell Mr. Skinner as soon as he gets back."

. . .

Felix Skinner was in fact already back from lunch at the time of Philip Swallow's phone call. He was, to be precise, in a basement storeroom on the premises of Lecky, Windrush and Bernstein. He was also, to be even more precise, in Gloria, who was bent forwards over a pile of cardboard boxes, divested of her skirt and knickers, while Felix, with his pinstripe trousers round his ankles, and knees flexed in a simian crouch, copulated with her vigorously from behind. Their relationship had ripened rapidly since the morning, warmed by several gin and tonics and a large carafe of Valpolicella over lunch. In the taxi afterwards, Felix's exploring hands encountered no defence— quite the contrary, for Gloria was a warm-blooded young woman, whose husband, an engineer with the London Electricity Board, was working the night shift. Accordingly, when they got into the lift of the Lecky, Windrush and Bernstein building, Felix pressed the button to go down rather than up. The storeroom in the basement had served him on similar occasions before, as Gloria guessed but did not remark upon. It was hardly a romantic bower of bliss, the concrete floor being too cold and dirty to lie down on, but their present posture suited them both, since Gloria did not have to look at Felix's horrible teeth or inhale his breath, which now reeked of garlic as well as Gauloises, while he could admire, as he held her hips, the way her plump white cheeks bulged between the constriction of suspender belt and stockings.

"Stockings!" he groaned. "How did you know I adored stockings and suspenders?"

"I didn't knowwwww!" she gasped. "Oh! oh! oh!" Gloria felt the boxes shift and slide underneath her as Felix thrust harder and faster. "Look out!" she cried.

"What?" Felix, his eyes shut tight, was concentrating on his orgasm.

"I'm falling!"

"I'm coming!"

"OH!"

"AH!"

They came and fell together in a heap of crushed cardboard and spilled books. Dust filled the air. Felix rolled on to his back and sighed with satisfaction. "That was bloody marvellous, Gloria. The earth moved, as they say."

Gloria sneezed. "It wasn't the earth, it was all these parcels." She rubbed her knee. "I've laddered my stocking," she complained. "What are they going to think upstairs?"

She looked at Felix for some response, but his attention had been distracted by the books that had fallen out of the broken boxes. He was on all fours, his trousers still fettering his ankles, staring at the books with astonishment. They were identical copies, in pale blue jackets. Felix opened one and extracted a small printed slip.

"My God," he said. "No wonder poor old Swallow never got a single review."

. . .

The day before he left for Vancouver, Rudyard Parkinson received a letter from Felix Skinner and a copy of *Hazlitt and the Amateur Reader*. "*Dear Rudyard*," said the letter, "*We published this book last year, but it was largely ignored by the press—unjustly in my view. Accordingly, we are sending out a fresh batch of review copies this week. If you yourself could possibly arrange to review it somewhere, that would be marvellous. I know how busy you are, but I have a hunch that the book might take your fancy. Yours ever, Felix*."

Rudyard Parkinson curled his lip over this missive and glanced at the book with lukewarm interest. He had never heard of Philip Swallow, and a first book by a redbrick professor did not promise much. As he riffled the pages, however, his attention was caught by a quotation from an essay of Hazlitt's entitled "On Criticism": "*A critic does nothing nowadays who does not try to torture the most obvious expression into a thousand meanings . . . His object indeed is not to do justice to his author, whom he treats with very little ceremony, but to do himself homage, and to show his acquaintance with all the topics and resources of criticism*." Hmmm, thought Rudyard Parkinson, there might be some ammunition here to use against Morris Zapp. He slipped the book into his briefcase, along with his passport and his red, white and blue airticket.

The journey to Vancouver was not a comfortable one. To make a little profit on the trip, he was travelling economy class, for the host University was paying his expenses based on first-class fares. This proved to be a mistake. First he had an altercation at Heathrow with a pert girl at the check-in desk who refused to accept his overnight case as cabin baggage. Then, when he boarded the aircraft he found that he was most unluckily seated next to a mother with a small child on her lap, which cried and wriggled and spat half-masticated food all over Rudyard Parkinson for most of the long and wearisome flight. He began bitterly to repent of the vanity which had prompted him to accept this perfectly useless degree, flying ten thousand miles in three days just for the pleasure of dressing up in unfamiliar robes, hearing a short and probably inaccurate panegyric in his honour, and exchanging small talk afterwards with a crowd of boring Canadian nonentities at some ghastly reception or banquet where they would all no doubt drink iced rye whisky throughout the meal.

In the event, there was wine at the dinner following the degree ceremony and, Rudyard Parkinson had to admit, rather good wine—Pouilly Fuissé '74 with the fish, and a really remarkable Gevrey Chambertin '73 with the filet steak. The conversation at table was as banal as he had feared, but he did have an interesting exchange at the reception beforehand with another of the honorary graduands, Jacques Textel, the Swiss anthropologist and UNESCO bureaucrat, who genially toasted him with a dry martini.

"Congratulations," he said. "I know I'm only here because the University is hoping to squeeze some money out of UNESCO, but you're being honoured for your own work."

"Nonsense, your degree was thoroughly deserved," anyone else would have replied; but Rudyard Parkinson, being Rudyard Parkinson, merely smirked and fluffed out his whiskers.

"You've no idea how many honorary degrees I've collected since I became ADG," said Textel.

"ADG?"

"Assistant Director General."

"Do you find it interesting work?"

"As an anthropologist, yes. The Paris HQ is like a tribe. Has its own rituals, taboos, order of precedence . . . Fascinating. As an administrator, it drives me crazy." Textel deftly placed his empty glass on the tray of a passing waiter with one hand and took a full glass with the other. "Take this chair of literary criticism, for instance . . ."

"What's that?"

"You haven't heard about it? I'm surprised. Siegfried von Turpitz has—he rang me up at seven-thirty in the morning to ask me about it. I'd just dropped off to sleep, too, being jet-lagged after a flight from Tokyo . . ."

"What is this chair?" Rudyard Parkinson persisted.

Textel told him. "Interested?" he concluded.

"Oh, no," said Rudyard Parkinson, smiling and shaking his head. "I'm quite content."

"That's nice to hear," said Jacques Textel. "In my experience top academics are the least contented people in the world. They always think the grass is greener in the next field."

"I don't think the grass anywhere is greener than in the Fellows' Garden at All Saints," said Rudyard Parkinson smugly.

"I can believe that," said Jacques Textel. "Of course, whoever gets this UNESCO chair won't have to move anywhere."

"Won't he?"

"No, it's a purely conceptual chair. Apart from the salary, which is likely to be in the region of a hundred thousand dollars."

At that juncture a servant announced that dinner was served. Rudyard Parkinson was seated at some distance from Jacques Textel, and the latter was hustled away immediately after the meal to catch a plane to Peru, where he was due to open a conference on the preservation of Inca sites the following day. This separation was a cause of some concern to Rudyard Parkinson, who would have liked an opportunity to correct the impression he might have given that he was wholly lacking in personal interest in the UNESCO chair. The more he thought about it—and he thought about it for almost the entire duration of the flight back to London—the more attractive it seemed. He was so used to receiving invitations to apply for lavishly endowed chairs in North America that refusing them was by now a reflex action. They always tried to tempt him with the promise of teams of research assistants, for whom he would have no use at all (could research assistants write his reviews for him?) and generous travel grants that would allow him to fly to Europe as often as he wanted. ("But I already *am* in Europe," he would point out, if he took the trouble to reply at all.) This chair, however, was decidedly different. Perhaps he had dismissed it too hastily, even if UNESCO was an institution routinely sneered at in Oxford Common Rooms. Nobody was going to sneer at one hundred thousand dollars a year, tax-free, to be picked up without the trouble of moving one's books. The problem was, how to intimate these second thoughts without crawling too obviously to Textel. No doubt the post would be advertised in due course, but Rudyard Parkinson was experienced enough in such matters to know that the people who were appointed to top academic posts never actually applied for them before they were approached. That, of course, was what Textel had been doing—it was clear as daylight in retrospect—and he had muffed the opportunity. Rudyard Parkinson clenched his grip on the armrest of his seat with chagrin. Well, a discreet note to Textel could hint at a change of heart. But something more was needed, something like a campaign, a broadside, a manifesto—but subtle, indirect. What could be done?

Opening his briefcase to find a notepad on which to draft a letter to Textel, Rudyard Parkinson's eye fell upon the book by Philip Swallow. He took it out, and began to browse. Soon he began to read with close attention. A plan was forming itself in his mind. A long middle for the *TLS*. The English School of Criticism. How gratifying to encounter, in the dreary desert of contemporary criticism, an exponent of that noble tradition of humane learning, of robust common sense and simple enjoyment of great books . . . Professor Swallow's timely and instructive study . . . In contrast, the jargon-ridden lucubrations of Professor Zapp, in which the perverse paradoxes of fashionable Continental savants are, if possible, rendered even more pretentious and sterile . . . The time has come for those who believe in literature as the expression of universal and timeless human values to stand up and be counted . . . Professor Swallow has sounded a clarion call to action. Who will respond?

Something like that should do the trick, Rudyard Parkinson mused, gazing out of the window at the sun rising or setting somewhere or other over a horizon of corrugated cloud. Vancouver, of which he had in any case seen little except rainswept roads between the airport and the University, had already faded from his memory.

. . .

Philip Swallow set off for his Turkish lecture tour in a more than usually flustered state. He had been working up to the last minute on his lecture about Literature and History, Society, Philosophy, and Psychology, to the neglect of more mundane preparations, such as packing his suitcase. Hilary was sullen and uncooperative as, late on the eve of his departure, he hunted for clean underwear and socks. "You should have thought of this earlier," she said "You know I do my big wash tomorrow." "You knew I was leaving tomorrow," he said bitterly, "you might have deduced that I'd need some clean clothes to take with me." "Why should I give any thought to your needs? Do you give any thought to mine?" "What needs?" said Philip. "You can't imagine that I would have any, can you?" said Hilary. "I don't want to have a big argument," said Philip wearily. "I'd just like some clean socks and pants and vests. If that isn't too much to ask."

He was standing on the threshold of the drawing-room, holding a tangled bundle of soiled underwear which he had just excavated from the laundry basket. Hilary put down her novel with a thump, and snatched the bundle from his arms. She stomped out to the kitchen, leaving a trail of odd socks in her wake. "They'll have to be dried in the tumble-drier," she threw over her shoulder.

Philip went to his study to gather together the books and papers he would need. As usual, he wasted a great deal of time wondering which books to take on his journey. He had a neurotic fear of finding himself stranded in some foreign hotel or railway station with nothing to read, and in consequence always travelled with far too many books, most of which he brought home unread. Tonight, unable to decide between two late Trollope novels, he packed both, along with some poems by Seamus Heaney, a new biography of Keats and a translation of the *Divine Comedy* which he had been carrying around with him on almost every trip for the last thirty years without ever having made much progress in it. By the time he had completed this task, Hilary had retired to bed. He lay beside her, wakeful and restless, listening to the noise of the tumble-drier churning in the kitchen, like the engine of a ship. His mind anxiously reviewed a checklist of the things he should have packed: passport, money, tickets, traveller's cheques, lecture notes, sunglasses, Turkish phrasebook. They were all in his briefcase, but he had a feeling something was missing. He was catching the same early morning plane to Heathrow as Morris Zapp had taken, and wouldn't have much time to spare in the morning.

Philip seldom slept well before leaving on one of his trips abroad, but to-night he was particularly wakeful. Usually he and Hilary would make love on such occasions. There was an unspoken agreement between them to sink their differences in a valedictory embrace which, however perfunctory, at least had the effect of relaxing them sufficiently to send them both off to sleep for a few hours. But when Philip tried an exploratory caress or two on Hilary's humped form, she shook off his hand with a sleepy grunt of irritation. Philip tossed and turned, filled with resentment and self-pity. He postulated his death in an air crash on the way to Turkey, and imagined with grim satisfaction Hilary's guilt and self-reproach on hearing the news. The only drawback to this scenario was that it entailed his own extinction, a high price to pay to punish her for not washing his socks in good time. He essayed, instead, a compensatory amorous adventure in Turkey, but found this difficult, having no idea what Turkey, or Turkish women, looked like. Eventually he settled for a chance meeting with Angelica Pabst, who, since nobody seemed to know where she had come from, or departed to, might as well be encountered in Turkey as anywhere else. One of the many disappointments of the Rummidge conference had been his failure to follow up the friendly relations he had established with that very attractive young woman on the first evening. With the help of a fantasy in which he rescued Angelica from the clutches of political terrorists on a Turkish railway train, and was rewarded with rapturous sexual intercourse, Angelica being conveniently clad in nothing more than a diaphanous nightie at the time of this crisis, Philip dozed off, though he woke at frequent intervals in the course of the night, and felt more fatigued than rested when his alarm clock finally roused him at 5:30.

Five-thirty isn't really early enough, considering that the taxi has been ordered for six, as Philip quickly realizes, washing, dressing, and shaving himself with ill-coordinated limbs, groping in the drawers and wardrobes of the darkened bedroom for his travelling clothes, fumbling with the locks on his suitcase. Hilary makes no move to get up and assist him, or to make him a cup of coffee. He cannot really blame her, in view of the hour, but he does, nevertheless, blame her. At three minutes to six he is, in a manner of speaking, ready—unevenly shaven, with hair uncombed and shoes unpolished, but ready. Then he remembers the item missing from his mental checklist—lavatory paper. He searches in the kitchen cupboard for a fresh roll without success and with increasing panic, throwing aside packets of detergent, soap powder, paper napkins, washing-up liquid, Brillo pads, in the urgency of his quest. He bounds up the stairs, bursts into the bedroom, hits the light switch, and peremptorily questions Hilary's shrouded back.

"Where's the toilet paper?"

Hilary raises and twists her head, stupid with sleep. "Eh?"

"Toilet paper. I need to take some with me."

"We're out of it."

"*What?*"

"I was going to get some today."

Philip throws his arms into the air. "Marvellous! Bloody marvellous!"

"You could buy some yourself."

"At six o'clock in the morning?"

"The airport might—"

"And the airport might not. Or I might not have time."

"You can take what's left in the downstairs loo, if you like."

"Thanks very much," says Philip sarcastically. He thumps down the stairs, two steps at a time. There is half a roll of pink toilet tissue in the downstairs cloakroom, suspended from a cylindrical roller attached by a spring-loaded axle to a ceramic holder screwed to the wall. Philip fumbles with this apparatus, seeking to remove the toilet roll from the roller. The front doorbell shrills. Philip starts, the toilet roll falls off the roller and unwinds itself across the floor of the cloakroom with amazing rapidity. Philip swears, tries to roll the paper up again, abandons the attempt, opens the front door to the taxi-driver, indicates his suitcase, runs to his study, stuffs a wad of A4 Bank typing paper into his briefcase, runs back to the hall, shouts an angry, "Goodbye, then," up the stairs, snatches his raincoat from its hook and leaves the house, slamming the front door behind him.

"All right, sir?" says the taxi-driver, as Philip collapses in the back seat.

Philip nods. The driver lets in the clutch and engages bottom gear. The taxi begins to move—then stops abruptly, obedient to a cry from the direction of the house. For here comes Hilary, trotting down the garden path, in her nightie, just an old coat thrown over her shoulders, scarcely decent, clasping to her bosom an untidy bundle of socks and underclothing. Philip lowers the window of the taxi.

"You forgot to take them out of the drier," Hilary says breathlessly, bundling socks, singlets and Y-fronts through the window and on to his lap. The taxi-driver looks on with amusement.

"Thanks," says Philip grudgingly, as he clutches the clothes.

Hilary is grinning at him. "Goodbye, then. Have a safe journey." She bends forward and offers her face at the window for a kiss, lips pursed and eyes closed. Philip can hardly refuse to respond, and leans forward to administer a perfunctory peck.

But then an extraordinary thing happens. Hilary's old coat falls open, the neckline of her nightgown gapes, and Philip glimpses the curve of her right breast. It is an object he knows well. He made his first tactile acquaintance with it twenty-five years ago, tentatively fondling it, through the impeding upholstery of a Marks and Spencer's fisherman's knit jumper and a stoutly constructed Maidenform brassière, as he kissed its young postgraduate owner goodnight on the porch of her digs one night after a Film Society showing of *Battleship Potemkin*. He first set entranced eyes upon its naked flesh on his wedding night. Since then he must have seen and touched it (and its twin) several thousand times—stroked it and kneaded it and licked it and nuzzled it, watched it suckling his children and sucked its nipple himself on occasion—during which time it lost its pristine firmness and satin texture, grew fuller and heavier and less elastic, and became as familiar to him as an old cushion, comfortable but unremarkable. But such is the mystery of desire— the fickleness and unpredictability of its springs and motions—that this unexpected glimpse of the breast, swinging free inside the loose folds of the nightgown, in a shadowy gap from which rises to his nostrils a pleasant smell of warm bed and body, makes Philip suddenly faint with the longing to touch, suck, lick, nuzzle, etc. it again. He does not want to go to Turkey. He does not want to go anywhere at this moment, except back to bed with Hilary. But of course, he cannot. Is it only because he cannot that he wants to so much? All he can do is to press his lips on Hilary's more enthusiastically than he had intended—or than she expected, for she looks at him with a quizzical, affectionate, even tender regard as the taxi, at last, inexorably moves away. Philip looks back through the rear window. Hilary stoops to pluck from the gutter a stray sock, and waves it forlornly after him, like a makeshift favour.

. . .

Not many hours after Philip Swallow flew out of Heathrow on a Turkish Airlines DC10 bound for Ankara, Persse McGarrigle flew in on an Aer Lingus Boeing 737 from Shannon, for it was the day of the Royal Academy of Literature's prizegiving party.

The *Annabel Lee* was an old pleasure steamer that had once plied up and down the Thames estuary. Now repainted and refurbished, her paddles stilled and her smokestack unsullied, she was moored beside the Thames at Charing Cross Embankment, accommodating a restaurant, bars and reception rooms that could be hired for functions like this one. The London literati cooed their delight at the novelty of the venue as they alighted from their taxis or debouched from the Tube station and strolled along the Embankment. It was a fine May evening, with the river almost at flood, and a brisk breeze flapping the flags and pennants on the *Annabel Lee's* rigging. When they got on board, some were not so sure it was a good idea. There was a distinct sensation of movement under one's feet, and whenever a biggish craft passed on the river, its wash heaved the *Annabel Lee* up and down sharply enough to make the guests stagger on the plush red carpet of the main saloon. Soon, however, it was difficult to distinguish between the effect of the river and the effect of the booze. Persse had never been to a literary party before, but the main object seemed to be to drink as much as possible as fast as possible, while talking at the top of your voice and at the same time looking over the shoulder of the person you were talking to and smiling and waving at other people who were also drinking and talking and smiling and waving. As for Persse, he just drank, since he didn't know a soul. He stood on the fringe of the party, feeling throttled in an uncustomary collar and tie, shifting his weight from one foot to another, until it was time to push his way back to the bar for another drink. There were waiters circulating with red and white wine, but Persse preferred Guinness.

"Hallo, is that Guinness you're drinking?" said a voice at his shoulder. "Where did you get it?"

Persse turned to find a large, fleshy, pockmarked face peering covetously at his drink through horn-rimmed glasses.

"I just asked for it at the bar," said Persse.

"This wine is like horsepiss," said the man, emptying his glass into a potted plant. He disappeared into the crowd, and came back a few moments later, dragging a case of Guinness. "I don't usually like bottled beer," he said. "But Guinness, in my experience, is better bottled than draught in England. Different matter in Dublin."

"I'm much of your opinion," said Persse, as the man topped up his glass. "Would it be something to do with the water, I wonder."

They had a learned technical conversation about the brewing of stout ale, illustrated by frequent sampling, for some time before they got round to introducing themselves. "Ronald Frobisher!" Persse exclaimed. "I've read some of your books. Are you getting a prize this evening?"

"No, I'm presenting one—Most Promising First Novel. When I started writing fiction there didn't seem to be more than a couple of literary prizes, and they were only worth about a hundred quid each. Nowadays there are so many that it's difficult to avoid winning one if you manage to publish anything at all. Sorry, didn't mean to cast aspersions on your—"

"That's all right," said Persse. "I understand your feelings. As a matter of fact I haven't even published my poems yet."

"That's what I mean, see?" said Frobisher, opening another bottle of Guinness. He had an ingenious knack of using the top of one bottle to lever off the cap from another. "I mean, I don't begrudge you your money—good luck to you—but the situation is getting daft. There are people here tonight who make a *living* out of prizes, bursaries and what have you. I can see the day coming when there'll be a separate prize for every book that's published. Best First Novel about a graduate housewife living in Camden Town with two young children and a cat and an unfaithful husband who works in advertising. Best travel book by a man under twenty-nine who has been round the world using only scheduled bus services and one pair of jeans. Best—"

As Frobisher was warming to his theme, a young woman came up and told him that he would soon be making the presentation of the Most Promising First Novel prize. He put down his glass. "Look after the Guinness," he exhorted Persse, as he moved off.

Persse resumed drinking and shifting his weight from one foot to the other. But soon he saw a face that he recognized, and waved to it in the manner he had observed other guests using. Felix Skinner came over, trailing a buxom young woman with honey-coloured hair, and another couple. "Hallo, old man, what brings you here?" he said.

"I've come to collect a prize for my poetry."

"I say, have you really?" Skinner exposed his fangs in a yellow smile. "Many congratulations. Sorry about the Shakespeare–Eliot book, by the way. This is my secretary, Gloria." He pushed forward the buxom young woman who shook Persse's hand listlessly. Her face was pale. "When are we going, Felix?" she said. "I'm feeling seasick." "We can't leave yet, my dear, the prizes haven't been given out," said Felix, and turned to introduce the other couple. "Professor and Mrs. Ringbaum, from Illinois. Howard is one of our authors."

Howard Ringbaum nodded dourly at Persse. His wife smiled and hiccupped. "Thelma, cut it out," he said, apparently without moving his lips. "I can't help it," she said, winking at Persse. "You could try drinking less," said Ringbaum.

At the other end of the room someone banged on the table and began making a speech. "Frightful man, Ringbaum," Skinner whispered into Persse's ear. "We published one of his books about four years ago, I say published, we took the sheets for five hundred copies, had to remainder most of them, and on the strength of that he conned me into giving him and wife lunch today and I haven't been able to get rid of them since. *He* bores the pants off you and *she* seems to be some kind of nymphomaniac—kept playing footsie with me in the restaurant. Damned embarrassing with Gloria there, I can tell you."

At precisely that moment, Persse became aware of the presence of another's leg against his own. He turned to find Mrs. Ringbaum standing very close to him. "Are you really a poet?" she said breathily. The breath was heavily scented with gin.

"Yes, I am," said Persse.

"Would you write a poem to me," said Mrs. Ringbaum, "if I made it worth your while?"

"One can't produce poems to order, I'm afraid," he said. He took a step backwards, but Mrs. Ringbaum followed, glued to him like a ballroom-dancing partner.

"I don't mean money," she said.

"Thelma," said Howard Ringbaum querulously from behind her back, "am I allergic to anchovies?" He was holding up a small sandwich with a bite-shaped hole in it. Persse took advantage of this distraction to put Skinner between himself and Mrs. Ringbaum. "What was that you said about my book?" he asked Skinner.

"Oh, haven't you had my letter? No? That's Gloria, she's been getting a little bit slack, lately. Well, I'm afraid we had a very negative report on your proposal. Ah, I see Rudyard Parkinson is making the biography award."

A man with muttonchop whiskers and a plump, self-pleased countenance had mounted the platform and was addressing the assembled guests. It was a speech in praise of somebody's book, though the smirk hovering round his lips seemed somehow to twist and devalue the sentiments they uttered, and to solicit knowing titters from his audience.

"Rudyard Parkinson . . . You've read his books, haven't you, Howard?" said Thelma Ringbaum.

"Absolute crap," said Howard Ringbaum.

Persse opened himself another bottle of Guinness, using Ronald Frobisher's technique. "So you don't want to publish my book after all?" he said to Felix Skinner.

"'Fraid not, old man."

"What did your reader say about it, then?"

"Well, that it wouldn't do. Wasn't on. Didn't stand up. In a word."

"Who is he?"

"I'm afraid I can't tell you that," said Felix Skinner. "It's confidential."

There was a burst of applause, and flashlights blinked, as the biographer went up to receive his prize from Rudyard Parkinson. "He isn't here tonight, by any chance?" said Persse wistfully. "Because if he is, I'd like to fight him."

Felix Skinner laughed uncertainly. "No, no, he's a long way from London. But a very eminent authority, I assure you. Ah, Rudyard, how very good to see you. Marvellous speech!"

Rudyard Parkinson, who had yielded the platform to Ronald Frobisher, smirked and brushed his whiskers upwards with the back of his hand. "Oh, hallo Skinner. Yes, I thought it went down pretty well."

Felix Skinner performed introductions.

"This is a real privilege, Professor Parkinson," said Howard Ringbaum, holding on to Parkinson's hand and gazing raptly into his eyes. "I'm a great admirer of your work."

"Kind of you," Parkinson murmured.

"Howard! Howard, that's Ronald Frobisher," cried Thelma Ringbaum excitedly, pointing to the platform. "You remember, I was reading one of his books on the plane on the way over."

"I recommend your book on James Thomson to all my students," said Howard Ringbaum to Rudyard Parkinson, ignoring his wife. "I've written a few articles on the subject myself, and it would be a real pleasure to—"

"Ah yes, poor Frobisher," said Parkinson, who seemed to prefer this topic of conversation. "He was up at Oxford when I was a young Fellow, you know. I'm afraid he's burned himself out. Hasn't published a new novel for years."

"They're doing one of his books on the telly," said Gloria from somewhere behind and beneath them. All turned and looked at her with surprise. She was stretched out on a bench seat that followed the curve of the ship's side, with her shoes off and her eyes closed.

"Yes," said Parkinson, with a curl of his lip, "I daresay they are. I don't possess a television receiver myself."

A woman in the crowd in front of them turned and frowned, and someone else hissed, "Ssh!" Ronald Frobisher was giving a speech in a low undertone, his hands thrust deep into the pockets of his corduroy jacket, his spectacles owlishly opaque under the lights.

"I can't imagine that he has much to say that is worth straining one's ears for," murmured Parkinson. "As a matter of fact he looks distinctly squiffy to me."

"By the way," said Felix Skinner to him. "Did you, er, by any chance, get a book by, er, Philip Swallow, which I, er . . ."

"Yes, I did. Not at all bad. I've arranged to do it for the *TLS*, along with another book. Should be in tomorrow's issue. I think you'll be pleased."

"Oh, jolly good! I'm tremendously grateful."

"I think it has important implications," said Parkinson solemnly. "More than the author himself is aware of."

There was another burst of applause as Ronald Frobisher handed an envelope to a smiling young woman in a fringe and homespun smock. The chairman who had opened the proceedings returned to the platform. "Now a number of awards and bursaries for young poets," he announced. "That must be you," said Thelma Ringbaum to Persse. "Hurry up." Persse began to push his way towards the front.

"First, the Maud Fitzsimmons Bequest for the Encouragement of Anglo-Irish poetry," said the chairman. "Is Persse McGarrigle . . . ?"

"Here!" cried Persse from the floor. "Hold on, I'm coming." A gust of laughter greeted his appearance on the platform, which Persse belatedly attributed to the fact that he was still holding a bottle of Guinness in his hand.

"Congratulations," said the chairman, handing him a cheque. "I see you have brought your inspiration with you."

"My inspiration," said Persse emotionally, "is a girl called Angelica."

"And very nice too," said the chairman, giving him a gentle push towards the steps. "And the next award . . ."

When Persse got back to his point of origin, he found Ronald Frobisher in angry confrontation with Rudyard Parkinson. "What would you know about literary creation anyway, Parkinson?" Frobisher was demanding. "You're just a ponce for the Sunday papers. Once a ponce, always a ponce. I remember you poncing about the quad at All Saints—"

"Now, now, that's enough," said Felix Skinner, trying to interpose himself between the two men.

"Are they going to fight?" said Thelma Ringbaum excitedly.

"Shut up, Thelma," said Howard Ringbaum.

"Really Frobisher," said Parkinson, "this sort of behaviour is bad enough in one of your novels. In real life it's quite intolerable." He spoke disdainfully, but backed away at the same time. "Anyway, I wasn't the only reviewer who didn't care for the last novel you wrote, what was it, ten years ago?"

"Eight. But you were the only one who made that crack about my old Dad, Parkinson. I've never forgiven you for that." Holding an empty Guinness bottle by the neck, Frobisher made a lunge in Parkinson's direction. Someone screamed. Felix Skinner pinned Frobisher's arms to his sides, and Howard Ringbaum grabbed the back of his collar and pulled, throttling the novelist. Thinking that this was an unfair as well as excessive use of force, Persse laid a restraining hand upon Ringbaum. Thelma threw herself into the scuffle and kicked her husband enthusiastically on the ankle. He released Frobisher with a howl of pain, and turned indignantly upon Persse. The upshot of all this was that a few minutes later, Persse and Frobisher found themselves alone together on the Embankment, having been requested in pressing terms by the management of the *Annabel Lee* to leave the reception forthwith.

"Silly buggers," said Frobisher, straightening his tie. "Did they really think I was going to bottle that ponce? I just wanted to give him a fright."

"I think you succeeded," said Persse.

"Well, I'll just make sure," said Frobisher, "I'll scare the shit out of the lot of them." He disappeared down some dank steps to a lower level of the Embankment.

It was dark now, and Persse could not see what his companion was doing. Supporting his chin on his elbows, and his elbows on the Embankment wall, he gazed across the river at the floodlit concrete slabs of the Festival Hall and the National Theatre. Empty bottles, sandwich papers, handkerchiefs, cardboard boxes, cigarette ends and other testimony of the summer night drifted downstream, for the tide had turned. The lights of the *Annabel Lee* glanced and darted in golden reflections on the dark water. At her stern a female figure was leaning over the rail, being sick. Frobisher reappeared at Persse's side, breathing heavily and wiping his hands on a rag.

. . .

Inside the saloon there was a buzz of excitement over the incident. "It's like the fifties all over again," said someone. "There was always a chance of some writer taking a poke at a critic in those days. The pub next to the Royal Court was a good place to watch."

Rudyard Parkinson was not disposed to take the matter so lightly. "I'll see that Frobisher is expelled from the Academy for this outrage," he said, trembling a little. "If not, I shall resign myself."

"Quite right," said Felix Skinner. "Did anyone see where Gloria got to?"

"That Irish punk nearly broke my ankle," said Howard Ringbaum. "I'm going to sue somebody for this."

"Howard," said Thelma, "I think the boat's moving."

"Shut up, Thelma."

. . .

Very slowly the *Annabel Lee* began to drift away from the Embankment. The rope attaching the ship to the gangplank creaked with the strain, then snapped. Space appeared between the end of the gangplank and the side of the ship.

"I don't think you should have done that," said Persse.

"When I graduated at Oxford," said Ronald Frobisher, in a tone of fireside reminiscence, "my Mam and Dad came up for the ceremony. Parkinson was a Research Fellow at the same college. He'd tutored me for a term—a pompous bastard I thought he was even then, though admittedly he'd read a lot. Anyway, we bumped into him in the quad that day, so I introduced him to Mam and Dad. My Dad was a skilled worker, sand-moulder in a foundry, he had a wonderful touch, the management grovelled to him whenever they had a tricky job to be done. Of course, Parkinson knew fuck-all about that, and cared less. To him Dad was just a stupid prole in a cloth cap and best suit, to be patronized like mad. He twittered away and Dad got more and more nervous and kept coughing to hide his nervousness. Now it so happened that he'd not long ago had all his teeth out, common enough in a middle-aged working man, have 'em all out and be done with 'em, was the form of preventive dentistry favoured in our neighbourhood, and his false set didn't fit too well. To cut a long story short, he coughed the top set right out of his mouth. Caught them, too, and shoved them in his pocket. It was funny really, but Parkinson looked as if he was going to faint. Anyway, many years later I wrote a novel about a character based on my Dad—he was dead by then—and Parkinson reviewed it for one of the Sundays. He said, I remember the exact words, "*It's difficult to share the author's sentimental regard for the main character. That your dentures fit badly doesn't automatically guarantee that you are the salt of the earth.*" Now there was nothing about false teeth in the book. That was a completely private piece of spite. I've never forgiven Parkinson for that."

The ship had now moved some distance downstream from its original position. Gloria lifted her white face from the rail and stared across the water as if dimly recognizing them. Frobisher waved to her and, in a puzzled, hesitant fashion, she waved back.

"I still don't think you should have done it," said Persse. "They might hit a bridge."

"It's all right," said Frobisher, "I left one long rope tied that should hold her. I know a thing or two about boats. I used to work on narrowboats in my vacations when I was a student. The Staffordshire and Worcestershire Canal. Those were the days."

Faint cries and shrieks of alarm were audible from the ship. A door burst open and light flooded onto the deck. A man shouted across the water.

"I think we should move on," said Persse.

"Good idea," said Frobisher. "I'll buy you a drink. It's only"—he checked his watch—"five to nine." Then he clapped a hand to his brow. "Christ, I'm supposed to be doing a radio interview at nine!" He stepped into the road and waved down a passing taxi. "Bush House," he told the driver, and bundled Persse into the vehicle. They rolled together from one side of the back seat to the other as the cab made a rapid U-turn.

"Who is interviewing you?" Persse asked.

"Somebody in Australia."

"*In* Australia?"

"They can do amazing things these days, with satellites. Australian telly is going to show the serial of *Any Road Further* soon, so they want to do a tie-in radio interview for some arts programme."

"I don't think I've read *Any Road Further*," said Persse.

"That's not surprising. It only exists as a telly serial. What happens to Aaron Stonehouse when he becomes rich and famous and fed up, like me." He looked at his watch again. "The Aussies have booked some studio time at the BBC. They won't be pleased if I'm late."

Fortunately for Ronald Frobisher, there had been some delay in getting the line open from Australia, and he was safely ensconced in the studio by the time the voice of the producer in Sydney came through, surprisingly loud and clear. Persse sat in the control room with the sound engineer, listening and watching the proceedings with some fascination. The engineer explained the set-up to him. The producer was in Sydney, the interviewer in Cooktown, Queensland. The questions went from Cooktown to Sydney by wire, and from Sydney to London by the Indian Ocean and European satellites, and Ronald Frobisher's replies went back to Australia via the Atlantic and Pacific Ocean satellites. A short question-and-answer exchange girdled the world in about ten seconds.

Watching the head-phoned Ronald Frobisher through the big glass pane that sealed off the studio from the control room, Persse admired the ease with which the writer handled this unusual discourse situation, chatting to his interlocutor, a rather dim-sounding man called Rodney Wainwright, as if he were on the other side of the table instead of on the other side of the world. Wainwright asked him if Aaron Stonehouse was still an Angry Young Man. "Still angry, not so young," said Ronald. Was the novel dying? "Like all of us, it has been dying since the day it was born." When did he do most of his writing? "In the ten minutes after my first morning coffee break."

When the interview was over, Persse went out of the control room to meet him. "Well done," he said.

"Did it seem all right?" Frobisher looked pleased with himself.

The sound engineer called them back into the control room. "This is rather amusing," he said. "Listen."

The voices of Rodney Wainwright and his producer in Sydney, a man called Greg, were still coming from the speakers. They seemed to be old buddies.

"When are you coming to Sydney, then, Rod?"

"I don't know, Greg. I'm pretty tied up here. Got a conference paper to write."

"Time we had some beers together, sport, and checked out the talent on Bondi beach."

"Well, to tell you the truth, Greg, the talent is not so bad up here in Queensland."

"I bet the girls don't go topless."

There was a pause. "Well, only by private arrangement."

Greg chortled. "You should see Bondi these days, on a fine Sunday. It'd make your eyes pop out of your head."

The sound engineer smiled at Persse and Ronald. "Sydney have forgotten to close down the line," he said. "They don't realize that we can still hear them."

"Can they hear us?" said Persse.

"No, not unless I switch this mike on."

"You mean we're eavesdropping from twelve thousand miles away?" said Persse. "That's a queer thought."

"Ssh!" hissed Ronald Frobisher, holding up a finger. The conversation in Australia had turned to another topic—himself.

"I didn't like his last one," Rodney Wainwright was saying. "And that was, what, eight years ago?"

"More than eight," Greg agreed. "You think he's washed up?"

"I'm sure he is," said Rodney Wainwright. "He had absolutely nothing to say about postmodernism. He didn't seem to even understand the question."

Ronald Frobisher bent to switch on the sound engineer's mike, "You can stick your question about postmodernism up your arse, Wainwright," he said.

There was a stunned silence from the antipodes. Then, "Who said that?" Rodney Wainwright quavered.

"Jesus," said Greg.

"Jesus?"

"I mean, Jesus, the fucking line is still open," said Greg.

. . .

Two thousand miles away, in Turkey, it has been dark for some hours. The little row of terraced houses outside Ankara looks to Akbil Borak, as he bumps towards it in his Deux Chevaux along the service road from the main highway, rather like a ship, with lights shining from its cabin windows, moored on the edge of the dark immensity that is the central Anatolian plain. He stops the car, kills the engine, and climbs stiffly out. It has been a long day.

In the kitchen Oya has left him a little snack and black tea in a thermos. Having eaten well that evening, at the University's expense, he leaves the snack, but drinks the tea. Then he goes upstairs, treading softly on the narrow stairs so as not to wake Ahmed. "Is that you, Akbil?" Oya sleepily enquires from the bedroom. Akbil murmurs a reassuring reply, and goes into Ahmed's room, to gaze fondly at his sleeping son, and tuck a dangling arm under the blankets. Then he goes to the bathroom. Then he gets into bed and makes love to Oya.

Akbil Borak has sex with his wife almost every night, ordinarily (that is, when he is not having to sit up over the collected works of William Hazlitt). In Turkey, this past winter, there have been few other pleasures to indulge in. It is also, he believes, good for the health. Tonight, since he is tired, their congress is brief and straightforward. Akbil soon rolls off Oya with a sigh of satisfaction, and pulls the quilt up over his shoulders.

"Don't go to sleep, Akbil," Oya complains. "I want to hear about your day. Did Professor Swallow arrive safely?"

"Yes, the plane was only a little late. I went with Mr. Custer in the British Council car to meet him."

"What is he like?"

"Tall, thin, stooping. He has a fine silver beard."

"Is he a nice man?"

"I think so. A little nervous. Eccentric, you might say. He had a vest hanging out of his raincoat pocket."

"A vest?"

"A white undervest. Perhaps he took it off in the plane because he was too hot, I don't know. He fell down outside the airport."

"Oh dear! Had he been drinking on the airplane?"

"No, he put his foot in a pothole. You know how bad the roads are since the winter. This hole must have been half a metre deep, right outside the terminal building. I felt ashamed. We really have no idea how to make roads in this country."

"Is Professor Swallow married?"

"Yes, he has three children. But he did not seem interested in talking about them," said Akbil sleepily.

Oya pinched him. "Then what happened? After he fell down?"

"We picked him up, Mr. Custer and I, and dusted him down and drove him into Ankara. He was rather nervous on the drive, he kept ducking down behind the back of the driver's seat. You know that the highway to the airport is only paved on one side for certain stretches, so traffic moving in both directions uses the same side of the road. I suppose it is a bit alarming if you are not used to it."

"Then what happened?"

"Then we went to Anitkabir to lay a wreath on Ataturk's tomb."

"Whatever for?"

"Mr. Custer thought it would be a nice gesture. And a funny thing happened. I will tell you." Akbil suddenly shed his drowsiness at the memory, and propped himself up on one elbow to tell Oya the story. "You know it is quite an awe-inspiring experience, the first time you go to Anitkabir. To walk down that long, long concourse, with the Hittite lions and the other statues, and the soldiers standing guard on the parapets, so still and silent they look like statues themselves, but all armed. Perhaps I should not have told Professor Swallow that it was a capital offence to show disrespect to the memory of Ataturk."

"Well, so it is."

"I said it as a kind of joke. However he seemed to be very worried by the information. He kept saying, 'Is it all right if I blow my nose?' and 'Will the soldiers be suspicious of my limp?'"

"Does he have a limp?"

"Since he fell down at the airport he has a slight limp, yes. Anyway, Mr. Custer told him, 'Don't worry, just do exactly as I do.' So we march down the concourse, Mr. Custer in front carrying the wreath, and Professor Swallow and I following in step, under the eyes of the soldiers. We swung left into the Great Meeting Place, very smartly, just like soldiers ourselves, and approached the Hall of Honour. And then Mr. Custer had the misfortune to trip over a paving stone that was sticking up and, being impeded by the wreath, fell on to his hands and knees. Before I could stop him, Professor Swallow flung himself to the ground and lay prostrate like a Muslim at prayer."

Oya gasped and giggled. "And what happened next?"

"We picked him up and dusted him down again. Then we laid the wreath and visited the museum. Then we went back to the British Council office to discuss Professor Swallow's programme. He must be a man of immense learning."

"Why do you say that?"

"Well, you know that he has come here to lecture on Hazlitt because it was the centenary last year. The other lecture he offered was on Jane Austen, and only our fourth-year students have read her books. So we asked the British Council if he could possibly offer a lecture on some broader topic, such as Literature and History, or Literature and Society, or Literature and Philosophy . . ." Akbil Borak yawned and closed his eyes. He seemed to have lost the thread of his story.

"Well?" said Oya, poking him impatiently in the ribs with her elbow.

"Well, apparently the message was somewhat garbled in the telex transmission. It said, please would he give a lecture on Literature *and* History *and* Society *and* Philosophy *and* Psychology. And, do you know, he agreed. He has prepared a lecture on Literature and Everything. We had a good laugh about it."

"Professor Swallow laughed?"

"Well, Mr. Custer laughed the most," Akbil conceded.

"Poor Professor Swallow," Oya sighed. "I do not think he had a very nice day."

"In the evening it was better," said Akbil. "I took him to a kebab restaurant and we had a good meal and some raki. We talked about Hull."

"He knows Hull?"

"Strangely, he has never been there," said Akbil. "So I was able to tell him all about it."

He turned onto his side, with his back to Oya, and pulled the quilt over his shoulders. Accepting that he would not talk any more, Oya settled herself to sleep. She stretched out a hand to switch off the bedside lamp, but, an instant before her fingers reached the switch, the light went out of its own accord.

"Another power cut," she remarked to her husband. But he was already breathing deeply in sleep.

. . .

"The trouble is," said Ronald Frobisher, "that twat Wainwright and that ponce Parkinson are right about one thing. I've dried up. Been blocked on a novel for six years now. Haven't published one for eight." He gazed mournfully into his tankard of real ale. Persse was still on Guinness. They were in the saloon bar of a pub off the Strand. "So I earn a living from the telly. Adapting my own novels or other people's. The odd episode of *Z-Cars* or *The Sweeney*. The occasional 'Play for Today.'"

"It's strange that you can still write drama, but not fiction."

"Ah well, you see, I can do dialogue all right," said Frobisher. "And somebody else does the pictures. But with fiction it's the narrative bits that give the writing its individuality. Descriptions of people, places, weather, stuff like that. It's like ale that's been kept in the wood: the flavour of the wood permeates the beer. Telly drama's like keg in comparison: all gas and no flavour. It's style I'm talking about, the special, unique way a writer has of using language. Well, you're a poet, you know what I'm talking about."

"I do," said Persse.

"I had a style once," said Frobisher wistfully. "But I lost it. Or rather I lost faith in it. Same thing, really. Have another?"

"It's my round," said Persse, getting to his feet. But he was obliged to return from the bar emptyhanded. "This is very embarrassing," he said, "but I'm going to have to ask you for a loan. All I have is some Irish punts and a cheque for one thousand pounds. The barman refused to cash it."

"It's all right. Have another drink on me," said Frobisher, proffering a ten pound note.

"I'll borrow this off you if I may," said Persse.

"What are you going to spend it on, the thousand pounds?" Frobisher asked him when he returned with the drinks, gripping a packet of potato crisps between his teeth.

"Looking for a girl," said Persse indistinctly.

"Looking for the Grail?"

"A girl. Her name is Angelica. Have some crisps."

"No thanks. Nice name. Where does she live?"

"That's the problem. I don't know."

"Good-looking?"

"Beautiful."

"You know that American Professor's wife back at the party? She made a pass at me."

"She made a pass at me too," said Persse. Frobisher looked mildly disappointed by this information. He began to eat crisps in an abstracted sort of way. In no time at all there was nothing left in the bag except a few crumbs and grains of salt. "How did you come to lose faith in your style?" Persse enquired.

"I'll tell you. I can date it precisely from a trip I made to Darlington six years ago. There's a new university there, you know, one of those plateglass and poured-concrete affairs on the edge of the town. They wanted to give me an honorary degree. Not the most prestigious university in the world, but nobody else had offered to give me a degree. The idea was, Darlington's a working-class, industrial town, so they'd honour a writer who wrote about working-class, industrial life. I bought that. I was sort of flattered, to tell you the truth. So I went up there to receive this degree. The usual flummery of robes and bowing and lifting your cap to the vice-chancellor and so on. Bloody awful lunch. But it was all right, I didn't mind. But then, when the official part was over, I was nobbled by a man in the English Department. Name of Dempsey."

"Robin Dempsey," said Persse.

"Oh, you know him? Not a friend of yours, I hope?"

"Definitely not."

"Good. Well, as you probably know, this Dempsey character is gaga about computers. I gathered this over lunch, because he was sitting opposite me. 'I'd like to take you over to our Computer Centre this afternoon,' he said. 'We've got something set up for you that I think you'll find interesting.' He was sort of twitching in his seat with excitement as he said it, like a kid who can't wait to unwrap his Christmas presents. So when the degree business was finished, I went with him to this Computer Centre. Rather grand name, actually, it was just a prefabricated hut, with a couple of sheep cropping the grass outside. There was another chap there, sort of running the place, called Josh. But Dempsey did all the talking. 'You've probably heard,' he said, 'of our Centre for Computational Stylistics.' 'No,' I said, 'Where is it?' 'Where? Well, it's here, I suppose,' he said. 'I mean, I'm it, so it's wherever I am. That is, wherever I am when I'm doing computational stylistics, which is only one of my research interests. It's not so much a place,' he said, 'as a headed notepaper. Anyway,' he went on, 'when we heard that the University was going to give you an honorary degree, we decided to make yours the first complete corpus in our tape archive.' 'What does that mean?' I said. 'It means,' he said, holding up a flat metal canister rather like the sort you keep film spools in, 'It means that every word you've ever published is in here.' His eyes gleamed with a kind of manic glee, like he was Frankenstein, or some kind of wizard, as if he had me locked up in that flat metal box. Which, in a way, he had. 'What's the use of that?' I asked. 'What's the use of it?' he said, laughing hysterically. 'What's the *use*? Let's show him, Josh.' And he passed the canister to the other guy, who takes out a spool of tape and fits it on to one of the machines. 'Come over here,' says Dempsey, and sits me down in front of a kind of typewriter with a TV screen attached. 'With that tape,' he said, 'we can request the computer to supply us with any information we like about your ideolect.' 'Come again?' I said. 'Your own special, distinctive, unique way of using the English language. What's your favourite word?' 'My favourite word? I don't have one.' 'Oh yes you do!' he said. 'The word you use most frequently.' 'That's probably *the* or *a* or *and*,' I said. He shook his head impatiently. 'We instruct the computer to ignore what we call grammatical words—articles, prepositions, pronouns, modal verbs, which have a high-frequency rating in all discourse. Then we get to the real nitty-gritty, what we call the lexical words, the words that carry a distinctive semantic content. Words like *love* or *dark* or *heart* or *God*. Let's see.' So he taps away on the keyboard and instantly my favourite word appears on the screen. What do you think it was?"

"Beer?" Persse ventured.

Frobisher looked at him a shade suspiciously through his owlish spectacles, and shook his head. "Try again."

"I don't know, I'm sure," said Persse.

Frobisher paused to drink and swallow, then looked solemnly at Persse. "Grease," he said, at length.

"Grease?" Persse repeated blankly.

"*Grease. Greasy. Greased.* Various forms and applications of the root, literal and metaphorical. I didn't believe him at first, I laughed in his face. Then he pressed a button and the machine began listing all the phrases in my works in which the word *grease* appears in one form or another. There they were, streaming across the screen in front of me, faster than I could read them, with page references and line numbers. *The greasy floor, the roads greasy with rain, the grease-stained cuff, the greasy jam butty, his greasy smile, the grease-smeared table, the greasy small change of their conversation*, even, would you believe it, *his body moved in hers like a well-greased piston.* I was flabbergasted, I can tell you. My entire *oeuvre* seemed to be saturated in grease. I'd never realized I was so obsessed with the stuff. Dempsey was chortling with glee, pressing buttons to show what my other favourite words were. *Grey* and *grime* were high on the list, I seem to remember. I seemed to have a penchant for depressing words beginning with a hard 'g.' Also *sink, smoke, feel, struggle, run* and *sensual*. Then he started to refine the categories. The parts of the body I mentioned most often were *hand* and *breast*, usually one on the other. The direct speech of male characters was invariably introduced by the simple tag *he said*, but the speech of women by a variety of expressive verbal groups, *she gasped, she sighed, she whispered urgently, she cried passionately.* All my heroes have brown eyes, like me. Their favourite expletive is *bugger*. The women they fall in love with tend to have Biblical names, especially ones beginning with 'R'—*Ruth, Rachel, Rebecca*, and so on. I like to end chapters with a short moodless sentence."

"You remember all this from six years ago?" Persse marvelled.

"Just in case I might forget, Robin Dempsey gave me a printout of the whole thing, popped it into a folder and gave it to me to take home. 'A little souvenir of the day,' he was pleased to call it. Well, I took it home, read it on the train, and the next morning, when I sat down at my desk and tried to get on with my novel, I found I couldn't. Every time I wanted an adjective, *greasy* would spring into my mind. Every time I wrote *he said*, I would scratch it out and write *he groaned* or *he laughed*, but it didn't seem right—but when I went back to *he said*, that didn't seem right either, it seemed predictable and mechanical. Robin and Josh had really fucked me up between them. I've never been able to write fiction since."

He ended, and emptied his tankard in a single draught.

"That's the saddest story I ever heard," said Persse.

The lights in the pub dimmed and brightened. "Time, ladies and gents!" called the barman.

"Come on," said Frobisher. "I know a place where we can get a drink. In Soho."

. . .

At Darlington's Computer Centre, the strip-lighting burns late. The student users of the facility have gone home long ago, back to their digs and halls of residence, back to the distractions of the Union bar and the Union disco, leaving behind them the paper excreta of the day's labours: punched data cards in various colours, swathes of printout, dogends, and crumpled paper cups. The air has a stale, slightly singed odour, as if the electronic machinery has burned up all its natural sweetness. There are only two men left in the building. One, sitting in a glass-partitioned booth, peels the polyfilm wrapping from a cheese sandwich and eats it, thoughtfully observing the other man, who is hunched over a console in a corner of the main room.

"NOBODY SEEMS TO LIKE ME," Robin Dempsey types.

"WHAT MAKES YOU SAY THAT?" replies ELIZA.

"IN THE STAFF CANTEEN I WATCH MY COLLEAGUES COMING TOWARDS MY TABLE WITH THEIR TRAYS AND THEN VEERING AWAY WHEN THEY RECOGNIZE ME."

"WHY DO YOU THINK THEY DO THAT?"

"BECAUSE THEY DON'T WANT TO TALK TO ME."

"WHY DO YOU THINK THEY DON'T WANT TO TALK TO YOU?"

"BECAUSE THEY'RE AFRAID I WILL TALK TO THEM ABOUT MY RESEARCH

AND THEY CAN'T STAND THAT BECAUSE I DO MORE RESEARCH THAN THE REST
OF THEM PUT TOGETHER."

"TELL ME ABOUT YOUR RESEARCH."

Robin Dempsey types for an hour without stopping.

. . .

Persse had never been in Soho before. He was shocked, but also excited, by
the blatant attempts to arouse lust made from every quarter, appealing to
every sense. Striptease, peepshows, massage parlours, pornographic films, vid-
eos, books and magazines. The rhythmic beat of jungle rock throbbing from
the bottom of cellar stairs. Odours of fish and garlic steaming from ventilators. Tarts and touts lounging in doorways. The word *Sex* blazoned everywhere—on shopfronts, bookcovers, tee-shirts, in capitals and lower case, in
print, in neon, in bulbs, red, yellow, blue, vertically, horizontally, diagonally.

"Soho's been ruined," Ronald Frobisher was complaining. "Just one big
pornographic wasteland, it is now. All the nice little Italian groceries and
wine shops are getting pushed out." He stopped on the corner of an intersection, hesitating. "You can get lost, it changes so fast. This used to be a shop
selling coffee beans, I seem to remember." Now it was a shop selling pornographic literature. Persse peered inside. Men stood facing the wall-racks, silent and thoughtful, as if they were urinating, or at prayer. "They don't seem
to be having much fun in there," he remarked, as they moved on.

"No, well, it's not surprising, is it? I believe they throw them out if they
start wanking in the shop." Frobisher turned down a narrow side street and
stopped outside a doorway over which there was an illuminated sign: *"Club
Exotica."*

"Well I'm buggered," said Frobisher. "What's happened to the old 'Lights
Out'?"

"It seems to have been turned into a striptease place," said Persse, looking
at the photographs of the artistes displayed in a glass case on the wall outside:
Lola, Charmaine, Mandy.

"Coming in, boys?" said a squat, swarthy man from just inside the door.
"These girls will put some lead in your pencil."

"Ribbon in my typewriter is more what I need," said Frobisher. "What
happened to the 'Lights Out' club which used to be here?"

"I dunno," said the man with a shrug. "Come inside, see the show, you
won't regret it."

"No thanks. Come on, Persse."

"Just a minute." Persse leaned against the wall with both hands, feeling faint. One of the pictures was unmistakably a photograph of Angelica. She was naked, swathed in chains, with her arms pinioned behind her back. Her hair streamed out behind her. Her expression was one of simulated distress and fear. A red paper disc over her pubis bore the legend *"Censored,"* and a red strip across her breasts identified her as "Lily." A. L. Pabst. Angelica Lily Pabst.

"What's the matter, Persse?" said Frobisher. "Are you all right?"

"I want to go in here," said Persse.

"What?"

"That's right," said the doorkeeper, "the young man has the right idea."

"You don't want to go in there, it's just a rip-off," said Frobisher.

"Don't listen to him," said the doorkeeper. "It's only three pounds, and that includes your first drink."

"Look, if you really want to see a strip show, let me take you somewhere with a bit of class," said Frobisher. "I know a place in Brewer Street."

"No," said Persse. "It has to be this place."

"You know something?" said the doorman. "You got good taste. Not like this old man here."

"Who are you calling old?" Frobisher said truculently. Grumbling, he followed Persse down the steps just inside the doorway. Persse paid for them both with the change left from Frobisher's ten pound note. "I resent paying for this sort of thing," the writer said as they stumbled and groped their way to a vacant table. The Club Exotica was as dark as the sex cinema in Rummidge, except for a small stage where, bathed in pink light, and to the accompaniment of recorded disco music, a young woman, not Angelica, wearing only high boots with spurs, was vigorously riding a rocking horse. They sat down and ordered whisky. "I mean, if I want to see a bit of tit and bum, I only have to write it into a telly script," said Frobisher. "*'With a tantalizing smile, she slowly unbuttons her blouse.' 'Her robe slides to the floor; she is wearing nothing underneath.'* That sort of thing. Then a few weeks later, I sit back in the comfort of my own home and enjoy it. This looks like the kind of corny strip show where the girls are always pretending to be doing something else."

Ronald Frobisher's judgment appeared to be correct. A succession of "turns" followed the rocking-horse rider, in which nudity was displayed in various incongruous contexts—a fire station, an airliner, an igloo. Sometimes there would be more than one artiste involved, and there was a young man, muscular but clearly homosexual, who occasionally combined with the girls to mime some trite story or situation, usually wielding a whip or instrument of torture. There was no sign of Angelica.

The tables were arranged in arcs facing the stage. When anyone rose to leave the front row, someone moved forward from behind to take his place.

"You want to move up?" Frobisher asked.

Persse shook his head.

"Had enough?" Frobisher enquired hopefully.

"I want to wait till the end."

"The *end*? We'll be here all night. They just keep the acts going in rotation till closing time, you know."

"Well, we haven't seen them all, yet," said Persse.

The stage lights faded on the spectacle of a naked girl thrashing about like a fish in a net suspended from the flies. There was lukewarm applause from the audience. The curtains closed and from behind a faint clinking of chains carried to Persse's ears. He sat up and leaned forward, hardly able to draw a breath.

The recorded music this time was less bland, more symphonic rock than disco, with a lot of distorted electric guitar. The curtain rose to reveal a naked girl in exactly the posture of "Lily" in the photograph outside: naked, chained to a pasteboard rock, writhing and twisting in her bonds, mouth and eyes wide with fear, long hair streaming in a current of air blowing from a wind machine in the wings. But it was not Angelica. It was the girl on the rocking horse. Persse slumped back in his seat, not sure whether he was relieved or disappointed.

"Let's go," he said.

"Well, we might as well wait till this act is finished," said Frobisher. "As a matter of fact, it's the first one that has come within a mile of turning me on. Something to do with the way those chains dig into the flesh, I think."

Persse had to admit that the spectacle had an impact that the previous entertainment had lacked. The nudity, for once, was thematically appropriate. The lighting and sound were expressive: wave effects were projected on to the backcloth, and the sound of surf had been mixed with the guitar chords. Whoever had produced this item knew something about the Andromeda archetype, though in the end it was travestied. The young homosexual, dressed up as Perseus, or possibly St. George, arrived to rescue the sacrificial virgin, but was chased off the stage by another naked girl in a dragon mask, who proved to have amorous rather than violent designs upon the captive. The lights faded on a scene of lesbian lovemaking.

"Rather neat, that," said Frobisher, as they climbed the stairs to street level.

"Enjoy the show, boys?" said the doorkeeper.

"What happened to Lily?" Persse demanded.

"Who?"

Persse pointed at the photograph.

"Oh, you mean Lily Papps."

Frobisher guffawed. "Good name for a stripper."

"Is that what she calls herself?" Persse asked.

"Yeah, Lily Papps, with two pees. She left a few weeks back. We haven't got round to doing a photo of the new girl."

"What happened to Lily? Where can I find her?" said Persse.

The man shrugged. "Don't ask me. These girls—they come, they go. Mind you, Lily was special. Not just a nice body—she had a brain too. You know that dragon number? Good, eh? That was her own idea."

"Someone you know?" Frobisher enquired, as they walked away from the Club Exotica.

"It's the girl I told you about. The one I'm looking for."

Frobisher raised an eyebrow. "You didn't tell me she was a stripper."

"She's not really. I don't know why she's doing it. Money, I suppose. She's an educated girl. She's doing a PhD. She shouldn't be doing that sort of thing at all."

"Ah," said Frobisher. "I understand. You're going to track down this damsel and rescue her from the sordid life to which poverty has condemned her?"

"I'd like to do that," said Persse, "for her own sake."

"Not for your own?"

Persse hesitated. "Well, yes, I suppose so . . . Only it was a shock, seeing her picture in that place back there. I didn't know, you see." It was still hard for him to imagine the girl he remembered from the Rummidge conference, eagerly discussing structuralism, romance, the poetry of Keats, performing in a nude cabaret in some sordid Soho cellar. His soul recoiled from the idea, but after all it was not an irredeemable degradation. No doubt for Angelica, as for Bernadette, it was simply a job, a way of earning money—though why she should have to choose *that* way was a mystery. One day he would discover the answer. Meanwhile, he must trust Angelica, and his first impressions of her. "Yes," he said, lengthening his stride, "I want to find her for my own sake."

. . .

Philip Swallow woke suddenly in his hotel room in Ankara with all the symptoms of incipient diarrhoea. It was pitch dark. He groped for the lightswitch on the wall above his head and pressed it, with no result. Bulb gone, or power cut? Sweating, feverish, he tried to recall the geography of the room. His briefcase was on a dressing-table facing the end of the bed. About three yards to the right of that was the door to the bathroom. Carefully he got out of bed and, tightening his sphincter muscle, felt his way along the edge of the bed until he reached the foot of it. With his arms extended in front of him like a blind man, he searched for the dressing-table, but it was his big toe that located this piece of furniture first. Whimpering with pain, he delved in his briefcase for his makeshift toilet paper, and shuffled along the wall like a rock-climber until he came to the bathroom door. He tried the lightswitch inside without effect. A power cut, then. Sink to the left, toilet beyond it. Ah, there, thank God. He lowered himself on to the toilet seat and voided his liquefied bowels. A foul smell filled the darkness. It must have been the kebab, or, more likely, the salad that accompanied it. Still, at least he had managed to get to the loo in time, in spite of the power cut.

Philip began to wipe himself. When the lights came on of their own accord he found he was up to page five of his lecture on "The Legacy of Hazlitt."

2

Persse woke late the next morning, after a night of troubled dreams, with a dry mouth and a moderate headache. He lay on his back for some time, staring at the sprinkler nozzle, a metallic omphalos in the ceiling of his room at the YMCA, wondering what to do next. He decided to go back to the Club Exotica and make further enquiries about the whereabouts of "Lily."

Soho seemed distinctly less sinful in the late morning sunshine. Admittedly the pornshops and the sex cinemas were already open, and had a few devout customers, but their façades and illuminated signs had a faded, shamefaced aspect. The streets and pavements were busy with people with jobs to do: dustmen collecting garbage, messengers on scooters delivering parcels, suited executives with briefcases, and young men pushing wheeled racks of ladies' dresses. There were wholesome smells in the air, of vegetables, fresh bread and coffee. At a newsagents, Persse bought a copy of the *Guardian* and the *Times Literary Supplement.* "LONDON LITERATI ADRIFT" said a headline on the front page of the former. "RUDYARD PARKINSON ON THE ENGLISH SCHOOL OF CRITICISM" announced the cover of the latter.

By retracing the route he had taken with Ronald Frobisher the night before, Persse found the Club Exotica—only it wasn't the Club Exotica any more. That name, in tubular glass script, lay discarded on the pavement, trailing flex. Over the door two workmen were erecting another, larger sign, "PUSSYVILLE."

"What happened to the Exotica?" Persse asked them. One looked down at him and shrugged. The other, without looking, said, "Changed its name, dinnit?"

"Under new management?"

"I should fink so. The gaffer's inside now."

Persse descended the stairs and pushed through the quilted swing doors at the bottom. Inside, unshaded bulbs hanging from the ceiling cast a bleak light on stained carpet and shabby furniture. A vacuum cleaner whined among the tables. In the middle of the floor, a man in a striped suit was inspecting a young woman who was wearing only briefs and high-heeled shoes. The man carried a clipboard in his hand, and circled the girl in the manner of a used-car dealer scrutinizing a possible purchase for signs of rust. Along one wall other girls lolled in négligés, evidently awaiting the same appraisal.

"Yes?" said the man, catching sight of Persse. "Have you brought the new lights?"

"No," said Persse, modestly averting his eyes from the half-naked young woman. "I'm looking for a girl called Lily."

"Anybody here called Lily?" said the man.

After a moment's silence, a girl stood up at the end of the row. "I'm Lily," she said, with one hand on her hip, shooting a languorous glance at Persse from beneath a frizzy blonde hair-do.

"I'm afraid I don't know you," stammered Persse.

"You were never Lily," said the girl next to the blonde, tugging her back into her seat. "You just fancy 'im." Laughter rippled along the row of seats.

"She used to perform here," said Persse, "when it was the Club Exotica."

"Yeah, well, this isn't the Club Exotica any more. It's Pussyville, and I have to find twelve topless waitresses by Monday, so if you don't mind . . ." The man frowned at his clipboard.

"Who owned the Club Exotica?" Persse asked.

"Girls Unlimited," said the man, without looking up.

"It's in Soho Square," said the frizzy-haired blonde.

"I know," said Persse, "but thank you."

Five minutes' walk took him to Soho Square. Girls Unlimited was on the fourth floor of a building on the west side. After stating his business, he was admitted to the office of a lady called Mrs. Gasgoine. The room was carpeted in red, and furnished with white filing cabinets and tubular steel chairs and tables. There was a large map of the world on the wall. Mrs. Gasgoine was elegantly dressed in black, and smoking a cigarette in a holder.

"What can I do for you, Mr. McGarrigle?"

"I'm looking for a girl called Lily Papps. I believe she worked for you at the Club Exotica."

"We've sold our interest in the Club Exotica."

"So I understand."

"Are you a client of ours?"

"Client?"

"Have you hired our girls in the past?"

"Good Lord, no! I'm just a friend of Lily's."

Mrs. Gasgoine blew angry smoke through her nostrils. "You mean she was moonlighting with you."

"I suppose you could say that," replied Persse, remembering the glassy corridor in the sky at Rummidge, the snowscape under the moon, the quotations from Keats.

Mrs. Gasgoine extinguished her cigarette and twisted the holder to expel the stub. It fell into her ashtray like a spent bullet case. "This isn't a Missing Persons Bureau, Mr. McGarrigle, it's a business organization. Lily is one of our most versatile employees. She's been transferred to another job—something that came up at short notice."

"Where?"

"I'm not at liberty to tell you. It's part of our contract with our girls that we don't divulge their whereabouts to family or friends. Quite often, you see, they're running away from some complication at home."

"I don't even know where her home is!" Persse protested.

"And I don't know you from Adam, Mr. McGarrigle. You could be a private investigator, for all I know. I'll tell you what I'll do. If you would like to leave me your name and address, I'll forward it to Lily, and if she wants to, she can get in touch with you."

Persse hesitated, doubtful whether Angelica would respond if she knew he had discovered her secret. "Thanks, but I won't put you to that trouble," he said at length.

Mrs. Gasgoine looked as if all her suspicions were confirmed.

He left the premises of Girls Unlimited and looked for a bank at which to cash his cheque. On his way, he passed a window at the side of Foyle's bookshop in which an assistant was arranging some rather dusty-looking copies of *Hazlitt and the Amateur Reader* by Philip Swallow, flanking a blown-up photocopy of Rudyard Parkinson's review in the *TLS*. At the bank Persse took out most of his money in traveller's cheques. Then he went to a branch of Thomas Cook and booked himself a flight to Amsterdam. The only thing he could think of doing now was to look for Angelica's adoptive father.

. . .

He hadn't been in Amsterdam three hours before he met Morris Zapp. Persse was standing on one of the curved canal bridges in the old town, puzzling over his tourist map, when the American came up and slapped him on the back.

"Percy! I didn't know you were at the conference."

"What conference?"

Morris Zapp indicated the large plastic disc dangling from his lapel, which had his name printed inside a circular inscription, "VIIth International Congress of Literary Semioticians." On his other lapel was a bright enamel button which declared, "*Every Decoding Is Another Encoding.*" "I had it made at a customized button shop back home," he explained. "Everybody here is crazy about it. If I'd brought a gross with me I could have made a fortune. A Jap professor offered me ten dollars for this one. But if you're not at the Conference, what are you doing in Amsterdam?"

"A sort of holiday," said Persse. "I won a poetry prize." He found that he didn't want to confide in Morris about Angelica.

"No kidding! Congratulations!"

A thought struck Persse. "Angelica isn't at the conference by any chance?"

"Haven't seen her, but that doesn't mean she isn't here. The conference only opened yesterday, and there are hundreds of people. We're all in the Sonesta—great hotel. Where are you staying?"

"At a little pension near here."

"It wasn't such a big prize, then?"

"I'm trying to make it go a long way," said Persse. "Perhaps I'll drop in on your conference."

"Why not? I thought I might go to this afternoon's session myself. Meanwhile, how about some lunch? They have great Indonesian food here."

"Good idea," said Persse. The diversion was welcome, for he had had a discouraging morning. The Head Office of KLM had been courteous but discreet. They confirmed that a Hermann Pabst had been an executive director of the airline in the nineteen-fifties, but he had resigned in 1961 to take up a post in America, the details of which they were unable or unwilling to divulge. Persse was faced with the prospect of having to continue his search in America. He wondered how long his £1000 would last at this rate.

Morris Zapp seemed to have already mastered the spider's-web layout of the Amsterdam canals and streets. He led Persse confidently past a quayside flowermarket, over bridges, down narrow alleys, along busy shopping streets. "You know something?" he said, "I really like this place. It's flat, which means I can walk without getting pooped, it has good cigars that are very cheap, and wait till you see the nightlife."

"I was in Soho the other night," said Persse.

"Soho, schmoho," said Morris Zapp. "That's a kindergarten compared with what goes on in the *rosse buurt*."

They emerged from a narrow street into a broad square where tables and chairs were spread in the sun outside the cafés. Morris Zapp suggested an aperitif.

"Have we time? What about the conference?" said Persse.

Morris shrugged. "It doesn't matter if we miss a few papers. The only one I want to hear is von Turpitz's."

"Who is he?"

Morris Zapp beckoned to a waiter. "Gin OK? It's the *vin du pays*." Persse nodded. "Two Bols," Morris ordered, forking the air with his fingers. "Turpitz is a kraut who's into reception theory. Years ago he wrote a book called *The Romantic Reader*—why people killed themselves after reading *Werther* or made pilgrimages to the *Nouvelle Héloise* country . . . Not bad, but basically trad. literary history. Then Jauss and Iser at Kostanz started to make a splash with reception theory, and von Turpitz jumped on the bandwagon."

"Why do you want to hear him, then?"

"Just to reassure myself. He's a sort of rival."

"For a woman?"

"God, no. For a job."

"I thought you were satisfied where you are."

"Every man has his price," said Morris Zapp. "Mine is one hundred grand a year and no duties. Have you heard of something new called the UNESCO Chair of Literary Criticism?"

While Morris was telling Persse about it, the waiter brought them two glasses of neat, chilled gin. "You're supposed to drink it in one gulp," said Morris, sniffing his glass.

"I'm your man," said Persse, raising his own.

"Here's to us, then," said Morris. "May we both achieve everything we desire."

"Amen," said Persse.

They lunched well at an Indonesian restaurant where dark-skinned waiters in white turbans brought to their table a seemingly endless supply of spicy aromatic dishes of chicken, prawn, pork and vegetables. Morris Zapp had dined there the previous evening and appeared to have taken tuition in the menu. "This is peanut sauce," he said, eating greedily. "This is meat stewed in coconut milk, these are pieces of barbecued sucking pig. Have a prawn cracker."

"Will you be able to stay awake this afternoon?" Persse asked, as they heavily descended the stairs of the restaurant and made their way towards the Sonesta. The sky had clouded over, and the atmosphere had become sultry and oppressive, as if a storm was brewing.

"I aim to sleep through the first paper," said Morris. "Just wake me up when von Turpitz appears on the rostrum. You can't mistake him, he wears a black glove on one hand. Nobody knows why and nobody dares to ask him."

The Sonesta was a huge modern hotel grafted on to some old buildings in the Kattengat, including a Lutheran church, in the shape of a rotunda, which had been converted into a conference hall. "I hope it's been deconsecrated," Persse remarked, as they came in under the huge domed ceiling. A mighty organ, built of dark wood and decorated with gilt, and a carved pulpit projecting from the wall, were the only reminders of the building's original function.

"Reconsecrated, you mean," said Morris Zapp. "Information is the religion of the modern world, didn't you know that?"

Persse surveyed the rapidly filling concentric rows of seats, hoping against hope that he might see Angelica there, cool and self-possessed behind her heavy spectacles, with her stainless steel pen poised over her notebook. A man with a brown leathery face and hooded eyes bowed just perceptibly to Morris Zapp as he passed, accompanied by a sulky-looking youth in tight black trousers. "That's Michel Tardieu," Morris murmured. "He's another likely contender for the UNESCO chair. The kid is supposed to be his research assistant. You can tell how good he is at research by the way he wriggles his ass."

"Hallo, young man." Persse felt a light tap on his shoulder, and turned to find Miss Sybil Maiden standing behind him in a Paisley pattern frock, holding a folded fan in her hand.

"Why, hallo, Miss Maiden," he greeted her. "I didn't know you were interested in semiotics."

"I thought I should find out what it is all about," she replied. "One should never dismiss what one does not understand."

"And what do you think of it so far?"

Miss Maiden fluttered her fan. "I think it's a lot of tosh," she declared. "However, Amsterdam is a very charming city. Have you been to the Van Gogh museum? Those late landscapes from Arles! The cypresses are so wonderfully phallic, the cornfields positively brimming with fertility."

"I think we'd better sit down," said Persse. "They seem to be starting."

On every seat was a handout which looked at first sight like the blueprint for an electric power station, all arrows, lines and boxes, except that the boxes were labelled *tragedy, comedy, pastoral, lyric, epic* and *romance*. "A Semiotic Theory of Genre" was the title of the paper, delivered by a sweating Slav in stumbling English—with French, the official language of the conference. It was warm in the rotunda. From behind Persse came the regular swish of Miss Maiden's fan, punctuated by an occasional snort of incredulity or contempt. Persse's head felt as heavy as a cannonball. Every now and again, as he dozed off, it would loll forward and wake him up by a painful jerk on his neck ligaments. Eventually, he allowed his chin to sink on to his breast, and fell into a deep sleep.

. . .

Persse woke with a start from a dream in which he was delivering a paper about the influence of T. S. Eliot on Shakespeare from a pulpit in a chapel shaped like the inside of a jumbo jet. What had woken him was a thunderclap. The sky was dark behind the high windows of the rotunda, and the lights had been switched on. Rain drummed on the roof. He yawned and rubbed his eyes. On the rostrum, a man with a pale face and a skullcap of blond hair was speaking into the microphone in Germanically accented English, biting off the consonants and spitting them out as if they were pips, gesturing occasionally with a black-gloved hand. Persse shook his head in the manner of a swimmer clearing his ears of water. Although visually he had woken up, his dream seemed to be continuing on the audio channel. He pinched himself, and felt the sensation. He pinched Morris Zapp, snoozing beside him.

"Lay off, Fulvia," Morris Zapp mumbled. Then, opening his eyes, he sat up. "Ah, yeah, that's von Turpitz. How long's he been speaking?"

"I'm not sure. I've been asleep myself."

"Is his stuff any good?"

"I think it's very good," said Persse. Morris Zapp looked glum. "But then," Persse continued, "I'm biased. I wrote it."

"Huh?" Morris Zapp gaped.

Lightning flickered outside the windows and the lights inside the auditorium went out. There was a gasp of surprise and consternation from the audience, immediately drowned by a tremendous thunderclap overhead which made them all jump with fright. The lights came on again. Von Turpitz continued to read his paper in the same relentlessly precise accent, without pause or hesitation. He had evidently been speaking for some time, because he reached the end of his discourse about ten minutes later. He squared off the pages of his script, bowed stiffly to the chairman, and sat down to polite applause. The chairman invited questions. Persse stood up. The chairman smiled and nodded.

"I'd like to ask the speaker," said Persse, "if he recently read a draft outline of a book about the influence of T. S. Eliot on the modern reading of Shakespeare, submitted by me to the publishers Lecky, Windrush and Bernstein, of London."

The chairman looked puzzled. Von Turpitz looked stunned.

"Would you repeat the question, please?" the chairman asked.

Persse repeated it. A sussuration of whispered comment and speculation passed like a breeze around the auditorium. Von Turpitz leaned across to the chairman and said something into his ear. The chairman nodded, and bent forward to address Persse through the microphone. His identification disc dangled from his lapel like a medal. "May I ask, sir, whether you are an officially registered member of the Conference?"

"Well, no, I'm not . . ." said Persse.

"Then I'm afraid your question is out of order," said the chairman. Von Turpitz busied himself with his papers, as though this procedural wrangle had nothing to do with him.

"That's not fair!" Persse protested. "I have reason to think that Professor von Turpitz has plagiarized part of his paper from an unpublished manuscript of my own."

"I'm sorry," said the chairman. "I cannot accept a question from someone who is not a member of the Conference."

"Well *I'm* a member," said Morris Zapp, rising to his feet beside Persse, "so let me ask it: did Professor von Turpitz read McGarrigle's manuscript for Lecky, Windrush and Bernstein, or did he not?"

There was mild uproar in the auditorium. Cries of "Shame!" "Point of order, Mr. Chairman!" "Answer!" and "Let him speak!" with equivalent ejaculations in various other languages, could be distinguished in a general babble of conversation. The chairman looked helplessly at von Turpitz, who seized the microphone, delivered an angry speech in German, pointing a black finger menacingly at Persse and Morris Zapp, and then stalked off the platform.

"What did he say?" Morris demanded.

Persse shrugged. "I don't speak German."

"He said he wasn't going to stay here and be insulted," said Miss Maiden from behind them, "but he looked distinctly guilty to me. You were quite right to stand up for yourself against the Black Hand, young man."

"Yeah, this is going to get around," said Morris Zapp, rubbing his hands together. "This is not going to help von Turpitz's reputation one little bit. Come on, Percy, I'll buy you another Bols."

Morris's jubilation did not, however, last for long. In the bar he spotted a folded copy of the *Times Literary Supplement* sticking out of Persse's jacket pocket. "Is that the latest issue?" he asked. "Mind if I take a look at it?"

"I shouldn't if I were you," said Persse, who had read it on the plane to Amsterdam.

"Why not?"

"Well, it contains a rather unfriendly review of a book of yours. By Rudyard Parkinson."

"That asshole? The day I get a good review from him, I'll know I'm washed up. Let me see." Morris almost snatched the journal from Persse and, with trembling fingers, flicked through the pages until he located Parkinson's review. "But this is all about Philip Swallow's book," he said, frowning, as he ran his eyes up and down the columns of print.

"The bit about you is at the end," Persse said. "You're not going to like it."

Morris Zapp didn't like it. When he had finished reading the review, he was silent for a few moments, pale and breathing heavily. "It's a limey plot," he said at length. "Parkinson is pushing his own claim to the UNESCO chair under cover of praising Philip Swallow's pathetic little book on Hazlitt."

"Do you think so?" said Persse.

"Of course—look at the title: 'The English School of Criticism.' He should have called it 'The English School of Genteel Crap.' May I borrow this?" he concluded, standing up and stuffing the *TLS* into his pocket.

"Sure—but where are you going?"

"I'm gonna look over my paper for tomorrow morning—see if I can work in some cracks against Parkinson."

"I didn't know you were giving a paper."

"How else could I claim my conference expenses? It's the same paper that I gave at Rummidge, slightly adapted. It's a wonderfully adaptable paper. I aim to give it all over Europe this summer. You want to take a stroll round the town tonight?"

"All right," Persse said. They made arrangements to meet. As soon as Morris Zapp had disappeared, the lean leathery figure of Michel Tardieu slid into the vacant space beside Persse in the curved, upholstered bar alcove.

"A most dramatic intervention," he said, after introducing himself. "Do I infer that you are a specialist in the work of T. S. Eliot?"

"That's right," said Persse. "I did my Master's dissertation on him."

"You may be interested, then, in a conference some Swiss friends of mine are organizing this summer."

"I'm not sure what my movements will be this summer," said Persse.

"I expect to attend this conference myself," said Michel Tardieu, putting his hand on Persse's knee beneath the table.

"I'm looking for a girl, you see," said Persse.

"Ah," shrugged Tardieu, removing his hand. "*C'est la vie, c'est la narration*. Each of us is a subject in search of an object. Have you by any chance seen a young man in a black velvet suit?"

"No, I'm afraid I haven't," said Persse. "If you will excuse me, I have to go now."

Outside the Sonesta the sky was blue again, and the late-afternoon sun shone on a rinsed and gleaming city. Persse took a canal ride in one of the sleek Plexiglass-covered tourist launches that slid through the narrow waterways and threaded the bridges at what seemed reckless speed, almost grazing each other as they passed in opposite directions, crackling commentaries in four languages from their loudspeakers. Once he glimpsed a girl walking across a bridge a hundred yards ahead who, from that distance, looked like Angelica, but this, he knew, was a mirage produced by his own desire. When the boat reached the bridge, the girl had disappeared.

. . .

Later that evening, when the canals were long black mirrors laid flat between the trees and the streetlamps, Morris conducted Persse on a stroll around the red light district, a maze of little streets near the Nieuwemarkt. It was, as Morris had promised, a far more extraordinary and shocking spectacle than anything Soho offered, and almost too much for an innocent young man from County Mayo to comprehend. In each brightly lit window sat a prostitute, dressed for her trade in some slinky gown or filmy négligé, boldly eyeing the passersby for possible custom. These were veritably streets of sin, the objects of men's lust being frankly displayed like goods in a shop window. You had only to step inside and settle the price, and the woman would draw thick heavy curtains across the casement and satisfy your desire. Two things prevented this traffic in female flesh from seeming simply sordid. The first was that the interiors of the houses were spotlessly clean, and furnished in a cosy petitbourgeois style, with upholstered chairs, embroidered antimacassars, potted plants, and immaculate linen turned down on the bed that could usually be glimpsed at the rear. The second thing was that all the women were young and attractive, and in many cases were passing the time in the homely occupation of knitting.

"Why do they do it?" Persse wondered aloud to Morris Zapp. "They look such nice girls. They could be married and raising families instead of selling themselves like this." He did not like to catch the women's eyes, not so much because he feared falling under the spell of their allure as because he felt slightly ashamed to be observing their self-exposure while remaining safely wrapped in his own virtue.

Morris shrugged. "Maybe they're planning to settle down later. When they've made their pile."

"But who would marry a . . . girl who had done that for a living?"

Morris moved ahead of Persse on the narrow, crowded pavement, and tossed his reply back over his shoulder. "Perhaps he wouldn't know."

The streets were becoming increasingly crowded by pedestrians, most of whom seemed to be window-shopping tourists like themselves, rather than serious customers. There were even couples, courting or married, to be seen amid the throng, walking arm-in-arm, grinning and nudging each other, deriving a cheap erotic thrill from the ambience of sexual licence. For some reason this depressed Persse more than any other component of the scene, and made him feel sorrier for the girls in the windows.

And then he saw her, in a house with a low red door and the number 13 painted on it. Angelica. There was no question that it was Angelica. She was sitting in the little parlour, not at the window, but on a chaise-longue beside a standard lamp with a rose-coloured shade, and she was painting her nails with nail-varnish, concentrating so intently on the task that she did not look up as he stood on the pavement and stared in through the window, thunderstruck. Her long dark hair was loose about her shoulders and she wore a black dress of some shiny material cut low across her bosom. The nail varnish was scarlet. When she extended her hand to examine the effect under the lamp it looked as though she had dipped her fingers in fresh blood.

Persse walked on in a daze. He felt as though he were drowning, fighting for breath. He cannoned blindly into other, protesting pedestrians, stumbled over a kerb, heard a squeal of brakes, and found himself sprawled over the bonnet of a car whose driver, leaning out of the window, was shouting angrily at him in Dutch or German.

"'Tis pity she's a whore," Persse said to the driver.

"Percy, what the hell are you doing?" said Morris Zapp, materializing out of the crowd that was observing this incident with mild interest. "I've been looking all over for you." He took Persse's arm and steered him back to the pavement. "Are you OK? What d'you want to do?"

"I'd rather be on my own for a while, if you don't mind," Persse said.

"Ah ha! You saw something that took your fancy in one of those windows back there, huh? Well, I don't blame you, Percy, you're only young once. Just do me a favour, if the girl offers you a condom, forget the Pope, wear it for my sake, OK? I'd hate to be the occasion of your getting the clap. I think I'll go back to the hotel. *Ciao.*"

Morris Zapp squeezed Persse's bicep and waddled away. Persse retraced his steps, rapidly, purposefully. Morris had put an idea into his head, a way of relieving his feelings of bitterness, betrayal, disgust. He would burst into that cosy, rose-tinted little parlour and demand "*How much?*" How much did the elusive maiden he had wooed and pursued along the paths and corridors of Rummidge, without winning so much as a kiss, how much did she charge for opening her legs to a paying customer? Was there a discount for an old friend, for a poet, for a paid-up member of the Association of University Teachers? Rehearsing these sarcasms in his head, imagining Angelica starting up from the chaise-longue, white-faced, aghast, clutching at her heart, he pushed his way through the shuffling crowds of voyeurs until he found himself outside the house with the red door. Its curtains were drawn.

Persse felt physically sick. He leaned against the wall and dug his nails into the hard gritty surface. A group of British youths passed, four abreast, yelling a football song, dribbling an empty beer can before them. One caught Persse a glancing blow with his shoulder, but Persse made no protest. He felt numb, blank, not even anger was left.

The chanting of the English yobbos faded as they turned a corner and the street became momentarily quiet and empty. After a few minutes the red door opened and closed again behind a young man who stood for a moment, adjusting his tight black trousers. Persse recognized him as the companion of Michel Tardieu. He looked furtively to left and right, then sauntered off. Light fell across the pavement as the curtains were drawn back inside the front room. Persse moved out of the shadows and looked in. A pretty Eurasian girl in a white petticoat smiled at him encouragingly. Persse gaped at her. He examined the door of the house: red, and with number 13 painted on it. He had made no mistake. He returned to the window. The same girl smiled again, and with a sweep of her eyes and a tilt of her head invited him to enter. When he did so, she greeted him with a smile and some unintelligible words of Dutch.

"Excuse me," he said.

"You American?" she enquired. "You like to spend some time with me? Forty dollar."

"There was another girl in here just now," said Persse.

"She gone. She babysitter. Don't worry, I give you good time."

"Babysitter?" Hope, relief, self-reproach surged in Persse's breast.

"Yeah, I got kid upstairs. Don't worry, he sleeps, don't hear a thing."

"Angelica is your babysitter?"

"You mean Lily? She's a friend, helps me out sometimes. I told her to draw the curtain, but she don't bother."

"Where has she gone? Where can I find her?"

The girl shrugged, sulky. "I dunno. You want to spend some time with me or not? Thirty dollar."

Persse took a hundred-guilder note out of his wallet and put it down on the table. "Where can I find Lily?"

With the speed and dexterity of a prestidigitator, the girl picked up the note, folded it with the fingers of one hand, and tucked it into her décolletage. "She works at a cabaret, Blue Heaven, on the Achterburg Wal."

"Where's that?"

"Turn right at the end of the street, then over the bridge. You will see the sign."

"Thanks," said Persse.

He raced along the street like a hurley player, jinking through the crowds and the traffic, juggling the ball of his confused emotions. For one dizzy moment he thought he had discovered Angelica in some totally innocent, totally benevolent occupation, a secular sister of mercy ministering to the prostitutes of Amsterdam. That had been wishful thinking, of course. But if Angelica wasn't just a babysitter, she wasn't a whore either—how could he ever have dreamed that she was? His shame at having entertained such an idea, however plausible the circumstantial evidence, made him readier to accept the fact that she performed in nude revues. He couldn't approve of it, he hoped to persuade her to give it up, but it didn't fundamentally affect his feelings for her.

He swerved round the corner of the street and raced across the bridge; saw blue neon letters trembling in the black water, and leapt three steps at a time down to the canalside cobbles. Some people queuing for admission to the Blue Heaven turned their heads and stared as Persse came thudding up to the entrance and skidded to a halt, panting, in front of the foyer. It had an illuminated façade, rather like a small cinema, on which the programme was advertised in moveable letters. "LIVE SEX SHOW," it stated, in English. "SEE SEX ACTS PERFORMED ON STAGE. THE REAL FUCKY FUCKY." On the pillars supporting the entrance canopy there were photographic stills of the performance. In one of them Angelica, naked, kneeling, was being mounted from behind by a hairy young man, also naked, and grinning. She looked exactly as she had done in what he had thought, till now, was a hallucination in the Rummidge cinema. He turned on his heel and walked slowly away.

· · ·

What did Persse do next? He got drunk, of course, like any other disillusioned lover. He bought a half-litre of Bols in a stone bottle at a liquor store and went back to his pension and lay on the bed and drank himself into insensibility. He woke next morning under a burning electric light bulb, uncertain which was worse, the pain in his head or the taste in his mouth, though neither was a patch on the ache in his heart. He had an open return ticket to Heathrow. Without bothering to enquire into the availability of flights, he checked out of the pension and took a bus to Schiphol airport, staring vacantly out through the window at the depressing environs of Amsterdam; factories, service stations and greenhouses scattered over the flat and featureless landscape like jetsam on a beach from which the tide had gone out and never returned.

He secured a seat on the next plane to London, and sat for an hour in the lounge next to the departure gate, not reading, not thinking, just sitting; the vacancy and anonymity of the place, with its rows of plastic moulded seats facing a huge tinted window framing blank sky, suited the zero state of his mind and heart. The flight was called, he shuffled aboard, past mechanically nodding and smiling cabin staff, the plane rose into the air like a lift, he stared through a porthole at a cloudscape as flat and featureless as the landscape below. A tray of food wrapped in polyfilm was placed before him and he consumed its contents stolidly, without any sensation of taste or aroma. The plane dumped him on the ground again, and he walked through the endless covered ways of Heathrow, so long their lines seemed to meet at the horizon.

Only Club class seats were available on the next flight to Shannon, but he cashed another traveller's cheque and paid the extra without demur. What did he need to husband his money for now? His life was laid waste, his occupation gone. The summer stretched before him barren as a desert. He had two hours to wait before his flight was called. He dragged his feet to St. George's chapel. His petition was still pinned to the green baize board, curling slightly at the edges: "*Dear God, let me find Angelica.*" He ripped the paper from its securing thumbtack, and crumpled it in his fist. He went inside the chapel, and sat for an hour in the back pew, staring blankly at the altar. On his way out he left another petition on the noticeboard: "*Dear God, let me forget Angelica. Lead her from the life that degrades her.*"

He sat for another half an hour in another anonymous waiting area, and shuffled in line aboard another airplane, past mechanically nodding and smiling cabin crew, and took his seat. The airplane rose like a lift into the air and he stared through the porthole at another featureless prairie of cloud. Another tray of tasteless, odourless food was placed on his lap, with a complimentary half bottle of chilled claret, because he was travelling Club class. But this time there appeared to be some deviation from the monotonous routine of flight. Persse, sitting in the forward section of the plane, observed much coming and going of the cabin crew through the curtain that screened the door to the flight deck. It gradually penetrated his dulled and apathetic sensibility that the three hostesses were alarmed about something.

Sure enough, the captain came on the intercom to inform the passengers that the plane had burst a nosewheel tyre on takeoff, and they would therefore be making an emergency landing at Shannon, where fire and rescue services were standing by. A murmur of apprehension passed through the cabins at this announcement. As if he had heard it, the captain tried to reassure the passengers, explaining that he did not doubt that he would be able to land safely, but emergency procedures were obligatory following a tyre burst—in case, he added, there should be a further burst (which was perhaps explaining too much). Shortly before landing, the passengers would be instructed to take off their shoes and adopt the recommended posture for emergency landing. The cabin crew would demonstrate, and give advice and help where needed.

In fact the cabin crew themselves looked in need of advice and help. Seldom had Persse seen three young women who looked more frightened, and gradually their fear communicated itself to the passengers. The terror of the latter was intensified by some violent turbulence which the aircraft encountered as it began its descent. Though this had absolutely nothing to do with the burst tyre, some unmechanically-minded passengers drew the opposite conclusion and emitted small screams of fear or pious ejaculations as the aircraft bucked and staggered in the air. Some pored over the plastic cards giving safety instructions tucked into the back of every seat, with coloured diagrams of the plane's emergency exits, and unconvincing pictures of passengers gaily sliding down the inflatable chutes, like children on a playground slide. Others, operating on the belt-and-braces principle, rooted out life-jackets from beneath their seats and practised putting them on. The air hostesses ran distractedly up and down the aisle, dissuading people from inflating their life-jackets and fending off urgent orders for strong drink.

Indifferent to life himself, Persse observed the conduct of those around him with detached curiosity. His seat gave him a ringside view of the cabin crew. He saw the chief stewardess take a handmike from its recess near the galley and clear her throat preparatory to making an announcement. Her expression was solemn. "Ladies and gentlemen," she said, in a Kerry accent, "we have received a request from a passenger for a public recitation of the Act of Contrition. Is there a priest on board who would be willing to lead us in prayer?" She waited anxiously for a few moments, looking down the length of the plane (the curtain between the Club- and economy-class sections had been drawn back) for signs of a volunteer. Another hostess came forward from the economy section, shaking her head. "No luck, Moira," she murmured to the chief stewardess. "Wouldn't you know it, just when you need a priest, there isn't one. Not even a nun."

"What shall I do?" said Moira distractedly, her hand over the mike.

"You'll have to say the Act of Contrition yourself."

Moira looked frantic. "I've forgotten it," she whimpered. "I haven't been to confession since I went on the pill."

"Oh, Moira, you never told me you were on the pill."

"You do it, Brigid."

"Oh, I couldn't."

"Yes, you could. Didn't you tell me you were a Child of Mary?" The chief stewardess said into the microphone: "Since there doesn't appear to be a priest on board, stewardess Brigid O'Toole will lead us all in the Act of Contrition." She thrust the mike into the hands of the dismayed Brigid, who looked at it as if it was a snake that might bite her at any moment. The plane reared and dropped sickeningly. The two girls, thrown off-balance, clung together for support.

"In the name of the Father . . ." Moira prompted in a whisper.

"In the name of the Father and of the Son and of the Holy Ghost," Brigid croaked into the microphone. She clapped her hand over it and hissed: "My mind's gone blank. I can't remember the Act of Contrition."

"Well, say any prayer you like," Moira urged. "Whatever comes into your head."

Brigid shut her eyes tightly and held the microphone to her lips. "For what we are about to receive," she said, "may the Lord make us truly thankful."

Persse was still laughing when they landed, quite safely, at Shannon airport, ten minutes later. Brigid gave him a sheepish grin as he left the aircraft. "Sorry about the fuss, sir," she murmured.

"Not a bit of it," he said. "You gave me back an appetite for life."

He went to the Irish Tourist Board desk at the airport and enquired about renting a cottage in Connemara. "I want somewhere very quiet and isolated," he said. He had decided what to do with the rest of his prize money and the rest of his study leave. He would buy a second-hand car, fill the back seat with books and writingpaper and Guinness and his cassette player and Bob Dylan tapes, and spend the summer in some humble equivalent of Yeats's lonely tower, writing poetry.

While they were telephoning for him, he picked up a leaflet advertising the American Express card, and for want of anything else to do, filled in the application form.

. . . .

Philip Swallow settled his hotel bill and sat in the foyer with his packed bags beside him, waiting to be picked up by the British Council car—or, rather, Landrover, for such was the vehicle prudently favoured by the Council in Ankara. Philip had never seen such roads in a modern city, pitted and pot-holed like the surface of the moon. Whenever there was rain the roads flooded because the construction workers who laid them had disposed of all debris by throwing them into the drains, which were therefore permanently blocked.

The hotel manager passed Philip, smiled, stopped and bowed. "You go back to England tonight, Professor?"

"No, no. To Istanbul. By the night train."

"Ah!" The manager's face lit up with envy and pathos. "Istanbul is very beautiful."

"So I've heard."

"Very old. Very beautiful. Not like Ankara."

"Oh, I've enjoyed my stay in Ankara very much," said Philip. Such lies become second nature to the cultural traveller. He had not enjoyed his stay in Ankara at all, and would be glad to shake the dust of the place off his feet— and there was plenty of that, whenever it didn't happen to be raining.

Admittedly, things had improved after his first day: they could hardly have got worse. Akbil Borak had been very kind and attentive, even if his only two topics of conversation did seem to be Hull and Hazlitt. There was no doubt that he really did know an awful lot about Hazlitt—rather more than Philip himself, in fact; though it was a pity that he drew attention to their common familiarity with the Romantic essayist by referring to him as "Bill Hazlitt." Philip had been trying for days to think of a way of correcting this habit without appearing to be rude.

The other Turks he had met had been equally kind and hospitable. Al-most every evening there had been a party or dinner or reception for him, at one of the Universities or in someone's cramped, overfurnished apartment. At private parties there would be food and drink somehow scrounged or saved in spite of the endemic shortages—at what cost and domestic sacrifice Philip hated to think. Official receptions were discreetly supplied with booze by the British Council, largesse deeply appreciated by the Turks, who looked upon

Philip in consequence as a kind of lucky mascot. Not for a long time had the university teachers of English in Ankara had so many parties in such a short time. They turned up night after night, the same faces beaming with pleasure, shaking Philip's hand enthusiastically as if they had just met him for the first time. There was laughter and chatter and recorded music—sometimes dancing. Philip laughed and chatted and drank, and even on one occasion essayed a clumsy *pas de deux* with a lady professor of mature years who retained a remarkable aptitude for the belly-dance. This performance was greeted with loud applause, and described by a misty-eyed British Council officer who witnessed it as a breakthrough in Anglo-Turkish cultural relations. But in some deep core of himself, where raki and Embassy scotch could not reach, Philip felt lonely and depressed. He recognized the symptoms of his malaise because he had suffered from it before on his travels, though never so severely. It was a feeling that defined itself as a simple, insistent question: *Why am I here?* Why was he in Ankara, Turkey, instead of in Rummidge, England? It was a question that posed itself less sharply at parties than when he sat beside a lectern at the front of some dusty classroom facing rows of curious, swarthy young men and dark-eyed young women and listened to some Turkish professor introducing him at laborious length, punctiliously enumerating every academic distinction that could be squeezed from the reference books (Philip confidently expected one day to hear his O-level results being recited, if not his brilliant performance in the eleven-plus) while he himself nervously fingered the hastily rewritten opening pages of his lecture on Hazlitt; or when he lay upon his hotel bed in the slack hours between lecturing and partying and sightseeing (not that there was a great deal to see in Ankara once you had visited the Anitkabir and the Hittite museum, but the tireless Akbil Borak had made sure that he saw it all), picking out previously unread bits of the crumpled *Guardian* he had brought with him days before, and listening to the strains of foreign music and the sound of foreign tongues coming through the walls and the strident noise of traffic rising from the street. *Why am I here?* Hundreds, probably thousands of pounds of public money had been expended on bringing him to Turkey. Secretaries had typed letters, telex machines had chattered, telephone wires hummed, files thickened in offices in Ankara, Istanbul, London. Precious fossil fuel had been burned away in the stratosphere to propel him like an arrow from Heathrow to Esenboga. The domestic economies and digestions of the academic community of Ankara had been taxed to their limits in the cause of entertaining him. And for what purpose? So that he could bring the good news about Hazlitt, or Literature and History and Society and Psychology and Philosophy, to the young Turkish bourgeoisie, whose chief motive for studying English (so Akbil Borak had confided in a moment of raki-induced candour) was to secure a job as a civil servant or air hostess and to avoid the murderously factious social science faculties? When he was driven through the streets of Ankara, teeming with a vast anonymous impoverished proletariat, dressed in dusty cotton drab, toiling up and down the concrete hills with the dogged inscrutable persistence of ants, under the unsmiling surveillance of the omnipresent, heavily armed military, he could understand the modest pragmatism of the students' ambitions. But how would Hazlitt help them?

"Excuse me, sir." The hotel manager was back. "Will you be requiring dinner? The train to Istanbul does not leave for several hours."

"Oh, no thank you," said Philip. "I'm going out." The manager bowed and withdrew.

Custer, the British Council's cultural affairs officer, had invited Philip to a buffet supper at his apartment. "I won't pretend it's in your honour," he had explained. "We've got a string quartet from Leeds arriving in the afternoon. Got to lay on something for them, so you might as well come along. Nothing elaborate, you know, quite informal. There'll be a few other people there. Tell you what," he added, as if struck by a brilliant idea, "I'll invite Borak."

"I think he may have seen enough of me in the last few days . . ." Philip suggested.

"Oh no, he'd be offended if I didn't invite him. His wife, too. Hassim will collect you from the hotel about seven. Bring your luggage with you, and I'll run you down to the station at about ten to catch your train."

Recognizing the tall figure and melancholy moustache of Hassim, the Council driver, negotiating the revolving door, Philip stood up and carried his bags across the foyer. Hassim, who spoke no English, relieved him of his suitcase and led the way to the Landrover.

Of course, Philip reflected, as he climbed into the seat beside Hassim, and they jolted away, he might have felt quite differently about this trip if it hadn't been for that surprising spasm of desire for Hilary at the very moment of his departure from home. The warm promise of that glimpsed swaying breast had imprinted itself upon his mind, taunting and tormenting him as he lay awake in his narrow hotel bed, reinforcing the question, *Why am I here?* Sex with Hilary wasn't the greatest erotic sensation in the world, but at least it was something. A temporary release from tension. A little pleasant oblivion. Here in Turkey there wasn't a hope of erotic adventure. The friendly women he met were all married, with husbands in genial but watchful attendance. The dimpled, sloe-eyed girl students never seemed to be allowed closer than lecturing distance to him, unless they appeared in the rôle of daughters to one of the academic couples, and Philip had the feeling that to make a pass at one of *them* might provoke a diplomatic incident. Turkey was, on the surface anyway, a country of old-fashioned moral propriety.

The Landrover crawled forward amid congested traffic. There seemed to be a permanent traffic jam in the centre of Ankara—if this was the centre. Philip had acquired no sense of the geography of the city because it all looked the same to him—untreated concrete, cracked pavements, pitted roads, everything the colour of ash, scarcely a tree or blade of grass to be seen, in spite of its being spring. It was getting dark, now, and under their sparse and inadequate street lighting the streets grew deep and sinister shadows, except where kerosene lamps flared amid an improvised street market, with shawled women haggling over vegetables and kitchenware, or where bleak fluorescent light bounced through plateglass windows from the Formica tabletops of a smoke-filled working-men's café. Philip had the feeling that if Hassim were suddenly to stop the Landrover and pitch him out into the street, he would never be seen again—he would be dragged into the shadows, stripped and robbed of everything he possessed, murdered and flung into one of the blocked drains. He felt a long way from home. Why was he here? Was it, perhaps, time to call a halt to his travels, abandon the quest for intensity of experience he had burbled on about to Morris Zapp, hang up his lecture notes and cash in his traveller's cheques, settle for routine and domesticity, for safe sex with Hilary and the familiar round of the Rummidge academic year, from Freshers' Conference to Finals Examiners' Meeting, until it was time to retire, retire from both sex and work? Followed in due course by retirement from life. Was that it?

The Landrover stopped: they had arrived at a modern apartment block on one of the hills that ringed the city. Hassim gestured Philip into the lift and pressed the button for the sixth floor. Custer came to the front door of the apartment, flushed, in shirtsleeves, a glass in his hand. "Ah, there you are, come in, come in! Let me take your case. Go into the drawing-room and I'll bring you a drink. Gin and tonic? Borak's in there. By the way, it isn't a string quartet after all, it's a jazz quartet. London cocked up again."

Custer led him down a hall, opened a door and ushered Philip into the drawing-room, moderately full of people standing in groups with glasses in their hands. The first face that Philip focused on was Joy Simpson's.

. . .

Akbil Borak never ceased to be surprised by Philip Swallow's behaviour. On the day of his arrival the Englishman had twice abruptly measured his length upon the ground, and now, on the evening of his departure, he looked as if he was going to do it again, in Mr. and Mrs. Custer's drawing-room, for he stumbled on the threshold, and only saved himself from falling by grabbing at a chair-back for support. Heads turned all across the room, and there was a moment's embarrassed hush; then, seeing that there was nothing seriously amiss, the groups resumed their convivial chatter.

Akbil had been standing next to Oya, talking to the drummer from the jazz quartet and to Mrs. Simpson, the British Council librarian at Istanbul, a pleasant, if reserved lady, with shapely buttocks and beautiful blonde hair. Akbil was telling Mrs. Simpson about the shops in Hull, and mentally wondering whether the fair women of the north had golden pubic hair to match their heads, when Philip Swallow made his noisy entrance, crashing into the furniture near the door. Akbil hurried forward to offer assistance, but Philip, rising from his knees, shook off his hand and took a few uncertain steps towards Mrs. Simpson. His face was white. "*You!*" he whispered hoarsely, staring at Mrs. Simpson. She, too, had turned slightly pale, as well she might at this strange greeting. "Hallo," she said, holding her glass tightly with the fingers of both hands. "Alex Custer told me that you might drop in tonight. How are you enjoying Turkey?"

"You have met before, then?" said Akbil, glancing from one to the other.

"Briefly," said Mrs. Simpson. "Several years ago, in Genoa, wasn't it, Professor Swallow?"

"I thought you were dead," said Philip Swallow. He had not altered the direction of his gaze, or even blinked.

Oya clutched at Akbil's sleeve with excitement. "Oh, how is that?" she cried.

Mrs. Simpson frowned. "Oh dear, I suppose you read that list in the newspapers," she said to Philip Swallow. "It was issued prematurely by the Indian authorities. It caused a great deal of confusion and distress, I'm afraid."

"You mean you survived that crash?"

"I wasn't on the plane. I was supposed to be—this was about three years ago," she explained parenthetically to Akbil and Oya and the jazz drummer. "My husband was posted to India. I was going with him, but at the last moment my doctor said not to go, I was eight months pregnant and he thought it would be too risky, so John went alone, and I stayed behind with Gerard, our little boy, but somehow our names were left on the passenger list, or some passenger list. The plane crashed, landing in the middle of a storm."

"And your husband . . . ?" Oya quavered.

"There were very few survivors," said Mrs. Simpson simply, "and he wasn't one of them."

Oya was weeping copiously. "I pity you," she said, snuffling into a handkerchief.

"I thought you were dead," said Philip Swallow again, as if he had not heard this explanation, or, having heard it, had failed to take it in.

"But you see, Professor Swallow, she is not dead after all! She lives!" Oya gave a little clap of her hands and rose on to the tips of her toes, smiling through her tears. Akbil had the sense that his wife was supplying all the emotion that the two English should be exhibiting. The jazz drummer had slipped away unnoticed at some point in Mrs. Simpson's recital. "You should be happy," said Oya to Philip. "It is like a fairy story."

"I am of course very pleased to see Mrs. Simpson alive and well," he said. He seemed to have recovered his composure, though his face was still pale.

"And the art of pleasing consists in being pleased, as Bill Hazlitt says," Akbil struck in, rather neatly, he thought.

"But what are you doing in Ankara?" Philip asked Mrs. Simpson.

"I'm just here for a few days, for some meetings. I run the Council library in Istanbul."

"I'm going to Istanbul tonight," said Philip Swallow, with some signs of excitement.

"Oh? How long will you be staying there?"

"Three or four days. I go home on Friday."

"Unfortunately, I'm here till Friday."

Philip Swallow looked as if he couldn't believe this intelligence. He turned to Akbil. "Akbil, Alex Custer seems to have forgotten all about my drink, could you possibly . . . ?"

"Of course," said Akbil, "I will seek it."

"I will help you," said Oya. "Mrs. Simpson also needs a refill." She took Mrs. Simpson's glass and almost pushed Akbil towards the door.

"Why did you not stay with them?" Akbil muttered to Oya in Turkish. "They will think us rude."

"I have a feeling they wish to be alone," said Oya. "I think there is something between them."

"Do you think so?" Akbil was astonished. He looked back over his shoulder. Philip Swallow was certainly deep in conversation with Mrs. Simpson, who looked flustered for once. "That man never ceases to surprise me," he said.

. . .

Three hours later, Philip paced anxiously up and down the broad platform of Ankara's main railway station beside the tall coaches of the Ankara-Istanbul express. The train had a period air, vaguely reminiscent of thirties' thrillers, as did the whole scene. Wisps of smoke and steam drifted out of deep shadows into the bright glare of arc lights. A family of peasants had camped out for the night on a bench, surrounded by their bundles and baskets. The mother, suckling her baby, gazed impassively at the women in chic velvet trouser-suits who led caravans of porters bearing their matched suitcases towards the first class coaches. Uniformed officials clasping millboards strutted up and down, giving orders to menials and kicking beggars out of the way. The second- and third-class compartments were already full, exhaling odours of garlic, tobacco and perspiration from their ventilators; the passengers within, wedged tightly together, hip to hip, knee to knee, prepared themselves stoically for the night's long journey. From time to time a figure would dart from one of these coaches across the platform to a small kiosk that sold tea, fizzy drinks, pretzel-shaped bread and poisonous-looking sweets.

In the first-class compartments, where Philip had a berth, the atmosphere was more relaxed. Bottles clinked against glasses, and card parties were being organized, though the lights were almost too dim to see the cards by. There was an atmosphere of gossip and intrigue, of assignations made and bribes passed. At the end of the corridor there was a red glow from the small solid-fuel furnace which the sleeping-car attendant was vigorously stoking, sweat pouring off his brow.

"It supplies heat and hot water to the sleepers," Custer had explained, when seeing Philip off. "Looks rather primitive, but it's effective. It can get quite cold out on the plains at night, even in spring."

Philip managed to persuade Custer and Akbil Borak not to wait with him until the train departed. "There's no point, really," he assured them. "I'll be quite all right."

"One of the pleasantest things in the world is going on a journey," said Akbil Borak with a smile, "but I prefer to go by myself."

"Do you really?" said Custer. "I prefer company."

"No, no!" Borak laughed. "I was quoting Bill Hazlitt. The essay 'On going on a journey.'"

"Please don't wait," said Philip.

"Well," said Custer, "Perhaps I should get back and see to the jazz quartet."

"And I must collect my wife from your apartment, Mr. Custer," said Borak.

They shook Philip's hand and after exchanging the pleasantries usual on such occasions, took themselves off. Philip watched them go with relief. If Joy decided in the end to join him, she would not want to be seen doing so by Custer and Borak.

But that had been half an hour ago, and still she had not come.

"I can't possibly go back to Istanbul tonight," she had said, when he got her alone for a few minutes at Custer's party. "I've only just arrived in Ankara. My suitcase is still in the hall, unpacked."

"That makes it all the simpler," said Philip. "Just pick it up and leave with me." He ate her with his eyes, wolfing the features he had thought he would never see again, the softly waved blonde hair, the wide generous mouth, the slightly heavy chin.

"I've come here on Council business."

"You could make some excuse."

"Why should I?"

"Because I love you." The words came out without premeditation. She blushed and lowered her eyes. "Don't be ridiculous."

"I've never forgotten that night," he said.

"For heaven's sake," she murmured. "Not here. Not now."

"When then? I must talk to you."

"Ah, have you two introduced yourselves?" cried Mrs. Custer, coming up to them with a plate of canapés.

"We've met before, actually. In Genoa," said Joy.

"Really? Ah, well, that's the way, isn't it, when one is in the Council, one is always bumping into old acquaintances in the most unlikely places. And how are you, Joy? How are the children—Gerard, isn't it, and—"

"Mrs. Simpson was just telling me that Gerard is not at all well," said Philip. Joy stared at him.

"Oh dear! Nothing serous I hope?" Mrs. Custer said to Joy.

Philip's heart thumped as he waited for her reply.

"He had a bit of a temperature when I left," she said at length. "I may phone my girl later to see how he is."

Philip turned his head aside to conceal his triumph.

"Oh, yes, please do," said Mrs. Custer. "Use the phone in our bedroom, it's more private." She swept the room with a hostess's regard. "Oh dear, the saxophonist is browsing at our bookshelves—I always think that's a bad sign at a party, don't you? Do come and talk to him, Joy—will you excuse us, Professor Swallow?"

"Of course," said Philip.

He could not contrive to be alone with Joy for the rest of the evening. He watched her movements closely, but did not see her go into the Custers' bedroom. When it was time for him to leave for the station, well before the party was due to end, he was obliged to shake her formally by the hand in the presence of the other guests. "Goodbye, then," he said, trying to hold her gaze. "I hope your little boy is all right. Have you phoned yet?"

"Not yet," she said. "Goodbye, Professor Swallow."

And that was that. He shot her one brief, beseeching look, and left the apartment with Custer and Borak. He could only hope and pray that after he had gone she would have made the call to Istanbul and concocted some story about her child that would require her immediate return home.

Philip took another turn beside the wagon-lit and checked his watch against the station clock. There were only three minutes to go before the train was due to depart. The suspense was agonizing, yet he felt strangely exhilarated. The depression of the past week had lifted, was already forgotten. He was again a man at the centre of his own story—and what a story! He could still hardly believe that Joy was not dead, after all, but alive. Alive! That warm, breathing flesh that he had clasped in the purple-lit bedroom in Genoa was still warm, still breathed. He felt himself transformed by the miraculous reversal of fortune, lifted up as by a wave. He heard himself saying to her in the corner of the Custers' drawing-room, *"Because I love you,"* simply, sincerely, without hesitation, without embarrassment, like a hero in a film. He was not, after all, finished, washed up, ready for retirement. He was still capable of a great romance. Intensity had returned to experience. Where it would lead him to, he did not know, or care. He had a vague premonition of difficulties and pain ahead, to do with Hilary, the children, his career, but pushed them aside. All his mental energy was concentrated on willing Joy to reappear.

Doors slammed along the length of the train. Railway officials, posted at intervals along the platform like sentries, stiffened and looked to each other for signals. The minute hand of the station clock twitched forward. One minute to go.

Philip climbed reluctantly into the train, lowered the window of the door, and hung out of it, looking desperately in the direction of the ticket barrier. A uniformed official standing just beneath him looked to his left and right, then raised a whistle to his lips.

"Stop!" cried Philip, opening the door and jumping down on to the platform. He had seen a woman's figure suddenly appear at the ticket barrier, her fair hair catching the light of the arc lamps. The man with the whistle, protesting in Turkish, tried to push Philip back into the train; then, when this failed, to close the door. As they wrestled, Joy came running across the broad platform, swinging a small suitcase in one hand. Philip pointed, the official stopped struggling and indignantly adjusted his uniform. Philip gave him a large-denomination banknote. The man smiled and held the door open for them to board the train. The door slammed behind them. A whistle shrilled. The train jerked into motion. In the dimly-lit corridor curious faces peered out of doorways, as Philip propelled Joy towards his compartment. He ushered her inside and slid the door shut behind him.

"You came," he said. It was the first word either of them had spoken.

Joy sank on to the made-up bed, and closed her eyes. Her bosom rose and fell as she gulped air. "I have a ticket," she gasped. "But no berth."

"You can share this one," he said.

. . .

As the train rocked and rumbled through the night they made awkward but rapturous love on the narrow bunk bed, their sighs and cries muffled by the creaking and rattling of the rolling-stock. Afterwards they clung together and talked. Or rather Joy talked—jerkily, hesitantly at first, then more fluently—while Philip mostly listened, responding with phatic strokings and squeezings of her soft limbs.

"That was so lovely, it's the first time since John . . . Yes, I've had opportunities, but I've been so racked with guilt . . . I thought John being killed was a sort of punishment, you see. For being unfaithful to him. With you, of course—did you think I was promiscuous, or something? The only time, yes, does that surprise you? Why did I let you, yes, I often wondered about that. I never did anything so insane, before or since, until now, and this is different, anyway, since I know you, in a manner of speaking, and John isn't here to be hurt. But that first time, there I was, a happily-married woman, well fairly happy anyway, as happy as most wives are, and I gave myself to a total stranger who suddenly appeared out of nowhere in the middle of the night, as if you were a god or an angel or something and there was nothing I could do but submit. When I woke up the next morning I thought it had been a dream, but when I saw that John had left and your bags were in the hall, and realized that it had all really happened I nearly went mad. Well I may have seemed calm to you but I can tell you that I was on the verge of hysteria, I had to keep going into the bathroom and jabbing a pair of nail scissors into my hand so that the pain in my hand would stop me thinking about what I had done.

"Do you ever have a feeling when you're driving fairly fast, in heavy traffic, that the whole thing is extraordinarily precarious, though everyone involved seems to take it for granted? All the drivers in their cars and lorries look so bored, so abstracted, just wanting to get from A to B; yet all the time they're just inches, seconds, away from sudden death. It only needs someone to turn their steering-wheel a few inches this way rather than that, for everyone to start crashing into one another. Or you're driving along some twisty coastal road, and you realize that if you were to take your hands off the wheel for just a second you would go shooting off the edge into thin air. It's a frightening feeling, because you realize how easy it would be to do it, how quick, how simple, how irreversible. It seemed to me that I had done something like that, only I had swerved off the road into life, not death.

"I couldn't complain about John as a husband. He was a kind man, faithful as far as I know, doted on Gerard, worked hard at his career. By normal standards it was a successful marriage. The physical side was all right, as far as I could tell. I mean, I didn't have any experience to compare it with, and John didn't have much either. We met when we were students at university, and we lived together for several years before we got married, our parents were terribly shocked when they found out, but actually it meant that we were pretty innocent about sex, never having known anybody else that way. I sometimes had an uneasy suspicion that John had decided to, not consciously you know, but well decided to find himself a girl as soon as he could in his first year and settle into a steady relationship, so as not to be distracted from getting on with his studies by sex. I mean, it was just like being married, really, and when we actually *got* married it was a purely social event, an expensive party, there was no difference in our lives before and after. The honeymoon was just a foreign holiday. I remember feeling rather sad on our wedding night that it was all so familiar, that neither of us was nervous or shy, and I had a wicked thought that perhaps we should go out and find another couple in the same situation—the hotel was full of honeymooners—and exchange partners, or all get into bed together. I wasn't serious, it was just a thought, but I suppose it was symptomatic. I didn't mention it to John, he wouldn't have understood, he would have been hurt, thought I was getting at him. He was a conscientious lover, read up books about foreplay and so on, did his best to please me, and he did please me—I mean I never actually wanted to make love with him, not enough to take the initiative, I left that to him, but if he wanted to I usually enjoyed it.

"But somehow there was something missing. I always felt that. Passion perhaps. I never felt that John desired me passionately, or I him. I used to read about people making love in novels, and they seemed so ecstatic, so carried away. I never felt that. Then I would read sensible books about sex and marriage and the correspondence columns in the women's magazines and decide that the novels were lying, the writers were making it all up, that I was jolly lucky to be having sex at all, never mind whether it was ecstatic or not. And then, that night, you appeared, and for the first time in my life I knew what it was like to be desired, passionately."

Here there was a hiatus in Joy's monologue while Philip once more fervently demonstrated how well-founded this intuition had been. Some time later she resumed.

"While I was sitting on the sofa with John, opposite you, and he was chuntering on about phonetics and testing techniques and language laboratories, I could feel your desire coming from you like radioactivity, burning through my dressing-gown. It astonished me that John couldn't sense it himself, that he was so oblivious to it that he was going to go off and leave us alone together. I was fascinated, excited. I had no intention at that point of letting you make love to me, indeed I didn't think you would have the nerve to even make a pass. I was so sure of myself that I let John go off to Milan without a qualm. But when I came back into the living-room and you started to shake, I started to shake too—you noticed? And then when we were in the bedroom and you were shaking more than ever, it seemed to me that you were like the core of a nuclear reactor that's, what's the word, gone critical, that you would shake yourself to pieces, or melt a hole in the floor, consume yourself with your own passion, if I didn't do something."

"I had come back from the dead," Philip groaned, remembering. "You were life, beauty. I wanted to be reconnected to life. You healed me."

"I took my hands off the wheel," said Joy. "I went over the edge with you because I had never been wanted like that before."

. . . .

In the early morning, they sat face to face in the restaurant car, with their fingers entwined beneath the table, sipping glasses of hot black tea from their free hands, as the train trundled through the pleasant little towns and villages on the Asian shore of the Sea of Marmara. There was vegetation here—trees and shrubs and vines—between the houses. The landscape seemed positively lush after the arid heights of Ankara. A few early risers were out in their gardens, watering the plants, or enjoying a quiet smoke in the slanting light of the rising sun. They waved as the train passed.

"You never wrote to me," said Joy.

"I didn't know how to, without risking compromising you," said Philip. "I thought you wouldn't want me to, anyway. You seemed so cold that morning I left Genoa, I thought you wanted to forget the whole thing had happened."

"I did," said Joy, "but I found that was impossible."

"Then it wasn't long before I read in the newspaper that you were dead."

"Yes, I never thought of that. The papers did publish a correction."

"I must have missed it," said Philip. "Anyway, *you* could have written to me, especially when your husband . . . I mean, when you were . . ."

"Free? I didn't want to interfere with your life. I looked you up. I know all about you. You're married, with three children, Amanda, Robert and Matthew. Wife Hilary, *née* Broome, daughter of Commander and Mrs. A. J. Broome. I didn't want to break up your marriage."

"It's not much of a marriage," said Philip. "The children are all grown up, and Hilary's fed up. We nearly separated ten years ago. I think we should have done." The image of Hilary's breast had almost faded from his memory, expunged by the more recent, keener sensation of Joy's blunt, cylindrical nipples stiffening under his touch. "I've stood in Hilary's way," he said earnestly. "She'd do better on her own."

. . .

"This is where Asia meets Europe," said Joy, as a battered taxi rushed them across a vast, new-looking suspension bridge. Far below, huge tankers and a multitude of smaller craft churned the waters of the Bosphorus. To their right, green hills dotted with white houses rose steeply from the narrowing channel. To their left, domes and minarets punctuated the skyline of an immense city, behind which the water broadened out into a sea. "Sea of Marmara," Joy explained. "The Black Sea is at the other end of the Bosphorus."

"It's wonderful," said Philip. "This combination of water and sky and hills and architecture reminds me of Euphoria, the view I used to see every morning when I woke up and drew the curtains. It's the Bay Area of the ancient world."

"I tell you what we'll do," said Joy. "We'll take this cab down to the Galata bridge, and take a ferry boat up the Bosphorus to Bogazici, where I live. That's the best way to get your first impressions of Istanbul, from the water."

Philip squeezed her knee. "You are my Euphoria, my Newfoundland," he said.

. . .

Half an hour later they stood hand in hand on the deck of a white steamer as it surged up the Bosphorus, away from the teeming quayside. Joy pointed out the landmarks. "That's Santa Sophia, that's the Blue Mosque. I'll take you to see them later. The Golden Horn is behind the bridge. That's the Sea of Marmara, with all the wrecks."

"Why so many?"

"There's far too much traffic on the water here, the ships keep colliding, especially the big tankers. Sometimes they crash into the houses at the edge of the Bosphorus. I took an apartment well up in the hills."

"Am I going to stay with you?" Philip asked.

Joy frowned. "I don't think it would be a good idea. I have a Turkish girl living in, and the children would be inquisitive. There wouldn't be much privacy. I know a nice hotel not far away, I'll come and see you there. But you can eat with us, of course."

"But won't you be able to spend the night with me?" Philip pleaded. "I want to wake up in the morning and find you beside me."

"You can't have everything you want," she said, smiling.

The ferry boat stitched its way up the Bosphorus, stopping frequently at small wooden jetties that were like aquatic bus-stops. The boat would swerve inshore, pull up amid much foaming and rattling as the screws were reversed; passengers carrying shopping bags and briefcases briskly disembarked, new passengers scurried aboard, a bell rang, and in seconds, it seemed, they would be off again. The houses on the shore gradually took on a less antique aspect, the landscape in the background became boskier, as they proceeded. At one of the stops, which had a relaxed, seasidey air to it, Joy led him ashore, and they took a taxi to Joy's apartment, situated on a road that twisted steeply between walled gardens matted with flowering vines. Childish shrieks and cries were heard from the windows as Philip paid the taxi driver the fare for which Joy had bargained at the outset of their ride ("If you don't beat them down by at least half, you've been diddled," she had warned him). "The children are surprised to see me back home so soon," she said.

"What will you tell them?"

"Oh, that my meetings were cancelled, or something."

The children were already running down the garden steps to meet their mother, followed by a plump, smiling girl with small black eyes set in a round brown face like currants in a bun. "Be careful!" she cried. "Gerard! Miranda! Not so fast."

Philip recognized Gerard, who treated him to the same slightly hostile scrutiny that he remembered well from Genoa. Miranda, who looked about three years old, smiled rather sweetly when she was introduced.

"Have you got presents for us, Mummy?" Gerard asked.

Joy looked crestfallen. "Oh, dear, I didn't have time. I came home so unexpectedly."

"I've got something," said Philip. "Do you two like Turkish Delight?" He opened his briefcase and brought out a cardboard box packed with rose-hip and almond flavoured delight. "This comes from Ankara—I was told it's the best you can get."

"Are you sure you didn't mean to give that to someone else?" said Joy.

"Oh, no," said Philip, who had bought it for Hilary. "Anyway, I can always get some more here."

"Just one piece each for now, then." said Joy. "Give the box to Selina, and say thank you to Professor Swallow."

"Please call me Philip," he said.

"Thank you" said Gerard, rather grudgingly, his mouth full of Turkish delight.

"Thank you Flip," said Miranda.

"Well, show Philip the way, Miranda," said Joy.

The little girl put her sticky hand in Philip's and led him up the steep steps that led to the house. He found himself strangely taken with this child, her trusting eyes and ready smile. Later, as he sat with Joy on the balcony of her first floor apartment, he watched Miranda at play with her dolls in the garden below. They were drinking coffee (a pleasure so rare in Turkey it almost made one faint) and Joy was telling him in condensed form the story of her recent life. "Of course I could have stayed in England and lived on my widow's pension, but I thought that would be just too dreary, so I persuaded the Council to let me train as a librarian and to give me a job. They weren't too keen, but I was able to exert a certain amount of moral pressure. Anyway, I'm a good librarian."

"I'm sure you are," said Philip abstractedly, peering down into the garden. Miranda had seated her dolls in a semicircle and was earnestly talking to them. "I wonder what Miranda's telling her dolls."

"She's probably telling them about you," said Joy. "She's greatly taken with your beard."

"Is that so?" Philip laughed, and stroked his beard self-consciously. He felt ridiculously pleased. "She's a most attractive little girl, isn't she? Reminds me of someone, but I can't think who it is."

"Can't you?" Joy gave him a rather strange look.

"Well, it's not you . . ."

"No, it's not me."

"It must be your husband, I suppose, though I don't remember him very well."

"No, she doesn't take after John."

"Who then?"

"You," said Joy. "She takes after you."

. . .

Four days later, gazing down at the snow-crusted Alps from the window of a Turkish Airlines Boeing 727, Philip could still go hot and cold at the memory of that extraordinary moment, as the import of Joy's "*She takes after you*" sank in, and he realized that the little girl playing in the garden beneath him, a fragile assemblage of brown limbs and blonde hair and white cotton smock, scarcely bigger than the dolls she handled, was a child of his loins; that for the past three years, all unknown to him, this little fragment of flesh had been in existence, orbiting his conscious life in silence and obscurity, like an undiscovered star. "*What?*" he breathed. "You mean—Miranda is my . . . our . . . Are you sure?"

"Not sure, but you must admit the likeness is striking."

"But, but . . ." he groped for words, gasped for breath. "But you told me, that night, that you were, you know, that it would be all right."

"I lied. I was off the pill, John and I were trying to conceive again. I was afraid that if I told you, it would break the spell, you might stop. Wasn't that wicked of me?"

"No, it was lovely of you, wonderful of you, but, my God, why didn't you tell me?"

"At first I didn't know whether I was pregnant by you or by John. The shock of the crash brought on the birth. As soon as I saw Miranda's eyes, I knew she was yours. But what would have been the point of telling you?"

"I could have divorced Hilary and married you."

"Exactly. I told you this morning, I didn't want that."

"I'm going to anyway, now," said Philip.

Joy said nothing for a few moments. Then she said, not looking at him, but painting rings on the plastic-topped table, dipping her finger in a pool of spilled coffee: "When I heard that you were coming to Turkey, I decided to avoid meeting you, because I was afraid that it would end like this. I arranged to go to Ankara just over the days when you would be in Istanbul—Alex Custer had been on at me for some time to meet the people up there to discuss policy. I got hold of your schedule and worked it all out so that I would arrive in Ankara just as you left. But I miscalculated by just a few hours. When I got to the Custers, they told me you were coming that evening."

"It was fate," said Philip.

"Yes, I came to that conclusion myself," said Joy. "That's why I joined you on the train."

"You cut it jolly fine," said Philip.

"I wanted to give Fate a chance for second thoughts," said Joy.

. . .

Low cloud covered southern England. As the plane dipped through it, the sun disappeared like a light being switched off, and underneath the cloud it was raining. Moisture dribbled down the windows of the aircraft as it taxied on Heathrow's wet tarmac. Waiting in the stuffy, humid baggage hall, Philip felt himself wilting and shrinking as the intensity of the last few days leaked away. He sank onto a seat, allowed his eyelids to droop, and projected upon their inner surface a home movie of Istanbul, its sights, sounds and smells: churches and minarets, water and sky, the acres of slightly damp carpet under their stockinged feet as they gazed up at the dome of the Blue Mosque, the stained glass glowing like gems in the Palace Harem, the prison-like staircases of Istanbul University with an armed soldier on every landing, the labyrinthine alleys of the great covered bazaar, the waterside restaurant where the wash of a passing ship suddenly slopped through a low window and drenched a whole table of diners; the hotel where he and Joy made love in the afternoons while huge Russian tankers slid past the windows, so close they momentarily blocked out the light that filtered through the venetian blinds. When the sun shone full upon the window, he angled the blinds so that bars of white-hot light striped Joy's body, kindling her blonde pubic hair into flame. He called it the golden fleece, mindful that the Hellespont was not far away. When he kissed her there, his beard brushing her belly, he made a wry joke about the silver among the gold, conscious of the contrast between her beautiful, still youthful body and his scraggy, middle-aged one, but she stroked his head reassuringly. "You make me feel desirable, that's what matters." He nuzzled her, inhaling odours of shore and rockpool; the skin of her inner thighs was as tender as peeled mushrooms; she tasted clean and salty, like some mollusc from the sea. "Ah," she whimpered, "that's divine."

Philip opened his eyes to find his suitcase taking a lonely ride on the carousel. He snatched it up and, somewhat incommoded by the sexual arousal induced by his reverie, ran all the way to Terminal One to catch his connecting flight to Rummidge.

. . .

Up, briefly, into the sunshine again, in a noisy Fokker Friendship; then down again through the grey clouds to the sopping fields and gleaming motorways that ringed Rummidge airport. He was surprised and disconcerted to be met by Hilary. Usually he took a taxi home, and he had counted on solitude, during this last stage of his journey, to rehearse what he was going to say to her. But there she was, in her old beige raincoat, waving from the balcony of the terminal building, as he and his fellow passengers descended the steps from the aircraft and picked their way through the oily puddles on the apron.

Inside the terminal Hilary rushed up and kissed him enthusiastically. "Darling, how are you? I'm glad to see you back safe and sound, the most exciting things have been happening—did you see the review?"

"No," he said. "What review?"

"In the *TLS*. Rudyard Parkinson reviewed your Hazlitt book in the most glowing terms, nearly two whole pages."

"Good Lord," said Philip, feeling himself turning pink with pleasure. "That must be Morris's influence. I'll have to write and thank him."

"I don't think so, darling," said Hilary, "because Parkinson was frightfully rude about Morris's book in the same review. He did you together."

"Oh dear," said Philip, feeling an ignoble spasm of *Schadenfreude* at this news.

"And the *Sunday Times* and the *Observer* have asked for a photograph of you, and Felix Skinner—he's ever so excited about it—says that means they're going to review it too. All I could find was an old snap of you at the seaside in shorts, but I expect they'll only use the head."

"Good Lord," said Philip.

"And I've got something else to tell you. About me."

"What?"

"Let me go and get the car first, while you wait for your luggage."

"I've got something to tell you, too."

"Wait till I get the car."

When she brought the car round to the entrance to the terminal, Hilary offered to move over into the passenger seat, but Philip told her not to bother. She drove rather boisterously, revving the engine hard between gear changes, and pulling up sharply at traffic-lights. As the familiar suburban streets slipped past the windows, she told him her big news. "I've found a job, darling. Well, not a job, exactly, but something I really want to do, something really interesting. I've had a preliminary interview and I'm pretty sure they'll accept me for training."

"What is it, then?" said Philip.

Hilary turned and beamed at him. "Marriage Guidance," she said. "I don't know why I didn't think of it before." She returned her attention to the road, not a moment too soon. "I see," said Philip. "That should be very interesting."

"Absolutely fascinating. I can't wait to start the training." She glanced at him again. "You don't seem very enthusiastic."

"It's a surprise," said Philip. "I wasn't prepared for it. I'm sure you'll be very good at it."

"Well," said Hilary, "I feel I do know something about the subject. I mean, we've had our ups and downs, but we're still together after all these years, aren't we?"

"Yes," said Philip. "We are." He gazed out of the car window at the names of shops: Sketchleys, Rumbelows, Radio Rentals, Woolworths. Plateglass windows stacked with refrigerators, music centres, televisions.

"And what was it you wanted to tell me?" said Hilary.

"Oh, nothing," said Philip. "Nothing important."

PART IV

1

*whhhhheeeeeeeeeeeee*EEEEEEEEEEEEEEE*EEEEEEEEEEEEE!*

To some people, there is no noise on earth as exciting as the sound of three or four big fan-jet engines rising in pitch, as the plane they are sitting in swivels at the end of the runway and, straining against its brakes, prepares for takeoff. The very danger in the situation is inseparable from the exhilaration it yields. You are strapped into your seat now, there is no way back, you have delivered yourself into the power of modern technology. You might as well lie back and enjoy it. *Whhheeeeeeeeeeeeee!* And away we go, the acceleration like a punch in the small of the back, the grass glimpsed through the window flying backwards in a blur, and then falling out of sight suddenly as we soar into the sky. The plane banks to give us one last glimpse of home, flat and banal, before we break through the cloud cover and into the sunshine, the no-smoking sign goes off with a ping, and a faint clink of bottles from the galley heralds the serving of cocktails. *Whheeeeeeeeee!* Europe, here we come! Or Asia, or America, or wherever. It's June, and the conference season is well and truly open. In Oxford and Rummidge, to be sure, the students still sit at their desks in the examination halls, like prisoners in the stocks, but their teachers are able to flit off for a few days before the scripts come in for marking; while in North America the second semester of the academic year is already finished, papers have been graded, credits awarded, and the faculty are free to collect their travel grants and head east, or west, or wherever their fancy takes them. *Wheeeeeeeeee!*

The whole academic world seems to be on the move. Half the passengers on transatlantic flights these days are university teachers. Their luggage is heavier than average, weighed down with books and papers—and bulkier, because their wardrobes must embrace both formal wear and leisurewear, clothes for attending lectures in, and clothes for going to the beach in, or to the Museum, or the Schloss, or the Duomo, or the Folk Village. For that's the attraction of the conference circuit: it's a way of converting work into play, combining professionalism with tourism, and all at someone else's expense. Write a paper and see the world! I'm Jane Austen—fly me! Or Shakespeare, or T. S. Eliot, or Hazlitt. All tickets to ride, to ride the jumbo jets. *Wheeeeeeeeee!*

The air is thick with the babble of these wandering scholars' voices, their questions, complaints, advice, anecdotes. Which airline did you fly? How many stars does the hotel have? Why isn't the conference hall air-conditioned? Don't eat the salad here, they use human manure on the lettuce. Laker is cheap, but their terminal at LA is the pits. Swissair has excellent food. Cathay Pacific give you free drinks in economy. Pan Am are lousy timekeepers, though not as bad as Jugoslavian Airlines (its acronym JAT stands for "joke about time"). Qantas has the best safety record among the international airlines, and Colombia the worst—one flight in three never arrives at its destination (OK, a slight exaggeration). On every El Al flight there are three secret servicemen with guns concealed in their briefcases, trained to shoot hijackers on sight—when taking something from your inside pocket, do it slowly and smile. Did you hear about the Irishman who tried to hijack a plane to Dublin? It was already going there. *Wheeeeeeeeeeeeeee!*

Hijackings are only one of the hazards of modern travel. Every summer there is some kind of disruption of the international airways—a strike of French air-traffic controllers, a go-slow by British baggage handlers, a war in the Middle East. This year it's the worldwide grounding of the DC-10, following a crash at Chicago's O'Hare Airport on May 25th, when one of these planes shed an engine on takeoff and plunged to the ground, killing everyone on board. The captain's last recorded word was "Damn." Stronger expletives are used by travellers fighting at the counters of travel agencies to transfer their tickets to airlines operating Boeing 747s and Lockheed Tristars; or at having to accept a seat on some slow, clapped-out DC-8 with no movies and blocked toilets, flying to Europe via Newfoundland and Reykjavik. Many conferees arrive at their destinations this summer more than usually fatigued, dehydrated and harassed; the dying fall of the engines' *WHHHEEEEEEEEeeeeeeeeee*, as the power is finally switched off, is sweet music to their ears, but their chatter is undiminished, their demand for information insatiable.

How much should you tip? What's the best way to get downtown from the airport? Can you understand the menu? Tip taxis ten per cent in Bangladesh, five per cent in Italy; in Mexico it is not necessary, and in Japan the driver will be positively insulted if you do. Narita airport is forty kilometres from downtown Tokyo. There is a fast electric train, but it stops short of the city centre—best take the limousine bus. The Greek word for bus stop is *stasis*. The Polish word for scrambled eggs is *jajecznice*, pronounced "yighy-ehchneetseh," which is sort of onomatopoeic, if you can get your tongue round it. In Israel, breakfast eggs are served soft-boiled and cold—yuk. In Korea, they eat soup at breakfast. Also at lunch and dinner. In Norway they have dinner at four o'clock in the afternoon, in Spain at ten o'clock at night. In Tokyo the nightclubs close at 11:30 p.m., in Berlin they are only just beginning to open by then.

Oh, the amazing variety of *langue* and *parole*, food and custom, in the countries of the world! But almost equally amazing is the way a shared academic interest will overcome these differences. All over the world, in hotels, university residences and conference centres, in châteaux and villas and country houses, in capital cities and resort towns, beside lakes, among mountains, on the shores of seas cold and warm, people of every colour and nation are gathered together to discuss the novels of Thomas Hardy, or the problem plays of Shakespeare, or the postmodernist short story, or the poetics of Imagism. And, of course, not all the conferences that are going on this summer are concerned with English literature, not by any means. There are at the same time conferences in session on French medieval *chansons* and Spanish poetic drama of the sixteenth century and the German *Sturm und Drang* movement and Serbian folksongs; there are conferences on the dynasties of ancient Crete and the social history of the Scottish Highlands and the foreign policy of Bismarck and the sociology of sport and the economic controversy over monetarism; there are conferences on low-temperature physics and microbiology and oral pathology and quasars and catastrophe theory. Sometimes, when two conferences share the same accommodation, confusions occur: it has been known for a bibliographer specializing in the history of punctuation to sit through the first twenty minutes of a medical paper on "Malfunctions of the Colon" before he realized his mistake.

But, on the whole, academic subject groups are self-defining, exclusive entities. Each has its own jargon, pecking order, newsletter, professional association. The members probably meet only once a year—at a conference. Then, what a lot of hallos, howareyous, and whatareyouworkingons, over the drinks, over the meals, between lectures. Let's have a drink, let's have dinner, let's have breakfast together. It's this kind of informal contact, of course, that's the real *raison d'être* of a conference, not the programme of papers and lectures which has ostensibly brought the participants together, but which most of them find intolerably tedious.

Each subject, and each conference devoted to it, is a world unto itself, but they cluster together in galaxies, so that an adept traveller in intellectual space (like, say, Morris Zapp) can hop from one to another, and appear in Amsterdam as a semiologist, in Zürich as a Joycean, and in Vienna as a narratologist. Being a native speaker of English helps, of course, because English has become the international language of literary theory, and theory is what unites all these and many other conferences. This summer the topic on everyone's lips at every conference Morris attends is the UNESCO Chair of Literary Criticism, and who will get it. What kind of theory will be favoured—formalist, structuralist, Marxist or deconstructionist? Or will it go to some sloppily eclectic liberal humanist, or even to an antitheorist like Philip Swallow?

"Philip Swallow?" says Sy Gootblatt incredulously to Morris Zapp. It is the 15th of June, the eve of Bloomsday, halfway through the International James Joyce Symposium in Zürich, and they are standing at the bar of the crowded James Joyce Pub on Pelikanstrasse. It is a beautifully preserved, genuine Dublin pub, all dark mahogany, red plush and brass fittings, rescued from demolition at the hands of Irish property developers, transported in numbered parts to Switzerland, and lovingly reconstructed in the city where the author of *Ulysses* sat out the First World War, and died in the Second. Its ambience is totally authentic apart from the hygienic cleanliness of everything, especially the basement toilets where you could, if you were so inclined, eat your dinner off the tiled floors—very different from the foetid, slimy hellholes to be found at the bottom of such staircases in Dublin. "*Philip Swallow?*" says Sy Gootblatt. "You must be joking." Sy is an old friend of Morris's from Euphoric State, which he left some five years ago to go to Penn, switching his scholarly interests at the same time from Hooker to the more buoyant field of literary theory. He is good-looking in his slight, dark way, and a bit of a dandy, but small in stature; he keeps rising restlessly on the balls of his feet as if to see who is to be seen in the crowded room.

"I hope I'm joking," says Morris, "but somebody sent me a cutting from a London paper the other day which says he's being mentioned as an outsider candidate for the job."

"What are the odds—nine million to one?" says Sy, who remembers Philip Swallow chiefly as the author of a parlour game called Humiliation, with which he wrecked one of his and Bella's dinner parties many years ago. "He hasn't published anything worth talking about, has he?"

"He's having a huge success with a totally brainless book about Hazlitt," says Morris, "Rudyard Parkinson gave it a rave review in the *TLS*. The British are on this great antitheory kick at the moment and Philip's book just makes them roll onto their backs and wave their paws in the air."

"But they tell me Arthur Kingfisher is advising UNESCO on this appointment," says Sy Gootblatt. "And he's surely not going to recommend that they appoint someone hostile to theory?"

"That's what I keep telling myself," says Morris. "But these old guys do funny things. Kingfisher doesn't like to think that there is anyone around now who is as good as he used to be in his prime, and he might encourage the appointment of a schmo like Philip Swallow just to prove it."

Sy Gootblatt drains his glass of Guinness and grimaces. "Jesus, I hate this stuff," he says. "Shall we go someplace else? I found a bar on the other side of the river that sells Budweiser."

Pocketing their James Joyce Pub beermats as souvenirs, they push their way to the door—a proceeding which takes some time, as every few paces one or the other of them bumps into someone he knows. Morris! Sy! Great to see you! How's Bella? How's Désirée? Oh, I didn't know. What are you working on these days? Let's have a drink some time, let's have dinner, let's have breakfast. Eventually they are outside, on the sidewalk, in the mild evening. There are not many people about, but the streets have a safe, sedate air. The shop windows are brightly lit, filled with luxury goods to tempt the rich burghers of Zürich. The Swissair window has a copy display of dumpy little airplanes made out of white flower-heads, suspended from wires in the form of a mobile. They remind Morris of fancy wreaths. "A good name for the DC-10," he observes, "The Flying Wreath."

This black humour reflects his sombre mood. Things have not been going well for Morris lately. First there was the attack on his book by Rudyard Parkinson in the *TLS*. Then his paper did not go down at all well in Amsterdam. A claque of feminists, hired, he wouldn't be surprised to learn, by his ex-wife, heckled him as he developed his analogy between interpretation and striptease, shouting "Cunts are beautiful!" when he delivered the line, "*staring into that orifice we find that we have somehow overshot the goal of our quest.*" Young McGarrigle, to whom he might have looked for some support, or at least sympathy, in that crisis, had unaccountably disappeared from Amsterdam, leaving no message. Then there was this report that Philip Swallow was being considered for the UNESCO chair—preposterous, but seeing it in print somehow made it seem disturbingly plausible.

"Who sent you the cutting?" Sy asks.

Morris doesn't know. In fact it was Howard Ringbaum, who spotted the item in the London *Sunday Times* and sent it anonymously to Morris Zapp, guessing correctly that it would cause him pain and anxiety. But who inspired the mention of Philip Swallow's name in the newspaper? Very few people know that it was Jacques Textel, who had received from Rudyard Parkinson a copy of his review article, "The English School of Criticism," together with a fawning covering letter, which Textel, irritated by Parkinson's pompous complacency at Vancouver, had chosen to misinterpret as expressing Parkinson's interest in promoting Philip Swallow's candidacy for the UNESCO chair rather than his own. It was Textel who had leaked Philip's name to his British son-in-law, a journalist on the *Sunday Times*, over lunch in the splendid sixth-floor restaurant at the Place Fontenoy; and the son-in-law, who had been ordered to write a special feature on "The Renaissance of the Redbrick University" and was rather short of facts to support this proposition, had devoted a whole paragraph of his article to the Rummidge professor whose recent book had caused such a stir and whose name was being mentioned in connection with the recently mooted UNESCO Chair of Literary Criticism—causing Rudyard Parkinson to choke on his kedgeree when he opened that particular issue of the *Sunday Times* in the Fellows' breakfast-room at All Saints.

Morris and Sy walk across the bridge over the Limmat. The bar that Sy discovered at lunchtime turns out to be in the middle of the red light quarter at night-time. Licenced prostitutes stand on the street corners, one per corner, in the methodical Swiss way. Each is dressed and made up in an almost theatrical fashion, to cater for different tastes. Here you have the classic whore, in short red skirt, black net stockings and high heels; there, a wholesome Tyrolean girl in dirndl skirt and embroidered bodice; and further on, a kinky model in a skin-tight leather jump suit. All look immaculately clean and polished, like the toilets of the James Joyce Pub. Sy Gootblatt, whose wife Bella is visiting her mother in Maine at this time, eyes these women with covert curiosity. "How much do you think they charge?" he murmurs to Morris.

"Are you crazy? Nobody pays to get laid at a conference."

Morris has a point. It's not surprising, when you reflect: men and women with interests in common—more than most of them have with their spouses—thrown together in exotic surroundings, far from home. For a week or two they are off the leash of domesticity, living a life of unwonted self-indulgence, dropping their towels on the bathroom floor for the hotel maid to pick up, eating in restaurants, drinking in outdoor cafés late into the summer nights, inhaling the aromas of coffee and caporals and cognac and bougainvillea. They are tired, overexcited, a little drunk, reluctant to break up the party and retire to solitary sleep. After a lifetime of repressing and sublimating libido in the interests of intellectual labour, they seem to have stumbled on that paradise envisioned by the poet Yeats:

> *Labour is blossoming or dancing where*
> *The body is not bruised to pleasure soul,*
> *Nor beauty born out of its own despair,*
> *Nor blear-eyed wisdom out of midnight oil.*

The soul is pleasured in the lecture theatre and seminar room, and the body in restaurants and night clubs. There need be, apparently, no conflict of interests. You can go on talking shop, about phonetics, or deconstruction, or the pastoral elegy or sprung rhythm, while you are eating and drinking and dancing or even swimming. Academics do amazing things under the shock of this discovery, things their spouses and colleagues back home would not believe: twist the night away in discothèques, sing themselves hoarse in beer cellars, dance on café tables with flowers gripped in their teeth, go midnight bathing in the nude, patronize fairgrounds and ride the giant roller-coasters, shrieking and clutching each other as they swoop down the shining rails, *whheeeeeeeeeeeee!* No wonder they quite often end up in each other's beds. They are recovering the youth they thought they had sacrificed to learning, they are proving to themselves that they are not dryasdust swots after all, but living, breathing, palpitating human beings, with warm flesh and blood, that stirs and secretes and throbs at a lover's touch. Afterwards, when they are back home, and friends and family ask if they enjoyed the conference, they say, oh yes, but not so much for the papers, which were pretty boring, as for the informal contacts one makes on these occasions.

Of course, these conference affairs are not without their incidental embarrassments. You may, for instance, be sexually attracted to someone whose scholarly work you professionally disapprove of. At the Vienna conference on Narrative, some weeks after the James Joyce Symposium in Zürich, Fulvia Morgana and Sy Gootblatt find themselves in the same crowd in a wine cellar in Michaelerplatz one evening, catching each other's eyes with increasing frequency across the scored and stained trestle table, as the white wine flows. At a convenient opportunity, Sy slides onto the bench beside Fulvia and introduces himself. In the din of the crowded cellar he only catches her first name, but that is all he needs. Their friendship ripens rapidly. Fulvia is staying at the Bristol, Sy at the Kaiserin Elisabeth. The Bristol having the more stars, they spend the night together there. Not till morning, after a very demanding night, which made Sy think wistfully of the Zürich whores (at least with them you could presumably call the plays yourself) does Sy get hold of Fulvia's second name and identify her as the raving Marxist poststructuralist whose essay on the stream-of-consciousness novel as an instrument of bourgeois hegemony (oppressing the working classes with books they couldn't understand) he has rubbished in a review due to appear in the next issue of *Novel*. Sy spends the rest of the conference sheepishly escorting Fulvia around the Ring, dodging into cafés whenever he sees anyone he knows, and nodding solemnly at Fulvia while she holds forth about the necessity of revolution with her mouth full of *Sachertorte*.

At Heidelberg, Désirée Zapp and Ronald Frobisher find adultery virtually thrust upon them by the social dynamics of the conference on *Rezeptionsästhetik*. The only two creative writers present, they find themselves constantly together, partly by mutual choice, since they both feel intimidated by the literary critical jargon of their hosts, which they both think is probably nonsense, but cannot be quite sure, since they do not fully understand it, and anyway they can hardly say so to the faces of those who are paying their expenses, so it is a relief to say so to each other; and partly because the academics, privately bored and disappointed by the contributions of Désirée Zapp and Ronald Frobisher to the conference, increasingly leave them to amuse each other. Siegfried von Turpitz, who invited them both, and might have been expected to concern himself with their entertainment, decided early on that the conference was a failure and after a couple of days discovered that he had urgent business in another European city. So Désirée and Ronald find themselves frequently alone together, walking and talking, walking along the Philosophenweg above the Neckar or rambling through the gardens and on the battlements of the ruined castle, and talking, as professional writers will talk to each other, about money and publishers and agents and sales and subsidiary rights and being blocked. And although not irresistibly attracted to each other, they are not exactly unattracted either, and neither wishes to appear in the eyes of the other timidly afraid of sexual adventure. Each has read the other's work in advance of meeting at the conference, and each has been impressed by the forceful and vivid descriptions of sexual intercourse to be found in those texts, and their common assumption that any encounter between a man and a woman not positively repelled by each other will end up sooner or later in bed. In short, each has attributed to the other a degree of libidinous appetite and experience that is in fact greatly exaggerated, and this mutual misapprehension nudges them closer and closer towards intimacy; until one warm night, a little tipsy after a good dinner at the Weinstube Schloss Heidelberg, with its terrace right inside the courtyard of the floodlit castle, as they totter down the cobbled hill together towards the baroque roofs of the old town, Ronald Frobisher stops in the shadow of an ancient wall, enfolds Désirée in his arms and kisses her.

Then of course there is no way of not going to bed together. Both know the inevitable conclusion of a narrative sequence that begins thus—to draw back from it would imply frigidity or impotence. There is only one consideration that cools Ronald Frobisher's ardour as he lies naked under the sheets of Désirée's hotel bed and waits for her to emerge from the bathroom, and it is not loyalty to Irma (Irma went off sex some years ago, following her hysterectomy, and has intimated that she has no objection to Ronald seeking carnal satisfaction elsewhere, providing it is nothing deeply emotional, and she and her friends never hear about it). Unknown to Ronald, an identical thought is troubling Désirée as she disrobes in the bathroom, performs her ablutions and fits her diaphragm (she has ideological and medical objections to the Pill). Getting into bed beside Ronald in the darkened room, she does not immediately turn to him, nor he to her. They lie on their backs, silent and thoughtful. Désirée decides to broach the matter, and Ronald clears his throat preparatory to doing the same.

{ "I was thinking—"
{ "It occurred to me—"

{ "Sorry."
{ "Sorry."

"What were you going to say?"

"No, please—you first."

"I was going to say," says Désirée, in the darkness, "that before we go any further, perhaps we ought to come to an understanding."

"Yes!" says Ronald, eagerly, then changes his intonation to the interrogative: "Yes?"

"What I mean is . . ." Désirée stops. "It's difficult to say without sounding as if I don't trust you."

"It's only natural," says Ronald. "I feel just the same."

"You mean, you don't trust me?"

"I mean there's something I might say to you which might imply that I didn't trust you."

"What is it?"

"It's . . . hard to say."

"I mean," says Désirée. "I've never done it with a writer before."

"Exactly!"

"And what I'm trying to say is . . ."

"That you don't want to read about it in a novel one of these days? Or see it on television."

"How did you guess?"

"I had the same thought."

Désirée claps her hands. "So we can agree that neither of us will use this as material? Whether it's good or bad?"

"Absolutely. Scout's honour."

"Then let's fuck, Ronald," says Désirée, rolling on top of him.

. . .

Whheeeeeeeeeeeeeeeeee! The spin-drier cycle of Hilary Swallow's washing machine makes a sound not unlike a jetplane, especially when she punches the button to stop the motor, and the piercing whine of the rotating drum dies away, falling in pitch, just like the engines of a jumbo jet when the pilot finally cuts them at the end of a long journey. The similarity does not strike Hilary, as she opens the windowed hatch at the front of the appliance, and lifts out a plaited tangle of damp, compacted clothing, for the sound made by a jet engine is less familiar to her than it is to her husband, who is not present to remark upon the likeness, but is in fact in Greece. Philip's absence is a source of understandable grievance in Hilary, as she hangs out his shirts, pants, vests and socks in the garden, for it seems as if he is only at home these days long enough to empty his suitcase of soiled linen, and pack it with freshly laundered shirts and underwear, before he is off on his travels again.

"Look, I'm sorry," Philip had said to her this last time, "but Digby Soames is begging me to go to Greece. I think someone else must have dropped out at the last moment."

"But why does it have to be you? You've only just come back from Turkey."

"Yes, I know, but I feel I should help the Council out if I can."

The facts of the matter are rather different. As soon as he got back from Istanbul, Philip was on the phone to Digby Soames begging him to fix him,

Philip, up as soon as possible with another lecture tour, conference, or sum-mer school—anything, as long as it was in south-east Europe. He had already arranged with Joy to meet her in Israel during Morris Zapp's conference on the Future of Criticism, but that wasn't till August, and he felt that he couldn't wait that long to see her again.

"Hmm," said Digby Soames. "It's an awkward time for Europe, the academic year is almost over. You wouldn't be interested in Australia by any chance?"

"No, Australia's too far. Greece would be handy."

"Handy for what?" said Digby Soames suspiciously.

"I'm doing some research on the classical background to English poetry," Philip improvised. "I just want an excuse to go to Greece."

"Well, I'll see what I can do," said Digby Soames.

What he was able to do was to arrange a few lectures in Salonika and Athens. "It won't be a proper specialist tour," he warned. "We'll pay your fares but no subsistence. You'll probably get fees for your lectures, though."

Philip flew to Salonika via Munich, gave his lectures, and met Joy by ar-rangement in Athens. While Hilary is hanging out the washing in her back garden in St. John's Road, Rummidge, Philip and Joy are having a late break-fast on the sunny balcony of their hotel room, with a view of the Acropolis.

"Will your wife divorce you, then?" says Joy, buttering a croissant.

"If I choose the right moment," says Philip. "I went home with every inten-tion of telling her about us, but when she announced that she wanted to be a marriage counsellor, it just seemed too cruel. I thought it might destroy her morale before she's even started. Perhaps they wouldn't even have taken her on. You can imagine what people might say—physician heal thyself, and so on."

Joy bites into her croissant and chews meditatively. "What are your plans?"

"I thought," says Philip, squinting in the sun at the Acropolis, already teeming with tourists like a block of cheese being devoured by black ants, "that we might hire a car and drive to Delphi."

"I don't mean this weekend, idiot, I mean long-term plans. About us."

"Ah," says Philip. "Well, I thought I wouldn't say anything to Hilary until she's well settled into her training for marriage guidance. I think that when she feels she's got a purpose in life, she'll be quite happy to agree to a divorce."

"And then what?"

"Then we get married, of course."

"And settle where? Not Rummidge, presumably."

"I haven't thought that far ahead," says Philip. "I think I could probably get a job somewhere else, America perhaps. My stock has gone up rather surprisingly, you know, just lately. One of the Sundays even mentioned my name in connection with this UNESCO Chair of Literary Criticism."

"Would that be in Paris?" says Joy. "I wouldn't mind living in Paris."

"It can be anywhere you like, apparently," says Philip. "But it's wishful thinking, anyway. They'd never appoint me. I can't think how my name got into the paper."

"You never know," says Joy.

. . .

Far away in Darlington, Robin Dempsey has also been reading the Sunday papers.

"HALLO, HOW ARE YOU FEELING TODAY?" says ELIZA.

"TERRIBLE," Robin Dempsey types.

"WHAT EXACTLY DO YOU MEAN BY TERRIBLE?"

"ANGRY. INCREDULOUS. JEALOUS."

"WHAT HAS CAUSED YOU TO HAVE THESE FEELINGS?"

"SOMETHING I READ IN THE NEWSPAPER ABOUT PHILIP SWALLOW."

"TELL ME ABOUT PHILIP SWALLOW."

Robin Dempsey types for twenty-five minutes without stopping, until Josh Collins wanders over from his glass-walled cubicle, nibbling a Kit-Kat, upon which Robin stops typing and covers the computer with its plastic hood.

"Want some?" says Josh, offering a piece of the chocolate-covered biscuit.

"No, thank you," says Robin, without looking at him.

"Getting some interesting stuff from ELIZA, are you?"

"Yes."

"You don't think you're overdoing it?"

"Overdoing what?" says Robin coldly.

"No offence, only you're in here morning, noon and night, talking to that thing."

"It doesn't interfere with you, does it?"

"Well, I have to *be* here."

"You'd be here anyway. You're always here."

"I used to like having the place to myself occasionally," says Josh, going rather red. "To work on my own programs in peace. I don't mind telling you," he continues (it is the longest conversation Josh has ever had with anyone). "That it fair gives me the creeps to see you hunched over that VDU, day in and day out. You're becoming dependent upon it."

"I'm simply doing my research."

"It's called transference. I looked it up in a psychology book."

"Rubbish!" shouts Robin Dempsey.

"If you ask me, you need a proper psychiatrist," says Josh Collins, trembling with anger. "You're off your trolley. That thing"—he points a quivering finger at ELIZA—"Can't really talk, you know. It can't actually *think*. It can't answer questions. It's not a bloody *oracle*."

"I know perfectly well how computers work, thank you," says Robin Dempsey, rising to his feet. "I'll be back after lunch."

He leaves the room in a somewhat flustered state, omitting to switch off the VDU. Josh Collins lifts up the plastic hood and reads what is written on the screen. He frowns and scratches his nose.

. . .

Delphi, like the Acropolis, is crawling with tourists, but the site is proof against their intrusion, as Philip and Joy agree, taking a breather halfway up the steep climb from the road, and looking down on the Sacred Plain far below, where the Pleistos winds through multitudinous olive groves to the Gulf of Corinth.

"It's sublime," she says. "I'm so glad we came."

"Apparently the ancients thought this was the centre of the world," says Philip, consulting his guidebook. "There was a stone on this site called the *omphalos*. The navel of the earth. I suppose that great cleft between the mountains was the vagina."

"You've got a one-track mind," says Joy.

"Is that fair?" says Philip. "Last night I sucked your ten toes, individually."

"There's no need to tell everyone in Delphi," says Joy, blushing charmingly.

"Give me a kiss."

"No, not here. The Greeks don't approve of people kissing in public."

"Not many Greeks about," he comments, which is true enough. The coaches that line the road below them have brought tourists of almost every nation except Greeks. Nevertheless Philip is surprised and somewhat disconcerted to be greeted, in the sanctuary of Apollo, by an elderly lady wearing a broad-brimmed straw hat tied under her chin with a chiffon scarf, and carrying a shooting stick.

"Sybil Maiden," she reminds him. "I attended the conference you organized at Rummidge."

"Oh, yes," says Philip. "How are you?"

"Very well, thank you. The heat is rather trying, but I have just cooled my brow at the Kastalian spring—most refreshing. This is also a great help." She pulls apart the handles of her shooting stick and, planting the point in a crevice between two ancient blocks of stone, seats herself on the little leather hammock at the top of the implement. "They laughed at me at first. Now everybody on the course wants one."

"What course is that?"

"Literature, Life and Thought in Ancient Greece. We have come from Athens for the day by charabanc—or so I call it, to the intense amusement of my fellow students, most of whom are Americans. They are all at the splendidly preserved stadium, further up the hill, running round the race track."

"Running? In this heat?" Joy exclaims.

"Jogging, I believe they call it. It seems to be an epidemic psychological illness afflicting Americans these days. A form of masochism, like the *flagellantes* in the Middle Ages. You are Mrs. Swallow, I presume?"

"Yes," says Philip.

"No," says Joy simultaneously.

Miss Maiden glances sharply from one to the other. "There used to be an inscription on the wall of the temple here, '*Know thyself.*' But they did not deem it necessary to add, '*Know thy wife . . .*'"

"Joy and I hope to marry one day," Philip explains, in some confusion. "My personal life is in a transitional state at the moment. I'd be grateful if you would not mention our meeting here to any mutual acquaintance in England."

"I am no tittle-tattle, Professor Swallow, I assure you. But I suppose you have to protect your reputation, now you are so much in the public eye. I read a very flattering item about you in one of the Sunday newspapers recently."

"Oh, that . . . I don't know where the journalist got the idea that I was in the running for the UNESCO chair. It was the first I'd heard of it."

"Ah yes, the Siege Perilous!" Miss Maiden holds up a hand to command their attention, and begins to recite in a high, vatic chant:

> "*O brother,*
> *In our great hall there stood a vacant chair*
> *Fashioned by Merlin ere he passed away,*
> *And carven with strange figures; and in and out*
> *The figures, like a serpent, ran a scroll*
> *Of letters in a tongue no man could read.*
> *And Merlin called it, 'The Siege Perilous,'*
> *Perilous for good and ill; 'for there,' he said,*
> *'No man could sit but he should lose himself.'*"

Miss Maiden drops her hand, and cocks her head interrogatively in Philip's direction. "Well, Professor Swallow?"

"It sounds like Tennyson," he says. "Is it from 'The Holy Grail,' in the *Idylls?*"

"Bravo!" exclaims Miss Maiden. "I respect a man who can recognize a quotation. It's a dying art." She dabs her brow with a dainty pocket handkerchief. "Everybody was talking about this UNESCO chair at Amsterdam recently. A most tedious conference in other respects."

"You seem to travel about the world a great deal, Miss Maiden," Joy observes.

"It keeps me young, my dear. I like to know what's going on in the world of scholarship. Who's in, who's out."

"And who," says Joy impulsively, "do *you* think will get the UNESCO Chair?"

Miss Maiden closes her eyes and seems to sway on the fulcrum of her shooting stick as she considers the question. "The most surprising person," she says in a slurred voice. "It always is in these cases."

Fearing that she is about to faint, Philip steps forward to lend his support, but Miss Maiden suddenly opens her eyes and straightens up. "I think I'll go back to the charabanc," she says. "It's air-conditioned. So nice to have met you both."

"Are you sure you can manage the steps on your own?" says Philip.

"Perfectly well, thank you," says Miss Maiden. "Goodbye, goodbye!"

They watch her carefully descend the winding steps towards the road where fleets of sightseeing buses are drawn up.

"Strange old girl," says Philip. "But you've got to admire her spirit."

"The most surprising person could be you," says Joy.

· · ·

In Darlington, it is a fine summer evening. The raw, unfinished campus looks almost attractive in the mellow evening light, though nothing can make the Computer Centre look other than an ugly prefabricated hut. Through its open windows carry the sounds of summer pursuits, the *pock pock* of tennis balls bandied to and fro on the nearby courts, the occasional cry of *Howzat?* from the playing fields, and the sounds of guitars and harmonicas from an impromptu al fresco singalong down by the artificial lake. The two men inside are, however, oblivious to these noises. One watches the other, who watches a screen. The dialogue represented there reads as follows:

R.D.: I'M NOT FEELING ANY BETTER.

ELIZA: WHY IS THAT?

R.D.: THIS BUSINESS ABOUT PHILIP SWALLOW.

ELIZA: TELL ME ABOUT PHILIP SWALLOW.

R.D.: I ALREADY TOLD YOU ABOUT HIM.

ELIZA: IS THERE ANYTHING YOU WOULD LIKE TO ADD TO YOUR PREVIOUS
REMARKS?

R.D.: SWALLOW EPITOMIZES THE UNFAIRNESS OF LIFE TO ME. AT RUMMIDGE
HE GOT THE SENIOR LECTURESHIP I SHOULD HAVE GOT. THEN HE GOT
THE CHAIR THERE BY A LUCKY FLUKE. NOW HE'S HAVING A GREAT
SUCCESS WITH THIS PATHETIC BOOK ABOUT HAZLITT.

ELIZA: TELL ME ABOUT HAZLITT.

R.D.: I'M NOT INTERESTED IN HAZLITT. I HAVEN'T EVEN READ SWALLOW'S
ROTTEN BOOK. I DON'T NEED TO. I SAT THROUGH ENOUGH TEDIOUS
EXAMINERS MEETINGS WITH HIM TO KNOW WHAT IT'S LIKE. THE IDEA
OF HIS BEING A SERIOUS CANDIDATE FOR THE UNESCO CHAIR IS
PREPOSTEROUS.

ELIZA: I WOULDN'T SAY THAT.

It is this last line of the dialogue that Robin Dempsey has been staring at, transfixed, for the last ten minutes. Its appearance made the hairs on the back of his neck bristle, for it is of an entirely different order from anything ELIZA has produced until now: not a question, not a request, not a statement about something already mentioned in the discourse, but an expression of *opinion*. How can ELIZA have opinions? How can she know anything about the UNESCO Chair that Robin himself doesn't know, or hasn't told her? Robin is almost afraid to ask. At last, slowly and hesitantly, he types:

WHAT DO YOU KNOW ABOUT IT?

Instantly ELIZA replies:

MORE THAN YOU THINK.

Robin turns pale, then red. He types:

ALL RIGHT, IF YOU'RE SO CLEVER, TELL ME WHO WILL GET THE UNESCO CHAIR

The screen remains blank. Robin smiles and relaxes. Then he realizes that he has forgotten to indicate the end of his message with a punctuation mark. He presses the period key. On the screen, the letters rippling from left to right faster than thought, appears a name:

PHILIP SWALLOW.

Robin Dempsey's chair keels over and crashes to the floor as he starts to his feet and staggers backwards, staring aghast at the screen. His face is ashen. Josh Collins comes out of his glass cubicle.

"Anything wrong?"

But Dempsey stumbles past him, out of the building, without a word, his eyes fixed, like a man walking in his sleep. Josh Collins watches him leave, then goes across to the computer terminal, and reads what is written there. If Josh Collins ever smiled, one might say he was smiling to himself.

. . .

After the Joyce Conference in Zürich, Morris returns to his luxurious nest on the shores of Lake Como. The days pass pleasantly. In the mornings he reads and writes; in the afternoons he takes a siesta, and deals with correspondence until the sun has lost some of its heat. Then it is time for a jog through the woods, a shower, a drink before dinner, and a game of poker or backgammon afterwards in the drawing-room. He retires early to bed, where he falls to sleep listening to rock music on his transistor radio. It is a restful, civilized régime. Only his correspondence keeps him conscious of the anxieties, desires and conflicts of the real world.

There is, for instance, a letter from Désirée's lawyers requesting a reply to their previous communication concerning college tuition fees for the twins, and a letter from Désirée herself threatening to visit him at the Rockefeller villa and make a public scene if he doesn't come through with the money pretty damn quick. It seems that she is in Europe for the summer: the letter is postmarked Heidelberg—uncomfortably close. There is another letter from his own lawyer advising him to pay up. Grudgingly, Morris complies. There is a cable, reply paid, from Rodney Wainwright, begging for another extension of the deadline for the submission of his paper for the Jerusalem conference. Morris cables back, "BRING FINISHED PAPER WITH YOU TO CONFERENCE" since it is too late now to strike Rodney Wainwright from the programme.

There is a letter, handwritten on Rummidge English Department notepaper, from Philip Swallow, confirming his acceptance of Morris's invitation to participate in the Jerusalem conference, and asking if he can bring a "friend" with him.

"You'll never guess who it is. You remember Joy, the woman I told you about, whom I met in Genoa, and thought was dead? Well, she wasn't killed in that plane crash after all—she wasn't on the plane, though her husband was. I met her by chance in Turkey, and we're madly in love with each other. Hilary doesn't know yet. When the time is right, I'll ask Hilary for a divorce. I think you know our marriage has been a lost cause for quite some time. Meanwhile, Jerusalem would be an ideal opportunity for Joy and I to get together. Naturally I will pay for her accommodation. (Please reserve us a double room at the Hilton.)"

This missive gives Morris no pleasure at all. "Madly in love," forsooth! Is this language appropriate to a man in his fiftieth year? Hasn't he learned by now that this whole business of being "in love" is not an existential reality, but a form of cultural production, an illusion produced by the mutual reflections of a million rosetinted mirrors: love poems, pop songs, movie images, agony columns, shampoo ads, romantic novels? Apparently not. The letter reads like the effusion of some infatuated teenager. Morris will not admit to himself that there may be a trace of envy in this harsh assessment. He prefers to identify his response as righteous indignation at being more or less compelled to collude in the deception of Hilary. For a man who claims to believe in the morally improving effects of reading great literature, Philip Swallow (it seems to Morris) takes his marriage vows pretty lightly.

There is a brief letter from Arthur Kingfisher, courteously acknowledging Morris's last and enclosing a Xerox copy of his keynote address to the Chicago conference on the Crisis of the Sign. Morris immediately fires back a reply asking if Arthur Kingfisher could by any chance contemplate taking part in the Jerusalem conference on the Future of Criticism. Morris is convinced that if he can only get Arthur Kingfisher to himself for a week or so, he will be able to cajole, wheedle and flatter the old guy into seeing his own irresistible eligibility for the UNESCO chair. He spends a whole day in the composition of this letter, emphasizing the exclusiveness of the conference, a small group of select scholars, not so much a conference as a symposium, setting out the attractions of the Jerusalem Hilton as a venue, alluding delicately to Arthur Kingfisher's half-Jewish ethnic origins, and drawing attention to the many optional sightseeing expeditions that have been arranged for the participants. Recalling that Fulvia Morgana had mentioned that at Chicago Arthur Kingfisher was inseparable from a beautiful Asian chick, Morris makes it clear that the invitation to Jerusalem includes any companion he cares to bring with him. As a final incentive he hints that the conference might run to a Concorde flight for the transatlantic leg of the journey, having checked this out first by a long-distance phone call to his Israeli friend Sam Singerman, who is co-organizer of the conference, and has raised the financial backing for it from a British supermarket chain whose Zionist chairman has been persuaded that the event will enhance Israel's international cultural prestige. "There'll be no problem about getting Kingfisher's fare," Sam assures Morris. "We can have as much money as we want. The only condition is that we've got to call it the Pricewize International Symposium on the Future of Criticism."

"That's all right," says Morris. "We can live with that. As long as we don't have to give Green Stamps with every lecture." He addresses and seals the letter to Arthur Kingfisher, and goes out on to the balcony of his room to stretch his limbs. It is late afternoon, and a hazy golden light falls on the mountains and the lake. Time for his jog.

Morris changes into his red silk running shorts and Euphoric State sweatshirt and Adidas training shoes, and drops his letter into the mail box in the hall on his way out of the villa. Some other residents sunning themselves on the terrace smile and wave as he trots briskly through the villa gardens. As soon as he is out of sight, he slows to a more deliberate pace. Even so, the sweat pours from his brow and the loudest noise he can hear is the rasp of his own breathing. His footsteps are muffled by the dead pine needles that carpet the footpath. He always takes the same route—a mile-long circuit through the woods, uphill from the villa, downhill coming back, which usually takes him about thirty-five minutes. He is determined one day to do the whole thing without stopping, but this evening, as usual, he is obliged to stop at the top of the incline about halfway round, to recover his breath. He leans against a tree, his chest heaving, looking up through the branches above his head to the hazy blue of the sky.

Then everything goes black.

2

whhhhhhhhhhhhhhhhhhheeeeeeeeee!

The wind whistled softly through the reeds at the edge of Lough Gill. Persse McGarrigle squinted anxiously at the sky. Overhead it was as blue as his own eyes, but the horizon looked ominously dark. The students of the Celtic Twilight Summer School, two days out from their base at Limerick on a literary sightseeing tour, did not, however, look so far. They were in ecstasies at the sunlight glinting on the ruffled waters of the lake, the reeds bowing gracefully in the breeze, the green hills encircling the lough, and the purple, whaleshaped outline of Ben Bulben in the background. Mostly middle-aged Americans, collecting credits for their part-time degree courses back home or combining a European vacation with cultural self-improvement, they jumped down from the bus with cries of delight, and waddled up and down the shore, clicking and whirring with their cameras, watched indulgently by a cluster of Sligo boatmen wearing waders and filthy, tattered Aran sweaters. Rocking gently beside a little wooden jetty were three weathered-looking rowing boats which had been hired to take the students across to the Lake Isle of Innisfree, subject of W. B. Yeats's most frequently anthologized poem.

"*I will arise and go now, and go to Innisfree,*'" an overweight matron in tartan Bermuda shorts and dayglo pink tee-shirt recited aloud in the accents of Brooklyn, with a knowing smile in Persse's direction. For the past two summers Persse had acted as tutor on this course, directed by Professor McCreedy, and being at a loose end since his disillusioning experience in Amsterdam, had agreed to do so again this summer. "*And a small cabin build there, of clay and wattles made.*' Do we get to see the cabin, Mr. McGarrigle?"

"I don't think Yeats actually got around to building it, Mrs. Finklepearl," said Persse. "It was more of a dream than a reality. Like most of our dearest ambitions."

"Oh, don't say that, Mr. McGarrigle. I believe in looking at the bright side of everything."

"Are we going in those little boats?"

Persse turned to face the addresser of this question with surprise and even pleasure, for it was the first word he had spoken in Persse's hearing since the summer school began.

"It's not far, Mr. Maxwell."

"They don't even have motors."

"The men are very strong rowers," Persse assured him. But Mr. Maxwell relapsed into gloomy silence. He was dressed more formally than most of the party, in herringbone sports jacket and worsted trousers, and wore the kind of sunglasses that went darker and lighter according to circumstances. In the bright dazzle off the lake, his eyes were two opaque black discs. Maxwell was a bit of a mystery man—a teacher at some small Baptist college in the Deep

South, who gave the impression in seminars that the level of discussion was too jejune to tempt his participation, and was consequently feared and disliked by the other students.

"You're not gonna chicken out of the boat-ride, are you, Mr. Maxwell?" Mrs. Finklepearl taunted him.

"I can't swim," he said shortly.

"Me neither!" cried Mrs. Finklepearl. "But nuttin' is gonna stop me going to the Lake Isle of Innisfree. *'Nine bean-rows will I have there, a hive for the honey-bee.'* I think I'll just get my zipper from the bus, though. This breeze is kinda chilly."

Persse encouraged her to do so, in spite of knowing that this garment was made of scarlet and lime-green nylon, with royal blue piping. He strolled over to the group of boatmen. "Shouldn't there be four boats?" he enquired.

"Paddy Malone's boat is holed," said one of the men. "But sure we'll manage fine with the three. They can all squeeze in."

"What about the weather?" said Persse, surveying the sky again. "It's very dark over to the west."

"The weather will hold for another two hours," he was assured. "As long as you can see Ben Bulben, you've no need to worry." This advice was hardly disinterested, as Persse well knew, for the boatmen stood to lose half their fee, not to mention tips, if the trip were cancelled. But his misgivings were overruled by Professor McCreedy, who was afraid of disappointing the students. "Let us not delay, however," he urged. "Round them up and get them into the boats."

So into the boats they got, amid much laughter and shouted advice and badinage, the ungainly American matrons in their gaudy windcheaters and plastic peeptoe sandals clambering into the rowboats held steady by the grinning boatmen standing in the shallow water. Persse found himself in the prow of his boat with knees pressed against Maxwell's, sitting opposite. There were thirty-six people in the party—twelve to a boat, plus two oarsmen. It was too many. The boats were low in the water—Persse could touch its surface without stretching.

At first, all went well. The oarsmen pulled strongly, and a kind of race developed between the boats, each group urging on its crew. The wavelets dashing against the bows caused only a slight, rather agreeable spray to sprinkle the passengers. But then, as the shore receded and flattened behind them, and the low outline of the Isle of Innisfree rose in front of them, the light seemed to thicken and the wind grew stronger. Persse anxiously surveyed the horizon, which was much nearer than it had been earlier. He could no longer see Ben Bulben. The sun disappeared behind a dark cloud and the colour of the water changed instantly from blue to black, flecked with whitecaps. The boats began to pitch and toss, and to ship large dollops of cold water, causing the passengers to utter shrill cries of alarm and distress. Persse, sitting at the prow, was soon soaked to his skin.

"Better turn back!" he shouted to the two oarsmen in his boat.

One of them shook his head "Can't risk turning in this squall," he cried. "We're over halfway there, anyhow."

The island, however, still looked dismally distant, shrouded by a shower of rain that swept rapidly towards them across the intervening water, and passed over the boats like a whiplash, stinging the faces of the passengers. They were all so wet now that they no longer bothered to complain when a wave slopped over the side. Their silence was an indication of how frightened they all were, gripping the gunwales, up to their ankles in water, watching the faces of the two oarsmen for reassurance. These two rowed grimly on in the teeth of the wind, their task made harder by the weight of water in the boat. There was no bailing implement aboard, though one or two passengers made feeble efforts to improvise with their shoes and sunhats.

Whether it was because their craft was leakier than the others, or its load heavier, or the oarsmen weaker, Persse observed that their boat was falling behind the other two. Mrs. Finklepearl, her eyes closed, was crooning the words of "The Lake Isle of Innisfree" to herself, like a prayer or mantra:

"And I shall have some peace there, for peace comes dropping slow, Dropping from the veils of morning to where the cricket sings . . ."

A particularly big wave broke over the bow and the recitation ended abruptly in a gurgle and a sob. Maxwell's lenses had turned transparent in the murky light and his pale grey eyes were eloquent of pure terror. He clutched at Persse's arm with a grip as tight as the Ancient Mariner's. "Are we sinking?" he screeched.

"No, no," said Persse. "We're fine. Safe as houses."

But his voice lacked conviction. The boat was dangerously low in the water—indeed it was beginning to look more like a bath than a boat. The veins stood out on the foreheads of the rowers, and their oars seemed almost to bend under the strain of keeping the waterlogged vessel in motion. The island was still more than a hundred yards away. The oarsmen looked at each other meaningfully and rested their oars. One called out to Persse, "I fear she's taken too much water, sir."

"I told you—we're sinking!" screamed Maxwell, clutching Persse still more tightly. "Save me!"

"For God's sake, control yourself man," protested Persse, struggling to free himself from the other's frantic grip.

"But I can't swim! I'll drown! Where are the other boats? Help! Help!"

"Can you only think of saving your own skin?" Persse exclaimed indignantly. "What about the ladies here?"

"You mustn't let me drown. I have a great sin on my conscience." Maxwell's face was contorted with fear and guilt. "This storm is God's judgment upon me."

"He's being very unfair to the rest of us, then," Persse snapped, peering through the rain at the shore of the island, which the other two boats seemed to have reached safely. "Let's shout 'Help' all together, ladies and gentlemen," he urged, to keep their spirits up. "One-two-three . . ."

"*Help!*" they all shouted in ragged chorus, all except Maxwell, who seemed to have abandoned hope. "Yes, it's God's judgment," he moaned. "To drown me in a lake in Sligo, the very place where I deceived the poor girl. I didn't know we'd be coming here when I signed up for the course."

"What girl was that?" said Persse.

"She was a chambermaid," sniffed Maxwell, tears or rain or lakewater running down his face and dripping from his nose. "In a hotel I was staying at, years ago, for the Yeats Summer School. My doctoral dissertation was on Celtic mythology in the early poems."

"The divil take your doctoral dissertation!" cried Persse. "What was the girl's name?"

"She was called Bernadette. I don't remember her second name."

"McGarrigle," said Persse. "The same as mine."

Maxwell's grip on Persse suddenly relaxed. He stared incredulously. "That's right. It *was* McGarrigle. How did you know?"

At that moment the boat slowly sank beneath them to the accompaniment of piteous cries from the rest of the passengers, who soon, however, found that they were floundering in only two feet of water, their vessel having fortunately drifted over a sandbank. The other boatmen waded out from the shore to carry the more elderly and infirm survivors of this shipwreck to dry land. Persse was obliged to carry Maxwell, who had flung his arms round Persse's neck as the boat went down, and refused to unclasp them.

"I've a good mind to hold your head under the water and drown you after all," Persse growled. "But drowning's too good for you. You ruined my cousin's life. Getting her with child and then deserting her."

"I'll make it up to her," whimpered Maxwell. "I'll marry her if you like."

"Huh, she wouldn't want to marry a spalpeen like yourself," said Persse.

"I'll make restitution. I'll make a settlement on her and the child."

"That's more like it," said Persse. "We'll have that put in writing by a Sligo solicitor tomorrow morning. Signed and sealed. I'll undertake to deliver it."

· · ·

Two days later, Persse flew from Dublin to Heathrow, carrying in his pocket a copy of the legal document, now lodged with a Sligo solicitor, in which Professor Sidney Maxwell, of Covenant College, Atlanta, Georgia, admitted paternity of Bernadette McGarrigle's son, Fergus, and guaranteed her an annual allowance that should be sufficient to permit her to retire from her present employment. Professor McCreedy had granted Persse twenty-four hours' leave from the summer school, and it was his intention to seek another interview with Mrs. Gasgoine, to ask her for Bernadette's address, or to forward his message. But when he got to the building in Soho Square, he found the office he had visited before occupied by a travel agency. "Girls Unlimited?" said the receptionist. "No, I never heard of it, but then I've only been here a couple of weeks. Gentleman looking for Girls Unlimited, Doreen, know anything about it? No, she don't either. You could try the video place on the ground floor." Persse tried the video place on the ground floor but they seemed to suspect him of being a policeman: first they offered him a bribe, and when he asked what it was for, they told him to get lost. Nobody in the entire building would admit to having known that Girls Unlimited ever existed, let alone its present whereabouts. Persse could think of nothing to do but return to Ireland and try advertising in newspapers, or perhaps show-business trade magazines.

He travelled back to Heathrow on the tube in a despondent mood, not only on account of his frustration over Bernadette, but because the journey had revived memories of Angelica. Not that she had been out of his mind for more than five minutes at a time all summer. The petition he had left in St. George's chapel on his last visit had not been answered—not the part that pertained to himself anyhow. "Dear God, let me forget Angelica." Would he ever forget that exquisite face and form? The dark hair falling in shining waves about her neck and shoulders at the Rummidge sherry party, or streaming on the wind as she spurned the footpath under her running shoes; her peat-dark eyes gravely attentive in the lecture-room, or dreamily enchanted by his snow poem under the moon? Or glazed and vacant in the obscene photograph outside the Blue Heaven? Persse shook his head irritably at that last image, angry that he had allowed it to rise into his consciousness, as he stepped off the train at Heathrow.

He discovered that he had a two-hour wait till the next plane to Dublin. A sign "To St. George's Chapel" caught his eye, and for want of anything better to do, he followed it. This time it led him not to the airport laundry, but to the bunker of liver-coloured brick beneath the black wooden cross. He pushed through the swing doors and descended the stairs to the hushed chapel below the ground.

His petition was still there, pinned to the green baize noticeboard: "*Dear God, let me forget Angelica. Lead her from the life that degrades her.*" But it had been annotated in a minute italic hand that Persse knew well—so well that his heart stopped beating for a moment, his lungs bulged with trapped breath, his vision blurred and he almost swooned.

"*Appearances can be misleading. Vide F.Q. II. xii. 66.*"

Persse recovered his balance, snatched the paper from the noticeboard, and ran with it to the nearest terminal building. He knocked aside protesting travellers in his eagerness to get to the bookstall. Did they have a copy of *The Faerie Queene* by Sir Edmund Spenser? No, they did not. Not even the Penguin edition? Not in any edition. Did they not realize *The Faerie Queene* was one of the jewels in the crown of English poetry? There was not much call for poetry at Heathrow. Sir could, if sir wished, try the other bookstalls in the airport, but his chances of success were slim. Persse ran from terminal to terminal, from bookstall to bookstall, loudly demanding a copy of *The Faerie Queene*. One assistant offered him Enid Blyton, another the latest issue of *Gay News*. He thrust his fingers through his curly hair in frustration. Obviously there was only one thing to do: go back to central London, where the bookshops would still, with any luck, be open.

As he hurried towards the exit of Terminal One with this intention, he was accosted by an eager female voice.

"Hallo there!"

Persse recognized Cheryl Summerbee, sitting on a stool behind a British Airways Information desk. He stopped and retraced his steps. "Hallo. How are you?" he said.

"Bored. I prefer working on check-in, especially when it's Terminal

Three—that's long-haul flights. There's more . . . scope. You're not wearing that lovely hat."

"Hat? Oh, you mean Professor Zapp's deerstalker. It's too warm for that."

"Are you over here for long?"

"No, just for the day. I'm going straight back to Ireland tonight. There's a summer school I've got to meet up with in Galway tomorrow."

Cheryl sighed wistfully. "I'd love to go to the west of Ireland. Is it very beautiful?"

"It is. Especially Connemara. I rented a cottage there these last few months . . . Look, Cheryl, I'd love to chat with you, but the fact is that I'm in a tearing hurry. I have to get back to London before the bookshops close."

"What book was it you wanted?"

"Oh, it's a book of poetry—a long poem called *The Faerie Queene*. I want to look up a reference very urgently."

"No problem," said Cheryl; and to Persse's astonishment she reached under the counter and pulled out a thick library edition of *The Faerie Queene*.

"God love you!" he exclaimed. "That's what I call service! I'll write to British Airways. I'll get you promoted."

"I shouldn't do that," said Cheryl. "It's my own book, for reading at slack times. We're not supposed to."

Persse, searching his pockets for the piece of paper with the reference on it, glanced at Cheryl with surprise. "*Your* book? I thought you went more for the Bills and Moon type of romance." He seemed to have lost the precious bit of paper. Damn.

"I used to," Cheryl agreed. "But I've grown out of that sort of book. They're all rubbish really, aren't they? Read one and you've read them all."

"Is that right?" Persse murmured abstractedly. He tried to recall the details of the reference written in Angelica's neat italic script. It was stanza sixty-something, and he was fairly sure that it was Book Two—but which canto? He riffled his way through each canto of Book Two, while Cheryl prattled on.

"I mean, they're not really romances at all, are they? Not in the true sense of romance. They're just debased versions of the sentimental novel of courtship and marriage that started with Richardson's *Pamela*. A realistic setting, an ordinary heroine that the reader can identify with, a simple plot about finding a husband, endless worrying about how far you should go with a man before marriage. Titillating but moral."

"Mmm, mmm," Persse muttered absently, flicking the pages of *The Faerie Queene* with moistened fingers.

"Real romance is a pre-novelistic kind of narrative. It's full of adventure and coincidence and surprises and marvels, and has lots of characters who are lost or enchanted or wandering about looking for each other, or for the Grail, or something like that. Of course, they're often in love too . . ."

"Ah!" Persse exclaimed, coming upon the episode of the Bower of Blisse, for he remembered Angelica mentioning to Morris Zapp the two girls whom Sir Guyon sees bathing in the fountain. His eyes zoomed in on stanza 66, and two words leapt off the page at him:

> *The wanton Maidens him espying stood*
> *Gazing a while at his unwonted guise;*
> *Then th'one her selfe low ducked in the flood*
> *Abash't that her a straunger did avise:*
> *But th'other rather higher did arise,*
> *And her two lily paps aloft displayed,*
> *And all, that might his melting hart entise*
> *To her delights, she unto him bewrayd:*
> *The rest hid vnderneath, him more desirous made.*

"Lily Papps!" Persse shouted joyfully. "There are two girls, not one. Lily and Angelica! They must be sisters—twins. A modest one and a bold one." He leaned across the counter and, cupping Cheryl's head between his two hands, stifled her still-continuing monologue with a smacking kiss.

"God bless you, Cheryl!" he said fervently. "For being in the right place at the right time with the right book. This is a great day for me, I can tell you."

Cheryl blushed deeply. Her squint increased and she seemed to experience some difficulty in breathing. In spite of these symptoms of stress, she managed to complete the sentence on which she was embarked before Persse interrupted her:

". . . in psychoanalytical terms, romance is the quest of a libido or desiring self for a fulfilment that will deliver it from the anxieties of reality but will still contain that reality. Would you agree with that?"

Persse now registered a long-overdue astonishment. He stared into Cheryl's eyes, which were a remarkably pretty shade of blue. "Cheryl—have you been going to night-school since I first met you?"

Cheryl blushed even more deeply, and dropped her eyes. "No," she said huskily.

"You're never telling me that those are your own ideas about romance and the sentimental novel and the desiring self?"

"The desiring self is Northrop Frye," she admitted.

"*You* have read Northrop *Frye*?" his voice rose in pitch like a jet engine.

"Well, not read, exactly. Somebody told me about it."

"Somebody? Who?" Persse felt a fresh quickening of inner excitement, the premonitory vibrations of another discovery. Who in the world was most likely to engage airline staff in casual conversation about the generic characteristics of romance?

"A customer. Her flight was delayed and we got chatting. She noticed I was reading a Bills and Moon romance under the counter, and she said what are you reading that rubbish for, well, not in so many words, she wasn't rude about it, but she started to tell me about the old romances, and how much more exciting and interesting they were. So I got her to write down the names of some books for me, to get from the library. *The Faerie Queene* was one of them. To be honest, I'm not getting on with it very well. I preferred *Orlando Furioso*, it's more amusing. She knew ever such a lot about books. I think she was in the same line of business as you."

Persse had scarcely dared to breathe in the course of this narrative. "A young woman, was she?" he said coaxingly.

"Yes, dark, good-looking, lovely long hair. A foreign sort of name, though you wouldn't have said so to hear her speak."

"Pabst, was it—the name?"

It was Cheryl's turn to look astonished. "That's right, it was."

"When was it that you were talking to her?"

"Just the other day. Monday."

"Do you remember where she was going?"

"She was flying to Geneva, but she said she was going on to Lausanne. Do you know her then?"

"Know her? I love her!" Persse exclaimed. "When is the next plane to Geneva?"

"I don't know," said Cheryl, who had now gone very pale.

"Look it up for me, there's a good girl. She didn't happen to mention where she was staying in Lausanne? The name of a hotel?"

Cheryl shook her head. It seemed to take her a long time to find the flight information. "Come on, Cheryl, you found *The Faerie Queene* for me quicker than this," Persse teased. Then to his astonishment, a tear rolled down her cheek and splashed on to the page of the open timetable. "What's the matter, for the love of God?"

Cheryl blew her nose on a paper tissue, straightened her shoulders and smiled at him professionally. "Nothing," she said. "Our next flight to Geneva is at 19:30. But there's a Swissair flight at 15:45 which you might catch if you run."

He ran.

. . .

Persse had scarcely recovered his breath before the Swissair Boeing 727 was airborne. He blessed the impulse that had made him apply for the American Express card, which made flying almost as simple as catching a bus. He could recall the elaborate preparations for his first flight, not so many years ago, from Dublin to Heathrow, entailing the withdrawal of a thick roll of banknotes from his Post Office savings account, and the paying over of the same across the counter of the Aer Lingus office in O'Connell Street weeks before the date of his departure. Now he had only to wave the little green and white plastic rectangle in the air to be wafted to Switzerland at five minutes' notice.

At Geneva airport, Persse changed the money he had on him into francs, and took the bus into the centre of the city, where he transferred immediately onto an electric train to Lausanne. It was a warm, breathless evening. The train ran out along the shores of the lake, its surface smooth and pearl-pink, like stretched satin, in the glow of the setting sun, which struck rosily on the peaks of distant mountains on the other side of the water. Fatigued by the long day's travelling, and all its emotional excitements, rocked gently by the swaying motion of the train, Persse fell asleep.

He woke suddenly to find the train halted on the outskirts of a large town. It was quite dark, and there was a full moon reflected on the surface of Lac Léman, some distance below the railway track. Persse had no idea where he was, and his compartment was empty of other passengers whom he might have asked. After about five minutes, the train moved slowly forward and pulled into a station. Loudspeakers whispered the name, "*Lausanne, Lausanne.*" He alighted, apparently the only person to do so, and climbed the steps to the station entrance. He paused in its colonnaded portico for a moment to take his bearings. Before him was a forecourt, with taxis drawn up. A driver cocked an interrogative eyebrow. Persse shook his head. He would have a better chance of spotting Angelica, or being spotted by her, if he explored the town on foot.

There was an air of excitement and gaiety on the streets of Lausanne this evening that surprised Persse, who had always thought of the Swiss as a rather disciplined and decorous people. The pavements were thronged with strollers, many of whom were dressed rather theatrically in the fashions of yesteryear. An early twenties' look seemed to be all the rage in Lausanne this season: tailored, long-skirted costumes for the women, suits with waistcoats and small, narrow lapels for the men. Smiling faces turned outwards from café terraces beneath strings of coloured lights. Hands pointed and waved. A babble of multi-lingual conversation rose from the tables and mingled with the remarks of the parading pedestrians, so that to Persse's ears, pricked for a possible greeting from Angelica, the effect was rather like that of twisting the tuning knob of a powerful radio set at random, picking up snatches of one foreign station after another. *"Bin gar keine Russin, stamm' aus Litauen, echt deutsch . . . Et O ces voix d'enfants, chantant dans la coupole! . . . Poi s'ascose nel foco che gli affina . . ."* Though he was a poor linguist, and spoke only English and Irish with any fluency, these fragments of speech seemed strangely familiar to Persse's ears, as did the words of a song carrying from an open casement, rendered in an operatic tenor:

> *Frisch weht der Wind*
> *Der Heimat zu*
> *Mein Irisch Kind,*
> *Wo weilest du?*

Persse stopped under the window to listen. Somewhere in the neighbouring streets, a clock struck nine, with a dead sound on the final stroke, though by Persse's watch it was twenty-five minutes past the hour. A woman in long skirts, hanging on the arm of a man wearing a silk hat and opera cloak, brushed past him saying to her escort, "And when we were children, staying at the archduke, my cousin's, he took me out on a sled, and I was frightened." Persse wheeled round and stared after the couple, wondering if he was dreaming or delirious. A young man thrust a card into his hand: *"Madame Sosostris, Clairvoyante. Horoscope and Tarot. The Wisest Woman in Europe."*

"Stetson!"

Persse looked up from his dazed inspection of the card to see a man dressed in the uniform of an officer in the First World War, Sam Browne and puttees, bearing down upon him, swagger-stick raised. "You who were with me in the ships at Mylae! That corpse you planted last year in your garden, has it begun to sprout?" Persse backed away in alarm. A group of people in a nearby beergarden, dressed in modern casual clothes, laughed and applauded. The madman in uniform rushed past Persse and lost himself in the crowd. Soon Persse heard him accosting someone else, crying "Stetson!" The clock struck nine again. A line of men dressed in identical striped business suits and bowler hats, and clasping rolled umbrellas, marched in step along the pavement, each man with his eyes fixed on the ground before his feet. They were followed by a laughing, jolly crowd of revellers in jeans and summer frocks who carried the bewildered Persse along with them until he found himself back near the station again. He saw a neon sign, "English Pub," and made towards it, but the place was so crowded that he couldn't even squeeze through the door. A poster outside announced: "Beer at 1922 prices tonight, 8–10." From within came, every few minutes, a gruff exclamation, "HURRY UP PLEASE IT'S TIME!" followed by the groans and pleas of those still waiting to be served. Persse felt the pressure of a hand on his shoulder, and turned to confront a brown, leathery countenance, hooded eyes and a reptilian smile.

"Professor Tardieu!" he exclaimed, glad to see a familiar face, even this one.

The other shook his head, still smiling. "*Je m'appelle Eugenides*," he said. "*Négotiant de Smyrne. Goûtez la marchandise, je vous prie.*" He withdrew his hand from his jacket pocket and offered on his open palm a few shrivelled currants.

"For the love of God," Persse pleaded, "tell me what is going on here."

"I believe it is called street theatre," said Tardieu, in his immaculate English. "But you must have read about it in the conference programme?"

"What conference?" said Persse. "I've only just arrived here."

Tardieu stared at him for a moment, then burst into prolonged laughter.

. . .

At Tardieu's suggestion, they took the funicular down to the little port of Ouchy, and shared a snack of *perches du lac* and dry white wine outside a harbourside tavern. From the bar inside came the pleasant whining of a mandoline—for the "Waste Land" happening extended this far.

"Every three years, the *T. S. Eliot Newsletter* organizes an international conference on the poet's work in some place with which he was associated," Tardieu explained. "St Louis, London, Cambridge Mass.—last time it was East Coker. I'm afraid we rather overwhelmed that charming little village. This year it is the turn of Lausanne. As you undoubtedly know, Eliot composed the first draft of *The Waste Land* here while recovering from a nervous breakdown in the winter of 1921–2."

"'By the waters of Léman I sat down and wept.'" Persse quoted.

"Just so. My own belief is that the crisis was precipitated by the poet's inability to accept his latent homosexuality . . . In principle I disapprove of this kind of insistence on the biographical origins of the literary text, but I was persuaded by some friends here to take in the conference on my way back from Vienna, and I must admit that the idea of acting out *The Waste Land* on the streets of Lausanne was very imaginative. Most diverting."

"Who are the performers?" asked Persse.

"Mostly students at the University here, with the addition of a few volunteers from among the conferees, like myself—and Fulvia Morgana over there." Michel Tardieu nodded in the direction of a tawny-haired, Roman-nosed lady in a clinging, sequin-studded black dress, sitting at a table with a small, slight, Jewish-looking man. "'Belladonna, the Lady of Situations.' The man is Professor Gootblatt of Penn. He looks as if he wishes he were elsewhere, don't you think?"

The name "Fulvia" made Persse, for a reason he could not for the moment identify, think of Morris Zapp.

"Is Morris Zapp at this conference?"

"No. He was expected at the Vienna conference on Narrative last week, but he did not arrive. He was the subject of a narrative retardation as yet unexplained," said Tardieu. "But you, young man, what are you doing in Lausanne, if you did not know about the conference?"

"I'm looking for a girl."

"Ah, yes, I remember." Tardieu sighed reminiscently. "That was the trouble with my research assistant, Albert. He was always looking for a girl. Any girl, in his case. The ungrateful boy—I had to let him go. But I miss him."

"The girl I'm looking for must be at this conference," said Persse. "Where is it being held? What time is the first session tomorrow?"

"*Mais, c'est finie!*" Tardieu exclaimed. "The conference is over. The street theatre was the closing event. Tomorrow we all disperse."

"What!" Persse jumped to his feet, dismayed. "Then I must start looking for her at once. Where can I get a list of all the hotels in Lausanne?"

"But there are hundreds, my friend. You will never find her that way. What is the young lady's name?"

"You won't have heard of her, she's just a graduate student. Her name is Angelica Pabst."

"Of course, I know her well."

"*You do?*" Persse sat down again.

"*Mais oui*! She attended my lectures last year at the Sorbonne."

"And *is* she attending the conference?"

"Indeed she is. Tonight she was the Hyacinth Girl. You remember:

> *You gave me hyacinths first a year ago;*
> *They called me the hyacinth girl."*

"Yes, yes," Persse nodded impatiently. "I know the poem well. But where can I find her?"

"She was wandering about the streets, in a long white dress, with her arms full of hyacinths. Very charming, if one likes that dark, rather overripe kind of feminine beauty."

"I do," said Persse. "Have you any idea where she is staying?"

"Our Swiss hosts have, with characteristic efficiency, supplied a list of conferees' accommodations," said Tardieu, taking a folded paper from his breast pocket. He ran a long brown finger down a list. "Ah, yes, here it is. Pabst A., Mademoiselle. Pension Bellegarde, Rue de Grand-Saint-Jean."

"Where is that?"

"I will show you," said Tardieu, gesturing to a waiter for the bill. "It seems a modest lodging for one whose father is extremely rich."

"Is he?"

"I understand he is executive president of one of the American airlines."

"How well do you know Angelica?" Persse asked the French professor, as the funicular drew them back to the town.

"Not very well. She came to the Sorbonne for a year, as an occasional postgraduate student. She used to sit in the front row at my lectures, gazing at me through thick-rimmed spectacles. She always had a notebook open and a pen in her hand, but I never saw her write anything. It piqued me, I must say. One day, as I was going out of the lecture theatre, I stopped in front of her and made a little joke. 'Excuse me, mademoiselle,' I said, 'but this is the seventh lecture of mine that you have attended and your notebook remains blank. Have I not uttered a single word that was worth recording?' Do you know what she said? 'Professor Tardieu, it is not what you say that impresses me most, it is what you are silent about: ideas, morality, love, death, things . . . This notebook'—she fluttered its vacant pages—'is the record of your profound silences. *Vos silences profonds.*' She speaks excellent French. I went away glowing with pride. Later I wondered whether she was mocking me. What do you think?"

"I wouldn't venture an opinion," said Persse, recalling one of Angelica's remarks at Rummidge: "*You have to treat these professors carefully. You have to flatter them a bit.*" He asked Tardieu if he had met Angelica's sister.

"Sister? No, is there a sister?"

"I'm pretty sure that there is."

"This is the street."

As they turned the corner, Persse suddenly panicked at the realization that he did not know what he was going to say to Angelica. That he loved her, of course—but she knew that already. That he had misjudged her? But she knew that as well, though he hoped she hadn't guessed how grievously. In all the excitement of pursuing her, or her double, across Europe, he had never thought to prepare himself with an appropriate speech for the moment of meeting. He almost hoped that she was still on the streets of Lausanne with her arms full of hyacinths, so that he would have time to sit in the pension's lounge and prepare himself before she returned.

Tardieu halted in front of a house with a small painted sign under a light over the door, "*Pension Bellegarde*." "Here you are," he said. "I wish you goodnight—and success."

"You won't come in?" Persse found himself absurdly nervous of meeting Angelica alone.

"No, no, my presence would be superfluous," said Tardieu. "I have performed my narrative function for tonight."

"You've been most helpful," said Persse.

Tardieu smiled and shrugged. "If one is not a subject or an object, one must be a helper or an opponent. You I help. Professor Zapp I oppose."

"Why do you oppose him?"

"You have perhaps heard of a UNESCO chair in literary criticism?"

"Oh, that."

"Yes, that. *Au revoir*."

They shook hands, and Persse felt a small pellet-like object pressed into his palm. As the other walked away, Persse tilted his hand towards a streetlamp and discovered a solitary currant adhering to it. He nibbled the currant, turned, took a deep breath, and rang the doorbell of the pension.

A middle-aged woman in a neat, dark dress opened the door. "*Oui monsieur?*"

"*Je cherche une jeune femme*," Persse stammered. "Miss Papps. I mean, Miss Pabst. I understand that she is staying here."

"Ah! Mademoiselle Pabst!" The woman smiled, then frowned. "Alas, she has departed."

"Oh, no!" Persse groaned. "You mean she's gone for good?"

"*Pardon?*"

"She has checked out—left Lausanne?"

"*Oui, m'sieu.*"

"When did she leave?"

"Half an hour ago."

"Did she say where she was going?"

"She asked about trains to Genève."

"Thanks." Persse turned and sprinted back down the street.

He ran all the way to the station, using the middle of the road, since the pavements were still crowded, cheered on by onlookers who evidently thought he was part of the street theatre, though he couldn't recall anyone actually running in *The Waste Land*—it was a rather ambulatory poem. He used such thoughts to distract himself from the stitch in his side and his chagrin at having missed Angelica by so small a margin. He dashed into the station and yelled at the first person he saw an interrogative "*Genève?*" The man pointed towards a staircase and Persse leapt down the stairs three at a time. But he had been misled, or mistaken: the train was drawn up beside the opposite platform, separated from him by another line. He heard doors slamming and a whistle shrilled. There was no time to retrace his steps—his only chance of catching the train was to cross the tracks and board it from this side. He glanced up and down the line to check that it was clear, but as he made to step down, a pair of uniformed arms closed around him and dragged him back from the brink.

"*Non non, m'sieu! C'est défendu de traverser!*"

Persse struggled momentarily, then, as the train moved smoothly out of the station, desisted. In one of the compartments he glimpsed the back of a girl's dark head that might have been Angelica. "Angelica!" he yelled despairingly, and futilely. The official released his grip on Persse and regarded him disapprovingly.

"When is the next train to Geneva?" Persse asked. "*A quelle heure le train prochain pour Genève?*"

"*Demain,*" said the man with righteous satisfaction. "*A six heures et demi.*"

As Persse came out into the station colonnade, a taxi driver cocked an interrogative eyebrow. This time he accepted the ride. "Pension Bellegarde," he said, and slumped back, exhausted, in the back seat.

The light over the front door of the pension was out, and the landlady took longer to answer Persse's ring. She looked surprised to see him back again.

"I'd like a room for the night, please."

She shook her head. "I am sorry, *m'sieu*, we are full."

"But you can't be!" Persse protested. "Miss Pabst has only just left. Can't I have the room she vacated?"

The woman pointed to her wristwatch. "It is late *m'sieu*. The room must be cleaned, the linen changed. That cannot be done tonight."

"Madame," said Persse fervently, "let me have the room exactly as it is, and I'll pay you double."

The landlady was clearly suspicious of this offer from a luggageless, wild-eyed, scruffy-looking foreigner, but when he explained that the young lady who had occupied the room was the object of his sentimental attachment, she smiled rosily and said he could have the room as it stood for half-price.

The room was under the steep eaves of the house, with a small dormer window that afforded a glimpse of the lake far below. The window was shut and the air inside the room heavy with the scent of a large bunch of hyacinths, crushed and wilting in the waste basket. The room showed all the signs of a recent hasty departure. Persse picked up a still-damp towel from the floor beneath the washbasin and held it to his cheek. He swallowed the dregs of water at the bottom of a glass tumbler as reverently as if it were communion wine. He carefully unfolded a crumpled paper tissue left on the dressing table, uncovering at its core the faint impression of a pair of red lips, to which he pressed his own. He slept naked between sheets that were still creased and wrinkled from contact with Angelica's lovely limbs, and inhaled from the pillow under his head the lingering fragrance of her shampoo. He fell asleep in a delirium of sweet sensation and poignant regret and physical exhaustion.

On waking the next morning, he made two precious discoveries underneath the hyacinths in the waste basket: a pair of nylon tights with a hole in one knee, which he tucked away into an inside pocket next to his heart, and a scrap of paper with a telephone number and "TAA 426 *Dep. 22:50 arr 06:20*" written on it in a neat italic hand, which he took immediately to the payphone in the hall downstairs. He dialled the number and was answered by a female voice.

"Transamerican Airways."

"Can you tell me the destination of your flight 426 that left Geneva at 22:50 last night?"

"Yes sir, flight 426 to New York and Los Angeles should have left at that time last night. But due to a technical problem the flight was postponed till this morning. We had to charter another plane."

"When did it leave?"

"It departs in one hour from now, at 09:30 hours, sir."

"Is there a vacant seat?"

"Plenty, sir, but you'd better hurry."

Persse thrust a generous quantity of francs into the hand of his bewildered landlady and ran down the hill to the taxi-rank in front of the station.

"Geneva airport," he gasped, collapsing into the back seat. "As fast as you can."

The route to the airport was mostly motorway, and the taxi passed everything on it. They arrived at the International Departures terminal at nine o'clock precisely. Persse gave all his remaining francs to the driver, who seemed well satisfied. He ran headlong at the automatic doors, which opened just in time to prevent him from crashing through their plate glass. Two Transamerican employees, a man and a girl, chatting idly behind the deserted check-in desk, looked up in surprise as Persse charged up to the counter.

"Do you have a passenger Pabst on Flight 426?" he demanded. "Miss Angelica Pabst?"

The man tapped on his computer terminal and confirmed that Miss Pabst had indeed checked in for the flight and was booked through to Los Angeles.

"Give me a ticket to Los Angeles, please, and a seat as near to Miss Pabst as possible."

Though the flight had technically closed, and the passengers were already boarding, the man got permission to issue Persse with a ticket—it helped that Persse had no luggage. The pair responded eagerly to the urgency of the transaction: while the man filled out the ticket and credit-card slip, the girl allocated him a seat. "You're in luck, sir," she said, studying her computer screen. "There's an empty seat right next to Miss Pabst."

"That's grand!" said Persse. He had a vision of himself, the last to board the plane, walking up the aisle and slipping into the seat next to Angelica while her head was turned to look out of the window, saying, quietly—saying what? *"Hallo. Long time no see. Going far? Did you [holding up the laddered tights] forget these?"* Or better still, saying nothing, just waiting to see how long it would take before she looked down and recognized his scuffed shoes, or the back of his hand on the seat arm between them, or simply felt the vibrations of excitement and expectancy flowing from his heart, and turned to look at him.

"Here's your Amex card, sir," said the man. "Could I see your passport?"

"Sure." Persse glanced at his watch. It was 9:15.

The man flicked open the passport, frowned, and thumbed through the pages very deliberately. "I can't find your visa, sir," he said at length.

Persse now knew, if he did not know before, what a cold sinking feeling was like. "Oh, Jaysus! Do I need a visa?"

"You can't fly to the United States without a visa, sir."

"I'm sorry, I didn't know."

The man sighed, and slowly tore Persse's ticket and American Express slip into small pieces.

3

*whhheeee*ᴇᴇᴇᴇᴇᴇᴇ*EEEEEEEE!* The scream of jet engines rises to a crescendo on the runways of the world. Every second, somewhere or other, a plane touches down, with a puff of smoke from scorched tyre rubber, or rises into the air, leaving a smear of black fumes dissolving in its wake. From space, the earth might look to a fanciful eye like a huge carousel, with planes instead of horses spinning round its circumference, up and down, up and down. *Whhheeeeeeeeeee!*

It's late July now, and schools as well as colleges and universities have begun their summer vacations. Conference-bound academics must compete for airspace with holidaymakers and package tourists. The airport lounges are congested, their floors are littered with paper cups, the ashtrays are overflowing and the bars have run out of ice. Everyone is on the move. In Europe, northerners head south for the shadeless beaches and polluted waters of the Mediterranean, while southerners flee to the chilly inlets and overcast mountains of Scotland and Scandinavia. Asians fly west and Americans fly east. Ours is a civilization of lightweight luggage, of permanent disjunction. Everybody seems to be departing or returning from somewhere. Jerusalem, Athens, Alexandria, Vienna, London. Or Ajaccio, Palma, Tenerife, Faro, Miami.

At Gatwick, pale-faced travellers in neatly pressed frocks and safari suits, anxiously clutching their passports and airtickets, hurry from the Southern Region railway station to the Air Terminal, struggling against a tide of their sunburned and crumpled counterparts flowing in the opposite direction, festooned with wickerwork baskets, dolls in folk costume, straw sombreros and lethal quantities of duty-free cigarettes and liquor.

Persse McGarrigle is carried along by the departing current. It is nearly a week since the débâcle at Geneva airport, during which time he has flown home to Ireland, found a substitute for himself on the Celtic Twilight Summer School and got himself a visa to the United States. Now he is on his way to Los Angeles, to look for Angelica, by Skytrain, the walk-on, no-reservation service that posters all over London inform him is the cheapest way to travel to the States. But the Laker check-in counters are ominously deserted. Has he made a mistake about the departure time? No. Alas, the Skytrain has been suspended owing to the grounding of the DC-10, the Laker staff explain to Persse with regret, sympathy and a certain incredulity. Is it possible that there is anyone left in the entire world who hasn't heard about the grounding of the DC-10? I haven't been reading the papers lately, he says apologetically, I've been living in a cottage in Connemara, writing poetry. What's the quickest way for me to get to Los Angeles? Well, they say, you could take the helicopter to Heathrow, though it will cost you, and try the big nationals. Or you could go from here by Braniff to Dallas/Fort Worth, they have onward connections to LA. Persse gets the last standby seat on a Boeing 747 painted bright orange, which takes him to an airport so immense you cannot see its perimeter at under two thousand feet, baking like an enormous biscuit in a temperature of 104° Farenheit; shivers for three hours in a smoked-glass terminal building air-conditioned to the temperature of iced Coke; and flies on to California in a Western Airlines Boeing 707.

It is dark by the time they begin their descent to Los Angeles, and the city is an awe-inspiring sight from the air—a glimmering gridiron of light from horizon to horizon—but Persse, who has been travelling continuously for twenty-two hours, is too tired to appreciate it. He has tried to sleep on the two planes, but they kept waking him up to give him meals. Long-distance flying, he decides, is rather like being in hospital in that respect, and it wouldn't have surprised him unduly if one of the hostesses had slipped a thermometer into his mouth between meals. He had scarcely had the strength to rip open the plastic envelope containing his cutlery for the last dinner he was offered.

He staggers out of the terminal into the warm Californian night, and stands dazedly on the pavement as cars and buses sweep by in an endless procession. A man strides to the edge of the kerb and waves down a minibus with "*Beverly Hills Hotel*" emblazoned on its side, which promptly swerves to a halt and springs open its door with a hiss of compressed air. The man gets in and Persse follows. The ride is free, the hotel room staggeringly expensive—clearly way out of Persse's usual class of accommodation, but he is too tired to quibble or to contemplate searching for a cheaper alternative. A porter insists on taking his ridiculously small sports grip, which is all the luggage he has, and leading him down long, carpeted corridors decorated with a design of huge, slightly sinister green leaves above the dado, and shows him into a handsome suite with a bed as big as a football pitch. Persse takes off his clothes and crawls into the bed, falls asleep instantly, wakes up only three hours later, 2 a.m. local time but 10 a.m. by his body clock, and tries to make himself drowsy again by studying the entries under "Pabst" in the Los Angeles telephone directory. There are twenty-seven of them altogether and none of them is called Hermann.

. . .

But where is Morris Zapp? His non-appearance at Vienna excited little interest—people often fail to show up at conferences they have provisionally applied for. But at Bellagio there is considerable concern. Morris Zapp never returned from his jog in the woods that afternoon, after writing his letter to Arthur Kingfisher. The letter is recovered from the outgoing mailbox in the villa's lobby and confiscated by the police as a possible source of clues to his disappearance; it is opened and perused and puzzled over and filed away and forgotten; it is never mailed and Arthur Kingfisher never knows that he was invited to the Jerusalem conference. Search parties are sent into the woods, and there is talk of dragging the lake.

A few days later, Désirée, vacationing at Nice, gets a telephone call in her hotel room from the Paris *Herald-Tribune*. A young, rather breathless American male voice.

"Is that Mrs. Désirée Zapp?"

"Not any longer."

"I beg your pardon ma'am?"

"I used to be Mrs. Désirée Zapp. Now I'm Ms. Désirée Byrd."

"The wife of Professor Morris Zapp?"

"The ex-wife."

"The author of *Difficult Days*?"

"Now you're talking."

"We just had a telephone call, Mrs. Zapp—"

"Ms. Byrd."

"Sorry, Ms. Byrd. We just had an anonymous telephone call to say that your husband has been kidnapped."

"*Kidnapped?*"

"That's right ma'am. We've checked it out with the Italian police and it seems to be true. Professor Zapp went out jogging from a villa in Bellagio three days ago and never returned."

"But why in God's name would anybody want to kidnap Morris?"

"Well, the kidnappers are demanding half a million dollars in ransom."

"*What?* Who do they think is going to pay that sort of money?"

"Well, *you* I guess, ma'am."

"They can go fuck themselves," says Désirée, putting down the phone.

Soon the young man is back on the line. "But isn't it true, Mrs. Zapp—Ms. Byrd—that you received half a million dollars for the film rights alone of *Difficult Days?*"

"Yeah, but I earned that money and I sure as hell didn't earn it to buy back a husband I said good riddance to years ago."

Désirée bangs down the phone. Almost immediately it rings again. "I have nothing further to say," she snaps.

There is silence for a moment, then a heavily accented voice says, "Ees dat Signora Zapp?"

· · ·

Persse has breakfast in a pleasant room on the ground floor of the Beverly Hills called the Polo Lounge, which is full of people who look like film stars and who, it gradually dawns upon him, *are* film stars. The breakfast costs as much as a three-course dinner in the best restaurant in Limerick. His American Express Card will take care of the bill, but Persse is getting worried at the thought of the debits he is totting up on the Amex computer. A few days' living in this place would see off the remainder of his bank balance, but there's no point in checking out till noon. He goes back to his palatial suite and telephones the twenty-seven Pabsts in the directory without finding one who will admit to having a daughter called Angelica. Then, cursing himself for not having thought of the expedient earlier, he works his way through the head offices of the airlines in the Yellow Pages, asking for Mr. Pabst, until, at last, the telephonist at Transamerican says, "Just one moment, I'll put you through to Mr. Pabst's secretary."

"Mr. Pabst's office," says a silky Californian voice.

"Oh, could I speak to Mr. Pabst?"

"I'm sorry, he's in a meeting right now. Can I take a message?"

"Well, it's a rather personal matter. I really want to see him myself. Urgently."

"I'm afraid that won't be possible today. Mr. Pabst has meetings all the morning and he's flying to Washington this afternoon."

"Oh dear, this is terrible. I've flown all the way from Ireland to see him."

"Did you have an appointment, Mr. . . ."

"McGarrigle. Persse McGarrigle. No, I don't have an appointment. But I must see him." Then, "It's about his daughter," he risks.

"Which one?"

Which one! Persse clenches the fist of his free hand and punches the air in triumph. "Angelica," he says. "But Lily, too, in a way."

There is a thoughtful silence at the other end of the line. "Can I come back to you about this Mr. McGarrigle?"

"Yes, I'm staying at the Beverly Hills Hotel," says Persse.

"The Beverly Hills, right." The secretary sounds impressed. Ten minutes later the phone rings again. "Mr. Pabst can see you for a few minutes at the airport, just before his plane leaves for Washington," she says. "Please be at the Red Carpet Club in the Transamerican terminal at 1:15 this afternoon."

"I'll be there," says Persse.

. . .

Morris Zapp hears the telephone ringing in the next room. He does not know where he is because he was knocked out with some sort of injection when they kidnapped him, and when he woke up, God knew how many hours later, he was blindfolded. From the sounds of birdsong and the absence of traffic noise beyond the walls of his room he deduces that he is in the country; from the coolness of the air around his legs, still clothed in red silk running shorts, that he is in the mountains. He complained bitterly about the blindfold until his captors explained that if he happened to see any of them they would be obliged to kill him. Since then, his main fear has been that his blindfold will slip down accidentally. He has asked them to knock on the door before they come into his room so that he can warn them of such an eventuality. They come in to give him his meals, untying his hands for this purpose, or to lead him to the john. They will not allow him outdoors, so he has to exercise by walking up and down his small, narrow bedroom. Most of the time he spends lying on the bunk bed, racked by a monotonous cycle of rage, self-pity and fear. As the days have passed, his anxieties have become more basic. At first he was chiefly concerned about the arrangements for the Jerusalem conference. Later, about staying alive. Every time the telephone rings in the next room, he feels an irrational spasm of hope. It is the chief of police, the military, the U.S. Marines. *"We know where you are, you are completely surrounded. Release your prisoner unharmed and come out with your hands on your heads."* He has no idea what the telephone conversations are actually about, since they are conducted in a low murmur of Italian.

One of Morris's guards, the one they call Carlo, speaks English and from him Morris has gathered that he has been kidnapped not by the Mafia, nor by the henchmen of some rival contender for the UNESCO chair, such as von Turpitz, but by a group of left-wing extremists out to combine fund-raising with a demonstration of anti-American sentiment. The Rockefeller Villa and its affluent life-style evidently struck them as an arrogant flaunting of American cultural imperialism (even though, as Morris pointed out, it was used by scholars from all nations) and the kidnapping of a well-connected resident as an effective form of protest which would also have the advantage of subsidizing future terrorist adventure. Somehow—Morris cannot imagine how, and Carlo will not tell him—they traced the connection between the American professor who went jogging at 5:30 every afternoon along the same path through the woods near the Villa Serbelloni, and Désirée Byrd, the rich American authoress reported in *Newsweek* as having earned over two million dollars in royalties and subsidiary rights from her novel *Difficult Days*. The only little mistake they made was to suppose that Morris and Désirée were still married. Morris's emphatic statement that they were divorced clearly dismayed his captors.

"But she got plenty money, yeah?" Carlo said, anxiously. "She don' wan' you to die, huh?"

"I wouldn't count on it," Morris said. That was Day Two, when he was still capable of humour. Now it is Day Five and he doesn't feel like laughing any more. It is taking them a long time to locate Désirée, who is apparently no longer to be found in Heidelberg.

The telephone conversation in the next room comes to an end, and Morris hears footsteps approaching and a knock on his door. "Come in," he croaks, fingering his blindfold.

"Well," says Carlo, "we finally located your wife."

"Ex-wife," Morris points out.

"She sure is some tough bitch."

"I told you," says Morris, his heart sinking. "What happened?"

"We put our ransom demand to her . . ." says Carlo.

"She refused to pay?"

"She said, 'How much do I have to pay to make you keep him?'"

Morris began to weep, quietly, making his blindfold damp. "I told you it was useless asking Désirée to ransom me. She hates my guts."

"We shall have to make her pity you."

"How are you going to do that?" says Morris anxiously.

"Perhaps if she receives some little memento of you. An ear. A finger . . ."

"For Christ's sake," Morris whimpers.

Carlo laughs. "A leetle joke. No, you must send her a message. You must appeal to her tender feelings."

"She hasn't got any tender feelings!"

"It will be a test of your eloquence. The supreme test."

. . .

"Yeah, there were two babies on that KLM flight, twin girls," says Hermann Pabst. "Nobody ever did discover how they were smuggled on board. All the women passengers were questioned on arrival at Amsterdam, and the stewardesses as well, of course. It was in all the papers, but you would have been too young to remember that."

"I was a baby myself at the time."

"Right," says Hermann Pabst. "I have some cuttings at home, I could let you have copies." He scribbles a note on a memo pad inside his wallet. He is a big, thickset man, with pale blond hair going white, and a face that has turned red rather than brown in the Californian sunshine. They are sitting in the bar of the Red Carpet Club, Pabst drinking Perrier water and Persse a beer. "I worked for KLM in those days, I was on duty the day the plane landed with those two little stowaways. They were parked in my office for a while, cute little things. Gertrude—my wife—and me, we had no children, not by choice, something to do with Gertrude's tubes" (he pronounces the word in the American way as "toobs"). "Now they can do an operation, but in those days . . . anyhow, I called her up, I said "Gertrude, congratulations, you just had twins." I decided to adopt those kids as soon as I set eyes on them. It seemed . . ." He gropes for a word.

"Providential?" Persse suggests.

"Right. Like they'd been sent from above. Which, in a way, they had. From 20,000 feet." He takes a swig of Perrier water and glances at his watch.

"What time does your plane leave?" Persse asks him.

"When I tell it to," says Hermann Pabst. "It's my own private jet. But I have to watch the time. I'm attending a reception at the White House this evening."

Persse looks suitably impressed. "It's very good of you to give me your time, sir. I can see that you are a very busy man."

"Yeah, I done pretty well since I came to the States. I gotta plane, a yacht, a ranch near Palm Springs. But let me tell you something, young man, ya can't buy love. That was where I went wrong with the girls. I spoiled them, smothered them with presents—toys, clothes, horses, vacations. They both rebelled against it in different ways, soon as they became teenagers. Lily ran wild. She discovered boys in a big way, then dope. She got in with a bad crowd at high school. I guess I handled it badly. She ran away from home at sixteen. Well there's nothing new about that, not in California. But it broke Gertrude's heart. Didn't do mine a lot of good either. I have high blood pressure, mustn't smoke, scarcely any drink"—he gestured to the Perrier water. "After a coupla years we traced Lily to San Francisco. She was living in some crummy commune, shacked up with some guy, or guys, making money by, would you believe, acting in blue movies. We brought her back home, tried to make a fresh start, sent her to a girls' college in the East with Angie, the best, but it didn't work out. Lily went to Europe for a vacation study programme and never came back. That was six years ago."

"And Angelica?"

"Oh, Angie," Hermann Pabst sighs. "She rebelled in a different way, the opposite way. She became an egghead. Spent all her time reading, never dated boys. Looked down at me and her mother because we weren't cultured—well, I admit it, I never did have much time for reading, apart from the *Wall Street Journal* and the aviation trade magazines. I tried to catch up with those *Reader's Digest* Condensed Books, but Angelica threw them in the trash can and gave me some others to read that I just couldn't make head or tail of. She got straight 'A's for every course she took at Vassar, and graduated Summa Cum Laude, then she insisted on going to England to do another Bachelor's course at Cambridge, then she told her mother and me she was going to Yale graduate school to do complete literature, or somethin'."

"Comp. Lit.? Comparative Literature?"

"That's it. Says she wants to be a college teacher. What a waste! I mean, there's a girl with looks, brains, everything. She could marry anybody she liked. Someone with power, money, ambition. Angie could be a President's wife."

"You're right, sir," says Persse. He has not thought it prudent to reveal his own matrimonial ambitions with respect to Angelica. Instead, he has represented himself to Mr. Pabst as a writer researching a book on the behavioural patterns of identical twins, who happened to meet Angelica in England, and wanted to learn more of her fascinating history.

"What makes it worse, she refuses to let me pay her fees through graduate school. She insists on being independent. Earned her tuition by grading papers for her Professor at Yale—can you imagine it? When I make more money in a single week than he does in a year. There's only one thing she'll accept from me, and that's a card that gives her free travel on Transamerican airlines anywhere in the world."

"She seems to make good use of it," says Persse. "She goes to a lot of conferences."

"Conferences! You said it. She's a conference freak. I told her the other day, 'If you didn't spend so much time going to conferences, Angie, you would have gotten your doctorate by now, and put all this nonsense behind you.'"

"The other day? You saw Angelica the other day?" says Persse as casually as he can manage. "Is she here in Los Angeles, then?"

"Well, she was. She's in Honolulu right now."

"Honolulu?" Persse echoes him, dismayed. "Jaysus!"

"And I'll give you three guesses why she's there."

"Another conference?"

"Right. Some conference on John."

"John? John who?"

Pabst shrugs. "Angie didn't say. She just said she was going to a conference on John, University of Hawaii."

"Could it have been 'Genre'?"

"That's it." Pabst looked at his watch. "I'm sorry, McGarrigle, but I have to leave now. You can walk me to the plane if you have any more questions." He picks up his sleek burgundy leather briefcase, and Persse his scuffed sports bag. They walk out of the air-conditioned building into the smog-hazed sunshine.

"Does Angelica have any contact with her sister, these days?" Persse asks.

"Yeah, that's what she came home to tell me," says Mr. Pabst. "She's been studying in Europe these last two years, on a Woodrow Wilson scholarship. Living in Paris, mostly, but travelling around, and always on the lookout for her sister. Finally tracked her down to some nightclub in London. Lily is working as some kind of exotic dancer, apparently. I suppose that means she takes her clothes off, but at least it's better than blue movies. Angie says Lily is happy. She works for some kind of international agency that sends her all over, to different jobs. Both my girls seem determined to see the world the hard way. I don't understand them. But then, why should I? They're not my flesh and blood, after all. I did my best for them, but somewhere along the line I blew it."

They walk out onto a tarmac parking area for private planes of every shape and size, from tiny one-engined, propeller-driven lightweights, fragile as gnats, to executive jets big as full-size airliners. A group of young men, squatting in the shade of a petrol tanker, rise to their feet expectantly as Hermann Pabst approaches, holding up handwritten signs that say "Denver," "Seattle," "St. Louis," "Tulsa." "Sorry, boys," says Pabst, shaking his head.

"Who are they?" Persse asks.

"Hitchhikers."

Persse looks back wonderingly over his shoulder. "You mean they thumb rides in airplanes?"

"Yup. It's the modern way to hitchhike: hang about the executive jet parks."

Hermann Pabst's private plane is a Boeing 737 painted in the purple, orange and white livery of Transamerican Airlines. Its engines are already whining preparatory to departure, *whheeeeeeeeeeee!* They shake hands at the bottom of the mobile staircase that has been wheeled up to the side of the aircraft.

"Goodbye Mr. Pabst, you've been very kind."

"Goodbye, McGarrigle. And good luck with your study. It's a very interesting subject. People are surprisingly ignorant about twins. Why, Angelica gave me a novel to read once, that had identical twins of different sexes. I didn't have the patience to go on with it."

"I don't blame you," says Persse.

"Where shall I send those cuttings?"

"Oh—University College, Limerick."

"Right. So long."

Hermann Pabst strides up the steps, gives a final wave and disappears inside the aircraft. The steps are wheeled away from the plane and the door swings shut behind him. Persse puts his fingers in his ears as the engine noise rises in pitch and volume, and the plane slowly taxis towards the runway. *WHHHEEEEEEEEEEEEEE!* It disappears out of sight behind a hangar, then, a few minutes later, rises into the air and flies out over the sea before it banks and turns back towards the east. Persse picks up his grip and walks slowly back towards the little group squatting in the shade of the petrol tanker.

"Hi," says one of the young men.

"Hi," says Persse squatting down beside him. He takes a piece of foolscap from his bag and writes on it, in large letters, with a felt-tip pen, the word, "HONOLULU."

. . .

The telephone rings in Désirée's hotel room on the Promenade des Anglais. The man from Interpol sits up sharply, puts on his headphones, switches on his recording apparatus, and nods to Désirée. She picks up the phone.

"Ees dat Signora Zapp?"

"Speaking."

"I 'ave message for you, please."

After a pause and a crackle, Désirée hears Morris's voice. "Hallo, Désirée, this is Morris."

"Morris," she says, "where the hell are you? I've had just about . . ." But Morris is speaking on regardless, and it dawns on Désirée that she is listening to a tape-recording.

". . . I'm OK physically, I'm being well looked after, but these guys are serious and they're losing patience. I explained to them that we're not married any more and as a special concession they've agreed to halve the ransom money to a quarter of a million dollars. Now, I know that's a lot of money, Désirée, and God knows you don't owe me anything, but you're the only person I know who can lay hands on that kind of dough. It says in *Newsweek* that you've made two grand from *Difficult Days*—these guys clipped it. Get me out of this and I'll pay the quarter of a million back to you, if it takes me the rest of my life. At least I'll *have* a life.

"What you've got to do is this. If you agree to pay the ransom, put a small ad in the next issue of the Paris *Herald-Tribune*—you can phone it in, pay by credit card—saying 'The lady accepts,' right? Got it? 'The lady accepts.' Then arrange to draw from the bank a quarter of a million dollars in used, unmarked bills, and await instructions about handing them over. Needless to say, you mustn't bring the police into this. Any police involvement and the deal is off and my life will be in peril."

While Morris has been speaking, the telephone exchange has traced the call, and police cars are tearing through the streets of Nice, their sirens braying, to surround a call-box in the old town, in which they find the receiver off the hook and propped up in front of a cheap Japanese cassette recorder, from which the voice of Morris Zapp can still be heard plaintively pleading.

The next day, Désirée places a small ad in the Paris *Herald-Tribune*: "*The lady offers ten thousand dollars.*"

"I think you're being very generous," says Alice Kauffman, on the line from Manhattan to Nice, her voice gluey with the surreptitious mastication of cherry-liqueur chocolates.

"So do I," says Désirée, "but I figured ten grand is a sum Morris might just seriously attempt to pay back. And it might look bad if something happened to him without my lifting a finger."

"You're right, honey, you're so right," says Alice Kauffman, little kissing noises punctuating her words as she licks the tips of her fingers. "People are apt to get emotional about a situation like this, even women who are theoretically liberated. It might have an adverse effect on your sales if he died on you. Perhaps you should offer twenty grand."

"Would it be tax-deductible?" Désirée asks.

. . .

"What kind of woman is this?" Carlo demands of Morris. "Who ever heard of anybody bargaining with kidnappers?"

"I warned you," says Morris Zapp.

"And ten thousand dollars she offers! It's an insult."

"*You* feel insulted! How do you think *I* feel?"

"You will have to record another message."

"It's no use, unless you're prepared to lower your price. Suppose you come down to one hundred thousand?"

Blindfolded Morris hears a hiss of sharply intaken breath.

"I'll talk to the others about it," Carlo says. Ten minutes later he comes back with the tape recorder. "One hundred thousand dollars is our final offer," he says. "Tell her, and tell her good. Make sure she understands."

"It's not so simple," says Morris. "Every decoding is another encoding."

"What?"

"Never mind. Give me the tape recorder."

. . .

"Look at it this way, Désirée." Morris's voice crackles in the telephone while outside, beneath the balcony of her room overlooking the sea, police cars go hee-hawing along the Promenade des Anglais in search of the call-box it is coming from. "One hundred thousand dollars is less than one-twentieth of your royalties from *Difficult Days*, which incidentally I thought was an absolutely wonderful book, a knockout, truly—less than four per cent. Now, although I take absolutely no credit for that achievement, I mean it was entirely your own creative genius, it is nevertheless true, in a sense, that if I hadn't been such a lousy husband to you all those years you wouldn't have been able to write the book. I mean you wouldn't have had the pain to express. You could say I made you a feminist. I opened your eyes to the oppressed state of modern American women. Don't you think that, viewed in that light, I'm entitled to some consideration in the present circumstances? I mean, you pay your agent ten per cent for doing less."

"The nerve," says Alice Kauffman, when Désirée recounts this new development on the transatlantic telephone. "I'd be inclined to let him rot. What are you going to do?"

"I'm offering twenty-five grand," says Désirée. "It's getting kind of interesting, like a Dutch auction. I wonder what the reserve is on Morris."

. . .

Persse sits on the narrow, crowded strip of beach in front of the Waikiki Sheraton, and tots up the sums on the pale blue American Express counterfoils that have accumulated in his wallet. He calculates that he has just about enough money in his bank account in Limerick to cover the total, but he will have to go into debt to get home. If he hadn't been lucky enough to get a free ride from Los Angeles to Honolulu on a plane chartered by a TV film crew, his finances would be in an even worse state.

It is hot, very hot, on the beach, in spite of the trade winds in which the palm trees sway and rustle overhead, and Persse feels unrefreshed by the swim he has just taken in an ocean that was like warm milk to the touch and almost as cloudy to the eye. The distant surf had tempted him, but he didn't like to leave his belongings unattended on the beach. He feels a distinct pang of nostalgia for the bracing, crystal-clear waters of Connemara, and its rock-strewn tidal beaches of firm-packed sand, where seabirds were often his only company earlier this summer. Here the sand is yielding and coarse-grained, and along the scarcely changing margin of the lukewarm sea plods an endless procession of humanity, in bikinis, trunks, Bermuda shorts and tank tops, the young and beautiful, the old and unlovely, the slim and the thin and the obese, the tanned and the freckled and the burned. Most of these people carry some form of food or drink in their hands—hamburgers, hot-dogs, ice-creams, soft drinks, even cocktails. The island is full of noises: twanging Hawaiian muzak from the hotel loudspeakers, rock music from toted transistor radios, the hum of air-conditioners and the thud of piledrivers laying the foundations for new hotels. Every two or three minutes, a jumbo jet rises into the air from the airport some miles to Persse's right and hangs, apparently almost motionless, above the bay, above the skyscraper hotels, the shimmying palms, the hired surfboards and outrigged canoes, the shopping centres and the parking lots, before turning east or west; and from its windows those who are departing look down, with varying degrees of envy or relief, upon those who have just arrived.

When Persse himself arrived the previous evening, he took a taxi immediately to the University, but all the administrative buildings were closed, and he wandered round the campus, which resembled a large botanical garden with sculpture exhibits, asking people at random for the Genre Conference without success, until a security guard advised him to go home before he got mugged. He returned early next morning, after spending the night in a cheap lodging-house, only to be informed that the conference had ended the day before, and that all the participants had dispersed, including the organizers who might conceivably have known where Angelica had gone. All the University Information Office could offer him was a copy of the conference programme, which included a tantalizing reference to a paper on "Comic Epic Romance from Ariosto to Byron—Literature's Utopian Dream of Itself" which Angelica had apparently delivered, and to which an Italian Professor called Ernesto Morgana and a Japanese called Motokazu Umeda had responded. How he would have loved to hear that!

Clutching this useless souvenir of Angelica's passage, Persse took the bus down to Waikiki and, glimpsing a strip of blue sea between two huge hotels, made for the beach to relieve his frustration with some exercise, and to contemplate his next move. There doesn't seem to be any sensible alternative to returning home. Persse sighs and buttons his wallet back into the breast pocket of his shirt.

Then his attention is caught by a strikingly incongruous figure among the sun-oiled, half-naked vacationers paddling along at the edge of the water. It is an elderly lady wearing a sprigged blue muslin dress, the full skirt of which has been elegantly gathered up and dovetailed to expose a modest extent of bare white leg. She is carrying a matching parasol to shade her face. Persse leaps to his feet and runs forward to greet her.

"Miss Maiden! Fancy seeing you here!"

"Hallo, young man! The surprise is mutual, but a pleasant one I'm sure. Are you staying at the Sheraton?"

"Good heavens, no, but there seems to be no way of getting to the beach in this place without walking through some hotel lobby."

"I am staying at the Royal Hawaiian, which I am told is very exclusive, though what counts as vulgar in Honolulu I cannot imagine," says Miss Maiden. "Are you sitting somewhere? I feel the need of a rest and perhaps a drink. They have something called slush here which in spite of its name is rather refreshing."

"Are you here for the Genre Conference?" is Persse's first question, when they have seated themselves at the counter of the Sheraton's outdoor soda-fountain, with two gigantic paper cups full of raspberry-flavoured crushed ice before them.

"No, this is simply a holiday, pure indulgence without any self-improvement. It's a place I've always wanted to visit. 'Hawaii Five-O' is one of my favourite TV programmes. I'm afraid the reality is a little disappointing. It generally is, I find, since the invention of colour television. Are you on holiday here yourself, young man?"

"Not exactly. I'm looking for a girl."

"A natural ambition, but haven't you come rather a long way for that purpose?"

"It's a particular girl that I'm looking for—Angelica Pabst—perhaps you remember her at the Rummidge conference."

"But how very extraordinary! I met her just a few days ago."

"You met Angelica?"

"On this very beach. I recognized her, though I couldn't remember her name. I'm afraid I'm losing my memory for names as I get older. Your own, for instance, just this moment escapes me, Mr. er—"

"McGarrigle. Persse McGarrigle."

"Ah yes, she mentioned you."

"She did? Angelica? How?"

"Oh, fondly, fondly."

"What did she say?"

"I can't remember, exactly, I'm afraid."

"Please try," Persse begs her. "It's very important to me."

Miss Maiden frowns with concentration, sucking vigorously on her straw and making a gurgling sound in her paper cup. "It was something about names. When she reminded me that she was called Angelica Pabst, I ventured to say that she deserved a more euphonious second name, and she laughed and asked me if I thought 'McGarrigle' would sound any better."

"She did?" Persse is ecstatic. "Then she loves me!"

"Were you in any doubt about it?"

"Well, she's been running away from me ever since I first met her."

"Ah, a young woman likes to be wooed before she is won."

"But I can never get near enough to her to start wooing," says Persse.

"She's putting you to the test."

"She certainly is. I was on the point of giving up and going back to Connemara."

"No, you mustn't do that. Never give up."

"Like the Grail knights?"

"Oh, but they were such boobies," says Miss Maiden. "All they had to do was to ask a question at the right moment, and they generally muffed it."

"Did Angelica happen to tell you where she was going next? Back to Los Angeles?"

"I think it was Tokyo."

"Tokyo?" Persse wails. "Oh, Jaysus!"

"Or was it Hong Kong? One of those Far Eastern places, anyway. She was going to some conference or other."

"That goes without saying," sighs Persse. "The question is, which conference?"

"If I were you, I should go to Tokyo and look for her."

"There are a lot of people in Tokyo, Miss Maiden."

"But they are very *little* people, are they not? Miss Pabst would stand out in the crowd, head and shoulders above everybody else. What a magnificent figure of a gal!"

"Indeed she is," Persse agreed ardently.

"I'm afraid she must have thought me very rude—I just couldn't keep my eyes off her as she was towelling herself. She had been swimming, you see— I met her wading out of the sea, wearing a two-piece bathing suit, her hair wet and her limbs gleaming."

"Like Venus," Persse breathes, closing his eyes to picture the scene more vividly.

"Quite so, the analogy struck me also. She has the most beautiful tan, which is very becoming with dark hair and eyes I always think. I observe that you have the same fair skin as myself, which burns and peels at the slightest exposure—your nose, if you will excuse my mentioning it, is already looking rather red; I would advise you to get yourself a hat—but Miss Pabst has skin like brown silk, a flawless, even tan. Except for a birthmark rather high up on the left thigh—have you noticed that? Shaped rather like an inverted comma."

"I have not had," says Persse, blushing, "the privilege of seeing Angelica in a bathing costume. I'm not sure I could bear it. I should be tempted to fight every man on the beach who looked at her."

"Well, you would certainly have had your work cut out that day. She was being ogled from all sides."

"Don't tell me," Persse begs. "There was a time when I thought she was a striptease dancer—it nearly broke my heart."

"That charming young woman a striptease dancer? How could that be?"

"It was a case of mistaken identity. It turned out to be her sister."

"Oh? Has she a sister?"

"Her twin sister, Lily, it was." How long ago it seems that he pursued Angelica's shadow through the stews of London and Amsterdam. The memory of Girls Unlimited makes him think of Bernadette and reminds him that he is still carrying around, undelivered, the document signed by Maxwell. In all the excitement of getting back onto Angelica's trail, he has forgotten all about Bernadette. How was that? He traces it back to the encounter with Cheryl Summerbee at Heathrow—Cheryl, whom he last saw inexplicably weeping over her timetable of flights to Geneva. What strange, unpredictable creatures women are!

And now, here is Miss Maiden surprising him with an unwonted sign of feminine fragility. She looks pale and sways on her stool as if about to faint. "Are you all right, Miss Maiden?" he asks anxiously, steadying her with his hand on her arm.

"The heat," she murmurs. "I'm afraid it is too much for me in the middle of the day. If you would give me your arm, I think I will go back to my hotel and lie down."

. . .

By chance, Fulvia and Ernesto Morgana fly into Milan airport at about the same time, she from Geneva, he from Honolulu. They meet in the baggage hall and embrace with style, kissing on both cheeks.

"Oh!" exclaims Fulvia. "You are very bristly, *carissimo!*"

"*Scusi*, my dearest, but it was a long flight and you know I don't like to shave on aeroplanes, in case of sudden turbulence."

"Of course, my love," Fulvia assures him. Ernesto uses an old-fashioned cut-throat razor. "Did you have a good conference?" she asks.

"Very enjoyable, thank you. Honolulu is extraordinary. The post-industrial society at play. You must go some time. And you?"

"The Narrative Conference was boring but Vienna was charming. At Lausanne it was the other way round. Oh, there are my bags coming— quick!"

Fulvia has left her bronze Maserati in the airport carpark, and drives them both home in it. "Did you meet anyone interesting?" she asks, pulling into the fast lane and flashing her headlights at a laggard Fiat.

"Well, the Signorina Pabst, to whose paper I was responding, turned out to be amazingly young and amazingly beautiful, as well as a most acute critic of Ariosto."

"Did you sleep with her?"

"Unfortunately her interest in me was purely professional. Was Professor Zapp at Vienna?"

"He was expected, but did not arrive, for some reason. I met a friend of his called Sy Gootblatt."

"Did you sleep with him?"

Fulvia smiles. "If you did not sleep with Miss Pabst, I did not sleep with Mr. Gootblatt."

"But I really didn't sleep with her!" Ernesto protests. "She's not that kind of girl."

"Are there still girls who are not that kind of girl? All right, I believe you. So who did you sleep with?"

Ernesto shrugs. "Just a couple of whores."

"How banal, Ernesto."

"Two at the same time," he says defensively. "So how was Mr. Gootblatt?"

"Mr. Gootblatt looked promising, but proved to lack both imagination and stamina. Unfortunately it turned out that we were both going on from Vienna to Lausanne, so we had to keep up pretences for another week. I did not invite him to visit us."

Ernesto nods as if this is all he wanted to know.

When they are indoors, and have showered and changed their clothes, they exchange gifts. Ernesto has bought Fulvia earrings and a brooch decorated with uncultured pearls, and Fulvia has bought Ernesto a silver-mounted riding crop. He mixes a dry martini for both of them, and they sit facing each other in the off-white drawing-room, Ernesto sorting through the mail which has accumulated in their absence, and Fulvia with a stack of neatly folded newspapers and magazines at her side. "It is a relief to ignore the news while one is away," she observes, "but there is such a lot of catching up to do when one returns home." She peels the top paper from the pile and scans the headlines. Her mouth falls open and her eyes stare. "Ernesto," she says in a quiet but steely tone.

"Yes, my love," he replies absently, ripping open envelopes with a paper knife.

"Did you by any chance tell any of our political friends about Morris Zapp? I mean about his being married to Désirée Byrd, the novelist?"

Ernesto, startled by his wife's tone of voice, looks up. "I might have mentioned it to Carlo, I suppose. Why do you ask?"

"Carlo is a young fool," says Fulvia, leaping to her feet and flinging the newspaper into Ernesto's lap. "He will get us all thrown into jail if you don't act at once. Morris Zapp has been kidnapped!"

. . .

They burst into Morris's bedroom in the middle of the night, waking him up. The blankets are ripped from the bed and he is jerked to his feet. Hands adjust and tighten his blindfold. Somebody roughly forces his feet into his Adidas. "Where are we going?" he quavers. "Shut up," says Carlo. "Has Désirée paid up?" "Quiet." Carlo sounds angry. Morris is shaking. He knows that this is it: either deliverance or death. Someone is rolling his sleeve up and dabbing at his forearm with a wet swab. "Don't move, or you'll get hurt." Surely they don't bother to give people an anaesthetic before bumping them off? It must be deliverance. Unless of course it's a lethal injection. He feels the prick of a needle. "Are you—" he begins, but before he can finish the sentence everything goes black.

. . .

The next sensation he becomes aware of is of a sharp rock digging into his right buttock, and cool air round his knees. Then the sound of birdsong. His hands are free. He pulls off his blindfold and blinks in a light that seems dazzling, but which, as his eyes accommodate, he perceives to be a delicate pink dawn sky, latticed with pine branches. He is lying on rough ground at the foot of a tall, straight tree. He sits up, and puts a hand to his throbbing head. His pale legs, protruding from the red silk running shorts, seem a long way off, and hardly to belong to him, but they bend at the knee when he wills them to, and, turning to lean against the tree for support, he struggles to his feet. He draws deep, intoxicating breaths of the pure, pine-scented air into his lungs. Free! Alive! God bless Désirée! His eyes begin to focus properly. He is in a forest, on a hillside. Through the trees he can see a grey strip of road. He stumbles down the hill towards it, grasping at tree trunks for support, falling once and grazing his leg.

The road is narrow and badly paved. It does not look as if much traffic passes on it. Morris hobbles across to the other side and stands on the grass verge, looking over a low wall into a deep valley between mountains. He can see the road ribboning beneath him for miles in long parallel loops. There is not a sign of human habitation.

Morris begins to limp slowly downhill. After a few minutes, he stops. Behind the birdsong, from far, far below, there comes a sweet mechanical sound, the faint burr of a distant vehicle. He looks over the edge of the road again, and sees a small dot climbing up the winding road towards him, moving rapidly along the straights and slowing to take the hairpin bends, occasionally disappearing behind a clump of trees, and shooting into visibility again, a faint squeal of tyres now accompanying the growl of the engine. It is a powerful GT coupé, driven with skill and verve. When it reaches the stretch of road directly beneath him, Morris identifies it as a bronze Maserati.

As the car comes round the final bend, Morris steps into the road and waves it down. The Maserati sprints towards him, then stops abruptly, spraying gravel from its tyres. A deeply tinted window sinks into the door on the driver's side, and the head of Fulvia Morgana, her tawny hair held in a silk scarf, appears in the aperture. Her eyebrows are arched in astonishment above her Roman nose.

"Why, Morris!" she says. "What are you doing here? People have been looking all over for you."

. . .

In Japanese language no articles. No "*a*," no "*the*." In Japanese inn (*ryokan*) where Persse takes room (because cheaper than Western-style hotel) not many articles either. No chair, no bed. Just matting, one cushion and small low table. At night maid lays out bedding on floor. Walls and doors are made of paper pasted on wood. No lock on sliding door. Maid brings meals to room, kneels to serve Persse seated on cushion before table. Noise of slurping audible through paper walls on all sides. In Japan polite to make noise when eating— signifies enjoyment. Communal bathroom where naked men soap and rinse themselves squatting on dwarf milking stools before climbing into large common bathtub to soak, floating languidly in steaming water, backs of heads resting on tiled rim of bath. Toilets like bidets hooded at one end and raised on plinth with footrests at each side: easy to pee in but other job trickier.

Persse wanders round Tokyo in a daze, not quite sure whether he is suffering more from culture shock or jet lag. He flew by night from Honolulu to

Tokyo, crossed the international date line and lost a whole day of his life. One minute it was 11:15 p.m. on Tuesday, the next it was 11:16 p.m. on Wednesday. When he arrived in Tokyo it was still night. The night seemed to go on for ever. It is hot in Tokyo, hotter than Honolulu and without the mitigation of the trade winds. As soon as Persse goes out into the street he breaks out in sweat and feels it trickling down his torso from under his arms. The Japanese, however, seem unperturbed and unperspiring, waiting patiently at the intersections for the traffic lights to change, or pressed uncomplainingly together in the subway train.

Persse travels back and forth across Tokyo on his quest. He enquires from the British Council and the United States Information Service and the Japanese Cultural Ministry about conferences being held in Tokyo at this time, and though there are several, on subjects as various as cybernetics, fish farming, Zen Buddhism, and economic forecasting, none of them seems likely to be of interest to Angelica. He has great hopes of a congress of science-fiction writers in Yokohama, but on investigation its membership turns out to be exclusively Asian and male.

To make up for this last disappointment, Persse treats himself to a steak dinner in a restaurant in the centre of Tokyo—a luxury he can ill afford, but he feels less dejected after consuming it with a few bottles of beer. Later he wanders through the streets off the Ginza, lined with small bars, whose pavements are crowded with harmlessly drunk Japanese businessmen evidently celebrating the fact that it is Friday. The night is close and humid, and suddenly it begins to rain. Persse dodges into the first bar he comes to, an establishment calling itself simply "*Pub*," and descends the stairs towards the sound of pop music of nineteen-sixties vintage, Simon and Garfunkel. Oriental faces turn and smile genially at him as he comes into a small L-shaped bar. He is the only Westerner present. A hostess shows him to a seat, takes his order for beer and puts a bowl of salted nuts in front of him. In the middle of the room two Japanese men in business suits are singing "Mrs. Robinson" in English into a microphone, a phenomenon which puzzles Persse for several reasons one of which he cannot instantly identify. The two men conclude their performance, receive friendly applause from the customers, and sit down among them. The chief puzzle, Persse realizes, is that they managed to produce a very creditable imitation of Simon and Garfunkel's guitar-playing without the advantage of possessing any visible instruments.

The hostess brings Persse his drink in a litre-sized bottle, and a large album full of pop song lyrics in various languages, all numbered. She motions him to choose one, and he points at random at number 77, "Hey Jude!" and returns the album to her, sitting back in the expectation of having his request performed by the two cabaret artists. But the hostess smiles, shakes her head, and gives the book back to him. She calls something to the barman and motions Persse to stand up, chattering to him in Japanese. "Sorry, I don't understand," says Persse. "Can't they sing, 'Hey Jude'? I don't mind—'A Hard Day's Night' will do." He points to song number 78. She calls out something to the barman again, he returns the book, she pushes it back into his hands. "Sorry, I don't understand," he says, embarrassed. The hostess gestures to him to sit down, to relax, not to worry, and she goes across to a group of men at a table in the opposite corner of the room. She returns with a youngish man dressed in a neat sports shirt with an Arnold Palmer monogram on the chest, and holding a small glass of liquor. He bows and smiles toothily.

"Are you American? British?" he says.

"Irish."

"Irish? That is very interesting. May I interpret for you? Which song do you wish to sing?"

"I don't wish to sing at all!" Persse protests. "I just came in here for a quiet drink."

The Japanese beams toothily and sits down beside him. "But this is *karaoke* bar," he says. "Everybody sings in *karaoke* bar."

Hesitantly, Persse repeats the word. "*Karaoke*—what does that mean?"

"Literally *karaoke* means 'empty orchestra.' You see, the barman provides the orchestra," he gestures towards the bar, at the back of which Persse now sees that there is a long shelf of music cassettes and a cassette deck, "And you provide the voice"—he gestures to the microphone.

"Oh, I see!" says Persse laughing and slapping his thigh. The Japanese laughs too, and calls something across to his friends, who also laugh. "So which song, please?" he says, turning back to Persse.

"Oh, I'll have to have a lot of beers before you get me up to that mike," he says.

"I sing with you," says the man, who has evidently had quite a few drinks himself this evening. "I also like Beatle songs. What is your name, please?"

"Persse McGarrigle. And what is yours?"

"I am Akira Sakazaki." He takes card from his breast pocket and gives it to Persse. It is printed in Japanese on one side and in English on the other.

Underneath his name there are two addresses, one that of a university English Department.

"Now I understand why you speak English so well," Persse says. "I'm a university teacher myself."

"Yes?" Akira Sakazaki's smile seems to fill his entire face with teeth. "Where do you teach?"

"Limerick. I'm afraid I haven't got a card to give you."

"Please write," says Akira, taking a ball pen from his pocket and putting a paper napkin in front of Persse. "Your name is very difficult for Japanese." When Persse obliges, Akira takes the paper napkin to the microphone and says into it, "Ladies and gentlemen, Professor Persse McGarrigle of University College, Limerick, Ireland, will now sing, 'Hey Jude.'"

"No he won't," says Persse, signalling to the barman for another beer.

Akira evidently translates his announcement into Japanese, for there is a volley of applause from the other customers, and smiles of encouragement in Persse's direction. He begins to weaken. "Have you any Dylan songs in that book?" he asks.

They have some of the most popular ones, "Tambourine Man" and "Blowin' in the Wind" and "Lay, Lady, Lay." Persse doesn't really need the album with the lyrics, since he knows these songs off by heart, and frequently sings them in the bath, but undoubtedly his performance is enhanced by having the original backing tracks as accompaniment. He sings "Tambourine Man," nervously at first, but gradually warming to the task, and putting on a plausible imitation of Dylan's nasal whine. The applause is rapturous. He sings "Blowin' in the Wind" and "Lay, Lady, Lay" as encores. At Akira's earnest request, he sings "Hey Jude" in duet with him. They yield the floor at last to a young girl who sings, shyly, but with perfect timing, Diana Ross's version of "Baby Love."

Akira introduces Persse to his circle of friends, explaining that they are all translators, who meet once a month in this bar, "to let the hair down and put the knees up." The Japanese beams proudly as he displays these idioms to Persse. All the translators give him their cards except one who is asleep or drunk in the corner. Most of them are technical and commercial translators, but, learning that Persse is a teacher of English literature, they politely make literary conversation. The man sitting on Persse's left, who translates maintenance manuals for Honda motorcycles, volunteers the information that he recently saw a play by Shakespeare performed by a Japanese company, entitled, "The Strange Affair of the Flesh and the Bosom."

"I don't think I know that one," says Persse politely.

"He means, *The Merchant of Venice*," Akira explains.

"Is that what it's called in Japan?" says Persse with delight.

"Some of the older translations of Shakespeare in our country were rather free," says Akira apologetically.

"Do you know any other good ones?"

"Good ones?" Akira looks puzzled.

"Funny ones."

"Oh!" Akira beams. It seems not to have occurred to him before that "The Strange Affair of the Flesh and the Bosom" is amusing. He ponders. "There is, 'Lust and Dream of the Transitory World,'" he says. "That is—"

"No, don't tell me—let me guess," says Persse. "*Anthony and Cleopatra*?"

"*Romeo and Juliet*," says Akira. "And 'Swords of Freedom' . . ."

"*Julius Caesar*?"

"Correct."

"You know," says Persse, "there's the makings of a good parlour game here. You could make up your own . . . like, 'The Mystery of the Missing Handkerchief' for *Othello*, or 'A Sad Case of Early Retirement' for *Lear*." He calls for another round of drinks.

"When I translate English books," says Akira, "I always try to get as close as possible to the original titles. But sometimes it is difficult, especially when there is a pun. For example, Ronald Frobisher's *Any Road*—"

"Ronald Frobisher—have you translated him?"

"I am presently translating his novel, *Could Try Harder*. Do you know it?"

"Know it? I know *him*."

"Really? You know Mr. Frobisher? But that is wonderful! You must tell me all about him. What kind of man is he?"

"Well," says Persse. "He's very nice. But rather irascible."

"Irascible? That is a new word to me."

"It means, easily angered."

"Oh yes, of course, he was Angry Young Man." Akira nods delightedly, and calls the attention of his friends to the fact that Persse is acquainted with the distinguished British novelist whose work he is translating. Persse recounts how Frobisher set the London *literati* adrift on the Thames, a story received with great pleasure by all, though they seem a little disappointed that the ship did not actually float out to sea and sink.

"You must know a lot of English writers," says Akira.

"No, Ronald Frobisher is the only one," says Persse. "Do you translate many?"

"No, only Mr. Frobisher," says Akira.

"Well," says Persse. "It's a small world. Do you have that saying in Japan?"

"Narrow world," says Akira. "We say, 'It's a narrow world.'"

At this point, the man who was asleep in the corner wakes up, and is introduced to Persse as Professor Motokazu Umeda, a colleague of Akira's. "He is translator of Sir Philip Sidney," says Akira. "He will know more of the old Shakespeare titles."

Professor Umeda yawns, rubs his eyes, accepts a whisky, and, when Persse's interest has been explained to him, comes up with "The Mirror of Sincerity" (*Pericles*), "The Oar Well-Accustomed to the Water" (*All's Well That Ends Well*) and "The Flower in the Mirror and the Moon on the Water" (*The Comedy of Errors*).

"Oh, that one beats them all!" exclaims Persse. "That's really beautiful."

"It is a set phrase," Akira explains. "It means, that which can be seen but cannot be grasped."

"Ah," says Persse with a pang, suddenly reminded of Angelica. That which can be seen but which cannot be grasped. His euphoria begins rapidly to ebb away.

"Excuse me," says Professor Motokazu Umeda, offering Persse his card, printed in Japanese on one side and English on the other. Persse stares at the name, which now rings a distant, or not so distant, bell.

"Were you by any chance at a conference in Honolulu recently?" he asks.

. . .

"Morris called me as soon as he got back to the villa," says Désirée. "At first he was hysterical with gratitude, it was like being licked all over your face by your dog when you get back home from a trip, I could almost hear his tail wagging on the other end of the line. Then when it sank in that I hadn't paid over any money, he turned very nasty, more like the Morris I remembered, accused me of being mean and callous and putting his life in jeopardy."

"Tsk, tsk," says Alice Kauffman on the other end of the telephone line, a sound like the rustling of empty chocolate wrappers.

"I told him, I was prepared to pay up to forty thousand dollars for his release, I was already collecting the notes together and stashing them away right here in the hotel safe, and it wasn't my fault if the kidnappers decided to let him go for nothing."

"Did they?"

"Apparently. They must have got scared that the police would find them, or something. The police are all on my side, incidentally, they think I broke down the kidnappers' morale by bargaining with them. I'm getting very good press here. 'The Novelist with Nerves of Steel,' they call me in the magazines. I told Morris that, and it didn't make him any sweeter . . . Anyway, I'm going to put the whole story into my book. It's a wonderful inversion of the normal power relationships between men and women, the man finding himself totally dependent on the generosity of the woman. I might change the ending."

"Yeah, let the sonofabitch die," says Alice Kauffman. "Where is he now, anyway?"

"Jerusalem. Some conference or other he's organizing. Another thing he's sore about is that a fink called Howard Ringbaum whom Morris specifically excluded from the conference took advantage of his temporary disappearance to get himself accepted by the other organizer. You'd think Morris would have better things to think about, wouldn't you, a man back from the edge of the grave, you might say?"

"That's men for you, honey," says Alice Kauffman. "Speaking of which, how's the book coming along?"

"I'm hoping this new idea will get it moving again," says Désirée.

* * *

According to Motokazu Umeda, who responded to her paper at Honolulu, Angelica intended to travel on to Seoul, via Tokyo, to attend a conference on Critical Theory and Comparative Literature to which, it was rumoured, various big Parisian guns had been lured by the promise of a free trip to the Orient. Persse, now beyond all thoughts of prudent budgeting, waves his magic green-and-white card again, and takes wing to Seoul by Japanese Airlines. On the plane he meets another Helper, a beautiful Korean girl in the adjacent seat, who is drinking vodka and smoking Pall Malls as if her life depends on consuming as much duty free as possible for the duration of the flight. The vodka makes her loquacious and she explains to Persse that she is going home from the States for her annual visit to her family and will not be able to indulge in alcohol or tobacco for the next two weeks. "Korea is a modern country on the surface," she says, "but underneath it's very traditional and conservative, especially as regards social behaviour. I can tell you, when I first went to the States I couldn't believe my eyes—kids being cheeky to their parents, young people kissing in public—the first time I saw that I fainted.

Then smoking and drinking—at home it's considered insulting for a young unmarried woman to smoke in front of her elders. If my parents knew that I was not only smoking in front of my elders, but living with one of them, I guess they'd disown me. So I have to play the part of the good little Korean girl for the next two weeks, not smoking, refusing strong drink, speaking only when spoken to." She reaches up and presses the service button above her head to order another vodka. "Now my parents want me to come home and get married to a guy they have lined up for me—yes, we still have arranged marriages in Korea, believe it or not. My father can't understand why I keep putting him off. 'You want to get married, don't you?' he says 'Settle down, have children?' What can I tell him?"

"That you're already engaged?" Persse suggests.

"Ah, but I'm not," says the girl sadly. Her name is Song-Mi Lee, and she seems, to judge from the names she casually lets drop, to move in high academic circles in the United States. She tells him that the conference on Critical Theory and Comparative Literature will almost certainly be held at the Korean Academy of Sciences, a purpose-built conference and study centre just outside Seoul. He can take a taxi from the city centre, but must be sure to agree the fare first and should refuse to pay more than 700 won. Later, after they have landed, he sees her in the Arrivals hall of the airport, demurely smiling and amazingly sober, being greeted with bouquets by proud parents in tailored Western clothes.

It is the monsoon season in Korea, and Seoul is wet and humid, a concrete wilderness of indistinguishable suburbs ringing a city centre whose inhabitants are apparently so terrorized by the traffic that they have decided to live under the ground in a complex of subways lined with brightly lit shops. Persse takes a taxi to the Korean Academy of Sciences, a complex of buildings in oriental-modernist style set at the feet of low wooded hills, but the conference on Critical Theory and Comparative Literature has, he is hardly surprised to learn, finished and its participants have dispersed—some on a sightseeing tour of the south. So Persse takes a train which trundles through a sopping and unrelievedly green landscape of paddy fields and tree-topped hills swathed in mist, to the resort town of Kyong-ju, site of many ancient monuments, temples and modern hotels, and an artificial lake on which floats, like a gigantic bathtoy, a fibreglass pleasureboat in the shape of a white duck, disembarking from which Persse meets, not Angelica, but Professor Michel Tardieu, in the company of three smiling Korean Professors, all called

Kim. Angelica, he learns from Tardieu, was indeed at the conference, but did not join the sightseeing tour. Tardieu seems to remember that she was going on to another conference, in Hong Kong.

. . .

Now it is mid-August, and Morris Zapp's conference on the Future of Criticism in Jerusalem is in full swing. Almost everybody involved agrees that it is the best conference they have ever attended. Morris is smug. The secret of his success is very simple: the formal proceedings of the conference are kept to a bare minimum. There is just one paper a day actually delivered by its author, early in the morning. All the other papers are circulated in Xeroxed form, and the remainder of the day is allocated to "unstructured discussion" of the issues raised in these documents, or, in other words, to swimming and sunbathing at the Hilton pool, sightseeing in the Old City, shopping in the bazaar, eating out in ethnic restaurants, and making expeditions to Jericho, the Jordan valley, and Galilee.

The Israeli scholars, a highly professional and fiercely competitive group, are disgruntled with this arrangement, since they have been looking forward to attacking each other in the presence of a distinguished international audience, and the tourist attractions of Jerusalem and environs naturally have less novelty for them. But everybody else is delighted, with the exception of Rodney Wainwright, who still has not finished his paper. The only finished paper he has in his luggage is one by Sandra Dix, submitted to him just before he left Australia as part of her assessment in English 351. It is entitled "Matthew Arnold's Theory of Culture," and it begins:

> *According to Matthew Arnold culture was getting to know, on the matters that most concerned you, the best people. Matthew Arnold was a famous headmaster who wrote "Tom Brown's Schooldays" and invented the game of Rugby as well as the Theory of Culture. If I don't get a good grade for this course I will tell your wife that we had sex in your office three times this semester, and you wouldn't let me out when there was a fire drill in case somebody saw us leaving the room together . . .*

Rodney Wainwright goes hot and cold every time he thinks of this term-paper, to which he awarded a straight "A" without a moment's hesitation, and which he has brought with him to Israel in case Bev or some colleague should happen to go through his desk drawers while he is away and find it. But he goes even hotter and colder when he thinks of his own conference paper, still stalled at, "*The question is, therefore, how can literary criticism . . .*" If only he had completed it in time! Then it could have been photocopied and circulated like most of the other contributions to the conference, and it wouldn't have mattered if it had been unconvincing, or even unintelligible, because nobody is seriously reading the papers anyway—you keep coming across them in the Hilton waste baskets . . . But because he hadn't a finished text to give Morris Zapp when he arrived, Rodney Wainwright has been allocated one of the "live," formal sessions—yes, he has been accorded the privilege of delivering his paper in person, on, in fact, the penultimate morning of the conference, for he was obliged to ask for as much grace as possible.

It's not surprising, therefore, that Rodney Wainwright is unable to throw himself enthusiastically into the giddy round of pleasure that his fellow-conferees are enjoying. While they are at the poolside, or at the bar, or within the walls of the Old City, or in the air-conditioned bus, he is sitting at his desk behind drawn blinds in his room at the Hilton, sweating and groaning over his paper—or if he is not, he is guiltily aware that he ought to be. His colleagues' carefree high spirits add gall to his own misery, and as the week passes with no progress on his paper, and professional humiliation looming ever nearer, his resentment of their euphoric mood focuses upon one man in particular: Philip Swallow. Philip Swallow, with his theatrical silver beard and his braying Pommie voice and his unaccountably dishy mistress. What does she see in him? It must be the randy old goat's appetite for sex, because they seem to have a lot of that: Rodney Wainwright happens to occupy the room next to theirs and is not infrequently disturbed, working on his paper in the watches of the night, or in the middle of the afternoon, by muffled cries of pleasure audible when he presses his ear to the party wall; and if he should go out onto his balcony in the cool of the evening to stretch his cramped limbs, the chances are that Philip Swallow and his Joy will be on the adjacent balcony, clasped tenderly together, Joy rhapsodizing about the sunset reflected on the roofs and domes of the Old City, while Philip fondles her tits under her négligé. Rodney surprised Joy sunbathing topless on her balcony one morning when she evidently expected him to be at the formal paper session, and he has to admit that the tits would be well worth fondling. Not quite as spectacular as Sandra Dix's, perhaps, but then Sandra Dix seemed to derive little pleasure from having them fondled by Rodney Wainwright, or indeed, from any aspect of his sexual performance, insisting on chewing gum throughout intercourse, and breaking silence only to ask if he wasn't finished yet. For such meagre erotic reward has he risked domestic catastrophe in Cooktown, which makes it all the more aggravating to face professional disgrace in Jerusalem to the accompaniment of loudly voiced orgasmic bliss from the next room.

How does Philip Swallow do it? After screwing his blonde bird into the small hours, he is up bright and early for a swim in the hotel pool, never misses the morning lecture, is always first on his feet with a question when the speaker sits down, and signs up unfailingly for every sightseeing excursion on offer. It is as if the man has been given ten days to live and is determined to pack every instant with sensation, sublime or gross. No sooner have they all returned from retracing the Way of the Cross or inspecting the Dome of the Rock or visiting the Wailing Wall, than Philip Swallow is organizing a party to eat stuffed quail at an Arab restaurant hidden away in some crooked alley of the Old City which has been particularly recommended to him by one of the Israelis, setting off afterwards in a taxi with Joy and other dedicated hedonists to find a discothèque that is functioning clandestinely on the Sabbath. Yes, while Jerusalem is hushed in holy silence, the streets deserted and the shops all shut, Philip Swallow is bopping away under the strobe lights to the sound of the Bee Gees, his silver beard beaded with perspiration, his eyes fixed on Joy's nipples bouncing under her cheesecloth blouse as she twitches to the same rhythm. Rodney Wainwright knows because he squeezed into the taxi himself at the last moment, rather than return to the solitary contemplation of his unfinished paper, though he does not dance, and sits gloomily on the edge of the dancefloor all evening, drinking overpriced beer and also watching Joy's nipples bounce.

The next morning, Rodney does not hear Philip Swallow go whistling down the corridor for his early morning swim, so perhaps at last his excesses are taking their toll. But after breakfast he is down in the lobby with Joy, looking only a little pale and drawn under his tan, all ready for the day's outing—it is a free day (free, that is, from even a single formal lecture) and an excursion has been arranged to the Dead Sea and Masada.

Rodney Wainwright knows that he ought to give this outing a miss, because his paper is due to be delivered the next morning, and it is still no further forward than when he arrived. He ought to spend the day alone in his room at the Hilton, with a carafe of iced water, working on it. But he knows all too well that he will fritter the day away, tearing up one draft after another, distracted by envious speculation about the fun the others will be having, especially Philip Swallow. Rodney Wainwright accordingly constructs a cunning plot against himself, whereby he will leave the composition of his paper to the last possible moment, viz., tonight, and thus force himself to finish it by the sheer, inexorable pressure of diminishing time.

The sun blazes down out of a cloudless blue sky on the brown, barren landscape. Even inside the air-conditioned bus it is warm. When they step down onto the parking lot of a bathing station on the shore of the Dead Sea, the heat is like the breath of a furnace. They change into their swimming costumes and float—it is impossible to swim—in a dense liquid—you could hardly call it water—the temperature and consistency of soup, so highly seasoned with chemicals that it burns your tongue and throat if you happen to swallow a drop. Afterwards, they are urged by their guide, Sam Singerman, the resident Israeli professor, to cover themselves with the black mud on the beach, which allegedly has health-giving properties; but of the party only Philip and Joy, followed by Morris Zapp and Thelma Ringbaum, have the nerve to do so, daubing each other hilariously with handfuls of the black goo, which dries rapidly in the sun so that they resemble naked aborigines. They rinse the mud off under the shower heads at the back of the beach and Rodney Wainwright follows them into the hot spring baths, which are so agreeable that they keep the others waiting in the bus while they dry and change, a delay for which Thelma Ringbaum is bitterly reproached by her husband.

Masada is, if it is possible, even hotter. After lunch in the inevitable cafeteria, a form of catering that Israel seems to have made its own, they take the cable car up to the ruined fortifications on the heights where the Jewish army of Eleazar committed collective suicide rather than surrender to the Romans in 73 A.D. "I'd rather commit suicide myself than come up here again," remarks an irreverent visitor, passing into the cable car that Rodney is leaving. The air is certainly no cooler up here—the cable car seems only to have brought them closer to the sun, which beats down relentlessly on the rock and rubble. The tourists stagger about in the heat, barely able to lift their cameras to eye level, looking for scraps of shade behind broken escarpments. Philip Swallow and Joy, hand-in-hand, descend some steps carved in the rock, which curve round the western face of the mountain to a little observation platform that is out of the sun. As they stand at the parapet, looking out over an immense panorama of stony hills and waterless valleys, Philip slides his arm round Joy's waist. My God, even in this heat he's still thinking about sex,

Rodney says to himself, wiping the perspiration from his face with his rolled-up shirt sleeve. Then Philip Swallow happens to turn in his direction and frowns.

"Enjoying yourself?" he says in a distinctly challenging tone.

"What? Eh?" says Rodney Wainwright, startled. He has hardly exchanged a word with the Englishman all the conference.

"Having a good look? Or should I say, wank?"

"Philip," Joy murmurs protestingly.

Rodney feels himself blushing hectically. "I don't know what you're talking about," he blusters.

"I'm just about sick and tired of being followed about by you wherever we go," says Philip Swallow.

Joy makes to move off, but Philip detains her, tightening his grip around her waist. "No," he says, "I want to have it out with Mr. Wainwright. You told me yourself he spied on you at the hotel the other day."

"I know," says Joy, "but I hate scenes."

"It's the heat," says Rodney to Joy, tapping his own forehead illustratively. "He doesn't know what he's saying."

"I bloody well do know," says Philip Swallow. "I'm saying you're some kind of pervert. A voyeur."

"'Ullo, our Dad!"

They all turn round to face a bronzed young man wearing jeans, tee-shirt and a gold stud in one ear, who has approached them by the staircase on the far side of the platform. Now it is Philip Swallow's turn to look embarrassed. He springs apart from Joy as if he had been burned. "Matthew!" he exclaims. "What in God's name are you doing here?"

"Working in a kibbutz further up the Jordan," says the young man. "I hitched out here as soon as I finished me A-Levels, didn't I?"

"Oh yes," says Philip, "it comes back to me now."

"Haven't been quite with it this summer, have you, Dad?" says the young man, looking curiously at Joy.

"Won't you introduce me, Philip?" she says.

"What? Oh, yes, of course," says Philip Swallow, plainly flustered. "This is my son, Matthew. This is, er, Mrs. Simpson, she's at the conference I'm attending."

"Oh, uh," says Matthew.

Joy extends her hand. "How d'you do, Matthew?"

"Perhaps you would like to go back to the cable car with Mr. Wainwright, Mrs. Simpson," says Philip Swallow quickly. "While I catch up with my son's news."

Joy Simpson looks stunned, as if she had received an unexpected slap in the face. She stares at Philip Swallow, opens her mouth to speak, closes it again, and walks away in silence, followed by Rodney Wainwright grinning insanely to himself. He catches her up at the top of the steps. "Do you want to look in at the Museum or go straight back down?" he says.

"I can find my own way back, thank you very much," she says coldly, standing aside to let him pass.

Philip Swallow seems to go into shock after this episode. As the party boards the bus to return home he complains in Rodney Wainwright's hearing of feeling feverish, and spends the entire journey with his eyes closed and an expression of suffering on his face, but Joy is silent and unsympathetic, sitting beside him with her own eyes inscrutable behind dark glasses. In the evening Philip does not come down to join the others, who, showered and changed into clean clothes, are gathering in the lobby to go off to a barbecue in Sam Singerman's garden. Rodney hears Joy telling Morris Zapp that Philip has a temperature. "Heat stroke, I wouldn't be surprised," he says, "It sure was hot as hell out there. Too bad he'll miss the barbecue. You wanna come on your own?" "Why not?" says Joy. Morris Zapp catches Rodney Wainwright's eye as he hovers a few yards away. "You coming, Wainwright?" Rodney gives a sickly grin: "No, I think I'll stay in and look over my paper for tomorrow."

All two and three-quarter pages of it, he thinks bitterly, going off to the elevator, *Schadenfreude* at Philip Swallow's discomfiture and indisposition overshadowed by his own approaching ordeal. Tonight is the night. Make or break. Finish the paper or bust. He lets himself into his room and turns on the desk lamp. He takes out his three dogeared, sweat-stained pages of typescript and reads them through for the ninety-fourth time. They are good pages. The prolegomena moves smoothly, confidently, to define the point at issue. "*The question is, therefore, how can literary criticism . . .*" Then there is nothing: blank page, white space—or a black hole which seems to have swallowed up his capacity for constructive thought.

The trouble is that Rodney Wainwright's imaginative projection of himself stepping up to the lectern the next morning with only two and three-quarter pages of typescript to last him for fifty minutes, is so vivid, so particular in every psychosomatic symptom of terror, that it hypnotizes him, it paralyses thought, it renders him less capable than ever of continuing with the composition of his paper. He sees himself pausing at the end of his two and three-quarter pages, taking a sip of water, looking at his audience, their faces upturned patiently, expectantly, curiously, restlessly, impatiently, angrily, pityingly . . .

In desperation, he helps himself to an extravagantly priced miniature bottle of whisky from the refrigerator in his room, and thus stimulated, begins to write something, anything, using a blue ballpen and sheets of Hilton notepaper. Fuelled by more miniatures, of gin, vodka, and cognac, his hand flies across the page with a will of its own. He begins to feel more optimistic. He chuckles to himself, twisting the tops off miniatures of Benedictine, Cointreau, Drambuie, with one hand, while the other writes on. He hears Joy Simpson return from the barbecue and let herself into the nextdoor room. He breaks off from composition for a moment to press his ear against the party wall. Silence. "No shagging tonight, eh, sport?" he shouts hilariously at the wall, as he staggers back to his desk, and snatches up a fresh sheet of paper.

Rodney Wainwright wakes in the morning to find his throbbing head reposing on top of the desk amid a litter of empty miniatures and sheets of paper covered with illegible gibberish. He sweeps the bottles and the paper into the waste basket. He showers, shaves, and dresses carefully, in his light-weight suit, a clean shirt, and tie. Then he kneels down beside his bed and prays. It is the only resource left to him now. He needs a miracle: the inspiration to extemporize a lecture on the Future of Criticism for forty-five of the fifty minutes allocated to him. Rodney Wainwright, never a deeply religious man, who has not in fact raised his mind and heart to God since he was nine, kneels in the holy city of Jerusalem, and prays, diplomatically, to Jehovah, Allah and Jesus Christ, to save him from disgrace and ruin.

The lecture is due to begin at 9:30. At 9:25, Rodney presents himself in the conference room. Outwardly he appears calm. The only sign of the stress within is that he cannot stop smiling. People remark on how cheerful he looks. He shakes his head and smiles, smiles. His cheek muscles are aching from the strain, but he cannot relax them. Morris Zapp, who is to chair his lecture, is anxiously conferring with Joy Simpson. Philip Swallow is apparently worse—his temperature won't go down, he has pains in his joints, and is gasping for breath. She has called a doctor to see him. Morris Zapp nods sympathetically, frowning, concerned. Rodney, overhearing this intelligence, beams at them both. They stare back at him. "I'm going back to our room to see if the doctor has come," says Joy.

"Right, let's get this show on the road," says Morris to Rodney.

Rodney sits grinning at the audience while Morris Zapp introduces him. Still smiling broadly, he takes his three typewritten pages to the lectern, smooths them down and squares them off. With lips curled in an expression of barely suppressed mirth, he begins to speak. The audience, inferring from his countenance that his discourse is supposed to be witty, titter politely. Rodney turns over to page three, and glimpses the abyss of white space at the foot of it. His smile stretches a millimetre wider.

At that moment there is a disturbance at the back of the room. Rodney Wainwright glances up from his script: Joy Simpson has returned, and is in whispered consultation with Sam Singerman in the back row. Other heads in their vicinity are turned, and talking to each other, wearing worried expressions. Rodney Wainwright falters in his delivery, goes back to the beginning of the sentence—his last sentence. *"The question is, therefore, how can literary criticism . . ."* The hum of conversation in the audience swells. A few people are leaving the room. Rodney stops and looks enquiringly at Morris Zapp, who frowns and raps on the table with his pen.

"Could we please have some quiet in the audience so that Dr. Wainwright can continue with his paper?"

Sam Singerman stands up in the back row. "I'm sorry, Morris, but we've had some rather disturbing information. It seems that Philip Swallow has suspected Legionnaire's Disease."

Somewhere in the audience a woman screams and faints. Everyone else is on their feet, pale, aghast, tightlipped with fear, or shouting for attention. Legionnaire's Disease! That dreaded and mysterious plague, still not fully understood by the medical profession, that struck down a congress of the American Legion at the Bellevue Stratford hotel in Philadelphia three years ago, killing one in six of its victims. It is what every conferee these days secretly fears, it is the VD of conference-going, the wages of sin, retribution for all that travelling away from home and duty, staying in swanky hotels, egotripping, partying, generally overindulging. Legionnaire's Disease!

"I don't know about anyone else," says Howard Ringbaum, in the front row, "but I'm checking out of this hotel right now. Come on, Thelma."

Thelma Ringbaum does not stir, but everybody else does—indeed there is something of a stampede to the exit. Morris turns to Rodney and spreads his hands apologetically. "It looks like we'll have to abandon the lecture. I'm very sorry."

"It can't be helped," says Rodney Wainwright, who has at last been able to stop smiling.

"It must be really disappointing, after all the work you've put into it."

"Oh well," says Rodney, with a philosophical shrug of his shoulders.

"We could try and fix another time later today," says Morris Zapp, taking out a fat cigar and lighting it, "but somehow I think this is curtains for the conference."

"Yes, I'm afraid so," says Rodney, slipping his three typewritten sheets back into their file cover.

Thelma Ringbaum comes up to the platform. "Do you think it's really Legionnaire's Disease, Morris?" she asks anxiously.

"No, I think that it's heat-stroke and the doctor's being paid by the Sheraton," says Morris Zapp. Thelma Ringbaum stares at him in wonder, then giggles. "Oh, Morris," she says, "You make a joke of everything. But aren't you a teeny bit worried?"

"A man who has been through what I've been through recently has no room left for fear," says Morris Zapp, with a flourish of his cigar.

This doesn't seem to be true of the rest of the conferees, however. Within an hour, most of them are in the hotel lobby with their bags packed, waiting for a bus that has been hired to take them to Tel Aviv, where they will catch their return flights. Rodney Wainwright mingles with the throng, receiving their condolences for having had his lecture interrupted. "Oh well," he says, shrugging his shoulders philosophically. "What about Philip?" he overhears Morris Zapp asking Joy Simpson, who also has her bags packed. "Who's going to look after him?"

"I can't risk staying," she says. "I have to think of my children."

"You're just abandoning him?" says Morris Zapp, his eyebrows arched above his cigar.

"No, I phoned his wife. She's flying out by the next plane."

Morris Zapp's eyebrows arch even higher. "Hilary? Was that a good idea?"

"It was Philip's idea," says Joy Simpson. "He asked me to phone her. So I did."

Morris Zapp carefully inspects the end of his cigar. "I see," he says at length.

Immediately, there is another diversion (it is only eleven a.m., but already it is easily the most eventful day of Rodney Wainwright's life). A tall, athletic young man, with a mop of red, curly hair, a round freckled face and a snub nose peeling from sunburn, wearing dusty blue jeans and carrying a canvas sports bag, comes into the Hilton lobby under the disapproving stare of the doorman, and greets Morris Zapp.

"Percy!" Morris exclaims, grasping the newcomer by his shoulders and giving him a welcoming shake. "How are you? What are you doing in Jerusalem? You're just too late for the conference, Philip Swallow has caught the Black Death and we're all running away."

The young man looks round the lobby. "Is Angelica here?"

"Al Pabst? No, she isn't. Why?"

The young man's shoulders slump. "Oh, Jaysus, I was sure I'd find her here."

"She never signed up for this conference, as far as I know."

"It must be the only one, then," says the young man bitterly. "I've pursued that girl around the world from one country to another. Europe, America, Asia. I've spent all my savings and had my American Express card withdrawn for non-payment of arrears. I had to work my passage from Hong Kong to Aden, and hitchhiked across the desert and nearly died of thirst. And never a sight nor sound of her have I had since she gave me the slip at Rummidge."

Morris Zapp sucks on his cigar. "I didn't realize you were so interested in the girl," he says. "Why don't you just write to her?"

"Because nobody knows where she lives! She's always moving on from one conference to another."

Morris Zapp ponders. "Don't despair, Percy. I'll tell you what to do: come to the next MLA. Anybody who's a conference freak is sure to be at the MLA."

"When is that?"

"December. In New York."

"Jaysus," wails the young man. "Must I wait that long?"

Rodney Wainwright leans forward and touches him on the arm. "Excuse me, young man," he says, "but would you mind very much not taking the Lord's name in vain?"

. . .

At the University of Darlington, it is deep summer vacation. The campus is largely deserted. The lecture rooms are silent save for the flies that buzz at the windows; the common rooms and corridors are empty and eerily clean. The rooms of the faculty are locked, and in the Departmental offices underemployed secretaries knit and gossip and bluetack to the walls brightly coloured picture postcards sent to them from Cornwall or Corfu by their more fortunate friends. Only in the Computer Centre has nothing changed since the summer term ended and the vacation began. There sit the two men in their familiar attitudes, like cat and mouse, spider and fly, the one crouched over his computer console, the other watching from his glass cubicle, his hand moving rhythmically from a bag of potato chips to his mouth and back again.

Robin Dempsey seems to have grown old in his swivel seat—Persse McGarrigle would scarcely recognize the thickset, broadshouldered, vigorous man who had accosted him at the Rummidge sherry party. These shoulders are hunched now, the blue suit hangs limply from them over a wasted torso, the jaw sags rather than thrusts, and the small eyes seem even smaller, set even closer together, than before. The atmosphere is charged. There is a tension in the room, like static electricity, a sense of things moving to a crisis. The only sounds are the tapping of Robin Dempsey's fingers on the keyboard of his computer terminal, and the crunching of Josh Collins's potato chips.

Josh Collins screws up the empty bag and tosses it into the waste basket, without taking his eyes off Robin Dempsey. Now there is only one sound in the room. Very quietly, stealthily, Josh Collins leaves his glass cubicle and tiptoes towards the hunched, frenziedly typing figure of Robin Dempsey. Robin Dempsey suddenly stops typing, and Josh Collins freezes in unison, but he is close enough to read what is printed on the screen:

I CAN'T GO ON LIKE THIS I'M OBSESSED WITH PHILIP SWALLOW MORN-
ING NOON AND NIGHT ALL I CAN THINK ABOUT IS HIM GETTING THE
UNESCO CHAIR I CAN'T BEAR THE THOUGHT OF IT BUT I CAN'T STOP
THINKING ABOUT IT THE WHOLE WORLD SEEMS TO CONSPIRE AGAINST
ME IF I FORGET HIM FOR A MOMENT I'M SURE TO OPEN A JOURNAL AND
SEE SOME SYCOPHANTIC REVIEW OF HIS BLOODY BOOK OR AN ADVER-
TISEMENT FOR IT FULL OF QUOTATIONS SAYING IT'S THE GREATEST
THING SINCE SLICED BREAD AND THIS MORNING I GOT A LETTER FROM
MY SON DESMOND HE'S IN ISRAEL WORKING ON A KIBBUTZ HE SAID
MATTHEW SWALLOW THAT'S SWALLOW'S BOY IS OUT HERE WITH ME
YESTERDAY HE MET HIS DAD WITH HIS ARM ROUND A GOOD-LOOKING
BLONDE BIRD HE WAS AT SOME CONFERENCE IN JERUSALEM AT LEAST
THAT WAS HIS STORY YOU SEE WHAT I MEAN SWALLOW IS HAVING IT
ALL WAYS SEX AND FAME AND FOREIGN TRAVEL ITS NOT FAIR I CAN'T
STAND IT I'M GOING CRAZY WHAT SHALL I DO

Robin Dempsey pauses, hesitates for a moment, then presses the query key:

?

Instantly ELIZA replies:

SHOOT YOURSELF.

Robin Dempsey stares, gapes, trembles, whimpers, covers his face with his hands. Then he hears from behind him a snigger, a splutter of suppressed laughter, and swivels round on his seat to find Josh Collins grinning at him. Robin Dempsey looks from the grinning face to the computer's screen, and back again.

"You—" he says in a choked voice.

"Just a little joke," says Josh Collins, raising his hands in a pacifying gesture.

"You've been tampering with ELIZA," says Robin Dempsey getting slowly to his feet.

"Now, now," says Josh Collins, backing away. "Keep calm."

"*You* made ELIZA say Swallow would get the UNESCO chair."

"You provoked me," says Josh Collins. "It's your own fault."

With a cry of rage, Robin Dempsey hurls himself upon Josh Collins. The two men grapple with each other, lurching round the room and banging into the equipment. They fall to the ground and roll across the floor, shouting and screaming abuse. One of the machines, jolted by a flying elbow or knee, stutters into life and begins to disgorge reams of printout which unfurls itself and becomes entangled in the wrestlers' flailing limbs. The printout consists of one word, endlessly repeated:

ERROR ERROR ERROR ERROR ERROR ERROR ERROR ERROR ERROR ER-
ROR ERROR ERROR ERROR ERROR ERROR ERROR ERROR ERROR ERROR
ERROR ERROR ERROR ERROR ERROR ERROR ERROR ERROR ERROR ER-
ROR ERROR ERROR ERROR ERROR ERROR ERROR ERROR ERROR ERROR
ERROR ERROR ERROR ERROR ERROR ERROR

PART V

1

The Modern Language Association of America is not, to British ears at any rate, a very appropriately named organization. It is as concerned with literature as with language, and with English as well as with those Continental European languages conventionally designated "modern." Indeed, making up by far the largest single group in the membership of the MLA are teachers of English and American literature in colleges and universities. The MLA is a professional association, which has some influence over conditions of employment, recruitment, curriculum development, *etc.*, in American higher education. It also publishes a fat quarterly, closely printed in double columns, devoted to scholarly research, known as *PMLA*, and a widely-used annual bibliography of work published in book or periodical form in all of the many subject areas that come within its purview. But to its members the MLA is best known, and loved, or hated, for its annual convention. Indeed, if you pronounce the acronym "MLA" to an American academic, he will naturally assume that you are referring not to the Association as such, nor to its journal or its bibliography, but to its convention. This is always held over three days in the week between Christmas and New Year, either in New York or in some other big American city. The participants are mostly, but not exclusively American, since the Association has funds to bring distinguished foreign scholars and creative writers to take part, and less distinguished ones can sometimes persuade their own universities to pay their fares, or may be spending the year in the United States anyway. In recent years the average attendance at this event has been around ten thousand.

The MLA is the Big Daddy of conferences. A megaconference. A three-ring circus of the literary intelligentsia. This year it is meeting in New York, in two adjacent skyscraper hotels, the Hilton and the Americana, which, enormous as they are, cannot actually sleep all the delegates, who spill over into neighbouring hotels, or beg accommodation from their friends in the big city. Imagine ten thousand highly-educated, articulate, ambitious, competitive men and women converging on mid-Manhattan on the 27th of December, to meet and to lecture and to question and to discuss and to gossip and to plot and to philander and to party and to hire or be hired. For the MLA is a market as well as a circus, it is a place where young scholars fresh from graduate school look hopefully for their first jobs, and more seasoned academics sniff the air for better ones. The bedrooms of the Hilton and the Americana are the scene not only of rest and dalliance but of hard bargaining and rigorous interviewing, as chairmen of departments from every state in the Union, from Texas to Maine, from the Carolinas to California, strive to fill the vacancies on their faculty rolls with the best talent available. In the present acute job shortage, it's a buyer's market, and some of these chairmen have such long lists of candidates to interview that they never get outside their hotel rooms for the duration of the convention. For them and for the desperate candidates kicking their heels and smoking in the corridors, waiting their turn to be scrutinized, the MLA is no kind of fun; but for the rest of the members it's a ball, especially if you like listening to lectures and panel discussions on every conceivable literary subject from "Readability and Reliability in the Epistolary Novel of England, France and Germany" to "Death, Resurrection and Redemption in the Works of Pirandello," from "Old English Riddles" to "Faulkner Concordances," from "Rationalismus und Irrationalismus im 18. Jahrhundert" to "Nueva Narrativa Hispanoamericana," from "Lesbian-Feminist Teaching and Learning" to "Problems of Cultural Distortion in Translating Expletives in the work of Cortazar, Sender, Baudelaire and Flaubert."

There are no less than six hundred separate sessions listed in the official programme, which is as thick as the telephone directory of a small town, and at least thirty to choose from at any hour of the day from 8:30 a.m. to 10:15 p.m., some of them catering to small groups of devoted specialists, others, featuring the most distinguished names in academic life, attracting enough auditors to fill the hotels' biggest ballrooms. The audiences are, however, restless and migratory: people stroll in and out of the conference rooms, listen a while, ask a question, and move on to another session while speakers are still speaking; for there is always the feeling that you may be missing the best show of the day, and a roar of laughter or applause from one room is quite likely to empty the one next door. And if you get tired of listening to lectures and papers and panel discussions, there is plenty else to do. You can attend the cocktail party organized by the Gay Caucus for the Modern Languages, or the Reception Sponsored by the American Association of Professors of Yiddish, or the Cash Bar Arranged in Conjunction with the Special Session on Methodological Problems in Monolingual and Bilingual Lexicography, or the Annual Dinner of the American Milton Society, or the Executive Council of the American Boccaccio Association, or the meetings of the Marxist Literary Group, the Coalition of Women in German, the Conference on Christianity and Literature, the Byron Society, the G. K. Chesterton Society, the Nathaniel Hawthorne Society, the Hazlitt Society, the D. H. Lawrence Society, the John Updike Society, and many others. Or you can just stand in the lobby of the Hilton and meet, sooner or later, everyone you ever knew in the academic world.

Persse McGarrigle is standing there, on the third morning of the conference, rubbing the warmth back into his hands, half-frozen by the bitterly cold wind blowing down the Avenue of the Americas, when he is greeted by Morris Zapp.

"Hi, Percy! How are ya liking the MLA?"

"It's . . . I can't find a word for it."

Morris Zapp chuckles expansively. He is wearing his loudest check sports jacket, and toting a huge cigar. He is obviously in his element. Every few seconds somebody comes up and slaps him on the shoulder or shakes his hand or kisses him on his cheek. "Morris, how *are* you? What are you working on? Where are you staying? Let's have a drink some time, let's have dinner, let's have breakfast." Morris shouts, waves, kisses, signals with his eyebrows, scribbles appointments in his diary, while contriving to advise Persse on which lectures to catch and which to avoid, and to ask him if he has seen any sign of Al Pabst.

"No," sighs Persse dejectedly. "She's not listed in the programme."

"That doesn't mean a thing, lots of people sign up after the programme has gone to press."

"The Convention Office doesn't have her name among the late registrations," says Persse. "I'm afraid she hasn't come."

"Don't despair, Percy, some people sneak in without registering, to save the fee."

"That's my own case," Persse confesses. He is still paying off the cost of his trip round the world, and it has been a struggle to raise the money to get here; how he is going to get home is a problem he hasn't yet faced.

"You want to cruise around the various meetings, looking out for the subjects that are likely to interest her."

"That's what I've been doing."

"Whatever you do, don't miss the forum on 'The Function of Criticism,' 2:15 this afternoon in the Grand Ballroom."

"Are you speaking?"

"How did you guess? This is the big one, Percy. Arthur Kingfisher is moderator. The buzz is that he's going to decide who is his favoured candidate for the UNESCO Chair today. Sam Textel is here, ready to take the good news back to Paris. This forum is like a TV debate for Presidential candidates."

"Who else is speaking?"

"Michel Tardieu, von Turpitz, Fulvia Morgana and Philip Swallow."

Persse registers surprise. "Is Professor Swallow in the same league as the rest of you?"

"Well, originally they invited Rudyard Parkinson, but he missed his plane—we just got a call from London. He was trying to put us in our place by only turning up for the last day of the Convention. Serves him right. Philip Swallow was here for the Hazlitt Society, so they drafted him in as a substitute for Parkinson. He was born lucky, Philip. He always seems to fall on his feet."

"He didn't have Legionnaire's Disease after all, then?"

"Nuh. As I thought, it was just heat-stroke. He'd been reading an article about Legionnaire's Disease in *Time* magazine and frightened himself into reproducing the symptoms. Hilary flew out to Israel to look after him quite unnecessarily. However, it had the effect of bringing them together again. Philip decided he was getting to the age when he needed a mother more than a mistress. Or maybe Joy did. But you didn't know Joy, did you?"

"No," says Persse. "Who was she?"

"It's a long story, and I must get my head together for the forum this afternoon. Look, the MLA executive are giving a party tonight, in the penthouse suite. If you wanna go, come along to my room at about ten tonight, OK? Room 956. *Ciao!*"

. . .

An immense audience was gathered in the Grand Ballroom to hear the forum on "The Function of Criticism." There must have been well over a thousand people sitting on the rows of gilt-painted, plush-upholstered chairs, and hundreds more standing at the back and along the sides of the vast, chandelier-hung room, attracted not only by the interest of the subject and the distinction of the speakers, but also by the rumoured involvement of the event in the matter of the UNESCO Chair. Persse, sitting near the front, and twisting round in his seat to scrutinize the audience for a sign of Angelica, was confronted by a sea of faces turned expectantly towards the platform where the five speakers and their chairman sat, each with a microphone and a glass of water before them. A roar of conversation rose to the gold and white ceiling, until Arthur Kingfisher, lean, dark-eyed, hook-nosed, white-maned, silenced the crowd with a tap of his pencil on his microphone. He introduced the speakers: Philip Swallow, who, Persse noted with surprise, had shaved off his beard, and seemed to regret it, fingering his weak chin with nervous fingers like an amputee groping for a missing limb; Michel Tardieu, pouchy and wrinkled, in a scaly brown leather jacket that was like some extrusion of his own skin; von Turpitz, scowling under his skullcap of pale, limp hair, dressed in a dark business suit and starched shirt; Fulvia Morgana, sensational in black velvet dungarees worn over a long-sleeved tee-shirt of silver lamé, her fiery hair lifted from her haughty brow by a black velvet sweatband studded with pearls; Morris Zapp in his grossly checked sports jacket and roll-neck sweater, chewing a fat cigar.

Philip Swallow was the first to speak. He said the function of criticism was to assist in the function of literature itself, which Dr. Johnson had famously defined as enabling us better to enjoy life, or better to endure it. The great writers were men and women of exceptional wisdom, insight, and understanding. Their novels, plays and poems were inexhaustible reservoirs of values, ideas, images, which, when properly understood and appreciated, allowed us to live more fully, more finely, more intensely. But literary conventions changed, history changed, language changed, and these treasures too easily became locked away in libraries, covered with dust, neglected and forgotten. It was the job of the critic to unlock the drawers, blow away the dust, bring out the treasures into the light of day. Of course, he needed certain specialist skills to do this: a knowledge of history, a knowledge of philology, of generic convention and textual editing. But above all he needed enthusiasm, the love of books. It was by the demonstration of this enthusiasm in action that the critic forged a bridge between the great writers and the general reader.

Michel Tardieu said that the function of criticism was not to add new interpretations and appreciations of *Hamlet* or *Le Misanthrope* or *Madame Bovary* or *Wuthering Heights* to the hundreds that already existed in print or to the thousands that had been uttered in classrooms and lecture theatres, but to uncover the fundamental laws that enabled such works to be produced and understood. If literary criticism was supposed to be knowledge, it could not be founded on interpretation, since interpretation was endless, subjective, unverifiable, unfalsifiable. What was permanent, reliable, accessible to scientific study, once we ignored the distracting surface of actual texts, were the deep structural principles and binary oppositions that underlay all texts that had ever been written and that ever would be written: paradigm and syntagm, metaphor and metonymy, mimesis and diegesis, stressed and unstressed, subject and object, culture and nature.

Siegfried von Turpitz said that, while he sympathized with the scientific spirit in which his French colleague approached the difficult question of defining the essential function of criticism in both its ontological and teleological aspects, he was obliged to point out that the attempt to derive such a definition from the formal properties of the literary art-object as such was doomed to failure, since such art-objects enjoyed only an as it were virtual existence until they were realized in the mind of a reader. (When he reached the word "reader" he thumped the table with his black-gloved fist.)

Fulvia Morgana said that the function of criticism was to wage undying war on the very concept of "literature" itself, which was nothing more than an instrument of bourgeois hegemony, a fetichistic reification of so-called aesthetic values erected and maintained through an élitist educational system in order to conceal the brutal facts of class oppression under industrial capitalism.

Morris Zapp said more or less what he had said at the Rummidge conference.

While they were speaking, Arthur Kingfisher looked more and more depressed, slumped lower and lower in his chair, and seemed to be almost asleep by the time Morris had finished. He roused himself from this lethargy to ask if there were any questions or comments from the floor. Microphones had been placed at strategic intervals in the aisles to allow members of the vast audience to make themselves heard, and several delegates who had not been able to insinuate themselves into any other session of the convention took this opportunity to deliver prepared diatribes on the function of criticism. The speakers made predictable rejoinders. Kingfisher yawned and glanced at his watch. "I think we have time for one more question," he said.

Persse was aware of himself, as if he were quite another person, getting to his feet and stepping into the aisle and up to a microphone placed directly under the platform. "I have a question for all the members of the panel," he said. Von Turpitz glared at him and turned to Kingfisher. "Is this man entitled to speak?" he demanded. "He is not wearing an identification badge." Arthur Kingfisher brushed the objection aside with a wave of his hand. "What's your question, young man?" he said.

"I would like to ask each of the speakers," said Persse, "What follows if everybody agrees with you?" He turned and went back to his seat.

Arthur Kingfisher looked up and down the table to invite a reply. The panel members however avoided his eye. They glanced instead at each other, with grimaces and gesticulations expressive of bafflement and suspicion. "What follows is the Revolution," Fulvia Morgana was heard to mutter; Philip Swallow, "Is it some sort of trick question?" and von Turpitz, "It is a fool's question." A buzz of excited conversation rose from the audience, which Arthur Kingfisher silenced with an amplified tap of his pencil. He leaned forward in his seat and fixed Persse with a beady eye. "The members of the forum don't seem to understand your question, sir. Could you re-phrase it?"

Persse got to his feet again and padded back to the microphone in a huge, expectant silence. "What I mean is," he said, "What do you *do* if everybody agrees with you?"

"Ah." Arthur Kingfisher flashed a sudden smile that was like sunshine breaking through cloud. His long, olive-complexioned face, worn by study down to the fine bone, peered over the edge of the table at Persse with a keen regard. "That is a very good question. A very in-ter-est-ing question. I do not remember that question being asked before." He nodded to himself. "You imply, of course, that what matters in the field of critical practise is not truth but difference. If everybody were convinced by your arguments, they would have to do the same as you and then there would be no satisfaction in doing it. To win is to lose the game. Am I right?"

"It sounds plausible," said Persse from the floor. "I don't have an answer myself, just the question."

"And a very good question too," chuckled Arthur Kingfisher. "Thank you, ladies and gentlemen, our time is up."

The room erupted with a storm of applause and excited conversation. People jumped to their feet and began arguing with each other, and those at the back stood on their chairs to get a glimpse of the young man who had asked the question that had confounded the contenders for the UNESCO Chair and roused Arthur Kingfisher from his long lethargy. "Who is he?" was the question now on every tongue. Persse, blushing, dazed, astonished at his own temerity, put his head down and made for the exit. The crowd at the doors parted respectfully to let him through, though some conferees patted his back and shoulders as he passed—gentle, almost timid pats, more like touching for luck, or for a cure, than congratulations.

. . .

That afternoon there was a brief but astonishing change in the Manhattan weather, unprecedented in the city's meteorological history. The icy wind that had been blowing straight from the Arctic down the skyscraper canyons, numbing the faces and freezing the fingers of pedestrians and streetvendors, suddenly dropped, and turned round into the gentlest warm southern breeze. The clouds disappeared and the sun came out. The temperature shot up. The hardpacked dirty snow piled high at the edge of the sidewalks began to thaw and trickle into the gutters. In Central Park squirrels came out of hibernation and lovers held hands without the impediment of gloves. There was a rush on sunglasses at Bloomingdales. People waiting in line for buses smiled at each other, and cab-drivers gave way to private cars at intersections. Members of the MLA Convention leaving the Hilton to walk to the Americana, cringing in anticipation of the cold blast on the other side of the revolving doors, sniffed the warm, limpid air incredulously, threw open their parkas, unwound their scarves and snatched off their woolly hats. Fifty-nine different people consciously misquoted T. S. Eliot's "East Coker," declaiming "*What is the late December doing/With the disturbance of the spring?*" in the hearing of the Americana's bell captain, to his considerable puzzlement.

In Arthur Kingfisher's suite at the Hilton, whither he repaired with Song-Mi Lee to rest after the forum, the central heating was stifling. "I'm going to open the goddam window," he said. Song-Mi Lee was doubtful. "We'll freeze," she said.

"No, it's a lovely day. Look—there are people on the sidewalk down there without topcoats." He struggled with the window fastenings: they were stiff, because seldom used, but eventually he got a pane open. Sweet fresh air gently billowed the net drapes. Arthur Kingfisher took deep breaths down into his lungs. "Hey, how d'you like this? The air is like wine. Come over here and breathe." Song-Mi came to his side and he put his arm round her. "You know something? It's like the halcyon days."

"What are they, Arthur?"

"A period of calm weather in the middle of winter. The ancients used to call them the halcyon days, when the kingfisher was supposed to hatch its eggs. Remember Milton—'*The birds sit brooding on the calmèd wave*'? The bird was a kingfisher. That's what 'halcyon' means in Greek, Song-Mi: kingfisher. The halcyon days were kingfisher days. My days. Our days." Song-Mi leaned her head against his shoulder and made a small, inarticulate noise of happiness and agreement. He was suddenly filled with an inexpressible tenderness towards her. He took her in his arms and kissed her, pressing her supple slender body against his own.

"Hey," he whispered as their lips parted. "Can you feel what I feel?"

With tears in her eyes, Song-Mi smiled and nodded.

. . .

Meanwhile, in other rooms, windowless and air-conditioned, the convention ground on remorselessly, and Persse paced the corridors and rode the elevators in search of Angelica, slipping into the back of lectures on "Time in Modern American Poetry" and "Blake's Conquest of Self" and "Golden Age Spanish Drama," putting his head round the door of seminars on "The Romantic Rediscovery of the Daemon," "Speech Act Theory" and "Neoplatonic Iconography." He was walking away in a state of terminal disappointment from a forum on "The Question of Postmodernism," when he passed a door to which a handwritten notice hastily scrawled on a sheet of lined notepaper had been thumbtacked. It said: "*Ad Hoc Forum on Romance*." He pushed open the door and went in.

And there she was. Sitting behind a table at the far end of the room, reading in a clear, deliberate voice from a sheaf of typewritten pages to an audience of about twenty-five people scattered over the dozen rows of chairs, and to three young men seated beside her at the table. Persse slipped into a seat in the back row. God, how beautiful she was! She wore the severe, scholarly look that he remembered from the lecture-room at Rummidge—heavy, dark-rimmed glasses, her hair drawn back severely into a bun, a tailored jacket and white blouse her only visible clothing. When she glanced up from her script, she seemed to be looking straight at him, and he smiled tentatively, his heart pounding, but she continued without a change of tone or expression. Of course, he recollected, with her reading glasses on he would be just a vague blur to her.

It was some time before Persse became sufficiently calm to attend to what Angelica was saying.

"Jacques Derrida has coined the term 'invagination' to describe the complex relationship between inside and outside in discursive practises. What we think of as the meaning or 'inside' of a text is in fact nothing more than its externality folded in to create a pocket which is both secret and therefore desired and at the same time empty and therefore impossible to possess. I want to appropriate this term and apply it, in a very specific sense of my own, to romance. If epic is a phallic genre, which can hardly be denied, and tragedy the genre of castration (we are none of us, I suppose, deceived by the self-blinding of Oedipus as to the true nature of the wound he is impelled to inflict upon himself, or likely to overlook the symbolic equivalence between eyeballs and testicles) then surely there is no doubt that romance is a supremely invaginated mode of narrative.

"Roland Barthes has taught us the close connection between narrative and sexuality, between the pleasure of the body and the 'pleasure of the text,' but in spite of his own sexual ambivalence, he developed this analogy in an overly masculine fashion. The pleasure of the classic text, in Barthes' system, is all foreplay. It consists in the constant titillation and deferred satisfaction of the reader's curiosity and desire—desire for the solution of enigma, the completion of an action, the reward of virtue and the punishment of vice. The paradox of our pleasure in narrative, according to this model, is that while the need to 'know' is what impels us through a narrative, the satisfaction of that need brings pleasure to an end, just as in psychosexual life the possession of the Other kills Desire. Epic and tragedy move inexorably to what we call, and by no accident, a 'climax'—and it is, in terms of the sexual metaphor, an essentially *male* climax—a single, explosive discharge of accumulated tension.

"Romance, in contrast, is not structured in this way. It has not one climax but many, the pleasure of this text comes and comes and comes again. No sooner is one crisis in the fortunes of the hero averted than a new one presents itself; no sooner has one mystery been solved than another is raised; no sooner has one adventure been concluded than another begins. The narrative questions open and close, open and close, like the contractions of the vaginal muscles in intercourse, and this process is in principle endless. The greatest and most characteristic romances are often unfinished—they end only with the author's exhaustion, as a woman's capacity for orgasm is limited only by her physical stamina. Romance is a multiple orgasm."

Persse listened to this stream of filth flowing from between Angelica's exquisite lips and pearly teeth with growing astonishment and burning cheeks, but no one else in the audience seemed to find anything remarkable or disturbing about her presentation. The young men seated at the table beside her nodded thoughtfully, and fiddled with their pipes, and made little notes on their scratchpads. One of them, wearing a sports jacket of Donegal tweed, and with a soft voice that seemed to match it, thanked Angelica for her talk and asked if there were any questions.

"Most impressive, didn't you think?" whispered a female voice into Persse's ear. He turned to find a familiar white-coiffed figure beside him.

"Miss Maiden! Fancy meeting you here!"

"You know I can't resist conferences, young man. But wasn't that a brilliant performance? If only Jessie Weston could have heard it."

"I can understand that it would appeal to you," said Persse. "It was a bit too near the knuckle for my taste." Somebody in the audience was asking Angelica if she would agree that the novel, as a distinct genre, was born when the epic, as it were, fucked the romance. She gave the suggestion careful consideration. "You know who she is, don't you?" he whispered to Miss Maiden.

"Of course I know, she's Miss Pabst, your young lady."

"No, I mean who she *was*. As a baby."

"As a baby?" Miss Maiden looked at him with a queer expression, at once fearful and expectant. One of the young men at the table said, if the organ of epic was the phallus, of tragedy the testicles, and of romance the vagina, what was the organ of comedy? Oh, the anus, Angelica replied instantly, with a bright smile. Think of Rabelais . . .

"You remember those twin girls, six weeks old, who were found in an airplane in 1954?" Persse hissed.

"Why should I remember them?"

"Because you found them, Miss Maiden." He took from his wallet a folded photocopy of a newspaper cutting sent to him by Hermann Pabst. "Look, '*Twin girls found in KLM Stratocruiser*'—and here's your name: '*discovered in the plane's toilet by Miss Sybil Maiden of Girton College*.' You could have knocked me down with a feather when I saw that."

The cutting seemed to have the same effect on Miss Maiden, for she toppled off her chair in a dead faint. Persse caught her just before she hit the ground. "Help!" he cried. People hurried to his assistance. By the time Miss Maiden had recovered, Angelica had disappeared.

. . .

Persse ran distractedly through the Hilton lobby, took the slow and express lifts at random to various floors, prowled along carpeted corridors, searched the bars and restaurants and shops. After nearly an hour, he found her, changed into a flowing dress of red silk, with her hair, freshly washed, all loose and shining about her shoulders. She was about to step into an elevator on the seventeenth floor as its doors slid open to let him out.

This time there was no hesitation in his actions. This time she would not escape. Without a word, he took her in his arms and kissed her long and passionately. For a moment she stiffened and resisted, but then she suddenly relaxed and yielded to his fierce embrace. He felt the long, soft line of her body from bosom to thigh moulding itself to his. They seemed to melt and fuse together. Time held its breath. He was dimly aware of the lift doors opening and closing again, of people stepping in and out. Then, when the landing was empty and silent once more, he drew his lips away from hers.

"At last I've found you!" he panted.

"So it seems," she gasped.

"I love you!" he cried. "I need you! I want you!"

"Okay!" she laughed. "All *right*! Your room or mine?"

"I haven't got a room," he said.

Angelica hung a *Do Not Disturb* sign on the outside of the door before locking and chaining it from inside. It was now late afternoon and already dark. She switched on a single, heavily-shaded table lamp which shed a soft golden glow on the bed, and drew the curtains across the window. Her dress sank with a whisper to the floor. She stepped out of it, and put her hands behind her back to release the catch of her brassiere. Her breasts poured out like honey. They swung and trembled as she stooped to strip off tights and briefs. The beauty of her bosom moved him almost to tears; the bold bush of black hair at her crotch startled and roused him. He turned away modestly to take off his own clothes, but she came up behind him and ran her cool soft fingers down his chest and belly, brushing his rigid, rampant sex. "Don't, for the love of God," he groaned, "or I won't answer for the consequences." She chuckled, and led him by the hand to the bed. She lay down on her back, with her knees slightly raised, and smiled at him with her dark, peat-pool eyes. He parted her thighs like the leaves of a book, and stared into the crack, the crevice, the deep romantic chasm that was the ultimate goal of his quest.

Like most young men's first experience of sexual intercourse, Persse's was as short as it was sweet. As soon as he was invaginated, he came, tumultuously. With Angelica's assistance and encouragement, however, he came twice more in the hours that followed, less precipitately, and in two quite different attitudes; and when he could come no more, when he was only a dry, straining erection, with no seed to expel, Angelica impaled herself upon him and came again and again and again, until she toppled off, exhausted. They lay sprawled across the bed, sweating and panting.

Persse felt ten years older, and wiser. He had fed on honey-dew and drunk the milk of paradise. Nothing could be the same again. Was it possible that in due course they could put on their clothes and go out of the room and behave like ordinary people again, after what had passed between them? It must always be so between lovers, he concluded: their knowledge of each other's nightside was a secret bond between them. "You'll have to marry me now, Angelica," he said.

"I'm not Angelica, I'm Lily," murmured the girl beside him.

He whipped over on to all fours, crouched above her, stared into her face. "You're joking. Don't joke with me, Angelica."

She shook her head. "No joke."

"You're Angelica."

"Lily."

He stared at her until his eyes bulged. The dreadful fact was that he had no idea whether she was Angelica lying or Lily telling the truth.

"There's only one way to tell the difference between us," she said. "We both have a birth mark on the thigh, like an inverted comma. Angie's is on the left thigh, mine on the right." She turned on to her side to point out the small blemish, pale against her tan, on her right thigh. "When we stand hip to hip in our bikinis, it looks like we're inside quotation marks. Have you seen Angelica's birthmark?"

"No," he said bitterly. "But I've heard about it." He felt suddenly ashamed of his nakedness, rolled off the bed, and hurriedly put on his underpants and trousers. "Why?" he said. "Why did you deceive me?"

"I never could resist a guy who was really hungry for it," said Lily.

"You mean, if any total stranger comes up and kisses you, you immediately drop everything and jump into bed with him?"

"Probably. But I figured who you were. Angie has talked to me about you. Why do you feel so sore about it, anyway? We made it together beautifully."

"I thought you were the girl I love," said Persse. "I wouldn't have made love to you otherwise."

"You mean, you were saving yourself for Angie?"

"If you like. You stole something that didn't belong to you."

"You're wasting your time, Persse, Angie is the archetypal pricktease."

"That's a despicable thing to say about your sister!"

"Oh, she admits it. Just like I admit I'm a slut at heart."

"That I won't attempt to deny," he said sarcastically.

"Oh, really?"

"Yes, really. The things you did."

"You seemed to dig them."

"I should have realized. No decent girl would have even conceived of them."

"Oh Persse—don't say that!" she suddenly cried, in a tone of real dismay.

"Why?" He went hot and cold.

"Because I *am* joking. I *am* Angelica!"

He flew to the bed. "Darling, I didn't mean it! It was beautiful, what we did, I—" He broke off. "What are you grinning at?"

"What about the birthmark? You forgot the birthmark." She twitched her right hip cheekily.

"You mean, you are Lily after all?"

"What do you think, Persse?"

He sank down on to a seat and covered his face with his hands. "I think you're trying to drive me mad, whoever you are."

He was aware of the girl pulling a coverlet from the bed and wrapping herself in it. She shuffled over and put a bare arm round his shoulder. "Persse, I'm trying to tell you that you're not really in love with Angelica. If you can't be sure whether the girl you just screwed is Angelica or not, how can you be in love with her? You were in love with a dream."

"Why do you want to tell me that?" he mumbled.

"Because Angie loves somebody else," she said.

Persse dropped his hands from his face. "Who?"

"A guy called Peter, they're getting married in the spring. He's associate professor at Harvard, very bright according to Angie. They met at some conference in Hawaii. She's hoping to get a college job in the Boston area, and Peter fixed it so she could give a paper at this convention to show off her paces. Angie heard that you were here looking for her, and she felt bad about it because she played some trick on you in England, right? She asked me to break it to you gently that she was already engaged. I did my best, Persse. Sorry if it lacked subtlety."

Persse went to the window, pulled back the curtain, and stared down at the brightly lit avenue below, and the cars and buses stopping and starting and turning at the intersection with 54th Street. He leaned his forehead against the cool glass. He was silent for several minutes. Then he said: "I feel hungry."

"That's more like it," said Lily. "I'll call room service. What would you like to eat?"

Persse glanced at his watch. "I'm going to a party, I'll get some grub there."

"The penthouse party? I'll see you there," said Lily. "Peter is taking Angie and me. This is their room, actually. I was just using it to change in."

Persse unchained the door of the room. "Does Peter know what you do for a living?" he asked. "I saw your photograph in Amsterdam once. Also in London."

"I've retired from that," she said. "I decided to go back to school, after all. Columbia. I live in New York, now."

"When you used to work for Girls Unlimited," said Persse, "did you come across a girl called Bernadette? Her professional name was Marlene."

Lily reflected for a moment, then shook her head. "No. It was a big organization."

"If you should ever come across her, tell her to get in touch with me."

Persse took the elevator down to the ninth floor and found the door of room 956 open. Inside, Morris Zapp was sitting on the bed, eating nuts and drinking bourbon and watching television. "Hi, Percy, come in," he said. "All ready for the party?"

"I could do with a shower," said Persse. "Could I possibly use your bathroom?"

"Sure, but there's somebody in there right now. Sit down and fix yourself a drink. That was a real curveball of a question you threw at us this afternoon."

"I didn't mean to make things difficult for you," said Persse apologetically, helping himself to the bourbon. "I don't know what came over me, to tell you the truth."

"It didn't make any difference. It was very obvious that Kingfisher wasn't interested in what I was saying."

"Are you disappointed?" Persse sat down on a chair from which he had an oblique view of the TV screen. A naked couple who might have been himself and Lily an hour earlier were twisting and writhing on a bed.

"Nuh, I think I finally kicked the ambition habit. Ever since I was kidnapped, just being alive has seemed enough." Suddenly the screen went blank, and a legend appeared: "*Dial 3 to order the movie of your choice.*" Another film, this time about cowboys, commenced. "They give you five minutes of a movie for free, to get you interested," Morris explained. "Then if you want to watch the whole thing, you call and have them pipe it to your room and charge it."

"Everything on tap," said Persse shaking his head. "Oh brave new world!"

"Right, you can get anything you want by telephone in this city: Chinese food, massage, yoga lessons, acupuncture. You can even call up girls who will talk dirty to you for so much a minute. You pay by credit card. But if you're into deconstruction, you can just watch all these trailers in a row as if it was one, free, avant-garde movie. Mind you," he added pensively, "I've rather lost faith in deconstruction. I guess it showed this afternoon."

"You mean every decoding is not another encoding after all?"

"Oh it is, it is. But the deferral of meaning isn't infinite as far as the individual is concerned."

"I thought deconstructionists didn't believe in the individual."

"They don't. But death is the one concept you can't deconstruct. Work back from there and you end up with the old idea of an autonomous self. I can die, therefore I am. I realized that when those wop radicals threatened to deconstruct *me*."

The bathroom door opened and out came a lady in a towelling bathrobe and a cloud of fragrant steam. "Oh!" she exclaimed, surprised at seeing Persse.

"Good evening, Mrs. Ringbaum," he said, getting to his feet.

"Have we met before?"

"At a party on the Thames last spring. The *Annabel Lee*."

"I don't remember much about that party," said Mrs. Ringbaum, "except that Howard got into a fight with Ronald Frobisher, and the boat started drifting down the river."

"It was Ronald Frobisher who set it adrift, as a matter of fact," said Persse.

"*Was* it? I'll tackle him about that this evening."

"Is Ronald Frobisher here—at the MLA?" exclaimed Persse.

"Everybody is at the MLA," said Morris Zapp. "Everybody you ever knew." He was now watching a film about boxing.

"Everybody except Howard," said Thelma, with her head inside the wardrobe. "Howard is stuck in Illinois because he's been barred for life by the airlines for soliciting sex in flight from a hostess."

"I'm sorry to hear that," said Persse.

"It doesn't bother me," said Thelma with a chuckle. "I left that fink back in September, the best thing I ever did." She shook out a black cocktail dress and held it up in front of herself, standing before a full-length mirror. "Shall I wear this tonight, honey?"

"Sure," said Morris, without taking his eyes off the TV. "It looks great."

"Shall I go to the bathroom to put it on, or is this young man going to do the decent thing and wait in the hall?"

"Percy, go take that shower while Thelma is dressing," said Morris. "Borrow my electric razor if you need a shave. And by the way, in case your Irish Catholic conscience is shocked by the set-up here, I should tell you that Thelma and I are thinking of getting married."

"Congratulations," said Persse.

"Our romance started in Jerusalem," Thelma confided, smiling fondly at Morris. "Howard never even noticed. He was too busy plotting to have sex with me in one of those cable cars at Masada."

. . .

When Persse had showered and shaved, the three of them took an express elevator to the highest public floor in the hotel, and then a man with a key admitted them to a small private lift that took them up to the penthouse suite. This was a huge, magical, split-level, glassed-in space which afforded breathtaking views of Manhattan at night. It was already crowded and loud with chatter, but the mood of the company was relaxed and euphoric. It helped that the only drink available was champagne. Arthur Kingfisher had donated a dozen cases. "He must have something really important to celebrate," commented Ronald Frobisher, who had commandeered one of the cases. He filled Persse's glass and introduced him to a lean, shrewd-eyed, red-haired woman in a green trouser-suit. "Désirée Byrd, Section 409, 'New Directions in Women's Writing,'" he said. "I'm Section 351, 'Tradition and Innovation in Postwar British Fiction.' Strictly speaking I'm just the Tradition bit. We were talking about that extraordinary spell of fine weather this afternoon."

"I'm afraid I missed it," said Persse, "I was indoors the whole afternoon."

"It was amazing," said Désirée Byrd. "I was in my agent's apartment talking about my new book. I was really depressed about it—I mean, it's virtually finished, but I'd completely lost faith in it. I was saying to Alice, 'Alice, I've decided I'm not a real writer after all. *Difficult Days* was a fluke, this new book is just a mess,' and she was saying, 'No, no, you mustn't say that,' and I said, 'Just let me read you some bits and you'll see what I mean,' and she said 'OK, but I'm going to open the window for a minute, it's so hot in here.'

So she opens the window—imagine opening a window in Manhattan in the middle of winter, I thought she must be crazy—and suddenly this extraordinarily sweet warm air comes drifting into the room, and I started to read at random from my manuscript. 'Well,' I said after a page or two, 'that isn't too bad, actually.' 'It's tremendous,' said Alice. I said, 'It's not typical, though. Listen to this.' And I read out some more. When I finished, Alice said, 'Fantastic,' and I said, 'Well, perhaps it's not all that bad.' And, you know—it wasn't. It really wasn't. Well, you can guess what happened. The more I looked for lousy passages, the more enthusiastic Alice became, and the more I came to believe that *Men* is perhaps quite a good book after all."

"Marvellous," said Ronald Frobisher. "I had a similar experience. I was sitting in Washington Square at the same time, thinking about Henry James and basking in this extraordinary sunshine, when suddenly the first sentence of a novel came into my head."

"Which novel?" said Désirée.

"My next novel," said Ronald Frobisher. "I'm going to write a new novel."

"What's it going to be about?"

"I don't know yet, but I feel somehow that I've got my style back. I can sense it in the rhythm of that sentence."

"By the way," said Persse, "I met your Japanese translator last summer."

"Akira Sakazaki? He just sent me his translation of *Could Try Harder*—it looks like a bride's prayerbook. Bound in white, with a mauve silk marker." He refilled Persse's glass.

"I'd better get some grub inside me before I drink any more of this," said Persse. "Excuse me."

He was helping himself to the splendid buffet supper spread out along one wall when a long arm, encased in a charcoal-grey worsted sleeve, very greasy around the wrist, reached over his shoulder and twitched the last remaining slice of smoked salmon away from the platter under his nose. Persse turned round indignantly to find Felix Skinner's yellow fangs grinning at him. "Sorry, old man, but I've a fatal weakness for this stuff." He dropped the slice of smoked salmon on to a plate already heaped with assorted foods. "What are you doing at the MLA?"

"I might ask you the same question," said Persse coolly.

"Oh, scouting for talent, testing the market, you know. Did you get my letter, by the way?"

"No," said Persse.

Felix Skinner sighed. "That's Gloria, she'll have to go . . . Well, we got a second opinion on your proposal, and we've decided to commission the book after all."

"That's marvellous!" exclaimed Persse. "Will there be an advance?"

"Oh, yes," said Felix Skinner. "Well, a small one," he added cautiously.

"Could I have it now?" said Persse.

"Now? Here?" Felix Skinner looked taken aback. "It's not normal practise. We haven't even signed a contract."

"I need two hundred dollars to get back to London," said Persse.

"I suppose I could give you that on account," said Felix Skinner grudgingly. "I happened to go to the bank this afternoon." He took two $100 bills from his wallet and passed them to Persse.

"Thanks a million," said Persse. "Your good health." He drained his glass, which was refilled in an absent-minded fashion by a shortish dark-haired man standing nearby with a bottle of champagne in his hand, talking to a tallish dark-haired man smoking a pipe. "If I can have Eastern Europe," the tallish man was saying in an English accent, "you can have the rest of the world." "All right," said the shortish man, "but I daresay people will still get us mixed up."

"Are they publishers too?" Persse whispered.

"No, novelists," said Felix Skinner. "Ah, Rudyard!" he cried, turning to greet a new arrival. "So you got here at last. You know young McGarrigle, I think. You were sadly missed at the forum this afternoon. What happened?"

"A disgraceful incident," said Rudyard Parkinson, puffing out his muttonchop whiskers so that he resembled an angry baboon. "I was just going through passport control at Heathrow—I was already late because I'd had a row with some impertinent chit at the check-in desk—when I was whisked off into a room by two thugs and subjected to a humiliating body-search and a third-degree grilling. I missed my plane in consequence."

"Good Lord, whatever did they do that for?" said Felix Skinner.

"They claimed it was mistaken identity. No excuse whatever, of course. Do I look like a smuggler? I made an official complaint. I shall very probably sue."

"I don't blame you," said Felix Skinner. "But was it worth coming so late?"

Parkinson began to mutter something about there being some people whom he wanted to meet, Kingfisher, Textel of UNESCO, and so on. Persse scarcely attended. Into his mind at the mention of "Heathrow" had swum the image of Cheryl Summerbee as he had last seen her, crying over her timetable; and it darted through him with the speed of an arrow, that Cheryl loved him. Only his infatuation with Angelica had prevented him from perceiving it earlier. As the consciousness of this fact sank in, Cheryl became endowed, to his mind's eye, with an aura of infinite desirability. He must go to her at once. He would take her in his arms, and wipe away her tears, and whisper in her ear that he loved her too. He turned away from Skinner and Parkinson, spilling some of his champagne in the process, only to confront Angelica and Lily, each hanging on to an arm of the dark young man in the Donegal tweed jacket who had chaired the forum on Romance. He identified Lily by her red silk dress. Angelica was still wearing her tailored jacket and white blouse. "Hallo, Persse," she said. "I'd like you to meet my fiancé."

"Glad to meet you," said the young man, smiling, "Peter McGarrigle."

"No, it's *Persse* McGarrigle," he said. "*You're* Peter something."

"McGarrigle," the young man laughed. "I've the same name as you. We're probably related somehow."

"Were you ever at Trinity?" said Persse.

"Indeed I was."

"I'm afraid I did you out of a job once, then," said Persse. "When they appointed me at Limerick, they thought they were appointing you. It's been on my conscience ever since."

"It was the best day's work anyone ever did for me," said Peter. "I came to the States in consequence, and I've done very well here." He smiled fondly at Angelica, and she squeezed his arm.

"No hard feelings, Persse?" she said.

"No hard feelings."

"I heard you were at my paper this afternoon. What did you think of it?" She looked at him anxiously, as though his opinion really mattered.

He was saved from having to reply by the sound of someone rapping on a table nearby. The party hubbub subsided. A man in a sleek pale grey suit was making a speech from halfway up the flight of stairs that connected the two levels of the penthouse suite. "Who is it?" Felix Skinner could be heard enquiring. "Jacques Textel," Rudyard Parkinson hissed in his ear.

"As most of you know," Jacques Textel was saying, "UNESCO intends to found a new chair of literary criticism tenable anywhere in the world, and I think it's no secret that we have been seeking the advice of the doyen of the subject, Arthur Kingfisher, as to how to fill this post. Well, ladies and gentlemen, I have news for you." Textel paused, teasingly, and Persse looked round the room, picking out the faces, tense and expectant, of Morris Zapp, Philip

Swallow, Michel Tardieu, Fulvia Morgana and Siegfried von Turpitz. "Arthur has just told me," said Jacques Textel, "that he is prepared to come out of retirement and allow his own name to go forward for the chair."

There was a collective gasp from the listeners, and a storm of applause, mingled with some expressions of a cynical and disapproving nature.

"Of course," said Textel, "I can't speak for the appointing committee, of which I am merely the chairman. But I should be surprised if there is any serious rival candidate to Arthur."

More applause. Arthur Kingfisher, standing just below Textel, held up his hands. "Thank you, friends," he said. "I know that some people might say that it is unusual for an assessor to put himself forward for the post on which he is advising; but when I agreed to act I thought I was finished as a creative thinker. Today I feel as if I have been given a new lease of life, which I would like to put at the service of the international scholarly community, through the good offices of UNESCO.

"To those friends and colleagues who may have been thinking that their claims to this chair are as good as mine, I will only say that in three years' time it will be up for grabs again." More applause, mingled with laughter, some hollow. "Finally, I would like to share with you a particular personal happiness. Song-Mi?" Arthur Kingfisher reached out and took the hand of Song-Mi Lee, gently pulling her up onto the step with himself. "This afternoon, ladies and gentlemen, this beautiful young lady, my companion and secretary for many years, agreed to become my wife." Cheers, shrieks, whistles, applause. Arthur Kingfisher beams. Song-Mi Lee smiles shyly. He kisses her. More applause.

But who is this little white-haired old lady who steps primly forward to confront the great literary theorist?

"Congratulations, Arthur," she says.

He stares, recognizes, starts back. "Sybil!" he exclaims, amazed. "Where have you come from? Where have you been? It must be thirty years . . ."

"Twenty-seven, Arthur," she says. "Just the age of your daughters."

"Daughters—what daughters?" says Arthur Kingfisher, loosening his necktie as if he is choking.

"Those lovely twin girls—there." She points dramatically to Angelica and Lily, who look at each other in amazement. Pandemonium among the audience. Sybil Maiden raises her voice above the hubbub. "Yes, Arthur, you remember when you took my long-preserved virginity during that summer school at Aspen, Colorado, in the summer of 'fifty-three? I thought I was too old to conceive children, but it proved otherwise." Now there is a breathless hush in the room, as all ears are strained to catch every word of this astonishing story. "A few weeks after we had parted, I discovered that I was pregnant—I, a respectable middle-aged spinster, fellow of Girton College, pregnant—and by a married man, for your wife was still alive then. What could I do but try to conceal the truth? Luckily I was starting a year's sabbatical in America. I was supposed to be working at the Huntington. Instead, I hid myself in the wilds of New Mexico, gave birth to the twins in the spring of 'fifty-four, smuggled them aboard a plane to Europe in a Gladstone bag— I travelled first class to get extra cabin baggage allowance, and there were no luggage searches and X-rays in those days—took the bag to the toilet as soon as we were airborne, and claimed to have found the babies there. Naturally, no one suspected that I, a supremely respectable spinster aged forty-six, could have been their mother. For twenty-seven years I have been carrying this guilty secret around with me. In vain have I tried to distract myself with travel. In the end it was through travel that I was brought face to face with my own grown-up children. Girls—can you ever forgive your mother for abandoning you?" She throws a piteous look in the direction of Angelica and Lily, who run to her side, and sweep her on to Arthur Kingfisher. "Mother!" "Daddy!" "My babies!" "My girls!" Poor Song-Mi Lee is in danger of being brushed aside, until Angelica stretches out a hand and pulls her into the reunited family circle. "Our second step-mother," she says, embracing her.

Everybody in the room, it seems, is embracing, laughing, crying, shouting. Désirée and Morris Zapp are kissing each other on both cheeks. Ronald Frobisher is shaking hands with Rudyard Parkinson. Only Siegfried von Turpitz looks cross and sulky. Persse grabs his hand and pumps it up and down. "No hard feelings," he says, "Lecky, Windrush and Bernstein are going to publish my book after all." The German pulls his hand away irritably, but Persse has not finished shaking it, and the black glove comes off, revealing a perfectly normal, healthy-looking hand underneath. Von Turpitz goes pale, hisses, and seems to shrivel in stature, plunges his hand in his jacket pocket, and slinks from the room, never to be seen at an international conference again.

Lily came across to Persse. "We're all going on somewhere we can dance," she said. "You want to come?"

"No thanks," said Persse.

"We could just go back to the room, if you like," she said. "You and me."

"Thanks," said Persse, "but I ought to be on my way."

He left the party a few minutes later, at the same time as Philip Swallow. The Englishman's eye was moist. "I know what it's like to discover that you have a child you never dreamt existed," he said, as they waited for the main elevator. "I found I had a daughter like that, once. Then I lost her again." The lift doors opened and they entered it.

"How was that?"

"It's a long story," said Philip Swallow. "Basically I failed in the role of romantic hero. I thought I wasn't too old for it, but I was. My nerve failed me at a crucial moment."

"That's a pity," said Persse politely.

"I wasn't equal to the woman in the case."

"Joy?"

"Yes, Joy," said Philip Swallow with a sigh. He didn't seem surprised that Persse knew the name. "I had a Christmas card from her, she said she's getting married again. Hilary said, 'Joy? Do we know someone called Joy?' I said, 'Just someone I met on my travels.'"

"Hilary is your wife?"

"Yes. She's a marriage counsellor. Jolly good at it, too. She helped the Dempseys get back together. Do you remember Robin Dempsey—he was at the Rummidge conference."

"I'm glad to hear that," said Persse. "He didn't seem very contented when I met him."

"Had some kind of a breakdown last summer, I understand. Janet took pity on him. This is my floor, I think. Goodnight."

"Goodnight."

Persse watched Philip Swallow walking down the corridor, swaying a little with fatigue or drink, until the lift doors closed.

. . .

Persse walked through the Hilton lobby and out into the cold, crisp night. The temperature had returned to normal, and a raw biting wind was blowing down the Avenue of the Americas again. He began to walk in the direction of the YMCA. A black youth sped towards him a few inches above the broad sidewalk. But what Persse had at first taken for winged feet turned out to be attached to roller skates, and what looked like a helmet was a woolly hat worn over a transistor radio headset. Persse, mindful of New York mugging stories, and of the fact that he was carrying two hundred dollars in cash, stopped and tensed in readiness to defend himself. The young man, however, wore a friendly aspect. He smiled to himself and rolled his eyes up into his head; his movements had a rhythmic, choreographed quality, and his approach to Persse was delayed by many loops and arabesques on the broad pavement. He was clearly dancing to the unheard melodies in his earphones. He held a sheaf of leaflets, and as he passed he deftly thrust one into Persse's hand. Persse read it by the light of a shop window.

"Lonely? Horny? Tired of TV? We have the answers," it proclaimed. *"Girls Unlimited offers a comprehensive service for the out-of-town visitor to the Big Apple. Escorts, masseuses, playmates. Visit our Paradise Island Club. Take a jacuzzi bath with the bathmate of your choice. Have her give you a relaxing massage afterwards. Let it all hang out at our nude discothèque. Too lazy to leave your hotel room? Our masseuses will come to you. Or perhaps you just want some spicy pillow talk to get yourself off . . . to sleep. Dial 74321 and share your wildest fantasies with . . ."*

Persse ran back to the Hilton lobby and pressed a dime into the nearest payphone. He dialled the number and a familiar voice said, somewhat listlessly: "Hallo, naughty boy, this is Marlene. What's on your mind?"

"Bernadette," said Persse. "I've got some important information for you."

2

On the last day of the year, Persse McGarrigle flew into Heathrow on a British Airways jumbo jet. Having only hand-baggage with him, his scuffed and shabby canvas grip, he was one of the first of the passengers to pass through customs and passport control. He went straight to the nearest British Airways Information desk. The girl sitting behind it was not Cheryl. "Yes?" she said. "Can I help you?"

"You can indeed," he said. "I'm looking for a girl called Cheryl. Cheryl Summerbee. She works for British Airways. Can you tell me where I can find her?"

"We're not supposed to answer that sort of question," said the girl.

"Please," said Persse. "It's important." He put all a lover's urgency into his voice.

The girl sighed. "Well, I'll see what I can do," she said. She pushed the buttons on her telephone and waited silently for an answer. "Oh, hallo Frank," she said at length. "Is Cheryl Summerbee on shift this morning? Eh? *What*? No, I didn't. Oh. You don't? I see. All right, then. No, nothing. 'Bye." She put the phone down and looked at Persse, curiously and with a certain compassion. "Apparently she got the sack yesterday," she said.

"What!" Persse exclaimed. "Whatever for?"

The girl shrugged. "Apparently she tried to get her own back on some bolshie passenger by marking his boarding card 'S,' for suspected smuggler. The Excise boys did him over and he complained."

"Where is she, then? How can I find out her address?"

"Frank said she's gone abroad."

"Abroad?"

"She said she was fed up with the job anyway and this was her chance to travel. She'd been saving up, apparently. That's what Frank said."

"Did she say where she was going?"

"No," said the girl. "She didn't. Can I help you, madam?" She turned aside to help another enquirer.

Persse walked slowly away from the Information desk and stood in front of the huge Departures flutterboard, with his hands in his pockets and his bag at his feet. New York, Ottawa, Johannesburg, Cairo, Nairobi, Moscow, Bangkok, Wellington, Mexico City, Buenos Aires, Baghdad, Calcutta, Sidney . . . The day's destinations filled four columns. Every few minutes the board twitched into life, and the names flickered and chattered and tumbled and rotated before his eyes, like the components of some complicated mechanical game of chance, a gigantic geographical fruit machine, until they came to rest once more. On to the surface of the board, as on to a cinema screen, he projected his memory of Cheryl's face and figure—the blonde, shoulder-length hair, the high-stepping gait, the starry, unfocused look of her blue eyes—and he wondered where in all the small, narrow world he should begin to look for her.

NICE WORK

To Andy and Marie, in friendship and gratitude

AUTHOR'S NOTE

Perhaps I should explain, for the benefit of readers who have not been here before, that Rummidge is an imaginary city, with imaginary universities and imaginary factories, inhabited by imaginary people, which occupies, for the purposes of fiction, the space where Birmingham is to be found on maps of the so-called real world.

I am deeply grateful to several executives in industry, and to one in particular, who showed me around their factories and offices, and patiently answered my often naive questions, while this novel was in preparation.

Upon the midlands now the industrious muse doth fall,
The shires which we the heart of England well may call.

DRAYTON: *Poly-Olbion*
(EPIGRAPH TO *Felix Holt the Radical,* BY GEORGE ELIOT)

"Two nations; between whom there is no intercourse and no sympathy; who are as ignorant of each other's habits, thoughts and feelings, as if they were dwellers in different zones, or inhabitants of different planets; who are formed by a different breeding, and fed by different food, and ordered by different manners . . ."

"You speak of—" said Egremont hesitatingly.

BENJAMIN DISRAELI: *Sybil; or, the Two Nations*

PART I

If you think . . . that anything like a romance is preparing for you, reader, you were never more mistaken. Do you anticipate sentiment, and poetry, and reverie? Do you expect passion, and stimulus, and melodrama? Calm your expectations, reduce them to a lowly standard. Something real, cool and solid lies before you; something unromantic as Monday morning, when all who have work wake with the consciousness that they must rise and betake themselves thereto.

CHARLOTTE BRONTË: PRELUDE TO *Shirley*

1

Monday January 13th, 1986. Victor Wilcox lies awake, in the dark bedroom, waiting for his quartz alarm clock to bleep. It is set to do this at 6:45. How long he has to wait he doesn't know. He could easily find out by groping for the clock, lifting it to his line of vision, and pressing the button that illuminates the digital display. But he would rather not know. Supposing it is only six o'clock? Or even five? It could be five. Whatever it is, he won't be able to get to sleep again. This has become a regular occurrence lately: lying awake in the dark, waiting for the alarm to bleep, worrying.

Worries streak towards him like enemy spaceships in one of Gary's video games. He flinches, dodges, zaps them with instant solutions, but the assault is endless: the Avco account, the Rawlinson account, the price of pig-iron, the value of the pound, the competition from Foundrax, the incompetence of his Marketing Director, the persistent breakdowns of the core blowers, the vandalising of the toilets in the fettling shop, the pressure from his divisional boss, last month's accounts, the quarterly forecast, the annual review . . .

In an effort to escape this bombardment, perhaps even to doze awhile, he twists onto his side, burrows into the warm plump body of his wife, and throws and arm round her waist. Startled, but still asleep, drugged with Valium, Marjorie swivels to face him. Their noses and foreheads bump against each other; there is a sudden flurry of limbs, an absurd pantomime struggle. Marjorie puts up her fists like a pugilist, groans and pushes him away. An object slides off the bed on her side and falls to the floor with a thump. Vic knows what it is: a book entitled *Enjoy Your Menopause*, which one of Marjorie's friends at the Weight Watchers' club has lent her, and which she has been reading in bed, without much show of conviction, and falling asleep over, for the past week or two. On retiring to bed Vic's last action is normally to detach a book from Marjorie's nerveless fingers, tuck her arms under the covers and turn out her bedside lamp, but he must have neglected the first of these chores last night, or perhaps *Enjoy Your Menopause* was concealed under the coverlet.

He rolls away from Marjorie, who, now lying on her back, begins to snore faintly. He envies her that deep unconsciousness, but cannot afford to join her in it. Once, desperate for a full night's sleep, he had accepted her offer of a Valium, sluicing it down with his usual nightcap, and moved about the next morning like a diver walking on the seabed. He made a mistake of two percentage points in a price for steering-boxes for British Leyland before his head cleared. *You shouldn't have mixed it with whisky*, Marjorie said. *You don't need both*. Then I'll stick to whisky, he said. *The Valium lasts longer*, she said. Too bloody long, if you ask me, he said. I lost the firm five thousand pounds this morning, thanks to you. *Oh, it's my fault, is it?* she said, and her lower lip began to tremble. Then to stop her crying, anything to stop that, he had to buy her the set of antique-look brass fire-irons she had set her heart on for the lounge, to give an extra touch of authenticity to the rustic stone fireplace and the imitation-log gas fire.

Marjorie's snores become louder. Vic gives her a rude, exasperated shove. The snoring stops but, surprisingly, she does not wake. In other rooms his three children are also asleep. Outside, a winter gale blusters against the sides of the house and swishes the branches of trees to and fro. He feels like the captain of a sleeping ship, alone at the helm, steering his oblivious crew through dangerous seas. He feels as if he is the only man awake in the entire world.

The alarm clock cheeps.

Instantly, by some perverse chemistry of his body or nervous system, he feels tired and drowsy, reluctant to leave the warm bed. He presses the Snooze button on the clock with a practised finger and falls effortlessly asleep. Five minutes later, the alarm wakes him again, cheeping insistently like a mechanical bird. Vic sighs, hits the Off button on the clock, switches on his bedside lamp (its dimmer control turned low for Marjorie's sake) gets out of bed and paddles through the deep pile of the bedroom carpet to the *en suite* bathroom, making sure the connecting door is closed before he turns on the light inside.

Vic pees, a task requiring considerable care and accuracy since the toilet bowl is low-slung and tapered in shape. He does not greatly care for the dark purplish bathroom suite ("Damson," the estate agent's brochure had called the shade) but it had been one of the things that attracted Marjorie when they bought the house two years ago—the bathroom, with its kidney-shaped handbasin and gold-plated taps and sunken bath and streamlined loo and bidet. And, above all, the fact that it was *"en suite." I've always wanted an en suite bathroom*, she would say to visitors, to her friends on the phone, to, he wouldn't be surprised, tradesmen on the doorstep or strangers she accosted in the street. You would think *"en suite"* was the most beautiful phrase in any language, the lengths Marjorie went to introduce it into her conversation. If they made a perfume called *En Suite*, she would wear it.

Vic shakes the last drops from his penis, taking care not to sprinkle the shaggy pink nylon fitted carpet, and flushes the toilet. The house has four toilets, a cause of concern to Vic's father. *FOUR toilets?* he said, when first shown over the house. *Did I count right?* What's the matter, Dad? Vic teased. Afraid the water table will go down if we flush them all at once? *No, but what if they start metering water, eh? Then you'll be in trouble.* Vic tried to argue that it didn't make any difference how many toilets you had, it was the number of times you flushed them that mattered, but his father was convinced that having so many toilets was an incitement to unnecessary peeing, therefore to excessive flushing.

He could be right, at that. At Gran's house, a back-to-back in Easton with an outside toilet, you didn't go unless you really had to, especially in the winter. Their own house in those days, a step up the social ladder from Gran's, had its own indoor toilet, a dark narrow room off the half-landing that always niffed a bit, however much Sanilav and Dettol his mother poured into the bowl. He remembered vividly that yellowish ceramic bowl with the trademark "Challenger," the big varnished wooden seat that was always pleasantly warm to the bum, and a long chain dangling from the high cistern with a sponge-rubber ball, slightly perished, on the end of it. He used to practise heading, flicking the ball from wall to wall, as he sat there, a constipated schoolboy. His mother complained of the marks on the distemper. Now he is the proud owner of four toilets—damson, avocado, sunflower and white, all centrally heated. Probably as good an index of success as any.

He steps onto the bathroom scales. Ten stone two ounces. Quite enough for a man only five feet five and a half inches tall. Some say—Vic has overheard them saying it—that he tries to compensate for his short stature by his aggressive manner. Well, let them. If it wasn't for a bit of aggression, he wouldn't be where he is now. Though how long he will stay there is far from certain. Vic frowns in the mirror above the handbasin, thinking again of last month's accounts, the quarterly forecast, the annual review . . . He runs hot water into the dark purple bowl, lathers his face with shaving foam from an aerosol can, and begins to scrape his jaw with a safety razor, using a Wilkinson's Sword blade. Vic believes fervently in buying British, and has frequent rows with his eldest son, Raymond, who favours a disposable plastic razor manufactured in France. Not that this is the only bone of contention between them, no, not by a long chalk. The principal constraint on the number of their disagreements is, indeed, the comparative rarity of their encounters, Raymond invariably being asleep when Vic leaves for work and out when he returns home.

Vic wipes the tidemark of foam from his cheeks and fingers the shaven flesh appraisingly. Dark brown eyes stare back at him. Who am I?

He grips the washbasin, leans forward on locked arms, and scans the square face, pale under a forelock of lank brown hair, flecked with grey, the two vertical furrows in the brow like a clip holding the blunt nose in place, the straight-ruled line of the mouth, the squared-off jaw. You know who you are: it's all on file at Division.

Wilcox: Victor Eugene. *Date of Birth*: 19 Oct. 1940. *Place of Birth*: Easton, Rummidge, England. *Education*: Endwell Road Primary School, Easton; Easton Grammar School for Boys; Rummidge College of Advanced Technology. MI Mech. Eng. 1964. *Marital Status*: married (to Marjorie Florence Coleman, 1964). *Children*: Raymond (*b.* 1966), Sandra (*b.* 1969), Gary (*b.* 1972). *Career*: 1962–64, apprentice, Vanguard Engineering; 1964–66, Junior Production Engineer, Vanguard Engineering; 1966–70, Senior Engineer, Vanguard Engineering; 1970–74 Production Manager, Vanguard Engineering; 1974–78, Manufacturing Manager, Lewis & Arbuckle Ltd; 1978–80,

Manufacturing Director, Rumcol Castings; 1980–85, Managing Director, Rumcol Castings. *Present Position*: Managing Director, J. Pringle & Sons Casting & General Engineering.

That's who I am.

Vic grimaces at his own reflection, as if to say: come off it, no identity crises, please. Somebody has to earn a living in this family.

He shrugs on his dressing-gown, which hangs from a hook on the bathroom door, switches off the light, and softly re-enters the dimly lit bedroom. Marjorie has, however, been woken by the sound of plumbing.

"Is that you?" she says drowsily; then, without waiting for an answer, "I'll be down in a minute."

"Don't hurry," says Vic. *Don't bother* would be more honest, for he prefers to have the kitchen to himself in the early morning, to prepare his own simple breakfast and enjoy the first cigarette of the day undisturbed. Marjorie, however, feels that she must put in an appearance downstairs, however token, before he leaves for work, and there is a sense in which Vic understands and approves of this gesture. His own mother was always first up in the mornings, to see husband and son off to work or college, and continued the habit almost till the day she died.

As Vic descends the stairs, a high-pitched electronic squeal rises from below. The pressure of his foot on a wired pad under the staircarpet has triggered the burglar alarm, which Raymond, amazingly, must have remembered to set after coming in at God knows what hour last night. Vic goes to the console beside the front door and punches in the numerical code that disarms the apparatus. He has fifteen seconds to do this, before the squeal turns into a screech and the alarm bell on the outside wall starts yammering. All the houses in the neighbourhood have these alarms, and Vic admits that they are necessary, with burglaries increasing in frequency and boldness all the time, but the system they inherited from the previous owners of the house, with its magnetic contacts, infra-red scanners, pressure pads and panic buttons, is in his opinion over-elaborate. It takes about five minutes to set it up before you retire to bed, and if you come back downstairs for something you have to cancel it and start all over again. *The sufferings of the rich*, Raymond sneered when Vic was complaining of this one day—Raymond, who despises his parents' affluence while continuing to enjoy its comforts and conveniences, such as rent-free centrally heated accommodation, constant hot water, free laundry service, use of mother's car, use of TV, video recorder, stereo system, etcetera etcetera. Vic feels his blood pressure rising at the thought of his eldest son, who dropped out of university four months ago and has not been usefully occupied since, now swaddled in a duvet upstairs, naked except for a single gold earring, sleeping off last night's booze. Vic shakes his head irritably to rid his mind of the image.

He opens the inner front door that leads to the enclosed porch and glances at the doormat. Empty. The newspaper boy is late, or perhaps there is no paper today because of a strike. An infra-red scanner winks its inflamed eye at him as he goes into the lounge in search of reading matter. The floor and furniture are littered with the dismembered carcasses of the *Mail on Sunday* and the *Sunday Times*. He picks up the Business Section of the *Times* and takes it into the kitchen. While the kettle is boiling he scans the front page. A headline catches his eye: "LAWSON COUNTS THE COST AS TAX HOPES FADE."

> *Nigel Lawson, the Chancellor, is this weekend closeted with his Treasury team assessing the danger to his economic strategy from last week's rise in interest rates, and the sharp rise in unemployment.*

So what else is new?

The kettle boils. Vic makes a pot of strong tea, puts two slices of white bread in the toaster, and opens the louvres of the venetian blinds on the kitchen window to peer into the garden. A grey, blustery morning, with no frost. Squirrels bound across the lawn like balls of fluff blown by the wind. Magpies strut from flowerbed to flowerbed, greedily devouring the grubs that he turned up in yesterday's gardening. Blackbirds, sparrows, robins, and other birds whose names Vic doesn't know, skip and hop about at a discreet distance from the magpies. All these creatures seem very much at home in Vic's garden, although it is only two miles from the city centre. One morning not long ago he saw a fox walking past this same window. Vic tapped on the pane. The fox stopped and turned his head to look at Vic for a moment, as if to say, *Yes?* and then proceeded calmly on his way, his brush swaying in the air behind him. It is Vic's impression that English wildlife is getting streetwise, moving from the country into the city where the living is easier—where there are no traps, pesticides, hunters and sportsmen, but plenty of well-stocked garbage bins, and housewives like Marjorie, softhearted or softheaded enough to throw their scraps into the garden, creating animal soup-kitchens. Nature is joining the human race and going on the dole.

Vic has eaten his two slices of toast and is on his third cup of tea and his first cigarette of the day when Marjorie shuffles into the kitchen in her dressing-gown and slippers, a scarf over her curlers, her pale round face puffy with sleep. She carries the *Daily Mail*, which has just been delivered.

"Smoking," she says, in a tone at once resigned and reproachful, condensing into a single word an argument well-known to both of them. Vic grunts, the distillation of an equally familiar rejoinder. He glances at the kitchen clock.

"Shouldn't Sandra and Gary be getting up? I won't waste my breath on Raymond."

"Gary doesn't have school today. The teachers are on strike."

"*What?*" he says accusingly, his anger at the teachers somehow getting displaced onto Marjorie.

"Industrial action, or whatever they call it. He brought a note home on Friday."

"Industrial *in*action, you mean. You don't see teachers out on the picket line, in the cold and the rain, have you noticed? They're just sitting around in their warm staff rooms, chewing the fat, while the kids are sent home to get into mischief. That's not action. It's not an industry, either, come to that. It's a profession and it's about time they started to act like professionals."

"Well . . ." says Marjorie placatingly.

"What about Sandra? Is the Sixth Form College taking 'industrial action' too?"

"No, I'm taking her to the doctor's."

"What's the matter with her?"

Marjorie yawns evasively. "Oh, nothing serious."

"Why can't she go on her own? A girl of seventeen should be able to go to the doctor's without someone to hold her hand."

"I don't go in with her, not unless she wants me to. I just wait with her."

Vic regards his wife suspiciously. "You're not going shopping with her afterwards?"

Marjorie blushes. "Well, she needs a new pair of shoes . . ."

"You're a fool, Marje!" Vic exclaims. "You spoil that girl something rotten. All she thinks about is clothes, shoes, hairstyles. What kind of A-Levels do you think she's going to get?"

"I don't know. But if she doesn't want to go to University . . ."

"What does she want to do, then? What's the latest?"

"She's thinking of hairdressing."

"Hairdressing!" Vic puts as much contempt into his voice as he can muster.

"Anyway, she's a pretty girl, why shouldn't she enjoy clothes and so on, while she's young?"

"Why shouldn't *you* enjoy dressing her up, you mean. You know you treat her like a doll, Marje, don't you?"

Rather than answer this question, Marjorie reverts to an earlier one. "She's been having trouble with her periods, if you must know," she says, imputing a prurient inquisitiveness to Vic, although she is well aware that such gynaecological disclosures are the last thing he wants, especially at this hour of the morning. The pathology of women's bodies is a source of great mystery and unease to Vic. Their bleedings and leakages, their lumps and growths, their peculiarly painful-sounding surgical operations—scraping of wombs, stripping of veins, amputation of breasts—the mere mention of such things makes him wince and cringe, and lately the menopause has added new items to the repertory: the hot flush, flooding, and something sinister called a bloat. "I expect he'll put her on the pill," says Marjorie, making herself a fresh pot of tea.

"What?"

"To regulate her periods. I expect Dr. Roberts will put Sandra on the pill."

Vic grunts again, but this time his intonation is ambiguous and uncertain. He has a feeling that his womenfolk are up to something. Could the real purpose of Sandra's visit to the doctor's be to fix her up with contraception? With Marjorie's approval? He knows he doesn't approve himself. Sandra having sex? At seventeen? With whom? Not that spotty youth in the army surplus overcoat, what's his name, Cliff, not him for God's sake. Not with anyone. An image of his daughter in the act of love, her white knees parted, a dark shape above her, flashes unbidden into his head and fills him with rage and disgust.

He is conscious of Marjorie's watery blue eyes scanning him speculatively over the rim of her teacup, inviting further discussion of Sandra, but he can't face it, not this morning, not with a day's work ahead of him. Not at any time, to be honest. Discussion of Sandra's sex-life could easily stray into the area of his and Marjorie's sex-life, or rather the lack of it, and he would rather not go into that. Let sleeping dogs lie. Vic compares the kitchen clock with his watch and rises from the table.

"Shall I do you a bit of bacon?" says Marjorie.

"No, I've finished."

"You ought to have a cooked breakfast, these cold mornings."

"I haven't time."

"Why don't we get a microwave? I could cook you a bit of bacon in seconds with a microwave."

"Did you know," says Vic, "that ninety-six per cent of the world's microwave ovens are made in Japan, Taiwan or Korea?"

"Everybody we know has got one," says Marjorie.

"Exactly," says Vic.

Marjorie looks unhappily at Vic, uncertain of his drift. "I thought I might price some this morning," she says. "After Sandra's shoes."

"Where would you put it?" Vic enquires, looking round at the kitchen surfaces already cluttered with numerous electrical appliances—toaster, kettle, coffee-maker, food-processor, electric wok, chip-fryer, waffle-maker . . .

"I thought we could put the electric wok away. We never use it. A microwave would be more useful."

"Well, all right, price them but don't buy. I can get one cheaper through the trade."

Marjorie brightens. She smiles, and two dimples appear in her pasty cheeks, still shiny from last night's application of face cream. It was her dimples that first attracted Vic to Marjorie twenty-five years ago, when she worked in the typing pool at Vanguard. These days they appear infrequently, but the prospect of a shopping expedition is one of the few things that are guaranteed to bring them out.

"Just don't expect *me* to eat anything cooked in it," he says.

Marjorie's dimples fade abruptly, like the sun going behind a cloud. "Why not?"

"It's not proper cooking, is it? My mother would turn in her grave."

Vic takes the *Daily Mail* with him to the lavatory, the one at the back of the house, next to the tradesmen's entrance, with a plain white suite, intended for the use of charladies, gardeners and workmen. By tacit agreement, Vic customarily moves his bowels in here, while Marjorie uses the guest cloakroom off the front hall, so that the atmosphere of the *en suite* bathroom remains unpolluted.

Vic smokes a second cigarette as he sits at stool, and scans the *Daily Mail*. Westland and Heseltine are still making the headlines. STOP THE NO. 10 WHISPERS. MAGGIE'S BID TO COOL OFF BATTLE. He flicks through the inside pages. MURDOCH FACING UNION CLASH. THE IMAM'S CALL TO PRAYER MAKES THE VICAR TALK OF BEDLAM. HEARTACHE AHEAD FOR THE BRIDE WHO MARRIED TWICE. WE'RE IN THE SUPER-LEAGUE OF NATIONS. Hang about.

Britain is back in the Super-League of top industrial nations, it is claimed today. Only Germany, Holland, Japan and Switzerland can now match us for economic growth, price stability and strong balance of payments, says Dr. David Lomax, the Natwest's economic adviser.

"Match" presumably means "beat." And since when was *Holland* an industrial superpower? Even so, it must be all balls, a mirage massaged from statistics. You only have to drive through the West Midlands to see that if we are in the Super-League of top industrial nations, somebody must be moving the goalposts. Vic is all in favour of backing Britain, but there are times when the *Mail*'s windy chauvinism gets on his tits. He takes a drag on his cigarette and taps the ash between his legs, hearing a faint hiss as it hits the water. 100 M.P.G. FAMILY CAR LOOKING GOOD IN TESTS.

Trials have been started by British Leyland of their revolutionary lightweight aluminium engine for a world-beating family car capable of 100 miles per gallon.

When was the last time we were supposed to have a world-beating aluminium engine? The Hillman Imp, right? Where are they now, the Hillman Imps of yesteryear? In the scrapyards, every one, or nearly. And the Linwood plant a graveyard, grass growing between the assembly lines, corrugated-iron roofs flapping in the wind. A car that nobody wanted to buy, built on a site chosen for political not commercial reasons, hundreds of miles from its component suppliers. He turns to the City Pages. HOW TO GET UP A HEAD OF ESTEEM.

What has been designated Industry Year has got off to a predictably silly start. Various bodies in Manufacturing Industry are working themselves into one of their regular lathers about the supposed low social esteem bestowed upon engineers and engineering.

Vic reads this article with mixed feelings. Industry Year is certainly a lot of balls. On the other hand, the idea that society undervalues its engineers is not.

It is 7:40 when Vic emerges from the lavatory. The tempo of his actions begins to accelerate. He strides through the kitchen, where Marjorie is listlessly loading his soiled breakfast things into the dishwasher, and runs up the stairs. Back in the *en suite* bathroom, he briskly cleans his teeth and brushes his hair. He goes into the bedroom and puts on a clean white shirt and a suit. He has six business suits, which he wears in daily rotation. He used to think five was enough, but acquired an additional one after Raymond wisecracked, "If that's the charcoal grey worsted, it must be Tuesday." Today it is the turn of the navy blue pinstripe. He selects a tie diagonally striped in dark tones of red, blue and grey. He levers his feet into a pair of highly polished black calf Oxfords. A frayed lace snaps under too vigorous a tug, and he curses. He rummages in the back of his wardrobe for an old black shoe with a suitable lace and uncovers a cardboard box containing a brand-new clock radio, made in Hong Kong, sealed in a transparent plastic envelope and nestling in a polystyrene mould. Vic sighs and grimaces. Such discoveries are not uncommon at this time of year. Marjorie has a habit of buying Christmas presents early, hiding them away like a squirrel, and then forgetting all about them.

When he comes downstairs again, she is hovering in the hall.

"Who was the clock radio for, then?"

"What?"

"I found a brand-new clock radio at the back of the wardrobe."

Marjorie covers her mouth with her hand. "Sst! I *knew* I'd got something for your Dad."

"Didn't we give him a Christmas present, then?"

"Of course we did. You remember, you rushed out on Christmas Eve and got him that electric blanket . . . Never mind, it will do for next year."

"Hasn't he already got a clock radio? Didn't we give him one a few years ago?"

"Did we?" says Marjorie vaguely. "Perhaps one of the boys would like it, then."

"What they need is a clock with a bomb attached to it, not a radio," says Vic, patting his pockets, checking for wallet, diary, keyring, calculator, cigarettes and lighter.

Marjorie helps him on with his camelhair overcoat, a garment she persuaded him to buy against his better judgment, for it hangs well below his knees and, he thinks, accentuates his short stature, as well as making him look like a prosperous bookie. "When will you be home?" she enquires.

"I don't know. You'd better keep my dinner warm."

"Don't be too late."

She closes her eyes and tilts her face towards him. He brushes her lips with his, then jerks his head in the direction of the first floor. "Get that idle shower out of bed."

"They need sleep when they're growing, Vic."

"Raymond's not *growing*, for Christ's sake. He stopped growing years ago, unless he's growing a beer belly, which wouldn't surprise me."

"Well, Gary's still growing."

"Make sure he does some homework today."

"Yes, dear."

Vic is quite sure she has no intention of carrying out his instructions. If she hadn't arranged to take Sandra to the doctor's Marjorie would probably go back to bed herself, now, with a cup of tea and the *Daily Mail*. A few weeks before, he'd returned home soon after getting to work because he'd left some important papers behind, and found the house totally silent, all three children and their mother sound asleep at 9:30 in the morning. No wonder the country is going to the dogs.

Vic passes through the glazed porch and out into the open air. The cold wind ruffles his hair and makes him flinch for a moment, but it is refreshing after the stale warmth of the house, and he takes a deep breath or two on his way to the garage. As he approaches the garage door it swings open as if by magic—in fact by electricity, activated by a remote-control device in Vic's pocket—a feat that never fails to give him a deep, childlike pleasure. Inside, the gleaming dark blue Jaguar V12, Registration Number VIC 100, waits beside Marjorie's silver Metro. He backs the car out, shutting the garage door with another touch on the remote control. Marjorie has now appeared at the lounge window, clutching her dressing-gown across her bosom with one hand and waving timidly with the other. Vic smiles conciliatingly, puts the automatic gear lever into Drive, and glides away.

Now begins the best half-hour of the day, the drive to work. In fact it is not quite half-an-hour—the journey usually takes twenty-four minutes, but Vic wishes it were longer. It is an interval of peace between the irritations of home and the anxieties of work, a time of pure sensation, total control, effortless superiority. For the Jaguar is superior to every other car on the road, Vic is convinced of that. When Midland Amalgamated headhunted him for the MD's job at Pringle's they offered him a Rover 3500 Vanden Plas, but Vic stuck out for the Jaguar, a car normally reserved for divisional chairmen, and to his great satisfaction he had got one, even though it wasn't quite new. It had to be a British car, of course, since Pringle's did so much business with the local automotive industry—not that Vic has ever driven a foreign car: foreign cars are anathema to him, their sudden invasion of British roads in the 1970s marked the beginning of the region's economic ruin in his view—

but he has to admit that you don't have a lot of choice in British cars when it comes to matching the top-of-the-range Mercedes and BMWs. In fact the Jag is just about the only one that can really wipe the smiles off their drivers' faces, unless you're talking Rolls-Royce or Bentley.

He pauses at the T-junction where Avondale Road meets Barton Road, on which the rush-hour traffic is already beginning to thicken. The driver of a Ford Transit van, though he has priority, hangs back respectfully to let Vic filter left. Vic nods his thanks, turns left, then right again, picking his way through the broad, tree-lined residential streets with practised ease. He is skirting the University, whose tall redbrick clock-tower is occasionally visible above trees and rooftops. Though he lives on its doorstep, so to speak, Vic has never been inside the place. He knows it chiefly as a source of seasonal traffic jams about which Marjorie sometimes complains (the University day begins too late and finishes too early to inconvenience Vic himself) and of distractingly pretty girls about whose safety he worries, seeing them walking to and fro between their halls of residence and the Students' Union in the evenings. With its massive architecture and landscaped grounds, guarded at every entrance by watchful security staff, the University seems to Vic rather like a small city-state, an academic Vatican, from which he keeps his distance, both intimidated by and disapproving of its air of privileged detachment from the vulgar, bustling industrial city in which it is embedded. His own *alma mater*, situated a few miles away, was a very different kind of institution, a dingy tower block, crammed with machinery and lab benches, overlooking a railway marshalling yard and a roundabout on the inner ring road. In his day a College of Advanced Technology, it has since grown in size and been raised to the status of a university, but without putting on any airs and graces. And quite right too. If you make college too comfortable nobody will ever want to leave it to do proper work.

Vic leaves the residential area around the University and filters into the traffic moving sluggishly along the London Road in the direction of the City Centre. This is the slowest part of his morning journey, but the Jaguar, whispering along in automatic, takes the strain. Vic selects a cassette and slots it into the four-speaker stereo system. The voice of Carly Simon fills the interior of the car. Vic's taste in music is narrow but keen. He favours female vocalists, slow tempos, lush arrangements of tuneful melodies in the jazz-soul idiom. Carly Simon, Dusty Springfield, Roberta Flack, Dionne Warwick, Diana Ross, Randy Crawford and, more recently, Sade and Jennifer Rush. The subtle inflexions of these voices, honeyed or slightly hoarse, moaning and whispering of women's love, its joys and disappointments, soothe his nerves and relax his limbs. He would of course never dream of playing these tapes on the music centre at home, risking the derision of his children. It is a very private pleasure, a kind of musical masturbation, all part of the ritual of the drive to work. He would enjoy it more, though, if he were not obliged to read at the same time, in the rear windows of other cars, crude reminders of a more basic sexuality. YOUNG FARMERS DO IT IN THEIR WELLIES. WATER SKIERS DO IT STANDING UP. HOOT IF YOU HAD IT LAST NIGHT. It, it, it. Vic's knuckles are white as he grips the steering wheel. Why should decent people have to put up with this crap? There ought to be a law.

Now Vic has reached the last traffic lights before the system of tunnels and flyovers that will conduct him without further interruption through the centre of the city. A red Toyota Celica draws up beside him, then inches forward as its driver rides his clutch, evidently intending a quick getaway. The lights turn to amber and the Toyota darts forward, revealing, wouldn't you know it, a legend in its rear window, HANG GLIDERS DO IT IN MID AIR. Vic waits law-abidingly for the green light, then presses the accelerator hard. The Jaguar surges forward, catches the Toyota in two seconds, and sweeps effortlessly past—Carly Simon, by happy coincidence, hitting a thrilling crescendo at the very same moment. Vic glances in his rear-view mirror and smiles thinly. Teach him to buy a Jap car.

It won't, of course. Vic is well aware of the hollowness of his small victory, a huge thirsty 5.3-litre engine pitted against the Toyota's economical 1.8. But never mind common sense for the moment, this is the time of indulgence, suspended between home and work, the time of effortless motion, cushioned in real leather, insulated from the noise and fumes of the city by the padded coachwork, the tinted glass, the sensuous music. The car's long prow dips into the first tunnel. In and out, down and up. Vic threads the tunnels, switches lanes, swings out onto a long covered ramp that leads to a six-lane expressway thrust like a gigantic concrete fist through the backstreets of his boyhood. Every morning Vic drives over the flattened site of his Gran's house and passes at chimney-pot level the one in which he himself grew up, where his widower father still stubbornly lives on in spite of all Vic's efforts to persuade him to move, like a sailor clinging to the rigging of a sinking ship—buffeted, deafened and choked by the thundering torrent of traffic thirty yards from his bedroom window.

Vic swings on to the motorway, going north-west, and for a few miles gives the Jaguar its head, moving smoothly up the outside lane at 90, keeping a watchful eye on the rear-view mirror, though the police rarely bother you in the rush hour, they are as eager as anyone to keep the traffic flowing. To his right and left spreads a familiar landscape, so familiar that he does not really see it, an expanse of houses and factories, warehouses and sheds, railway lines and canals, piles of scrap metal and heaps of damaged cars, container ports and lorry parks, cooling towers and gasometers. A monochrome landscape, grey under a low grey sky, its horizons blurred by a grey haze.

. . .

Vic Wilcox has now, strictly speaking, left the city of Rummidge and passed into an area known as the Dark Country—so called because of the pall of smoke that hung over it, and the film of coaldust and soot that covered it, in the heyday of the Industrial Revolution. He knows a little of the history of this region, having done a prize-winning project on it at school. Rich mineral deposits were discovered here in the early nineteenth century: coal, iron, limestone. Mines were sunk, quarries excavated, and ironworks sprang up everywhere to exploit the new technique of smelting iron ore with coke, using limestone as a flux. The fields were gradually covered with pitheads, found-ries, factories and workshops, and rows of wretched hovels for the men, women and children who worked in them: a sprawling, unplanned, industrial conurbation that was gloomy by day, fearsome by night. A writer called Thomas Carlyle described it in 1824 as *"A frightful scene . . . a dense cloud of pestilential smoke hangs over it forever . . . and at night the whole region becomes like a volcano spitting fire from a thousand tubes of brick."* A little later, Charles Dickens recorded travelling *"through miles of cinder-paths and blazing furnaces and roaring steam engines, and such a mass of dirt, gloom and misery as I never before witnessed."* Queen Victoria had the curtains of her train window drawn when she passed through the region so that her eyes should not be offended by its ugliness and squalor.

The economy and outward appearance of the area have changed consider-ably since those days. As the seams of coal and iron were exhausted, or be-came unprofitable to work, mining and smelting diminished. But industries based on iron—casting, forging, engineering, all those kinds of manufactur-ing known generically as "metal-bashing"—spread and multiplied, until their plant met and merged with the expanding industrial suburbs of Rummidge. The shrinkage of heavy industry, and the development of new forms of energy, have reduced the visible pollution of the air, though the deadlier fumes of leaded petrol exhaust, drifting from the motorways with which the whole area is looped and knotted, thicken the characteristic grey haziness of the Midlands light. Nowadays the Dark Country is not noticeably darker than its neighbouring city, and of country there is precious little to be seen. Foreign visitors sometimes suppose that the region gets its name not from its environmental character but from the complexions of so many of its inhabitants, immigrant families from India, Pakistan and the Caribbean, drawn here in the boom years of the fifties and sixties, when jobs were plentiful, and now bearing the brunt of high unemployment.

All too soon it is time to slow down and leave the motorway, descending into smaller-scale streets, into the congestion of traffic lights, roundabouts, T-junctions. This is West Wallsbury, a district dominated by factories, large and small, old and new. Many are silent, some derelict, their windows starred with smashed glass. Receiverships and closures have ravaged the area in recent years, giving a desolate look to its streets. Since the election of the Tory Government of 1979, which allowed the pound to rise on the back of North Sea oil in the early eighties and left British industry defenceless in the face of foreign competition, or (according to your point of view) exposed its inefficiency (Vic inclines to the first view, but in certain moods will admit the force of the second), one-third of all the engineering companies in the West Midlands have closed down. There is nothing quite so forlorn as a closed factory—Vic Wilcox knows, having supervised a shutdown himself in his time. A factory is sustained by the energy of its own functioning, the throb and whine of machinery, the clash of metal, the unceasing motion of the assembly lines, the ebb and flow of workers changing shifts, the hiss of airbrakes and the growl of diesel engines from wagons delivering raw materials at one gate, taking away finished goods at the other. When you put a stop to all that, when the place is silent and empty, all that is left is a large, ramshackle shed—cold, filthy and depressing. Well, that won't happen at Pringle's, hopefully, as they say. Hopefully.

. . .

Vic is very near his factory now. A scarlet neon sign, *Susan's Sauna*, subject of many nudge-nudge jokes at work, but to Vic merely a useful landmark, glows above a dingy shop-front. A hundred yards further on, he turns down Coney Lane, passes Shopfix, Atkinson Insulation, Bitomark, then runs alongside the railings that fence the Pringle site until he reaches the main entrance. It is a long fence, and a large site. In its heyday, in the post-war boom, Pringle's employed four thousand men. Now the workforce has shrunk to less than a thousand, and much of the plant is in disuse. There are buildings and annexes that Vic has never been inside. It is cheaper to let them rot than to clear them away.

Vic hoots impatiently at the barrier; the security man's face appears at the window and flashes an ingratiating smile. Vic nods grimly back. Bugger was probably reading a newspaper. His predecessor had been fired at Vic's insistence just before Christmas when, returning unexpectedly to the factory at night, he found the man watching a portable TV instead of the video monitors he was paid to watch. It looks as though this one is not much of an improvement. Perhaps they should employ another security firm. Vic makes a mental note to raise the matter with George Prendergast, his Personnel Director.

The barrier is raised and he drives to his personal parking space next to the front entrance of the office block. He checks the statistics of his journey on the digital dashboard display. Distance covered: 9.8 miles. Journey time: 25 mins. 14 secs. Average for the morning rush hour. Petrol consumption: 17.26 m.p.g. Not bad—would have been better if he hadn't put the Toyota in its place.

Vic pushes through the swing doors to the reception lobby, a reasonably impressive space, its walls lined with light oak panelling installed in a more prosperous era. The furniture is looking a bit shabby, though. The clock on the wall, an irritating type with no numbers on its face, suggests that the time is just before half-past eight. Doreen and Lesley, the two telephonist-receptionists, are taking off their coats behind the counter. They smile and simper, patting their hair and smoothing their skirts.

"Morning Mr. Wilcox."

"Morning. Think we could do with some new chairs in here?"

"Oh yes, Mr. Wilcox, these are ever so hard."

"I didn't mean *your* chairs, I mean for visitors."

"Oh . . ." They don't know quite how to react. He is still Mr. New Broom, slightly feared. As he pushes through the swing doors and walks down the corridor towards his office, he can hear them spluttering with stifled laughter.

"Good morning, Vic." His secretary, Shirley, smirks from behind her desk, self-righteous at being at her post before the boss, even though she is at this moment inspecting her face in a compact mirror. She is a mature woman with piled hair of an improbable yellow hue, and a voluptuous bosom on which her reading glasses, retained round her neck by a chain, rest as upon a shelf. Vic inherited her from his predecessor, who had evidently cultivated an informal working relationship. It was not with any encouragement from himself that she began to address him as Vic, but he was obliged to concede the point. She had worked for Pringle's for years, and Vic was heavily dependent on her know-how while he eased himself into the job.

"Morning, Shirley. Make us a cup of coffee, will you?" Vic's working day is lubricated by endless cups of instant coffee. He hangs up his camelhair coat in the anteroom that connects his office with Shirley's, and passes into the former. He shrugs off the jacket of his suit and drapes it over the back of a chair. He sits down at his desk and opens his diary. Shirley comes in with coffee and a large photograph album.

"I thought you'd like to see Tracey's new portfolio," she says.

Shirley has a seventeen-year-old daughter whose ambition is to be a photographic model, and she is forever thrusting glossy pictures of this well-developed young hussy, crammed into skimpy swimsuits or revealing underwear, under Vic's nose. At first, he suspected her of trying to curry favour by pandering to his lust, but later came to the conclusion that it was genuine parental pride. The silly bitch really couldn't see that there was anything dubious about turning your daughter into a pin-up.

"Oh yes?" he says, with scarcely concealed impatience. Then, as he opens the portfolio: "Good Christ!"

The pouting, weak-chinned face under the blonde curls is familiar enough, but the two huge naked breasts, thrust towards the camera like pink blancmanges tipped with cherries, are a new departure. He turns the stiff, polythene-covered pages rapidly.

"Nice, aren't they?" says Shirley fondly.

"You let someone take pictures of your daughter like this?"

"I was there sort of thing. In the studio."

"I'll be frank with you," says Vic, closing the album and handing it back. "I wouldn't let *my* daughter."

"I don't see the harm," says Shirley. "People think nothing of it nowadays, topless sort of thing. You should have seen the beach at Rhodes last summer. And even television. If you've got a beautiful body, why not make the most of it? Look at Sam Fox!"

"Who's he?"

"She. Samantha Fox. You *know!*" Incredulity raises Shirley's voice an octave. "The top Page Three girl. D'you know how much she earned last year?"

"More than me, I don't doubt. And more than Pringle's will make this year, if you waste any more of my time."

"Oh, you," says Shirley roguishly, adept at receiving reprimands as if they are jokes.

"Tell Brian I want to see him, will you?"

"I don't think he's in yet."

Vic grunts, unsurprised that his Marketing Director has not yet arrived. "As soon as he is, then. Let's do some letters in the meantime."

The telephone rings. Vic picks up the receiver. "Wilcox."

"Vic?"

The voice of Stuart Baxter, chairman of Midland Amalgamated's Engineering and Foundry Division, sounds faintly disappointed. He was hoping, no doubt, to be told that Mr. Wilcox wasn't in yet, so that he could leave a message for Vic to ring back, thus putting him on the defensive, knowing that his divisional chief knew that he, Vic, hadn't been at his desk as early as him, Stuart Baxter. Vic becomes even more convinced that this was the motive for the call as it proceeds, because Stuart Baxter has nothing new to communicate. They had the same conversation the previous Friday afternoon, about the disappointing figures for Pringle's production in December.

"There's always a downturn in December, Stuart, you know that. With the long Christmas holiday."

"Even allowing for that, it's well down, Vic. Compared to last year."

"And it's going to be well down again this month, you might as well know that now."

"I'm sorry to hear you say that, Vic. It makes life very difficult for me."

"We haven't got the foundry on song, yet. The core blowers are always breaking down. I'd like to buy a new machine, fully automated, to replace the lot."

"Too expensive. You'd do better to buy in from outside. It's not worth investing in that foundry."

"The foundry has a lot of potential. It's a good workforce. They do nice work. Any road, it's not just the foundry. We're working on a new production model for the whole factory—new stock control, new purchasing policy. Everything on computer. But it takes time."

"Time is what we haven't got, Vic."

"Right. So why don't we both get back to work now, instead of nattering on like a couple of housewives over the garden fence?"

There is a momentary silence on the line, then a forced chuckle, as Stuart

Baxter decides not to take offence. Nevertheless he *has* taken offence. It was probably a foolish thing to say, but Vic shrugs off any regret as he puts the receiver down. He is not in the business of ingratiating himself with Stuart Baxter. He is in the business of making J. Pringle & Sons profitable.

Vic flicks a switch on his telephone console and summons Shirley, whom he had gestured out of the office while Baxter was talking, to take some letters. He leafs through the file of correspondence in his In-tray, the two vertical lines in his brow above the nose drawing closer together as he concentrates on names, figures, dates. He lights a cigarette, inhales deeply, and blows two plumes of smoke through his nostrils. Outside the sky is still overcast, and the murky yellow light that filters through the vertical louvres of the window blinds is hardly enough to read by. He switches on his desk lamp, casting a pool of light on the documents. Through walls and windows comes a muffled compound noise of machinery and traffic, the soothing, satisfying sound of men at work.

2

And there, for the time being, let us leave Vic Wilcox, while we travel back an hour or two in time, a few miles in space, to meet a very different character. A character who, rather awkwardly for me, doesn't herself believe in the concept of character. That is to say (a favourite phrase of her own), Robyn Penrose, Temporary Lecturer in English Literature at the University of Rummidge, holds that "character" is a bourgeois myth, an illusion created to reinforce the ideology of capitalism. As evidence for this assertion she will point to the fact that the rise of the novel (the literary genre of "character" *par excellence*) in the eighteenth century coincided with the rise of capitalism; that the triumph of the novel over all other literary genres in the nineteenth century coincided with the triumph of capitalism; and that the modernist and postmodernist deconstruction of the classic novel in the twentieth century has coincided with the terminal crisis of capitalism.

Why the classic novel should have collaborated with the spirit of capitalism is perfectly obvious to Robyn. Both are expressions of a secularised Protestant ethic, both dependent on the idea of an autonomous individual self who is responsible for and in control of his/her own destiny, seeking happiness and fortune in competition with other autonomous selves. This is true of the novel considered both as commodity and as mode of representation. (Thus Robyn in full seminar spate.) That is to say, it applies to novelists themselves as well as to their heroes and heroines. The novelist is a capitalist of the imagination. He or she invents a product which consumers didn't know they wanted until it was made available, manufactures it with the assistance of purveyors of risk capital known as publishers, and sells it in competition with makers of marginally differentiated products of the same kind. The first major English novelist, Daniel Defoe, was a merchant. The second, Samuel Richardson, was a printer. The novel was the first mass-produced cultural artefact. (At this point Robyn, with elbows tucked into her sides, would spread her hands outwards from the wrist, as if to imply that there is no need to say more. But of course she always has much more to say.)

According to Robyn (or, more precisely, according to the writers who have influenced her thinking on these matters) there is no such thing as the "self" on which capitalism and the classic novel are founded—that is to say, a finite, unique soul or essence that constitutes a person's identity; there is only a subject position in an infinite web of discourses—the discourses of power, sex, family, science, religion, poetry, etc. And by the same token, there is no such thing as an author, that is to say, one who originates a work of fiction *ab nihilo*. Every text is a product of intertextuality, a tissue of allusions to and citations of other texts; and, in the famous words of Jacques Derrida (famous to people like Robyn, anyway), "*il n'y a pas de hors-texte*," there is nothing outside the text. There are no origins, there is only production, and we produce our "selves" in language. Not "*you are what you eat*" but "*you are what you speak*" or, rather "*you are what speaks you*," is the axiomatic basis of Robyn's philosophy, which she would call, if required to give it a name, "semiotic materialism." It might seem a bit bleak, a bit inhuman ("antihumanist, yes; inhuman, no," she would interject), somewhat deterministic ("not at all; the truly determined subject is he who is not aware of the discursive formations that determine him. Or her," she would add scrupulously, being among other things a feminist), but in practise this doesn't seem to affect her behaviour very noticeably—she seems to have ordinary human feelings, ambitions, desires, to suffer anxieties, frustrations, fears, like anyone else in this imperfect world, and to have a natural inclination to try and make it a better place. I shall therefore take the liberty of treating her as a character, not utterly different in kind, though of course belonging to a very different social species, from Vic Wilcox.

Robyn rises somewhat later than Vic this dark January Monday. Her alarm clock, a replica of an old-fashioned instrument purchased from Habitat, with an analogue dial and a little brass bell on the top, rouses her from a deep sleep at 7:30. Unlike Vic, Robyn invariably sleeps until woken. Then worries rush into her consciousness, as into his, like clamorous patients who have been waiting all night for the doctor's surgery to open; but she deals with them in a rational, orderly manner. This morning she gives priority to the fact that it is the first day of the winter term, and that she has a lecture to deliver and two tutorials to conduct. Although she has been teaching now for some eight years, on and off, although she enjoys it, feels she is good at it, and would like to go on doing it for the rest of her life if possible, she always feels a twinge of anxiety at the beginning of a new term. This does not disturb her self-confidence: a good teacher, like a good actress, should not be immune from stage fright. She sits up in bed for a moment, doing some complicated breathing and flexing of the abdominal muscles, learned in yoga classes, to calm herself. This exercise is rendered easier to perform by the fact that Charles is not lying beside her to observe and ask ironic questions about it. He left the previous evening to drive to Ipswich, where his own term is due to begin today at the University of Suffolk.

And who is Charles? While Robyn is getting up, and getting ready for the day, thinking mostly about the nineteenth-century industrial novels on which she has to lecture this morning, I will tell you about Charles, and other salient facts of her biography.

. . .

She was born, and christened Roberta Anne Penrose, in Melbourne, Australia, nearly thirty-three years ago, but left that country at the age of five to accompany her parents to England. Her father, then a young academic historian, had a scholarship to pursue post-doctoral research into nineteenth-century European diplomacy at Oxford. Instead of returning to Australia, he took a post at a university on the South Coast of England, where he has been ever since, now occupying a personal Chair. Robyn has only the dimmest memories of the country of her birth, and has never had the opportunity to refresh or renew them, Professor Penrose's characteristic response to any suggestion that the family should revisit Australia being a shudder.

Robyn had a comfortable childhood, growing up in a pleasant, unostentatious house with a view of the sea. She attended an excellent direct-grant grammar school (which has since gone independent, much to Robyn's disgust) where she was Head Girl and Captain of Games and which she left with four A grades at A-Level. Though urged by the school to apply for a place at Oxbridge, she chose instead to go to Sussex University, as bright young people often did in the 1970s, because the new universities were considered exciting and innovatory places to study at. Under the umbrella of a degree course in English Literature, Robyn read Freud and Marx, Kafka and Kierkegaard, which she certainly couldn't have done at Oxbridge. She also set about losing her virginity, and accomplished this feat without difficulty, but without much pleasure, in her first term. In her second, she was recklessly promiscuous, and in her third she met Charles.

(Robyn kicks off the duvet and gets out of bed. She stands upright in her long white cotton nightgown from Laura Ashley, scratches her bottom through the cambric, and yawns. She goes to the window, treating the rugs spread on the sanded and waxed pine floorboards as stepping-stones, pulls back the curtain, and peers out. She looks up at the grey clouds scudding across the sky, down at a vista of narrow back gardens, some neat and trim with goldfish ponds and brightly painted play equipment, others tatty and neglected, cluttered with broken appliances and discarded furniture. It is an upwardly mobile street of nineteenth-century terraced cottages, where house-proud middle-class owners rub shoulders with less tidy and less affluent working-class occupiers. A gust of wind rattles the sash window and the draught makes Robyn shiver. She has not double-glazed the house in order to preserve its architectural integrity. Clutching herself, she skips to the door from rug to rug, like a Scottish country dancer, across the landing and into the bathroom, which has smaller windows and is warmer.)

The Sussex campus, with its tastefully harmonised buildings in the modernist-Palladian style, arranged in elegant perspective at the foot of the South Downs a few miles outside Brighton, was much admired by architects, but had a somewhat disorienting effect on the young people who came to study there. Toiling up the slope from Falmer railway station, you had the Kafkaesque sensation of walking into an endlessly deep stage set where apparently three-dimensional objects turned out to be painted flats, and reality receded as fast as you pursued it. Cut off from normal social intercourse with the adult world, relieved of inhibition by the ethos of the Permissive Society, the students were apt to run wild, indulging in promiscuous sex and experimenting with drugs, or else turned melancholy mad. Robyn's generation, coming up to university in the early 1970s, immediately after the heroic period of student politics, were oppressed by a sense of belatedness. There were no significant rights left to demand, no taboos left to break. Student demonstrations developed an ugly edge of gratuitous violence. So did student parties. In this climate, shrewd and sensitive individuals with an instinct for self-preservation looked around for a partner and pair-bonded. By living in what their parents called sin, they nailed their colours to the mast of youthful revolt, while enjoying the security and mutual support of old-fashioned matrimony. Sussex, some longhaired, denim-clad veteran of the sixties complained, was looking more and more like a housing estate for first-time buyers. It was full of couples holding hands and plastic carrier bags that were as likely to contain laundry and groceries as books and revolutionary pamphlets. One of these couples consisted of Robyn and Charles. She had looked around, and chosen him. He was clever, personable, and, she thought, probably loyal (she had not been proved wrong). It was true that he had been educated at a public school, but he managed to disguise this handicap very well.

(Robyn, her white nightdress billowing round her hips, sits on the loo and pees, mentally rehearsing the plot of Mrs. Gaskell's *Mary Barton* (1848). Rising from the toilet, she pulls the nightdress over her head and steps into the bath, not first pulling the chain of the toilet because that would affect the temperature of the water coming through the showerhead on the end of its flexible tube, with which she now hoses herself down. She palpates her breasts as she washes, checking for lumps. She steps from the bath, stretching for a towel in one of those ungainly, intimate postures so beloved of Impressionist painters and deplored by the feminist art historians Robyn admires. She is tall and womanly in shape, slender of waist, with smallish round breasts, heavier about the hips and buttocks.)

In their second year, Robyn and Charles moved off campus and set up house in a small flat in Brighton, commuting to the University by local train. Robyn took an active part in student politics. She ran successfully for the Vice-Presidentship of the Student Union. She organized an all-night telephone counselling service for students in despair about their grades or love-lives. She spoke frequently in the Debating Society in favour of progressive causes such as abortion, animal rights, state education and nuclear disarmament. Charles led a more subdued and private life. He kept the flat tidy while Robyn was out doing good works, and always had a cup of cocoa or a bowl of soup ready for her when she returned home, tired but invariably triumphant. At the end of the first term of her third year, Robyn resigned from all her commitments in order to prepare for Finals. She and Charles worked hard and, despite the fact that they were pursuing the same course, without rivalry. In their Final Examinations, Robyn obtained a First—her marks, she was unofficially informed, were the highest ever achieved by a student in the School of European Studies in its short history—and Charles an extremely high Upper Second. Charles was not jealous. He was used to living in the shade of Robyn's achievements. And in any case his degree was good enough to earn him, as Robyn's did for her, a Major State Studentship to do post-graduate research. The idea of doing research and pursuing an academic career was common ground to both of them; indeed they had never considered any alternative.

They had got used to living in Brighton, and saw no reason to uproot themselves, but one of their tutors took them aside and said, "Look, this place hasn't got a proper research library, and it's not going to get one. Go to Oxbridge." He had seen the writing on the wall: after the oil crisis of 1973 there wasn't going to be enough money to keep all the universities enthusiastically created or expanded in the booming sixties in the style to which they had become accustomed. Not many people perceived this quite so soon.

(Robyn, a dressing-gown over her underclothes and slippers on her feet, descends the short dark staircase to the ground floor and goes into her narrow and extremely untidy kitchen. She lights the gas stove, and makes herself a breakfast of muesli, wholemeal toast and decaffeinated coffee. She thinks about the structure of Disraeli's *Sybil; or, the Two Nations* (1845), until the sound of the *Guardian* dropping onto the doormat sends her scurrying to the front door.)

So Robyn and Charles went to Cambridge to do their PhDs. Intellectually it was an exciting time to be a research student in the English Faculty. New ideas imported from Paris by the more adventurous young teachers glittered like dustmotes in the Fenland air: structuralism and poststructuralism, semiotics and deconstruction, new mutations and graftings of psychoanalysis and Marxism, linguistics and literary criticism. The more conservative dons viewed these ideas and their proponents with alarm, seeing in them a threat to the traditional values and methods of literary scholarship. Battle was joined, in seminars, lectures, committee meetings and the review pages of scholarly journals. It was revolution. It was civil war. Robyn threw herself enthusiastically into the struggle, on the radical side naturally. It was like the sixties all over again, in a new, more austerely intellectual key. She subscribed to the journals *Poètique* and *Tel Quel* so that she could be the first person on the Trumpington Road to know the latest thoughts of Roland Barthes and Julia Kristeva. She forced her mind through the labyrinthine sentences of Jacques Lacan and Jacques Derrida until her eyes were bloodshot and her head ached. She sat in lecture theatres and nodded eager agreement as the Young Turks of the Faculty demolished the idea of the author, the idea of the self, the idea of establishing a single, univocal meaning for a literary text. All this of course took up a great deal of time and delayed the completion of Robyn's thesis on the nineteenth-century industrial novel, which had to be constantly revised to take the new theories into account.

Charles was not quite so committed to the new wave. He supported it, naturally—otherwise he and Robyn could hardly have continued to co-habit— but in a more detached spirit. He chose a subject for his PhD—the idea of the Sublime in Romantic poetics—which sounded reassuringly serious to the traditionalists and off-puttingly dry to the Young Turks, but which neither party knew much about, so Charles was not drawn into the front-line contro- versy in his own research. He delivered his dissertation on time, was awarded his doctorate, and was lucky enough to obtain a lectureship in the Compara- tive Literature Department at the University of Suffolk, "the last new job in Romanticism this century," as he was wont to describe it, with justifiable hyperbole.

(Robyn scans the front-page headline of the *Guardian*, "LAWSON DRAWN INTO FRAY OVER WESTLAND," but does not linger over the text beneath. It is enough for her to know that things are going badly for Mrs. Thatcher and the Tory party; the details of the Westland affair do not engage her interest. She turns at once to the Women's page, where there is a Posy Simmonds strip cartoon adroitly satirising middle-aged, middle-class liberals, an article on the iniquities of the Unborn Children (Protection) Bill, and a report on the struggle for women's liberation in Portugal. These she reads with the kind of pure, trance-like attention that she used to give, as a child, to the stories of Enid Blyton. A column entitled "Bulletin" informs her that Marilyn French will be discussing her new book, *Beyond Power: Women, Men and Morals,* at a public meeting to be held later in the week in London, and it crosses Robyn's mind, not for the first time, that it is a pity she lives so far from the metropo- lis where such exciting events are always happening. This thought reminds her of why she is living in Rummidge, namely her job, and makes her guiltily aware that time is passing. She puts her soiled breakfast things in the sink, already crammed with the relics of last night's supper, and hurries upstairs.)

Charles' success in landing a job provoked in Robyn the first twinge of jealousy, the first spasm of pique, to mar their relationship. She had grown used to being the dominant partner, the teachers' favourite, the Victrix Ludorum. Her grant had expired, and she was still some way off completing her PhD dissertation. However, she had her sights fixed on higher things than the University of Suffolk, a new "plateglass" university with a reputation for student vandalism. Her supervisor and other friends in the Faculty encouraged her to think that she would get an appointment at Cambridge eventually if she could hang on. She hung on for two years, existing on fees for supervising undergraduates and an allowance from her father. She finished, at last, her thesis, and was awarded her PhD. She competed successfully for a post-doctoral research fellowship at one of the less fashionable women's colleges. It was for three years only, but it was a promising stepping-stone to a proper appointment. She got a contract to turn her thesis on the Industrial Novel into a book, and settled enthusiastically to the task. Her personal life did not change much. Charles continued to live with her in Cambridge, commuting by car to Ipswich to teach his classes, and staying there for a night or two each week.

Then, in 1981, all hell broke loose in the Cambridge English Faculty. An extremely public row about the denial of tenure to a young lecturer associated with the progressive party opened old wounds and inflicted new ones on this always thin-skinned community. Long-standing friendships were broken, new enmities established. Insults and libel suits were exchanged. Robyn was almost ill with excitement and outrage. For a few weeks the controversy featured in the national and even international press, up-market newspapers carrying spicy stories about the leading protagonists and confused attempts to explain the difference between structuralism and poststructuralism to the man on the Clapham omnibus. To Robyn it seemed that critical theory had at last moved to its rightful place, centre-stage, in the theatre of history, and she was ready to play her part in the drama. She put her name down to speak in the great debate about the state of the English Faculty that was held in the University Senate; and in the *Cambridge University Reporter* for 18th February, 1981, occupying a column and half of small print, sandwiched between contributions from two of the University's most distinguished professors, you may find Robyn's impassioned plea for a radical theorisation of the syllabus.

(Robyn straightens the sheet on the bed, shakes and spreads the duvet. She sits at her dressing-table and vigorously brushes her hair, a mop of copper-coloured curls, natural curls, as tight and springy as coiled steel. Some would say her hair is her finest feature, though Robyn herself secretly hankers after something more muted and malleable, hair that could be groomed and styled according to mood—drawn back in a severe bun like Simone de Beauvoir's, or allowed to fall to the shoulders in a Pre-Raphaelite cloud. As it is, there is not much she can do with her curls except, every now and again, crop them brutally short just to demonstrate how inadequately they represent her character. Her face is comely enough to take short hair, though perfectionists might say that the grey-green eyes are a little close-set, and the nose and chin are a centimetre longer than Robyn herself would have wished. Now she rubs moisturiser into her facial skin as protection against the raw wintry air outside, coats her lips with lip-salve, and brushes some green eyeshadow on her eyelids, pondering shifts of point of view in Charles Dickens' *Hard Times* (1854). Her simple cosmetic operations completed, she dresses herself in opaque green tights, a wide brown tweed skirt and a thick sweater loosely knitted in muted shades of orange, green and brown. Robyn generally favours loose dark clothes, made of natural fibres, that do not make her body into an object of sexual attention. The way they are cut also disguises her smallish breasts and widish hips while making the most of her height: thus are ideology and vanity equally satisfied. She contemplates her image in the long looking-glass by the window, and decides that the effect is a little too sombre. She rummages in her jewellery box where brooches, necklaces and earrings are jumbled together with enamel lapel badges expressing support for various radical causes—*Support the Miners, Crusade for Jobs, Legalise Pot, A Woman's Right To Choose*—and selects a silver brooch in which the CND symbol and the Yin sign are artfully entwined. She pins it to her bosom. She takes from the bottom of her wardrobe a pair of calf-length fashion boots in dark brown leather and sits on the edge of the bed to pull them on.)

When the dust settled in Cambridge, however, it seemed that the party of reaction had triumphed. A University committee charged to investigate the case of the young lecturer determined that there had been no administrative malpractice. The man himself departed to take up a more remunerative and prestigious post elsewhere, and his friends and supporters fell silent, or retired, or resigned and took jobs in America. One of the latter group, somewhat the worse for drink at his farewell party, advised Robyn to get out of

Cambridge too. "This place is finished," he said, meaning that Cambridge would be a less interesting place for his own absence from it. "Anyway, you'll never get a job here, Robyn. You're a marked woman."

Robyn decided she would not put this gloomy prediction to further test. Her research fellowship was coming to an end, and she could not bear the prospect of "hanging on" for another year as a freelance supervisor of undergraduates, sponging on her parents. She began to look for a university job outside Cambridge.

But there were no jobs. While Robyn had been preoccupied with the issues of contemporary literary theory and its repercussions on the Cambridge English Faculty, the Conservative Government of Mrs. Thatcher, elected in 1979 with a mandate to cut public spending, had set about decimating the national system of higher education. Universities everywhere were in disarray, faced with swingeing cuts in their funding. Required to reduce their academic staff by anything up to 20 per cent, they responded by persuading as many people as possible to take early retirement and freezing all vacancies. Robyn considered herself lucky to get a job for one term at one of the London colleges, deputising for a woman lecturer on maternity leave. There followed an awful period of nearly a year when she was unemployed, searching the back pages of the *Times Higher Educational Supplement* in vain every week for lectureships in nineteenth-century English Literature.

The previously unthinkable prospect of a non-academic career now began to be thought—with fear, dismay and bewilderment on Robyn's part. Of course she was aware, cognitively, that there was a life outside universities, but she knew nothing about it, nor did Charles, or her parents. Her younger brother, Basil, in his final year of Modern Greats at Oxford, spoke of going into the City when he graduated, but Robyn considered this was just talk, designed to ward off *hubris* about his forthcoming examinations, or an Oedipal teasing of his academic father. When she tried to imagine herself working in an office or a bank, her mind soon went blank, like a cinema screen when the projector breaks down or the film snaps. There was always schoolteaching, of course, but that would entail the tiresome business of acquiring a Postgraduate Certificate of Education, or else working in the independent sector, to which she had ideological objections. In any case, teaching English literature to schoolchildren would only remind her daily of the superior satisfactions of teaching it to young adults.

Then, in 1984, just when Robyn was beginning to despair, the job at

Rummidge came up. Professor Philip Swallow, Head of the English Department at Rummidge University, had been elected Dean of the Arts Faculty for a three-year term; and since the duties of this office, added to his Departmental responsibilities, drastically reduced his contribution to undergraduate teaching, he was by tradition allowed to appoint a temporary lecturer, at the lower end of the salary scale, as what was quaintly termed "Dean's Relief." Thus a three-year lectureship in English Literature was advertised, Robyn applied, was interviewed along with four other equally desperate and highly qualified candidates, and was appointed.

Glory! Jubilation! Huge sighs of relief. Charles met Robyn off the train from Rummidge with a bottle of champagne in his hand. The three years stretching ahead seemed like a long time, then, worth buying a little house in Rummidge for (Robyn's father lent her the money for the deposit) rather than paying rent. Besides, Robyn had faith that, somehow or other, she would be kept on when her temporary appointment came to an end. She was confident that she could make her mark on the Rummidge Department in three years. She knew she was good, and it wasn't long before she privately concluded that she was better than most of her colleagues—more enthusiastic, more energetic, more productive. When she arrived she had already published several articles and reviews in academic journals, and shortly afterwards her much-revised thesis appeared under the imprint of Lecky, Windrush and Bernstein. Entitled *The Industrious Muse: Narrativity and Contradiction in the Industrial Novel* (the title was foisted on her by the publishers, the subtitle was her own) it received enthusiastic if sparse reviews, and the publishers commissioned another book provisionally entitled, *Domestic Angels and Unfortunate Females: Woman as Sign and Commodity in Victorian Fiction.* She was a popular and conscientious teacher, whose optional courses on women's writing were over-subscribed. She performed her share of administrative duties efficiently. Surely they couldn't just let her go at the end of the three years?

(Robyn goes into her long narrow living-room, formed by knocking down the dividing wall between the front and back parlours of the little house, which also serves as her study. There are books and periodicals everywhere— on shelves, on tables, on the floor—posters and reproductions of modern paintings on the walls, parched-looking potted plants in the fireplace, a BBC micro and monitor on the desk, and beside it sheaves of dot-matrix type-script of early chapters of *Domestic Angels and Unfortunate Females* in various drafts. Robyn picks her way across the floor, putting her shapely boots down carefully in the spaces between books, back numbers of *Critical Inquiry* and *Women's Review*, LP albums by Bach, Philip Glass and Phil Collins (her musical tastes are eclectic) and the occasional wineglass or coffee cup, to the desk. She lifts from the floor a leather Gladstone bag, and begins to load it with the things she will need for the day: well-thumbed, much underlined and annotated copies of *Shirley, Mary Barton, North and South, Sybil, Alton Locke, Felix Holt, Hard Times*; her lecture notes—a palimpsest of holograph revisions in different-coloured inks, beneath which the original typescript is scarcely legible; and a thick sheaf of student essays marked over the Christmas vacation.

Returning to the kitchen, Robyn turns down the thermostat of the central heating and checks that the back door of the house is locked and bolted. In the hall she wraps a long scarf round her neck and puts on a cream-coloured quilted cotton jacket, with wide shoulders and inset sleeves, and lets herself out by the front door. Outside, in the street, her car is parked, a red six-year-old Renault Five with a yellow sticker in its rear window, *"Britain Needs Its Universities."* It was formerly her parents' second car, sold to Robyn at a bargain price when her mother replaced it. It runs well, though the battery is getting feeble. Robyn turns the ignition key, holding her breath as she listens to the starter's bronchial wheeze, then exhales with relief as the engine fires.)

Three years didn't seem such a long time when one of them had elapsed, and although Robyn was satisfied that she was highly valued by her colleagues, the talk at the University these days was all of further cuts, of tightening belts, deteriorating staff–student ratios. Still, she was optimistic. Robyn was naturally optimistic. She had faith in her star. Nevertheless, the future of her career was a constant background worry as the days and weeks of her appointment at Rummidge ticked away like a taxi meter. Another was her relationship with Charles.

What was it, exactly, this relationship? Hard to describe. Not a marriage, and yet more like marriage than many marriages: domesticated, familiar, faithful. There was a time, early in their days at Cambridge, when a brilliant and handsome research student from Yale made a determined pitch for Robyn, and she had been rather dazzled and excited by the experience (he wooed her with a heady mixture of the latest postfreudian theoretical jargon and devastatingly frank sexual propositions, so she was never quite sure whether it was Lacan's symbolic phallus he was referring to or his own real one). But in the end she pulled back from the brink, conscious of Charles' silent but reproachful figure hovering on the edge of her vision. She was too honest to deceive him and too prudent to exchange him for a lover whose interest would probably not last very long.

When Charles obtained his post at Suffolk, there had been a certain amount of pressure from both sets of parents for them to get married. Charles was willing. Robyn indignantly rejected the suggestion. "What are you implying?" she demanded from her mother. "That I should go and keep house for Charles in Ipswich? Give up my PhD and live off Charles and have babies?" "Of course not, dear," said her mother. "There's no reason why you shouldn't still have your own career. If that's what you want." She managed to imbue this last phrase with a certain pitying incomprehension. She herself had never aspired to a career, finding complete satisfaction in acting as her husband's typist and research assistant in the time she had left over from gardening and housekeeping. "Certainly it's what I want," said Robyn, so fiercely that her mother let the subject drop. Robyn had a reputation in the family for being strong-willed, or, as her brother Basil less flatteringly put it, "bossy." There was a much-told tale of her Australian infancy that was held to be prophetic in this respect—about how at the age of three she had, by the sheer force of her will, compelled her uncle Walter (who was taking her for a walk to the local shops at the time) to put all the money he had on his person into a charity collecting-box in the shape of a plaster-of-Paris boy cripple; as a result of which the uncle, too embarrassed to admit to this folly and borrow from his relatives, had run out of petrol on the way back to his sheep station. Robyn herself, needless to say, interpreted this anecdote in a light more favourable to herself, as anticipating her later commitment to progressive causes.

Charles found a *pied-à-terre* in Ipswich and continued to keep his books and most of his other possessions in the flat at Cambridge. Naturally they saw less of each other, and Robyn was aware that this did not cause her to repine as much as perhaps it should have done. She began to wonder if the relationship was not, very very slowly, dying a natural death, and whether it would not be sensible to terminate it quickly. She put this calmly and rationally to Charles one day, and calmly and rationally he accepted it. He said that although he was personally quite happy with things as they were, he understood her doubts and perhaps a trial separation would resolve them one way or the other.

(Robyn drives her red Renault zigzag across the south-west suburbs of Rummidge, sometimes with the flow of rush-hour traffic, sometimes against—though the rush hour is almost over. It is 9:20 a.m. as Robyn reaches the broad tree-lined streets that border the University. She takes a short cut down Avondale Road, and passes the five-bedroom detached house of Vic Wilcox without a glance, for she does not know him from Adam, and the house is outwardly no different from any of the other modern executive dwellings in this exclusive residential district: red brick and white paint, "Georgian" windows, a tarmac drive and double garage, a burglar alarm prominently displayed on the front elevation.)

So Charles moved his books and other possessions to Ipswich, which Robyn found rather inconvenient, since she was in the habit of borrowing his books, and occasionally his sweaters. They remained good friends, of course, and called each other up frequently on the telephone. Sometimes they met for lunch or a theatre in London, on neutral ground, and both looked forward to these meetings as if they were occasions of almost illicit pleasure. Neither was short of opportunities to form new relationships, but somehow neither of them could be bothered to do so. They were both busy people, preoccupied with their work—Robyn with her supervisions and the completion of her PhD, Charles with the demands of his new job—and the thought of having to adjust to another partner, to study their interests and minister to their needs, wearied them in anticipation. There were so many books and periodicals to be read, so many abstruse thoughts to be thought.

There was sex of course, but although both of them were extremely interested in sex, and enjoyed nothing better than discussing it, neither of them, if the truth be told, was quite so interested in actually having it, or at any rate in having it very frequently. They seemed to have burned up all their lust rather rapidly in their undergraduate years. What was left was sex in the head, as D. H. Lawrence called it. He had meant the phrase pejoratively, of course, but to Robyn and Charles D. H. Lawrence was a quaint, rather absurd figure, and his fierce polemics did not disturb them. Where else would the human subject have sex but in the head? Sexual desire was a play of signifiers, an infinite deferment and displacement of anticipated pleasure which the brute coupling of the signifieds temporarily interrupted. Charles himself was not an imperious lover. Calm and svelte, stealthy as a cat in his movements, he seemed to approach sex as a form of research, favouring techniques of foreplay so subtle and prolonged that Robyn occasionally dozed off in the middle of them, and would wake with a guilty start to find him still crouched studiously over her body, fingering it like a box of index cards.

During their trial separation, Robyn became deeply involved in a Women's Group at Cambridge who met regularly but informally to discuss women's writing and feminist literary theory. It was an article of faith with this circle that women must free themselves from the erotic patronage of men. That is to say, it was not true, as every novel, film, and TV commercial implied, that a woman was incomplete without a man. Women could love other women, and themselves. Several members of the group were lesbians, or tried hard to be. Robyn was quite sure she was not; but she enjoyed the warmth and companionship of the group, the hugging and kissing that accompanied their meetings and partings. And if her body occasionally craved a keener sensation, she was able to provide it herself, without shame or guilt, theoretically justified by the writings of radical French feminists like Hélène Cixous and Luce Irigaray, who were very eloquent on the joys of female autoeroticism.

Robyn had two casual heterosexual encounters at this time, both one-night stands after rather drunken parties, both unsatisfactory. She took no new live-in lover, and as far as she was aware, neither did Charles. So then it became a question, what was the point of separation? It was just costing them a lot of money in phone calls and train tickets to London. Charles moved his books and sweaters back to Cambridge and life went on much as before. Robyn continued to give much of her time and emotional energy to the Women's Group, but Charles did not object; after all, he considered himself a feminist too.

But when, two years later, Robyn was appointed to Rummidge, they had to split up again. It was impossible to commute from Rummidge to Ipswich or *vice versa*. The journey, by road or rail, was one of the most tedious and inconvenient it was possible to contrive in the British Isles. To Robyn, it seemed a providential opportunity to make another—this time decisive— break with Charles. Much as she liked him, much as she would miss his companionship, it seemed to her that the relationship had reached a dead end. There was nothing new in it to be discovered, and it was preventing them from making new discoveries elsewhere. It had been a mistake to get together again—a symptom of their immaturity, their enslavement to Cambridge. Yes (she swelled with the certainty of this insight) it had been Cambridge, not desire, that had reunited them. They were both so obsessed with the place, its gossip and rumours and intrigues, that they wanted to spend every possible moment together there, comparing notes, exchanging opinions: who was in, who out, what X said about Y's review of P's book about Q. Well, she was sick and tired of the place, tired of its beautiful architecture housing vanity and paranoia, glad to exchange its hothouse atmosphere for the real if smoky air of Rummidge. And to make the break with Cambridge somehow entailed breaking finally with Charles. She informed him of this conclusion, and with his usual calm he accepted it. Later she wondered if he was counting on her not sticking to her resolution.

Rummidge was a new leaf, a blank page, in Robyn's life. She had at the back of her mind the thought that some new male companion might figure in it. But no such person manifested himself. All the men in the University seemed to be married or gay or scientists, and Robyn had no time or energy to look further afield. She was fully stretched preparing her classes, on a whole new range of subjects, marking her essays, researching *Domestic Angels and Unfortunate Females*, and making herself generally indispensable to the Department. She was fulfilled and happy, but, occasionally, a little lonely. Then sometimes she would pick up the telephone and natter to Charles. One day she rashly invited him to stay for a weekend. She had in mind a purely platonic visit—there was a guestroom in the little house; but in the event, perhaps inevitably, they ended up in bed together. And it was nice to have someone else caress your body, and release the springs of pleasure hidden within it, instead of having to do the job yourself. She had forgotten how nice it was, after so long an interval. It seemed, after all, that they were indispensable to each other; or, if that was putting it too strongly, they fulfilled a mutual need.

They did not go back to "living together" even in the purely conceptual sense of many academic couples they knew, separated by their jobs. When Charles came to visit, he did so as a guest, and when he departed he left no possessions behind him. However, on these occasions they invariably slept together. An odd relationship, undoubtedly. Not a marriage, not a living-together, not an affair. More like a divorce in which the two parties occasionally meet for companionship and sexual pleasure without strings. Robyn is not sure whether this is wonderfully modern and liberated of them, or rather depraved.

. . .

So these are the things that are worrying Robyn Penrose as she drives through the gates of the University, with a nod and a smile to the security man in his little glass sentry box: her lecture on the Industrial Novel, her job future, and her relationship with Charles—in that order of conspicuousness rather than importance. Indeed, her uneasiness about Charles scarcely counts as a conscious worry at all; while the worry about the lecture is, she is well aware, a trivial and mechanical one. It is not that she does not know what to say, it is that there is not enough time to say all she knows. After all, she worked on the nineteenth-century industrial novel for something like ten years, and even after publishing her book she went on accumulating ideas and insights about the subject. She has boxes full of notes and file cards on it. She probably knows more about the nineteenth-century industrial novel than anyone else in the entire world. How can all that knowledge be condensed into a fifty-minute lecture to students who know almost nothing about it? The interests of scholarship and pedagogy are at odds here. What Robyn likes to do is to deconstruct the texts, to probe the gaps and absences in them, to uncover what they are *not* saying, to expose their ideological bad faith, to cut a cross-section through the twisted strands of their semiotic codes and literary conventions. What the students want her to do is to give them some basic facts that will enable them to read the novels as simple straightforward reflections of "reality," and to write simple, straightforward, exam-passing essays about them.

Robyn parks her car in one of the University's landscaped car parks, lugs her Gladstone bag from the front passenger seat, and makes her way to the English Department. Her gait is deliberate and stately. She holds her head erect, her red-gold curls like a torch burning in the grey, misty atmosphere. You would not think her unduly burdened with worries, if you watched her crossing the campus, smiling at people she knows, her eyes bright, her brow unfurrowed. And indeed, she carries them lightly, her worries. She has youth, she has confidence, she regrets nothing.

She passes into the foyer of the Arts Block. Its stairs and passages are crowded with students; the air is loud with their shouts and laughter as they greet each other on the first day of the new term. Outside the Department Office she meets Bob Busby, the Department's representative on the local committee of the Association of University Teachers, pinning a sheet of paper to the AUT noticeboard. The notice is headed "ONE DAY STRIKE—WED. JAN-UARY 15TH." Unbuttoning her coat, and unwinding her scarf, she reads over his shoulder: "*Day of Action . . . protest against cuts . . . erosion of salaries . . . pickets will be mounted at every entrance to the University . . . volunteers should give their names to Departmental representatives . . . other members are asked to stay away from the campus on the Day of Action.*"

"Put me down for picketing, Bob," says Robyn.

Bob Busby, who is having trouble digging a drawing-pin out of the noticeboard, swivels his black beard towards her. "Really? That's jolly decent of you."

"Why?"

"Well, you know, a young temporary lecturer . . ." Bob Busby looks slightly embarrassed. "No one would blame you if you wanted to keep a low profile."

Robyn snorts indignantly. "It's a matter of principle!"

"Right then. I'll put you down." He resumes work on the drawing-pin.

"Good morning, Bob. Good morning, Robyn."

They turn to face Philip Swallow, who has evidently just arrived, since he is wearing his rather grubby anorak and carrying a battered briefcase. He is a tall, thin, stooped man, with silvery grey hair, deeply receding at the temples, curling over his collar at the back. Robyn has been told that he once had a beard, and he is forever fingering his chin as if he missed it.

"Oh, hallo, Philip," says Bob Busby. Robyn merely says, "Hallo." She is always uncertain how to address her Head of Department. "Philip" seems too familiar, "Professor Swallow" too formal, "Sir" impossibly servile.

"Had a good vac, both of you? All set to return to the fray? Jolly good." Philip Swallow utters these platitudes without waiting for, or appearing to expect, a reply. "What are you up to, Bob?" His face falls as he reads the heading of the notice. "Do you really think a strike is going to do any good?"

"It will if everyone rallies round," says Bob Busby. "Including those who voted 'Against' in the ballot."

"I was one of them, I don't mind admitting," says Philip Swallow.

"Why?" Robyn boldly interjects. "We must *do* something about the cuts. Not just accept them as if they're inevitable. We must protest."

"Agreed," says Philip Swallow. "I just doubt the effectiveness of a strike. Who will notice? It's not as if we're like bus drivers or air traffic controllers. I fear the general public will find they can get along quite well without universities for a day."

"They'll notice the pickets," says Bob Busby.

"A very sticky wicket," says Philip Swallow.

"Pickets. I said, they'll notice the pickets," says Bob Busby, raising his voice against the surrounding hubbub.

"Hmm, mounting pickets, are we? Going the whole hog." Philip Swallow shakes his head, looking rather miserable. Then, with a slightly furtive glance at Robyn, "Have you got a moment?"

"Yes, of course." She follows him into his office.

"Have a good vac?" he says again, divesting himself of his coat.

"Yes, thanks."

"Do sit down. Go anywhere interesting? North Africa? Winter sports?" He grins encouragingly, as if to intimate that a positive reply would cheer him up.

"Good Lord, no."

"I hear they have very cheap packages to the Gambia in January."

"I couldn't afford the time, even if I had the money," says Robyn. "I had a lot of marking to catch up on. Then I was interviewing all last week."

"Yes, of course."

"What about you?"

"Oh, well, I, er, don't do admissions any more. Used to, of course—"

"No," says Robyn, smiling. "I mean, did *you* go anywhere interesting?"

"Ah. I had an invitation to a conference in Florida," says Philip Swallow wistfully. "But I couldn't get a travel grant."

"Oh dear, what a shame," says Robyn, without being able to work up much genuine compassion for this misfortune.

According to Rupert Sutcliffe, the most senior member of the Department, and its most pertinacious gossip, there was a time not so long ago when Philip Swallow was forever swanning around the globe on some conference jaunt or other. Now it seems that the cuts have clipped his wings. "And quite right, too," Rupert Sutcliffe declared. "A waste of time and money, in my opinion, those conferences. *I've* never attended an international conference in my life." Robyn nodded polite approval of this abstention, while privately guessing that Rupert Sutcliffe had not been embarrassed by a large number of invitations. "Mind you," Sutcliffe added, "I don't think it's just lack of funds that has kept him at home lately. I have a hunch that Hilary read him the riot act."

"Mrs. Swallow?"

"Yes. He used to get up to all kinds of high jinks on those trips, by all accounts. I suppose I ought to tell you: Swallow has a bit of a weakness where women are concerned. Forewarned is forearmed." Sutcliffe tapped the side of his long nose with his index finger as he uttered these words, dislodging his spectacles and causing them to crash into his tea-cup—for this conversation took place in the Senior Common Room, not long after Robyn's arrival at Rummidge. Looking at Philip Swallow now, as he seats himself in a low, upholstered chair facing her, Robyn has difficulty in recognising the jet-set philanderer of Rupert Sutcliffe's description. Swallow looks tired and care-worn and slightly seedy. She wonders why he has invited her into his office. He smiles nervously at her and combs a phantom beard with his fingers. Suddenly a portentous atmosphere has been established.

"I just wanted to say, Robyn . . . As you know, your present appointment is a temporary one."

Robyn's heart leaps with hope. "Yes," she says, interlocking her hands to stop them from trembling.

"For three years only. You're a third of the way into your second year, with another full year still to run from next September." He states these facts slowly and carefully, as if they might somehow have slipped her mind.

"Yes."

"I just wanted to say that, we would of course be very sorry to lose you, you've been a tremendous asset to the Department, even in the short time you've been here. I really mean that."

"Thank you," says Robyn dully, untwining her fingers. "But?"

"But?"

"I think you were going to say something beginning with *But*."

"Oh. Ah. Yes. But I just wanted to say that I, we, shouldn't at all blame you if you were to start applying for jobs elsewhere now."

"There aren't any other jobs."

"Well, not at this moment in time, perhaps. But you never know, something may turn up later in the year. If so, perhaps you should go in for it. I mean, you shouldn't feel under any obligation to complete the three years of your contract here. Much as we should regret losing you," he says again.

"What you mean is: there's no chance of my being kept on after the three years are up."

Philip Swallow spreads his hands and shrugs. "No chance at all, as far as I can see. The University is desperate to save on salaries. They're talking about another round of early retirements. Even if someone were to leave the Department, or drop dead—even if you were to, what's the expression, take out a contract on one of us"—he laughs to show that this is a joke, displaying a number of chipped and discoloured teeth, set in his gums at odd angles, like tombstones in a neglected churchyard—"even then, I very much doubt whether we should get a replacement. Being Dean, you see, I'm very aware of the financial constraints on the University. Every day I have the Heads of other Departments in here bellyaching about lack of resources, asking for replacements or new appointments. I have to tell them that the only way we can meet our targets is an absolute freeze. It's very hard for young people in your position. Believe me, I do sympathise."

He reaches out and puts a hand comfortingly on Robyn's pair. She looks at the three hands with detachment, as if they are a still life. Is this the long-delayed, much-heralded pass? Is there a promotions-and-appointments couch somewhere in the room? It seems not, for Philip Swallow immediately removes his hand, stands up and moves to the window. "It's no fun being Dean, these days, I can tell you. All you do is give people bad news. And, as Shakespeare observed, the nature of bad news infects the teller."

"When it concerns the fool or coward." Robyn recklessly recites the next line from *Anthony and Cleopatra*, but fortunately Philip Swallow appears not to have heard. He is staring down gloomily into the central quadrangle of the campus.

"I feel as if, by the time I retire, I shall have lived through the entire life-cycle of post-war higher education. When I was a student myself, provincial universities like Rummidge were a very small show. Then in the sixties, it was all expansion, growth, new building. Would you believe our biggest grouse in the sixties was about the noise of construction work? Now it's all gone quiet. Won't be long before they're sending in the demolition crews, no doubt."

"I'm surprised you don't support the strike, then," says Robyn tartly. But Philip Swallow evidently thinks she said something entirely different.

"Exactly. It's like the Big Bang theory of the universe. They say that at a certain point it will stop expanding and start contracting again, back into the original primal seed. The Robbins Report was our Big Bang. Now we've gone into reverse."

Robyn glances surreptitiously at her watch.

"Or perhaps we've strayed into a black hole," Philip Swallow continues, evidently enchanted with his flight of astronomical fancy.

"If you'll excuse me," says Robyn, getting to her feet. "I have to get ready for a lecture."

"Yes, yes, of course. I'm sorry."

"It's all right, only I—"

"Yes, yes, my fault entirely. Don't forget your bag." With smiles, with nods, with evident relief that an awkward interview is over, Philip Swallow ushers her out of his office.

Bob Busby is still busy at his bulletin board, rearranging old notices around the new one, like a fussy gardener tidying a flower bed. He cocks an inquisitive eyebrow at Robyn as she passes.

"Is it your impression that Philip Swallow is a bit hard of hearing?" she asks him.

"Oh yes, it's been getting worse lately," says Bob Busby. "It's high-frequency deafness, you know. He can hear vowels but not consonants. He tries to guess what you say to him from the vowels. Usually he guesses what he happens to be thinking about himself, at the time."

"It makes conversation rather a hit-or-miss affair," says Robyn.

"Anything important, was it?"

"Oh no," says Robyn, disinclined to share her disappointment with Bob Busby. She smiles serenely and moves on.

There are several students slouching against the wall, or sitting on the floor, outside her room. Robyn gives them a wry look as she approaches, having a pretty good idea of what they want.

"Hallo," she says, by way of a general greeting as she fishes for her door key in her coat pocket. "Who's first?"

"Me," says a pretty, dark-haired girl wearing an outsize man's shirt like an artist's smock over her jeans and sweater. She follows Robyn into her room. This has the same view as Philip Swallow's, but is smaller—indeed, rather too small for all the furniture it contains: a desk, bookcases, filing cabinets, a table and a dozen or so unstacked stacking chairs. The walls are covered with posters illustrative of various radical causes—nuclear disarmament, women's liberation, the protection of whales—and a large reproduction of Dante Gabriel Rossetti's painting, "The Lady of Shalott," which might seem incongruous unless you have heard Robyn expound its iconic significance as a matrix of male stereotypes of the feminine.

The girl, whose name is Marion Russell, comes straight to the point. "I need an extension for my assessed essay."

Robyn sighs. "I thought you might." Marion is a persistent defaulter in this respect, though not without reason.

"I did two jobs in the vac, you see. The Post Office, as well as the pub in the evenings."

Marion does not qualify for a maintenance grant because her parents are well off, but they are also estranged, from each other and from her, so she is obliged to support herself at university with a variety of part-time jobs.

"You know we're only supposed to give extensions on medical grounds."

"Well, I did get a terrible cold after Christmas."

"I don't suppose you got a medical certificate?"

"No."

Robyn sighs again. "How long do you want?"

"Ten days."

"I'll give you a week." Robyn opens a drawer in her desk and takes out the appropriate chit.

"Thanks. Things will be better this term. I've got a better job."

"Oh?"

"Fewer hours, but better pay."

"What is it?"

"Well, it's sort of . . . modelling."

Robyn stops writing and looks sharply at Marion. "I hope you know what you're doing."

Marion Russell giggles. "Oh it's nothing like that."

"Like what?"

"You know. Porn. Vice."

"Well, that's a relief. What is it you model, then?"

Marion Russell drops her eyes and blushes slightly. "Well, it's sort of underwear."

Robyn has a vivid mental image of the girl before her, now so pleasantly and comfortably dressed, sheathed in latex and nylon, the full fetishistic ensemble of brassière, knickers, suspender belt and stockings with which the lingerie industry seeks to truss the female body, and having to parade at some fashion show in front of leering men and hardfaced women from department stores. Waves of compassion and outrage fuse with delayed feelings of self-pity for her own plight, and society seems for a moment a huge conspiracy to exploit and oppress young women. She feels a choking sensation in her chest, and a dangerous pressure in her tear-ducts. She rises and clasps the astonished Marion Russell in her arms.

"You can have two weeks," she says, at length, sitting down and blowing her nose.

"Oh, thanks, Robyn. That's super."

Robyn is rather less generous with the next supplicant, a young man who broke his ankle falling off his motorbike on New Year's Eve, but even the least deserving candidate gets a few days' respite, for Robyn tends to identify with the students against the system that assesses them, even though she is herself part of the system. Eventually they are all dealt with, and Robyn is free to prepare for her lecture at eleven. She opens her Gladstone bag, pulls out the folder containing her notes, and settles to work.

3

The University clock strikes eleven, its chimes overlapping with the chimes of other clocks, near and far. All over Rummidge and its environs, people are at work—or not, as the case may be.

. . .

Robyn Penrose is making her way to Lecture Room A, along corridors and down staircases thronged with students changing classes. They part before her, like waves before the prow of a stately ship. She smiles at those she recognises. Some fall in behind her, and follow her to the lecture theatre, so that she appears to be leading a little procession, a female Pied Piper. She carries under one arm her folder of lecture notes, and under the other a bundle of books from which to read illustrative quotations. No young man offers to carry this burden for her. Such gallantry is out of fashion. Robyn herself would disapprove of it on ideological grounds, and it might be interpreted by other students as creeping.

. . .

Vic Wilcox is in a meeting with his Marketing Director, Brian Everthorpe, who answered Vic's summons at 9:30, complaining of contraflow holdups on the motorway, and whom Vic, himself dictating letters at 9:30, told to come back at eleven. He is a big man, which in itself doesn't endear him to Vic, with bushy sideboards and RAF-style moustache. He wears a three-piece suit with an old-fashioned watch-chain looped across his waistcoated paunch. He is the most senior, and the most complacent, member of the management team Vic inherited.

"You should live in the city, like me, Brian," says Vic. "Not thirty miles away."

"Oh, you know what Beryl is like," says Brian Everthorpe, with a smile designed to seem rueful.

Vic doesn't know. He has never met Beryl, said to be Everthorpe's second wife, and formerly his secretary. As far as he knows, Beryl may not even exist, except as an excuse for Brian Everthorpe's delinquencies. *Beryl says the kids need country air. Beryl was poorly this morning and I had to run her to the doctor's. Beryl sends her apologies—she forgot to give me your message.* One day, quite soon in fact, Brian Everthorpe is going to have to concentrate his mind on the difference between a wife and an employer.

. . .

In a café in a covered shopping precinct at the centre of Rummidge, Marjorie and Sandra Wilcox are sipping coffee, debating what colour shoes Sandra should buy. The walls of the café are covered with tinted mirrors, and soft syncopated music oozes from speakers hidden in the ceiling.

"I think a beige," says Marjorie.

"Or that sort of pale olive," says Sandra.

The shopping precinct is full of teenagers gathered in small clusters, smoking, gossiping, laughing, scuffling. They look at the goods in the shiny, illuminated shop windows, and wander in and out of the boutiques, but do not buy anything. Some stare into the café where Marjorie and Sandra are sitting.

"All these kids," says Marjorie disapprovingly. "Wagging it, I suppose."

"On the dole, more likely," says Sandra, suppressing a yawn, and checking her appearance in the mirrored wall behind her mother's back.

. . .

Robyn arranges her notes on the lectern, waiting for latecomers to settle in their seats. The lecture theatre resonates like a drum with the chatter of a hundred-odd students, all talking at once, as if they have just been released from solitary confinement. She taps on the desk with an inverted pencil and clears her throat. A sudden hush falls, and a hundred faces tilt towards her— curious, expectant, sullen, apathetic—like empty dishes waiting to be filled. The face of Marion Russell is absent, and Robyn cannot suppress a tiny, ignoble twinge of resentment at this ungrateful desertion.

. . .

"I've been looking at your expense account, Brian," says Vic, turning over a small pile of bills and receipts.

"Yes?" Brian Everthorpe stiffens slightly.

"It's very modest."

Everthorpe relaxes. "Thank you."

"I didn't mean it as a compliment."

Everthorpe looks puzzled. "Sorry?"

"I'd expect the Marketing Director of a firm this size to claim twice as much for overnight stays."

"Ah, well, you see, Beryl doesn't like being on her own in the house at night."

"But she has your kids with her."

"Not during term, old man. We send them away to school—have to, living in the depths of the country. So I prefer to drive back home after a meeting, no matter how far it is."

"Your mileage is pretty modest, too, isn't it?"

"Is it?" Brian Everthorpe, beginning to get the message, stiffens again.

. . .

"In the 1840s and 1850s," says Robyn, "a number of novels were published in England which have a certain family resemblance. Raymond Williams has called them 'Industrial Novels' because they dealt with social and economic problems arising out of the Industrial Revolution, and in some cases described the nature of factory work. In their own time they were often called 'Condition of England Novels,' because they addressed themselves directly to the state of the nation. They are novels in which the main characters debate topical social and economic issues as well as fall in and out of love, marry and have children, pursue careers, make or lose their fortunes, and do all the other things that characters do in more conventional novels. The Industrial Novel contributed a distinctive strain to English fiction which persists into the modern period—it can be traced in the work of Lawrence and Forster, for instance. But it is not surprising that it first arose in what history has called 'the Hungry 'Forties.'

"By the fifth decade of the nineteenth century the Industrial Revolution had completely dislocated the traditional structure of English society, bringing riches to a few and misery to the many. The agricultural working class, deprived of a subsistence on the land by the enclosures of the late eighteenth and early nineteenth centuries, thronged to the cities of the Midlands and the North where the economics of *laissez-faire* forced them to work long hours in wretched conditions for miserable wages, and threw them out of employment altogether as soon as there was a downturn in the market.

"The workers' attempt to defend their interests by forming trades unions was bitterly resisted by the employers. The working class met even stiffer resistance when they tried to secure political representation through the Chartist Movement."

Robyn glances up from her notes and sweeps the audience with her eyes. Some are busily scribbling down every word she utters, others are watching her quizzically, chewing the ends of their ballpoints, and those who looked bored at the outset are now staring vacantly out of the window or diligently chiselling their initials into the lecture-room furniture.

"The People's Charter called for universal male suffrage. Not even those far-out radicals could apparently contemplate the possibility of universal *female* suffrage."

All the students, even those who have been staring out of the window, react to this. They smile and nod or, in a friendly sort of way, groan and hiss. It is what they expect from Robyn Penrose, and even the rugby-playing boys in the back row would be mildly disappointed if she didn't produce this kind of observation from time to time.

. . .

Vic Wilcox asks Brian Everthorpe to stay for a meeting he has arranged with his technical and production managers. They file into the office and sit round the long oak table, slightly in awe of Vic, serious men in chain-store suits, with pens and pencils sticking out of their breast pockets. Brian Everthorpe takes a chair at the far end of the table, slightly withdrawn as if to mark his difference from the engineers. Vic sits at the head of the table, in his shirt-sleeves, half a cup of cold coffee at his right hand. He unfolds a sheet of computer printout.

"Does anybody know," he says, "how many different products this firm made last year?" Silence. "Nine hundred and thirty-seven. That's about nine hundred too many, in my opinion."

"You mean different specs, don't you? Not products," says the technical manager, rather boldly.

"All right, different specs. But every new specification means that we have to stop production, retool or reset the machines, stop a flow line, or whatever. That costs time, and time is money. Then the operatives are more likely to make mistakes when set-ups are constantly changing, and that leads to increased wastage. Am I right?"

. . .

"There were two climactic moments in the history of the Chartist Movement. One was the submission of a petition, with millions of signatures, to Parliament in 1839. Its rejection led to a series of industrial strikes, demonstrations, and repressive measures by the Government. This is the background to Mrs. Gaskell's novel *Mary Barton* and Disraeli's *Sybil*. The second was the submission of another monster petition in 1848, which forms the background to Charles Kingsley's *Alton Locke*. 1848 was a year of revolution throughout

Europe, and many people in England feared that Chartism would bring revolution, and perhaps a Terror, to England. Any kind of working-class militancy tends to be presented in the fiction of the period as a threat to social order. This is also true of Charlotte Brontë's *Shirley* (1849). Though set at the time of the Napoleonic wars, its treatment of the Luddite riots is clearly an oblique comment on more topical events."

. . .

Three black youths with huge, multicoloured knitted caps pulled over their dreadlocks like tea-cosies lean against the plateglass window of the shopping-precinct café, drumming a reggae beat on it with their finger-tips until shooed away by the manageress.

"I hear there was more trouble in Angleside at the weekend," says Marjorie, wiping the milky foam of the cappuccino from her lips with a dainty tissue.

Angleside is the black ghetto of Rummidge, where youth unemployment is 80 per cent, and rioting endemic. There are long queues in the Angleside Social Security office this morning, as every morning. The only job vacancies in Angleside are for interviewers in the Social Security office, where the furniture is screwed to the floor in case the clients should try to assault the interviewers with it.

"Or maybe oyster," says Sandra dreamily. "To go with my pink trousers."

. . .

"My point is simply this," says Vic. "We're producing too many different things in short runs, meeting small orders. We must rationalise. Offer a small range of standard products at competitive prices. Encourage our customers to design their systems around *our* products."

"Why should they?" says Brian Everthorpe, tipping his chair back on its rear legs and hooking his thumbs in his waistcoat pockets.

"Because the product will be cheap, reliable and available at short notice," says Vic. "If they want something manufactured to their own spec, OK, but we insist on a thumping great order or a high price."

"And if they won't play?" says Brian Everthorpe.

"Then let them go elsewhere."

"I don't like it," says Brian Everthorpe. "The small orders bring in the big ones."

The heads of the other men present have been swivelling from side to side, like spectators at a tennis match, during this argument. They look fascinated but slightly frightened.

"I don't believe that, Brian," says Vic. "Why should anybody order long when they can order short and keep their inventory down?"

"I'm talking about goodwill," says Brian Everthorpe. "Pringle's has a slogan—"

"Yes, I know, Brian," says Vic Wilcox. *"If it can be made, Pringle's will make it.* Well, I'm proposing a new slogan. *If it's profitable, Pringle's will make it."*

· · ·

"Mr. Gradgrind in *Hard Times* embodies the spirit of industrial capitalism as Dickens saw it. His philosophy is utilitarian. He despises emotion and the imagination, and believes only in Facts. The novel shows, among other things, the disastrous effects of this philosophy on Mr. Gradgrind's own children, Tom, who becomes a thief, and Louisa, who nearly becomes an adulteress, and on the lives of working people in the city of Coketown which is made in his image, a dreary place containing:

> *several streets all very like one another, and many more streets still more like one another, inhabited by people equally like one another, who all went in and out at the same hours, with the same sound upon the same pavements, to do the same work, and to whom every day was the same as yesterday and tomorrow, and every year the counterpart of the last and the next.*

"Opposed to this alienated, repetitive way of life, is the circus—a community of spontaneity, generosity and creative imagination. *'You mutht have us, Thquire,'* says the lisping circus master, Mr. Sleary, to Gradgrind. *'People mutht be amuthed.'* It is Cissie, the despised horserider's daughter adopted by Gradgrind, who proves the redemptive force in his life. The message of the novel is clear: the alienation of work under industrial capitalism can be overcome by an infusion of loving kindness and imaginative play, represented by Cissie and the circus."

Robyn pauses, to allow the racing pens to catch up with her discourse, and to give emphasis to her next sentence: "Of course, such a reading is totally inadequate. Dickens' own ideological position is riddled with contradiction."

The students who have been writing everything down now look up and smile wryly at Robyn Penrose, like victims of a successful hoax. They lay down their pens and flex their fingers, as she pauses and shuffles her notes preparatory to the next stage of her exposition.

· · ·

In Avondale Road, the Wilcox boys have risen from their beds at last and are making the most of their unsupervised occupancy of the house. Gary is eating a heaped bowl of cornflakes in the kitchen, while reading *Home Computer* propped up against the milk bottle and listening via the hall and two open doors to a record by UB40 playing at maximum volume on the music centre in the lounge. In his bedroom Raymond is torturing his electric guitar, which is plugged into an amplifier as big as an upended coffin, grinning fiendishly as he produces howls and wails of feedback. The whole house vibrates like a sounding-box. Ornaments tremble on shelves and glassware tinkles in sideboards. A tradesman who has been ringing at the front door for several minutes gives up and goes away.

. . .

"It is interesting how many of the industrial novels were written by women. In their work, the ideological contradictions of the middle-class liberal humanist attitude to the Industrial Revolution take on a specifically sexual character."

At the mention of the word "sexual," a little ripple of interest stirs the rows of silent listeners. Those who have been daydreaming or carving their initials into the desktops sit up. Those who have been taking notes continue to do so with even greater assiduousness. People cease to cough or sniff or shuffle their feet. As Robyn continues, the only interference with the sound of her voice is the occasional ripping noise of a filled-up page of A4 being hurriedly detached from its parent pad.

"It hardly needs to be pointed out that industrial capitalism is phallocentric. The inventors, the engineers, the factory owners and bankers who fuelled it and maintained it, were all men. The most commonplace metonymic index of industry—the factory chimney—is also metaphorically a phallic symbol. The characteristic imagery of the industrial landscape or townscape in nineteenth-century literature—tall chimneys thrusting into the sky, spewing ribbons of black smoke, buildings shaking with the rhythmic pounding of mighty engines, the railway train rushing irresistibly through the passive countryside—all this is saturated with male sexuality of a dominating and destructive kind.

"For women novelists, therefore, industry had a complex fascination. On the conscious level it was the Other, the alien, the male world of work, in which they had no place. I am, of course, talking about middle-class women, for all women novelists at this period were by definition middle-class. On the subconscious level it was what they desired to heal their own castration, their own sense of lack."

Some of the students look up at the word "castration," admiring the cool poise with which Robyn pronounces it, as one might admire a barber's expert manipulation of a cut-throat razor.

"We see this illustrated very clearly in Mrs. Gaskell's *North and South*. In this novel, the genteel young heroine from the south of England, Margaret, is compelled by her father's reduced circumstances to take up residence in a city called Milton, closely based on Manchester, and comes into social contact with a local mill-owner called Thornton. He is a very pure kind of capitalist who believes fanatically in the laws of supply and demand. He has no compassion for the workers when times are bad and wages low, and does not ask for pity when he himself faces ruin. Margaret is at first repelled by Thornton's harsh business ethic, but when a strike of workers turns violent, she acts impulsively to save his life, thus revealing her unconscious attraction to him, as well as her instinctive class allegiance. Margaret befriends some of the workers and shows compassion for their sufferings, but when the crunch comes she is on the side of the master. The interest Margaret takes in factory life and the processes of manufacturing—which her mother finds sordid and repellent—is a displaced manifestation of her unacknowledged erotic feelings for Thornton. This comes out very clearly in a conversation between Margaret and her mother, who complains that Margaret is beginning to use factory slang in her speech. She retorts:

> "*And if I live in a factory town, I must speak factory language when I want it. Why, Mamma, I could astonish you with a great many words you never heard in your life. I don't believe you know what a knobstick is.*"
>
> "*Not I, child. I only know it has a very vulgar sound; and I don't want to hear you using it.*"

Robyn looks up from the copy of *North and South* from which she has been reading this passage, and surveys her audience with her cool, grey-green eyes. "I think we all know what a knobstick is, metaphorically."

The audience chuckles gleefully, and the ballpoints speed across the pages of A4 faster than ever.

. . . .

"Any more questions?" says Vic Wilcox, looking at his watch.

"Just one point, Vic," says Bert Braddock, the Works Manager. "If we rationalise production like you say, will that mean redundancies?"

"No," says Vic, looking Bert Braddock straight in the eye. "Rationalisation will mean growth in sales. Eventually we'll need more men, not fewer." Eventually perhaps, if everything goes according to plan, but Braddock knows as well as Vic that some redundancies are inevitable in the short term. The exchange is purely ritual in function, authorising Bert Braddock to reassure anxious shop stewards if they start asking awkward questions.

Vic dismisses the meeting and, as the men file out, stands up and stretches. He goes to the window, and fiddles with the angle of the louvred blinds. Staring out across the car park, where silent, empty cars wait for their owners like patient pets, he ponders the success of the meeting. The telephone console on his desk buzzes.

"It's Roy Mackintosh, Wragcast," says Shirley.

"Put him on."

Roy Mackintosh is MD of a local foundry that has been supplying Pringle's with castings for many years. He has just heard that Pringle's is not reordering, and has phoned to enquire the reason.

"I suppose someone is undercutting us," he says.

"No, Roy," says Vic. "We're supplying ourselves now."

"From that old foundry of yours?"

"We've made improvements."

"You must have . . ." Roy Mackintosh sounds suspicious. After a certain amount of small talk, he says casually. "Perhaps I might drop by some time. I'd like to have a look at this foundry of yours."

"Sure." Vic does not welcome this proposal, but protocol demands a positive response. "Tell your secretary to fix it with mine."

Vic goes into Shirley's office, shrugging on the jacket of his suit. Brian Everthorpe, who is hanging over Shirley's desk, straightens up guiltily. Griping about the boss, no doubt.

"Hallo, Brian. Still here?"

"Just off." Smiling blandly, he tugs the points of his waistcoat down over his paunch and sidles out of the office.

"Roy Mackintosh wants to look round the foundry. When his secretary rings, put him off as long as you decently can. Don't want the whole world knowing about the KW."

"OK," says Shirley, making a note.

"I'm just going over there now, to see Tom Rigby. I'll drop into the machine shop on my way."

"Right," says Shirley, with a knowing smile. Vic's frequent but unpredictable visits to the shop floor are notorious.

. . .

Robyn's student, Marion Russell, wearing a long, shapeless black overcoat and carrying a plastic holdall, hurriedly enters a large building in the commerical centre of Rummidge and asks the security man at the desk for directions. The man asks to see inside her bag and grins at the contents. He motions her towards the lift. She takes the lift to the seventh floor and walks along a carpeted corridor until she comes to a room whose door is slightly ajar. The noises of men talking and laughing and the sound of champagne corks popping filter out into the corridor. Marion Russell stands at the threshold and peeps cautiously round the edge of the door, surveying the arrangement of people and furniture as a thief might case a property for ease of entry and swiftness of escape. Satisfied, she retraces her steps until she comes to a Ladies' cloakroom. In the mirror over the washbasins she applies pancake makeup, lipstick and eyeliner, and combs her hair. Then she locks herself in one of the cubicles, puts her bag on the toilet seat, and takes out the tools of her trade: a red satin basque with suspenders attached, a pair of black lace panties, black fishnet stockings and shiny highheeled shoes.

. . .

"The writers of the industrial novels were never able to resolve in fictional terms the ideological contradictions inherent in their own situation in society. At the very moment when they were writing about these problems, Marx and Engels were writing the seminal texts in which the political solutions were expounded. But the novelists had never heard of Marx and Engels—and if they had heard of them and their ideas, they would probably have recoiled in horror, perceiving the threat to their own privileged position. For all their dismay at the squalor and exploitation generated by industrial capitalism, the novelists were in a sense capitalists themselves, profiting from a highly commercialised form of literary production."

The campus clock begins to strike twelve, and its muffled notes are audible in the lecture theatre. The students stir restlessly in their seats, shuffling their papers and capping their pens. The spring-loaded clips of looseleaf folders snap shut with a noise like revolver shots. Robyn hastens to her conclusion.

"Unable to contemplate a political solution to the social problems they described in their fiction, the industrial novelists could only offer narrative solutions to the personal dilemmas of their characters. And these narrative solutions are invariably negative or evasive. In *Hard Times* the victimised worker Stephen Blackpool dies in the odour of sanctity. In *Mary Barton* the working-class heroine and her husband go off to the colonies to start a new life. Kingsley's Alton Locke emigrates after his disillusionment with Chartism, and dies shortly after. In *Sybil*, the humble heroine turns out to be an heiress and is able to marry her well-meaning aristocratic lover without compromising the class system, and a similar stroke of good fortune resolves the love stories in *Shirley* and *North and South*. Although the heroine of George Eliot's *Felix Holt* renounces her inheritance, it is only so that she can marry the man she loves. In short, all the Victorian novelist could offer as a solution to the problems of industrial capitalism were: a legacy, a marriage, emigration or death."

. . .

As Robyn Penrose is winding up her lecture, and Vic Wilcox is commencing his tour of the machine shop, Philip Swallow returns from a rather tiresome meeting of the Arts Faculty Postgraduate Studies Committee (which wrangled for two hours about the proposed revision of a clause in the PhD regulations and then voted to leave it unchanged, an expenditure of time that seemed all the more vain since there are scarcely any new candidates for the PhD in arts subjects anyway these days) to find a rather disturbing message from the Vice-Chancellor's office.

His secretary Pamela reads it off her memo pad: "The VC's PA rang to say could they have your nomination for the Industry Year Shadow Scheme."

"What in God's name is that?"

Pamela shrugs. "I don't know. I've never heard of it. Shall I ring Phyllis Cameron and ask her?"

"No, no, don't do that," says Philip Swallow, nervously fingering his beardless chin. "Last resort. Don't want to make the Arts Faculty look incompetent. We're in enough trouble already."

"I'm sure *I* never saw a letter about it," says Pamela defensively.

"No, no, my fault, I'm sure."

It is. Philip Swallow finds the VC's memorandum, its envelope still unopened, at the bottom of his In-tray, trapped between the pages of a brochure for Bargain Winter Breaks in Belgium which he had picked up from a local travel agency some weeks ago. His casual treatment of this missive is not entirely surprising, since its external appearance hardly conveys an idea of its august addresser. The brown manila envelope, originally despatched to the

University by an educational publishing firm, whose name and address, printed on the top lefthand corner, has been partially defaced, is creased and tattered. It has already been used twice for the circulation of internal mail and resealed by means of staples and Sellotape.

"Sometimes I think the VC takes his economy drive a little too far," says Philip, gingerly extracting the stencilled memorandum from its patched and disintegrating container. The document is dated 1st December, 1985. "Oh dear," says Philip, sinking into his swivel seat to read it. Pamela reads it with him, peering over his shoulder.

From: The Vice-Chancellor *To*: Deans of all Faculties

Subject: INDUSTRY YEAR SHADOW SCHEME
> As you are no doubt aware, 1986 has been designated Industry Year by the Government. The DES, through the UGC, have urged the CVCP to ensure that universities throughout the UK—

"He does love acronyms, doesn't he," Philip murmurs.
"What?" says Pamela.
"All these initials," says Philip.
"It's supposed to save paper and typing time," says Pamela. "We had a memo round about it. Acrowhatsits to be used whenever possible in University correspondence."

> —make a special effort in the coming year to show themselves responsive to the needs of industry, both in terms of collaboration in research and development, and the provision of well-trained and well-motivated graduates for recruitment to industry.
>
> A working party was set up last July to advise on this University's contribution to IY, and one of its recommendations, approved by Senate at its meeting of November 18th, is that each Faculty should nominate a member of staff to "shadow" some person employed at senior management level in local manufacturing industry, nominated through CRUM, in the course of the winter term.

"I don't remember it coming up at that meeting of Senate," says Philip. "Must have been passed without discussion. What's CRUM?"

"Confederation of Rummidge Manufacturers?" Pamela hazarded.

"Could be. Good try, Pam."

There is a widespread feeling in the country that universities are "ivory tower" institutions, whose staff are ignorant of the realities of the modern commercial world. Whatever the justice of this prejudice, it is important in the present economic climate that we should do our utmost to dispel it. The SS will advertise our willingness to inform ourselves about the needs of industry.

"The SS? Got his own stormtroopers, now, has he, the VC?"

"I think it stands for Shadow Scheme," says Pamela.

"Yes, I'm afraid you're probably right."

A Shadow, as the name implies, is someone who follows another person about all day as he goes about his normal work. In this way a genuine, inward understanding of that work is obtained by the Shadow, which could not be obtained by a simple briefing or organized visit. Ideally, the Shadow should spend an uninterrupted week or fortnight with his opposite number, but if that is impracticable, a regular visit of one day a week throughout the term would be satisfactory. Shadows will be asked to write a short report of what they have learned at the end of the exercise.

Action: Nominations to reach the VC's Office by Wednesday 8th January, 1986.

"Oh dear," says Philip Swallow, once more, when he has finished reading the memorandum.

Anxiety makes him want to pee. He hurries to the Male Staff toilet and finds Rupert Sutcliffe and Bob Busby already ensconced at the three-stall urinal.

"Ah, well met," says Philip, taking his place between them. In front of his nose dangles a hexagonal rubber handle suspended from a chain, installed a year or two earlier when the University removed all automatic flushing systems from its men's cloakrooms as an economy measure. Someone in the Works and Buildings Department, haunted by the thought of these urinals gushing pointlessly at regular intervals all through the hours of darkness, Sundays and public holidays, had hit on this means of reducing the University's water rate. "I need a volunteer," says Philip, and briefly explains the Shadow Scheme.

"Not my cup of tea, I'm afraid," says Rupert Sutcliffe. "What are you laughing at, Swallow?"

"Cup of pee. Very good, Rupert, I must admit."

"Tea. I said cup of *tea*," says Rupert Sutcliffe frostily. "Traipsing round a factory all day is not mine. I can't think of anything more wearisome." Buttoning up his fly (Sutcliffe's trousers date back to that era, and look it) he retreats to the washbasins on the other side of the room.

"Bob, what about you?" says Philip, swivelling his head in the opposite direction. Bob Busby has also concluded his business at the urinal, but is adjusting his dress with a great deal of fumbling and knee-flexing, as if his member is of such majestic size that it can be coaxed back into his Y-fronts only with the greatest difficulty.

"Quite impossible this term, Philip. With all the extra AUT work on top of everything else." Bob Busby stretches out a hand in front of Philip's face and pulls the chain. The cistern flushes, sending a fine spray over Philip's shoes and trouser bottoms, and the swinging handle released by Busby hits him on the nose. The protocol of chain-pulling in multiple-occupancy urinals has not been thought through by the Works and Buildings Department.

"Who shall I nominate, then?" says Philip Swallow plaintively. "I've got to have a name by 4:30 this afternoon. There isn't time to consult other Departments."

"Why not do it yourself?" Rupert Sutcliffe suggests.

"Don't be absurd. With all the work I have as Dean?"

"Well, the whole idea is pretty absurd," says Sutcliffe. "What has the Faculty of Arts to do with Industry Year, or Industry Year to do with the Faculty of Arts?"

"I wish you'd put that question to the Vice-Chancellor, Rupert," says Philip. "*What has the FA to do with IY, or IY with the FA?*"

"I'm sure I don't know what you're talking about."

"Just my little joke," says Philip to Sutcliffe's departing back. "Not much to joke about when you're Dean of sweet FA," he continues to Bob Busby, who is carefully combing his hair in the mirror. "It's responsibility without power. You know, I ought to be able to *order* one of you to do this shadow nonsense."

"You can't," says Bob Busby smugly. "Not without asking for nominations and holding a Department meeting to discuss it first."

"I know, and there isn't time."

"Why don't you ask Robyn Penrose?"

"The most junior member of the Department? Surely it wouldn't—"

"It's right up her street."

"Is it?"

"Of course—her book on the Victorian industrial novel."

"Oh, *that*. It's hardly the same . . . Still, it's a thought, Bob."

. . .

Later that day, much later, when Shirley and the other office staff have gone home, and Vic sits alone in the administration block, working in his darkened office by the light of a single desk lamp, he gets a call from Stuart Baxter.

"You've heard about Industry Year, Vic?"

"Enough to know it's a waste of time and money."

"I'm inclined to agree with you. But the Board feels that we've got to go along with it. Good PR for the Group, you know. Our chairman is dead keen. I've been asked to co-ordinate initiatives—"

"What do you want me to do?" Vic cuts in impatiently.

"I was coming to that, Vic. You know what a shadow is, don't you?"

When Stuart Baxter has finished telling him, Vic says: "No way."

"Why not, Vic?"

"I don't want some academic berk following me about all day."

"It's only one day a week, Vic, for a few weeks."

"Why me?"

"Because you're the most dynamic MD in the division. We want to show them the best."

Vic knows this compliment is totally insincere, but he has no wish to disown it. It could be useful to remind Stuart Baxter of it some time in the future.

"I'll think about it," he says.

"Sorry, Vic. I've got to tie it up now. Seeing the Chairman tonight at a function."

"Left it a bit late, haven't you?"

"To tell you the truth, my secretary fucked up. Lost the letter."

"Oh yes?" says Vic sceptically.

"I'd be very grateful if you'd co-operate."

"You mean, it's an order?"

"Don't be silly, Vic. We're not in the Army."

Vic keeps Baxter in suspense for a few moments, while he reviews the advantages of having him under an obligation. "About that automatic core blower . . ."

"Send me a Capex and I'll run it up the flagpole."

"Thanks," says Vic. "Will do."

"And the other?"

"All right."

"Great! The name of your shadow is Dr. Robin Penrose."

"A medic?"

"No."

"Not a shrink, for Christ's sake?"

"No, I understand he's a lecturer in English Literature."

"English *what?*"

"Don't know much else about him—only got the message this afternoon."

"Jesus wept."

Stuart Baxter chuckles. "Read any good books lately, Vic?"

PART II

Mrs. Thornton went on after a moment's pause: "Do you know anything of Milton, Miss Hale? Have you seen any of our factories? our magnificent warehouses?"

"No," said Margaret. "I have not seen anything of that description as yet."

Then she felt that, by concealing her utter indifference to all such places, she was hardly speaking the truth; so she went on: "I dare say, papa would have taken me before now if I had cared. But I really do not find much pleasure in going over manufactories."

ELIZABETH GASKELL: *North and South*

1

Ten days later, at eight-thirty in the morning of Wednesday, 22nd January, Robyn Penrose set off in a snowstorm and an ill humour to begin her stint as the University of Rummidge Faculty of Arts Industry Year Shadow, or URFAIYS as she was designated in memoranda emanating from the Vice-Chancellor's Office. One of these documents had informed her that she was to be attached to a Mr. Victor Wilcox, Managing Director of J. Pringle & Sons, for one day a week during the remainder of the winter term, and she had chosen Wednesdays for this undertaking since it was the day she normally kept free from teaching. By the same token it was a day she normally spent at home, catching up on her marking, preparation and research, and she bitterly resented having to sacrifice it. For this reason above all others she had come very close to declining Philip Swallow's proposal to nominate her for the Shadow Scheme. After all, if the University wasn't going to keep her on (Swallow's request had come, rather tactlessly, later in the very same day on which he had communicated this gloomy prognosis) why should she put herself out to oblige the University?

"*Exactly!*" said Penny Black the following evening, as she peeled off her jeans in the women's changing-room at the University Sports Centre. "I don't understand why you agreed to do it." Penny was a feminist friend of Robyn's from the Sociology Department, with whom she played squash once a week.

"I wish I hadn't, now," said Robyn. "I wish I'd told him to, to . . ."

"To stick his shadow scheme up his ass. Why didn't you?"

"I don't know. Well, I do, really. A little voice, a nasty, calculating little voice whispered in my ear that one day I'm going to need a reference from Swallow."

"You're right, honey. That's how they screw us, these men in authority. It's a power trip. Damn these hooks and eyes."

Penny Black fumbled with the fastenings of her bra, reversed around her waist like a belt. Succeeding, she rotated the garment, levered her formidable breasts into the cups and thrust her arms through the shoulderstraps. Latex smacked lustily against solid flesh. Playing squash was the only time Penny wore a bra—without it, as she said, her boozums would bounce from wall to wall faster than the ball.

"Oh, I wouldn't say that about Swallow," Robyn demurred. "To be fair, he doesn't seem to *have* much power. He was practically begging me to agree."

"So why didn't you bargain with him? Why didn't you say you'd be his fucking shadow if he'd give you tenure?"

"Don't be ridiculous, Penny."

"What's ridiculous?"

"Well, A, he's not in a position to give it to me, and B, I wouldn't stoop to that sort of thing."

"You British!" said Penny Black, shaking her head in despair. She herself was British, in fact, but having spent several years as a graduate student in California, where she had been converted to radical feminism, she now thought of herself as spiritually an American, and tried as far as possible to speak like one. "Well," she continued, pulling on a red Amazon sports shirt, "you'll just have to sweat out your hostility on the squash court." Her dark, tousled head popped out of the collar, a grinning Jill-in-the-box: "Pretend the ball is one of Swallow's."

A middle-aged grey-haired woman swathed in a bath-towel nodded a greeting to Robyn as she passed between the sauna and the showers. Robyn smiled radiantly back, hissing between her teeth, "For God's sake keep your voice down, Penny, that's his wife."

Charles was amused by this story when Robyn rang him up later that evening. But, like Penny, he was surprised Robyn had agreed to be nominated as Arts Faculty Shadow.

"It's not your sort of thing, is it?"

"Well, I *am* supposed to be an expert on the industrial novel. Swallow made a great point of that."

"But not in a *realist* sort of way. I mean, you're not suggesting that there's any possible *relevance*—"

"No, no, of course not," said Robyn, anxious to disown the taint of realism. "I'm just trying to explain the pressure that was put on me." She was beginning to feel that she had made a mistake, and allowed herself to be exploited. It was a rare sensation for Robyn, and all the more unpleasant for that.

This suspicion hardened into certainty in the days that followed. She woke on the morning appointed for her initiation into the Shadow Scheme with a heavy heart, which the weather did nothing to lighten. "Oh no," she groaned, pulling the bedroom curtain aside on a sky swirling with snow-flakes, like a shaken paperweight. A thin layer already covered the frost-hardened ground, and clung delicately to tree-branches, clothes-lines and back-garden bric-à-brac. She was tempted to use the weather as an excuse to postpone her visit to J. Pringle & Sons, but the work ethic that had carried her successfully through so many years of study and so many examinations now exerted its leverage on her conscience once more. She had already post-poned the exercise by one week, because of the AUT strike. Another cancel-lation would look bad.

Over breakfast (no *Guardian* was delivered, doubtless because of the snow) she pondered the question of what clothes to wear for the occasion. She possessed a boiler suit bought recently from Next, which seemed in theory appropriate, but it was bright orange, with a yellow flower appliquéd on the bib, and it might, she thought, lack dignity. On the other hand, she wasn't going to show excessive respect by wearing her olive-green tailored interview suit. What did a liberated woman wear to visit a factory? It was a nice semi-otic problem. Robyn was well aware that clothes do not merely serve the practical purpose of covering our bodies, but also convey messages about who we are, what we are doing, and how we feel. However, she did in the end let the weather partly determine her choice: a pair of elephant-cord trousers tucked Cossack-style into her high boots, and a chunky-knit cardigan with a shawl collar worn over a Liberty print blouse. On top of this outfit she wore her cream-coloured quilted cotton jacket and a Russian-style hat made of artificial fur. Thus attired, she ventured out into the blizzard.

The little Renault already looked sculpted out of snow, and the key would not turn in the frozen door-lock. She freed it with a patent squirt imported from Finland, and hastily discontinued, called Superpiss. Charles had given it to her for a joke, suggesting she use it as a visual aid to introduce Saussurean linguistics to first-year undergraduates, holding the tube aloft to demonstrate that what is onomatopoeia in one language community may be obscenity in another. The snow adhering to the car windows created a sepulchral gloom inside, and Robyn spent several minutes brushing it off before she attempted to start the engine. Amazingly, perversely, and rather to her regret (a flat battery would have been a cast-iron excuse to abort the visit) the engine fired. With the Rummidge *A to Z* open on the passenger seat beside her, she set off to find J. Pringle & Sons, somewhere on the other side of the city: the dark side of Rummidge, as foreign to her as the dark side of the moon.

· · ·

Because of the weather Robyn decides not to use the motorway, and, finding the residential backstreets treacherous and strewn with abandoned vehicles, she joins a long, slow-moving convoy of traffic on the Outer Ring—not a purpose-built road, this, but a motley string of suburban shopping streets and main roads, where the snow has already been churned into filthy curds and whey. She feels as if she is negotiating the entrails of the city in the slow, peristaltic procession. Stopping and starting, grinding forward in low gear, she passes shops, offices, tower blocks, garages, car marts, churches, fast-food outlets, a school, a bingo hall, a hospital, a prison. Shocking, somehow, to come across this last, a gloomy Victorian gaol in the middle of an ordinary suburb where double-decker buses pass and housewives with shopping bags and pushchairs go about their mundane business. Prison is just a word to Robyn, a word in a book or a newspaper, a symbol of something—the law, hegemony, repression (*"The prison motif in* Little Dorrit *is a metaphorical articulation of Dickens' critique of Victorian culture and society"—Discuss*). Seeing it there, foursquare in sootstreaked stone, with its barred windows, great studded iron door, and high walls trimmed with barbed wire, makes her think with a shudder of the men cooped up inside in cramped cells smelling of sweat and urine, rapists and pimps and wife-beaters and child-molesters among them, and her heart sinks under the thought that crime and punishment are equally horrible, equally inevitable—unless men should change, all become like Charles, which seems unlikely.

The convoy crawls on. More shops, offices, garages, takeaways. Robyn passes a cinema converted into a bingo hall, a church converted into a community centre, a Co-op converted into a Freezer Centre. This part of the city lacks the individual character of Robyn's own suburb, where health-food stores and sportswear boutiques and alternative bookshops have sprung up to cater for the students and liberal-minded yuppies who live there; and still more does it lack the green amenities of the residential streets around the University. There are few trees and no parks to be seen. There are occasional strips of terraced houses, whose occupants seem to have given up the unequal struggle against the noise and pollution of the Ring Road, and retreated to their back rooms, for the frontages are peeling and dilapidated and the curtains sag in the windows with a permanently drawn look. Here and there an effort has been made at renovation, but always in deplorable taste, "Georgian" bay windows or Scandinavian-style pine porches clapped on to the Victorian and Edwardian façades. The shops are either flashy or dingy. The windows of the former are piled with cheap mass-produced goods, banks of conjunctival TVs twitching and blinking in unison, blinding white fridges and washing-machines, ugly shoes, ugly clothes, and unbelievably ugly furniture, all plastic veneers and synthetic fabrics. The windows of the dingy shops are like cemeteries for unloved and unwanted goods—limp floral print dresses, yellowing underwear, flyblown chocolate boxes and dusty plastic toys. The people slipping and sliding on the pavements, spattered with slush by the passing traffic, look stoically wretched, as if they expect no better from life. A line from D. H. Lawrence—was it *Women in Love* or *Lady Chatterley?*—comes into Robyn's head, "*She felt in a wave of terror the grey, gritty hopelessness of it all.*" How she wishes she were back in her snug little house, tapping away on her word-processor, dissecting the lexemes of some classic Victorian novel, delicately detaching the hermeneutic code from the proairetic code, the cultural from the symbolic, surrounded by books and files, the gas fire hissing and a cup of coffee steaming at her elbow. She passes launderettes, hairdressers, betting shops, Sketchleys, Motaparts, Currys, a Post Office, a DIY Centre, a Denture Centre, an Exhaust Centre. An exhaustion centre is what she will soon be in need of. The city seems to stretch on and on—or is she going round and round the Ring Road in an endless loop? No, she is not. She is off the Ring Road. She is lost.

Robyn thinks she must be in Angleside, because the faces of the people slithering on the pavements or huddled miserably at bus-stops are mostly swarthy and dark-eyed, and the bright silks of saris, splashed with mud, gleam beneath the hems of the women's drab topcoats. The names on the shopfronts are all Asian. Nanda General Stores. Sabar Sweet Centre. Rajit Brothers Import Export. Punjabi Printers Ltd. Usha Saree Centre. Halted at a red light, Robyn consults her *A to Z*, but before she has found the place on the map, the lights have changed and cars are hooting impatiently behind her. She takes a left turn at random, and finds herself in an area of derelict buildings, burned out and boarded up, the site, she realizes, of the previous year's rioting. Caribbean faces now preponderate on the pavements. Youths in outsize hats, lounging in the doorways of shops and cafés, with hands thrust deep into their pockets, gossip and smoke, jog on the spot to keep warm, or lob snowballs at each other across the road, over the roofs of passing cars. How strange it is, strange and sad, to see all these tropical faces amid the slush and dirty snow, the grey gritty hopelessness of an English industrial city in the middle of winter.

Halted on the inside lane, Robyn catches the eye of a young West Indian with Rastafarian dreadlocks, hunched in the entrance of a boarded-up shop, and smiles: a friendly, sympathetic, anti-racist smile. To her alarm the young man immediately straightens up, takes his hands out of the pockets of his black leather jacket, and comes over to her car, stooping to bring his head level with the window. He mouths something through the glass which she cannot hear. The car in front moves forward a few yards, but when Robyn inches forward in turn the young man lays a restraining hand on the Renault's wing. Robyn leans across the passenger seat and winds the window down a little way. "Yes?" she says, her voice squeaky with suppressed panic.

"You want soom?" he says in a broad Rummidge accent.

"What?" she says blankly.

"You want soom?"

"Some what?"

"The weed, man, wudjerthink?"

"Oh," says Robyn, as the penny drops. "No thank you."

"Somethin' else? Smack? Speed? You nime it."

"No, really, it's very kind of you, but—" The car ahead moves forward again and the car behind hoots impatiently. "Sorry—I can't stop!" she cries and lets out the clutch. Mercifully the traffic progresses for fifty yards before it stalls again, and the Rasta does not pursue her further, but Robyn keeps a nervous eye on her rear-view mirror.

Robyn sees a roadsign to West Wallsbury, the area in which J. Pringle & Sons is situated, and gratefully follows it. But the snow, which has been slight in the past half-hour, suddenly begins to fall fast and furiously again, limiting her vision. She finds herself on a dual carriageway, almost a motorway, raised above the level of the neighbouring houses, and with no apparent exits. She is forced to go faster than she would choose by the intimidating bulk of lorries nudging up behind her, their radiator grilles looming like cliffs in her rear-view mirror, the drivers high above, out of sight. Every now and again one of these vehicles swings out and surges past, spattering her side windows with filth and making the little Renault stagger under the impact of displaced air. How can these men (of course they are all men) drive their juggernauts at such insane speeds in such dreadful conditions? Frightened, Robyn clings to the steering wheel like a helmsman in a storm, her head craned forward to peer past the flailing windscreen wipers at the road ahead, ribbed with furrows of yellow-brown slush. At the last possible moment, she glimpses a slip-road to her left and swerves down it. At the bottom there is a roundabout, which she circles twice, trying to make sense of the direction signs. She takes an exit at random and pulls up at the side of the road to consult her *A to Z*, but there are no street names visible which would enable her to orient herself. Seeing the glow of a red and yellow Shell sign ahead, she drives on and pulls into the forecourt of a self-service petrol station.

Inside the little shop, a doleful Asian youth wearing finger mittens, walled in behind racks of cheap digital watches, ballpoint pens, sweets, and music cassettes, shakes his head and shrugs when she asks him the name of the street. "Do you mean to say that you don't know the name of the street your own garage is in?" she says sharply, exasperation overcoming sensitivity to racial minorities.

"An't my garridge," says the youth in a broad Rummidge accent. "Oi juss work 'ere."

"Well, do you know if this is West Wallsbury?"

The youth admits that it is. Does he know the way to J. Pringle & Sons? He shakes his head again.

"Pringle's? I'll take you there."

Robyn turns to face a man who has just entered the shop: tall, heavily built, with bushy sideboards and moustache, a sheepskin coat open over his three-piece suit.

"With pleasure," he adds, smiling and looking Robyn up and down.

"If you would just show me the route on this map," says Robyn, without returning the smile, "I'd be most grateful."

"I'll take you. Just let me settle with Ali Baba here."

"I have a car of my own, thank you."

"I mean you can follow me."

"I couldn't put you to that trouble. If you would just—"

"No trouble, my love. I'm going there myself." Seeing the doubtful expression on Robyn's face, he laughs. "I work there."

"Oh well, in that case . . . Thank you."

"And what brings *you* to Pringle's?" says the man, as he signs his credit card slip with a flourish. "Going to work for us, too? Secretary?"

"No."

"Pity. But you're not a customer, I think?"

"No."

"So . . . what? Are you going to make me play twenty questions?"

"I'm from Rummidge University. I'm, er, taking part in, that is to say . . . I'm on a kind of educational visit."

The man freezes in the act of stowing away his wallet. "You're never Vic Wilcox's shadow?"

"Yes."

He gapes at her for a moment, then chortles and slaps his thigh. "My word, Vic's in for a surprise."

"Why?"

"Well, he was expecting . . . someone rather different. Older." He snorts with suppressed laughter. "Less attractive."

"Perhaps we should get on," says Robyn frostily. "I'm going to be very late."

"No wonder, in this weather. I'm a bit late myself. Motorway was a shambles. I'm Brian Everthorpe, by the way. Marketing Director at Pringle's." He produces a small card from his waistcoat pocket and presents it.

Robyn reads aloud: "Riviera Sunbeds. Daily and weekly rental."

"Oops, somebody else's card, got mixed up with mine," says Brian Everthorpe, exchanging the card with another. "Nice little business that, as a matter of fact, Riviera Sunbeds. I know the people. I can arrange a discount if you're interested."

"No thank you," says Robyn.

"You get a marvellous tan. Good as a trip to Tenerife, and a fraction of the cost."

"I never sunbathe," says Robyn. "It gives you skin cancer."

"If you believe the newspapers," says Brian Everthorpe, "everything nice is bad for you." He opens the door of the shop and a flurry of snow blows in. "That's my Granada over there by pump number two. Just get on my tail and stick to it, as the bee said to the pollen."

. . .

Brian Everthorpe led Robyn a tortuous route through streets lined with factories and warehouses, many of them closed down, some displaying "For Sale" or "For Lease" signs on them, some derelict beyond the hope of restoration, with snow blowing through their smashed windows. There was not a soul to be seen on the pavements. She was glad of Everthorpe's guidance, though she disliked his manners and resented his evident desire to stage-manage her arrival at Pringle's. At the entrance to the factory, he engaged the man controlling the barrier in some kind of argument, then got out of his car to speak to Robyn. She lowered her window.

"Sorry, but the security johnny insists that you sign the visitors' book. He's afraid Vic'll bawl him out otherwise. Bit of a martinet, Vic, I should warn you." His eye lit upon the little tube on the dashboard. "Superpiss! What's that for?" he chortled.

"It's for unfreezing car locks," said Robyn, hastily stowing it away in the glove compartment. "It's made in Finland."

"I'd rather use my own," said Brian Everthorpe, enjoying the joke hugely. "It costs nothing, and it's always on tap."

Robyn got out of the car and looked through railings across the car park to a brick office block and a tall windowless building behind it, a prospect almost as depressing as the prison she had seen that morning. Only the carpet of snow relieved its drabness, and that was being rolled up by a man driving a small tractor with a scoop on the front.

"Where are the chimneys?" she asked.

"What chimneys?"

"Well, you know. Great tall things, with smoke coming out of them."

Brian Everthorpe laughed. "We don't need 'em. Everything runs on gas or electricity." He looked at her quizzically. "Ever been inside a factory before?"

"No," said Robyn.

"I see. A virgin, eh? Factorywise, I mean." He grinned and stroked his whiskers.

"Where's the Visitors' Book?" Robyn enquired coldly.

After she had signed in, Brian Everthorpe directed her to the section of the car park reserved for visitors, and waited for her at the entrance to the Administration Block. He ushered her into an overheated wood-panelled lobby.

"This is Dr. Penrose," he said to the two women behind the reception desk. They gaped at her as if she was an alien from outer space, as she shook the snow from her fur cap and quilted jacket. "I'll tell Mr. Wilcox she's here," said Brian Everthorpe, and Robyn thought she saw him wink for some inscrutable reason. "Take a seat," he said, indicating a rather threadbare sofa of the kind Robyn associated with very old-fashioned cinema foyers. "I won't be a tick. Can I take your coat?" The way he looked her up and down made Robyn wish she had kept it on.

"Thanks, I'll keep it with me."

Everthorpe left, and Robyn sat down. The two women behind the reception desk avoided her eye. One was typing and the other was operating the switchboard. Every minute or so the telephone operator intoned in a bored sing-song, "J. Pringle & Sons good morning kin I 'elp yew?," and then, "Puttin' yew threw," or "Sorree, there's no reply." Between calls she murmured inaudibly to her companion and stroked her platinum-blonde hair-do as if it were an ailing pet. Robyn looked around the room. There were framed photographs and testimonials on the panelled walls, and some bits of polished machinery in a glass case. On a low table in front of her were some engineering trade magazines and a copy of the *Financial Times*. It seemed to her that the world could not possibly contain a more boring room. Nothing her eye fell upon aroused in her the slightest flicker of interest, except a bulletin board with removable plastic letters which declared, under the day's date: "*J. Pringle & Sons welcomes Dr. Robin Penrose, Rummidge University.*" Noticing that the two women were now looking at her, Robyn smiled and said, "It's Robyn with a 'y' actually." To her bewilderment they both dissolved into giggles.

2

Vic Wilcox was dictating letters to Shirley when Brian Everthorpe knocked and put his head round the door, grinning, for some reason, from sideburn to sideburn.

"Visitor for you, Vic."

"Oh?"

"Your shadow."

"He's late."

"Well, not surprising, is it, in this weather?" Brian Everthorpe came uninvited into the room. "The motorway was a shambles."

"You should move further in, Brian."

"Yes, well, you know what Beryl is like about the country . . . This shadow caper: what happens exactly?"

"You know what happens. He follows me about all day."

"What, everywhere?"

"That's the idea."

"What, even to the Gents?" Brian Everthorpe exploded with laughter as he uttered this question.

Vic looked wonderingly at him and then at Shirley, who arched her eyebrows and shrugged incomprehension. "You feeling all right, Brian?" he enquired.

"Quite all right, thanks, Vic, quite all right." Everthorpe coughed and wheezed and wiped his eyes with a silk handkerchief which he wore, affectedly, in his breast pocket. "You're a lucky man, Vic."

"What are you talking about?"

"Your shadow. But what will your wife say?"

"What's it got to do with Marjorie?"

"Wait till you see her."

"Marjorie?"

"No, your shadow. Your shadow's a bird, Vic!"

Shirley gave a little squeak of surprise and excitement. Vic stared speechlessly as Brian Everthorpe elaborated.

"A very dishy redhead. I prefer bigger boobs, myself, but you can't have everything." He winked at Shirley.

"Robin!" said Shirley. "It can be a girl's name, can't it? Though they spell it different. With a 'y' sort of thing."

"In the letter it was 'Robin' with an 'i,'" said Vic.

"An easy mistake," said Brian Everthorpe.

"Stuart Baxter said nothing about a woman," said Vic.

"I'll bring her in. Seeing's believing."

"Let me find that letter first," said Vic, riffling blindly through the papers in his Pending-tray, playing for time. He felt anger surging through his veins and arteries. A lecturer in English Literature was bad enough, but a *woman* lecturer in English Literature! It was a ludicrous mistake, or else a calculated insult, he wasn't sure which, to send such a person to shadow him. He wanted to rage and swear, to shout down the telephone and fire off angry memoranda. But something in Brian Everthorpe's demeanour restrained him.

"How old is she sort of thing?" Shirley asked Brian Everthorpe.

"I dunno. Young. In her thirties, I'd say. Shall I bring her in?"

"Go and find that letter, first," Vic said to Shirley. She went into her office, followed, to his relief, by Brian Everthorpe. Everthorpe was getting a lot of mileage out of the mix-up, trying to make him look foolish. Vic could imagine him spreading the story all round the works. *"You should have seen his face when I told him! I couldn't help laughing. Then he went spare. Shirley had to cover her ears . . ."* No, better to limit the damage, control his anger, make nothing of it, pretend he didn't mind.

He rose from his desk and went through the anteroom into Shirley's office. High up on one wall were some glazed panels. They were painted over, but someone had scraped away a small area of paint, exposing the clear glass. Shirley was peering through this spyhole, balanced precariously on top of a filing cabinet, steadied by the hand of Brian Everthorpe on her haunch. "Hmm, not a bad-looking wench," she was saying. "If you like that type."

"You're just jealous, Shirley," said Brian Everthorpe.

"Me, jealous? Don't be daft. I like her boots, mind."

"What in God's name are you doing up there?" Vic said.

Brian Everthorpe and Shirley turned and looked at him.

"A little dodge of your predecessor," said Brian Everthorpe. "He liked to look over his visitors before a meeting. Reckoned it gave him a psychological advantage." He removed his hand from Shirley's rump, and assisted her to the ground.

"I couldn't find that letter," she said.

"You mean you can see into reception from there?" said Vic.

"Have a dekko," said Brian Everthorpe.

Vic hesitated, then sprang onto the filing cabinet. He applied his eye to the hole in the paint and gazed, as if through a telescope already fixed and focused, at the young woman seated on the far side of the lobby. She had copper-coloured hair, cut short as a boy's at the back, with a mop of curls tilted jauntily forward at the front. She sat at her ease on the sofa, with her long, booted and pantalooned legs crossed at the ankles, but the expression on her face was bored and haughty. "I've seen her before," he said.

"Oh, where?" said Shirley.

"I don't know." She was like a figure in a dream that he could not quite recall. He stared at the topknot of red-gold curls, straining to remember. Then she yawned suddenly, like a cat, revealing two rows of white, even teeth, before she covered her mouth. She lifted her head as she did this, and seemed to look straight at him. Embarrassed, feeling too like a Peeping Tom for comfort, he scrambled to the floor.

"Let's stop playing silly buggers," he said, striding back into his office. "Show the woman in."

. . .

Brian Everthorpe threw open the door of Vic Wilcox's office and motioned Robyn across the threshold with a flourish. "Doctor Penrose," he announced, with a smirk.

The man who rose from behind a large polished desk on the far side of the room, and came forward to shake Robyn's hand, was smaller and more ordinary-looking than she had expected. The term "Managing Director" had suggested to her imagination some figure more grand and gross, with plump, flushed cheeks and wings of silver hair, a rotund torso sheathed in expensively tailored suiting, a gold tiepin and cufflinks, and a cigar wedged between manicured fingers. This man was stocky and wiry, like a short-legged terrier, his face was pale and drawn, with two vertical worry-lines scored into the brow above the nose, and the hank of dark, flat hair that fell forward across his brow had clearly never had the attention of an expert barber. He was in shirtsleeves, and the shirt did not fit him very well, the buttoned cuffs hanging down over his wrists, like a schoolboy's whose clothes had been purchased with a view to his "growing into" them. Robyn almost smiled with relief as she appraised his advancing figure—she already heard herself describing him to Charles or Penny as "a funny little man"—but the strength of his handshake, and the glint in his dark brown eyes, warned her not to underestimate him.

"Thanks, Brian," he said to the hovering Everthorpe. "I expect you've got work to do."

Everthorpe departed with obvious reluctance. "See you later, I hope," he said unctuously to Robyn, as he closed the door.

"Like some coffee?" said Wilcox, taking her coat and hanging it on the back of the door.

Robyn said she would love some.

"Have a seat." He indicated an upright armchair drawn up at an angle to his desk, to which he now returned. He flicked a switch on a console and said, "Two coffees, please, Shirley." He thrust a cigarette pack in her direction. "Smoke?"

Robyn shook her head. He lit one himself, sat down and swivelled his chair to face her. "Haven't we met before?" he said.

"Not that I'm aware of."

"I've a feeling I've seen you recently."

"I can't imagine where that would be."

Wilcox continued to stare at her through a cloud of smoke. If it had been Everthorpe, she would have dismissed this performance as a clumsy pass, but Wilcox seemed teased by some genuine memory.

"I'm sorry I'm a bit late," she said. "The roads were terrible, and I got lost."

"You're a week late," he said. "I was expecting you last Wednesday."

"Didn't you get my message?"

"About halfway through the morning."

"I hope I didn't inconvenience you."

"You did, as a matter of fact. I'd cancelled a meeting."

He did not lighten this rebuke with a smile. Robyn felt herself growing warm with resentment of his rudeness, mingled with the consciousness that her own conduct had not been entirely blameless. Her original plan for the previous Wednesday had been to put in an hour or two of picket duty very early in the morning, and then go on to her appointment at Pringle's. But on the picket line Bob Busby had pointed out to her that the Shadow Scheme was official University business and that she would be strike-breaking if she kept her appointment. Of course it was and of course she would! *Stupida!* She punched her head with her fist in self-reproach. She was inexperienced in the protocol of industrial action, but only too pleased to have an excuse to put off her visit to Pringle's for a week.

"I'm sorry," she said to Wilcox. "It was a bit chaotic at the University last Wednesday. We had a one-day strike on, you see. The switchboard wasn't operating normally. It took me ages to phone."

"That's where I saw you!" he exclaimed, sitting up in his chair, and pointing a finger at her like a gun. "You were standing outside the University gates at about eight o'clock in the morning, last Wednesday."

"Yes," said Robyn. "I was."

"I drive past there every day on my way to work," he said. "I was held up there last Wednesday. Put two minutes on my journey time, it did. You were holding a banner." He pronounced this last word as if it denoted something unpleasant.

"Yes, I was picketing."

What fun it had been! Stopping cars and thrusting leaflets through the drivers' windows, turning back lorries, waving banners for the benefit of local TV news cameras, cheering when a truck driver decided not to cross the picket line, thawing one's fingers round a mug of thermos-flask coffee, sharing the warm glow of camaraderie with colleagues one had never met before. Robyn had not felt so exalted since the great women's rally at Greenham Common.

"What were you striking about? Pay?"

"Partly. That and the cuts."

"You want no cuts and more pay?"

"That's right."

"Think the country can afford it?"

"Certainly," said Robyn. "If we spent less on defence—"

"This company has several defence contracts," said Wilcox. "We make gearbox casings for Challenger tanks, and con-rods for Armoured Personnel Carriers. If those contracts were cancelled, I'd have to lay off men. Your cuts would become ours."

"You could make something else," said Robyn. "Something peaceful."

"What?"

"I can't say what you should make," said Robyn irritably. "It's not my business."

"No, it's mine," said Wilcox.

At that moment his secretary came into the room with two cups of coffee, which she distributed in a pregnant silence, shooting curious, covert glances at each of them. When she had gone, Wilcox said, "Who were you trying to hurt?"

"Hurt?"

"A strike has to hurt someone. The employers, the public. Otherwise it has no effect."

Robyn was about to say, "The Government," when she saw the trap: Wilcox would find it easy enough to argue that the Government had not been troubled by the strike. Nor, as Philip Swallow had predicted, had the general public been greatly inconvenienced. The students' Union had supported the strike, and its members had not complained about a day's holiday from lectures. The University, then? But the University wasn't responsible for the cuts or the erosion of lecturers' salaries. Faster than a computer, Robyn's mind reviewed these candidates for the target of the strike and rejected them all. "It was only a one-day strike," she said at length. "More of a demonstration, really. We got a lot of support from other trade unions. Several lorry-drivers refused to cross the picket lines."

"What were they doing—delivering stuff?"

"Yes."

"I expect they came back the next day, or the next week?"

"I suppose so."

"And who paid for the extra deliveries? I'll tell you who," he went on when she did not answer. "Your University—which you say is short of cash. It's even shorter, now."

"They docked our salaries," said Robyn. "They can pay for the lorries out of that."

Wilcox grunted as if acknowledging a debating point, from which she deduced that he was a bully and needed to be stood up to. She did not think it necessary to tell him that the University administration had been obliged to circulate all members of staff with a memorandum asking them, if they had been on strike, to volunteer the information (since there was no other way of finding out) so that their pay could be docked. It was rumoured that the number of staff who had responded was considerably smaller than the number of participants in the strike claimed by the AUT. "Do you have many strikes here?" she asked, in an effort to shift the focus of conversation.

"Not any more," said Wilcox. "The employees know which side their bread is buttered. They look around this area, they see the factories that have closed in the past few years, they know how many people are out of work."

"You mean, they're afraid to strike?"

"Why should they strike?"

"I don't know—but if they wanted to. For higher wages, say?"

"This is a very competitive industry. A strike would plunge us deep into the red. The division could close us down. The men know that."

"The division?"

"The Engineering and Foundry Division of Midland Amalgamated. They own us."

"I thought J. Pringle & Sons were the owners."

Wilcox laughed, a gruff bark. "Oh, the Pringle family got out years ago. Took their money and ran, when the going was good. The company's been bought and sold twice since then." He took a brown manila folder from a drawer and passed it to her. "Here are some tree diagrams showing how we fit into the conglomerate, and the management structure of the company. D'you know much about business?"

"Nothing at all. But isn't that supposed to be the point?"

"The point?"

"Of the Shadow Scheme."

"I'm buggered if I know what the point is," said Wilcox sourly. "It's just a PR stunt, if you ask me. You teach English literature, don't you?"

"Yes."

"What's that? Shakespeare? Poetry?"

"Well, I do teach a first-year course that includes some—"

"We did *Julius Caesar* for O-Level," Wilcox interjected. "Had to learn great chunks of it by heart. Hated it, I did. The master was a toffee-nosed southerner, used to take the pi—used to make fun of our accents."

"My field is the nineteenth-century novel," said Robyn. "And women's studies."

"Women's studies?" Wilcox echoed with a frown. "What are they?"

"Oh, women's writing. The representation of women in literature. Feminist critical theory."

Wilcox sniffed. "You give degrees for that?"

"It's one part of the course," said Robyn stiffly. "It's an option."

"A soft one, if you ask me," said Wilcox. "Still, I suppose it's all right for girls."

"Boys take it too," said Robyn. "And the reading load is very heavy, as a matter of fact."

"Boys?" Wilcox curled a lip. "Nancy boys?"

"Perfectly normal, decent, intelligent young men," said Robyn, struggling to control her temper.

"Why aren't they studying something useful, then?"

"Like mechanical engineering?"

"You said it."

Robyn sighed. "Do I really have to tell you?"

"Not if you don't want to."

"Because they're more interested in ideas, in feelings, than in the way machines work."

"Won't pay the rent, though, will they—ideas, feelings?"

"Is money the only criterion?"

"I don't know a better one."

"What about happiness?"

"Happiness?" Wilcox looked startled, caught off balance for the first time.

"Yes, I don't earn much money, but I'm happy in my job. Or I would be, if I were sure of keeping it."

"Why aren't you?"

When Robyn explained her situation, Wilcox seemed more struck by her colleagues' security than by her own vulnerability. "You mean, they've got jobs for life?" he said.

"Well, yes. But the Government wants to abolish tenure in the future."

"I should think so."

"But it's essential!" Robyn exclaimed. "It's the only guarantee of academic freedom. It's one of the things we were demonstrating for last week."

"Hang about," said Wilcox. "*You* were demonstrating in support of the other lecturers' right to a job for life?"

"Partly," said Robyn.

"But if they can't be shifted, there'll never be room for you, no matter how much better than them you may be at the job."

This thought had crossed Robyn's mind before, but she had suppressed it as ignoble. "It's the principle of the thing," she said. "Besides, if it wasn't for the cuts, I'd have had a permanent job by now. We should be taking more students, not fewer."

"You think the universities should expand indefinitely?"

"Not indefinitely, but—"

"Enough to accommodate all those who want to do women's studies?"

"If you like to put it that way, yes," said Robyn defiantly.

"Who pays?"

"You keep bringing everything back to money."

"That's what you learn from business. There's no such thing as a free lunch. Who said that?"

Robyn shrugged. "I don't know. Some right-wing economist, I suppose."

"Had his head screwed on, whoever he was. I read it in the paper somewhere. There's no such thing as a free lunch." He gave his gruff bark of a laugh. "Someone always has to pick up the bill." He glanced at his watch. "Well, I suppose I'd better show you round the estate. Just give me a few minutes, will you?" He stood up, seized his jacket and thrust his arms into the sleeves.

"Aren't I supposed to follow you everywhere?" said Robyn, rising to her feet.

"I don't think you can follow me where I'm going," said Wilcox.

"Oh," said Robyn, colouring. Then, recovering her poise, she said, "Perhaps you would direct me to the Ladies."

"I'll get Shirley to show you," said Wilcox. "Meet me back here in five minutes."

. . .

Jesus wept! Not just a lecturer in English literature, not just a *woman* lecturer in English literature, but a trendy lefty feminist lecturer in English literature! A *tall* trendy leftist feminist lecturer in English literature! Vic Wilcox scuttled into the Directors' Lavatory as if into a place of sanctuary. It was a large, dank, chilly room, empty at this moment, which had been lavishly appointed, in more prosperous times, with marble washbasins and brass taps, but was now badly in need of redecoration. He stood at the urinal and peed fiercely at the white ceramic wall, streaked with rusty tear-stains from the corroding pipes. What the hell was he going to do with this woman every Wednesday for the next two months? Stuart Baxter must be off his trolley, sending someone like that. Or was it a plot?

It was strange, strange and ominous, that he had seen her before, outside the University last week. Her hair, glowing like a brazier through the early-morning mist, her high boots and her cream-coloured quilted jacket with its exaggerated shoulders, had drawn his gaze as he sat impatiently in a line of cars while the pickets argued with the driver of an articulated wagon that was trying to enter the University. She had been standing on the pavement, holding some silly banner—*"Education Cuts Are Not Comic,"* or something like that—talking and laughing excitedly with a big-bosomed woman stuffed into a scarlet ski-suit and pink moon boots, and he remembered thinking to himself: so it's finally happened—designer industrial action. The two women, the copperhead in particular, had seemed to epitomise everything he most detested about such demonstrations—the appropriation of working-class politics by middle-class style. And now he was stuck with her for two months.

There was a marble-topped table in the centre of the flagged floor, bearing, like an altar, a symmetrical arrangement of clothes brushes and men's toiletries that Vic had never seen anyone disturb since he came to Pringle's. In his anger and frustration, he picked up a long, curved clothes brush and banged it down hard on the surface of the table. It broke in half.

"Shit!" said Vic, aloud.

As if on cue, a cistern flushed and the door of one of the WC cubicles opened to reveal the emerging figure of George Prendergast, the Personnel Director. This was not a total surprise, since Prendergast suffered from

Irritable Bowel Syndrome and was frequently to be encountered in the Directors' Lavatory, but Vic had thought he was alone, and felt rather foolish standing there with the stump of the clothes brush, like an incriminating weapon, in his fist. For the sake of appearances, he picked up another brush and began swatting at the sleeves and lapels of his suit.

"Smartening yourself up for your Shadow, Vic?" said Prendergast jocularly. "I hear she's quite a, er, that is . . ." Catching sight of Vic's expression, he faltered into silence. His pale blue eyes peered anxiously at Vic through thick rimless spectacles. He was the youngest of the senior management team and rather overawed by Vic.

"Have you seen her?" Vic demanded.

"Well, no, not actually seen, but Brian Everthorpe says—"

"Never mind what Brian Everthorpe says, he's only interested in the size of her tits. She's a women's libber, if you don't mind, a bloody Communist too, I shouldn't be surprised. She had one of those CND badges on. What in the name of Christ am I—" He stopped, struck by a sudden thought. "George— can I borrow your phone?"

"Of course. Something wrong with yours?"

"No, I just want to make a private call. Give me a couple of minutes, will you? Brush yourself down while you're waiting. Here." He thrust the clothes brush into the bewildered Prendergast's hand, patted him on the shoulder, and made tracks for the Personnel Director's Office by a circuitous route that did not take him past his own.

"Mr. Prendergast's just popped out," said his secretary.

"I know," said Vic, striding past her and shutting the door of Prendergast's room behind him. He sat down at the desk and dialled Stuart Baxter's private number. Luckily he was in.

"Stuart—Vic Wilcox here. My shadow's just arrived."

"Oh yes? What's he like?"

"She, Stuart, she. You mean you didn't know?"

"Honest to God," said Stuart Baxter, when he had finished laughing, "I had no idea. Robyn with a 'y,' well, well. Is she good-looking?"

"That's the only thing anybody seems to be interested in. My managers are poncing about like gigolos and the secretaries are beside themselves with jealousy." This was admittedly an exaggeration, but he wanted to emphasise the potentially disruptive effect of Robyn Penrose's presence. "Christ knows what will happen when I take her onto the shop floor," he said.

"So she *is* good-looking."

"Some might say so, I suppose. More to the point, she's a Communist."

"What? How d'you know?"

"Well, a left-winger, anyway. You know what those university types are like, on the arts side. She's a member of CND."

"That's not a crime, Vic."

"No, but we do have MoD contracts. She's a security risk."

"Hmm," said Stuart Baxter. "Not exactly secret weapons you're making, are they, Vic? Gearbox casings for tanks, engine components for trucks . . . Any of your people had to be vetted? Have you signed the Official Secrets Act?"

"No," Vic admitted. "But it's better to be safe than sorry. I think you ought to get her taken off the scheme."

After a brief pause for thought, Stuart Baxter said, "No can do, Vic. There'd be the most almighty row if we appeared to be sabotaging an Industry Year project simply because this bird is a member of CND. I can just see the headlines—RUMMIDGE FIRM SLAMS DOOR ON RED ROBYN. If you catch her stealing blueprints, let me know, and I'll do something about it."

"Thanks a lot," said Vic flatly. "You're a great help."

"Why be so negative, about it, Vic? Relax! Enjoy the girl's company. I should be so lucky." Stuart Baxter chuckled, and put down the phone.

3

"Well—what did you make of it?" Vic Wilcox demanded, an hour or so later, when they were back in his office after what he had referred to as "a quick whistle round the works."

Robyn sank down on to a chair. "I thought it was appalling," she said.

"Appalling?" He frowned. "What d'you mean, appalling?"

"The noise. The dirt. The mindless, repetitive work. The . . . everything. That men should have to put up with such brutalising conditions—"

"Now just a minute—"

"Women, too. I did see women, didn't I?" She had a blurred memory of brown-skinned creatures vaguely female in shape but unsexed by their drab, greasy overalls and trousers, working alongside men in some parts of the factory.

"We have a few. I thought you were all for equality?"

"Not equality of oppression."

"*Oppression?*" He gave a harsh, derisive laugh. "We don't force people to work here, you know. For every unskilled job we advertise, we get a hundred applicants—more than a hundred. Those women are glad to work here—go and ask 'em if you don't believe me."

Robyn was silent. She felt confused, battered, exhausted by the sense-impressions of the last hour. For once in her life, she was lost for words, and uncertain of her argumentative ground. She had always taken for granted that unemployment was an evil, a Thatcherite weapon against the working class; but if this was employment then perhaps people were better off without it. "But the noise," she said again. "The dirt!"

"Foundries are dirty places. Metal is noisy stuff to work with. What did you expect?"

What *had* she expected? Nothing, certainly, so like the satanic mills of the early Industrial Revolution. Robyn's mental image of a modern factory had derived mainly from TV commercials and documentaries: deftly edited footage of brightly coloured machines and smoothly moving assembly lines, manned by brisk operators in clean overalls, turning out motor cars or transistor radios to the accompaniment of Mozart on the sound track. At Pringle's there was scarcely any colour, not a clean overall in sight, and instead of Mozart there was a deafening demonic cacophony that never relented. Nor had she been able to comprehend what was going on. There seemed to be no logic or direction to the factory's activities. Individuals or small groups of men worked on separate tasks with no perceptible relation to each other. Components were stacked in piles all over the factory floor like the contents of an attic. The whole place seemed designed to produce, not goods for the outside world, but misery for the inmates. What Wilcox called the machine shop had seemed like a prison, and the foundry had seemed like hell.

. . .

"There are two sides to our operation," he had explained, when he led her out of the office block and across a bleak enclosed courtyard, where footsteps had scored a diagonal path through the snow, towards a high windowless wall of corrugated iron. "The foundry, and the machine shop. We also do a bit of assembly work—small engines and steering assemblies, I'm trying to build it up—but basically we're a general engineering firm, supplying components to the motor industry mostly. Parts are cast in the foundry or brought in and then we machine 'em. The foundry was allowed to go to pot in the seventies and Pringle's started purchasing from outside suppliers. I'm trying to make our foundry more efficient. So the foundry is a cost-centred operation, and the engineering side is profit-centred. But if all goes well, in time we should be able to sell our castings outside and make a profit on them too. In fact we've got to, because a really efficient foundry will produce more castings than we can use ourselves."

"What exactly is a foundry?" said Robyn, as they reached a small, scarred wooden door in the corrugated-iron wall. Wilcox halted, his hand on the door. He stared at her incredulously.

"I told you I didn't know anything about . . ." She was going to say "industry," but it occurred to her that this admission would come oddly from an expert on the Industrial Novel. "This sort of thing," she concluded. "I don't suppose *you* know a lot about literary criticism, do you?"

Wilcox grunted and pushed open the door to let her through. "A foundry is where you melt iron or other metal and pour it into moulds to make castings. Then in the machine shop we mill and grind them and bore holes in them so that they can be assembled into more complex products, like engines. Are you with me?"

"I think so," she said coldly. They were walking along a broad corridor between glass-partitioned offices, lit by bleak fluorescent strip lighting, where sallow-faced men in shirtsleeves stared at computer terminals or pored over sheets of printout.

"This is production control," said Wilcox. "I don't think there'd be much point trying to explain it to you now."

Some of the men in the offices looked up as they passed, nodded to Wilcox and eyed Robyn curiously. Few smiled.

"We should really have started at the foundry," said Wilcox, "since that's the first stage of our operation. But the quickest way to the foundry is through the machine shop, especially in this weather. So you're seeing the production process in reverse." He pushed through another battered-looking swing door and held it open for her. She plunged into the noise as into a tank of water.

The machine shop was an enormous shed with machines and work benches laid out in a grid pattern. Wilcox led her down the broad central aisle, with occasional detours to left and right to point out some particular operation. Robyn soon gave up trying to follow his explanations. She could hardly hear them because of the din, and the few words and phrases that she did catch—"tolerances to five thou," "cross-boring," "CNC machine," "indexes round"—meant nothing to her. The machines were ugly, filthy and surprisingly old-fashioned in appearance. The typical operation seemed to be that the man took a lump of metal from a bin, thrust it into the machine, closed some kind of safety cage, and pulled a lever. Then he opened the cage, took out the part (which now looked slightly different) and dropped it into another bin. He did all this as noisily as possible.

"Does he do the same thing all day?" she shouted to Wilcox, after they had watched one such man at work for some minutes. He nodded. "It seems terribly monotonous. Couldn't it be done automatically?"

Wilcox led her to a slightly quieter part of the shop floor. "If we had the capital to invest in new machines, yes. And if we cut down the number of our operations—for the part he's making it wouldn't be worth automating. The quantities are too small."

"Couldn't you move him to another job occasionally?" she said, with a sudden burst of inspiration. "Move them all about, every few hours, just to give them a change?"

"Like musical chairs?" Wilcox produced a crooked smile.

"It seems so awful to be standing there, hour after hour, doing the same thing, day after day."

"That's factory work. The operatives like it that way."

"I find that hard to believe."

"They don't like being shunted about. You start moving men about from one job to another, and they start complaining, or demanding to be put on a higher grade. Not to mention the time lost changing over."

"So it comes back to money again."

"Everything does, in my experience."

"Never mind what the men want?"

"They prefer it this way, I'm telling you. They switch off, they daydream. If they were smart enough to get bored, they wouldn't be doing a job like this in the first place. If you want to see an automated process, come over here."

He strode off down one of the aisles. The blue-overalled workers reacted to his passage like a shoal of minnows in the presence of a big fish. They did not look up or catch his eye, but there was a perceptible tremor along the work benches, a subtle increase in the carefulness and precision of their movements as the boss passed. The foremen behaved differently. They came hurrying forward with obsequious smiles as Wilcox stopped to ask about a bin of components with "WASTE" chalked on the side, or squatted beside a broken-down machine to discuss the cause with an oily-pawed mechanic. Wilcox made no attempt to introduce Robyn to anyone, though she was aware that she was an object of curiosity in these surroundings. On all sides she saw glazed abstracted eyes click suddenly into sharp focus as they registered her presence, and she observed sly smiles and muttered remarks being exchanged between neighbouring benches. The content of these remarks she could guess all too easily from the pin-ups that were displayed on walls and pillars everywhere, pages torn from softporn magazines depicting glossy-lipped naked women with bulging breasts and buttocks, pouting and posturing indecently.

"Can't you do something about these pictures?" she asked Wilcox.

"What pictures?" He looked around, apparently genuinely puzzled by the question.

"All these pornographic pin-ups."

"Oh, those. You get used to them. They don't register, after a while."

That, she realized, was what was peculiarly degrading and depressing about the pictures. Not just the nudity of the girls, or their poses, but the fact that nobody was looking at them, except herself. Once these images must have excited lust—enough to make someone take the trouble to cut them out and stick them up on the wall; but after a day or two, or a week or two, the pictures had ceased to arouse, they had become familiar—faded and tattered and oil-stained, almost indistinguishable from the dirt and debris of the rest of the factory. It made the models' sacrifice of their modesty seem poignantly vain.

"There you are," said Wilcox. "Our one and only CNC machine."

"What?"

"Computer-numerically controlled machine. See how quickly it changes tools?"

Robyn peered through a Perspex window and watched things moving round and going in and out in sudden spasms, lubricated by spurts of a liquid that looked like milky coffee.

"What's it doing?"

"Machining cylinder heads. Beautiful, isn't it?"

"Not the word I'd choose."

There was something uncanny, almost obscene, to Robyn's eye, about the sudden, violent, yet controlled movements of the machine, darting forward and retreating, like some steely reptile devouring its prey or copulating with a passive mate.

"One day," said Wilcox, "there will be lightless factories full of machines like that."

"Why lightless?"

"Machines don't need light. Machines are blind. Once you've built a fully computerised factory, you can take out the lights, shut the door and leave it to make engines or vacuum cleaners or whatever, all on its own in the dark. Twenty-four hours a day."

"What a creepy idea."

"They already have them in the States. Scandinavia."

"And the Managing Director? Will he be a computer too, sitting in a dark office?"

Wilcox considered the question seriously. "No, computers can't think. There'll always have to be a man in charge, at least one man, deciding what should be made, and how. But these jobs"—he jerked his head round at the rows of benches—"will no longer exist. This machine here is doing the work that was done last year by twelve men."

"O brave new world," said Robyn, "where only the managing directors have jobs."

This time Wilcox did not miss her irony. "I don't like making men redundant," he said, "but we're caught in a double bind. If we don't modernise we lose competitive edge and have to make men redundant, and if we *do* modernise we have to make men redundant because we don't need 'em any more."

"What we should be doing is spending more money preparing people for creative leisure," said Robyn.

"Like women's studies?"

"Among other things."

"Men like to work. It's a funny thing, but they do. They may moan about it every Monday morning, they may agitate for shorter hours and longer holidays, but they need to work for their self-respect."

"That's just conditioning. People could get used to life without work."

"Could *you*? I thought you enjoyed your work."

"That's different."

"Why?"

"Well, it's nice work. It's meaningful. It's rewarding. I don't mean in money terms. It would be worth doing even if one wasn't paid anything at all. And the conditions are decent—not like this." She swept her arm round in a gesture that embraced the oil-laden atmosphere, the roar of machinery, the crash of metal, the whine of electric trolleys, the worn, soiled ugliness of everything.

"If you think this is rough, wait till you see the foundry," said Wilcox, with a grim smile, and set off again at his brisk terrier's trot.

. . .

Even this warning did not prepare Robyn for the shock of the foundry. They crossed another yard, where hulks of obsolete machinery crouched, bleeding rust into their blankets of snow, and entered a large building with a high vaulted roof hidden in gloom. This space rang with the most barbaric noise Robyn had ever experienced. Her first instinct was to cover her ears, but she soon realized that it was not going to get any quieter, and let her hands fall to her sides. The floor was covered with a black substance that looked like soot, but grated under the soles of her boots like sand. The air reeked with a sulphurous, resinous smell, and a fine drizzle of black dust fell on their heads from the roof. Here and there the open doors of furnaces glowed a dangerous red, and in the far corner of the building what looked like a stream of molten lava trickled down a curved channel from roof to floor. The roof itself was holed in places, and melting snow dripped to the floor and spread in muddy puddles. It was a place of extreme temperatures: one moment you were shivering in an icy draught from some gap in the outside wall, the next you felt the frightening heat of a furnace's breath on your face. Everywhere there was indescribable mess, dirt, disorder. Discarded castings, broken tools, empty canisters, old bits of iron and wood, lay scattered around. Everything had an improvised, random air about it, as if people had erected new machines just where they happened to be standing at the time, next to the debris of the old. It was impossible to believe that anything clean and new and mechanically efficient could come out of this place. To Robyn's eye it resembled nothing so much as a medieval painting of hell— though it was hard to say whether the workers looked more like devils or the damned. Most of them, she observed, were Asian or Caribbean, in contrast to the machine shop where the majority had been white.

Wilcox led her up a twisted and worn steel staircase to a prefabricated office perched on stilts in the middle of the building, and introduced her to the general manager, Tom Rigby, who looked her up and down once and then ignored her. Rigby's young assistant regarded her with more interest, but was soon drawn into a discussion about production schedules. Robyn looked around the office. She had never seen a room that had such a forlorn, unloved look. The furniture was dirty, damaged and mismatched. The lino on the floor was scuffed and torn, the windows nearly opaque with grime, and the walls looked as if they had never been repainted since the place was constructed.

Fluorescent strip lighting relentlessly illuminated every sordid detail. The only splash of colour in the drab decor was the inevitable pin-up, on the wall above the desk of Rigby's young assistant: last year's calendar, turned to the page for December, depicting a grinning topless model tricked out in fur boots and ermine-trimmed bikini pants. Apart from her, the only item in the room that didn't look old and obsolete was the computer over which the three men were crouched, talking earnestly.

Bored, she stepped outside, onto a steel gallery overlooking the factory floor. She surveyed the scene, feeling more than ever like Dante in the Inferno. All was noise, smoke, fumes and flames. Overalled figures, wearing goggles, facemasks, helmets or turbans, moved slowly through the sulphurous gloom or crouched over their inscrutable tasks beside furnaces and machines.

"Here—Tom said you'd better put this on."

Wilcox had appeared at her side. He thrust into her hands a blue plastic safety helmet with a transparent visor.

"What about you?" she asked, as she put it on. He shrugged and shook his head. He hadn't even got a coat or overall to cover his business suit. Some kind of macho pride, presumably. The boss must appear invulnerable.

"Visitors have to," said Tom Rigby. "We're responsible, like."

A very loud hooter started bleating frantically, and made Robyn jump.

Rigby grinned: "That's the KW, they've got it going again."

"What was the matter with it?" said Wilcox.

"Just a valve, I think. You should show her." He jerked his head in Robyn's direction. "Something worth seeing, the KW, when she's on song."

"What's a KW?" Robyn asked.

"Kunkel Wagner Automatic Moulding Line," said Wilcox.

"The boss's pride and joy," said Rigby. "Only installed a few weeks back. You should show her," he said again to Wilcox.

"All in due course," said Wilcox. "The pattern shop first."

The pattern shop was a haven of relative peace and quiet, reminiscent of cottage industry, a place where carpenters fashioned the wooden shapes that contributed the first stage of the moulding process. After that she saw men making sand moulds, first by hand, and then with machines that looked like giant waffle-irons. It was there that she saw women working alongside the men, lifting the heavy-looking mouldings, reeking of hot resin, from the machines, and stacking them on trolleys. She listened uncomprehendingly to Wilcox's technical explanations about the drag and the cope, core boxes and coffin moulds. "Now we'll have a dekko at the cupola," he shouted. "Watch your step."

The cupola turned out to be a kind of gigantic cauldron erected high in one corner of the building where she had earlier noticed what looked like volcanic lava trickling downwards. "They fill it up continuously with layers of coke and iron—scrap-iron and pig-iron—and limestone, and fire it with oxygenated air. The iron melts, picking up the correct amount of carbon from the coke, and runs out of the taphole at the bottom." He led her up another tortuous steel staircase, its steps worn and buckled, across improvised bridges and ricketty gangways, up higher and higher, until they were crouching next to the very source of the molten metal. The white-hot stream flowed down a crudely-fashioned open conduit, passing only a couple of feet from Robyn's toecaps. It was like a small pinnacle in Pandemonium, dark and hot, and the two squatting Sikhs who rolled their white eyeballs and flashed their teeth in her direction, poking with steel rods at the molten metal for no discernible purpose, looked just like demons on an old fresco.

The situation was so bizarre, so totally unlike her usual environment, that there was a kind of exhilaration to be found in it, in its very discomfort and danger, such as explorers must feel, she supposed, in a remote and barbarous country. She thought of what her colleagues and students might be doing this Wednesday morning—earnestly discussing the poetry of John Donne or the novels of Jane Austen or the nature of modernism, in centrally heated, carpeted rooms. She thought of Charles at the University of Suffolk, giving a lecture, perhaps, on Romantic landscape poetry, illustrated with slides. Penny Black would be feeding more statistics on wife-beating in the West Midlands into her data-base, and Robyn's mother would be giving a coffee morning for some charitable cause in her Liberty-curtained lounge with a view of the sea. What would they all think if they could see her now?

"Something funny?" Wilcox yelled in her ear, and she realized that she was grinning broadly at her own thoughts. She straightened her features and shook her head. He shot her a suspicious glance, and continued his commentary: "The molten metal is received into that holding furnace down there. Its temperature is regulated electrically, so we only use what we need. Before I installed it, they had to use all the iron they melted, or else waste it." He stood up abruptly, and without explanation or offer of assistance, set off on the descent to the factory floor. Robyn followed as best she could, her high-heeled boots skidding on the slippery surfaces, polished by generations of men grinding black sand underfoot. Wilcox waited impatiently for her at the bottom of the final staircase. "Now we can have a look at the KW," he said, marching off again. "Better hurry, or they'll soon be knocking off for lunch."

"I thought the man in the office, Mr. Rigby, said it was a new machine," was Robyn's first comment, when they stood before its massive bulk. "It doesn't look new."

"It's not *new*," said Wilcox. "I can't afford to buy machines like that brand new. I got it second-hand from a foundry in Sunderland that closed down last year. A snip, it was."

"What does it do?"

"Makes moulds for cylinder blocks."

"It seems quieter than the other machines," said Robyn.

"It's not running at the moment," Wilcox said, with a pitying look. "What's up?" he demanded, addressing the back of a blue-overalled worker who was standing beside the machine.

"Fookin' pallet's jammed," said the man, without turning his head. "Fitter's workin' on it."

"Watch your language," said Wilcox. "There's a lady present."

The man turned round and looked at Robyn with startled eyes. "No offence," he muttered.

The hooter recommenced its strident blasts.

"Right—here we go," said Wilcox.

The workman manipulated some knobs and levers, closed a cage, stood back, and pressed a button on a console. The huge complex of steel shuddered into life. Something moved forward, something turned over, something began to make a most appalling noise, like a pneumatic drill greatly amplified. Robyn covered her ears. Wilcox jerked his head to indicate that they should move on. He led her up some stairs to a steel gallery from which he said they would get a bird's-eye view of the operation. They overlooked a platform on which several men were standing. A moving track brought to the platform, from the machine that was making the appalling noise, a series of boxes containing moulds shaped out of black sand (though Wilcox called it green). The men lowered core moulds made of orange sand into the boxes, which were turned over and joined to boxes containing the other half of the moulds (the bottom half was the drag, the top the cope—the first bit of jargon she had managed to master) and moved forward on the track to the casting area. Two men brought the molten metal from a holding furnace to the moulds. It was contained in huge ladles suspended from hoists which they guided with push-button controls on the end of electric cables, held in one hand. The other hand grasped a kind of huge steering wheel attached to the side of the ladle, which they turned to tip the molten metal into the small holes in the mould-boxes. The two men, working in rotation, turn and turn about, moved with the slow deliberate gait of astronauts or deep-sea divers. She couldn't see their features, because they wore facemasks and goggles—not without reason, for when they tipped the ladles to pour, white-hot metal splashed like pancake batter and sparks flew through the air.

"Do they do that job all day?" Robyn asked.

"All day, every day."

"It must be frightfully hot work."

"Not so bad in winter. But in summer . . . the temperature can go up to a hundred and twenty Fahrenheit down there."

"Surely they could refuse to work in conditions like that?"

"They could. The office staff start whingeing if it gets above eighty. But those two are men." Wilcox gave this noun a solemn emphasis. "The track makes a ninety-degree turn down there," he went on, shooting out an arm to point, "and the castings go into a cooling tunnel. And the end of it, they're still hot, but hard. The sand gets shaken off them at the knockout."

The knockout was aptly named. It certainly stunned Robyn. It seemed to her like the anus of the entire factory: a black tunnel that extruded the castings, still encased in black sand, like hot, reeking, iron turds, onto a metal grid that vibrated violently and continuously to shake off the sand. A gigantic West Indian, his black face glistening with sweat, bracing himself with legs astride in the midst of the fumes and the heat and the din, dragged the heavy castings from the grid with a steel rod, and attached them to hooks on a conveyor belt by which they were carried away, looking now like carcasses of meat, to another stage of the cooling process.

It was the most terrible place she had ever been in in her life. To say that to herself restored the original meaning of the word "terrible": it provoked terror, even a kind of awe. To think of being that man, wrestling with the heavy awkward lumps of metal in that maelstrom of heat, dust and stench, deafened by the unspeakable noise of the vibrating grid, working like that for hour after hour, day after day . . . That he was black seemed the final indignity: her heart swelled with the recognition of the spectacle's powerful symbolism. He was the noble savage, the Negro in chains, the archetype of exploited humanity, quintessential victim of the capitalist-imperialist-industrial system. It was as much as she could do to restrain herself from rushing forward to grasp his hand in a gesture of sympathy and solidarity.

. . .

"You have a lot of Asians and Caribbeans working in the foundry, but not so many in the other part," Robyn observed, when they were back in the peaceful calm and comparative luxury of Wilcox's office.

"Foundry work is heavy work, dirty work."

"So I noticed."

"The Asians and some of the West Indians are willing to do it. The locals aren't any more. I've no complaints. They work hard, especially the Asians. It's like poetry, Tom Rigby says, when they're working well. Mind you, they have to be handled carefully. They stick together. If one walks out, they all walk out."

"It seems to me the whole set-up is racist," said Robyn.

"Rubbish!" said Wilcox angrily. He pronounced it "Roobish"—it was a word in which his Rummidge accent was particularly noticeable. "The only race trouble we have is between the Indians and the Pakis, or the Hindus and the Sikhs."

"You just admitted blacks do all the worst jobs, the dirtiest, hardest jobs."

"Somebody's got to do them. It's supply and demand. If we were to advertise a job today—a labouring job in the foundry—I guarantee we'd have two hundred black and brown faces at the gates tomorrow morning, and maybe one white."

"And what if you advertise a skilled job?"

"We have plenty of coloureds in skilled jobs. Foremen, too."

"Any coloured managers?" Robyn asked.

Wilcox fumbled for a cigarette, lit it, and exhaled smoke through his nostrils like an angry dragon. "Don't ask me to solve society's problems," he said.

"Who is going to solve them, then," said Robyn, "if it isn't people with power, like you?"

"Who said I have power?"

"I should have thought it was obvious," said Robyn with an airy gesture that embraced the room and its furnishings.

"Oh, I have a big office, and a secretary, and a company car. I can hire and, with a bit more difficulty, fire people. I'm the biggest cog in this particular machine. But a small cog in a much bigger one—Midland Amalgamated. They can get rid of me whenever they like."

"Isn't there something called a golden handshake?" Robyn enquired drily.

"A year's salary, two if I was lucky. That doesn't last for ever, and it's not easy to psych yourself up to get another job after you've been given the push. I've seen it happen to a lot of good MDs that got fired. It wasn't their fault, usually, that the firm was doing badly, but they had to carry the can. You can have the greatest ideas in the world for improving competitive edge, but you have to rely on other people to carry them out, from senior managers down to labourers."

"Perhaps if everybody had a stake in the business, they would work better," said Robyn.

"How d'you mean?"

"Well, if they had a share in the profits."

"And in the losses, too?"

Robyn pondered this awkward point. "Well," she shrugged, "that's the trouble with capitalism, isn't it? It's a lottery. There are winners and losers."

"It's the trouble with life," said Wilcox, looking at his watch. "We'd better get some lunch."

. . .

Lunch was, in its way, as obnoxious to the senses as everything else in the factory. Rather to Robyn's surprise, there were no special eating arrangements for management. "Pringle's used to have a Directors' Dining Room, with their own cook," Wilcox explained as he led her through the drab corridors of the administration block, and out across a yard where fresh snow was already covering the footpath that had been cleared. "I used to have lunch there occasionally when I worked for Lewis & Arbuckle—marvellous grub, it was. And there was a separate restaurant for middle management, too. All that went by the board with the first wave of redundancies. Now there's just the canteen."

"Well, it's more democratic," said Robyn approvingly.

"Not really," said Wilcox. "My senior managers go to the local pub, and the men prefer to bring their own snap. So it's mostly technical and clerical who eat here." He ushered her into a dismal canteen with strip lighting, Formica-topped tables and moulded plastic stacking chairs. The windows were steamed over, and there was a smell in the air that reminded Robyn nauseatingly of school dinners. The food was predictably stodgy—steak pie or fish fried in batter, chips, boiled cabbage and tinned peas, sponge pudding and custard—but it was astonishingly cheap: 50p for the whole menu. Robyn wondered why more workmen didn't take advantage.

"Because they'd have to take off their overalls," said Wilcox, "and they can't be bothered. They'd rather sit on the factory floor and eat their snap, without even washing their hands. You don't want to get too sentimental about the operatives, you know," he went on. "They're a pretty crude lot. They seem to like dirt. We put new toilets in the fettling shop last November. In two weeks they were all vandalised. Disgusting it was, what they did to those toilets."

"Perhaps it was a form of revenge," said Robyn.

"Revenge?" Wilcox stared. "Revenge against who? Me, for giving them new toilets?"

"Revenge against the system."

"What system?"

"The factory system. It must generate enormous resentment."

"Nobody forces them to work here," said Wilcox, stabbing the crust of his steak pie with a fork.

"That's what I mean, it's the return of the repressed. It's unconscious."

"Oh? Who says?" Wilcox enquired, cocking his eyebrow.

"Freud, for one," said Robyn. "Sigmund Freud, the inventor of psycho-analysis."

"I know who you mean," said Wilcox sharply. "I'm not completely solid between the ears, you know, even if I do work in a factory."

"I wasn't implying that you were," said Robyn, flushing. "Have you read Freud, then?"

"I don't get much time for reading," said Wilcox, "but I've a rough idea what he was about. Said everything came down to sex, didn't he?"

"That's a rather over-simplified way of putting it," said Robyn, disinterring some overcooked fish from its carapace of orange batter.

"But basically right?"

"Well, not entirely wrong," said Robyn. "The early Freud certainly thought libido was the prime mover of human behaviour. Later he came to think the death instinct was more important."

"The death instinct—what's that?" Wilcox arrested the transfer of a morsel of meat to his mouth to put this question.

"It's hard to explain. Essentially it's the idea that unconsciously we all long for death, for non-being, because being is so painful."

"I often feel like that at five o'clock in the morning," said Wilcox. "But I snap out of it when I get up."

. . .

Not long after they got back to Wilcox's office, Brian Everthorpe appeared at the door. His face was flushed and his waistcoat seemed perceptibly tighter than ever across his paunch.

"Hallo, Vic. We were expecting you down at the Man in the Moon. But no doubt you had a nice *tête-à-tête* lunch somewhere a bit more upmarket, eh? The King's Head, was it?" He leered at Robyn, and masked a belch with the back of his hand.

"We ate in the canteen," said Wilcox coldly.

Everthorpe fell back a pace, in exaggerated astonishment. "You never took her to that hole, Vic?"

"Nothing wrong with it," said Wilcox. "It's clean and it's cheap."

"How did you enjoy the food?" Everthorpe enquired of Robyn. "Not exactly cordon blue, is it?"

Robyn sat down in an armchair. "It's part of the factory, I suppose."

"Very diplomatic. Next time—there will be a next time, I hope? Next time, get Vic to take you to the King's Head Carvery. If he won't, I will."

"Did you want to see me about something?" said Wilcox impatiently.

"Yes, a little idea I've had. I think we ought to have a calendar. You know, something to give customers at the end of the year. Great advertisement for the firm. It's up there on the wall three hundred and sixty-five days a year."

"What kind of calendar?" said Wilcox.

"Well, you know, the usual sort of thing. Birds with boobs." He glanced at Robyn and winked. "Tasteful, you know, nothing crude. Like the Pirelli calendar. Collectors' items they are, you know."

"Are you off your trolley?" said Wilcox.

"I know what you're going to say," said Everthorpe, holding up his pink, fleshy palms placatingly. "'We can't afford it.' But I wasn't thinking of hiring the Earl of Lichfield and a lot of London models. There's a way we can get it done cheap. You know Shirley has a daughter who does modelling?"

"Wants to do it, you mean."

"Tracey's got what it takes, Vic. You should see her portfolio."

"I have. She looks like a double helping of pink blancmange, and about as exciting. Did Shirley put you up to this?"

"No, Vic, it was my own idea," said Everthorpe, looking hurt. "Of course, I've discussed it with Shirley. She's all in favour."

"Yes, I bet she is."

"My idea is, we use the same girl—Tracey, that is—for each month, but with different backgrounds according to the season."

"Very original. Won't the photographer have his own ideas?"

"Ah, but that's where the other part of my plan comes in. You see, I belong to a photographic club—"

"Excuse me," said Robyn, standing up. The two men, who had temporarily forgotten her presence in the heat of argument, turned their heads and looked at her. She addressed herself to Everthorpe. "Do I understand that you're proposing to advertise your products with a calendar that degrades women?"

"It won't degrade them, my dear, it will . . ." Everthorpe groped for a word.

"Celebrate them?" Robyn helped him out.

"Exactly."

"Yes, I've heard that one before. But you *are* proposing to use pictures of naked women, or one naked woman—like the pin-ups that are plastered all over the factory?"

"Well, yes, but classier. Good taste, you know. None of your *Penthouse*-style crotch shots. Just tit and bum."

"What about a bit of prick and bum, too?" said Robyn.

Everthorpe looked satisfyingly taken aback. "Eh?" he said.

"Well, statistically, at least ten percent of your customers must be gay. Aren't they entitled to a little porn too?"

"Ha, ha," Everthorpe laughed uneasily. "Not many queers in our line of business, are there, Vic?"

Wilcox, who was following this conversation with amused interest, said nothing.

"Or what about the women who work in the offices where these calendars are stuck up?" Robyn continued. "Why should they have to look at naked women all the time? Couldn't you dedicate a few months of the year to naked men? Perhaps you'd like to pose yourself, along with Tracey?"

Vic Wilcox guffawed.

"I'm afraid you've got it wrong, darling," said Everthorpe, struggling to retain his poise. "Women aren't like that. They're not interested in pictures of naked men."

"*I* am," said Robyn. "I like them with hairy chests and ten-inch pricks." Everthorpe gaped at her. "You're shocked, aren't you? But you think it's perfectly all right to talk about women's tits and bums and stick pictures of them up all over the place. Well, it isn't all right. It degrades the women who pose for them, it degrades the men who look at them, it degrades sex."

"This is all very fascinating," said Wilcox, looking at his watch, "but I've got a meeting in here in about five minutes' time, with my technical manager and his staff."

"I'll talk to you later," said Brian Everthorpe huffily. "When there's less interference."

"I'm afraid it's a non-starter, Brian," said Wilcox.

"Stuart Baxter didn't think so," said Everthorpe, fluffing out his side-boards with the back of his hand.

"I don't give a monkey's what Stuart Baxter thinks," said Wilcox.

"I'll talk to you again, when your shadow, or your guardian angel, or whatever she is, will let me get a word in edgewise." Everthorpe strode out of the office.

Robyn, whose legs felt suddenly weak as the adrenalin drained out of her, sat down. Wilcox, who had been frowning after the departing figure of Everthorpe, turned and almost smiled. "I quite enjoyed that," he said.

"You agree with me, then?"

"I think we'd make ourselves a laughing-stock."

"I mean about the principle. The exploitation of women's bodies."

"I don't have much time for that sort of thing myself," said Wilcox. "But some men never grow up."

"You could do something about it," said Robyn. "You're the boss. You could ban all pin-ups from the factory."

"I could, if I was completely barmy. All I need is a wildcat strike over pin-ups."

"You could set an example, at least. There's one of those girlie calendars in your secretary's office."

"Is there?" Wilcox looked genuinely surprised. He jumped up from his swivel chair and went into the adjoining office. A few moments later he returned, scratching his chin thoughtfully. "Funny, I never noticed it. Gresham's Pumps gave it to us."

"Are you going to take it down, then?"

"Shirley says the Gresham's buyer likes to see it on the wall when he visits. No point offending a customer."

Robyn tossed her head scornfully. She was disappointed, having glimpsed the possibility of returning from this expedition into the cultural heart of darkness with some creditable achievement to report to Charles and Penny Black.

Wilcox turned on some lights above the board table on the other side of the room. He went to the window, where the daylight was already fading, and looked out between the vertical louvres of the blind. "It's snowing again. Maybe you should be on your way. The roads will be difficult."

"It's only half past two," said Robyn. "I thought I was supposed to stay with you all day."

"Suit yourself," he said, with a shrug. "But I warn you, I work late."

While Robyn was hesitating, the office began to fill up with men wearing drab suits and dull ties and with the pasty complexions that seemed to be common to everybody who worked in the factory. They came in diffidently, nodded respectfully to Wilcox, and looked askance at Robyn. They sat down at the table, and took out of their pockets packets of cigarettes, lighters and calculators, placing these objects carefully in front of them as if they were necessary equipment for some game they were about to play.

"Where shall I sit?" said Robyn.

"Anywhere you like," said Wilcox.

Robyn took a seat at the opposite end of the table from Wilcox. "This is Dr. Robyn Penrose, of Rummidge University," he said. As though given permission to stare at her, the men all turned their heads simultaneously in her direction. "You've all heard of Industry Year, I suppose. And you all know what a shadow is. Well, Dr. Penrose is my Industry Year Shadow." He looked round the table as if daring anyone to smile. No one did. He explained the Shadow Scheme briefly, and concluded, "Just carry on as if she wasn't there."

This they seemed to find no difficulty in doing, once the meeting started. The subject was Wastage. Wilcox began by stating that the percentage of products rejected by their own inspectors was five per cent, which he considered far too high, and another one per cent was returned by customers. He listed various possible causes—defective machines, careless workmanship, poor supervision, faulty lab tests—and asked the head of each department to identify the main cause of waste in their own area. Robyn found the discussion hard to follow. The managers spoke in cryptic, allusive utterances, using technical jargon that was opaque to her. The adenoidal whine of their accents dulled her hearing, and the smoke of their cigarettes made her eyes smart. She grew bored, and gazed out of the window, at the fading winter light and the fluttering descent of the snow. The snow was general all over Rummidge, she mused, playing variations on a famous passage by James Joyce to divert herself. It was falling on every part of the dark, sprawling conurbation, on the concrete motorways, and the treeless industrial estates, falling softly upon the lawns of the University campus and, further westward, upon the dark mutinous waters of the Rummidge–Wallsbury Canal. Then suddenly she was listening with attention again.

They were discussing a machine that was continually breaking down. "It's the operative's fault," one of the managers was saying. "He's just not up to the job. He doesn't set the indexes properly, so it keeps jamming."

"What's his name?" Wilcox demanded.

"Ram. He's a Paki," said one.

"No, he's not, he's Indian," said another.

"Well, whatever. Who can tell the difference? They call him Danny. Danny Ram. He was moved on to the job when we were short-handed last winter, and up-graded from labourer."

"Let's get rid of him, then," said Wilcox. "He's causing a bottleneck. Terry—see to it, will you?"

Terry, a heavily built man smoking a pipe, took it out of his mouth and said, "We haven't got a basis to fire him."

"Rubbish. He's been trained, hasn't he?"

"I'm not sure."

"Check it out. If he hasn't, train him, even if he can't grasp it. Are you with me?"

Terry nodded.

"Then each time he fails to set the machine properly, you give him a proper warning. On the third warning, he's fired. Shouldn't take more than a fortnight. All right?"

"Right," said Terry, putting his pipe back between his teeth.

"The next question," said Wilcox, "is quality control in the machine shop. Now I've got some figures here—"

"Excuse me," said Robyn.

"Yes, what is it?" said Wilcox, looking up impatiently from his spreadsheet.

"Do I understand that you are proposing to pressure a man into making mistakes so that you can sack him?"

Wilcox stared at Robyn. There was a long silence, such as falls over a saloon bar in a Western at moments of confrontation. Not only did the other men not speak; they did not move. They did not appear even to breathe. Robyn herself was breathing rather fast, in short, shallow pants.

"I don't think it's any of your business, Dr. Penrose," said Wilcox at last.

"Oh, but it is," said Robyn hotly. "It's the business of anyone who cares for truth and justice. Don't you see how wrong it is, to trick this man out of his job?" she said, looking round the table. "How can you sit there, and say nothing?" The men fiddled uneasily with their cigarettes and calculators, and avoided meeting her eye.

"It's a management matter in which you have no competence," said Wilcox.

"It's not a management matter, it's a moral issue," said Robyn.

Wilcox was now pale with anger. "Dr. Penrose," he said, "I think you've got the wrong idea about your position here. You're a shadow, not an inspector. You're here to learn, not to interfere. I must ask you to keep quiet, or leave the meeting."

"Very well, I'll leave," said Robyn. She gathered up her belongings in a strained silence, and left the room.

"Meeting over?" said Shirley, with a bright, meaningless smile.

"No, it's still going on," said Robyn.

"You're leaving early, then? I don't blame you, in this weather. Coming back tomorrow, are you?"

"Next week," said Robyn. "Every Wednesday—that's the arrangement." She was very doubtful whether this arrangement would continue, but it suited her purpose to conceal the row that had just occurred. "Do you know a worker in the factory called Danny Ram?" she asked, in a casual tone of voice.

"Can't say I do. What's his job?"

"I'm not sure. He operates some kind of machine."

"Well, most of them do, don't they?" said Shirley, with a laugh. "Quite a change for you, isn't it, this kind of place? After the University, I mean."

"Yes, quite a change."

"This Ram a friend of yours, is he?" Shirley's curiosity, and perhaps suspicion, had been aroused.

"No, but I think he's the father of one of my students," Robyn improvised.

"You could ask Betty Maitland in Accounts," said Shirley. "Two doors along the corridor."

"Thanks," said Robyn.

Betty Maitland very obligingly looked up Danny Ram on the payroll (his name was actually Danyatai Ram) and told Robyn that he worked in the foundry. Since the only way she knew to the foundry was the route of her guided tour earlier that day, she was obliged to retrace it.

In the machine shop, without Victor Wilcox to escort her, Robyn was as conspicuous in her high-fashion boots, her cord breeches and her cream-coloured quilted jacket, as some rare animal, a white doe or a unicorn, would have been in the same place. Wolf-whistles and catcalls, audible in spite of the mechanical din, followed her as she hurried through the factory. The more the men whistled, the more ribald their remarks, the faster she walked; but the faster she walked, the more of a sexual object, or sexual quarry, she became, twisting and turning between the rows of benches (for she soon lost her bearings), stumbling over piles of metal parts, skidding on the oily floor, her cheeks as red as her hair, the wings of her nostrils white, her eyes fixed steadfastly ahead, refusing to meet the gaze of her tormentors. *"'Allo, darlin', lookin' for me? Fancy a bit of that, Enoch? Show us yer legs! Coom over 'ere and 'old me tool, will yow?"*

At last she found the exit at the far end of the enormous shed, and burst out into a dark courtyard, littered with the hulks of abandoned machinery, which she remembered from the morning. She paused for a moment under a feeble electric light to recover her self-possession, drawing the clean cold air into her lungs, before plunging once more into the third circle of this industrial inferno. With no daylight at all penetrating to the interior of the foundry, it looked more hellish than ever, its furnaces glowing fiercely in the smoky gloom. Here the workers were fewer than in the machine shop, and shyer—perhaps because they were mostly Asian. They avoided her glance, and turned away at her approach, as though her presence vaguely alarmed them. "Danny Ram?" she called after them. "Do you know where Danny Ram works?" They shook their heads, rolled their eyes, grinned nervously, and went about their inscrutable business. At last she came across a white man, nonchalantly lighting his cigarette from a twelve-inch flame shooting out of a gas jet, who was prepared to answer her question. "Danny Ram?" he said, holding his head aslant to avoid being scorched, "Yeah, I know 'im. Woi?"

"I have a message for him."

"'E's over theer," said the man, straightening up, and pointing to a thin, rather depressed-looking Asian standing beside a complicated piece of machinery. It was making so much noise, and absorbing his attention so completely, that he didn't register Robyn's approach.

"Mr. Ram?" she said, touching his sleeve.

He started and swivelled round. "Yes?" he mouthed, staring.

"I have some important information for you," she shouted.

"Information?" he repeated wonderingly. "Who are you, please?"

Fortunately the machine came to the end of its cycle at this point and she was able to continue in a more normal tone of voice. "It doesn't matter who I am. The information is confidential, but I think you ought to know. They're going to try and sack you." The man began to tremble slightly inside his overalls, which were stiff with grease and dirt. "They're going to keep finding fault with your work, and giving you warnings, so they can sack you. Understand? Forewarned is forearmed. Don't tell anyone I told you." She smiled encouragingly, and extended her hand. "Goodbye."

The man wiped his hands ineffectually on his hips and gave her a limp handshake. "Who are you?" he said. "How do you know this?"

"I'm a shadow," said Robyn. The man looked mystified, and slightly awestruck, as if he thought the word denoted some kind of supernatural messenger. "Thank you," he said.

. . .

To avoid running the gauntlet of the machine shop again, Robyn made her way back to the car park by going round the outside of the building, but the paths were covered with drifting snow and the going was difficult. She got lost in the labyrinth of yards and passageways that separated the numerous buildings, many of them apparently disused or derelict, that covered the factory site, and there was nobody around to direct her. At last, after about twenty minutes' wandering, her feet soaking wet inside her leaking boots, and her leg muscles aching from wading through the snow, she arrived at the car park outside the administration block, and found her car. She brushed a thick layer of snow from its windows, and, with a sigh of relief, got behind the wheel. She turned the ignition key. Nothing happened.

"Fuck," said Robyn, aloud to herself, alone in the middle of the frozen car park. "Bum. Tit."

If it was the battery it must have finally given up the ghost, because there wasn't even the faintest wheeze or whisper from the starter motor. Whatever it was, she could do nothing about it herself, since she hadn't the remotest idea what went on under the bonnet of the Renault. She got wearily out of the car and tramped across the car park to the reception lobby, where she asked the receptionist with peroxided hair if she could phone the AA. While she was dialling, Wilcox passed in the corridor beyond, saw her, checked, and came in.

"Still here?" he said, lifting an eyebrow.

Robyn nodded, holding the receiver to her ear.

"She's phoning the AA," said the peroxide blonde. "Car won't start."

"What's the problem?" said Wilcox.

"Nothing happens when I turn the key. It's completely dead."

"Let's have a look at it," said Wilcox.

"No, no," said Robyn. "Please don't bother. I'll manage."

"Come on." He jerked his head in the direction of the car park. "You won't get the AA to come for hours on a day like this."

The engaged tone bleeping in Robyn's ear confirmed the good sense of this judgment, but she put down the receiver reluctantly. The last thing she wanted at this juncture was to be under an obligation to Wilcox.

"Don't you want to get your overcoat?" she asked, as they passed through the swing doors into the freezing outside air.

Wilcox shook his head impatiently. "Where's your car?"

"The red Renault over there."

Wilcox set off in a straight line, indifferent to the snow that covered his thin black shoes and clung to his trouser bottoms.

"Why did you buy a foreign car?" he said.

"I didn't buy it, my parents gave it to me, when they changed it."

"Why did they buy it, then?"

"I don't know. Mummy liked it, I suppose. It's a good little car."

"So's the Metro. Why not buy a Metro if you want a small car? Or a Mini? If everybody who bought a foreign car in the last ten years had bought a British one instead, there wouldn't be seventeen per cent unemployment in this area." He made a sweeping gesture with his arm that took in the wilderness of derelict factories beyond the perimeter fence.

As a subscriber to *Marxism Today*, Robyn had suffered occasional qualms of guilt because she didn't cycle to work instead of driving, but she had never been attacked for owning a foreign car before. "If British cars were as good as foreign ones, people would buy them," she said. "But everyone knows they're hopelessly unreliable."

"Rubbish," said Wilcox. *Roobish.* "They used to be, I grant you, some models, but now our quality control is as good as anybody's. Trouble is, people love to sneer at British products. Then they have the gall to moan about the unemployment figures." His breath steamed, as though his anger were condensing in the frigid air. "What does your father drive?" he said.

"An Audi," said Robyn.

Wilcox grunted contemptuously, as if he had expected no better.

They came up to the Renault. Wilcox told her to get in and release the bonnet catch. He opened the bonnet and disappeared behind it. After a moment or two she heard him call, "Turn the ignition key," and when she did so, the engine fired.

Wilcox lowered the bonnet and pushed it shut with the palm of his hand. He came to the driver's window, brushing snow from his suit.

"Thank you very much," said Robyn. "What was it?"

"Loose electrical connection," he said. "Looked as if someone had pulled out the HT lead, actually."

"Pulled it out?"

"I'm afraid we get a bit of vandalism here, and practical joking. Was the car locked?"

"Maybe not every door. Anyway, thanks very much. I hope you won't catch cold," she said, encouraging him to leave. But he lingered by the window, inhibiting her from winding it up.

"I'm sorry if I was a bit sharp at the meeting this afternoon," he said gruffly.

"That's all right," said Robyn; though it wasn't all right, she told herself, it wasn't all right at all. She fiddled with the choke button to avoid having to look at him.

"Only sometimes you have to use methods that look a bit dodgy, for the good of the firm."

"I don't think we should ever agree about that," said Robyn. "But this is hardly the time or the place . . ." Out of the corner of her eye she saw a man in a white coat floundering through the snow towards them, and in some intuitive way this increased her anxiety to be off.

"Yes, you'd better be on your way. I'll see you next Wednesday, then?"

Before Robyn could reply, the man in the white coat had called out, "Mr. Wilcox! Mr. Wilcox!" and Wilcox turned to face him.

"Mr. Wilcox, you're wanted in the foundry," said the man breathlessly, as he came up. "There's been a walkout."

"Goodbye," said Robyn, and let out the clutch. The Renault shot forward and slewed from side to side in the snow as she drove fast towards the gates. In her rear-view mirror she saw the two men hurrying back towards the administration block.

PART III

"People mutht be amuthed. They can't be alwayth a learning, nor yet they can't be alwayth a working. They an't made for it."

CHARLES DICKENS: *Hard Times*

1

"The drive back was quite horrendous," said Robyn. "Swirling snow. Roads like skating-rinks. Abandoned cars strewn all over the place. It took me two and a half hours to get home."

"God," said Charles sympathetically.

"I felt absolutely exhausted and filthy—my feet were soaking wet, my clothes reeked of that ghastly factory, and my hair was full of soot. All I wanted was to wash my hair and take a long, hot bath. I'd just eased myself into it—oh, what bliss!—when the doorbell rang. Well, I thought, too bad, I'm not going to answer it. I couldn't imagine who it could be, anyway. But the bell went on ringing and ringing. I began to think perhaps it was a real emergency. Anyway, after a while I couldn't stand it any longer, lying there and listening to the bloody bell, so I got out of the bath, dried myself after a fashion, put on a bathrobe, and went downstairs to open the door. Who d'you think it was?"

"Wilcox?"

"How clever of you to guess. He was in a towering rage, pushed his way into the house most rudely, and didn't even bother to wipe his feet. They were covered in snow, and left great wet footprints on the hall carpet. When I took him into the living-room he even had the cheek to look round and say to himself, loud enough for me to hear, 'What a tip!'"

Charles laughed. "Well, you must admit, dear, you aren't the world's tidiest housekeeper."

"I never claimed to be," said Robyn. "I have more important things to do than housework."

"Oh, absolutely," said Charles. "What did Wilcox want, then?"

"Well, it was about Danny Ram, of course. It seems that as soon as I left he told his workmates what the management were up to, and they all walked out in protest. It was pretty silly of him, actually. I mean, it didn't take Wilcox long to work out who had tipped him off."

"So Wilcox had come straight round to complain?"

"More than complain. He demanded that I go back to the factory next morning and tell Danny Ram and his mates that I'd made a mistake, and that there was no plot to sack him."

"Good Lord, what a nerve! Would you move over a bit?"

Robyn, who was lying naked, face down on the bed, wriggled over towards the centre of the mattress. Charles, who was also naked, knelt astride her legs and poured aromatic oil from Body Shop onto her shoulders and down her spine. Then, capping the bottle carefully, he put it aside and began working the oil into Robyn's neck and shoulders with his long, supple, sensitive fingers. Charles had come to stay for the weekend following Robyn's visit to Pringle's, and this was their customary way of rounding off Saturday evening, after an early film at the Arts Laboratory followed by an excellent cheap supper at one of the local Asian restaurants. It began as a real massage, and turned almost imperceptibly into an erotic one. Robyn and Charles were into nonpenetrative sex these days, not because of AIDS (which to heterosexuals was only a cloud on the horizon, no bigger than a man's hand, in the winter of 1986) but for reasons both ideological and practical. Feminist theory approved, and it solved the problem of contraception, Robyn having renounced the pill on health grounds and Charles regarding condoms as unaesthetic (though Robyn, like the thoroughly liberated young woman she was, always had a packet handy should the need arise). At the moment they were still at the non-erotic stage of the massage. The bedroom was dimly lit and cosily warm, the radiators being supplemented by an electric fire. Robyn supported her head, turned sideways, on a pillow, and conversed with Charles over her shoulder, as he rubbed and stroked.

"You refused, I presume?" said Charles.

"Well, yes, at first."

"Only at first?"

"Well, after a while he stopped trying to bully me, when he saw that it wouldn't do any good, and began to use real arguments. He said that if the walkout settled into a strike, the whole factory would be brought to a standstill. The Asian workers are very clannish, he said, and very stubborn. Once they get an idea into their heads, it's hard to shift it."

"Racist talk," said Charles.

"Well, I know," said Robyn. "But they're so Neanderthal in that respect, the whole management, that after a while you only notice the grosser examples of prejudice. Anyway, Wilcox said a strike could drag on for weeks. The foundry would stop supplying the machine shop. The whole factory would grind to a halt. Midland Amalgamated might decide to cut their losses by closing it down altogether. Then hundreds of men would be thrown out of work, with no hope of getting another job. All because of me, was the implication. Of course, I told him it was his fault in the first place. If he hadn't plotted to trick Danny Ram out of his job, none of it would have happened."

"Quite," said Charles, running the edges of his hands up and down Robyn's vertebrae.

"He had got me a bit worried, though, I must admit. I mean, I'd only intended to put Danny Ram on his guard, not to provoke a major industrial dispute."

"Did Wilcox admit he was in the wrong?"

"Well, exactly, that was crucial. I said to him, look, you're asking me to lie, to say something I said was untrue, when it wasn't. What are *you* going to do?"

"And what did he say?"

"'Anything, within reason.' So I said, all right, I want an admission that it's immoral to get rid of a worker the way you proposed to get rid of Danny Ram, and I want an undertaking that you won't do it again. Well, he looked pretty sick at that, but he swallowed hard, and agreed. So I reckon I achieved something at the end of the day. But what a day!"

"Do you trust him to keep his word?"

Robyn considered this for a moment. "Yes, I do, as a matter of fact."

"In spite of the way he was going to treat the Indian?"

"He honestly didn't see it was immoral, you know, until I protested. It's not uncommon, apparently, to get rid of people like that. There's no procedure for remedial training. If someone's promoted to a higher-level job, and they're not up to it, there's no way of dealing with the problem. Don't you think that's incredible?"

"Not really, it applies to several full professors I can think of at Suffolk," said Charles. "Except you can't fire them."

Robyn sniggered. "I know what you mean . . . Anyway, I got him to agree to fix up Danny Ram with some special training."

"Did you, by golly!" Charles paused in his ministrations, with a hand on each of Robyn's firm round buttocks. "You really are a remarkable girl, Robyn."

"Woman," Robyn corrected him, but without rancour. She was pleased with the success of her story and the heroic role she had fashioned for herself in it. She had concealed from Charles some qualms of conscience about collaborating in the cover-up about Danny Ram. As a piece of action in a Victorian novel she might have judged it harshly as a case of one bourgeois supporting another when the chips were down, but she had persuaded herself that it was for the greater good of the factory workers—not to save Wilcox's skin—that she had lied; and the conditions she had imposed on Wilcox were a guarantee of her good faith.

"So that was the story we agreed on: I would tell Danny Ram that I'd got the wrong end of the stick at the meeting, and misunderstood the discussion, which was *really* about the need to give him special training, not to sack him."

"And did you?" Charles now dismounted from his position astride Robyn's legs in order to massage them. He kneaded the backs of her thighs and stroked the muscles of her calves, he flexed her ankles, scratched the soles of her feet and, gently parting the interstices of her toes, moistened the hollow spaces between them with with his oiled fingers.

"Absolutely. The next morning at seven-thirty sharp, Wilcox was at my door again, with his enormous Jaguar, to drive me to the factory. He didn't say a word to me for the whole journey. Rushed me into his office, with the secretaries and so on all skipping out of his way like frightened rabbits, and goggling at me as if I was some kind of terrorist he'd put under citizen's arrest. Then he and two of his cronies took me to a special meeting with the Asian foundry workers, in the canteen. There must have been about seventy of them, including Danny Ram, in their ordinary clothes, not overalls. Danny Ram gave me a scared kind of smile when I came in. There were some whites there too. Wilcox said they were shop stewards come to observe, deciding whether to make the strike official. So I said my piece to Danny, but really to all of them. I must say it stuck in my throat when I had to apologise, but I went through with it. Then we withdrew into another room, the canteen manageress's office I think it was, while the Asians deliberated. After about twenty minutes they sent a delegation to say that they were prepared to go back to work providing Danny was guaranteed his job back after retraining and on condition they were given five minutes paid washing-up time at the end of their shift. Then they went out and Wilcox and his cronies went into a huddle. Wilcox was furious, he said the washing-up time business had nothing to do with the original dispute, and that the shop stewards had put them up to it, but the other two said that the workers had to get something out of the walkout or they'd lose face, so they should settle. After a while Wilcox agreed to offer two minutes, and finally settled for three, but with ill-grace I must say. After all, I *had* lied to get him off the hook, and I didn't like doing it, but I didn't get a word of thanks, or any other kind of word. He stalked out of the room after the meeting without so much as a goodbye. The Personnel Manager drove me back to the University, an incredibly boring man who talked to me all the time about his Irritable Bowel Syndrome. I got back to the University just in time for a ten o'clock tutorial on *Middlemarch*. It was a rather weird feeling, actually. I thought it must be like coming off a night shift. The day was just starting for the Department, the students were still yawning and rubbing the sleep out of their eyes, but I felt as if I had been up for hours and hours. I suppose I was emotionally drained by the drama of the meeting and the negotiations. I had a ridiculous urge to tell the students all about it, but of course I didn't. I don't think it was one of my better tutorials, though. My mind was on other things."

Robyn fell silent. The massage had reached its erotic stage. Without being prompted, she rolled over on to her back. Charles' practised index finger gently probed and stroked her most sensitive parts. Quite soon she reached a very satisfying climax. Then it was Charles' turn.

Robyn's massage technique was more energetic than Charles'. She splashed oil all down his back and began to pummel him vigorously with the edges of her palms. "Ow! Ooh!" he exclaimed pleasurably, as the rather plump cheeks of his buttocks vibrated under this assault.

"You've got a horrible pimple on your bottom, Charles," she said. "I'm going to squeeze it."

"Oh, no, don't," he groaned. "You hurt so when you do that." But the note of protest was partly feigned.

Robyn pinched the pimple between her two forefingers and pressed hard. Charles yelled and his eyes filled with water. "There, all gone," said Robyn, swabbing away the residue of the pimple with a piece of cotton wool. She stopped pummelling, and began to stroke and smooth the backs of his thighs.

Charles stopped whimpering into his pillow. He closed his eyes and his breathing became regular. "Will you go back next week?" he murmured. "To the factory, I mean?"

"I shouldn't think so," said Robyn. "Turn over, Charles."

2

At about the same time that evening, Vic Wilcox was restively watching television with his younger son, Gary, in the lounge of the five-bedroomed, four-lavatoried neo-Georgian house on Avondale Road. Marjorie was upstairs in bed, reading *Enjoy Your Menopause*, or, more likely, had already fallen asleep over it. Raymond was out boozing somewhere with his cronies, and Sandra was at a disco with the spotty Cliff. Gary was too young to go out on a Saturday night and Vic was . . . not too old, of course, but disinclined. He did not care for the noisy, false bonhomie of pubs and clubs; he had always regarded the cinema as primarily a convenience for courting couples in the winter months, and had ceased to patronise it shortly after getting married; and he had never been a theatre- or concert-goer. When he worked for Vanguard, he and Marjorie had belonged to a rather gay crowd of other young managers and their wives, who used to meet regularly in each other's houses on Saturday nights; but it turned out that there was a lot of hanky-panky going on at those parties, or after them, or in between them, and the circle eventually broke up in an atmosphere of scandal and recrimination. Since those days, Vic had moved on and up the career ladder to a point where he seemed to have no friends any more, only business acquaintances, and all social life was an extension of work. His idea of pleasure on a Saturday night was to sit in front of the telly, with a bottle of scotch conveniently to hand, watching "Match of the Day," and discussing the finer points of the game with his younger son.

But this winter there was no "Match of the Day," owing to a dispute between the Football League and the TV companies. The Football League had got greedy and demanded a hugely increased fee for broadcasting rights, and the TV companies had called their bluff. Vic's satisfaction at the administration of this business lesson was tempered by a sense of personal deprivation. Football on television was about the only form of escape he had left, and it was also one of the few topics on which he could hold a reasonably amicable conversation with his sons. When Raymond was a kid, he used to take him to watch Rummidge City, but gave that up when, at some time in the nineteen-seventies, football grounds were entirely taken over by tribes of foul-mouthed juvenile delinquents. Now even televised soccer was denied him, and he was obliged to sit with Gary on a Saturday night watching old films and TV dramas that were either boring or embarrassing.

The one they were watching now looked as if it was just about to change from being boring to being embarrassing. The hero and heroine were dancing cheek to cheek to a stereo in the girl's apartment. You could tell by the kind of music, and the look of dreamy lust on their faces, that before long they would be in bed together, with nothing on, writhing about under the bedcovers, or even on top of the bedcovers, uttering the usual obligatory moans and sighs. The decline of soccer and the increase of explicit sex in the media seemed to be reciprocally related symptoms of national decline, though Vic sometimes thought he was the only one who had noticed the coincidence. You saw things on television nowadays that would have been under-the-counter pornography when he was a lad. It made family viewing an anxious and uncomfortable business. "You don't want to watch any more of this, do you?" he said to Gary, with affected casualness.

"It's all right," said Gary, slumped in an armchair, without taking his eyes from the screen. His hand moved rhythmically from a bag of potato crisps to his mouth and back again.

"Let's see what's on the other channels."

"No, Dad, don't!"

Overriding Gary's protest, Vic played a short scale on the buttons of the remote control. The other channels were showing: a documentary about sheepdogs, a repeat of an American detective series about (Vic remembered it) a murdered prostitute, and another feature film the hero and heroine of which were already in bed together and wrestling energetically under the bedcovers. Vic quickly switched back to the first channel, where the girl was now slowly unbuttoning her blouse in front of a mirror while the man looked lasciviously over her shoulder. It was only a matter of time, Vic thought, before he scored a pornographic jackpot, simulated copulation on all four channels simultaneously.

"You don't want to watch any more of this crap," he said, pressing the Off button.

"Oh, *Dad!*"

"Anyway, it's time you were in bed," said Vic. "It's gone half past eleven."

"It's Saturday, Dad," Gary whined.

"No matter. You need a lot of sleep at your age."

"You just want to watch it on your own, don't you?" said Gary slyly.

Vic gave a derisive laugh. "Watch that rubbish? No, I'm off to bed, and so are you."

Vic was now obliged to follow his son upstairs to bed, though he wasn't sleepy and would, indeed, left to himself, have gone on watching the film, just to keep himself up to date on the decline of public decency. To add to his irritation, Marjorie was still awake when he got to the bedroom, and seemed disposed to talk. She chattered away through the open door of the bathroom as he brushed his teeth, about redecorating the lounge and buying loose covers for the three-piece suite; and when he came back into the bedroom to put on his pyjamas she asked him if he liked her new nightdress. It was a semi-transparent effort in peach-coloured nylon, with narrow shoulder straps and a deeply plunging neckline that revealed a considerable expanse of Marjorie's pale, freckled bosom. The dark circles round her flat nipples showed through the thin material like two stains. There was something else unfamiliar about her appearance, though he couldn't put his finger on it.

"A bit flimsy for this weather, isn't it?" he said.

"But do you like it?"

"It's all right."

"It's supposed to be the *Dynasty* look."

Vic grunted. "Don't talk to me about television."

"Why, what've you been watching?"

"The usual crap." Vic climbed into bed and switched off his bedside lamp. "You're very talkative tonight," he remarked. "Is the Valium losing its effect?"

"I haven't taken it yet," said Marjorie, turning off the lamp on her side. Her reason became all too clear when she laid a hand on his thigh under the bedclothes. At the same moment he became aware that she had drenched herself in a powerful scent, and realized that she had looked different sitting up in bed because she wasn't wearing curlers. "Vic," she said. "It's a long time since we . . . you know."

He pretended not to understand. "What?"

"You *know*." Marjorie rubbed his thigh with the back of her hand. It was something she used to do in their courting days, giving him a hard-on like a bar of pig-iron. Now his member didn't even stir.

"I thought you'd gone off it," he muttered.

"It was only a phase. Part of the change of life. It says so in the book." She switched on her bedside lamp and reached for *Enjoy Your Menopause*.

"For God's sake, Marjorie!" he grumbled. "What are you doing?"

"Where are my glasses . . . ? Ah, yes, here it is. Listen. '*You may feel a revulsion against marital relations for a while. This is quite normal, and nothing to worry about. With time, and patience, and an understanding partner, your lib, libby—*'"

"Libido," said Vic. "Freud invented it before he discovered the death instinct."

"'*Your libido will return, stronger than ever.*'" Marjorie replaced the book on the bedside table, took off her glasses, turned out the light, and sank down in the bed beside him.

"You mean, you've got it back?" Vic asked flatly.

"Well, I don't know," she said. "I mean, I won't, will I, not till we try? I think we ought to give it a try, Vic."

"Why?"

"Well, it's natural for married couples. You used to want to . . ." There was a dangerous quaver in Marjorie's voice.

"Everything comes to an end," he said desperately. "We're getting on."

"But we're not old, Vic, not that old. The book says—"

"Fuck the book," said Vic.

Marjorie began to cry.

Vic sighed, and turned on his bedside lamp. "Sorry, love," he said. "Only you can't expect me to suddenly . . . get all interested, out of the blue. I thought we were past all that. So we're not—good—but give me time to readjust. OK?"

Marjorie nodded, and blew her nose daintily on a paper tissue.

"I have my own problems, you know," he said.

"I know, Vic," said Marjorie. "I know you have a lot of worries at work."

"That silly bitch from the University has caused me no end of trouble . . . then there's Brian Everthorpe with his daft idea of a calendar, which he claims Stuart Baxter approves of. Why is Brian Everthorpe in Stuart Baxter's confidence, I'd like to know?"

"As long as it's not me," Marjorie sniffed.

He leaned over and planted a dry kiss on her cheek, before turning out the light again. "'Course it's not you," he said.

But of course it was. It was years since he had felt any unforced desire for

Marjorie, and now he couldn't even force it. When she seemed to be going off sex because of her time of life he'd been secretly relieved. The buxom, dimpled girl he'd married had become a middle-aged podge with tinted hair and too much make-up. Her roly-poly body embarrassed him when he happened to see it naked, and as for her mind, well that was almost as embarrassing when she exposed it. It would be futile to complain of this, for there was no way she could change herself, become clever and witty and sophisticated, any more than she could become tall and slim and athletic. He had married Marjorie for what she was, a simple, devoted, docile young woman, with the kind of plump good looks that quickly run to fat, and he was in honour bound to put up with her. Vic had old-fashioned ideas about marriage. A wife was not like a car: you couldn't part-exchange her when the novelty wore off, or the bodywork started to go. If you discovered you'd made a mistake, too bad, you just had to live with it. The one thing you couldn't do, he thought grimly, was make love to it.

Even that arrogant, interfering women's libber from the University was more of a turn-on than poor old Marjorie. If her ideas were barmy, at least they were ideas, whereas Marjorie's idea of an idea was something she had about wallpaper or loose covers. Of course she was young, which always helped, and good-looking in a way, if you liked that type of hairstyle, with the neck shaved like a boy's, which he didn't, and ignored the ridiculous Cossack's get-up. She'd looked a bit more normal in her bathrobe, when he drove round to her house that evening in a cold fury, taking hair-raising risks with the Jaguar in the ice and snow, and practically battered her door down.

He'd gone with no other intention than to scare the shit out of her and relieve his own feelings. He meant to tell her that the Shadow Scheme was cancelled, and that he would be telling the University the reason why. It was only when he came face to face with her that he'd thought of persuading her to undo the damage she'd caused instead. It was probably a stroke of luck that she was having a bath at the time. It put her at a disadvantage, not being properly dressed.

Vic's memory presented to him with surprising vividness the image of Robyn Penrose, her copper curls damp, her feet bare, swathed in a white towelling bathrobe that gaped as she stooped to light the gas fire in her cluttered living-room, giving him a glimpse of a gently sloping breast and the profile of a pink nipple, for she appeared to have nothing on under the robe. To his surprise, and almost dismay, his penis stiffened at the recollection. At the same moment, Marjorie, reaching probably for his hand, to give it a friendly squeeze, found his penis instead, giggled and murmured, "Ooh, you are interested after all, then?"

Then he had no option but to go through with it, though as Marjorie gasped and grunted beneath him he was only able to come by imagining he was doing it to Robyn Penrose, sprawled on the rug in front of her gas fire, her bathrobe cast aside to reveal that indeed she was wearing nothing underneath it, yes, that was sweet revenge on the silly stuck up cow for making him Brian Everthorpe's butt and interrupting his meetings with damnfool questions and telling tales on the shopfloor and nearly destroying six months' patient coaxing of the foundry back to efficiency—yes, that was good, to have her there on the floor amid the incredible litter of books and dirty coffee cups and wineglasses and album sleeves and copies of *Spare Rib* and *Marxism Today*, stark naked, her bush as fiery red as her topknot, thrashing and writhing underneath him like the actresses in the TV films, moaning with pleasure in spite of herself as he thrust and thrust and thrust.

When he rolled off Marjorie she gave a sigh—whether of satisfaction or relief, he couldn't tell—pulled down her nightdress, and waddled off to the bathroom. He himself felt only guilt and depression, like he used to feel as a lad when he wanked off. That he'd been able to make love to his wife only by whipping up crude fantasies about a woman he had every reason to detest was bad enough; but the bitterest thought was that, had she known what he'd done, Robyn Penrose would have nodded smugly at so complete a confirmation of her feminist prejudices. So far from having had his revenge, Vic felt that he had suffered a moral defeat. It had not been a good week, he reflected gloomily, listening to Marjorie sloshing water about in the bidet, and then filling a glass at the sink to help swallow her Valium. He nearly called out to her to bring one for him, too.

As Marjorie came back into the bedroom, the noise of the front door closing made him spring upright in the bed. "Is that Sandra?" he said.

"I expect so, what's the matter?"

"I forgot all about her."

It was his usual practise to wait up until Sandra came in on a Saturday night, partly to reassure himself that she had got home safely, and partly to see Cliff, the acne ace, off the premises. But because Gary had manoeuvred him into going to bed early, he had forgotten all about his daughter.

"She's all right. Cliff always sees her home."

"That's what I'm worried about. He's probably downstairs now." He threw back the covers and fumbled under the bed for his slippers.

"Where are you going?" Marjorie said.

"Downstairs."

"Leave them alone for heaven's sake, Vic," said Marjorie, with a surprising show of spirit. "You'll make yourself look ridiculous. They're only having a cup of coffee or something. Don't you trust your own daughter?"

"I don't trust that Cliff," Vic said. But after a few moments' hesitation, sitting on the edge of the bed, he got slowly back under the blankets and turned out the light for, it felt like, the ninety-seventh time that night. "Youths like him are only interested in one thing," he said.

"Cliff's all right. Anyway, you're a fine one to talk." Marjorie sniggered, and nudged him with her elbow. "You didn't half go it just now."

Vic said nothing, thankful that the darkness concealed the expression on his face.

"It was nice, though, wasn't it?" Marjorie murmured drowsily.

Vic grunted a vague assent which appeared to satisfy her. The Valium, coming on top of the unwonted sexual exercise, soon worked its effect. Marjorie's breathing became deep and regular. She was asleep.

Vic must have dozed off himself. He was woken by a sound like the beating of his own heart, and when he checked his alarm clock the digital display showed the time to be one-fifteen. The heart beat, he quickly realized, was actually the throb of the bass notes on a record someone was playing on the music centre in the lounge. A clip from the film he'd watched earlier that evening replayed itself in his head, with Sandra and Cliff standing in for the infatuated couple dancing cheek to cheek. He levered himself out of bed, groped for his slippers and, as his eyes accommodated to the darkness, took his dressing-gown from behind the bathroom door and quietly left the bedroom. The landing and front hall were dark, but a dim light over the burglar-alarm control box guided him down the stairs. He could hear the sound of music, though no light was visible under the lounge door. He opened it and went in.

Vic felt like a white explorer who had stumbled on a cave where some nomadic tribe had bivouacked for the night. The only light in the room came from the gas flames licking round the imitation logs in the hearth, casting a fitful illumination over half-a-dozen figures sprawled in a semi-circle on the floor. He switched on the main ceiling light. Six young men, one of them

Raymond, with cans of lager and smouldering cigarettes in their fists, blinked and gaped up at him.

"'Ullo, Dad," said Raymond, with the vague geniality that was the usual sign that he had been drinking.

"What's going on?" Vic demanded, tugging the cord of his dressing-gown tight.

"Jus' brought a few of the lads back," said Raymond.

Vic had seen them all before at one time or another, though he didn't know their names, since Raymond never bothered to introduce them, nor did they seem capable of introducing themselves. They did not get to their feet now, or show any other sign of respect or discomfiture. They reclined on the floor in the shabby overcoats and Doc Marten boots that they never seemed to take off, and gaped apathetically at him from under their sticky punk haircuts. Like Raymond, they were all college dropouts, or youths who hadn't been able to summon up the energy even to start college. They lived on the dole and on their parents, and spent their time drinking in pubs or pricing amplifiers in the Rummidge music stores; for they all played electric guitars of various shapes and sizes, and nourished the fantasy of forming a "band" one day, in spite of the fact that none of them could read music and the collective noise they made was so dire that they could seldom find anywhere to rehearse. Just to look at them made Vic want to start campaigning for the restoration of National Service, or the workhouse, or transportation—anything to encourage these idle young sods to get off their backsides and into some honest work.

"Where's Sandra?" he asked Raymond. "Did she come in?"

"Gone t' bed. Came in a while ago."

"And whatsisname?"

"Cliff went home." As usual, Raymond did not look Vic in the eye as he spoke, but down at his own feet, rocking his head slightly to the rhythm of the music. Vic looked round the room, feeling self-conscious now, standing there in his pyjamas and dressing-gown—garments he was fairly confident none of these youths had worn since attaining the age of puberty. "That my lager?" he enquired, feeling mean even as he uttered the question.

"Yeah, d'you mind?" said Raymond. "I'll replace it when I get me next giro."

"I don't mind you drinking the lager," said Vic, "as long as you don't puke all over the carpet."

"That was Wiggy," said Raymond, recognising the allusion to an incident some months earlier. "He doesn't go around with us any more."

"Learned some sense, has he?"

"Nah. He got married." Raymond grinned and glanced slyly at his friends, who seemed to find this idea as amusing as he did. They belched and guffawed, or shook their shoulders in silent laughter.

"God help his wife, is all I can say," said Vic. He stepped over several pairs of outstretched legs to reach the stereo, and turned down the volume and bass controls. "Keep this low," he said, "or you'll wake your mother."

"A'right," said Raymond mildly, though he knew as well as Vic that only a bomb would wake Marjorie now. He added, as Vic made his way to the door, "Turn the light out, will you, Dad?"

As he climbed the stairs, Vic thought he heard the sound of stifled laughter coming from the lounge. It was a sound he was getting increasingly tired of.

. . .

The following morning Vic, while engaged in cleaning the road salt off the underside of his car with a pressure hose in the front drive, saw several of last night's nomads leave, and by dint of staring hard even compelled two of them to mutter a greeting. Under an agreement negotiated some time ago, Raymond was allowed to have friends to stay in the house overnight only on condition that they slept in his room. This clause, intended to limit the number of his guests, had quite failed of its intended effect since, however many there were, they all somehow managed to squeeze themselves into the available space, curled up on the floor in sleeping bags or wrapped in their overcoats in (as Vic imagined the scene) a snoring, farting, belching heap. From this foetid nest they would emerge, singly and at intervals, in the course of Sunday morning, to pee, not always accurately, in one of the lavatories of the house, and help themselves lavishly to cornflakes in the kitchen, before sloping off to their next pub rendezvous. As usual, Raymond was the last to rise this morning; indeed, he was still having his breakfast when Vic drove off to fetch his father for lunch.

Since Vic's elder sister, Joan, had married a Canadian and gone to live in Winnipeg twenty-five years ago, the responsibility of looking after their parents had fallen to him. Mr. Wilcox Senior had retired in 1975 after working all his life, first as a toolmaker, later as a stores supervisor, for one of the largest engineering companies in Rummidge. Vic's mother had died six years later, of cancer, but Mr. Wilcox insisted on staying on in the terraced house in Ebury

Street he had married into, old-fashioned and inconvenient as it was. Bringing him round to Avondale Road for Sunday lunch was a regular ritual.

Every time Vic drove down Ebury Street, it seemed a little more dejected, but on this overcast January Sunday, with a slow thaw in progress, it seemed especially depressing. Decay had set in at each end of the street, as if the molars had been the first to go in a row of teeth, and was creeping slowly towards the middle, where a few of the long-term residents, like his father, still remained stubbornly rooted. Some of the houses were squats, some were boarded up, and others were occupied by poor immigrants. To this latter group Mr. Wilcox had a curiously divided attitude. Those he knew personally he spoke of in terms of the warmest regard; the rest he anathematised as "bloody blacks and coloureds" who had brought the neighbourhood down. Vic had tried on several occasions to explain to his father that their presence in Ebury Street was an effect, not a cause—that the cause was the expressway striding over the rooftops only thirty yards away on its great bulging concrete legs—but without success. Come to think of it, he had never succeeded in changing his father's mind about anything.

Vic drew into the gutter, still clogged with dirty packed snow, and parked outside number 59. Some Caribbean children throwing slushy snowballs at each other desisted for a moment to stare at the big shiny car, as well they might. The Jaguar seemed almost obscenely opulent alongside the bangers parked in this street, old rust-eaten Escorts and Marinas sagging on their clapped-out shock-absorbers. Vic would have felt more comfortable driving Marjorie's Metro, but he knew that his father got a kick out of being collected in the Jag. It was a message to the neighbours: *Look, my son is rich and successful. I'm not like you, I don't have to live on this shit-heap. I can move out any time I like. I just happen to like living in my own house, the house I've always lived in.*

Vic knocked on the front door. His father opened it almost immediately, neatly dressed in his Sunday best: a checked sports jacket with grey flannels, a woolly cardigan under the jacket, collar and tie, and brown shoes gleaming like freshly gathered conkers. His thin grey hair was slicked down with haircream, which, Vic reflected, thinking of Raymond's friends, seemed to be coming back into fashion—not that fashion had anything to do with Mr. Wilcox's use of it.

"I'll just get my coat," he said, "I was airing it. D'you want to come in?"

"I might as well," said Vic.

The air seemed almost as damp and chill in the hall as outside on the pavement. "You ought to let me put central heating in this house," Vic said, as he followed the dark shape of his father—short and broad-shouldered like his own, but with less flesh on the bones—down the hall. Correctly predicting the reply, he silently mouthed it in unison.

"I don't 'old with central 'eating."

"You wouldn't have to air your clothes in front of the kitchen stove."

"It's bad for the furniture."

Somewhere Mr. Wilcox had picked up the idea that central heating dried up the glue in furniture, causing it eventually to collapse and disintegrate. The fact that Vic's furniture was still intact after many years in a centrally heated environment had not shaken this conviction, and of course it could not be pointed out to Mr. Wilcox that his own furniture, mostly bought from the Co-op in the nineteen-thirties, was in any case hardly worth careful preservation.

The back kitchen was at least cosy and warm, which was just as well, since Mr. Wilcox virtually wintered in it, sitting in his highbacked armchair facing the stove, with the TV perched precariously on top of the sideboard and a pile of the old books and magazines he bought from jumble sales within easy reach. The door of the solid-fuel boiler was open, and in front of it a navy-blue overcoat was slumped like a drunk over the back of an upright chair. Mr. Wilcox closed the door of the boiler with a bang, and Vic helped him on with the coat.

"You could do with a new one," he said, noticing the threadbare cuffs.

"You can't get material like this any more," said Mr. Wilcox. "That thing you've got on doesn't look as if it's got any warmth in it."

Vic was wearing a quilted gilet over a thick sweater. "It's warmer than it looks," he said. "Nice for driving—leaves your arms free."

"How much was it?"

"Fifteen pounds," said Vic, halving the actual price.

"Good God!" Mr. Wilcox exclaimed.

Whenever his father asked him the price of anything, Vic always halved it. This formula, he found, ensured that the old man was agreeably scandalised without being really upset.

"Picked up an interesting book yesterday," said Mr. Wilcox, brandishing a volume with limp red covers, somewhat soiled and creased. "Only cost me fivepence. 'Ave a look."

The book was the *AA Guide to Hotels and Restaurants 1958*. "Bring it with you, Dad," said Vic. "We'd better be on our way, or the dinner'll spoil."

"Did you know, in 1958 you could get bed and breakfast in a one-star hotel in Morecambe for seven-and-six a night?"

"No, Dad, I didn't."

"How much d'you reckon it would cost now. Seven quid?"

"Easily," said Vic. "More like twice that."

"I don't know how folk manage these days," said Mr. Wilcox, with gloomy satisfaction.

. . .

Sunday lunch, or dinner as Vic called it in deference to his father, hardly varied through the year, also in deference to Mr. Wilcox: a joint of beef or lamb, with roast potatoes and sprouts or peas, followed by apple crumble or lemon meringue pie: Once Marjorie had experimented with *coq au vin* from a recipe in a magazine, and Mr. Wilcox had sighed unhappily as his plate was put before him and said afterwards that it was very nice but he had never been much of a one for foreign food and there was nothing like the good old English roast. Marjorie had taken the hint.

After lunch they sat in the lounge and Mr. Wilcox diverted himself and, he fondly supposed, the rest of the family, by reading aloud extracts from the *AA Guide to Hotels and Restaurants*, and inviting them to guess the 1958 rate for a week's half board at the best hotel in the Isle of Wight or the price of bed and breakfast at a class A boarding house in Rhyl. "I don't even know what seven-and-six *means*, Grandpa," said Sandra irritably, while Gary had to be restrained from giving his grandfather a patronising lecture on inflation. Sandra and Gary squabbled over the TV, Sandra wanting to watch the *Eastenders* omnibus and Gary wanting to play a computer game. He had a black-and-white set of his own upstairs, but the game required colour. When Vic upheld Sandra's claim, Gary sulked and said it was time he had a colour set of his own. Mr. Wilcox asked how much the set in the living-room cost and Vic, looking fiercely at the rest of the family, said two hundred and fifty pounds. Marjorie was reading, with great concentration and hardly moving her lips at all, a mail-order brochure that had come with her credit-card account and kept proposing to purchase various items of useless gadgetry—a keyring that bleeped when you whistled for it, an alarm clock that stopped bleeping if you shouted at it, an inflatable neck-pillow for sleeping on aeroplanes, a battery-operated telescopic tie-rack, a thermostatically controlled waxing machine for removing unwanted hair, and a jacuzzi conversion kit for the bathtub—until Mr. Wilcox's relentless quiz about 1958 hotel prices reminded her of summer holidays and she began to go through the Sunday papers and the TV guides cutting out coupons for brochures. Sandra said she was sick of family holidays and why didn't they buy their own apartment in Spain or Majorca, then they could all go separately and stay with their friends, a proposal enthusiastically backed up by Raymond, who came in from the kitchen, where he had been eating his warmed-up lunch because as usual he had come in from the pub too late to sit down at table. He also asked Vic if he would lend him and his mates two hundred and fifty pounds to have a "demo tape" of their band made, a request Vic had the satisfaction of turning down flat. Caught in the crossfire between a parent who regarded all nonessential expenditure as a form of moral turpitude and a wife and children who would spend his annual salary five times over if given the chance, Vic gave up the attempt to read the Sunday papers and relieved his feelings by going outside and shovelling away the slush on the front drive. Nothing depressed him more than the thought of summer holidays: a fortnight of compulsory idleness, mooning about in the rain in some dreary English seaside resort, or looking for a bit of shade on a sweltering Mediterranean beach. Weekends were bad enough. By this point on a Sunday afternoon he was itching to get back to the factory.

3

For Robyn and Charles weekends were for work as well as recreation, and the two activities tended to blend into each other at certain interfaces. Was it work or recreation, for instance, to browse through the review pages of the *Observer* and the *Sunday Times*, mentally filing away information about the latest books, plays, films, and even fashion and furniture (for nothing semiotic is alien to the modern academic critic)? A brisk walk in Wellington boots to feed the ducks in the local park was, however, definitely recreation; and after a light lunch (Robyn cooked the omelettes and Charles dressed the salad), they settled down for a few hours' serious work in the congested living-room study, before it would be time for Charles to drive back to Suffolk. Robyn had a stack of essays to mark, and Charles was reading a book on Deconstruction which he had agreed to review for a scholarly journal. The gas fire hissed and popped in the the hearth. A harpsichord concerto by Haydn tinkled quietly on the stereo. Outside, as the light faded from the winter sky, melting snow dripped from the eaves and trickled down the gutters. Robyn, looking up from Marion Russell's overdue assessed essay on *Tess of the D'Urbervilles* (which was actually not at all bad, so perhaps the modelling job was turning out to be a sensible decision), caught Charles' abstracted gaze and smiled.

"Any good?" she enquired, nodding at his book.

"Not bad. Quite good on the de-centring of the subject, actually. You remember that marvellous bit in Lacan?" Charles read out a quotation: "*I think where I am not, therefore I am where I think not . . . I am not, wherever I am the plaything of my thought; I think of what I am wherever I don't think I am thinking.*'"

"Marvellous," Robyn agreed.

"There's quite a good discussion of it in here."

"Isn't that where Lacan says something interesting about realism?"

"Yes: '*This two-faced mystery is linked to the fact that the truth can be evoked only in that dimension of alibi in which all "realism" in creative works takes its virtue from metonymy.*'"

Robyn frowned. "What d'you think that *means*, exactly? I mean, is 'truth' being used ironically?"

"Oh, I think so, yes. It's implied by the word 'alibi,' surely? There is no 'truth,' in the absolute sense, no transcendental signified. Truth is just a rhetorical illusion, a tissue of metonymies and metaphors, as Nietzsche said. It all goes back to Nietzsche, really, as this chap points out." Charles tapped the book on his lap. "Listen. Lacan goes on: '*It is likewise linked to this other fact that we accede to meaning only through the double twist of metaphor when we have the unique key: the signifier and the signified of the Saussurian formula are not at the same level, and man only deludes himself when he believes that his true place is at their axis, which is nowhere.*'"

"But isn't he making a distinction there between 'truth' and 'meaning'? Truth is to meaning as metonymy is to metaphor."

"How?" It was Charles' turn to frown.

"Well, take Pringle's, for example."

"Pringle's?"

"The factory."

"Oh, that. You seem quite obsessed with that place."

"Well, it's uppermost in my mind. You could represent the factory realistically by a set of metonymies—dirt, noise, heat and so on. But you can only grasp the *meaning* of the factory by metaphor. The place is like hell. The trouble with Wilcox is that he can't see that. He has no metaphorical vision."

"And what about Danny Ram?" said Charles.

"Oh, poor old Danny Ram, I don't suppose he has any metaphorical vision either, otherwise he couldn't stick it. The factory to him is just another set of metonymies and synecdoches: a lever he pulls, a pair of greasy overalls he wears, a weekly pay packet. That's the truth of his existence, but not the meaning of it."

"Which is . . . ?"

"I just told you: hell. Alienation, if you want to put it in Marxist terms."

"But—" said Charles. But he was interrupted by a long peal on the doorbell.

"Who on earth can that be?" Robyn wondered, starting to her feet.

"Not your friend Wilcox, again, I hope," said Charles.

"Why should it be?"

"I don't know. Only you made him sound a bit . . ." Charles, uncharacteristically, couldn't find the epithet he wanted.

"Well, you needn't look so apprehensive," said Robyn, with a grin. "He won't eat you." She went to the window and peeped out at the front porch. "Good Lord!" she exclaimed. "It's Basil!"

"Your brother?"

"Yes, and a girl." Robyn did a hop, skip and jump across the cluttered floor and went to open the front door, while Charles, displeased at the interruption, marked his place in the book and stowed it away in his briefcase. The little he knew about Basil did not suggest that deconstruction was a likely topic of conversation in the next hour or two.

Basil's decision to go into the City, announced to an incredulous family in his last undergraduate year at Oxford, had not been an idle threat. He had joined a merchant bank on graduating and after only three years' employment was already earning more than his father, who had related this fact to Robyn at Christmas with a mixture of pride and resentment. Basil himself had not been at home for Christmas, but skiing in St. Moritz. It was in fact some time since Robyn had seen her brother, because, for their parents' sake, they deliberately arranged their visits home to alternate rather than coincide, and they had little desire to meet elsewhere. She was struck by the change in his appearance: his face was fatter, his wavy corn-coloured hair was neatly trimmed, and he seemed to have had his teeth capped—all presumably the results of his new affluence. Everything about him and his girlfriend signified money, from their pastel-pale, luxuriously thick sheepskin coats that seemed to fill the threshold when she opened the front door, to the red C-registration BMW parked at the kerb behind Charles' four-year-old Golf. Underneath the sheepskin coats Basil was wearing an Aquascutum cashmere sports jacket, and his girlfriend, whose name was Debbie, an outfit remarkably like one designed by Katherine Hamnett illustrated in that day's *Sunday Times*. This classy attire was explained partly by the fact that they had been to a hunt ball in Shropshire the previous evening, and had decided on impulse to call in on their way back to London.

"A hunt ball?" Robyn repeated, with a raised eyebrow. "Is this the same man whose idea of a good night out used to be listening to a punk band in a room over a pub?"

"We all have to grow up, Rob," said Basil. "Anyway, it was partly business. I made some useful contacts."

"It was a real lark," said Debbie, a pretty pale-faced girl with blonde hair cut like Princess Diana's, and a figure of almost anorexic slimness. "Held in a sorter castle. Just like a horror film, wonnit?" she said to Basil. "Suits of armour and stuffed animals' heads and everyfink."

At first Robyn thought that Debbie's Cockney accent was some sort of joke, but soon realized that it was authentic. In spite of her Sloaney clothes and hair-do, Debbie was decidedly lower-class. When Basil mentioned that she worked in the same bank as himself, Robyn assumed that she was a secretary or typist, but was quickly corrected by her brother when he followed her out to the kitchen where she was making tea.

"Good Lord, no," he said. "She's a foreign-exchange dealer. Very smart, earns more than I do."

"And how much is that?" Robyn asked.

"Thirty thousand, excluding bonuses," said Basil, his arms folded smugly across his chest.

Robyn stared. "Daddy said you were getting disgustingly rich, but I didn't realize just how disgusting. What do you do to earn that sort of money?"

"I'm in capital markets. I arrange swaps."

"Swaps?" The word reminded her of Basil when he was her kid brother, a gangling boy in scuffed shoes and a stained blazer, sorting conkers or gloating over his stamp collection.

"Yes. Suppose a corporate has borrowed *x* thousands at a fixed rate of interest. If they think that interest rates are going to fall, they could execute a swap transaction whereby we pay them a fixed rate and they pay us LIBOR, that's the London Interbank Offered Rate, which is variable . . ."

While Basil told Robyn much more than she wanted to know, or could understand, about swaps, she busied herself with the teacups and tried to conceal her boredom. He was anxious to assure her that he was only earning less than Debbie because he had started later. "She didn't go to University, you see."

"No, I thought she probably didn't."

"Not many spot dealers are graduates, actually. They've usually left school at sixteen and gone straight into the bank. Then somebody sees that they've got what it takes and gives them a chance."

Robyn asked what it took.

"The barrow-boy mentality, they call it. Quick wits and an appetite for non-stop dealing. Bonds are different, you have to be patient, spend a long time preparing a package. There are lulls. I couldn't last for half-an-hour in Debbie's dealing room—fifty people with about six telephones in each hand shouting across the room things like '*Six hundred million yen 9th of January!*' All day. It's a madhouse, but Debbie thrives on it. She comes from a family of bookies in Whitechapel."

"Is it serious, then, between you and Debbie?"

"What's serious?" said Basil, showing his capped teeth in a bland smile. "We don't have anybody else, if that's what you mean."

"I mean, are you living together?"

"Not literally. We both have our own houses. It makes sense to have a mortgage each, the way property prices are going up in London. How much did you pay for this place, by the way?"

"Twenty thousand."

"Good God, it would fetch four times that in Stoke Newington. Debbie bought a little terraced house there two years ago, just like this, for forty thousand, it's worth ninety now . . ."

"So property governs sexuality in the City these days?"

"Hasn't it always, according to Saint Karl?"

"That was before women liberated themselves."

"Fact is, we're both too knackered after work to be interested in anything more energetic than a bottle of wine and a hot bath. It's a long day. Twelve hours—sometimes more if things get lively. Debbie is usually at her desk by seven."

"Whatever for?"

"She does a lot of business with Tokyo . . . So we tend to work hard on our own all week and live it up together at the weekend. What about you and Charles? Isn't it time you got hitched?"

"Why d'you say that?" Robyn demanded.

"I was thinking, as we saw you through your front window from the pavement, that you looked just like some comfortably married couple."

"We're not into marriage."

"I say, do people still say 'into' like that, up here in the rust belt?"

"Don't be a metropolitan snob, Basil."

"Sorry," he said, with a smirk that showed he wasn't. "You've been very faithful, anyway."

"We don't have anyone else, if that's what you mean," she said drily.

"And how's the job?"

"In jeopardy," said Robyn, leading the way back to the living-room. Debbie, perched on the arm of Charles' chair, her hair falling over her eyes, was showing him a little gadget like a pocket quartz alarm clock.

"Is Lapsang Suchong all right?" Robyn asked, setting down the tea tray, and thinking to herself that Debbie probably favoured some brand advertised on television by chimps or animated teapots, brewed so strong you could stand the teaspoon up in it.

"Love it," said Debbie. She really was a very difficult person to get right.

"Very interesting," said Charles politely, handing Debbie's gadget back to her. It apparently informed her of the state of the world's principal currencies twenty-four hours a day, but as it only worked within a fifty-mile radius of London its liquid-crystal display was blank.

"I get ever so nervy when I'm outside of the range," she said. "At home I sleep with it under my pillow, so if I wake in the middle of the night I can check on the yen–dollar rate."

"So what's this about your job?" Basil asked Robyn.

Robyn explained briefly her situation, while Charles provided a more emotive gloss. "The irony is that she's easily the brightest person in the Department," he said. "The students know it, Swallow knows it, the other staff know it. But there's nothing anybody can do about it, apparently. That's what this government is doing to the universities: death by a thousand cuts."

"What a shame," said Debbie. "Why doncher try somethink else?"

"Like the money market?" Robyn enquired sardonically, though Debbie seemed to take the suggestion seriously.

"No, love, it's too late, I'm afraid. You're burned out at thirty-five, they reckon, in our game. But there must be something else you could do. Start a little business!"

"A business?" Robyn laughed at the absurdity of the idea.

"Yeah, why not? Basil could arrange the finance, couldn't you darl?"

"No problem."

"And you can get a government grant, forty quid a week and free management training for a year, too," said Debbie. "Friend of mine did it after she was made redundant. Opened a sports shoe boutique in Brixton with a bank loan of five thousand. Sold out two years later for a hundred and fifty grand and went to live in the Algarve. Has a chain of shops out there now, in all them time-share places."

"But I don't want to run a shoe shop or live in the Algarve," said Robyn. "I want to teach women's studies and poststructuralism and the nineteenth-century novel and write books about them."

"How much do you get for doing that?" Basil asked.

"Twelve thousand a year, approximately."

"Good God, is that all?"

"I don't do it for the money."

"No, I can see that."

"Actually," said Charles, "there are a great many people who live on half that."

"I'm sure there are," said Basil, "but I don't happen to know any of them. Do you?"

Charles was silent.

"I do," said Robyn.

"Who?" said Basil. "Tell me one person you know, I mean *know*, not just know of, somebody you talked to in the last week, who earns less than six thousand a year." His expression, both amused and belligerent, reminded Robyn of arguments they used to have when they were younger.

"Danny Ram," said Robyn. She happened to know that he earned a hundred and ten pounds a week, because she had asked Prendergast, the Personnel Director at Pringle's.

"And who's Danny Ram?"

"An Indian factory worker." Robyn derived considerable satisfaction from uttering this phrase, which seemed a very effective putdown of Basil's arrogant cynicism; but of course she then had to explain how she came to be acquainted with Danny Ram.

"Well, well," said Basil, when she had finished a brief account of her experiences at Pringle's, "So you've done your bit to make British industry even less competitive than it is already."

"I've done my bit to bring some social justice to it."

"Not that it will make any difference in the long run," said Basil. "Companies like Pringle's are batting on a losing wicket. Maggie's absolutely right—the future for our economy is in service industries, and perhaps some hi-tech engineering."

"Finance being one of the service industries?" Charles enquired.

"Naturally," said Basil, smiling. "And you ain't seen nothing yet. Wait till the Big Bang."

"What's that?" said Robyn.

Basil and Debbie looked at each other and burst out laughing. "I don't believe it," said Basil. "Don't you read the newspapers?"

"Not the financial pages," said Robyn.

"It's some kind of change in the rules of the Stock Exchange," said Charles, "that will allow people like Basil to make even more money than they do already."

"Or lose it," said Basil. "Don't forget there's an element of risk in our job. Unlike women's studies or critical theory," he added, with a glance at Robyn. "That's what makes it more interesting, of course."

"It's just a glorified form of gambling, isn't it?" said Charles.

"That's right. Debbie gambles with a stake of ten to twenty million pounds every day of the week, don't you my sweet?"

"'Sright," said Debbie. "Course, it's not like having a flutter on a horse. You don't *see* the money, and it's not yours anyway, it's the bank's."

"But twenty million!" said Charles, visibly shaken. "That's nearly the annual budget of my University."

"You should see Debbie at work, Charles," said Basil. "It would open your eyes. You too, Rob."

"Yeah, why not?" said Debbie. "I could probably fix it."

"It might be interesting," said Charles, rather to Robyn's surprise.

"Not to me, I'm afraid," she said.

Basil glanced at his watch, extending his wrist just long enough to show that it was a Rolex. "Time we were off."

He insisted that they went outside into the slushy street to admire his BMW. It had a sticker in the rear window saying BOND DEALERS DO IT BACK TO BACK. Robyn asked what it meant.

Debbie giggled. "Back to back is like a loan that's made in one currency and set against an equal loan in another."

"Oh, I see, it's a metaphor."

"What?"

"Never mind," said Robyn, hugging herself against the damp chill of the evening.

"It's also a joke," said Basil.

"Yes, I see that a joke is intended," said Robyn. "It must rather pall on people following you down the motorway."

"Nobody stays that close for long," said Basil. "This is a very fast car. Well, goodbye, sister mine."

Robyn submitted to a kiss on the cheek from Basil, then from Debbie. After a moment's hesitation and a little embarrassed laugh, Debbie brushed Charles' cheek with her own, and jumped into the passenger seat of the car. Charles and Basil waved vaguely to each other as they parted.

"You don't really want to visit that bank, do you?" Robyn said to Charles, as they returned to the house.

"I thought it might be interesting," said Charles. "I thought I might write something about it."

"Oh well, that's different," said Robyn, closing the front door and following Charles back into the living room. "Who for?"

"I don't know, *Marxism Today* perhaps. Or the *New Statesman*. I've been thinking lately I might try and supplement my income with a little freelance journalism."

"You've never done anything like that before," said Robyn.

"There's always a first time."

Robyn stepped over the soiled tea things on the floor and crouched by the gas fire to warm herself. "What did you make of Debbie?"

"Rather intriguing."

"Intriguing?"

"Well, so childlike in many ways, but handling millions of pounds every day."

"I'm afraid Mummy will consider Debbie what she calls 'common'—if Basil ever dares take her home."

"You rather gave the impression that you thought her common yourself."

"Me?" said Robyn indignantly.

"You patronised her terribly."

"Nonsense!"

"You may not think so," said Charles calmly. "But you did."

Robyn did not like to be accused of snobbery, but her conscience was not entirely easy. "Well, what can you talk about to people like that," she said defensively. "Money? Holidays? Cars? Basil's just as bad. He's become quite obnoxious, as a matter of fact."

"Mmm."

"Don't let's ever become rich, Charles," said Robyn suddenly anxious to mend the little breach that had opened up between them.

"I don't think there's any danger of that," Charles said, rather bitterly, Robyn thought.

PART IV

"I know so little about strikes, and rates of wages, and capital, and labour, that I had better not talk to a political economist like you."

"Nay, the more reason," said he eagerly. "I shall be only too glad to explain to you all that may seem anomalous or mysterious to a stranger; especially at a time like this, when our doings are sure to be canvassed by every scribbler who can hold a pen."

ELIZABETH GASKELL: *North and South*

1

The following Wednesday morning, Robyn found herself back in Vic Wilcox's office, rather to her own surprise, and certainly to Wilcox's, to judge from the expression on his face as Shirley ushered her in.

"You again?" he said, looking up from his desk.

Robyn did not advance into the room, but stood just inside the door, stripping off her gloves. "It's Wednesday," she said. "You didn't send a message telling me not to come."

"I didn't think you'd have the nerve to show your face in this place again, to tell you the truth."

"I'll go away, if you like," said Robyn, with one glove off and one on. "Nothing would please me more."

Wilcox resumed flicking through the contents of a file that was open on his desk. "Why did you come then?"

"I agreed to come every Wednesday for the rest of this term. I wish I hadn't, but I did. If you want to cancel the arrangement, that's fine by me."

Wilcox looked at her in a calculating kind of way. After a long pause he said, "You might as well stay. They might send me somebody even worse."

His rudeness was provocation enough to walk out, but Robyn hesitated.

She had already expended a lot of time and energy in the past couple of days wondering whether to go back to Pringle's, expecting from hour to hour a message from Wilcox or the VC's office that would settle the question. No message had come. Penny Black, whose advice she had sought after squash on Monday evening, had urged her to go back—"if you don't, he'll think he's won"—so she had gone back. And now the voice of prudence counselled her to stay. Wilcox evidently hadn't lodged a formal complaint about her conduct the previous Wednesday, but if she resigned from the Shadow Scheme it would all come out. Though she wasn't ashamed of her intervention on behalf of Danny Ram (and Penny had been deeply impressed) there had been, she privately acknowledged, something slightly Quixotic about it, and she didn't relish the prospect of having to explain and justify it to Philip Swallow or the VC. She came further into the room and peeled off her remaining glove.

"As long as one thing is understood," said Wilcox. "Everything you see or hear while you're shadowing me is confidential."

"All right," said Robyn.

"Don't take your coat off yet—we may be going out." He spoke to Shirley on his intercom: "Phone Foundrax and ask if Norman Cole can spare me a few minutes this morning, will you?"

. . .

For once, Wilcox himself put on an overcoat, an expensive-looking camelhair garment that, like most of his clothes, seemed designed for a man with longer arms and legs. In the lobby they ran into Brian Everthorpe, swaggering in from the car park, huffing and puffing and rubbing his pink hands together. Robyn hadn't seen him since the previous Wednesday—mercifully he hadn't been present at the meeting with the Asian workers, though he must have heard about it.

"Hallo, Vic, I see your beautiful shadow is back, she must be a glutton for punishment. How are you, my dear? Get home all right last week, did you?"

"I managed," Robyn said coldly. Something knowing about his grin made her suspect that he had been responsible for tampering with her car.

"Bad on the motorway was it this morning, Brian?" said Wilcox, glancing at his watch.

"Terrible."

"I thought so."

"Always the same, Wednesday mornings."

"See you," said Wilcox, slicing through the swing doors.

Robyn followed him outside. After the weekend's partial thaw, the weather had turned bitterly cold again. The remnants of last week's blizzard had frozen into corrugated patches of ice on the car park, but Wilcox's Jaguar was just outside the office block, in a bay that had been neatly scraped clean and dry. The car was long and low and luxuriously upholstered. When Wilcox turned the ignition key, a female vocalist sang out with startling clarity and resonance, as if she were concealed, complete with orchestra, in the back seat-well: "*Maybe I'm a dreamer, maybe just a fool—*" Wilcox, evidently embarrassed to have his musical tastes thus revealed, snapped off the stereo system with a quick movement of his hand. The car glided away, ice crackling under its tyres. As he drove, he explained the background to the morning's business, an appointment with the Managing Director of a firm called Foundrax, situated not far away.

Pringle's and Foundrax both supplied a manufacturer of diesel-powered pumps, Rawlinson's, with components—Pringle's with cylinder blocks, Foundrax with cylinder heads. Recently Rawlinson's had asked Pringle's to drop their prices by five per cent, claiming that they had had a quote from another firm at that level. "Of course, they may be bluffing. They're almost certainly bluffing about the size of the discount. Prices ought to be going up, not down, what with the cost of pig-iron and scrap these days. But competition is so ferocious it's possible another company is trying to get some of the action by offering a silly price. The question is, how silly? And who are they? That's why I'm going to see Norman Cole. I want to find out if Rawlinson's are asking for the same sort of reduction on his cylinder heads."

The offices of the Foundrax factory had, like Pringle's, an air of being embalmed in an earlier era, the late fifties or early sixties. There was the same dull reception foyer done out in light oak veneer and worn-looking splay-legged furniture, the same trade magazines spread on the low tables, the same (it seemed to Robyn's inexpert eye) bits of polished machinery in dusty display cases, the same permanent waves on the heads of the secretaries, including the one who, casting curious glances at Robyn, escorted them to Norman Cole's office. Like Wilcox's, this was a large, colourless room, with an executive desk on one side, and on the other a long board table at which he invited them to sit.

Cole was a portly, bald-headed man who blinked a great deal behind his glasses, and smoked a pipe—or rather he poked, scraped, blew into, sucked on and frequently applied burning matches to a pipe. Not much smoke was produced by all this activity. He exuded instead a rather false air of bonhomie. "Ha, ha!" he exclaimed, when Wilcox explained Robyn's presence. "I'll believe you, Vic. Thousands wouldn't." He turned to Robyn: "And what is it you do at the University, Miss er . . ."

"Doctor," said Wilcox, "she's Dr. Penrose."

"Oh, on the medical side, are you?"

"No, I teach English Literature," said Robyn.

"And women's studies," said Wilcox, with a grimace.

"I don't go in for women's studies, ha, ha," said Cole. "But I like a good book. I'm on *The Thorn Birds* at the moment." He looked expectantly at Robyn.

"I'm afraid I haven't read it," said Robyn.

"So how's business, Norman?" Wilcox said.

"Mustn't grumble," said Cole.

The conversation about trade continued desultorily for some minutes. The secretary brought in a tray with coffee and biscuits. Vic raised the topic of some charity fund-raising function the two men were involved in. Cole glanced at his watch. "Anything special I can do for you, Vic?"

"No, I'm just making a few calls to give this young lady an idea of the scope of our business," said Vic. "We won't take up any more of your time. Oh, while I'm here—you haven't had a letter from Rawlinson's buyer lately, by any chance?"

Cole lifted an eyebrow and blinked at Robyn.

"It's all right," said Wilcox. "Dr. Penrose understands that nothing we say goes beyond these four walls."

Cole took out of his pocket an implement like a miniature Swiss Army knife, and began to poke at the bowl of his pipe. "No," he said. "Not to my knowledge. What would it be about?"

"Asking for a reduction on your prices. In the order of five per cent."

"I don't recollect anything," said Cole. He interrupted his excavations to flick a switch on his telephone console and ask his secretary to bring in the Rawlinson file. "Having some trouble with Rawlinson's, then, Vic?"

"Someone's trying to undercut us," Wilcox said. "I'd like to know who it is."

"A foreign firm, perhaps," Cole suggested.

"I don't believe a foreign firm could do it cheaper," said Wilcox. "Why would they bother, anyway? The quantities are too small. What are you thinking of? Germany? Spain?"

Cole unscrewed the mouthpiece of his pipe and peered into the barrel. "I'm just guessing in the dark," he said. "Far East, perhaps, Korea."

"No," said Wilcox, "by the time you added on the cost of shipping it wouldn't make sense. It's another British company, you can bet on that."

The secretary brought in a thick manila file and laid it reverently on Norman Cole's desk. He glanced inside. "No, nothing untoward there, Vic."

"How much are you asking for your cylinder heads, as a matter of interest?"

Norman Cole exposed two rows of nicotine-stained teeth in a broad grin. "You wouldn't expect me to answer that, Vic."

Vic returned the smile with a visible effort. "I'll be off, then," he said, getting to his feet and holding out his hand.

"Taking your shadow with you?" said Cole, grinning and blinking.

"What? Oh. Yes, of course," said Wilcox, who had clearly forgotten Robyn's existence.

"You can leave her here if you like, ha, ha," said Cole, shaking Wilcox's hand. He shook Robyn's hand as well. "*The Fourth Protocol*, that's another good one," he said. "Have you read it?"

"No," said Robyn.

When they were outside in the car, Wilcox said, "Well, what did you make of Norman Cole?"

"I didn't think much of his literary taste."

"He's an accountant," said Wilcox. "Managing Directors in this business are either engineers or accountants. I don't trust accountants."

"He did seem a bit shifty," said Robyn. "All that fiddling with his pipe is an excuse to avoid eye contact."

"Shifty is the word," said Wilcox. "I began to get suspicious when he started talking about Korea. As if anyone in Korea would be interested in Rawlinson's business."

"You think he's hiding something, then?"

"I think he may be the mysterious third party," said Wilcox, as he swung the Jaguar out of the Foundrax car park and slotted into a gap in the traffic on the main road, between a yellow van conveying Riviera Sunbeds and a Dutch container truck.

"You mean the one offering a five per cent reduction?"

"Supposed to be offering five per cent. He might only be offering four."

"But why would he do that? You said nobody could make a profit at that price."

"There could be all kinds of motives," said Wilcox. "Perhaps he's desperate for orders, even loss-making orders, just to keep his factory turning over for the next few weeks, hoping things will improve. Perhaps he's nursing some plot, like to get all the Rawlinson's business for himself and then, next time they re-order, increase the prices without having to bother about competition from us." He gave a dry bark of a laugh. "Or perhaps he knows he's for the high jump and couldn't care less what his figures look like."

"How will you find out?"

Wilcox considered the question for a moment, then reached for a telephone receiver mounted under the dashboard. "Go and see Ted Stoker at Rawlinson's," he said, handing her the instrument. "Phone Shirley for me, will you? It'll save me having to stop."

Robyn, who had never even seen a car phone before, found it rather fun to use.

"I'm afraid Mr. Wilcox is out at the moment," Shirley intoned in a secretarial sing-song.

"I know," said Robyn, "I'm with him."

"Oh," said Shirley. "Who did you say you were?"

"Robyn Penrose. The shadow." She could not suppress a smile as she identified herself—it sounded like the name of a comic-book character. Superman. Spiderwoman. The Shadow. She passed on Wilcox's instruction to arrange a meeting with Ted Stoker, the Managing Director of Rawlinson's, that afternoon if possible.

"You used me as a pretext to see Norman Cole, didn't you?" Robyn said, as they cruised along the road, waiting for Shirley to call back.

"You came in useful," he said with a quiet grin. "Don't mind, do you? You owe me after last week."

A few minutes later Shirley rang back to say she had fixed an appointment for three o'clock. "Have a nice trip," she said with, Robyn thought, a slightly bitchy intonation. Wilcox made a U-turn through a gap in the road's central reservation, and began driving briskly in the opposite direction.

"Where are we going?" Robyn asked.

"Leeds."

"What—today? There and back?"

"Why not?

"It seems a long way."

"I like driving," said Wilcox.

Robyn could understand why, given the power and comfort of the big car. The wind of their passage was the loudest noise inside its upholstered shell as they sailed up the motorway in the fast lane. Outside, the frostbound fields and skeletal trees cowered under a steely shield of cloud. There was a kind of pleasure in being warm and mobile in a cold and lifeless landscape. Robyn asked if they could have some music, and Wilcox switched on the radio and invited her to tune it. She found some Mozart on Radio Three, and settled back in her seat.

"Like that sort of music, do you?" he said.

"Yes. Don't you?"

"I don't mind it."

"But you prefer Randy Crawford?" she said slyly, having spotted the empty cassette box in the dashboard recess.

Wilcox looked impressed, evidently supposing that she had identified by ear the snatch of song heard earlier that morning. "She's all right," he said guardedly.

"You don't find her a little bland?"

"Bland?"

"Sentimental, then."

"No," he said.

Somewhere on the outskirts of Manchester he pulled off the motorway and drove to a pub he knew for lunch. It was an undistinguished modern building situated on a roundabout next to a petrol station, but it had a restaurant attached to it done out in mock-Tudor beams and stained imitation oak furniture and enough reproduction antique brassware to stock a gift shop in Stratford-upon-Avon. Each table bore an electric lamp fashioned in the shape of a carriage lantern, with coloured glass panels. The menus were huge laminated cards that garnished every dish with epithets designed to tickle the appetite: *"succulent," "sizzling," "tender," "farm-fresh,"* etc. The clientèle were mostly businessmen in three-piece suits laughing boisterously and blowing cigarette smoke in each other's faces, or talking earnestly and confidentially to well-dressed young women who were more probably their secretaries than their wives. In short, it was the kind of establishment that Robyn would normally have avoided like the plague.

"Nice place, this," said Wilcox, looking around him with satisfaction. "What will you have?"

"I think I'll have an omelette," said Robyn.

Wilcox looked disappointed. "Don't stint yourself," he said. "Lunch is on the firm."

"All right," said Robyn. "I'll have a half of luscious avocado pear with tangy French dressing to start, and then I'll have golden-fried ocean-fresh scampi and a crisp farmhouse side salad. Oh, and a home-baked wholemeal roll coated with tasty sesame seeds."

If Wilcox perceived any irony in her pedantic recitation of the menu, he did not betray it. "Some chips as well?" he enquired.

"No thanks."

"Anything to drink?"

"What are you having?"

"I never drink in the middle of the day. But don't let that stop you."

Robyn accepted a glass of white wine. Wilcox ordered a mixture of Perrier water and orange juice to go with his succulent char-grilled rump steak and golden crisp french-fried potatoes. Few of the other diners were so abstemious—bottles of red wine cradled in wickerwork baskets, and bottles of white sticking up like missiles from enormous ice buckets, were much in evidence on or between the tables. Even without alcohol, though, Wilcox became relaxed, almost expansive over the meal.

"If you really want to understand how business works," he said, "you shouldn't be following me around, you should be shadowing somebody who runs his own small company, employing, say, fifty people. That's how firms like Pringle's begin. Somebody gets an idea of how to make something cheaper or better than anybody else, and sets up a factory with a small team of employees. Then if all goes well he takes on more labour and brings his sons into the business to take over when he retires. But either the sons aren't interested, or they think to themselves: why risk all our capital in this business, when we could sell out to a bigger company and invest the money in something safer? So the firm gets sold to a conglomerate like Midland Amalgamated, and some poor sod like me is brought in to run it on a salary."

"Late capitalism," said Robyn, nodding.

"What's late about it?"

"I mean, that's the era we're living in, the era of late capitalism." This was a term much favoured in *New Left Review*; post-modernism was said to be symbiotically related to it. "Big multinational corporations rule the world," she said.

"Don't you believe it," said Wilcox. "There'll always be small companies." He looked round the restaurant. "All the men in here are working for firms like Pringle's, and I bet there's not one of them who wouldn't rather be running his own business. A few of them will do it, and then, after a few years, they'll sell out, and the whole process starts again. It's the cycle of commerce," he said rather grandiloquently. "Like the cycle of the seasons."

"Would you prefer to be running your own business, then?"

"Of course."

When Robyn asked him what kind of business, he glanced around in a slightly conspiratorial fashion, and lowered his voice. "Tom Rigby—you remember, the general manager of the foundry—Tom and I have an idea for a little gadget, a kind of spectrometer, for giving instant readout of the chemical composition of the molten metal, straight onto the shop floor. If it worked, it would save having to take samples to the lab for analysis. Every foundry in the world would have to have one. Nice little business, that could be."

"Why don't you do it, then?"

"I have a mortgage, a wife and three idle children to support. Like most of these poor buggers."

Following Wilcox's sweeping glance at the other diners, Robyn observed how the deportment of the secretaries being entertained by their bosses had mutated under the influence of drink from a demure reserve over the starter to giggling irresponsibility by the time the dessert was served. She was less amused by their waiter's evident assumption that she herself was Wilcox's secretary, being set up for seduction. He referred to her throughout the meal as "the young lady," winked and smirked when Wilcox suggested another glass of wine, and recommended something "sweet and lovely" for dessert.

"I wish you'd drop a hint to that young man that I'm not your dolly-bird," Robyn said at last.

"What?" said Wilcox, so startled by the suggestion that he nearly choked on his portion of home-made orchard-fresh apple pie.

"Haven't you noticed the way he's carrying on?"

"I thought he was just queer. Waiters often are, you know."

"I think he's hoping for a big tip."

"He'll get a big surprise, then," said Wilcox grimly, and nearly bit the unfortunate waiter's head off when he urged them to round off their meal "with a *relaxing* liqueur." "Just coffee, and bring the bill with it," he growled. "I've got an appointment in Leeds at three."

Robyn was rather sorry that she had raised the subject, not so much for the waiter's sake as because Wilcox now relapsed into sulky silence, evidently feeling that he had somehow been compromised or made to look foolish. "Thanks for the meal," she said conciliatorily, though in truth the scampi had tasted of nothing except the oil in which they had been fried, and the cheese-cake had glued her tongue to the roof of her mouth.

"Don't thank me," Wilcox said ungraciously. "It's all on expenses."

. . .

The drive over the still snow-covered wastes of the Pennines on the rolling M62 was spectacular. "Oh look, that's the way to Haworth!" Robyn exclaimed, reading a roadsign. "The Brontës!"

"What are they?" Wilcox asked.

"Novelists. Charlotte and Emily Brontë. Have you never read *Jane Eyre* and *Wuthering Heights*?"

"I've heard of them," said Wilcox guardedly. "Women's books, aren't they?"

"They're about women," said Robyn. "But they're not women's books in the narrow sense. They're classics—two of the greatest novels of the nineteenth century, actually." There must, she reflected, be millions of literate, intelligent people like Victor Wilcox walking about England who had never read *Jane Eyre* or *Wuthering Heights*, though it was difficult to imagine such a state of cultural deprivation. What difference did it make, never to have shivered with Jane Eyre at Lowood school, or throbbed in the arms of Heathcliff with Cathy? Then it occurred to Robyn that this was a suspiciously humanist train of thought and that the very word *classic* was an instrument of bourgeois hegemony. "Of course," she added, "they're often read simply as wish-fulfilment romances, *Jane Eyre* especially. You have to deconstruct the texts to bring out the political and psychological contradictions inscribed in them."

"Eh?" said Wilcox.

"It's hard to explain if you haven't read them," said Robyn, closing her eyes. The lunch, the wine, and the cushioned warmth of the car had made her drowsy, and disinclined to demonstrate an elementary deconstructive reading of the Brontës. Soon she dropped off to sleep. When she awoke, they were in the car park of Rawlinson and Co.

. . .

Another drab reception lobby, another interval spent leafing through trade magazines with titles like *Hydraulic Engineering* and *The Pump*, another walk down lino-tiled corridors behind a high-heeled secretary, another managing director rising from behind his polished executive desk to shake their hands and have Robyn's presence explained to him.

"Dr. Penrose understands that everything we say is confidential," Wilcox said.

"If it's all right by you, Vic, it's all right by me," said Ted Stoker with a smile. "I've got nothing to hide." He sat down and plonked two hands the size of hams on the surface of his desk as if to prove the point. He was a tall, heavily-built man with a face composed of pachydermatous folds and wrinkles from amongst which two small, pale and rheumy eyes looked out with lugubrious humour. "What can I do for you?"

"You sent us a letter," said Wilcox, taking a paper out of his briefcase.

"Yes, we did."

"I think there was a typing error in it," said Wilcox. "It says you're looking for a reduction of five per cent on our prices for cylinder blocks."

Stoker looked at Robyn and grinned. "He's a caution," he said, jerking his head in Wilcox's direction. "You're a caution, Vic," he repeated, turning back to Wilcox.

"There's no mistake?"

"No mistake."

"Five per cent is ridiculous."

Stoker shrugged his massive shoulders. "If you can't do it, there's others who can."

"What others?"

Stoker turned to Robyn again. "He knows I can't tell him that," he said, grinning with delight. "You know I can't tell you that, Vic."

Robyn acknowledged Stoker's asides with the thinnest of smiles. She didn't relish the role of stooge, but she couldn't quite see how to get out of it. Stoker was in control of this conversational game.

"Is it a foreign firm?" Wilcox said.

Stoker wagged his head slowly from side to side. "I can't tell you that either."

"I could bite the bullet and come down by two per cent on the four-bore," said Wilcox, after a pause.

"You're wasting your time, Vic."

"Two and a half."

Stoker shook his head.

"We've been doing business together for a long time, Ted," said Vic reproachfully.

"It's my duty to accept the lowest bid, you know that." He winked at Robyn. "He knows that."

"The quality won't be as good," said Wilcox.

"The quality is fine."

"You're already sourcing from them, then?" Wilcox asked quickly.

Stoker nodded, then looked as if he wished he hadn't. "The quality is fine," he repeated.

"Whoever it is can't be making any money out of it," said Wilcox.

"That's their problem. I have my own."

"Business not so good, eh?"

Ted Stoker addressed his answer to Robyn. "We sell a lot to the third world," he said. "Irrigation pumps, mostly. The third world is broke. The banks won't lend them any more money. Our Nigerian order book is down fifty per cent on last year."

"That's terrible," said Robyn.

"It is," said Ted Stoker. "We may have to go on to short time."

"I mean for the third world."

"Oh, the third world . . ." Stoker shrugged off the insoluble problems of the third world.

Wilcox was busy with his calculator while this conversation was going on. "Three per cent," he said, looking up. "That's my last offer. I just can't go any lower. Say yes to three per cent and I'll tear your arm off."

"Sorry, Vic," said Ted Stoker. "You're still two per cent adrift of what I'm offered elsewhere."

When they were back in the car, Robyn said, "Why were you doing those calculations if you were already prepared to come down by three per cent?"

"To fool him into thinking he'd pressured me into it, got himself a bargain. Not that it did fool him. He's a shrewd old bugger, is Ted Stoker."

"He didn't tell you who the other company were."

"I didn't expect him to. I just wanted to see his expression when I asked him."

"And what did it tell you?"

"He's not bluffing. There really is somebody offering four or five per cent below our price. More important, they're already supplying Rawlinson's. That means I can find out who they are."

"How?"

"I'll get a couple of our reps to sit in a car outside Rawlinson's and make a note of the name on every wagon that goes into the place. They can sit there all week if necessary. With a bit of luck we'll be able to find out who's delivering cylinder blocks and where from."

"Is it worth going to such lengths?" Robyn asked. "How much is this business actually worth?"

Wilcox thought for a moment. "Not all that much," he admitted. "But it's the principle of the thing. I don't like to be beaten," he said, pressing the accelerator so that the Jaguar surged forward with a squeal of tyres. "If the mystery supplier turns out to be Foundrax, I'll make Norman Cole rue the day."

"How?"

"I'll blast him. I'll attack his other customers."

"You mean assault them?" said Robyn, shocked.

Wilcox guffawed, the first full-blooded laugh she had heard from him. "What d'you think we are—the Mafia?"

Robyn flushed. His melodramatic talk of setting men to spy on Rawlinson's had misled her.

"No, I mean attack 'em with low prices," said Wilcox, "take his business away. Tit for tat, only our tit will be a lot more than his tat. He won't know what hit him."

"I don't see the point of all this jockeying and intriguing and undercutting," said Robyn. "No sooner do you get an advantage in one place than you lose it in another."

"That's business," said Wilcox. "I always say it's like a relay race. First you're ahead, then you drop the baton and someone else takes the lead, then you catch up again. But there's no finishing line. The race never ends."

"So who gains in the end?"

"The consumer gains," said Wilcox piously. "At the end of the day, somebody gets a cheaper pump."

"Why don't you—all of you, you and Norman Cole and Ted Stoker— why don't you put your heads together and *make* a cheaper pump instead of squabbling over a few per cent here or there?"

"What would happen to competition?" said Wilcox. "You've got to have competition."

"Why?"

"You've just got to. How did you get to where you are?"

"What?"

"How did you become a university lecturer? By doing better than other people in exams, right?"

"Actually, I'm opposed to competitive examinations," said Robyn.

"Yes, you would be," said Wilcox. "Having done all right out of them, you can afford to be."

This observation made Robyn angry, but she could not think of a satisfactory reply. "I'll tell you what it reminds me of, your precious competition," she said. "A lot of little dogs squabbling over bones. Foundrax has stolen the Rawlinson's bone from you, so while they're chewing on that one you're going to steal another bone from them."

"We don't know it's Foundrax, yet," said Wilcox, ignoring the analogy. "Mind if I smoke?"

"I'd rather you didn't," said Robyn. "Could I have Radio Three on?"

"I'd rather you didn't," said Wilcox.

The rest of the journey passed in silence.

. . .

On the following Monday morning, Rupert Sutcliffe put his head round Robyn's door in the middle of a tutorial to say she was wanted on the telephone. As part of the economy drive, telephones capable of communicating with the outside world had been removed from the offices of all but the most senior members of the University, and consequently a good deal of expensive academic and secretarial time was wasted running up and down the corridor to and from the phone in the Department Office. Pamela, the Department Secretary, usually avoided interrupting a class, but apparently she wasn't in the office when this call came through, and Sutcliffe, who was, had thought fit to fetch Robyn. "It sounded important," he said to her in the corridor. "Somebody's secretary. I thought it might be your publisher." But it wasn't her publisher's secretary who spoke when she picked up the phone. It was Shirley.

"Mr. Wilcox for you," she said. "I'm putting you through."

"It's Foundrax," Wilcox said, without any preliminaries. "I thought you'd like to know. Two of our reps sat in a car outside Rawlinson's for two days and a night, nearly froze to death they said, but they got the name on every wagon that went in. The likeliest was a Midlands firm called GTG. My transport manager used to work for them, luckily, so he gave his old mates a buzz and soon found out what they were delivering to Rawlinson's. Guess what? Four-bore cylinder blocks from Foundrax."

"Have you brought me to the phone just to tell me that?" Robyn enquired icily.

"Don't you have your own phone?"

"No, I don't. Furthermore, I was in the middle of a tutorial."

"Oh, sorry," said Wilcox. "Why didn't your secretary tell Shirley?"

"I don't have a personal secretary," said Robyn. "We have one secretary between fifteen of us, and she isn't in the office at the moment. She's probably in the store-room steaming open letters so we can reuse the envelopes. Is there anything else you'd like to know, or can I go back to my tutorial now?"

"No, that's all," said Wilcox. "I'll see you on Wednesday, then."

"Goodbye," said Robyn, and put the phone down. She turned to find that Philip Swallow had wandered into the office, holding a paper in his hand rather helplessly as if he were looking for Pamela.

"Hallo, Robyn," he said. "How are you?"

"Cross," she said. "That man Wilcox I'm supposed to be shadowing seems to think he owns me."

"Yes, it is depressing weather," Swallow said, nodding. "How's that shadow business going by the way? The VC was asking me only the other day."

"Well, it's going."

"The VC is looking forward to your report. He takes a personal interest in the scheme."

"Perhaps he'll take a personal interest in keeping me on, then," said Robyn. She smiled as she said this, from which Swallow evidently inferred that she had made a joke.

"Ha, ha, very good," he said. "I must remember to tell him that."

"I hope you will," said Robyn. "I must dash now, I'm in the middle of a tutorial."

"Yes, yes, of course," said Swallow. "*Tutorial*" was one of the words he still recognized without too much difficulty, perhaps because it had a lot of vowels in it.

. . .

When Robyn Penrose rang off, Vic Wilcox replaced the telephone receiver on its cradle slowly and deliberately, as if trying to convince some invisible observer that that was what he had intended to do. In fact, he prided himself on being a fast gun when it came to using the phone—quick to snatch up the instrument as soon as it rang, and the first to put it down when the conversation had served its purpose. He had a theory that this gave you a psychological advantage over a business adversary. Robyn Penrose wasn't a business adversary, but he didn't like the sensation of having been put in his place by her abrupt termination of his call. Somehow he had miscalculated, supposing that she would be as elated as himself at having solved the mystery of Rawlinson's supplier. He had expected congratulations and had received instead a flea in his ear.

He shook his head, as if he could physically dismiss these irritating thoughts, but they lingered, retarding his progress through the files on his desk. He tried to picture the context in which Robyn Penrose had received his call. Where was the telephone to which she had been called? How far had she walked to come to it? What would she have been doing in the tutorial? He could summon up only the vaguest images to answer these questions. Nevertheless, he began to develop some dim appreciation of why she might not have been overjoyed to receive his news. This did nothing to improve his humour. When Shirley brought him the fruits of that morning's dictation to sign he complained about the layout of one of the letters and told her to do it again.

"I always do quotations that way," she said. "You never complained before."

"Well, I'm complaining now," he said. "Just do it again, will you?"

Shirley went off muttering about some people being impossible to please. Then Brian Everthorpe, who had been off sick the previous Thursday and Friday, came huffing and puffing into Vic's office, having picked up a rumour about the Foundrax–Rawlinson's affair. Vic briefly filled him in.

"Why didn't you tell me you were going to see Ted Stoker?" he said. "I would have come with you."

"There wasn't time. I fixed it up on the spur of the moment, straight after seeing Norman Cole. Did it all through Shirley on the car phone. You weren't available," he lied, though it was a safe lie, since Brian Everthorpe seldom was available when you wanted him.

"Took your shadow with you, though, I hear," said Everthorpe.

"She happened to be with me at the time," said Vic. "It was her day."

"Sounds more like it was yours," said Everthorpe with a leer. "You're a dark horse, Vic."

Vic ignored this remark. "Anyway, as you gathered, we found out that Norman Cole is undercutting us on cylinder blocks at Rawlinson's by five per cent."

"How can he do it at that price?"

"I don't think he can for long."

"What are we going to do—go after him?"

"No," said Vic.

"No?" Everthorpe's bushy eyebrows shot up.

"We'd make ourselves look weak, fighting with Foundrax for the Rawlinson account. Like little dogs squabbling over a bone. Not much meat on the Rawlinson bone, when you work it out. Let Norman Cole have it. Let him choke on it."

"You're going to let him get away with poaching on our business?"

"I'll drop a hint that I know what his game is. That'll worry him. I'll let him twist in the wind a while."

"Looks to me like we're twisting in the wind."

"Then I'll hit him."

"With what?"

"I haven't decided yet."

"That doesn't sound like you, Vic."

"I'll let you know," said Vic coldly. "Feeling better, are you?"

"What?"

"Weren't you off sick last week?"

"Oh, yes! That's right." Brian Everthorpe's illness had evidently not engraved itself on his memory. "Touch of flu."

"I expect you've got a lot of work to catch up on, then." Vic opened a file to signify that the interview was over.

A little later he phoned Stuart Baxter and told him he wanted to let Brian Everthorpe go.

"Why, Vic?"

"He's no good. He's idle. He's stuck in old grooves. He doesn't like me and I don't like him."

"He's been with the company a long time."

"Exactly."

"He won't go without a fight."

"I'll enjoy that."

"He'll want a hefty golden handshake."

"It'll be money well spent."

Stuart Baxter was silent for a moment. Vic heard the rasp and snick of a cigarette lighter at the other end of the line. Then Baxter said, "I think you should give Brian a chance to adjust."

"Adjust to what?"

"To you, Vic, to you. It's not easy for him. I suppose you know he had hopes of your job?"

"I can't think why," said Vic.

Stuart Baxter sighed. Vic imagined plumes of smoke jetting from his nostrils. "I'll think about it," he said at last. "Don't do anything hasty, Vic."

For the second time that day Vic heard the click of a telephone receiver being put down before he was able to replace his own. He frowned at the instrument, wondering why Stuart Baxter was so protective towards Brian Everthorpe. Perhaps they were both Masons. Vic himself wasn't—he had been approached once, but couldn't bring himself to go through all the mumbo-jumbo of initiation.

Shirley came back into the office with the retyped letter. "Is that all right?" she said, with a surprisingly obsequious smile.

"That's fine," he said, scanning the document.

"I believe Brian mentioned to you his idea for a Pringle's calendar," she said, hovering at his shoulder.

"Yes," Vic said, "he did."

"He said you weren't keen."

"That's putting it mildly."

"It would be a great chance for Tracey," said Shirley wistfully.

"A great chance to degrade herself," said Vic, handing her the letter.

"What d'you mean?" said Shirley indignantly.

"You really want pictures of your daughter in the altogether stuck up on walls for anybody to look at?"

"I don't see the harm . . . What about art galleries?"

"Art galleries?"

"They're full of nudes. Old masters."

"That's different."

"I don't see why."

"You don't get blokes going into an art gallery and staring at a picture of Venus or whatever and nudging each other in the ribs saying, '*I wouldn't mind going through her on a Saturday night.*'"

"Ooh!" gasped Shirley, averting her face.

"Or taking the picture home to wank off with," Vic continued remorselessly.

"I'm not listening," Shirley said, retreating rapidly to her office. "I don't know what's got into you."

No more do I, Vic Wilcox thought to himself, feeling slightly ashamed of his outburst, as the door closed behind her. It was in fact several weeks before he realized that he was in love with Robyn Penrose.

2

The winter term at Rummidge was of ten weeks' duration, like the autumn and summer terms, but seemed longer than the other two because of the cheerless season. The mornings were dark, dusk came early, and the sun seldom broke through the cloud cover in the brief interval of daylight. Electric lights burned all day in offices and lecture rooms. Outside, the air was cold and clammy, thick with moisture and pollution. It drained every colour and blurred every outline of the urban landscape. You could hardly see the face of the clock at the top of the University's tower, and the very chimes sounded muffled and despondent. The atmosphere chilled the bones and congested the lungs. Some people attributed the characteristic adenoidal whine of the local dialect to the winter climate, which gave everybody runny noses and blocked sinuses for months on end and obliged them to go about with their mouths open like fish gasping for air. At this time of the year it was certainly hard to understand why human beings had ever settled and multiplied in such a cold, damp, grey place. Only work seemed to provide an answer. No other reason would make anyone come here, or having come, stay. All the more grim, there-fore, was the fate of the unemployed of Rummidge and environs, condemned to be idle in a place where there was nothing much to do, except work.

Robyn Penrose was not unemployed—yet. She had plenty of work: her teaching, her research, her administrative duties in the Department. She had survived the previous winter by surrendering herself to work. She drove to and fro between her cosy little house and her warm, well-lit room at the University, ignoring the dismal weather. At home she read, she took notes, she distilled her notes into continuous prose on her word-processor, she marked essays; at the University she lectured, she gave seminars and tutorials, she counselled stu-dents, interviewed applicants, drew up reading-lists, attended committee meetings, and marked essays. Twice a week she played squash with Penny Black, a form of recreation unaffected by the climate—or, indeed, any other aspect of the environment: swiping and sweating and panting in the brightly lit cubic court down in the bowels of the Sports Centre one might have been anywhere—in Cambridge, or London, or the South of France. The steady grind of intellectual work, punctuated by brief explosions of indoor physical exercise—that was the rhythm of Robyn's first winter at Rummidge.

But this year the winter term was different. Every Wednesday she left her familiar milieu, and drove across the city (by a quicker and more direct route than she had followed on her first visit) to the factory in West Wallsbury. In a way she resented the obligation. It was a distraction from her work. There were always so many books, so many articles in so many journals, waiting to be read, digested, distilled and synthesised with all the other books and ar-ticles she had read, digested, distilled and synthesised. Life was short, criti-cism long. She had her career to think of. Her only chance of staying in academic life was to build up an irresistibly impressive record of research and publication. The Shadow Scheme contributed nothing to that—on the contrary, it interfered with it, taking up the precious one day a week she had kept free from Departmental duties.

But this irritation was all on the surface. The Shadow Scheme was something to grumble about, to Charles, to Penny Black, something handy to blame for getting behind with other tasks. At some deeper level of feeling and reflection she derived a subtle satisfaction from her association with the factory, and a certain sense of superiority over her friends. Charles and Penny led their lives, as she had done, wholly within the charmed circle of academia. She now had this other life on one day of the week, and almost another identity. The designation "Shadow," which had seemed so absurd initially, began to acquire a suggestive resonance. A shadow was a kind of double, a *Doppelgänger*, but it was herself she duplicated at Pringle's, not Wilcox. It was as if the Robyn Penrose who spent one day a week at the factory was the shadow of the self who on the other six days a week was busy with women's studies and the Victorian novel and post-structuralist literary theory—less substantial, more elusive, but just as real. She led a double life these days, and felt herself to be a more interesting and complex person because of it. West Wallsbury, that wilderness of factories and warehouses and roads and roundabouts, scored with overgrown railway cuttings and obsolete canals like the lines on Mars, itself seemed a shadowland, the dark side of Rummidge, unknown to those who basked in the light of culture and learning at the University. Of course, to the people who worked at Pringle's, the reverse was true: the University and all it stood for was in shadow—alien, inscrutable, vaguely threatening. Flitting backwards and forwards across the frontier between these two zones, whose values, priorities, language and manners were so utterly disparate, Robyn felt like a secret agent; and, as secret agents are apt to do, suffered occasional spasms of doubt about the righteousness of her own side.

"You know," she mused aloud to Charles one day, "there are millions of people out there who haven't the slightest interest in what we do."

"What?" he said, looking up from his book, and marking his place in it with his index finger. They were sitting in Robyn's study–living-room on another Sunday afternoon. Charles' weekend visits had become more frequent of late.

"Of course they don't *know* what we do, but even if one tried to explain it to them they wouldn't understand, and even if they understood what we were doing they wouldn't understand why we were doing it, or why anybody should pay us to do it."

"So much the worse for them," said Charles.

"But doesn't it bother you at all?" Robyn said. "That the things we care so passionately about—for instance, whether Derrida's critique of metaphysics lets idealism in by the back door, or whether Lacan's psychoanalytic theory is phallogocentric, or whether Foucault's theory of the episteme is reconcilable with dialectical materialism—things like that, which we argue about and read about and write about endlessly—doesn't it worry you that ninety-nine point nine per cent of the population couldn't give a monkey's?"

"A what?" said Charles.

"A monkey's. It means you don't care a bit."

"It means you don't give a monkey's fuck."

"Does it?" said Robyn, with a snigger. "I thought it was a monkey's nut. I should have known: 'fuck' is much more poetic in Jakobson's terms—the repetition of the 'k' as well as the first vowel in 'monkey' . . . No wonder Vic Wilcox looked startled when I said it the other day."

"Did you pick it up from him?"

"I suppose so. Though he doesn't use that kind of language much, actually. He's a rather puritanical type."

"The protestant ethic."

"Exactly . . . Now I've forgotten what I was saying."

"You were saying they don't go in much for poststructuralism at the factory. Hardly surprising, is it?"

"But doesn't it worry you at all? That most people don't give a . . . damn about the things that matter most to us?"

"No, why should it?"

"Well, when Wilcox starts getting at me about arts degrees being a waste of money—"

"Does he do that often?"

"Oh yes, we argue all the time . . . Anyway, when he does that, I find myself falling back on arguments that I don't really believe any more, like the importance of maintaining cultural tradition, and improving students' communicative skills—arguments that old fogies like Philip Swallow trot out at the drop of a hat. Because if I said we teach students about the perpetual sliding of the signified under the signifier, or the way every text inevitably undermines its own claim to a determinate meaning, he would laugh in my face."

"You can't explain poststructuralism to someone who hasn't even discovered traditional humanism."

"Precisely. But doesn't that make *us* rather marginal?"

There was a silence while Charles pondered this question. "Margins imply a centre," he said at length. "But the idea of a centre is precisely what poststructuralism calls into question. Grant people like Wilcox, or Swallow for that matter, the idea of a centre, and they will lay claim to it, justifying everything they do by reference to it. Show that it's an illusion, a fallacy, and their position collapses. We live in a decentred universe."

"I know," said Robyn. "But who pays?"

"Who pays?" Charles repeated blankly.

"That's always Wilcox's line. *'Who pays?' 'There's no such thing as a free lunch.'* I expect he'd say there's no such thing as a free seminar on deconstruction. Why should society pay to be told people don't mean what they say or say what they mean?"

"Because it's true."

"I thought there was no such thing as truth, in the absolute sense."

"Not in the absolute sense, no." Charles looked exasperated. "Whose side are you on, Robyn?"

"I'm just being Devil's Advocate."

"They don't pay us all that much, anyway," said Charles, and resumed reading his book.

Robyn caught sight of the title, and pronounced it aloud: "*The Financial Revolution*! What on earth are you reading that for?"

"I told you, I'm going to write an article about what's going on in the City."

"Are you really? I'd no idea you were serious about that. Isn't it terribly boring?"

"No, it's very interesting, actually."

"Are you going to go and watch Basil's Debbie at work?"

"I might." Charles smiled his feline smile. "Why shouldn't I be a shadow too?"

"I didn't think you could ever get interested in business."

"This isn't business," said Charles, tapping his book. "It's not about buying and selling real commodities. It's all on paper, or computer screens. It's abstract. It has its own rather seductive jargon—arbitrageur, deferred futures, floating rate. It's like literary theory."

Pringle's was definitely a business dealing in real commodities and running it was not in the least like doing literary theory, but it did strike Robyn sometimes that Vic Wilcox stood to his subordinates in the relation of teacher to pupils. Though she could seldom grasp the detailed matters of engineering and accounting that he dealt with in his meetings with his staff, though these meetings often bored and wearied her, she could see that he was trying to *teach* the other men, to coax and persuade them to look at the factory's operations in a new way. He would have been surprised to be told it, but he used the Socratic method: he prompted the other directors and the middle managers and even the foremen to identify the problems themselves and to reach by their own reasoning the solutions he had himself already determined upon. It was so deftly done that she had sometimes to temper her admiration by reminding herself that it was all directed by the profit-motive, and that beyond the walls of Vic Wilcox's carpeted office there was a factory full of men and women doing dangerous, demeaning and drearily repetitive tasks who were mere cogs in the machine of his grand strategy. He was an artful tyrant, but still a tyrant. Furthermore, he showed no reciprocal respect for her own professional skills.

A typical instance of this was the furious argument they had about the Silk Cut advertisement. They were returning in his car from visiting a foundry in Derby that had been taken over by asset-strippers who were selling off an automatic core moulder Wilcox was interested in, though it had turned out to be too old-fashioned for his purpose. Every few miles, it seemed, they passed the same huge poster on roadside hoardings, a photographic depiction of a rippling expanse of purple silk in which there was a single slit, as if the material had been slashed with a razor. There were no words on the advertisement, except for the Government Health Warning about smoking. This ubiquitous image, flashing past at regular intervals, both irritated and intrigued Robyn, and she began to do her semiotic stuff on the deep structure hidden beneath its bland surface.

It was in the first instance a kind of riddle. That is to say, in order to decode it, you had to know that there was a brand of cigarettes called Silk Cut. The poster was the iconic representation of a missing name, like a rebus. But the icon was also a metaphor. The shimmering silk, with its voluptuous curves and sensuous texture, obviously symbolised the female body, and the elliptical slit, foregrounded by a lighter colour showing through, was still more obviously a vagina. The advert thus appealed to both sensual and sadistic impulses, the desire to mutilate as well as penetrate the female body.

Vic Wilcox spluttered with outraged derision as she expounded this interpretation. He smoked a different brand, himself, but it was as if he felt his whole philosophy of life was threatened by Robyn's analysis of the advert. "You must have a twisted mind to see all that in a perfectly harmless bit of cloth," he said.

"What's the point of it, then?" Robyn challenged him. "Why use cloth to advertise cigarettes?"

"Well, that's the name of 'em, isn't it? Silk Cut. It's a picture of the name. Nothing more or less."

"Suppose they'd used a picture of a roll of silk cut in half—would that do just as well?"

"I suppose so. Yes, why not?"

"Because it would look like a penis cut in half, that's why."

He forced a laugh to cover his embarrassment. "Why can't you people take things at their face value?"

"What people are you referring to?"

"Highbrows. Intellectuals. You're always trying to find hidden meanings in things. Why? A cigarette is a cigarette. A piece of silk is a piece of silk. Why not leave it at that?"

"When they're represented they acquire additional meanings," said Robyn. "Signs are never innocent. Semiotics teaches us that."

"Semi-what?"

"Semiotics. The study of signs."

"It teaches us to have dirty minds, if you ask me."

"Why d'you think the wretched cigarettes were called Silk Cut in the first place?"

"I dunno. It's just a name, as good as any other."

"'Cut' has something to do with the tobacco, doesn't it? The way the tobacco leaf is cut. Like 'Player's Navy Cut'—my uncle Walter used to smoke them."

"Well, what if it does?" Vic said warily.

"But silk has nothing to do with tobacco. It's a metaphor, a metaphor that means something like, 'smooth as silk.' Somebody in an advertising agency dreamt up the name 'Silk Cut' to suggest a cigarette that wouldn't give you a sore throat or a hacking cough or lung cancer. But after a while the public got used to the name, the word 'Silk' ceased to signify, so they decided to have an advertising campaign to give the brand a high profile again. Some bright spark in the agency came up with the idea of rippling silk with a cut in it. The original metaphor is now represented literally. But new metaphorical connotations accrue—sexual ones. Whether they were consciously intended or not doesn't really matter. It's a good example of the perpetual sliding of the signified under the signifier, actually."

Wilcox chewed on this for a while, then said, "Why do women smoke them, then, eh?" His triumphant expression showed that he thought this was a knock-down argument. "If smoking Silk Cut is a form of aggravated rape, as you try to make out, how come women smoke 'em too?"

"Many women are masochistic by temperament," said Robyn. "They've learned what's expected of them in patriarchal society."

"Ha!" Wilcox exclaimed, tossing back his head. "I might have known you'd have some daft answer."

"I don't know why you're so worked up," said Robyn. "It's not as if you smoke Silk Cut yourself."

"No, I smoke Marlboros. Funnily enough, I smoke them because I like the taste."

"They're the ones that have the lone cowboy ads, aren't they?"

"I suppose that makes me a repressed homosexual, does it?"

"No, it's a very straightforward metonymic message."

"Metowhat?"

"Metonymic. One of the fundamental tools of semiotics is the distinction between metaphor and metonymy. D'you want me to explain it to you?"

"It'll pass the time," he said.

"Metaphor is a figure of speech based on similarity, whereas metonymy is based on contiguity. In metaphor you substitute something *like* the thing you mean for the thing itself, whereas in metonymy you substitute some attribute or cause or effect of the thing for the thing itself."

"I don't understand a word you're saying."

"Well, take one of your moulds. The bottom bit is called the drag because it's dragged across the floor and the top bit is called the cope because it covers the bottom bit."

"*I* told *you* that."

"Yes, I know. What you didn't tell me was that 'drag' is a metonymy and 'cope' is a metaphor."

Vic grunted. "What difference does it make?"

"It's just a question of understanding how language works. I thought you were interested in how things work."

"I don't see what it's got to do with cigarettes."

"In the case of the Silk Cut poster, the picture signifies the female body metaphorically: the slit in the silk is *like* a vagina—"

Vic flinched at the word. "So you say."

"All holes, hollow spaces, fissures and folds represent the female genitals."

"Prove it."

"Freud proved it, by his successful analysis of dreams," said Robyn. "But the Marlboro ads don't use any metaphors. That's probably why you smoke them, actually."

"What d'you mean?" he said suspiciously.

"You don't have any sympathy with the metaphorical way of looking at things. A cigarette is a cigarette as far as you are concerned."

"Right."

"The Marlboro ad doesn't disturb that naive faith in the stability of the signified. It establishes a metonymic connection—completely spurious of course, but realistically plausible—between smoking that particular brand and the healthy, heroic, outdoor life of the cowboy. Buy the cigarette and you buy the life-style, or the fantasy of living it."

"Rubbish!" said Wilcox. "I hate the country and the open air. I'm scared to go into a field with a cow in it."

"Well then, maybe it's the solitariness of the cowboy in the ads that appeals to you. Self-reliant, independent, very macho."

"I've never heard such a lot of balls in all my life," said Vic Wilcox, which was strong language coming from him.

"Balls—now that's an interesting expression . . ." Robyn mused.

"Oh no!" he groaned.

"When you say a man 'has balls,' approvingly, it's a metonymy, whereas if you say something is a 'lot of balls,' or 'a balls-up,' it's a sort of metaphor. The metonymy attributes value to the testicles whereas the metaphor uses them to degrade something else."

"I can't take any more of this," said Vic. "D'you mind if I smoke? Just a plain, ordinary cigarette?"

"If I can have Radio Three on," said Robyn.

. . .

It was late by the time they got back to Pringle's. Robyn's Renault stood alone and forlorn in the middle of the deserted car park. Wilcox drew up beside it.

"Thanks," said Robyn. She tried to open the door, but the central locking system prevented her. Wilcox pressed a button and the locks popped open all round the car.

"I hate that gadget," said Robyn. "It's a rapist's dream."

"You've got rape on the brain," said Wilcox. He added, without looking at her: "Come to lunch next Sunday."

The invitation was so unexpected, and issued so off-handedly, that she wondered whether she had heard correctly. But his next words confirmed that she had.

"Nothing special," he said. "Just the family."

"Why?" she wanted to ask, if it wouldn't have sounded horribly rude. She had resigned herself to giving up one day a week to shadowing Wilcox, but she didn't want to sacrifice part of her precious weekends as well. Neither would Charles.

"I'm afraid I have someone staying with me this weekend," she said.

"The Sunday after, then."

"He stays most weekends, actually," said Robyn.

Wilcox looked put out, but after a moment's hesitation he said, "Bring him too, then."

To which there was nothing Robyn could say except, "All right. Thank you very much."

. . .

Vic let himself into the administration block. The solid wooden inner door was locked, as well as the glass swing doors. Only a low-wattage security light illuminated the reception lobby, making it look shabbier than ever. The office staff, including Shirley, had all gone home. So, it seemed, had the other directors.

He always liked being alone in the building. It was a good time to work. But this evening he didn't feel like working. He went into his office without switching on any lights, making his way by the dim illumination that filtered through the blinds from the car park. He slung the jacket of his suit over the back of his swivel chair, but instead of sitting down at the desk, he slumped into an armchair.

Of course, she was bound to have a boyfriend, a lover, wasn't she—an attractive, modern young woman like Robyn Penrose? It stood to reason. Why then had he been so surprised, why had he felt so . . . disappointed, when she mentioned the man who stayed with her at weekends? He hadn't supposed she was a virgin, for God's sake, not the way she talked about penises and vaginas without so much as a blush; nor that she was a lezzie, in spite of the cropped hair. But there was something about her that was different from the other women he knew—Marjorie, Sandra, Shirley and her Tracey. Dress, for instance. Whereas they dressed (or, in the case of Tracey, undressed) in a way which said, *Look at me, like me, desire, marry me,* Robyn

Penrose turned herself out as if entirely for her own pleasure and comfort. Stylishly, mind—none of your women's lib regulation dungarees—but without a hint of coquetry. She wasn't forever fidgeting with her skirt or patting her hair or stealing glances at herself in every reflecting surface. She looked a man boldly in the eye, and he liked that. She was confident—arrogant at times—but she wasn't vain. She was the most independent woman he had ever met, and this had made him think of her as somehow unattached and—it was a funny word to float into his mind, but, well, *chaste*.

He recalled a painting he had seen once at the Rummidge Art Gallery, on a school outing—it must have been more than thirty years ago, but it had stuck in his memory, and arguing with Shirley the other day about nudes had revived it. A large oil painting of a Greek goddess and a lot of nymphs washing themselves in a pond in the middle of a wood, and some young chap in the foreground peeping at them from behind a bush. The goddess had just noticed the Peeping Tom, and was giving him a really filthy look, a look that seemed to come right out of the picture and subdue even the schoolboys who stared at it, usually all too ready to snigger and nudge each other at the sight of a female nude. For some reason the painting was associated in his mind with the word "chaste," and now with Robyn Penrose. He pictured her to himself in the pose of the goddess—tall, white-limbed, indignant, setting her dogs on the intruder. There was no place in the picture for a lover or husband—the goddess needed no male protector. That was how he had thought of Robyn Penrose, too, and she had said nothing to suggest the contrary until today, which had made it all the more upsetting.

Upsetting? What right or reason had he to feel upset about Robyn Penrose's private life? It's none of your business, he told himself angrily. Business is your business. He thumped his head with his own fists as if to knock some sense into it, or the nonsense out of it. What in God's name was he doing, the managing director of a casting and engineering company with a likely deficit this month of thirty thousand pounds, sitting in the dark, woolgathering about Greek goddesses? He should be at his desk, working on the plan to computerise stock and purchasing.

Nevertheless he remained slumped in his armchair, thinking about Robyn Penrose, and about having her to lunch next Sunday. It had been an unpremeditated act, that had surprised himself almost as much as it had evidently surprised her. Now he regretted it. He should have taken the opportunity, when she mentioned her boyfriend, to let the matter drop. Why had he persisted—why, for God's sake, had he invited the boyfriend too, whom he hadn't the slightest wish to meet? He was sure to be another highbrow, without Robyn Penrose's compensating attractions. The lunch would be a disaster: the certainty of this pierced him like a self-administered dagger-blow. It would be the first worry to rush into his head tomorrow morning, and every morning until Sunday. And his anxiety would communicate itself to Marjorie, who always got into a panic anyway when they were entertaining. She would probably drink too much sherry out of nervousness and burn the dinner or drop the plates. Then imagine her making small talk with Robyn Penrose—no, it was too painful to imagine. What would they discuss? The semiotics of loose covers? Metaphor and metonymy in wallpaper patterns? While his father entertained the boyfriend with the retail price index for 1948, and his children sneered and sulked on the sidelines in their usual fashion? The social nightmare he had conjured up so appalled him that he seriously contemplated phoning Robyn Penrose at once to cancel the invitation. He could easily invent an excuse—a forgotten engagement for next Sunday, say. But that would only be a postponement. Having pressed the invitation upon her, he would have to go through with it, and the sooner it was got over with, the better. Probably Robyn Penrose felt the same way.

Vic literally writhed in his armchair as he projected the likely consequences of his own folly. He loosened his collar and tie, and kicked off his shoes. He felt stifled—the central heating was set far too high considering the building was empty (and even in the throes of his private anxieties he made a mental note to have the thermostat turned down at night—it could save hundreds on the energy bill). He closed his eyes. This seemed to calm him. His mind went back over the argument with Robyn Penrose in the car, about Silk Cut. She was clever, you had to admit, even if her theories were half-baked. A vagina indeed! Admittedly, some people did call it a slit sometimes. And clit of course was like *slit* and *cut* run together . . . *Silk slit clit cut cunt* . . . Silk Cunt . . . That was one she hadn't thought of! Nice name for a packet of fags. Vic smiled faintly to himself as he dropped off.

• • •

He woke oppressed with a sense that he had made a terrible mistake about something, and immediately he remembered what it was: inviting Robyn Penrose to lunch next Sunday. At first he thought he must be in bed at five o'clock in the morning, but his clothes and his posture in the armchair soon reminded him where he was. He sat up stiffly and yawned. He glanced at his watch, pressing the button to illuminate the digital display. Nine twenty-three. He must have been asleep for nearly two hours. Marjorie would be wondering where the hell he was. Better phone her.

As he got to his feet and moved towards the desk he was arrested by a strange, muffled sound. It was very faint, but his hearing was sharp, and the building otherwise totally quiet. It seemed to be coming from the direction of Shirley's office. Still in his socks, he moved stealthily across the carpeted floor and through the communicating anteroom into Shirley's office. This was dark, save for the light seeping through the blinds from the car park, and quite empty. The sound, however, was slightly more audible here. There was nothing particularly sinister about a noise at this time of night, but Vic was curious to identify it. Perhaps one of the other directors was working late after all. Or it might be the security man, though usually he only patrolled the outside of the buildings, and in any case why would he be talking or moaning to himself? For that was what the noise sounded like—indistinguishable human speech or someone moaning with pain or—

Suddenly he knew what the sound was, and where it was coming from—from the reception lobby on the other side of the partition wall, with its painted-over windows. His eye flew to the spyhole scratched in the paint, where a spot of light shone faintly like an old penny. Quietly and carefully he placed a chair so that he could climb onto the filing cabinet immediately below the hole. Even as he did so he recalled how he had spied on Robyn Penrose on her first visit, and realized with a guilty pang why he associated her with the picture in the Rummidge Art Gallery: he himself was the Peeping Tom in the foreground. He wondered if perhaps he was dreaming and whether, when he applied his eye to the spyhole, he would see Robyn Penrose, with the robes of a classical goddess slipping from her marbly limbs, glaring indignantly back at him.

What he actually saw, by the dim illumination of the security light, was Brian Everthorpe copulating with Shirley on the reception lobby sofa. He couldn't see Everthorpe's face, and the broad bum going up and down like a piston under his shirt tails between Shirley's splayed legs could have belonged to anyone, but he recognised the sideboards and the bald spot on the top of his head. He could see Shirley's face very clearly. Her eyes were shut and her mouth was open in a dark red O. It was Shirley who was making the noise Vic had heard. He climbed down quietly and carefully from the filing cabinet, went back into his own office and shut the connecting doors. He sat in his armchair and covered his ears.

. . .

He hadn't been dreaming, but he went about for the next few days as if he was in a dream. Marjorie remarked on his more than usually abstracted state. So did Shirley, whose eyes he dared not meet when she came into his office the morning after he had watched her and Brian Everthorpe making love. A lot of things had clicked into place when he set eyes on that tableau, a lot of puzzles had been cleared up: why Brian Everthorpe always seemed to know so much, so quickly, about what was going on at Pringle's, and why he had taken such a personal interest in the forwarding of Tracey's career as a model. How long the affair had been going on he had no way of knowing, but there had been something about Shirley's joyful abandonment that suggested it wasn't the first time Brian Everthorpe had had her on the reception lobby sofa. They were taking an extraordinary risk doing it there; though, on reflection, if the building was empty and the inner door of the entrance locked, they were fairly safe from interruption except by the security man, and no doubt Everthorpe had squared him. They must have come into the building by the back door from a restaurant or pub after Vic himself had fallen asleep in his office, or perhaps they had been holed up in Everthorpe's office waiting for everyone else to leave. Presumably they preferred the reception lobby to Everthorpe's office because of the sofa. Or perhaps the greater danger of discovery there added an extra excitement to their amours.

He had a sense of being on the edge of depths and mysteries of human behaviour he had never plumbed himself, and brooded on them with mixed feelings. He didn't approve of what Everthorpe and Shirley were up to. He'd never had any time for hanky-panky between married folk, especially when it was mixed up with work. By rights he ought to be feeling a virtuous indignation at their adultery and considering how he could use his knowledge to get rid of the pair of them. And yet he felt no such inclination. The fact was that he was ashamed of his own part in the episode. He could tell no one, including the culprits, about what he had witnessed without evoking the ludicrous and ignoble picture of himself standing in the dark in his socks on top of the filing cabinet, squinting through a peephole in the partition wall. And beyond that consideration was another, even more painful to contemplate. In spite of the fact that they were an unglamorous pair of lovers, Brian Everthorpe fat and balding, and Shirley past her prime, with double chin and dyed hair; in spite of the incongruous setting and undignified half-undressed state in which they had coupled, Everthorpe's trousers and underpants and Shirley's skirt, knickers and tights tossed carelessly over the tables and chairs and copies of *Engineering Today*; in spite of all that, it couldn't be denied that they had been transported by genuine passion. It was a passion Vic himself had not experienced for a very long time, and he was doubtful whether Marjorie ever had. Certainly his lovemaking had never drawn from Marjorie the cries of pleasure that had carried to his ears through a partition wall and across the space of two offices. Vic had never imagined that he would envy Brian Everthorpe anything, but he did now. He envied him the full-blooded fucking of a passionate woman, and the woman's full-throated hurrahs. It was a kind of defeat, and with the bitter taste of it in his mouth, he had no spirit to visit retribution on Brian Everthorpe. Vic did not speak to Stuart Baxter again about letting Everthorpe go.

The scene in the lobby replayed itself again and again in his head like a film—not one of the carefully edited and soft-focused bedroom scenes you saw on late-night television, but more like the peep-show he had watched once in a sordid booth in Soho in a moment of furtive curiosity, feeding 50p pieces into the machine to keep the flickering jerking naked figures in motion. Again and again he saw Brian Everthorpe's heaving buttocks, Shirley's splayed white knees, her red lips rounded in that O of pleasure, her long painted nails digging into Everthorpe's shoulders so hard Vic could see the indentations—though it was difficult in retrospect to distinguish what he had witnessed from what his overheated imagination had reconstructed. Sometimes he wondered whether he hadn't been dreaming after all, whether the whole episode wasn't a fantasy that had passed through his head as he dozed in his office armchair. He made a surreptitious examination of the reception lobby sofa, looking for corroborating evidence. He observed a few stains that could have been either semen or milky coffee, and discovered a crinkly black filament that might have been a pubic hair or a fibre from the upholstery, before a curious glance from one of the receptionists moved him on.

The approach of Sunday and its lunch did nothing to calm his state of mind. He badgered Marjorie continually about the menu, requesting a lamb joint rather than beef because it wouldn't suffer so much if she overcooked it, and requiring her to specify exactly what vegetables she proposed to serve. He expressed a preference for apple crumble for dessert rather than the less reliable lemon meringue pie which was Marjorie's other staple pudding. And he insisted on having a starter.

"We never have a starter," said Marjorie.

"There's always a first time."

"What's got into you, Vic? Anybody would think the Queen was coming."

"Don't be stupid, Marjorie. Starters are quite normal."

"In restaurants they may be. Not at home."

"In Robyn Penrose's home," said Vic, "they'd have a starter. I'd take a bet on it."

"If she's as stuck up as that—"

"She's not stuck up at all."

"I thought you didn't like her, anyway. You complained enough."

"That was at the beginning. We got off on the wrong foot."

"So you do like her, then?"

"She's all right. I don't like her or dislike her."

"Why invite her to lunch, then? Why make all this fuss?"

Vic was silent for a moment. "Because she's interesting, that's why," he said at length. "You can have an intelligent conversation with her. I thought it would make a change. I'm sick to death of our Sunday lunches, with the children squabbling and Dad wittering on about the cost of living and—" He cut short an unkind reflection on Marjorie's conversational accomplishments, and concluded limply, "I just thought it would make a change."

Marjorie, who had a cold, blew her nose. "What d'you want, then?"

"Eh?"

"For your precious starter."

"I don't know. I'm not a cook."

"And I'm not a starter cook."

"You don't have to cook starters. They can be raw, can't they? Have melon."

"You can't get melon at this time of year."

"Well, something else then. Smoked salmon."

"Smoked salmon! Do you know what it costs?"

"You don't usually care how much anything costs."

"*You* do, though. And so does your Dad."

Vic contemplated his father's likely comments on the price of smoked salmon, and withdrew the suggestion. "Avocado pear," he said, remembering that Robyn had seemed to enjoy this at the restaurant near Manchester. "You just cut it in half, take out the stone and fill the hole with oil and vinegar."

"Your Dad won't like it," said Marjorie.

"He needn't eat it, then," said Vic impatiently. He began to worry about the wine. It would have to be red to go with the lamb, of course, but should he get some white to go with the avocado and if so how dry should it be? Vic was no wine connoisseur, but he had somehow convinced himself that Robyn's boyfriend was, and would sneer at his choices.

"I could use those glass dishes I got in the Sales for the avocados," Marjorie conceded. This idea seemed to please her, and she accepted the idea of a starter.

"And tell Raymond I don't want him walking in from the pub in the middle of lunch this Sunday," said Vic.

"Why don't you tell him yourself?"

"He listens to you."

"He listens to me because you won't talk to him."

"I'd only lose my temper."

"You should make an effort, Vic. You don't talk to any of us. You're that wrapped up in yourself."

"Don't start on me," he said.

"I've lent him the money, any road."

"What money?"

"For their demo tape. For the band." Marjorie looked defiantly at him. "It's my own money, from my Post Office account."

At another time, in another mood, Vic would have had a blazing row with her. As it was, he merely shrugged and said, "More fool you. Don't forget paper serviettes."

Marjorie looked blank.

"For Sunday."

"Oh! I always have serviettes when we have guests."

"Sometimes we run out," said Vic.

Marjorie stared at him. "I've never known you give a second's thought to serviettes in your life before," she said. In her pale, tranquillised eyes, he saw, like something stirring indistinctly under water, a flicker of fear, a shadow of suspicion; and realized for the first time that she had grounds for these feelings.

3

Half of Vic's apprehension about the Sunday lunch was relieved when Robyn rang on the Saturday morning to say her boyfriend, Charles, had a cold, and wouldn't be coming to Rummidge that weekend after all. She herself arrived rather late, and they sat down at table almost immediately. There were paper serviettes at every place setting and, reposing in blue-tinted glass dishes, halves of avocado pear. These last excited much wonderment and derision from the children.

"What's this?" Gary demanded, sticking a fork into his half, and lifting it into the air.

"It's avocado, stupid," said Sandra.

"It's a starter," said Marjorie.

"We don't usually have a starter," said Raymond.

"Ask your father," said Marjorie.

All looked at Vic, including Robyn Penrose, who smiled, as if she recognised that the avocado was his personal tribute to her sophistication.

"I thought it would make a change," Vic said gruffly. "Don't eat it if you don't want to."

"Is it a fruit or a veg?" said his father, poking doubtfully at his portion.

"More like a vegetable, Dad," said Vic. "You pour oil and vinegar dressing into the hole and eat it with a spoon."

Mr. Wilcox scooped out a small spoonful of the yellow flesh and nibbled it experimentally. "Queer sort of taste," he said. "Like candle-grease."

"They cost five pounds each, Grandad," said Raymond.

"What!"

"Take no notice, Dad, he's having you on," said Vic.

"I wouldn't give you five pee for them, to be honest with you," said his father.

"They taste much nicer with the vinaigrette, Mr. Wilcox," said Robyn. "Won't you try some?"

"No thanks, love, olive oil doesn't agree with me."

"Gives you the squits, does it, Grandad?" said Gary.

"You're so vile, Gary," said Sandra.

"Aye, it does, lad," said Mr. Wilcox. "We used to call 'em the backdoor trots when I was a lad. That's because—"

"We know why, Dad, or we can guess," Vic interrupted him with an apologetic glance at Robyn, but she seemed to be amused rather than offended by this exchange. He began cautiously to relax.

Thanks to Robyn, the meal was not the social minefield he had feared. Instead of talking a lot herself and making the family feel ignorant, she drew them out with questions about themselves. Raymond told her about his band and Sandra told her about hairstyling and Gary told her about computer games and his father told her about how he and Vic's mother had married on thirty-five bob a week and hadn't considered themselves poor. Whenever the old man looked like getting onto the subject of "the immigrants," Vic managed to head him off by some provocative remark about the cost of living. Only Marjorie had defeated Robyn's social skills, absorbing all her questions with monosyllabic murmurs or faint, abstracted smiles. But that was Marjorie for you. She always kept herself in the background, or in the kitchen, when they had guests. But she'd served up a cracking good dinner, apart from the avocados, which were underripe and rather hard.

The nearest approach to a snag in the smooth running of the proceedings came when Robyn tried to take a hand in washing up after the meal, and Marjorie strongly resisted. For a moment there was a polite struggle of wills between the two women, but in the end Vic arranged a compromise by taking charge of the operation himself, conscripting the children to help. He proposed a short walk afterwards before it got dark, but Marjorie excused herself on the grounds that it was too cold, Raymond went off to rehearse with his mates in somebody's garage, Sandra curled up in front of the telly with an emery board to manicure her nails and watch *Eastenders*, and Gary implausibly pleaded a prior commitment to homework. Mr. Wilcox agreed to come out, but when Vic returned to the lounge after completing the washing up, he was asleep and snoring faintly in an armchair. Vic didn't wake him, or make any effort to persuade the other members of the family. A walk with Robyn on her own was what he had been secretly hoping for.

"I'd no idea your children were so grown-up," she said, as soon as they were clear of the house.

"We've been married twenty-three years. We started a family straight away. Marjorie was only too glad to give up work."

"What work was that?"

"Typing pool."

"Ah."

"Marje is no intellectual," said Vic, "as you probably noticed. She left school without any O-Levels."

"Does that bother her?"

"No. It bothers me, sometimes."

"Why don't you encourage her to do a course of some kind, then?"

"What—O-Levels? Marjorie? At her time of life?" His laughter rang out in the cold air, harsher than he had intended.

"It doesn't have to be O-Level. There are extra-mural courses she could do, or WEA. And the Open University has courses you can follow without doing the examinations."

"Marjorie wouldn't be up to it," said Vic.

"Only because you've made her think she isn't," said Robyn.

"Rubbish! Marjorie's perfectly content. She has a nice house, with an *en suite* bathroom and four lavatories, and enough money to go shopping whenever she feels like it."

"I think that's an unbelievably patronising thing to say about your own wife," said Robyn Penrose.

They walked on in silence for a while, as Vic considered how to respond to this rebuke. He decided to let it pass.

He led Robyn by an aimless route through the quieter residential streets. It was a cold, misty afternoon, with a low red sun glowing through the branches of the leafless trees. They met few other people: a lone jogger, a couple with a dog, some disconsolate-looking African students waiting at a bus stop. At every intersection, marking the nocturnal passage of marauding vandals, uprooted traffic bollards lay on their sides, with all their wiring exposed.

"It's my kids who should be worrying about getting qualifications," said Vic. "Raymond dropped out of university last year. Failed his first-year exams and the resits."

"What was he doing?"

"Electrical Engineering. He's clever enough, but never did any work. And Sandra says she doesn't want to go to university. Wants to be a hairdresser, or 'hairstylist,' as they call it."

"Of course, hair is very important in youth culture today," Robyn mused. "It's a form of self-expression. It's almost a new form of art."

"It's not a serious job, though, is it? *You* wouldn't do it for a living."

"There are lots of things I wouldn't do. I wouldn't work in a factory. I wouldn't work in a bank. I wouldn't be a housewife. When I think of most people's lives, especially women's lives, I don't know how they bear it."

"Someone has to do those jobs," said Vic.

"That's what's so depressing."

"But Sandra could do something better. I wish you'd talk to her, about going to university."

"Why should she take any notice of me?"

"She won't take any notice of *me*, and Marjorie isn't interested. You're nearer her age. She'd respect your advice."

"Does she know I shall probably be out of a job next year?" Robyn asked. "Not much of an advertisement for the academic life, is it? She'd probably make much more money out of hairdressing."

"Money isn't—" Vic pulled himself up.

"Everything?" Robyn completed his sentence, with arched eyebrows. "I never thought to hear you say that."

"I was going to say, money isn't something she understands," he lied. "None of my kids do. They think it comes out of the bank like water out of a tap—or it could if mean old Dad didn't keep his thumb over the spout."

"The trouble is, they've had it too easy. They've never had to work for their living. They take everything for granted."

"Right!" Vic agreed enthusiastically, then saw, too late, by her expression, that she was parodying him. "Well, it's true," he said truculently.

Their stroll had brought them to the landscaped site of the University's halls of residence, and Robyn proposed that they should turn in through the gates and walk round the lake.

"It's private, isn't it?" said Vic.

"Don't worry, I know the password," she said, mocking him again. "No, of course it's not. Anyone can walk around."

In the winter dusk the long buildings, backlit by a red sunset, looked like great liners at anchor, their lighted windows mirrored in the dark surface of the lake. A frisbee flew back and forth like a bat between a group of track-suited young men, who shouted each other's names as they threw. A couple stood on a curved wooden bridge throwing crusts to a splashing, fluttering throng of ducks and Canadian geese.

"I like this place," said Robyn. "It's one of the University's few architectural successes."

"Very nice," Vic agreed. "Too nice for students, if you ask me. I never did understand why they had to have these massive three-star hotels built especially for them."

"They've got to live somewhere."

"Most of 'em could live at home and go to their local colleges. Like I did."

"But leaving home is part of the experience of going to university."

"And a very expensive part, too," said Vic. "You could build a whole polytechnic for the price of this little lot."

"Oh, but polytechnics are such ghastly places," said Robyn. "I was interviewed for a job at one once. It seemed more like an overgrown comprehensive school than a university."

"Cheap, though."

"Cheap and nasty."

"I'm surprised you defend this élitist set-up, considering your left-wing principles." He gestured at the handsome buldings, the well-groomed grassy slopes, the artificial lake. "Why should my workers pay taxes to keep these middle-class youths in the style to which they're accustomed?"

"The universities are open to everyone," said Robyn.

"In theory. But all those cars in the car park back there—who do they belong to?

"Students," Robyn admitted. "I agree, our intake is far too middle-class. But it needn't be. Tuition is free. There are grants for those who need them. What we need to do is to motivate more working-class children to go to university."

"And kick out the middle-class kids to make room?"

"No, provide more places."

"And more landscaped halls of residence, with artificial lakes and ducks on them?"

"Why not?" said Robyn defiantly. "They enhance the environment. Better these halls than another estate of executive houses with Georgian windows, or is it Jacobean now? Universities are the cathedrals of the modern age. They shouldn't have to justify their existence by utilitarian criteria. The trouble is, ordinary people don't understand what they're about, and the universities don't really bother to explain themselves to the community. We have an Open Day once a year. Every day ought to be an open day. The campus is like a graveyard at weekends, and in the vacations. It ought to be swarming with local people doing part-time courses—using the Library, using the laboratories, going to lectures, going to concerts, using the Sports Centre—everything." She threw out her arms in an expansive gesture, flushed and excited by her own vision. "We ought to get rid of the security men and the barriers at the gates and let the people in!"

"It's a nice idea," said Vic. "But it wouldn't be long before you'd have graffiti sprayed all over the walls, the toilets vandalised and the Bunsen burners nicked."

Robyn let her arms fall back to her sides. "Who's being élitist now?"

"I'm just being realistic. Give the people polytechnics, with no frills. Not imitation Oxford colleges."

"That's an incredibly condescending attitude."

"We live in the age of the yob. Whatever they don't understand, whatever isn't protected, the yobs will smash, and spoil it for everybody else. Did you notice the traffic bollards on the way here?"

"It's unemployment that's responsible," said Robyn. "Thatcher has created an alienated underclass who take out their resentment in crime and vandalism. You can't really blame them."

"You'd blame them if you were mugged going home tonight," said Vic.

"That's a purely emotive argument," said Robyn. "But of course you support Thatcher, don't you?"

"I respect her," said Vic. "I respect anybody with guts."

"Even though she devastated industry round here?"

"She got rid of overmanning, restrictive practises. She overdid it, but it had to be done. Any road, my dad will tell you there was worse unemployment here in the thirties, and much worse poverty, but you didn't get youths beating up old-age pensioners and raping them, like you do now. You didn't get people smashing up roadsigns and telephone booths just for the hell of it. Something's happened to this country. I don't know why, or exactly when it happened, but somewhere along the line a lot of basic decencies disappeared, like respect for other people's property, respect for the old, respect for women—"

"There was a lot of hypocrisy in that old-fashioned code," said Robyn.

"Maybe. But hypocrisy has its uses."

"The homage vice pays to virtue."

"What?"

"Somebody said hypocrisy was the homage vice pays to virtue. Rochefoucauld, I think."

"He had his head screwed on, whoever it was," said Vic.

"You put it down to the decline of religion, then?" said Robyn, with a slightly condescending smile.

"Maybe," said Vic. "Your universities may be the cathedrals of the modern age, but do you teach morality in them?"

Robyn Penrose paused for thought. "Not as such."

As if on cue, a church bell began to toll plangently in the distance.

"Do you go to church, then?" she asked.

"Me? No. Apart from the usual—weddings, funerals, christenings. What about you?"

"Not since I left school. I was rather pious at school. I was confirmed. That was just before I discovered sex. I think religion served the same psychological purpose—something very personal and private and rather intense. Do you believe in God?"

"What? Oh, I don't know. Yes, I suppose so, in a vague sort of way." Vic, distracted by Robyn's casual reference to her discovery of sex, was unable to focus his mind on theological questions. How many lovers had she had, he wondered. "Do you?"

"Not the patriarchal God of the Bible. There are some rather interesting feminist theologians in America who are redefining God as female, but they can't really get rid of all the metaphysical baggage of Christianity. Basically I suppose I think God is the ultimate floating signifier."

"I'll buy that," said Vic, "even though I don't know what it means."

Robyn laughed. "Sorry!"

But Vic didn't resent her high-flown language. That she used it unselfconsciously in conversation with him, whereas she had spoken normal English to the rest of the family, he took as a kind of compliment.

. . .

When they returned to the house, Robyn declined to take off her coat and have a cup of tea. "I must be getting back," she said. "I have a lot of work to do."

"On a Sunday, love?" Mr. Wilcox protested.

"I'm afraid so. Marking essays, you know. I'm always behind. Thanks for the lovely lunch," she said to Marjorie, who gave a watery smile in acknowledgement. "Sandra—your father wants me to talk to you about the advantages of a university education."

"Oh, does he?" said Sandra, with a grimace.

"Perhaps you'd like to come and see me in the University one day?"

"All right," said Sandra, with a shrug. "I don't mind."

Vic longed to box his daughter's ears or pull her hair or smack her bottom, or better still, to do all three at once. "Say thank you, Sandra," he said.

"Thanks," she said sullenly.

Vic saw Robyn to her car. "Sorry about my daughter's manners," he said. "It's the Yobbish Tendency."

Robyn dismissed the matter with a laugh.

"I'll see you Wednesday, then," said Vic.

"All being well," she said, getting into her car.

Vic went back into the lounge. His father was alone in the room, thirstily sipping hot tea from the saucer. "Nice young wench, that," he observed. "What she call herself Robin for? Boy's name, innit?"

"It can be a girl's. They spell it with a 'y.'"

"Oh-ah. Wears her hair like a boy's too. Not one of them . . . you know, is she?"

"I don't think so, Dad. She's got a boyfriend, but he couldn't come today."

"I just wondered, seein' as how she's one o' them university dongs."

"Dons."

"Well, whatever. You get all kinds at them places."

"What do you know about universities, Dad?" Vic said, amused.

"I seen films on the telly. All sorts of queer folk, carrying on with each other something chronic."

"You don't want to believe everything you see on television, Dad."

"Aye, you're right there, son," said Mr. Wilcox.

. . .

When she got home, Robyn telephoned Charles. "How are you?" she said. He said he was fine. "What about your cold?" she said. It hadn't materialised, he said. "Beast," said Robyn, "I believe you made it up, just to get out of lunch at the Wilcoxes." How had it been, Charles asked, not denying the accusation.

"All right. You would have been bored stiff."

"But you weren't?"

"It was quite interesting to me to see Wilcox in his domestic setting."

"What was the house like?"

"Luxurious. Hideous taste. They actually have that reproduction of the black girl with the green complexion in the lounge. And the fireplace is unbelievable. It's one of those multicoloured rustic stone affairs, stretching all the way up to the ceiling, with all sorts of nooks and crannies for ornaments. Just to look at it makes you want to coil a rope round your waist and start scaling it. Of course they've got one of those *trompe l'oeil* gas fires, logs that burn from everlasting to everlasting, plus, would you believe, a set of antique brass fire-irons. It's like something by Magritte." She felt slightly ashamed, hearing herself going on in this Cambridgey way, but something inhibited her from telling Charles about the rather interesting conversation she had had with Vic Wilcox on their walk. It was easier to entertain him with amusing domestic vignettes of the Rummidge bourgeoisie. "Oh, and they've got four loos," she added.

"Did you have to go that often?" Charles giggled on the other end of the line.

"The old grandfather told me in a stage whisper. He was a bit of a racist, but otherwise rather sweet."

"What about the rest of the family?"

"Well, I couldn't get much out of Mrs. She seemed to be scared stiff of me."

"Well, you are rather scaring, Robyn."

"Nonsense."

"I mean to women who aren't intellectual. Did you talk a lot about literary theory?"

"Of course I didn't, what d'you take me for? I talked to everybody about their interests, but I couldn't discover what her interests were. Perhaps she hasn't got any. She seemed to me the classic downtrodden housewife whose occupation's gone once the children are grown up. The whole scene was like a Freudian sit-com, actually. The eldest son is still working through his Oedipus complex at the age of 22, by the look of it, and Wilcox has repressed incestuous feelings for his daughter which are displaced into constant nagging."

"Did you tell him that?"

"Are you joking?"

"Teasing," said Charles.

"Actually, I did tell him I thought he was oppressing his wife."

"And how did he take that?"

"I thought he was going to lose his temper, but he didn't."

"Ah, Robyn," Charles sighed along the line from Ipswich. "I wish I had your confidence."

"What do you mean?"

"You're a born teacher. You go around the world putting people straight, and instead of resenting it, they're grateful."

"I'm not sure Vic Wilcox was grateful," said Robyn. She sneezed suddenly and violently. "Damn. You may not have a cold, but I think I have."

· · ·

When Robyn Penrose didn't turn up at the appointed hour on the following Wednesday, Vic was surprised to find how much her absence disturbed him. He was unable to concentrate on chairing a meeting with the sales staff, and was corrected several times by his financial director over figures, much to the delight of Brian Everthorpe. At 10:30, after the meeting had broken up, he phoned Robyn's Department at the University, and was informed that she didn't normally come in on a Wednesday. He phoned her home number. It had rung about fifteen times, and he was just about to put the receiver down, when Robyn's voice croaked, "Hallo?"

She had a cold, probably flu. She sounded extremely cross. She had been asleep, she said.

"Then I'm sorry I disturbed you. But as you didn't send a message . . ."

"I don't have a bedside phone," she said. "I've come all the way downstairs to answer this call. You seem to make a habit of making inconvenient phone calls."

"I'm sorry," said Vic, mortified. "Go back to bed. Take some aspirin. Do you need anything?"

"Nothing except peace and quiet." She rang off.

Later in the day Vic arranged for a basket of fruit to be delivered by Rummidge's major department store, but phoned again almost immediately to cancel the order on reflecting that, to receive it, Robyn would have to get out of bed and go downstairs again.

The following Wednesday she returned, looking a little pale, a mite thinner perhaps, but recovered from the flu. Vic could not repress a grin of pleasure as she came through the door. Somehow, Robyn Penrose had changed, in the space of a few weeks, from being a nuisance and a pain in the neck, to being the person of all his acquaintance he was most glad to see. He counted the days between her visits to Pringle's. His weeks pivoted on Wednesdays rather than weekends. When Robyn was shadowing him he was aware that he performed particularly well. When she was absent he played to her imagined presence and silent applause. She was someone to whom he could confide his plans and hopes for the company, work through his problems and refine the solutions. He couldn't trust any of his staff with such speculative thoughts, and Marjorie wouldn't have had a clue what he was on about. Robyn didn't understand all the fine detail, but her quick wit soon grasped the general principles, and her detachment made her a useful judge. It was Robyn who had made him see the futility of a tit-for-tat policy towards Foundrax. He'd heard on the grapevine that Foundrax was having cash-flow problems—hardly surprising if they were supplying Rawlinson's at a loss. He would just wait for Foundrax to pull out, or fold altogether, then resume negotiations with Ted Stoker for a reasonable price. Brian Everthorpe didn't approve of this waiting game, but then he wouldn't, would he?

Vic tried not to think too much about Brian Everthorpe rogering Shirley on the reception lobby sofa. Having Robyn Penrose around helped with that, too. Her youthful complexion and lissom figure made Shirley look raddled and overblown in comparison. Shirley was jealous of Robyn, that was plain to see, and Brian Everthorpe was piqued by his inability to decide whether Vic was taking advantage of the situation. He was forever throwing out innuendoes about the intimate relationship between a man and his shadow.

When Robyn let slip that her temporary post at the University was called "Dean's Relief," he could hardly contain his glee. "What about an MD's Relief, eh Vic?" he said. "No need to slip round to Susan's Sauna, then, for a spot of executive's tonal treatment, eh? Have it laid on." If Robyn had shown any sign of being bothered by this, Vic would have taken Everthorpe aside and told him to leave it out; but she responded with stony indifference, and Vic wasn't averse to keeping Everthorpe guessing whether he and Robyn Penrose were having an affair, ridiculous as the idea was. Ridiculous, yet there was a kind of pleasure to be got from letting it float idly in the stream of one's thoughts, driving to and from work. He played Jennifer Rush a lot on the car stereo these days: her voice—deep, vibrant, stern, backed by a throbbing, insistent rhythm accompaniment—moved him strangely, enclosing his daydreaming in a protective wall of sound. She sang:

> *There's no need to run away*
> *If you feel that this is for real,*
> *'Cause when it's warm and straight from the heart,*
> *It's time to start.*

She sang:

> *Surrender! It's your only chance, surrender!*
> *Don't wait too long to realize*
> *That her eyes will say, "Forever."*

He played the cassette so often that he learned the lyrics by heart. The track he liked best was the last one of side two, "The Power of Love":

> *'Cause I am your lady*
> *And you are my man,*
> *Whenever you reach for me,*
> *I'll do all that I can.*
> *We're heading for something,*
> *Somewhere I've never been,*
> *Sometimes I am frightened,*
> *But I'm ready to learn*
> *About the power of love.*

One day, after sitting through a series of meetings with junior management about rationalising the company's operations, Robyn asked him whether he intended to explain the grand strategy to the workers as well. It hadn't occurred to Vic to do so, but the more he thought about the idea, the more he was taken with it. The men tended to see everything in terms of their own little bit of the factory's operations, and automatically assumed that any change in their work-patterns was an attempt by management to screw more work out of them without giving them more pay. Of course, this was broadly true. Given the bad old work practises the industry had inherited from the nineteen-sixties, it had to be. But if he could explain that the changes related to an overall plan, which would mean greater security and prosperity for everybody in the long term, he would be more likely to get their co-operation.

Vic went to see his Personnel Director about it. George Prendergast was sitting crosslegged on the floor in the middle of his office, with his hands on his knees.

"What are you doing?" Vic demanded.

"Breathing," said Prendergast, getting to his feet. "Yoga breathing exercises for my Irritable Bowel Syndrome."

"You look daft, if you don't mind my saying so."

"It helps, though," said Prendergast. "Your Shadow suggested it."

"Did she teach you herself?" Vic felt, absurdly, something like a stab of jealousy.

"No, I go to evening classes," said Prendergast.

"Yes, well, I should keep it to evening classes, if I was you," said Vic. "Don't want you levitating in the middle of the factory, it might be distracting for the operatives. And speaking of them, I've got a suggestion."

Prendergast was enthusiastic about the idea. "Worker education is very important these days," he said. "Dialogue between management and shop-floor is the name of the game." Prendergast was a graduate in Business Studies, and was fond of this sort of jargon.

"There won't be much dialogue about it," said Vic. "I'll give a speech, and tell 'em what we're going to do."

"Won't there be questions?"

"If there are, you can answer them."

"Perhaps I could arrange small group discussions at work stations afterwards," said Prendergast.

"Don't overdo it, we're not running an evening institute. Just set up a series of lunchtime meetings in the old transport shed, will you? Say three hundred at a time? Starting next Wednesday." He specified Wednesday so that Robyn Penrose would be present at the inaugural meeting.

Brian Everthorpe was sceptical about the idea, naturally, claiming that it would only unsettle the men and make them suspicious. "They won't thank you for taking up half their lunch hour, either."

"Attendance will be voluntary," said Vic, "except for directors."

Everthorpe's face fell. "You mean, we've got to be there at every meeting?"

"It's no use my banging on to the men about all pulling together if they know my directors are down at the Man in the Moon knocking back pints while I'm talking."

The following Wednesday, at one o'clock, Vic sat on a makeshift platform in the old transport shed, a gloomy hangar-like building, obsolete since the company started contracting out its transportation requirements, which was now used for large meetings on the factory site when the canteen was not available. He was flanked by his directors, sitting on moulded plastic chairs. A few rows of chairs and benches had been arranged on the floor, facing the platform, and he was surprised to see Shirley as well as Robyn sitting there. The mass of the audience stood in a great crowd behind these seats, beneath a haze of cigarette smoke and condensing breath. Though Vic had ordered the wall heaters to be turned on that morning, the atmosphere was still damp and chilly. His directors were sitting in their overcoats, but Vic was just in his suit, which he regarded as a kind of uniform that went with his job. He rubbed his hands together.

"I think I'll start," he muttered to Prendergast, who was sitting beside him. "Do you want me to introduce you?"

"No, they all know who I am. Let's get on with it. It's perishing in here."

He felt an unaccustomed spasm of nervousness as he stood up and stepped forward to the microphone that had been set up, with a couple of portable speakers, at the front of the platform. A hush fell over the assembly. He scanned their faces—expectant, sullen, quizzical—and wished he had prepared some joke to take the tension out of the moment. But he had never been one for jokes—he forgot funny stories five minutes after he'd been told them, perhaps because he seldom found them funny.

"You're supposed to start speeches with a joke," he began. "But I don't have one. I'll be honest with you: running this company is no joke." They laughed a little at that, so it seemed that he had broken the ice after all. "You all know me. I'm the boss. You may think I'm like God in this place, that I can do what I like. I can't. I can't do anything at all on my own."

He grew in confidence as he went on. The men listened to him attentively. There were only a few faces in the audience that looked thoroughly bored and mystified. Then, just as he was hitting his stride, all the faces broke into broad grins. There were cheers, hoots, shrill whistles and much laughter. Vic, who was not conscious of having said anything funny, faltered in his speech and stopped. He looked round and saw a young woman advancing towards him, obviously deranged because she was in her underwear. She was shivering from the cold, and her arms and shoulders were covered in goosepimples, but she smiled at him coyly.

"Mr. Wilcox?" she said.

"Go away," he said. "This is a meeting."

"I have a message for you," she said, flexing a leg sheathed in a fishnet stocking, and taking a folded paper out of her garter.

The crowd cheered. "Show us yer tits!" someone shouted. Another yelled, "Tek yer knickers off!"

The girl smiled and waved nervously at the audience. Behind her head Brian Everthorpe's grinning face bobbed like a red balloon.

"OFF, OFF, OFF!" roared the crowd.

"Get out of here!" Vic hissed.

"It won't take long," said the girl, unfolding the piece of paper. "Be a sport."

Vic grabbed her by the arm, intending to bustle her off the stage, but such a whoop went up that he let go as if he had been burned. Inclining her head towards the mike, the girl began to sing:

> *"Pringle bells, Pringle bells, Pringle all the day,*
> *Oh what fun it is to work the Victor Wilcox way!*
> *Oh, Pringle bells—"*

"Marion," said Robyn Penrose, who had suddenly appeared just below the front of the platform. "Stop that at once."

The girl looked down at her with blank astonishment. "Doctor Penrose!" she exclaimed. She thrust the message into Vic's hands, turned on her high heels, and fled.

"Hey, let's hear the rest of it!" Brian Everthorpe called after her. The audience hissed and groaned as the girl disappeared through a small door at the back of the shed. Robyn Penrose said to Vic, "Why don't you carry on?" and hastened after the girl before Vic could enquire into the magical power she seemed to have over her.

He tapped on the mike for attention. "As I was saying . . ." The men guffawed good-naturedly, and settled to hear him out.

. . .

After the meeting had dispersed, Vic found Robyn sitting in his office, reading a book.

"Thanks for getting rid of the girl," he said. "Know her, do you?"

"She's one of my students," said Robyn. "She has no grant and her parents won't pay for her maintenance, so she has to work."

"You call that work?"

"I disapprove of its sexist aspects, naturally. But it's quite well-paid, and it doesn't take up too much of her time. It's called a kisso-gram, apparently. She didn't get as far as the kiss today, of course."

"Thank Christ for that," said Vic, throwing himself in his swivel chair and taking out his cigarettes. "Or rather, thank *you*."

"It could have been worse. There's also something called a gorilla-gram."

"It was bad enough. Another minute, and the meeting would've collapsed."

"I could see that," said Robyn. "That's why I intervened."

"You saved my bacon," said Vic. "Can I buy you a drink and a sandwich? Haven't got time for a proper lunch, I'm afraid."

"A sandwich will be fine. Thanks. Marion was worried that she wouldn't get paid because she didn't finish the job. I said you'd make it up to her if necessary."

"Oh, you did, did you?"

"Yes." Robyn Penrose held him with her cool, grey-green eyes.

"All right," he said. "I'll pay her double if she can find out who set me up."

"I asked her that," said Robyn. "She said the customer's name is confidential. Only the boss of the agency knows. Have you no idea?"

"I have my suspicions," he said.

"Brian Everthorpe?"

"Right. It has his fingerprints all over it."

Vic did not take Robyn to the Man in the Moon or the King's Head, where they would be likely to meet his colleagues. Instead he drove a little further, to the Bag o' Nails, a quaint old pub built on ground riddled with disused mineshafts and subject to chronic subsidence which had twisted every line of the building out of true. Doors and windows had been re-made in the shape of rhomboids to fit the distorted frames, and the floor sloped so steeply you had to hang on to your glass to prevent it from sliding off the table.

"This is fun," said Robyn, looking about her as they sat down near the open fire. "I feel drunk already."

"What will you have?" he asked.

"Beer, I think, in a place like this. Half a pint of best bitter."

"And to eat?"

She glanced at the bar menu. "Ploughman's Lunch with Stilton."

He nodded approval. "They do a nice ploughman's here."

When he came back from the bar with their drinks, he said, "I've never bought draught bitter for a woman before."

"Then you must have had a very limited experience of life," she said, smiling.

"You're dead right," he replied, without returning the smile. "Cheers." He took a long swallow of his pint. "Sometimes when I'm lying awake in the small hours, instead of counting sheep, I count the things I've never done."

"Like what?"

"I've never skied, I've never surfed, I've never learned to play a musical instrument, or speak a foreign language, or sail a boat, or ride a horse. I've never climbed a mountain or pitched a tent or caught a fish. I've never seen Niagara Falls or been up the Eiffel Tower or visited the Pyramids. I've never . . . I could go on and on." He had been about to say, *I've never slept with a woman other than my wife*, but thought better of it.

"There's still time."

"No, it's too late. All I'm fit for is work. It's the only thing I'm any good at."

"Well, that's something. To have a job you like and be good at it."

"Yes, it's something," he agreed, thinking that in the small hours it didn't seem enough; but he didn't say that aloud either.

A silence fell. Robyn seemed to feel the need to break it. "Well," she said, looking round the pub, "Wednesdays won't be the same when term ends."

Alarm bells rang in Vic's head. "When's that then?"

"Next week."

"*What?* But Easter's weeks off!"

"It's a ten-week term," said Robyn. "This is week nine. I must say it's flown by."

"I don't know how you people justify your long holidays," he grumbled, to cover his dismay. Although he had always known the Shadow Scheme had a limited time-span, he had avoided calculating exactly when it would end.

"The vacations are not holidays," she said hotly. "You ought to know that. We do research, and supervise it, as well as teach undergraduates."

The arrival of their food excused him from answering. Robyn tucked into her ploughman's with relish. Vic took out his diary. "You've only got one more week, then?" he said. "It says here that I'm going to Frankfurt next Wednesday. I'd forgotten that."

"Oh well," she said. "In that case *this* is my last week. So let me buy you another drink."

"No it isn't," he said. "You have to come with me to Frankfurt."

"I can't," she said.

"It's only two days. One night."

"No, it's impossible. I have a lot of classes on a Thursday."

"Cancel them. Get somebody else to do them for you."

"That's easier said than done," she said. "I'm not a professor, you know. I'm the most junior member of staff."

"It's the terms of the Shadow Scheme," he said. "You have to follow me around all the time, for one day a week. If I happen to be in Frankfurt that day, then so must you."

"What are you going for?"

"There's a big machine-tool exhibition. I'm seeing some people who make automatic core blowers—I'm going to buy a new one instead of messing about with second-hand. It would be interesting for you. No dirty factories. We'd stay in a posh hotel. Get taken out for meals." It had suddenly become a matter of the greatest urgency and importance that Robyn Penrose should accompany him to Frankfurt. "They have restaurants on river boats," he said enticingly. "On the Rhine."

"The Main, isn't it?"

"The Main, then. I never was much good at geography."

"Who would pay my fare?"

"Don't worry about the fare. If your University won't pay, we will."

"Well, I'll see," said Robyn. "I'll think about it."

"I'll get Shirley to make reservations for you this afternoon."

"No, don't do that. Wait."

"They can always be cancelled," he said.

"I really don't think I can come," said Robyn.

Driving home later that afternoon, Robyn noticed that there was still some light left in the sky. In fact the streetlamps were only just coming on, each slender metal stalk tipped with a rosy blush that briefly preceded the yellow sodium glare. For a few moments these fairy lights bestowed a fragile beauty on the soiled tarmac, concrete and brick of West Wallsbury. Usually it was quite dark when she drove home from Pringle's. But it was the middle of March now. Spring was approaching, even if you couldn't feel it in the air. So, thank God, was the Easter vacation. Only one more week of nonstop preparation, lecturing, tutoring, marking. Interesting as it was, you could only keep up the pace for so long—rushing breathlessly from one literary masterpiece to another, from one group of anxious, eager, needy students to another. Besides, she was itching to get back to *Domestic Angels and Unfortunate Females*, which she'd hardly looked at this term, partly because of the Shadow Scheme. Not that she regretted her involvement in that, especially now that it was drawing to a close. It had been an interesting experience, and she had the satisfaction of knowing that she'd done a good PR job. From being hostile and bullying at the outset, Vic Wilcox had become, in the space of a couple of months, friendly and confiding, positively glad to see her at the factory on Wednesday mornings, and patently dismayed at the imminent termination of the Shadow Scheme. Once again she had proved herself invaluable. If Vic Wilcox was going to write a report too, she ought to come out of it well.

Robyn permitted herself a complacent smile, recalling the way she had despatched Marion Russell earlier that day, Vic's gratitude, and his eager insistence that she should accompany him to Frankfurt. That might be fun, actually, she reflected. Frankfurt was not a name that set the pulses racing, but she had never been there—in fact she hadn't been anywhere outside England for the past two years, so preoccupied had she been first with getting a job, then with trying to hang on to it. She felt a sudden pang of appetite for travel, the bustle of airports, the novelty of foreign tongues and foreign manners, clanging tramcars and pavement cafés. Spring might have already arrived in Frankfurt. But no, it wasn't possible. Thursday was a heavy teaching day for her, including two groups of the Women's Writing seminar, the most important classes of the week as far as she was concerned. She knew from experience that it would be impossible to find alternative hours at which all the students concerned could attend, such were the labyrinthine complexities and infinite permutations of their personal timetables. And no one else in the

Department was qualified to take these classes, even if they were willing to do so, which was unlikely. A pity. It would have been a nice break.

Robyn had made up her mind. Mentally she registered her regret, sealed her decision, and filed it away, with a memo to phone Vic Wilcox the next day.

. . .

Later that evening she received a surprising phone call from Basil. He said he was phoning from his office after everyone else had gone home. He sounded a little, but only a little, drunk.

"Have you seen Charles recently?" he asked.

"No, not very recently," she said. "Why?"

"Have you two split up, then?"

"No, of course not. He just hasn't been over lately. First he had a cold or thought he did, and then I had flu . . . what are you on about, Basil?"

"Did you know he's been seeing Debbie?"

"Seeing her?"

"Yes, *seeing* her. You know what I mean."

"I knew he was going to watch her at work."

"He's done more than that. He spent the night with her."

"You mean, he stayed in her house?"

"Yes."

"So what? He probably took her out to dinner and missed his last train and she put him up."

"That's what Debbie says."

"Well, then."

"You don't find it suspicious?"

"Of course not." The only thing she found slightly disturbing about the story was that Charles had said nothing about it to her on the telephone, but she did not admit this to Basil.

"Suppose I told you it happened twice."

"Twice?"

"Yes, once last week, and again last night. Missing one train is unfortunate, missing two looks suspicious, wouldn't you say?"

"How do you know all this, Basil? I thought you and Debbie never saw each other in midweek."

"Last Tuesday I phoned her at ten o'clock in the evening and Charles answered the phone. And last night I followed them."

"You *what?*"

"I knew he was up in town again, researching his stupid article or whatever it is. After work I followed them. First they went to a wine bar and then I saw them go into Debbie's house. I waited until the lights went out. The last light to go out was Debbie's bedroom."

"Well, it would be, wouldn't it?"

"Not necessarily. Not if he was sleeping in the guest room."

"Basil, you're being paranoid."

"Even paranoids have unfaithful girlfriends."

"I'm sure there's some perfectly simple explanation. I'll ask Charles—I'm seeing him this weekend."

"Well, that's a relief, anyway."

"Why?"

"Debbie claims she's going to stay with her parents this weekend. I was beginning to wonder. What do you women see in Charles anyway? He seems a cold fish to me."

"I don't want to discuss Charles' attractions with you, Basil," said Robyn, and rang off.

A little later, Charles rang. "Darling," he said, "do you mind terribly if I don't come this weekend after all?"

"Why?" Robyn said. To her surprise and annoyance she found she was trembling slightly.

"I want to write up my article on the City. There's a chap I knew at Cambridge who works for *Marxism Today* and he's really interested."

"You're not going to visit Debbie's mother, then?"

There was a brief, surprised silence. "Why should I want to do that?" Charles said.

"Basil just phoned me," said Robyn. "He says you stayed overnight with Debbie. Twice."

"Three times, actually," said Charles coolly. "Is there any reason why I shouldn't?"

"No, of course not. I just wondered why you hadn't mentioned it."

"It didn't seem important."

"I see."

"To tell you the truth, Robyn, I thought you were a teeny-weeny bit jealous of Debbie, and I didn't see the point of aggravating your hostility."

"Why should I be jealous of her?"

"Because of all the money she makes."

"I don't give a monkey's fuck how much money she makes," said Robyn evenly.

"She's been extraordinarily helpful to me over this article. That's why I've been staying with her—to talk at leisure. It's impossible while she's working—it's pandemonium in the dealing room. Unbelievable."

"You didn't sleep with her, then?"

Another pregnant pause. "Not in the technical sense, no."

"What do you mean, in the technical sense?"

"Well, I gave her a massage."

"You gave her a massage?" A vivid and unwelcome image presented itself to Robyn's consciousness, of Debbie's skinny, naked body squirming with pleasure under Charles' oily fingers.

"Yes. She was very tense. It's the nature of her work, of course, continuous stress . . . She suffers from migraines . . ."

While Charles was describing Debbie's symptoms, Robyn rapidly reviewed various questions of a casuistical nature. Did a masssage, their kind of massage, constitute infidelity, if administered to a third party? Could there, in fact, *be* infidelity between herself and Charles?

"I don't really want to know all these details," she said, interrupting him in mid-sentence. "I just wanted to get the basic facts straight. You and I have had an open relationship, with no strings, since I moved to Rummidge."

"That's what I thought," said Charles. "I'm glad to hear you confirm it."

"But Basil doesn't see things the same way."

"Don't worry about Basil. Debbie can handle Basil. I think she was a bit pissed off with him, actually. He tends to be over-possessive. I expect she was using me to make a point."

"You don't mind being used?"

"Well, I'm using her, in a way. For researching my article. And how are things with you?" he said, trying rather obviously to change the subject.

"Fine. I'm going to Frankfurt next week." She uttered this thought without premeditation, as it blossomed irresistibly in her head.

"Really! How's that?"

"The Shadow Scheme. Vic Wilcox is going to a trade fair on Wednesday, so I have to go with him."

"Well, that should be quite fun."

"Yes, that's what I thought."

"How long will you stay?"

"Just one night. In a posh hotel, Vic says."

"Shall I come over the weekend after that?"

"No, I don't think so."

"All right. You're not angry or anything, are you?"

"Of course not." She laughed rather shrilly. "I'll phone you."

"Oh, right." He sounded relieved. "Well, enjoy yourself in Frankfurt."

"Thanks."

"What will you do about your teaching, while you're away?"

"I'll ask Swallow's advice," she said. "After all, this shadow business was his idea."

· · ·

The next morning, after her ten o'clock lecture, Robyn knocked on Philip Swallow's door and asked if he could spare a few minutes.

"Yes, yes, come in," he said. He held a thick stencilled document in his hand and wore a haggard look. "You don't know what 'virement' means, I suppose?"

"Sorry, no. What's the context?"

"Well, this is a paper on resources for the next meeting of Principals and Deans. *'At present, resources are allocated to each Department for separate heads of expenditure without the possibility of virement.'"*

Robyn shook her head. "I've no idea. I've never come across the word before."

"Neither had I before the cuts. Then it suddenly started appearing on all kinds of documents—committee papers, working party reports, UGC circulars. The VC is particularly fond of it. But I still don't know what it means. It's not in the *Shorter Oxford Dictionary*. It's not in any of my dictionaries."

"How very peculiar," said Robyn. "Why don't you ask somebody who would know? The writer of that paper, for instance."

"The Bursar? I can't ask *him*. I've been sitting on committees with the Bursar for months solemnly discussing virement. I can't admit *now* that I have no idea what it means."

"Perhaps no one knows what it means, but they're afraid to admit it," Robyn suggested. "Perhaps it's a word invented by the Government to terrorise the universities."

"It certainly sounds nasty enough," said Philip Swallow. "*Virement . . .*" He stared unhappily at the stencilled document.

"The reason I wanted to see you . . ." Robyn prompted.

"Oh, yes, sorry," said Philip Swallow, wrenching his attention away from the mystery word.

"It's about the Shadow Scheme," she said. "Mr. Wilcox, the man I'm shadowing, is going to Frankfurt on business next Wednesday and he thinks I ought to go with him."

"Yes, I know," said Swallow. "He's been on the phone to me this morning."

"Has he?" Robyn tried to conceal her surprise.

"Yes. We've agreed that the University will pay half your expenses and his firm the other half."

"You mean, I can go?"

"He was very insistent that you should. He seems to take the terms of the Shadow Scheme very literally."

"What shall I do about my teaching on Thursday?" Robyn said.

"Oh, it's the usual rather heavy German cuisine," said Philip Swallow. "Pork and dumplings and sauerkraut, you know."

"No, my *teaching* on *Thursday*," Robyn said more loudly. "What shall I do about it? I'd rather not cancel classes in the last week of term."

"Quite," said Swallow, rather sharply, as if she had been responsible for the misunderstanding. "I've been looking at your timetable. You have quite a lot of teaching, don't you?"

"Yes, I do," said Robyn, pleased that he had noticed this.

"The ten o'clock lecture you can swap with one Bob Busby was going to give next term in the same course. And I'm going to ask Rupert Sutcliffe to take the third-year tutorial at three . . ." Robyn nodded, wondering who would be most dismayed by this news, Sutcliffe or the students. "The difficult ones are the two Women's Writing seminars at twelve and two," Swallow said. "There seems to be only one member of staff free at those hours. Me."

"Oh," said Robyn.

"What is the topic, actually?"

"The female body in contemporary women's poetry."

"Ah. I don't know a lot about that, I'm afraid."

"The students will have prepared reports," said Robyn.

"Well, of course, I don't mind just chairing a discussion, if that would . . ."

"That would be fine," said Robyn. "Thank you very much."

Swallow escorted her to the door. "Frankfurt," he said wistfully. "I attended a very lively conference there once."

PART V

"Some persons hold," he pursued, still hesitating, "that there is a wisdom of the Head, and that there is a wisdom of the Heart. I have not supposed it so; but, as I have said, I mistrust myself now. I have supposed the head to be all-sufficient. It may not be all-sufficient; how can I venture this morning to say it is!"

CHARLES DICKENS: *Hard Times*

1

It was, perhaps, inevitable that Victor Wilcox and Robyn Penrose would end up in bed together in Frankfurt, though neither of them set off from Rummidge with that intention. Vic was conscious only of wanting to have Robyn's company, and to give her a treat. Robyn was conscious only of wanting to be treated, and to be whisked away from her routine existence for an interval, however brief. But subconsciously other motives were in play. Vic's growing interest in Robyn was on the point of ripening into infatuation. Robyn's cool handling of Charles's relationship with Debbie concealed wounded pride, and she was ready to assert her own erotic independence. The trip to a foreign city, safe from the observation of friends and family, provided the perfect alibi, and a luxury hotel the perfect setting, for an *affaire* whose time had come. It hardly needed the extra incitements of the drama of the Altenhofer negotiations, Robyn's susceptibility to champagne, or the hotel disc-jockey's penchant for Jennifer Rush. As Robyn herself might have said, the event was over-determined.

. . .

Vic picked up Robyn from her house at 6:30 and drove swiftly through slumbering suburbs to the airport, with her silent and still half-asleep beside him. While he parked the car, she had a cup of coffee and started to come to life.

It was her first time in Rummidge Airport. The new-looking terminal impressed her with its stainless-steel and fibreglass surfaces, its vaulted roof, its electronic databoard announcing departures to half the capitals of Europe. Built (so Vic informed her) with the help of a grant from the EEC, it seemed like an interface between the scruffy, depressed English Midlands and a more confident, expansive world. Burly Rummidge businessmen toting overnight bags and burgundy leather briefcases with digital locks checked in nonchalantly for their flights to Zürich, Brussels, Paris, Milan, as if they did so every day of the week.

"Smoking or non-smoking?" the British Airways checker asked Vic, who hesitated and glanced at Robyn.

"I don't mind," she said accommodatingly.

"Non-smoking," he decided. "I can do without fags for an hour and a half."

Only an hour and a half! If one had the money, then, one could rise at six and be in Germany in time for breakfast. Quite a lot of money, though—she sneaked a look at her ticket and was appalled to see that the fare was £280000. Breakfast was included, however. They were travelling Club Class, and attentive stewardesses served them with a compote of apricots and pears, scrambled eggs and ham, rolls, croissants and coffee, and Dundee marmalade in miniature stoneware jars. Robyn, whose rare flights were undertaken on the cheapest tickets available, and usually spent sitting next to the lavatories in the bucking tail of the plane, trying to eat a trayful of tasteless pap with her knees under her chin, relished the standard of service. "You businessmen do yourselves proud," she said.

"Well, we deserve it," said Vic with a grin. "The country depends on us."

"My brother Basil thinks the country depends on merchant bankers."

"Don't talk to me about the City," said Vic. "They're only interested in short-term profits. They'd rather make a fast buck in foreign markets than invest in British companies. That's why our interest rates are so high. This machine I want will take three years to pay for itself."

"I never did understand stocks and shares," said Robyn. "And after listening to Basil, I'm not sure I want to."

"It's all paper," said Vic. "Moving bits of paper about. Whereas we *make* things, things that weren't there till we made 'em."

Sunlight flooded the cabin as the plane changed course. It was a bright, clear morning. Robyn looked out of the window as England slid slowly by beneath them: cities and towns, their street plans like printed circuits, scattered over a mosaic of tiny fields, connected by the thin wires of railways and motorways. Hard to imagine at this height all the noise and commotion going on down there. Factories, shops, offices, schools, beginning the working day. People crammed into rush-hour buses and trains, or sitting at the wheels of their cars in traffic jams, or washing up breakfast things in the kitchens of pebble-dashed semis. All inhabiting their own little worlds, oblivious of how they fitted into the total picture. The housewife, switching on her electric kettle to make another cup of tea, gave no thought to the immense complex of operations that made that simple action possible: the building and maintenance of the power station that produced the electricity, the mining of coal or pumping of oil to fuel the generators, the laying of miles of cable to carry the current to her house, the digging and smelting and milling of ore or bauxite into sheets of steel or aluminium, the cutting and pressing and welding of the metal into the kettle's shell, spout and handle, the assembling of these parts with scores of other components—coils, screws, nuts, bolts, washers, rivets, wires, springs, rubber insulation, plastic trimmings; then the packaging of the kettle, the advertising of the kettle, the marketing of the kettle to wholesale and retail outlets, the transportation of the kettle to warehouses and shops, the calculation of its price, and the distribution of its added value between all the myriad people and agencies concerned in its production and circulation. The housewife gave no thought to all this as she switched on her kettle. Neither had Robyn until this moment, and it would never have occurred to her to do so before she met Vic Wilcox. What to do with the thought was another question. It was difficult to decide whether the system that produced the kettle was a miracle of human ingenuity and co-operation or a colossal waste of resources, human and natural. Would we all be better off boiling our water in a pot hung over an open fire? Or was it the facility to do such things at the touch of a button that freed men, and more particularly women, from servile labour and made it possible for them to become literary critics? A phrase from *Hard Times* she was apt to quote with a certain derision in her lectures, but of which she had thought more charitably lately, came into her mind: "'*Tis aw a muddle.*" She gave up the conundrum, and accepted another cup of coffee from the stewardess.

. . .

Vic, meanwhile, was reflecting that he was sitting next to the best-looking woman on the plane, including the hostesses. Robyn had surprised him by appearing at the door of her little house dressed as he had never seen her dressed before, in a tailored two-piece costume, with matching cape, made out of a soft olive-green cloth that set off her coppery curls and echoed her grey-green eyes. "You look terrific," he said spontaneously. She smiled and stifled a yawn and said, "Thanks. I thought I'd try and dress the part."

But what was the part? The other passengers on the plane had clearly made up their minds. They were businessmen like himself, many of them on their way to the same trade fair, and he had intercepted their knowing, appraising glances at Robyn as she strode into the departure lounge at his side. She was his girlfriend, his mistress, his dolly-bird, his bit of spare, his nookie-cookie, thinly disguised as his secretary or PA, going with him to Frankfurt on the firm's expenses, nice work if you could fiddle it, lucky bastard. And the Germans would presumably think the same.

"How shall I explain you to the Germans?" he said. "I can't go through all that rigmarole about the Shadow Scheme every time I introduce you. I don't suppose they'd understand what I was on about anyway."

"I'll explain," she said. "I speak German."

"Go on! You don't!"

"*Ja, bestimmt. Ich habe seit vier jahren in der Schule die Deutsche Sprache studiert.*"

"What's that mean?"

"Yes, I do. I studied German for four years at school."

Vic stared in wonderment. "I wish I could do that," he said. "*Guten Tag* and *Auf Wiedersehen* are about the limits of my German."

"I'll be your interpreter, then."

"Oh, they all speak English . . . As a matter of fact," he said, struck by a thought, "it might be useful if you don't let on that you understand German when we meet the Altenhofer people."

"Why?"

"I've done business with Krauts before. Sometimes they talk German to each other in the middle of a meeting. I'd like to know what they're saying."

"All right," said Robyn. "But how will you explain what I'm doing there?"

"I'll say you're my Personal Assistant," said Vic.

. . .

Altenhofer's had sent a car to meet them at the airport. The driver was standing at the exit from Customs holding a cardboard sign with MR. WILCOX on it. "Hmm, giving us the treatment," said Vic, when he saw this.

"How much would this sale be worth to them?" Robyn asked.

"I'm hoping to get the machine for £150,000. *Guten Tag*," he said to the chauffeur. *"Ich bin Herr Wilcox."*

"This way, please sir," said the man, taking their bags.

"You see what I mean?" Vic murmured. "Even the bloody chauffeurs speak better English than I do."

The driver nodded approvingly when Vic gave the name of their hotel. It was on the outskirts of the city because it hadn't been possible to get an additional room for Robyn in the downtown hotel where he'd originally been booked. "But this one should be comfortable," said Vic. "It's pricey enough."

It was in fact the most luxurious hotel Robyn had ever entered as a guest, though the ambience was more like that of an exclusive country club, with a great deal of natural wood and exposed brick in the decor, and all kinds of facilities for recreation and body-maintenance: a beauty salon, a gymnasium, a sauna, a games room, and a swimming pool. *"Schwimmbad!"* Robyn exclaimed, seeing the direction sign. "If I'd known I'd have brought my costume."

"Buy one," said Vic. "There's a shop over there."

"What, just for one swim?"

"Why not? You'll use it again, won't you?"

While Vic was registering, she strolled over to the sports boutique on the other side of the lobby and flicked through a rack of bikinis and swimsuits. The more exiguous they were, the dearer they seemed to be. "Much too expensive," she said, coming back to the reception desk.

"Let me treat you," he said.

"No thanks. I want to see my room. I bet it's enormous."

It was. It had a monolithic bed, an immense leather-topped desk, a glass-topped coffee table, a TV, a minibar and a vast wardrobe system in which the few items of her modest luggage looked lost. She plucked a grape from the complimentary bowl of fruit on the coffee table. She switched on the radio at the bedside console and the strains of Schubert filled the room. She pressed another button and the net curtains, electrically operated, whirred apart to reveal, like a cinemascope establishing shot, landscaped grounds and an artificial lake. The bathroom, gleaming with sophisticated plumbing, had two washbasins carved out of what looked convincingly like marble, and was provided with more towels of diverse sizes than she could think of uses for. Behind the door were two towelling bathrobes sealed in polythene covers. Schubert filtered into the bathroom from an extension speaker. It was the only sound in the suite: double glazing, deep-pile carpets, and the heavy wooden door, absorbed all sound of the outside world. Two weeks here, she thought, and I could finish off *Domestic Angels and Unfortunate Females.*

The chauffeur had waited to take them into the centre of the city. Sitting in the back seat of the swift, silent Mercedes, Robyn was struck by the contrast between the streets of Frankfurt and their equivalents in poor old Rummidge. Everywhere here looked clean, neat, freshly painted and highly polished. There were no discarded chip cones, squashed fried-chicken cartons, dented lager cans, polystyrene hamburger containers or crumpled paper cups in the gutters. The pavements had a freshly rinsed look, and so had the pedestrians. The commercial architecture was sleek and stylish.

"Well, they had to rebuild from scratch after the war, didn't they," said Vic when she commented on this. "We pretty well flattened Frankfurt."

"The centre of Rummidge has been pretty well flattened too," said Robyn.

"Not by bombing."

"No, by the developers. But they haven't rebuilt it like this, have they?"

"Couldn't afford to. We won the war and lost the peace, as they say."

"Why did we?"

Vic pondered a moment. "We were too greedy and too lazy," he said. "In the fifties and sixties, when you could sell anything, we went on using obsolete machines and paid the unions whatever they asked for, while the Krauts were investing in new technology and hammering out sensible labour agreements. When times got harder, it paid off. They think they've got a recession here, but it's nothing like what we've got."

This was an unusually critical assessment of British industry, coming from Vic. "I thought you said our problem was we bought too many imports?" she said.

"That too. Where was that outfit of yours made, as a matter of interest?"

"I've no idea." She looked at the label inside the cape and laughed: "West Germany!"

"There you are."

"But it's nice, you said so yourself. Anyway, you can't talk. This cost me all of eighty-five pounds. You're just about to spend a hundred and fifty thousand on a German machine tool."

"That's different."

"No, it isn't. Why don't you buy a British machine?"

"Because we don't make one that will do the job," Vic said. "And that's another reason why we lost the peace."

. . .

The exhibition centre housing the trade fair was rather like an airport without aeroplanes: a vast multi-levelled complex of large halls, connected by long walkways and moving staircases, with bars and cafeterias dotted about the landings. They registered inside the entrance hall. Robyn put down on the form, "J. Pringle & Sons" under *Company* and "Personal Assistant to Managing Director" under *Position*, and received an identity card recording these false particulars.

Vic frowned at a plan of the exhibition. "We have to go through CADCAM," he said, adding for her benefit: "Computer-aided design and computer-aided manufacture." Robyn stored away the information for future reference: she intended to compose her URFAIYS report as far as possible in acronyms.

They threaded their way though a hot and crowded space where computers hummed and printers chattered and screeched on stands packed as close together as fairground booths, and passed into a larger, airier hall where the big machine tools were displayed, some in simulated operation. Wheels turned, crankshafts cranked, oiled pistons slid up and down, in and out, conveyor belts rattled round, but nothing was actually produced. The machines were odourless, brightly painted and highly polished. It was all very different from the stench and dirt and heat and noise of a real factory. More like a moving toyshop for grown men; and men in large numbers were swarming round the massive machines, squatting and bending and craning to get a better view of their intricacies. Robyn saw very few women about, except for professional models handing out leaflets and brochures. They wore skintight Lycra jumpsuits, heavy make-up and fixed smiles and looked as if they had been extruded from the Altenhofer automatic core-moulding machine.

The sales director of Altenhofer's, Herr Winkler, and his technical assistant, Dr. Patsch, welcomed Vic and Robyn warmly at the company's stand, and ushered them into a carpeted inner sanctum for refreshment. Champagne was offered, as well as coffee and orange juice.

"Coffee for me," said Vic. "I'll leave the bubbly till later."

Herr Winkler, a portly, smiling man, with small, perfectly shod feet and a springy step like a ballroom dancer, chuckled. "You wish to keep a clear head, of course. But your charming assistant . . . ?"

"Oh, she can drink as much as she likes," said Vic offhandedly, presumably to encourage the supposition that her presence on this occasion was purely decorative. He had already stripped her of her doctorate, introducing her to the Germans as "Miss Penrose." With her false identity card on her lapel, Robyn felt she had no option but to go along with the role assigned to her, and enjoy the fun of it. "I'm rather susceptible to champagne," she simpered. "I think I'd better mix it with orange juice."

"Ah, yes, the Buck Fizz, isn't it?" said Herr Winkler.

"Buck's Fizz, actually," she said, ever the teacher, even in disguise. "As distinct from Buck House, where the Queen lives."

"Buck's Fizz, Buck House—I must remember," said Herr Winkler, waltzing over to the drinks table. "Heinrich! a glass of Buck's Fizz for the lady! And coffee for Mr. Wilcox, who wishes to buy one of our beautiful machines."

"If the price is right," said Vic.

"Ha ha! Of course," Winkler chuckled. Dr. Patsch, tall, saturnine and dark-bearded, measured orange juice and sparkling wine into a champagne flute, holding it level with his eyes like a test-tube. Winkler snatched the drink from him and sashayed back to Robyn. He presented the glass to her with a slight bow and a perceptible click of his heels. "I am informed that your boss is a hard bargainer, Miss Penrose."

"Who told you that?" Vic said.

"My spies," said Dr. Winkler, beaming merrily. "We have all spies in business these days, do we not? Will you take cream in your coffee, Mr. Wilcox?"

"Black with sugar, please. Then I'd like to take a closer look at the machine you've got out there."

"Of course, of course. Dr. Patsch will explain everything to you. Then you and I will talk money, which is so much more complicated."

The next hour was rather tedious for Robyn and she had no difficulty in simulating bored incomprehension. They went out into the exhibition hall and examined the huge moulding machine at its phantom task. Dr. Patsch gave a detailed commentary on its operation in excellent English, and Vic seemed impressed. When they went back inside the stand to discuss terms, however, there appeared to be a wide gap between the asking price and Vic's limit. Winkler suggested that they adjourn for lunch, and pranced them out of the exhibition centre and across the road to a high-rise hotel of ostentatious luxury where a table had been reserved. It was the kind of restaurant where the first thing the waiters did was to take away the perfectly serviceable place settings already on the table and substitute more elaborate ones. Robyn submitted to being guided through the German menu by Dr. Winkler, and compensated herself by choosing the most expensive items on it, smoked salmon and venison. The wine was excellent. There was light conversation about differences between England and Germany in which Robyn avoided giving any impression of suspicious intelligence by attributing her every opinion to something she had read in a newspaper. But as the meal drew to its conclusion the talk turned back to the matter of business. "It's a beautiful machine," said Vic, puffing a cigar over the coffee and cognac. "It's exactly what I need. The trouble is, you want a hundred and seventy thousand pounds for it, and I'm only authorised to pay a hundred and fifty."

Dr. Winkler smiled, a shade desperately. "We might be able to arrange a small discount."

"How small?"

"Two per cent."

Vic shook his head. "Not worth talking about." He glanced at his watch. "I have another appointment this afternoon . . ."

"Yes, of course," said Winkler despondently. He motioned to a waiter for his bill. Vic excused himself and went off to the men's cloakroom. Winkler and Patsch exchanged some remarks in German to which Robyn listened attentively, while accepting a second cup of coffee from the waiter and indulging herself in a chocolate truffle. After a little while she stood up and, with a little charade of embarrassment, asked the way to the Ladies. She loitered outside the door until Vic emerged from the adjacent *Herren*.

"They're going to accept your price," she said.

His face brightened. "Are they? That's terrific!"

"But there's a catch in it, I think. Patsch said, *'We can't do it with a* something *system,'*—it sounded like *'semen,'* And Winkler said, *'Well, he hasn't specified semen.'*"

Vic frowned and pushed his fingers through his forelock. "The cunning bastards. They're going to try and fob me off with an electromechanical control system."

"What?"

"The machine we saw this morning has a Siemens solid-state control system with diagnostic panels for identifying faults. The older type is electromechanical—all switches and relays, and no diagnostic facility. Nowhere near as reliable. The Siemens system would add nearly twenty thousand to the total cost—exactly the margin we're haggling about. Nice work, Robyn." While he was talking Vic was moving back towards the restaurant.

"Wait for me," said Robyn. "I don't want to miss anything, but I must go to the loo."

When they returned to the restaurant, Robyn wondered whether Winkler and Patsch would have seen anything suspicious in their long absence, but Vic had had a story ready about phoning his divisional boss in England. "No dice, I'm afraid. My ceiling is still a hundred and fifty thousand."

"We have been discussing the problem," said Winkler with a genial smile. "After all, we think we can meet your requirements for that figure."

"Now you're talking," said Vic.

"Excellent!" Winkler beamed. "Let us have another cognac." He waved to the wine waiter.

"I'll send you a letter as soon as I get back," said Vic. "Let's just get the deal straight." He took a notebook from his inside pocket and leafed through it with a wetted finger till he reached a certain page. "It's your 22EX machine, right?"

"Correct."

"With Siemens solid-state systems."

Herr Winkler's smile faded. "I do not think we specified that."

"But the demonstration model in the exhibition has Siemens solid-state."

"Very likely," said Winkler with a shrug. "Our machines are available with a variety of control systems."

"The 22EX is also supplied with Klugermann electromechanical controls," said Dr. Patsch. "That is what we had in mind for the price."

"Then it's no deal," said Vic, closing his notebook and stowing it away. "I'm only interested in solid-state."

The wine waiter came up to the table. Winkler swatted him away irritably. Vic stood up and put his hand on the back of Robyn's chair. "Perhaps we shouldn't waste any more of your time, Mr. Winkler."

"Thanks for the lovely lunch," said Robyn, getting to her feet and giving a vacant smile of which she was rather proud.

"One moment, Mr. Wilcox. Sit down, please," said Winkler. "If you will excuse us, I should like to discuss further with my colleague."

Winkler and Patsch went off in the direction of the cloakrooms, deep in conversation. The former's step seemed to have lost some of its spring, and he collided clumsily with one of the waiters as he threaded his way through the tables.

"Well?" said Robyn.

"I think they might just bite the bullet," said Vic. "Winkler thought he had the deal sewn up. He can't bear the thought of it slipping out of his grasp at the last moment."

After five minutes, the Germans came back. Patsch was looking glum, but Winkler smiled gamely. "One hundred and fifty-five thousand," he said, "with Siemens solid-state. That is absolutely our final offer."

Vic took out his notebook again. "Let's not make any more mistakes," he said. "This is the 22EX with Siemens solid-state, for one hundred and fifty-five thousand, to be paid in sterling in stages as per your outline quotation: 25% with order, 50% on delivery, 15% on being commissioned by your engineers, and 10% after two months satisfactory operation, right?"

"Correct."

"Can you write out the new quotation and let me have it today?"

"It will be delivered to your hotel this afternoon."

"It's a deal, Mr. Winkler," said Vic. "I can find the odd five thousand from somewhere." He shook Winkler's hand.

"I was not misinformed about you, Mr. Wilcox," said Winkler, with a slightly weary smile.

They all shook hands again when they parted in the foyer of the hotel. "Goodbye, Miss Penrose," said Winkler. "Enjoy yourself in Frankfurt."

"*Auf Wiedersehen, Herr Winkler,*" she replied. "*Ich wurde mich freuen wenn der Rest meines Besuches so erfreulich wird wie dieses köstliche Mittagessen.*"

He gaped at her. "I did not know you speak German."

"You didn't ask me," she said, smiling sweetly.

"Goodbye, then," said Vic, taking Robyn's arm. "You'll be getting a letter next week. Then my technical people will be in touch." He hurried her away towards the revolving doors. "What did you say?" he muttered.

"I said I would be happy if the rest of my stay was as enjoyable as the delicious lunch."

"That was cheeky," he said, keeping his grinning face hidden from the Germans. As the door spun them into the open, he punched the air triumphantly, like a footballer who has scored a goal. "Turned the tables on the buggers!" he cried. "At a hundred and fifty-five, it's a snip!"

"Ssh! They'll hear you."

"They can't back out now. What do you want to do?"

"Haven't you got another appointment?"

"No, I invented that to concentrate their minds, I've got no more meetings till tomorrow. We could go and have a look at the Old Town if you like—it's all fake, mind. Or go on the river. Whatever you fancy. It's your treat. You deserve it."

"It's raining," Robyn observed.

He held out a hand and looked up at the sky. "So it is."

"Not much fun sightseeing in the rain. I think what I'd like to do is buy a swimming-costume and go back to that nice hotel and have a swim."

"Good idea. There's a taxi!"

· · ·

So they went back to the hotel by taxi and Robyn chose a blue and green one-piece swimming costume in the sports boutique and allowed Vic to pay for it. He bought a pair of trunks for himself at the same time. He was not a great enthusiast for this form of exercise, but he had no intention of letting Robyn out of his sight any longer than was necessary to change into a pair of trunks.

It was years since he had bought such a garment, and in the meantime either he had got bigger or swimming costumes had got smaller. Robyn's appearance when she emerged from the changing-room suggested that the latter was the case. Her pointed nipples were sharply embossed on the tight-fitting satiny cloth, and the bottom part of her costume was cut away so steeply that tendrils of red-gold hair crept out from under the fabric at the vee. He would have enjoyed all this more if he hadn't been so conscious of his genitals bulging like a bunch of grapes at the crotch of his own costume.

They had the pool to themselves, apart from a couple of kids splashing about at the shallow end. Robyn dived gracefully into the water, and began a tidy crawl up and down the length of the pool. He might have guessed she would be a good swimmer. He jumped in, holding his nose, and tailed her with his slower breaststroke. When she offered to race him, he stipulated the breaststroke, but she still beat him easily. She climbed out of the pool, water streaming from her long white flanks, and tried vainly to lever the cheeks of her buttocks under the skimpy costume with her thumbs. She stood at the end of the diving board, bounced once, twice, and somersaulted into the water with a great splash. She surfaced, laughing and spluttering, "*Made a hash of that!*" and hauled herself out to try again. Vic trod water and watched her, entranced.

There was a jacuzzi at one end of the pool, a foaming whirlpool of hot water that gently pummelled your muscles into a state of blissful relaxation. They sat in it up to their necks, facing each other like cartoon characters in a cannibal's pot. "I've never been in one of these before," said Vic. "It's magic."

"An item to tick off your list," said Robyn.

"What list?"

"The miss list. The list of things you've never done."

"Oh, yes," said Vic. He thought of another item, that she did not know about. Jennifer Rush burst into song inside his head:

> *There's no need to run away,*
> *If you feel that this is for real,*
> *'Cause when it's warm and straight from the heart,*
> *It's time to start.*

"We shouldn't stay in here too long," said Robyn. She clambered out and took a running dive into the pool. He clumsily followed suit, gasping with the shock of the cool water after the hot jacuzzi. Into the jacuzzi they went once more, and once more into the pool. Then they separated to shower and dry themselves. The locker-room was supplied with an abundance of towels, robes, track suits, soaps, shampoos, body lotions and talcum powders. They emerged pink, gleaming, and odoriferous from these ablutions, and ordered tea in the games room. They played table-tennis and Vic won the best of five games. Then he taught her how to play snooker, a heady experience. Apart from the occasional handshake, or a guiding hand placed on her arm, he had never touched her before. Now he encircled her with his arms, almost embraced her from behind, as he corrected her posture and adjusted her handling of the cue. Jennifer Rush murmured:

> *I hold on to your body,*
> *And feel each move you make,*
> *Your voice is warm and tender*
> *A love that I could not forsake.*

They explored the gymnasium and played with the exercise bicycle and the rowing-machine and a kind of inverted treadmill that looked as if it had been invented by the Spanish Inquisition, until they worked up such a sweat that it was necessary to go and shower again. They agreed to rest for an hour or so in their rooms.

Vic lay on his bed, feeling tired but relaxed after all the exercise, his eyes shut, his head a mere amplifier now for Jennifer Rush. The lobes of his brain were two spools on which her tape played and replayed in an endless loop.

But it makes you feel all right,
Just to think of doin' her right,
The road to choose is straight ahead in the end.
Surrender! It's your only chance, surrender!
Don't wait too long to realize
That her eyes will say "Forever."

He rose after an hour and shaved for the second time that day. In the mirror his hair looked as light and fluffy as a baby's from all the washing and drying. He parted it carefully, and combed it back, but the limp forelock fell forward inevitably across his forehead. Other men's hair didn't do that, he reflected irritably. Perhaps all his life he had been combing it the wrong way. He tried parting it on the other side, but it looked queer. Then he combed it forward without a parting at all, but it looked ridiculous. He rubbed some Vaseline into it, parted and combed it in the usual style. As soon as he moved, the forelock fell forward.

He put on a clean shirt and anxiously inspected his tie, which had got splashed with a bit of gravy at lunch. He dabbed at it with a wet face-flannel without much effect, except for creating a damp halo around the original spot. It was the only tie he had, though, and he could hardly wear an open-necked shirt with his striped suit. For the first time in his life, Vic wished he had brought more clothes with him on a business trip. Robyn, he felt sure, would have brought a change for the evening. *"I thought I'd dress the part."*

He was not disappointed. When he knocked on the door of her room at the appointed time, she appeared at the threshold wearing a dress he had never seen before, something silky and filmy and swirling, in a muted pattern of brown, blue and green, with different shoes and different earrings, even a different handbag, from the ones she'd worn earlier that day.

"You look wonderful," he said. His voice sounded strange to his own ears: it had assimilated some of the passionate timbre of Jennifer Rush. Robyn seemed to notice, for she blushed slightly, and rattled away in reply:

"Thanks—shall I come straight away? I'm ready, and hungry, believe it or not. Must be all that exercise."

"Do you want to go out somewhere to dinner? Or shall we eat here?"

"I don't mind," she said. "Do you know somewhere special?"

"No," he said. "Wherever we go will be crowded with people from the trade fair."

"Then let's eat here."

"Good," he said.

. . . .

Vic insisted on ordering champagne at dinner. "A celebration," he said. "We deserve it." He raised his glass. "Here's to the Altenhofer 22EX automatic core blower with Siemens solid-state diagnostic controls at the bargain price of a hundred and fifty-five thousand pounds."

"Here's to it," said Robyn, feeling the bubbles explode pleasantly in her nostrils as she drank. "Mmm, delicious!"

Robyn hadn't been joking when she told Herr Winkler that she was peculiarly susceptible to champagne. It had no perceptible effect on her at first, apart from tasting nice, so that she tended to drink more of it, more quickly, than she would another wine. Then, suddenly—woomph! She would be high as a kite. This evening she ordered herself to drink slowly, but somehow the bottle had emptied itself before they had finished their main course of trout *meunière*, and she weakly acquiesced in the ordering of a second. After all, why shouldn't she get a little high? She was in a holiday mood: carefree, hedonistic, glowing with physical wellbeing. Rummidge and its attendant worries seemed infinitely remote. The curved crystal-lit dining room, filled with the civilised sounds of tinkling glassware, the soft clash of cutlery on china plate, subdued laughter and conversation, might have been the cabin of a spaceship, with portholes behind the thick velvet curtains from which the Earth would look no bigger or more substantial than a milky-coloured balloon. There was no gravity here, and one breathed champagne bubbles. The sensation was exhilarating.

Across the table, Vic talked ramblingly about the difference the new machine would make to Pringle's competitive edge. She responded with phatic murmurs, not really attending. He hardly seemed to be attending himself. His dark eyes gazed intently at her from under the falling forelock. He was, after all, she thought, a not unattractive man, in spite of his short stature. If only he had clothes that fitted him properly, he could look quite handsome. He certainly looked better without any. She recalled his white, broad-shouldered torso in the pool that afternoon, the flat belly and sinewy arms, the masculine bulge under his briefs. Under the table she slipped off her shoe and briefly rubbed her foot against his calf, keeping a straight face with difficulty as she watched a startled question fill his eyes, like the face of a prisoner who comes to the door of his cell and grips the bars, only to discover that it is unlocked, and does not know whether the prospect of release is genuine or not. Robyn herself had not decided, she was suspended in time and space, but she teased him mischievously.

"I suppose if I hadn't been here, Herr Winkler would have fixed you up with a call-girl tonight. Isn't that what goes on at these trade fairs?"

"So they tell me," he said, gripping the bars more tightly. "I wouldn't know."

The waiter presented the bill, and Vic signed it. "What d'you want to do now?" he said. "A drink in the bar?"

"No more drink," she said. "I'd like to dance." She laughed at the look of dismay on his face. "There's a discothèque in the hotel—it said so in the lift."

"I can't do that sort of dancing."

"Anyone can do it after that much champagne," she said, getting a little unsteadily to her feet.

There turned out to be two discothèques in the hotel; one a booming, strobe-lit cell in the basement designed for young people, occupied at this hour only by the disc-jockey and the two children who had been in the swimming pool: and another, situated in an annexe to the bar, that was more like a nightclub, offering music of a less frenzied tempo to a more mature clientèle. Vic looked round with relief. "This is all right," he said. "There are even people dancing together."

"Together?"

"Holding on to each other, I mean. The way I learned to dance."

"Come on, then," she said. She took him by the hand and led him onto the floor. A song of sublime silliness and repetitive melody was in progress, sung by a female vocalist with a high-pitched girlish voice.

> *I'm in the mood for wooing, and doing*
> *The things we do so well together . . .*

Vic led off with a kind of modified quickstep, holding her at arm's length. Then Robyn executed a few jive twists and turns and broke away so that he was forced to jig up and down on his own, facing her across two yards of floor.

"Come back," he said, with comical pathos, shuffling his feet awkwardly, his torso rigid, his arms held stiffly at his side. "I can't do this."

"You're doing fine," she said. "Just let yourself go."

"I never let myself go," he said. "It's against my nature."

"Poor Vic!" She shimmied up to him and, as he reached for her like a drowning swimmer, backed away.

At last, after several records, she took pity on him. They sat down and ordered soft drinks. "Thanks, Vic, that was lovely," she said. "I haven't danced for ages."

"Don't you have balls at the University?" he said. "May balls." He dredged up the phrase as if it belonged to a foreign language.

"May balls are Cambridge. I believe they have dances at the Rummidge Staff Club, but I don't know anybody who goes to them."

The lights dimmed. Music of a slower tempo commenced. The couples on the dance floor drew together. A strange expression came over Vic's face that she could only describe as awe.

"This tune," he said hoarsely.

"You know it?"

"It's Jennifer Rush."

"You like her?"

He stood up. "Let's dance."

"All right."

It was a slow, smoochy ballad with an absurd, sentimental refrain about *I am your lady and you are my man* and *the power of love*, but it did amazing things for Vic's dancing. His limbs lost their stiffness, his movements were perfectly on the beat, he held her close, firmly but lightly, nudging her round the floor with his hips and thighs. He said nothing, and with her chin resting on his shoulder she couldn't see his face, but he seemed to be humming faintly to himself. She closed her eyes and yielded to the languorous rhythms of the silly, sexy tune. When the record finished she gave him a quick kiss on the lips.

"What was that for?" he said, startled out of his trance.

"Let's go to bed," said Robyn.

2

They do not speak to each other again until they are inside Robyn's room. Robyn has nothing to say, and Vic is speechless. As, hand in hand, they tread the carpeted corridors of the hotel, as they wait for the lift, and rise to the second floor, their states of mind are very different.

. . .

Robyn's mood is blithe. She feels mildly wanton, but not wicked. She sees herself not as seducing Vic but as putting him out of his misery. There is of course always a special excitement about the first time with a new partner. One never knows quite what to expect. Her heart beats faster than if she were going to bed with Charles. But she is not anxious. She is in control. Perhaps she feels a certain sense of triumph at her conquest: the captain of industry at the feet of the feminist literary critic—a pleasing tableau.

. . .

For Vic the event is infinitely more momentous, his mood infinitely more perturbed. The prospect of going to bed with Robyn Penrose is the secret dream of weeks come true, yet there is something hallucinatory about the ease with which his wish has been granted. He regards himself with wonderment led by the hand by this handsome young woman towards her bedroom, as if his soul is stumbling along out of step behind his body. In the mirrored wall of the lift he sees himself standing shoulder to shoulder beside Robyn, who is three inches taller. She catches his eye and smiles, lifts his hand and rubs it against her cheek. It is like watching a puppet being manipulated. He smiles tensely back into the mirror.

. . .

Robyn opens the door of her room, hangs the *Do Not Disturb* sign on the outside, and locks it from the inside. She kicks off her shoes, bringing her height down nearer to Vic's. He pushes her against the door and begins to kiss her violently, his hands clutching and groping all over her. Only passion, he feels, will carry him across the threshold of adultery, and this is what he supposes passion is like.

. . .

Robyn is surprised, and a little alarmed, by this behaviour. "Take it easy, Vic," she says breathlessly. "You don't have to tear the clothes off me."

"Sorry," he says, desisting at once. His arms drop to his sides. He looks at her humbly. "I haven't done this before."

"Oh, Vic," she says, "don't keep on saying that, it's too sad." She goes to the minibar and peers inside. "Good," she says, "there's a half bottle of champagne. You don't have to do anything if you don't want to."

"Oh, I want to," he says. "I love you."

"Don't be silly," she says, handing him the bottle. "That song has gone to your head. The one about the power of love."

"It's my favourite song," he says. "From now on it will be our song."

Robyn can hardly believe her ears.

. . .

Robyn holds out two glasses. Vic fills only one. "Not for me," he says.

Robyn looks at him over the rim of her glass. "You're not worried about being impotent, are you?"

"No," he says hoarsely. He is, of course.

"If it happens, it doesn't matter, OK?"

"I don't think it will be a problem," he says.

"You could just give me a massage, if you like."

"I want to make love," he says.

"Massage is a way of making love. It's gentle, tender, non-phallic."

"I'm a phallic sort of bloke," he says apologetically.

"Well, it's also a nice kind of foreplay," says Robyn.

The word "foreplay" gives him a tremendous hard-on.

. . .

Robyn puts her hands behind her back, undoes a catch on her dress, and pulls it over her shoulders. As she hangs it up in the wardrobe, she inspects the label. "'*Made in Italy*.' Failed the patriotic test again." She pulls her slip over her head. "'*Fabriqué en France*.' Dear, dear." This is her way of keeping the tone light. She glances at Vic, who is staring at her, still holding the champagne bottle. "Aren't you going to get undressed?" she says. "I feel a little shy standing here like this." She is wearing vest, pants, tights.

"Sorry," he says, struggling out of his jacket, wrenching at his tie, tearing off his shirt.

She picks the shirt up from the floor and searches for its label. "Ha! '*Made in Hong Kong*.'"

"Marjorie buys my shirts."

"No excuses . . . The suit seems to be British though." She hangs his jacket on a wooden valet. "All too British, if I may say so, Vic."

The only British-made garment Robyn is wearing is the last to come off. "I always buy my knickers at Marks and Spencer's," she says with a grin.

She stands before him, a naked goddess. Small, round breasts with pink, pointed nipples. A slender waist, broad hips, and gently curving belly. A tongue of fire at her crotch. He worships.

"You're beautiful," he says.

"Shall I make a terrible confession? I wish I had bigger breasts. Why? I ask myself. There's absolutely no reason except the grossest sexual stereotyping."

"Your breasts are beautiful," he says, kissing them gently.

"That's nice, Vic," she says. "You're getting the idea. Gently does it."

. . .

She turns back the sheets on the bed, places a bottle of oil to hand on the night table, switches off all the lights except one lamp. She lies down on the bed, and stretches out her hand. "Aren't you going to take your shorts off?" she says.

"Can we have that light out?"

"Certainly not."

He turns away from her to slip off his boxer shorts, then comes to the bed, shielding his erection with his hands.

. . .

"My, what a knobstick," she says.

"Why do you call it that?"

"Private joke." As quick as a lizard she darts out her tongue and licks his cock from root to tip.

"God Almighty," he says. "Can we skip the massage?"

"If you like," she says, beginning herself to be excited by the urgency of his desire. "Have you got a condom?"

. . .

Vic looks at her with blank dismay. "Aren't you on the pill or something?"

"No. Came off the pill for health reasons. And the coil."

"What shall we do? I haven't got anything."

"Fortunately I have. Pass that sponge-bag, will you?"

He passes her the sponge-bag. "Here we are," she says. "Shall I put it on for you?"

"Good God, no!" he exclaims.

"Why not?"

He laughs wildly. "All right."

Deftly she rolls the condom onto his penis. When she releases the teat it falls sideways like a limp forelock.

"I don't believe this," he says.

. . .

Ever the teacher, Robyn is, of course, trying to make a point, to demystify "love."

"I love you," he says, kissing her throat, stroking her breasts, tracing the curve of her hip.

"No, you don't, Vic."

"I've been in love with you for weeks."

"There's no such thing," she says. "It's a rhetorical device. It's a bourgeois fallacy."

"Haven't you ever been in love, then?"

"When I was younger," she says, "I allowed myself to be constructed by the discourse of romantic love for a while, yes."

"What the hell does that mean?"

"We aren't essences, Vic. We aren't unique individual essences existing prior to language. There is only language."

"What about this?" he says, sliding his hand between her legs.

"Language and biology," she says, opening her legs wider. "Of course we have bodies, physical needs and appetites. My muscles contract when you touch me there—feel?"

"I feel," he says.

"And that's nice. But the discourse of romantic love pretends that your finger and my clitoris are extensions of two unique individual selves who need each other and only each other and cannot be happy without each other for ever and ever."

"That's right," says Vic. "I love your silk cunt with my whole self, for ever and ever."

"Silly," she says, but smiles, not unmoved by this declaration. "Why do you call it that?"

. . .

"Private joke," he says, covering her body with his. "Do you think we could possibly stop talking now?"

. . .

"All right," she says. "But I prefer to be on top."

3

"Imagine," Robyn whispered. "He had never done it that way before."

"Really?" Penny Black whispered back. "How long did you say he had been married?"

"Twenty-two years."

"Twenty-two years in the missionary position? That's kind of perverted."

Robyn sniggered, a mite guiltily. She didn't like to expose Vic to Penny Black's ridicule, but she felt she had to confide in somebody. It was ten days since the expedition to Frankfurt, and she and Penny were having a sauna after their Monday evening game of squash, on the highest, hottest bench, and they were whispering because Philip Swallow's wife, wrapped modestly in a towel, was sitting on the lowest.

"Well, I don't think there's been a lot of sex in the marriage in recent years," said Robyn.

"I'm not surprised," said Penny.

Mrs. Swallow rose to her feet and went out of the sauna, nodding curtly to the two young women as she closed the door.

"Oh dear," said Robyn, "d'you think she thought we were talking about her and Swallow?"

"Never mind the Swallows," said Penny, "tell me about your fling with Wilcox. What possessed you?"

"I fancied him," said Robyn, cupping her chin in her hands, and supporting her elbows on her knees. "At that particular conjuncture, I fancied him."

"I thought you couldn't stand him? I thought he was a bully, a philistine and a male chauvinist."

"Well, he did seem a bit like that at first. In fact he's really quite decent, when you get to know him. And by no means stupid."

"That doesn't sound like enough reason to go to bed with him."

"I told you, Penny, that night I fancied him. You know how it is: you're in a strange place, you have a few drinks, a smooch on the dance floor . . ."

"Yeah, yeah, I know, I've taught Open University Summer School. But Robyn, for heaven's sake—a middle-aged factory owner!"

"Managing Director."

"Well, whatever . . . it's like rough trade."

"He wasn't a bit rough. On the contrary."

"I don't mean physically, I mean psychologically. I think the idea of this man's power and money is a turn-on for you. He's the antithesis of everything you stand for." Penny Black shook her head reproachfully. "I'm afraid it's the old female rape-fantasy rearing its ugly head again, Robyn. When Wilcox screwed you, it was like the factory ravished the university."

"Don't be absurd, Penny," said Robyn. "If anyone did any ravishing, it was me. The trouble is, he wants to make a great romance out of it. He insists that he's in love with me. I tell him I don't believe in the concept, but it doesn't make any difference. He keeps ringing me up and asking to meet. I don't know what to do."

"Tell him you're committed to Charles."

"The trouble is, I'm not. We're not seeing each other at the moment."

"Tell him you're a lesbian," said Penny, with a sly, sideways glance. "That should put him off."

Robyn laughed, a little self-consciously, and pressed her knees more closely together. She had a suspicion that Penny Black herself had tendencies of this kind. "He knows I'm not a lesbian," she said, "all too well."

"What does he have in mind?" said Penny. "Does he want to set you up as his mistress or something?" She chuckled. "Maybe you should consider it seriously, it might be useful when your job runs out."

"He claims he wants to marry me," said Robyn. "He's prepared to get a divorce and marry me."

"Wow! That's heavy!"

"It's quite ridiculous, of course."

"All because of a single fuck?"

"Well, three actually," said Robyn.

. . .

The first time he came almost as soon as she straddled him and bore down on him—came with a great groan, like a tree being torn out of the ground by the roots. A little later he was sufficiently hard again to allow her to reach an orgasm, but couldn't come himself until she helped him with the aid of a little massage oil. He wept at that, whether from mortification or gratitude or a mixture of both, she couldn't be sure. And in the early hours of the morning, with the grey dawn light just beginning to seep through the curtains, she woke to find his hand between her legs, and she rolled over onto her back and, still half asleep, let him have her in his own direct way, under the bedclothes, without a word exchanged—only inarticulate cries and moans to which she contributed her quota. When she woke again, in broad daylight, he had gone back to his own room, much to her relief. She gave him credit for unsuspected tact. They could carry on as if the events of the night were bracketed off from their normal relationship. Sober and wide awake, she had no wish to be reminded of them.

But at breakfast in the restaurant he looked at her from under his forelock with worried, doggy devotion, hardly responding to her small talk, eating little but drinking cup after cup of coffee and chainsmoking his Marlboros.

When they went back upstairs to pack he followed her into her room and asked what they were going to do. Robyn said she thought she might look at the Old Town while he did his business at the trade fair, and he said, I don't mean that, I mean what are we going to do about last night? And she said, we don't have to do anything about it, do we? We both got a bit carried away, but it was nice. Nice, he said, nice, is that all you can say about it? It was wonderful. All right, she said, to humour him, it was wonderful. I slept beautifully, did you? I hardly slept at all, he said, and he looked it. But it was wonderful, he said, especially the last time, we came together the last time, didn't we? Did we, she said, I don't really remember, I was half-asleep. Don't mock me, he said. I'm not mocking you, she said. It means nothing to you, I suppose, he said, it was just a, what do they call it, a one-night stand, I expect you do it all the time, but I don't. Neither do I, she said hotly, I haven't slept with anyone except Charles for years, and I'm not seeing Charles at the moment. Not that it's any of your business, she added. But a look of relief had come over his face. Well then, he said, so it was love. No it wasn't, she said, I keep telling you there's no such thing. Love, that sort of love, is a literary con-trick. And an advertising con-trick and a media con-trick. I don't believe that, he said. We must talk more. I'll meet you for lunch at the Plaza, where we ate yesterday.

· · ·

"So I ran away," said Robyn to Penny Black, after giving her a précis of this scene. "I phoned up the airport and found I could get back to Rummidge that morning via Heathrow on my ticket, and I took off."

"Without telling Wilcox?"

"I left a message for him at the Plaza. I couldn't face a sentimental inquest over lunch about the night before. And, you know, I was feeling frightfully guilty about missing my classes in the Department. I got back to Rummidge surprisingly early, because of the time difference. I took a taxi to the University and arrived just in time to take my second Women's Writing seminar. Swallow was very relieved to see me. The first group had given him a hard time over menstruation, I think—he was looking distinctly queasy. And I was able to take my third-year tutorial group back off Rupert Sutcliffe, to their great relief. So I went home that evening by bus quite pleased with myself. But of course, when I turned the corner of the street, there he was, waiting for me."

"Were you frightened?" Penny Black said. "Did you feel he might attack you?"

"Of course not," Robyn said. "Anyway, you can't feel really frightened of someone three inches shorter than you are."

. . .

As she approached her house, Vic got out of his car, his face white and tense. Why did you run off like that, he said. I had things to do in Rummidge, she said, rooting in her handbag for her keys. If I'd known how easy it was I'd have flown back yesterday evening, instead of staying overnight, it would have been better all round. Can I come in, he said. I suppose so, she said, if you must, but won't they be expecting you at home? Not yet, he said. I must talk to you. Alright, she said, as long as it's not about love and not about last night. You know that's what I want to talk about, he said. That's the condition, she said. Alright, he said, I suppose I have no choice.

She led him into the living-room and lit the gas fire. He looked round the room. You ought to get a woman in to clean for you, he said. I would never employ a woman to do my dirty work, she said, it's against my principles. Well a man then, he said, I believe they have male cleaners these days. I can't afford it, she said. I'll pay for it, he said, and she gave him a warning look. I like my house like it is, she said. It may look like chaos to you, but to me it's a filing system. I know exactly where everything is on the floor. A cleaning woman would tidy everything up, and then I'd be lost.

She offered to make a pot of tea, and he followed her out into the kitchen. He stared appalled at the heap of soiled dishes in the sink. Why don't you get a dishwasher, he said. Because I can't afford it, and no, you can't buy me one, she said. Anyway, I quite like washing up, it's therapeutic. You don't seem to need therapy very often, he said.

. . .

"Cheeky," Penny Black commented.

"I didn't mind," said Robyn. "I took it as a good sign, actually—that he was getting over his maudlin mood." She clambered down over the benches to splash water from a plastic bucket on the stove. Steam hissed angrily and the temperature rose a few degrees higher. She climbed back to her perch. "I tried to keep his mind off the love stuff by talking about the business side of the Frankfurt trip. But then I got a very unpleasant shock."

. . .

So when will you get this new toy of yours, then, she said, when they carried their tea back into the living-room. Oh, I should think six to nine months, he said. Could be twelve. That long, she said. It depends, he said, whether they've got something already built that's suitable or whether they have to start from scratch. I hope it won't be more than nine, he said, I have a hunch the recession has bottomed out. Business is going to pick up next year and with the new core blower coupled to the KW we'll be all set to exploit a rising market. I suppose you've got to produce more if the machine is to pay for itself, she said. Yes, he said, but there are savings on costs too. There'll be fewer breakdowns, less overtime to make up for breakdowns, and of course I'll be able to lose several men. What do you mean, lose, she said. Well, the new machine will replace half a dozen old ones, he said, so most of the operators will be redundant. But that's terrible, she said, if I'd known that, I'd never have helped you buy the wretched thing. But it stands to reason, he said, that's why you buy a CNC machine, to cut your labour costs. If I'd known it was going to cause redundancies, I'd never have had anything to do with it, she said. That's silly, he said, if you want to stay in business at all, you can't afford to be sentimental about a few men being laid off. Sentimental, she cried, look who's talking! The man whose knees go weak at the sound of Jennifer Rush, the man who believes in love at first fuck. That's different, he said, flinching at the word fuck, I'm talking about business, you don't understand. I understand that some men who have jobs today aren't going to have them this time next year, she said, thanks to you and me and Herr Winkler. Those old machines had to be renewed sooner or later, he said, they're always breaking down, and they're very tricky to operate, we're always having trouble with them, well, you know yourself . . . He faltered and stopped, seeing the expression in her face. Robyn stared at him. You don't mean to say that Danny Ram, operates one of those machines, she said. I thought you knew, he said.

. . .

"Well, you can imagine what a fool I felt," Robyn said. "After all the trouble I took back in January keeping Danny Ram's job for him, now I discovered I'd helped to lose it for him again."

"Sickening," Penny Black agreed. "How is it you didn't know?"

"I never knew exactly what job it was he had," said Robyn. "I mean, I don't know the names of all these machines, or what they do. I'm no engineer."

"Well I wouldn't brood on it," said Penny Black. "I bet Wilcox would have got rid of him anyway, as soon as your back was turned. He sounds like a real hard-nosed bastard."

"Hard-nosed and soft-centred. When he saw how upset I was he started to backtrack and pretend that it might not be necessary to lay men off after all, if things went very well, he said, they might be able to have a night shift—

imagine working at night in that place, it's bad enough in the daytime . . . but that's by the by. And then he said he would guarantee to find Danny Ram another job somewhere in the factory."

"Just to please you? At the expense of some other poor sod, presumably."

"Exactly. That's what I told him."

. . .

You're playing with people's lives as if they're things to be bought and sold and given away, she said. You're offering me Danny Ram's job as a sop, as a bribe, as a present, like other men give their mistresses strings of pearls. I don't want you to be my mistress, he said, I want you to be my wife. She gaped at him for a moment, then threw back her head and laughed. You're out of your mind, she said, have you forgotten that you're married already? I'll get a divorce, he said. I refuse to listen to any more of this, she said, I think you'd better go home, I have a lot of essays to mark. Term ends tomorrow. Listen to me, he said, my marriage has been dead for years, we have nothing in common any more, Marjorie and me. And what do you think *we* have in common, she demanded. Not a single idea, not a single value, not a single interest. Last night, he said. Oh, shut up about last night, she said. That was just a fuck, nothing more or less. I wish you wouldn't keep saying that, he said. Anybody would think it had never happened before, she said, the way you go on about it. It never did happen to me before, he said, not like that. Oh, shut up, she said, go away, go home, for God's sake. She sat up very straight in her armchair, closed her eyes, and did some yoga breathing exercises. She heard a floorboard creak as he got to his feet, and felt his presence like a shadow falling over her. When will I see you again, he said. I've no idea, she said, without opening her eyes. I don't see any reason why we should ever meet again except by accident. That ridiculous scheme is finished. I don't have to go to your ghastly factory ever again, thank God. I'll be in touch, he said, and taking advantage of her closed eyes, kissed her quickly on the lips. She was on her feet instantly, glaring at him from her full height, hissing: *Leave me alone!* All right, he said, I'm going. At the door, he turned and looked back at her. When you're angry, he said, you look like a goddess.

. . .

"A *goddess*?" Penny Black repeated wonderingly.

"That's what he said. Heaven knows what he was on about."

Penny Black shifted her weight from one massive haunch to the other, making her pendulous breasts tremble. Runnels of sweat ran down between them and vanished into the damp undergrowth at her crotch. "I must say,

Robyn, putting ideology aside for a moment . . . I mean, it's not every day of
the week a woman gets to be called a goddess."

"It's just a nuisance, as far as I'm concerned, a nuisance and an embarrassment. He keeps phoning me up, and he writes every day."

"What does he say?"

"I don't know. I put the phone down immediately and I throw the letters
away without reading them."

"Poor Vic!"

"Don't waste your pity on him—what about poor me? I can't get on with
my research."

"Poor lovesick Vic. Next thing you know, he'll be outside your house
serenading you."

"Playing his Jennifer Rush and Randy Crawford cassettes under my window." They giggled together. "No, but it isn't funny really," said Robyn.

"Does his wife know?"

"I think not," said Robyn, "But she must suspect something. And I had a
visit from his daughter today."

"His *daughter*?"

. . .

Sandra Wilcox had turned up in the Department without an appointment, but
Robyn happened to be in her room checking the proofs of a Finals paper at the
time. The girl was fashionably dressed all in black, with a mask of white make-
up, and her hair was expensively contrived to look as if she had just been elec-
trocuted. Oh, hallo Sandra, said Robyn, come in, aren't you at school today? I
had to go to the dentist's this afternoon, Sandra said. It wasn't worth going back
to school so I thought I'd drop in. Fine, said Robyn, what can I do for you? It's
not for me, it's my Dad, said Sandra. Why, what's the matter with him, said
Robyn anxiously. I mean it's my Dad who made me come, said Sandra. Oh I
see, said Robyn, with a light laugh, but she had given something away to the
girl, and it was a subtext of their conversation about the pros and cons of going
to university. Why not apply for admission in 1988, said Robyn, and take a year
off after leaving school to make up your mind? I could, I suppose, said Sandra,
I could get a job at Tweezers—I already work there Saturdays. Tweezers, Robyn
said, what's that? Unisex hairdressers, said Sandra. She looked round the room.
Have you read all these books, she said. Not all of them, Robyn said, but some
I've read several times. What for, said Sandra. You're not thinking of applying
for English, are you, Sandra, said Robyn. No, said Sandra. Good, said Robyn,

because there's a lot of re-reading in English. I thought I'd do psychology, if I did anything, said Sandra. I'm interested in the way people's minds work. I'm not sure psychology will help you there, said Robyn, it's mostly about rats as far as I can make out. You'd probably learn more about how people's minds work by reading novels. Like my parents, said Sandra. I'd love to know what makes them tick. My Dad is acting most peculiar, lately. Is he, said Robyn, in what way? He doesn't listen to a word anyone says to him, said Sandra, he goes about in a dream. He banged into another car the other day. Oh dear, I hope he wasn't hurt, said Robyn. No, it was just a bump, but it's the first accident he's ever had in twenty-five years' driving. Mum's worried about him, I can tell, her Valium consumption's gone up. Does your mother take Valium regularly? said Robyn. Does she, said Sandra, pick her up and shake her and she rattles. And now he's reading books, novels, he never did that in his life before. What kind of novels? said Robyn. My school copy of *Jane Eyre* for one, said Sandra, we're doing it for A-Level. I was looking for it everywhere the other day, it made me late for school. Eventually I found it under a cushion on his armchair in the lounge. What's he want with *Jane Eyre* at his age?

. . .

"He's obviously trying to study your interests," said Penny Black. "It's rather touching, in a way."

"Touched, you mean," said Robyn. "What shall I do? Next thing you know, I'll have Mrs. Wilcox in my office, stoned on Valium, begging me not to entice her husband away from her. I feel as if I'm getting dragged into a classic realist text, full of causality and morality. How can I get out of it?"

"I've had enough," said Penny Black, getting to her feet.

"I'm sorry, Penny," said Robyn, contritely.

"I mean, I've had enough of this heat. I'm going to shower."

"I'll come too." said Robyn. "But what shall I do?"

"You'd better run away again," said Penny Black.

4

So Robyn piled her books and her notes and her BBC micro in the back of the Renault, and locked up her little house and went to spend the remainder of the Easter vacation with her parents in their house with a view of the sea on the South Coast. She instructed Pamela, the Department Secretary, not to divulge her whereabouts to anybody except in the direst emergency, explaining that she wanted to get on with her research free from any distraction. She gave the same reason to her somewhat puzzled parents for descending upon them so abruptly and for so extended a visit. Her old bedroom was much as she had left it on going up to the University; the photos of David Bowie and The Who and Pink Floyd had been taken off the walls, and the wallpaper renewed, but the woodwork was still painted the rather violent pink she had chosen in late adolescence. She set up her word-processor on the scratched and stained desk where she had swotted for her A-Levels, under the window from which, when you looked up from your work, you could see the horizon of the English Channel ruled like a faint blue line between the roofs of two neighbouring houses.

She spent most of her time in this room, but when she went out into the town to shop, or just to stretch her legs, she couldn't help reflecting that although she was only a hundred and fifty miles from Rummidge, she might as well have been in another country. There was no visible industry here, and no visible working class. Black and brown faces were rare, mostly belonging to students from the University, or to tourists who came in motor coaches to stare at the fine old cathedral set serenely among green lawns and venerable trees. The shops were small, specialised, and served by suavely deferential staff. The customers seemed all to be wearing brand-new clothes from Jaeger and to be driving brand-new Volvos. The streets and gardens were well-groomed, the air soft and clean, smelling faintly of the sea. Robyn thought of Rummidge sprawled darkly and densely in the heart of England, with all its noise and fumes and ugliness, its blind-walled metal-bashing factories and its long, worm-like streets of tiny terraced houses crawling over the hills, its congested motorways and black canals, its hideous concrete core, awash with litter and defaced with graffiti, and she wondered whether it was by luck or cunning that the English bourgeoisie had kept the industrial revolution out of their favourite territory.

"You don't know what the real world is like down here," she told her parents at supper one day.

"Oh, but we do," said her father. "That's why we chose to stay. I could have had the Chair at Liverpool years ago. I went up there and walked about the streets for a morning, and I told the Vice-Chancellor, thanks very much, but I'd rather be a Reader all my life than move up here."

"I don't suppose you'll be sorry to leave Rummidge, will you dear?" said her mother.

"I shall be extremely sorry," said Robyn. "Especially if I can't get another job."

"If only something would turn up here," her mother sighed. "Your father could use his influence."

"On the contrary," said Professor Penrose, "I should have to declare my interest and have nothing to do with the appointment." Professor Penrose always spoke in a formal and deliberate manner, in an effort, Robyn sometimes thought, to disguise his Australian origins. "But the problem will not arise, I'm afraid. We're suffering the same cuts as everywhere else. There are no prospects of any new posts in the Arts Faculty, unless our UGC letter is very much better than expected."

"What letter is that?" Robyn asked.

"The UGC is going to announce, probably some time in May, the distribution of the available funds to each university, based on an assessment of their research record and the viability of their departments. There are rumours that one or two universities will be closed down completely."

"They wouldn't dare!" Robyn exclaimed.

"This Government is capable of anything," said Professor Penrose, who was a member of the SDP. "They are systematically destroying the finest university system in the world. Whatever happened to the spirit of the Robbins Report? Higher education for everyone who could benefit. Did I ever tell you," he said, smiling reminiscently at his daughter, "that someone once asked me if we called you Robyn after the Robbins report?"

"Many times, Daddy," said Robyn. "Needless to say I deplore the cuts, but don't you think, in retrospect, that the way Robbins was implemented was a mistake?"

Professor Penrose laid down his knife and fork and looked at Robyn over his spectacles. "What do you mean?"

"Well, was it a good idea to build so many new universities in parks on the outskirts of cathedral cities and county towns?"

"But why shouldn't universities be in nice places rather than nasty ones?" said Mrs. Penrose plaintively.

"Because it perpetuates the Oxbridge idea of higher education as a version of pastoral, a privileged idyll cut off from ordinary living."

"Nonsense," said Professor Penrose. "The new universities were carefully sited in places that, for one reason or another, had been left out of the development of higher education."

"That would make sense if they served their own communities, but they don't. Every autumn there's this absurd migration of well-heeled youth going from Norwich to Brighton or from Brighton to York. And having to be accommodated in expensive halls of residence when they get there."

"You seem to have acquired a very utilitarian view of universities, from your sojourn in Rummidge," said Professor Penrose, who was one of the very few people Robyn knew who used the word sojourn in casual conversation. Robyn made no answer. She was well aware that she had adopted some of the arguments of Vic Wilcox, but she had no intention of mentioning him to her parents.

When they were washing up, Mrs. Penrose asked Robyn if she would like to invite Charles down for the weekend.

"We're not seeing each other at the moment," she said.

"Oh dear, is it off again?"

"Is what off?"

"You know what I mean, dear."

"There was never anything 'on,' Mummy, if you mean, as I presume, getting married."

"I don't understand you young people," Mrs. Penrose sighed unhappily. "Charles is such a nice young man, and you have such a lot in common."

"Perhaps too much," said Robyn.

"What do you mean?"

"I don't know," said Robyn, who had spoken without premeditation. "It's just a bit boring when you agree about everything."

"Basil brought a most unsuitable girl down here," said Mrs. Penrose. "I do hope he doesn't intend to marry her."

"Debbie? When was that?"

"Oh, some time in February. You've met her, then?"

"Yes. I believe it's all off, as you would say."

"Oh, good, she was a frightfully common little thing, I thought." Robyn smiled secretly.

. . .

Basil himself confirmed Robyn's speculation when he came home for the Easter weekend. He was loudly pleased with himself, having just moved to a new job with a Japanese bank in the City at a greatly increased salary. "No, I'm not seeing Debbie any more," he said, "socially or professionally. Is Charles?"

"I don't know," said Robyn. "I'm incommunicado at the moment, trying to finish my book."

"What book is that?"

"It's on the image of women in nineteenth-century fiction."

"Does the world really need another book on nineteenth-century fiction?" said Basil.

"I don't know, but it's going to get one," said Robyn. "It's my chief hope of getting a permanent job somewhere."

When Basil went back to London on Easter Monday evening, peace and quiet returned to the house, and Robyn resumed work on her book. She made excellent progress. It was a house that respected scholarship. No radios played. The telephone bell was muted. The cleaning lady's vacuuming was strictly controlled. Professor Penrose worked in his study and Robyn worked in her bedroom, and Mrs. Penrose padded quietly to and fro between the two of them, bringing coffee and tea at appropriate intervals, silently setting the fresh cups down on their desks, and removing the soiled ones. To minimise distraction, Robyn denied herself her daily fix of the *Guardian*, and only the occasional late news on television brought her tidings of events in the great world: the American raid on Libya, riots in British prisons, violent confrontations between striking printers and police at Wapping. These public outrages and conflicts, which would normally have stirred her to indignation and perhaps action (signing a petition, joining a demonstration), hardly penetrated her absorbed concentration on the book. By the end of the vacation, it was three-quarters written in draft.

She drove back to Rummidge in buoyant mood. She felt pleased with what she had written, though she hankered for confirmation from some other person, some kindred spirit, some knowledgeable but sympathetic reader, someone like Charles. They had always relied on each other for such help. It was a pity, in the circumstances, that they were not seeing each other any more. Of course, nothing decisive or final had been said. There was no reason why she shouldn't ring him up when she got home, and ask if he would read her draft, no reason at all. It would not even be necessary to meet, though obviously it would be more convenient if he could come over for a weekend and read the manuscript there and then. Robyn decided she would phone Charles that evening.

When she got back to her house in Rummidge, there was a letter from Charles on the doormat, along with nine from Vic Wilcox which she threw straight into the waste-bin. She opened Charles' letter, which was quite bulky, at once, and read it standing in the kitchen with her outdoor coat still on. Then she took off her coat and made a cup of tea and sat down and read it again.

. . .

My dear Robyn,

I've tried to phone you several times without success, and the Secretary of your Department refuses for some reason to admit that she knows where you are, so I am writing to you—which is probably the best thing to do, anyway, in the circumstances. The telephone is an unsatisfactory medium for communicating anything important, allowing neither the genuine absence of writing nor the true presence of face-to-face conversation, but only a feeble compromise. A thesis topic there, perhaps? "Telephonic communication and affective alienation in modern fiction, with special reference to Evelyn Waugh, Ford Madox Ford, Henry Green . . ."

But I've finished with thesis topics. What I have to tell you is that I have determined upon a change of career. I'm going to become a merchant banker.

"Have you done laughing?" as Alton Locke says to his readers. I am of course rather old to be making such a change, but I feel quite confident that I can make a success of it and I'm very excited by the challenge. I think it's the first *risky* thing I've ever done in my life, and I feel a new man in consequence. I've got to undergo a period of training, of course, but even so I shall start at a higher salary than my present one, and after that, well, the sky's the limit. It's not just the money, though, that has led me to this decision, though I *am* rather fed up with the constant struggle to make ends meet, but a feeling that, as a university teacher, especially at a place like Suffolk, I've been left behind by the tide of history, stranded on the mudflats of an obsolete ideology.

You and I, Robyn, grew up in a period when the state was smart: state schools, state universities, state-subsidised arts, state welfare, state medicine—these were things progressive, energetic people believed in. It isn't like that any more. The Left pays lip-service to those things, but without convincing anybody, including themselves. The people who work in state institutions are depressed, demoralised, fatalistic. Witness the extraordinary meekness with which the academic establishment has accepted the cuts (has there been a single high-level resignation, as distinct from early retirements?). It's no use blaming Thatcher, as if she was some kind of witch who has enchanted the nation. She is riding the *Zeitgeist*. When trade unions offer their members discount subscriptions to BUPA, the writing is on the wall for old-style socialism. What the new style will be, I don't know, but I believe there is more chance of identifying it from the vantage-point of the City than from the University of Suffolk. The first thing that struck me about the City when I started observing Debbie at work was the sheer *energy* of the place, and the second was its democracy. A working-class girl like Debbie pulling down thirty-thousand-odd a year is by no means an anomalous figure. Contrary to the stereotype of the ex-public-school stockbroker, it doesn't matter what your social background is in the City these days, as long as you're good at your job. Money is a great leveller, upwards.

As to our universities, I've come to the conclusion that they are élitist where they should be egalitarian and egalitarian where they should be élitist. We admit only a tiny proportion of the age group as students and give them a very labour-intensive education (élitist), but we pretend that all universities and all university teachers are equal and must therefore have the same funding and a common payscale, with automatic tenure (egalitarian). This worked all right as long as the country was prepared to go on pumping more and more money into the system, but as soon as the money supply was reduced, universities could only balance their books by persuading people to retire early, often the very people they can least afford to lose. For those who remain the prospects are bleak: bigger classes, heavier work-loads, scant chances of promotion or of moving to a new job. You know as well as I do that, apart from the occasional chair, new appointments are always made, if they're made at all, at the bottom of the scale. I reckon I would be stuck in Suffolk for another fifteen years, possibly for ever, if I stayed in academic life. I don't think I could face that.

The opportunity to change direction came, curiously enough, from my developing these thoughts, or something like them, in the company of a big wheel in Debbie's bank, at a party she took me to. I began rather fancifully to propose the idea of privatising the universities, as a solution to their financial crisis, and as a way of promoting healthy competition. Staff could buy shares in their own universities and have a financial stake in their success. I was only half serious, in fact I was half pissed, but the big wheel was rather impressed. We need men with bold ideas like that, he said, to spot new investment opportunities. That's what started me thinking about a change of career. When I went to see the big wheel a few days later, he was very encouraging. He wants to set up a kind of strategic planning team within the bank, and the idea is that I will join it when I've acquired some basic experience in securities etc. I have to admit, in spite of the stuff about democracy above, that it helped that I was at Westminster, because his son is there. Also that I had Maths to A-Level.

But, you will ask, what about the ideas to which we have dedicated our lives for the last ten years, what about critical theory and all that? Well, I see no fundamental inconsistency. I regard myself as simply exchanging one semiotic system for another, the literary for the numerical, a game with high philosophical stakes for a game with high monetary stakes—but a *game* in each case, in which satisfaction comes ultimately from playing rather than winning, since there are no absolute winners, for the game never ends. Anyway, I have no intention of giving up reading. I don't see why deconstruction shouldn't be my hobby as other men have model railways or tropical fish as hobbies, and it will be easier to pursue without the anxiety of integrating it into one's work.

To be honest, I have had my doubts for some time about the pedagogic application of poststructuralist theory, doubts that I've suppressed, as a priest, I imagine, suppresses his theological doubts, hiding them away one by one until one day there is no space left in which to hide them and he finally admits to himself and to the world that he has lost his faith. There was a moment when we were talking in your house a couple of months ago, and you were putting the case against teaching poststructuralism as a kind of Devil's Advocate—do you remember? You wanted reassurance—your factory manager friend had got you rattled—so I told you what you wanted to hear, but it was a close thing. You were articulating so many of my own doubts that I nearly "came out" there and then.

Poststructuralist theory is a very intriguing philosophical game for very clever players. But the irony of teaching it to young people who have read almost nothing except their GCE set texts and *Adrian Mole*, who know almost nothing about the Bible or classical mythology, who cannot recognise an ill-formed sentence, or recite poetry with any sense of rhythm—the irony of teaching them about the arbitrariness of the signifier in week three of their first year becomes in the end too painful to bear . . .

So, I've resigned from Suffolk—taken severance, actually, they're desperate to lose staff, so I have a nice lump sum of £30,000 which I confidently expect to enhance by at least 25 per cent in the equity market by the end of the year. I'm moving in with Debbie, so living expenses will be modest. I hope you and I can still be friends. I shall always think of you with the greatest admiration and affection. Good luck in the future—if anyone deserves a tenured university job, it's you, Robyn.

Love, Charles

"You shit," Robyn said aloud, when she had finished reading the letter. "You utter shit." But the "utter" was a hyperbole. There were things in this letter which struck a nerve of reluctant assent, mixed up with things she found false and obnoxious. 'Twas all a muddle.

. . .

Meanwhile, Vic Wilcox was having a hard time, nursing his unrequited love. The weekdays were not so bad, when he could distract himself with work. He pushed on faster than ever with the rationalisation programme at Pringle's, harried his managers mercilessly, chaired endless meetings, doubled the frequency of his surprise swoops on the shop floor. You could almost hear the effect of all this pressure when you pushed through the door into the machine shop: more decibels clashing to a brisker rhythm. In the foundry, they started clearing a space for the new core blower, and Vic made this the occasion for a full-scale good housekeeping campaign. Under his personal supervision, the debris of years was swept away.

But there was a limit to the number of hours even Vic could work. There were still too many left over—driving to and from work, at home in the evenings and at weekends, and, above all, lying awake in the early morning in the darkened bedroom—when he couldn't keep his thoughts from Robyn Penrose and their night of love (for so he persisted in regarding it). There is no need to record these thoughts in detail. They were for the most part repetitive and predictable: a mixture of erotic fantasy and erotic reminiscence, wish-fulfilment and self-pity, accompanied by snatches of Jennifer Rush. But they made him more than usually silent and abstracted around the house. He was subject to fits of absent-mindedness. In the kitchen he washed up cups that had just been cleaned and dried. He would go to the garage for a tool and, when he got there, would have forgotten what he wanted it for. One morning he drove halfway to West Wallsbury, dimly registering that the traffic was unusually light, before he remembered that it was a Sunday morning and he was supposed to be picking up his father. One evening he went upstairs to change his trousers and proceeded mechanically to take off all his clothes and put on his pyjamas. It was only when he was about to get into bed that he snapped out of his reverie. Marjorie came into the room at this moment and stared at him. "What are you doing?" she said.

"I'm having an early night," he improvised, turning back the bedclothes.

"But it's only half-past eight!"

"I'm tired."

"You must be ill. Shall I call the doctor?"

"No, I'm just tired." He got into bed and closed his eyes to shut out Marjorie's worried frown.

"Vic, is there anything wrong?" she said. "Any trouble at work?"

"No," he said. "Work is fine. The factory is on song. We'll make a profit this month."

"Well, what's the matter then? You're not yourself. You've not been yourself since you went to Germany. D'you think you caught a bug or something?"

"No," said Vic. "I haven't got a bug." He had not told Marjorie that Robyn had accompanied him to Frankfurt.

"I'll get you an aspirin."

Vic heard her moving about the room, drawing the curtains, and telling Raymond to turn down his hi-fi because his father wasn't feeling well. To save a lot of argument, he swallowed the aspirin and, shortly afterwards, fell asleep. At three in the morning he was wide awake. With hours to go before the alarm, he played blue movies in his head featuring himself and Robyn Penrose, and crept guiltily to the *en suite* bathroom to seek a schoolboy's relief.

. . .

"Marjorie's worried about you," his father said the following Sunday evening, when Vic was driving him home after tea.

Vic feigned surprise. "Why?"

"She says you're not yourself. No more you are."

"I'm fine," said Vic. "When was this?"

"This afternoon, when you was out. What d'you want to go off on your own like that for?"

"You were asleep, Dad," he said. "And Marjorie doesn't like walking."

"You could've asked her."

Vic drove in silence.

"It isn't a wench, is it?" said his father.

"What?" Vic forced an incredulous laugh.

"You're not carryin' on with some young wench, are you? I seen it happen enough times," he went on rapidly, as if he feared having his question answered. "Bosses and their secretaries. It always gets round at work."

"My secretary is a pain in the arse," said Vic. "Anyway, she's made other arrangements."

"I'm glad to hear it. The game's not worth the candle, son, take my word for it. I seen it happen many a time, blokes that left their wives for a young wench. They ended up penniless, paying for two families out of one pay packet. Lost their homes, lost their furniture. Wives took it all. Think of that, Vic, next time some flighty piece makes eyes at you."

This time Vic did not have to force his guffaw.

"You can laugh," said Mr. Wilcox huffily, "but you wouldn't be the first one what's made a fool of himself for a pretty face or a trim figure. It don't last though. It don't last."

"Not like furniture?"

"Definitely."

This conversation, absurd as it was, had the effect of putting Vic on his guard. He wrote his letters to Robyn at work, in the lunch break when Shirley was out of the office, and posted them himself. He telephoned her from callboxes on the way to and from work. Not that these efforts to communicate succeeded, but they relieved his pent-up feelings somewhat, and his secret remained safe.

Marjorie, though, was plainly disturbed. Her shopping developed a manic intensity. She brought home a new dress or pair of shoes every day, and as often as not exchanged them the next. She had her hair done in a new style and wept for hours at the result. She started a diet that consisted entirely of grapefruit and abandoned it after three days. She bought an exercise bicycle and could be heard puffing and wheezing behind the door of the guest bedroom where it had been erected. She rented a sunbed from the Riviera Sunbed company, who delivered and collected at home, and lay under it in a two-piece swimsuit and dark glasses, anxiously gripping a kitchen timer in case the built-in time switch failed, in mortal terror of overcooking herself. Vic realized that she was doing all this to make herself attractive to him, probably following the advice of some trashy woman's magazine. He was touched, but in a distant, detached way. Marjorie looked at him from the far side of his obsession, with dumb affection and concern, like a dog on the hearth. He felt as if he had only to stretch out his hand and she would jump all over him, licking his face. But he could not do it. Awake in the early hours of the morning, he no longer sought the animal comfort of her body's warmth. He lay on the edge of the mattress, as far as possible from the humped, Valium-drugged shape that groaned and whimpered in its sleep, wondering how to get back in touch with Robyn Penrose.

PART VI

The story is told. I think I now see the judicious reader putting on his spectacles to look for the moral. It would be an insult to his sagacity to offer directions. I only say, God speed him in the quest!

CHARLOTTE BRONTË: *Shirley*

1

The new term began with a spell of fine weather. Students disported themselves on the lawns of the campus, the young girls in their bright summer dresses sprouting like crocuses in the warm sunshine. There were laughter and music in the air, and dalliance under the trees. Some tutors elected to hold their classes outdoors, and sat cross-legged on the grass, discoursing on philosophy or physics to little groups of reclining ephebes, as they did in the Golden Age. But this idyllic appearance was deceptive. The students were apprehensive about their forthcoming examinations, and the world of uncertain employment that lay beyond that threshold. The staff were apprehensive about the forthcoming UGC letter, and its implications for their future. For Robyn, though, the letter was her last hope of a reprieve. If Rummidge, and more particularly its English Department, received strong support from the University Grants Committee, there was just a chance, Philip Swallow told her, a sliver of a chance, that when Rupert Sutcliffe retired the following year (not an early retirement—on the contrary, Swallow tartly observed, it was if anything overdue), they would be allowed to fill the vacancy.

Because she had worked on her book up till the last moment of the vacation, Robyn was less well prepared than usual for her teaching, and the first week was hectic. She was obliged to sit up late each night, urgently refreshing her memory of *Vanity Fair* and *The Picture of Dorian Gray* and *The Rainbow* and "The Waste Land" and *1984*, texts on which she had rashly committed herself to giving tutorials all in the same week, not to mention revising a lecture on Virginia Woolf and reading Dorothy Richardson's *Pointed Roofs* for the first time in her life for her Women's Writing seminars. This gruelling work-load made it easier, however, to forget Charles and his apostasy. As to Vic Wilcox, her abrupt flight from Rummidge a month before seemed to have had the desired effect, for he no longer pestered her by letter or telephone. Robyn suddenly found herself liberated from the attentions of the two men who had laid claim to her affective life in the recent and long-term past. She was her own woman once more. If this consciousness did not kindle the glow of satisfaction that might have been expected—if, perversely, she felt a little lonely and neglected by the end of the week—this was no doubt because she had been overworking.

Saturday offered a welcome social diversion. A friend of Philip Swallow's, Professor Morris Zapp, had touched down briefly in Rummidge on his way from the West Coast of the United States to somewhere else, and the Swallows were giving a party for him to which Robyn was invited. She was familiar with his publications: originally a Jane Austen specialist in the Neo-Critical close-reading tradition, he had converted himself (rather opportunistically, Robyn thought) into a kind of deconstructionist in the nineteen-seventies, and enjoyed an international reputation in both guises. He was also something of a local legend at Rummidge, having steered the Department safely through the student revolution of '69, when he had exchanged posts with Philip Swallow. The two men had swapped more than their jobs, according to Rupert Sutcliffe, who whispered to Robyn that there had been an affair between Zapp and Hilary Swallow at the same time that Swallow was carrying on with Zapp's then wife Désirée, subsequently famous as the author of *Difficult Days* and *Men*, big best-selling books written in a mode Robyn sometimes called "vulgar feminism." She was curious to meet Professor Zapp.

Robyn arrived a little late at the Swallows' modernised Victorian villa, and their living-room was already crowded, but she had no difficulty in identifying the guest of honour as she glanced through the window on her way up the garden path to the front porch. He was wearing a seersucker jacket in canary yellow with a bold blue check, and was smoking a cigar the size of a small zeppelin. He was bulky rather than big, with grizzled, receding hair, a wrinkled, sun-tanned face, and a grey moustache that drooped downwards at each end rather lugubriously, perhaps because at that moment he was having his ear bent by Bob Busby.

Philip Swallow opened the door to Robyn and ushered her into the living-room. "Let me introduce you to Morris," he said. "He needs rescuing."

Robyn obediently followed Swallow as he pushed his way through the throng and nudged Bob Busby away from Morris Zapp with a light shoulder-charge. "Morris," he said, "this is Robyn Penrose, the girl I was telling you about."

"Girl, Philip? Girl? Men have been castrated for less at Euphoric State. You mean woman. Or lady. Which do you prefer?" he said to Robyn, as he shook her hand.

"Person would be fine," said Robyn.

"Person, right. Are you going to get this person a drink, Philip?"

"Yes, of course," said Swallow, looking flustered. "Red or white?"

"Why don't you get her a proper drink?" said Zapp, who appeared to have a tumbler of neat scotch in his fist.

"Well, er, of course, if . . ." Swallow looked even more flustered.

"White will be fine," said Robyn.

"I always know when I'm in England," said Morris Zapp, as Philip Swallow went off, "because when you go to a party, the first thing anyone says to you is, 'Red or white?' I used to think it was some kind of password, like the Wars of the Roses were still going on or something."

"Are you here for long?" Robyn asked.

"I'm going to Dubrovnik tomorrow. Ever been there?"

"No," said Robyn.

"Neither have I. I'm breaking a rule: never attend a conference in a Communist country."

"Isn't that a rather bigoted rule?" Robyn said.

"There's nothing political about it, it's just that I've heard such terrible things about East European hotels. But they tell me Yugoslavia is half-Westernised, so I thought, what the hell, I'll risk it."

"It seems a long way to travel for a conference."

"There's more than one. After Dubrovnik I go to Vienna, Geneva, Nice and Milan. Milan is a private visit," he said, brushing the ends of his moustache upwards with the back of his hand. "Looking up an old friend. But the rest are conferences. You been to any good ones lately?"

"No, I'm afraid I missed the UTE conference this year."

"If that's the one I attended here in '79, then you did well to avoid it," said Morris Zapp. "I mean real conferences, international conferences."

"I couldn't afford to go to one of those," said Robyn. "Our overseas conference fund has been cut to the bone."

"Cuts, cuts, cuts," said Morris Zapp, "that's all anyone will talk about here. First Philip, then Busby, now you."

"That's what life is like in British universities these days, Morris," said Philip Swallow, presenting Robyn with a glass of rather warm Soave. "I spend all my time on committees arguing about how to respond to the cuts. I haven't read a book in months, let alone tried to write one."

"Well, I have," said Robyn.

"Read one or written one?" said Morris Zapp.

"Written one," said Robyn. "Well, three-quarters of it, anyway."

"Ah, Robyn," said Philip Swallow, "you put us all to shame. What shall we do without you?" He shuffled off, shaking his head.

"You leaving Rummidge, Robyn?" said Morris Zapp.

She explained her position. "So you see," she concluded, "this book is very important to me. If by any chance there should be a job advertised in the next twelve months, I ought to stand a fair chance of getting it, with two books to my credit."

"You're right," said Morris Zapp. "There are full professors at large in this country who have published less." His eye strayed in the direction of Philip Swallow. "What's your book about?"

Robyn told him. Morris Zapp vivaed her briskly about its contents and methodology. The names of prominent feminist critics and theorists crackled between them like machinegun fire: Elaine Showalter, Sandra Gilbert, Susan Gubar, Shoshana Felman, Luce Irigaray, Catherine Clement, Susan Suleiman, Mieke Bal—Morris Zapp had read them all. He recommended an article in the latest issue of *Poetics Today* which she hadn't seen. Finally he asked her if she had made arrangements to publish her book in America.

"No, my British publishers distributed my first book in the States themselves—the one on the industrial novel. I suppose the same will happen with this one."

"Who are they?"

"Lecky, Windrush and Bernstein."

Morris Zapp pulled a face. "They're terrible. Didn't Philip tell you what they did to him? Lost all his review copies. Sent them out a year late."

"Oh, dear," said Robyn.

"How many did you sell in America?"

"I don't know. Not many."

"I'm a reader for Euphoric State University Press," said Morris Zapp. "Send me your manuscript and I'll have a look at it."

"That's extremely kind of you," said Robyn, "but I already have a contract with Lecky, Windrush and Bernstein."

"If Euphoric State make an offer for the American rights, it would be in their interest to go along with it," said Morris Zapp. "They could sell them the camera-ready copy. Of course, I may not like it. But you look like a smart girl to me."

"Person."

"Person, sorry."

"How shall I get the manuscript to you?"

"Could you drop it here tomorrow morning before eight-thirty?" said Morris Zapp. "I'm catching the 9:45 shuttle to Heathrow."

Robyn left the party early. Philip Swallow intercepted her as she wormed her way through the crowded hall on her way to the front door. "Oh, leaving so soon?" he said.

"Professor Zapp has kindly offered to look at my work-in-progress. It's still on floppy discs, so I'm going home to print it out."

"What a pity, you should have brought him," said Philip Swallow.

"Who?"

"That young man of yours from Suffolk."

"Oh, Charles! I'm not seeing Charles any more. He's become a merchant banker."

"*Has* he? How very interesting." Philip Swallow swayed slightly on his feet, whether from inebriation or fatigue she couldn't tell, and supported himself against the wall with a locked arm, which had the effect of barring her progress. Over his shoulder Robyn saw Mrs. Swallow regarding them suspiciously. "Isn't it extraordinary how interesting money has become lately? Do you know, I've suddenly started reading the business pages in the *Guardian* after thirty years of skipping straight from the arts pages to the sports reports."

"I can't say it interests me much," said Robyn, ducking under Swallow's arm. "I must go, I'm afraid."

"I suppose it started when I bought some British Telecom shares," said Swallow, swivelling on his heel and following her to the front door. "Do you know, they're worth twice what I paid for them now?"

"Congratulations," said Robyn. "How much profit have you made?"

"Two hundred pounds," said Swallow. "I wish I'd bought more, now. I'm wondering whether to apply for British Gas. D'you think your young man would advise me?"

"He's not my young man," said Robyn. "Why don't you write and ask him?"

. . .

Robyn sat up all night printing out her book. She considered the effort would be worthwhile if she could secure the endorsement of a prestigious imprint like Euphoric State University Press. Besides, there was something about Morris Zapp that inspired hope. He had blown into the jaded, demoralised atmosphere of Rummidge University like an invigorating breeze, intimating that there were still places in the world where scholars and critics pursued their professional goals with zestful confidence, where conferences multiplied and grants were to be had to attend them, where conversation at academic parties was more likely to be about the latest controversial book or article than about the latest scaling-down of departmental maintenance grants. She felt renewed faith in her book, and her vocation, as she crouched, yawning and red-eyed, over her computer.

Even at draft speed, it took a long time to spew out her sixty thousand words, and it was nearly eight-fifteen in the morning when she finished the task. She drove quickly through the deserted Sunday streets to deliver her manuscript. It was a bright sunny morning, with a strong wind that was stripping the cherry-blossom from the trees. A taxi trembled at the kerb outside the Swallows' house. In the front porch Hilary Swallow, in a dressing-gown, was saying goodbye to Morris Zapp, while Philip, carrying Morris Zapp's suitcase, hovered anxiously halfway down the garden path, like a complaisant cuckold seeing off the lover of the night before. But whatever passion there might have been between Zapp and Mrs. Swallow had cooled long ago, Robyn inferred, from the merely amicable way they brushed each other's cheeks. Indeed, it was difficult to imagine these three almost elderly figures being involved in a sexual intrigue at all.

"Come on, Morris!" Swallow called out. "Your taxi's waiting." Then he swung round and caught sight of Robyn. "Good Lord—Robyn! What are you doing here at this hour of the morning?"

As she was explaining all over again, Morris Zapp came waddling down the garden path, an open Burberry flapping round his knees. "Hiya Robyn, howya doin'?" He drew a cigar like a long-barrelled weapon from an inside pocket and clamped it between his teeth.

"Here's the manuscript."

"Great, I'll read it as soon as I can." He lit his cigar, shielding the flame against the wind.

"It's unfinished, as I told you. And unrevised."

"Sure, sure," said Morris Zapp. "I'll let you know what I think. If I like it, I'll call you, if I don't I'll mail it back. Is your phone number on the manuscript?"

"No," said Robyn, "I'll give it to you."

"Do that. Haven't you noticed that in the modern world good news comes by telephone and bad news by mail?"

"Now that you mention it," said Robyn, scribbling her phone number on the outside of the package.

"Morris, the taxi," said Philip Swallow.

"Relax, Philip, he's not going to run away—are you, driver?"

"No sir," said the taxi-driver, from behind his wheel, "it's all the same to me."

"There you are," said Morris Zapp, stuffing Robyn's manuscript into a briefcase bulging with books and periodicals.

"I mean, the meter is ticking over."

"So what?"

"I'm afraid I've become a bit obsessive about waste since becoming Dean," Philip Swallow sighed. "I can't help it."

"Well, hang in there, Philip," said Morris Zapp. "Or as you Brits say, keep your pecker up." He wheezed with laughter and coughed cigar smoke. "You should come back to Euphoric State for a visit some time. It would do you good to watch us spending money."

"Are you going to stay there till you retire?" said Philip Swallow.

"Retire? I hate the sound of that word," said Morris Zapp. "Anyway they've just discovered that compulsory retirement is unconstitutional, it's a form of ageism. And why should I move? I have a contract with Euphoric State that says nobody in the humanities is to be paid more than me. If they want to hire some hotshot from one of the Ivy League schools at an inflated salary, they have to pay me at least one thousand dollars more than he's getting."

"Why restrict it to the humanities, Morris?" said Swallow.

"You have to be realistic," said Zapp. "Guys that can cure cancer, or blow up the world, deserve a little more than us literary critics."

"I've never heard such modesty from your lips before," said Swallow.

"Ah well, we all mellow as we get older," said Morris Zapp, clambering into the cab. "*Ciao*, folks."

Blossom swirled in the road like confetti as the taxi drew away. They stood on the edge of the pavement and waved until the car turned the corner.

"He's fun, isn't he?" said Robyn.

"He's a rogue," said Philip Swallow. "An amiable rogue. I'm surprised that he wanted to see your book."

"Why?"

"He can't stand feminists, usually. They've given him such a rough time in the past, at conferences and in reviews."

"He seemed well up in the literature."

"Oh, Morris is always well up, you have to grant him that. I wonder what his game is, though . . ."

"You don't think he would plagiarise my book, do you?" said Robyn, who had heard of such things happening.

"I shouldn't think so," said Philip Swallow. "He'd find it rather difficult to pass off a piece of feminist criticism as his own work. Will you come in for a cup of coffee?"

"Thanks, but I've been up all night, printing off my book. All I want to do at this moment is fall into bed."

"As you wish," said Philip Swallow, walking her to her car. "How are you getting on with your report, by the way?"

"Report?"

"On the Shadow Scheme."

"Oh, that. I'm a bit behind with that, actually," said Robyn. "I've been working flat out on my book, you see."

"Yes," said Philip Swallow, "I suppose you might as well leave it until after the next stage, now."

. . .

Robyn didn't understand this remark of Philip Swallow's, but she attributed the obscurity of its reference to his deafness, and was too tired at the time to try and sort it out. She went home and slept until late afternoon, and when she woke she had forgotten all about the matter. It wasn't until she arrived at the University the following morning, and saw Vic Wilcox talking to Philip Swallow on the crowded landing outside the English Department office, that she remembered it again, with instant misgivings. Vic, standing with his hands clasped behind his back in his dark business suit and polished black leather shoes, with the students in their bright loose clothes swirling and fluttering round him, looked like a crow that had strayed into an aviary for exotic birds. Even Philip Swallow, dressed in a crumpled beige linen jacket and scuffed Hush Puppies, looked dashingly casual in comparison. Swallow, spotting Robyn, beckoned.

"Ah, there you are," he said. "I discovered your shadow outside your door, 'alone and palely loitering.' Apparently he's been here since nine o'clock."

"Hallo, Robyn," said Vic.

Robyn ignored him. "What do you mean, *my* shadow?" she said to Swallow.

"Ah, that explains it," he said, nodding.

"What do you mean, my shadow?" Robyn repeated, raising her voice against the surrounding babble.

"Yes, the second stage of the Shadow Scheme. We talked about it yesterday."

"I didn't know what you were referring to," said Robyn. "And I still don't," she added, though she could now have made a good guess.

Philip Swallow looked helplessly from one to the other. "But I thought Mr. Wilcox . . ."

"I wrote to you about it," Vic said to Robyn, with a hint of smugness.

"The letter must have gone astray," said Robyn. Across the landing, beside the Third Year noticeboard, she saw Marion Russell staring at them, as if she was trying to place Vic Wilcox.

"Oh dear," said Swallow. "So you weren't expecting Mr. Wilcox this morning?"

"No," said Robyn, "I wasn't expecting him any morning."

"Well," said Swallow, "in the vacation—I think you were away at the time—Mr. Wilcox wrote to the VC suggesting a follow-up to the Shadow Scheme. It seems that he was so impressed by the experiment"—Swallow exposed his tombstone teeth to Vic in a complacent smile—"that he thought it should be continued, in reverse so to speak."

"Yes, me shadowing you, for a change," said Vic. "After all, if the idea is to improve relations between industry and the University, it should be a two-way process. We in industry," he said piously, "have a lot to learn too."

"No way," said Robyn.

"Jolly good," said Swallow, rubbing his hands.

"I said I WON'T DO IT," Robyn shouted.

"Why not?" Philip Swallow looked worried.

"Mr. Wilcox knows," said Robyn.

"No I don't," said Vic.

"It's not fair on the students, with the examinations coming up. He'd have to sit in on my classes."

"I'd just be a fly on the wall," said Vic, "I wouldn't interfere."

"I really don't think the students would object, Robyn," said Philip Swallow. "And it's only one day a week."

"One day a week?" said Robyn. "I'm surprised Mr. Wilcox can spare a whole day away from his factory. I thought he was indispensable."

"Things are running smoothly at the moment," said Vic. "And I have a lot of holidays owing to me."

"If Mr. Wilcox is giving up his holidays to this project, I really think that . . ." Swallow turned his slightly bloodshot eyes appealingly in Robyn's direction. "The VC is *most* enthusiastic."

Robyn thought of the impending UGC letter and the chance, slender as it was, that it might open the way to a permanent job for her at Rummidge. "I don't seem to have much choice, do I?" she said.

"Good!" said Philip Swallow, beaming with relief. "I'll leave you in Robyn's capable hands, then, Mr. Wilcox. Metaphorically speaking, of course. Ha, ha!" He shook hands with Vic and disappeared into the Departmental office. Robyn led Vic Wilcox along the corridor to her room.

"I consider this an underhand trick," she said, when they were alone.

"What d'you mean?"

"You're not trying to pretend, are you, that you're genuinely interested in finding out how University Departments of English operate?"

"Yes I am, I'm very interested." He looked round the room. "Have you read all these books?"

"When I first came to Pringle's, you expressed utter contempt for the kind of work I do."

"I was prejudiced," he said. "That's what this shadow scheme is all about, overcoming prejudice."

"I think you fixed this up as an excuse to see me," said Robyn. She hoicked her Gladstone bag onto the desk and began to unpack books, folders, essays.

"I want to see what you do," said Vic. "I'm willing to learn. I've been reading those books you mentioned, *Jane Eyre* and *Wuthering Heights*."

Robyn could not resist the bait. "And what did you think of them?"

"*Jane Eyre* was all right. A bit long-winded. With *Wuthering Heights* I kept getting in a muddle about who was who."

"That's deliberate, of course," said Robyn.

"Is it?"

"The same names keep cropping up in different permutations and different generations. Cathy the older is born Catherine Earnshaw and becomes Catherine Linton by marriage. Cathy the younger is born Catherine Linton, becomes Catherine Heathcliff by her first marriage to Linton Heathcliff, the son of Isabella Linton and Heathcliff, and later becomes Catherine Earnshaw by her second marriage to Hareton Earnshaw, so she ends up with the same name as her mother, Catherine Earnshaw."

"You should go on 'Mastermind,'" said Vic.

"It's incredibly confusing, especially with all the time-shifts as well," said Robyn. "It's what makes *Wuthering Heights* such a remarkable novel for its period."

"I don't see the point. More people would enjoy it if it was more straightforward."

"Difficulty generates meaning. It makes the reader work harder."

"But reading is the opposite of work," said Vic. "It's what you do when you come home from work, to relax."

"In this place," said Robyn, "reading is work. Reading is production. And what we produce is meaning."

There was a knock on the door, which slowly opened to the extent of about eighteen inches. The head of Marion Russell appeared around the edge of the door like a glove puppet, goggled at Robyn and Vic, and withdrew. The door closed again, and whispering and scuffling on the other side of it were faintly audible, like the sounds of mice.

"That's my ten o'clock tutorial," said Robyn.

"Is ten o'clock when you usually start work?"

"I never stop working," said Robyn. "If I'm not working here, I'm working at home. This isn't a factory, you know. We don't clock in and out. Sit in that corner and make yourself as inconspicuous as possible."

"What's this tutorial about, then?"

"Tennyson. Here, take this." She gave him a copy of Tennyson's *Poems*, a cheap Victorian edition with sentimental illustrations that she had bought from a second-hand bookshop as a student and used for years, until Ricks' Longman's Annotated edition was published. She went to the door and opened it. "Right, come in," she said, smiling encouragingly.

. . .

It was Marion Russell's turn to start off the tutorial discussion, by reading a short paper on a topic she had chosen herself from an old exam paper; but when the students filed into the room and seated themselves round the table, she was missing.

"Where's Marion?" Robyn asked.

"She's gone to the cloakroom," said Laura Jones, a big girl in a navy-blue track suit, who was doing Joint Honours in English and Physical Education, and was a champion shot putter.

"She said she didn't feel well," said Helen Lorimer, whose nails were painted with green nail-varnish to match her hair, and who wore plastic earrings depicting a smiling face on one ear and a frowning face on the other.

"She gave me her essay to read out," said Simon Bradford, a thin, eager young man, with thick-lensed spectacles and wispy beard.

"Wait a minute," said Robyn, "I'll go and see what's the matter with her. Oh, by the way—this is Mr. Wilcox, he's observing this class as part of an Industry Year project. I suppose you all know this is Industry Year, don't you?" They looked blankly at her. "Ask Mr. Wilcox to explain it to you," she said, as she left the room.

She found Marion Russell hiding in the staff women's lavatory.

"What's the matter, Marion?" she said briskly. "Pre-menstrual tension?"

"That man," said Marion Russell. "He was the one at the factory, wasn't he?"

"Yes."

"What's he doing here? Has he come to complain?"

"No, of course not. He's here to observe the tutorial."

"What for?"

"It's too complicated to explain now. Come along, we're all waiting for you."

"I can't."

"Why not?"

"It's too embarrassing. He's seen me in my knickers and stuff."

"He won't recognise you."

"Course he will."

"No he won't. You look entirely different." Marion Russell was wearing harem pants and an outsize teeshirt with Bob Geldof's face imprinted on it like the face of Christ on Veronica's napkin.

"What did you do your paper on?"

"The struggle between optimism and pessimism in Tennyson's verse," said Marion Russell.

"Come on, then, let's hear it."

If Vic had been explaining Industry Year to the other three students, he had been very brief, for the room was silent when Robyn returned with Marion Russell. Vic was frowning at his copy of Tennyson, and the students were watching him as rabbits watch a stoat. He looked up as Marion came in, but, as Robyn had predicted, his eyes signalled no flicker of recognition.

Marion began reading her paper in a low monotone. All went well until she observed that the line from "Locksley Hall," "*Let the great world spin for ever, down the ringing grooves of change,*" reflected the confidence of the Victorian Railway Age. Vic raised his hand.

"Yes, Mr. Wilcox?" Robyn's tone and regard were as discouraging as she could make them.

"He must have been thinking of trams, not trains," said Vic. "Train wheels don't run in grooves."

Simon Bradford gave an abrupt, high-pitched laugh; then, on meeting Robyn's eye, looked as if he wished he hadn't.

"D'you find that suggestion amusing, Simon?" she said.

"Well," he said, "trams. They're not very poetic, are they?"

"It said the Railway Age in this book I read," said Marion.

"What book, Marion?" said Robyn.

"Some critical book. I can't remember which one, now," said Marion, riffling randomly through a sheaf of notes.

"Always acknowledge secondary sources," said Robyn. "Actually, it's quite an interesting, if trivial, point. When he wrote the poem, Tennyson was under the impression that railway trains ran in grooves." She read out the footnote from her Longman's Annotated edition: "*When I went by the first train from Liverpool to Manchester in 1830 I thought that the wheels ran in a groove. It was a black night, and there was such a vast crowd round the train at the station that we could not see the wheels. Then I made this line.*'"

It was Vic's turn to laugh. "Well, he didn't make it very well, did he?"

"So, what's the answer?" said Laura, a rather literal-minded girl who wrote down everything Robyn said in tutorials. "Is it a train or a tram?"

"Both or either," said Robyn. "It doesn't really matter. Go on, Marion."

"Hang about," said Vic. "You can't have it both ways. '*Grooves*' is a whadyoucallit, metonymy, right?"

The students were visibly impressed as he brought out this technical term. Robyn herself was rather touched that he had remembered it, and it was almost with regret that she corrected him.

"No," said Robyn. "It's a metaphor. '*The grooves of change*' is a metaphor. The world moving through time is compared to something moving along a metal track."

"But the grooves tell you what kind of track."

"True," Robyn conceded. "It's metonymy inside a metaphor. Or to be precise, a synecdoche: part for whole."

"But if I have a picture of grooves in my head, I can't think of a train. It has to be a tram."

"What do the rest of you think?" said Robyn. "Helen?"

Helen Lorimer reluctantly raised her eyes to meet Robyn's. "Well, if Tennyson thought he was describing a train, then it's a train I s'pose," she said.

"Not necessarily," said Simon Bradford. "That's the Intentional Fallacy." He glanced at Robyn for approval. Simon Bradford had attended one of her seminars in Critical Theory the previous year. Helen Lorimer, who hadn't, and who had plainly never heard of the Intentional Fallacy, looked despondent, like the earring on her left ear.

There was a brief silence, during which all looked expectantly at Robyn.

"It's an aporia," said Robyn. "A kind of accidental aporia, a figure of undecidable ambiguity, irresolvable contradiction. We know Tennyson intended an allusion to railways, and, as Helen said, we can't erase that knowledge." (At this flattering paraphrase of her argument, Helen Lorimer's expression brightened, resembling her right earring.) "But we also know that railway trains don't run in grooves, and nothing that *does* run in grooves seems metaphorically adequate to the theme. As Simon said, trams aren't very poetic. So the reader's mind is continually baffled in its efforts to make sense of the line."

"You mean, it's a duff line?" said Vic.

"On the contrary," said Robyn, "I think it's one of the few good ones in the poem."

"If there's a question about the Railway Age in Finals," said Laura Jones, "can we quote it?"

"Yes, Laura," said Robyn patiently. "As long as you show you're aware of the aporia."

"How d'you spell that?"

Robyn wrote the word with a coloured felt-tip on the whiteboard screwed to the wall of her office. "*Aporia*. In classical rhetoric it means real or pretended uncertainty about the subject under discussion. Deconstructionists today use it to refer to more radical kinds of contradiction or subversion of logic or defeat of the reader's expectation in a text. You could say that it's deconstruction's favourite trope. Hillis Miller compares it to following a mountain path and then finding that it gives out, leaving you stranded on a ledge, unable to go back or forwards. It actually derives from a Greek word meaning 'a pathless path.' Go on, Marion."

A few minutes later, Vic, evidently encouraged by the success of his intervention over *"grooves,"* put up his hand again. Marion had been arguing, reasonably enough, that Tennyson was stronger on emotions than on ideas, and had quoted in support the lyrical outburst of the lover in *Maud*, "Come into the garden, Maud, For the black bat night has flown."

"Yes, Mr. Wilcox?" said Robyn, frowning.

"That's a song," said Vic. "'Come into the garden Maud.' My grandad used to sing it."

"Yes?"

"Well, the bloke in the poem is singing a song to his girl, a well-known song. It makes a difference, doesn't it?"

"Tennyson wrote 'Come into the garden, Maud,' as a poem," said Robyn. "Somebody else set it to music later."

"Oh," said Vic. "My mistake. Or is it an aporia?"

"No, it's a mistake," said Robyn. "I must ask you not to interrupt any more, please, or Marion will never finish her paper."

Vic lapsed into a hurt silence. He stirred restlessly in his seat, he sighed impatiently to himself from time to time in a way that made the students stall nervously in the middle of what they were saying, he licked his fingers to turn the pages of his book, and flexed it so violently in his hands that the spine cracked noisily, but he didn't actually interrupt again. After a while he seemed to lose interest in the discussion and to be browsing in the Tennyson on his own account. When the tutorial was over and the students had left, he asked Robyn if he could borrow it.

"Of course. Why, though?"

"Well, I thought if I have a read of it, I might have a better idea of what's going on next week."

"Oh, but we're not doing Tennyson next week. It's *Daniel Deronda*, I think."

"You mean, you've finished with Tennyson? That's it?"

"As far as this group is concerned, yes."

"But you never told them whether he was optimistic or pessimistic."

"I don't tell them what to think," said Robyn.

"Then how are they supposed to learn the right answers?"

"There are no right answers to questions like that. There are only interpretations."

"What's the point of it, then?" he said. "What's the point of sitting around discussing books all day, if you're no wiser at the end of it?"

"Oh, you're *wiser*," said Robyn. "What you learn is that language is an infinitely more devious and slippery medium than you had supposed."

"That's good for you?"

"Very good for you," she said, tidying the books and papers on her desk. "Do you want to borrow *Daniel Deronda* for next week?"

"What did he write?"

"He's not a he, he's a book. By George Eliot."

"Good writer, is he, this Eliot bloke?"

"He was a she, actually. You see how slippery language is. But, yes, very good. D'you want to swap *Daniel Deronda* for the Tennyson?"

"I'll take them both," he said. "There's some good stuff in here." He opened the Tennyson, and read aloud, tracing the lines with his blunt forefinger:

"Woman is the lesser man, and all thy passions, matched with mine,
Are as moonlight unto sunlight, and as water unto wine."

"I might have guessed you would lap up 'Locksley Hall,'" said Robyn.

"It strikes a chord," he said, turning the pages. "Why didn't you answer my letters?"

"Because I didn't read them," she said. "I didn't even open them."

"That wasn't very nice."

"I knew all too well what would be in them," she said. "And if you're going to get stupid and sentimental, and sick Tennyson all over me, I'm going to call off The Shadow Scheme Part Two right away."

"I can't help it. I keep thinking about Frankfurt."

"Forget it. Pretend it never happened. Would you like some coffee?"

"It must have meant something to you."

"It was an aporia," she said. "A pathless path. It led nowhere."

"Yes," he said bitterly. "It left me stuck on a ledge. I can't go forward, I can't go back."

Robyn sighed. "I'm sorry, Vic. Surely you can see that we're too different? Not to mention the fact that you have other ties."

"Never mind them," he said. "I can take care of them."

"We're from two different worlds."

"I could change. I already have changed. I've read *Jane Eyre* and *Wuthering Heights*. I've got rid of pin-ups at the factory, I've—"

"You've what?"

"We've been cleaning up the place—I took the opportunity to have the pin-ups taken off the walls."

"Won't they just put up new ones?"

"I got the unions to put it to a vote. The shop stewards weren't keen, but the Asian membership was overwhelmingly in favour. They're a bit prudish, you know."

"Well! I'm impressed," said Robyn. She smiled a benediction on him. This proved to be a mistake. To her dismay he seized her hand, and dropped to his knees beside her chair, in a posture reminiscent of one of the engravings in her old Tennyson *Poems*.

"Robyn, give me a chance!"

She snatched her hand away. "Get up, you fool!" she said.

At that moment there was a knock on the door and Marion Russell blundered breathlessly into the room. She stopped on the threshold and stared at Vic on his knees. Robyn slid off her chair and on to the floor. "Mr. Wilcox has dropped his pen, Marion," she said. "You can help us look for it."

"Oh," said Marion. "I'm afraid I can't, I've got a lecture. I came back for my bag." She pointed to a plastic shopping-bag full of books under the chair where she had been sitting.

"All right," said Robyn, "take it."

"Sorry." Marion Russell retrieved her bag, backed towards the door and, with a last stare, left the room.

"Right, that's it," said Robyn, as she got to her feet.

"I'm sorry, I got carried away," said Vic, dusting his knees.

"Please leave now," said Robyn. "I'll tell Swallow that I've changed my mind."

"Let me stay. It won't happen again." He looked embarrassed and helpless. She was reminded of when they had gone back to her room at the Frankfurt hotel and how he had sprung on her behind the door, and just as abruptly desisted.

"I don't trust you. I think you're a bit mad."

"I promise."

Robyn waited till he looked her in the eye before she spoke again. "No more references to Frankfurt?"

"No."

"No more love-stuff?"

He swallowed, and nodded glumly. "All right."

Robyn thought of the tableau they must have presented to Marion Russell, and giggled. "Come on, let's get some coffee," she said.

. . .

As usual at this hour of the morning, the Senior Common Room was crowded, and they had to join a short queue for coffee. Vic looked about him in a puzzled way.

"What's going on here?" he said. "Are these people having an early lunch?"

"No, just morning coffee."

"How long are they allowed?"

"Allowed?"

"You mean they can doss around here as long as they like?"

Robyn looked at her colleagues lounging in easy chairs, smiling and chatting to each other, or browsing through the newspapers and weekly reviews, as they drank their coffee and nibbled their biscuits. She suddenly saw this familiar spectacle through an outsider's eyes, and almost blushed. "We all have our own work to do," she said. "It's up to us how we do it."

"If you don't start till ten and you knock off for a coffee-break at eleven," said Vic, "I don't see where you find the time." He seemed to recognise no intermediate point in manners between self-abasement and truculence. The first having failed, he switched straight into the second.

Robyn paid for two cups of coffee and led Vic to a couple of vacant chairs beside one of the full-length windows that overlooked the central square of the campus. "Surprising as it may seem to you," she said, "a lot of the people in this room are working at this moment."

"You could've fooled me. What kind of work?"

"Discussing university business, settling committee agendas. Exchanging ideas about their research, or consulting about particular students. Things like that."

It was unfortunate that at this moment the Professor of Egyptology, who was sitting nearby, said very audibly to his neighbour, "How are your tulips this year, Dobson?"

"If I was in charge," said Vic, "I'd shut this place down and have that woman behind the counter going up and down the corridors with a trolley."

The Professor of Egyptology turned in his seat to stare at Vic.

"Scruffy lot, aren't they, the men in here? No ties, most of 'em. And look at that bloke over there, he's got his shirt hanging out."

"He's a very distinguished theologian," said Robyn.

"That's no excuse for looking as if he'd slept in his clothes," said Vic.

Philip Swallow approached them with a coffee cup in one hand and a thick sheaf of committee papers in the other. "May I join you?" he said. "How are you getting on, Mr. Wilcox?"

"Mr. Wilcox is scandalised by our lax habits," said Robyn. "Open-necked shirts and open-ended coffee-breaks."

"It wouldn't do in industry," said Vic. "People would take advantage."

"I'm not sure that some of our colleagues don't take advantage," said Swallow, looking round the room. "You do tend to see the same faces in here, taking their time over coffee."

"Well, you're the boss, aren't you?" said Vic. "Why don't you give them a warning?"

Philip Swallow gave a hollow laugh. "I'm nobody's boss. I'm afraid you're making the same mistake as the Government."

"What's that?"

"Why, supposing that universities are organized like businesses, with a clear division between management and labour, whereas in fact they're collegiate institutions. That's why the whole business of the cuts has been such a balls-up. Excuse my French, Robyn."

Robyn waved the apology aside.

"You see," said Philip Swallow, "when the Government cut our funding they obviously hoped to improve efficiency, get rid of overmanning, and so on, like they did in industry. Well, let's admit that there was room for some of that—it would be a miracle if there hadn't been. But in industry, management decides who shall be made redundant in the labour force, senior management decides who shall go from junior management, and so on. Universities don't have that pyramid structure. Everybody is equal in a sense, once they pass probation. Nobody can be made redundant against their will. Nobody will vote to make their peers redundant."

"I should think not," said Robyn.

"That's all very well, Robyn, but nobody will even vote for a change of syllabus that threatens to make anyone redundant. I wouldn't like to count the hours I've spent on committees discussing the cuts," said Philip Swallow wearily, "and in all that time I can't remember a single instance in which anybody admitted that there was any aspect of our existing arrangements that was dispensable. Everybody recognises that there have to be cuts, because the Government controls the purse-strings, but nobody will actually make them."

"Then you'll soon be bankrupt," said Vic.

"We would be already, if it wasn't for early retirements," said Swallow. "But of course the people who have volunteered to take early retirement are not always the people we can most afford to lose. And then the Government had to give us a lot of money to make the terms attractive. So we ended up paying people to go away and work in America or for themselves or not at all, instead of spending the money on bright young people like Robyn here."

"It sounds like a shambles," said Vic. "Surely the answer is to change the system. Give management more muscle."

"No!" said Robyn hotly. "That's not the answer. If you try to make universities like commercial institutions, you destroy everything that makes them valuable. Better the other way round. Model industry on universities. Make factories collegiate institutions."

"Ha! We wouldn't last five minutes in the marketplace," said Vic.

"So much the worse for the marketplace," said Robyn. "Maybe the universities are inefficient, in some ways. Maybe we do waste a lot of time arguing on committees because nobody has absolute power. But that's preferable to a system where everybody is afraid of the person on the next rung of the ladder above them, where everybody is out for themselves, and fiddling their expenses or vandalising the lavatories, because they know that if it suited the company they could be made redundant tomorrow and nobody would give a damn. Give me the University, with all its faults, any day."

"Well," said Vic, "it's nice work if you can get it." He turned his head and looked out of the full-length window, which was open to the warm day, at the central square of the campus.

Robyn followed the direction of his gaze with her own eyes. The students in their summer finery were scattered like petals over the green lawns, reading, talking, necking, or listening to their discoursing teachers. The sun shone upon the façade of the Library, whose glazed revolving doors flashed intermittently like the beams of a lighthouse as it fanned readers in and out, and shone upon the buildings of diverse shapes and sizes dedicated to Biological Sciences, Chemistry, Physics, Engineering, Education and Law. It shone on the botanical gardens, and on the sports centre and the playing fields and the running track where people would be training and jogging and exercising. It shone on the Great Hall where the University orchestra and choir were due to perform "The Dream of Gerontius" later in the term, and on the Student Union with its Council Chamber and committee rooms and newspaper offices, and on the privately endowed art gallery with its small but exquisite collection of masterpieces. It seemed to Robyn more than ever that the university was the ideal type of a human community, where work and play, culture and nature, were in perfect harmony, where there was space, and light, and fine buildings set in pleasant grounds, and people were free to pursue excellence and self-fulfilment, each according to her own rhythm and inclination.

And then she thought, with a sympathetic inward shudder, of how the same sun must be shining upon the corrugated roofs of the factory buildings in West Wallsbury, how the temperature must be rising rapidly inside the foundry; and she imagined the workers stumbling out into the sunshine at midday, sweatstained and blinking in the bright light, and eating their snap, squatting on oil-stained tarmac in the shade of a brick wall, and then, at the sound of a hooter, going back in again to the heat and noise and stench for another four hours' toil.

But no! Instead of letting them go back into that hell-hole, she transported them, in her imagination, to the campus: the entire workforce—labourers, craftsmen, supervisors, managers, directors, secretaries and cleaners and cooks, in their grease-stiff dungarees and soiled overalls and chain-store frocks and striped suits—brought them in buses across the city, and unloaded them at the gates of the campus, and let them wander through it in a long procession, like a lost army, headed by Danny Ram and the two Sikhs from the cupola and the giant black from the knockout, their eyes rolling white in their swarthy, soot-blackened faces, as they stared about them with bewildered curiosity at the fine buildings and the trees and flowerbeds and lawns, and at the beautiful young people at work or play all around them. And the beautiful young people and their teachers stopped dallying and disputing and got to their feet and came forward to greet the people from the factory, shook their hands and made them welcome, and a hundred small seminar groups formed on the grass, composed half of students and lecturers and half of workers and managers, to exchange ideas on how the values of the university and the imperatives of commerce might be reconciled and more equitably managed to the benefit of the whole of society.

Robyn became aware that Philip Swallow was talking to her. "I beg your pardon," she said, "I was daydreaming."

"The privilege of youth," he said, smiling. "I thought for a moment you might be getting a little hard of hearing, Robyn."

2

"The next question," said Philip Swallow, "is what we do about the Syllabus Review Committee's report."

"Throw it in the wastepaper basket," Rupert Sutcliffe suggested.

"It's easy for Rupert to sneer," said Bob Busby, who was Chairman of the Syllabus Review Committee, "but it's no easy matter, revising the syllabus. Everybody in the Department wants to protect their own special interests. Like all syllabuses, ours is a compromise."

"A thoroughly unworkable compromise, if I may say so," said Rupert Sutcliffe. "I calculate that it would entail setting a hundred and seventy-three different Finals papers every year."

"We haven't gone into the question of assessment yet," said Bob Busby. "We wanted to get the basic structure of courses agreed first."

"But assessment is vital," said Robyn. "It determines the students' whole approach to their studies. Isn't this an opportunity to get rid of final examinations altogether, and go over to some form of continuous assessment?"

"Faculty Board would never accept that," said Bob Busby.

"Quite right too," said Rupert Sutcliffe. "Continuous assessment should be confined to infant schools."

"I must remind you," said Philip Swallow wearily, "as I shall have to remind the full Department Committee in due course, that the object of this exercise is to economise on resources in the face of the cuts. Three colleagues will be leaving, for various reasons, at the end of this year. It's more than likely that there will be further losses next year. If we go on offering the present syllabus with fewer and fewer staff, individual teaching loads will rise to intolerable levels. The Syllabus Review Committee was set up to confront this problem, not to devise a new syllabus that all of us, in ideal circumstances, would like to teach."

"Rationalisation," said Vic from the far end of the table.

The others gathered in Philip Swallow's room, including Robyn, turned their heads and looked at Vic in surprise. He did not normally speak at the committee meetings to which he followed her—nor, since his first day, had he intervened in tutorials. On his weekly visits to the University he sat in the corner of her room, or at the back of the lecture theatre, quietly attentive, and followed her about the corridors and staircases of the Arts Faculty like a faithful dog. Sometimes she wondered what he was making of it all, but most of the time she simply forgot he was there, as she had done this morning. It was the fourth week of term, and they were attending a meeting of the Department Agenda Committee.

Like everything else in the Department, the Agenda Committee had a history, and a folklore, which Robyn had gradually pieced together from various sources. For decades the Head of Department had been a notorious eccentric called Gordon Masters, who spent every available moment pursuing field sports and had never been known to convene a Department Committee except for the annual Examiners' Meeting. As a result of the student demonstrations of 1969 (which had contributed to Masters' abrupt retirement in a disturbed mental condition) his successor, Dalton, was obliged by a new University statute to hold regular Department Committee meetings, but had cunningly defeated the democratic intention behind this rule by keeping the agenda of such meetings a secret unto himself. His colleagues were therefore able to raise important matters only under Any Other Business, and Dalton invariably contrived to spin out the discussion of his own agenda of yawn-inducing trivia for so long that by the time the meeting reached AOB it was no longer quorate. To counter this strategy, Philip Swallow, then a Senior Lecturer freshly energised by his exchange visit to America, had managed to secure the establishment of a new subcommittee called the Agenda Committee whose function was to prepare business for discussion by the full Department Committee. Swallow had inherited this apparatus when he himself became Head of Department following the sudden death of Dalton in a car accident, and he used the Agenda Committee as a kind of kitchen cabinet, to consider the Department's policy on any given issue, and how it might be presented to the full Department Committee with the minimum risk of contentious debate. The Agenda Committee consisted of himself as *de facto* chairman, Rupert Sutcliffe, Bob Busby, Robyn, and a student representative who seldom attended, and was absent on this occasion.

"Rationalisation is what you're talking about," said Vic. "Cutting costs, improving efficiency. Maintaining throughput with a smaller workforce. It's the same in industry."

"Well, that's an interesting thought," said Philip Swallow politely.

"Perhaps Mr. Wilcox would like to design a new syllabus for us," said Rupert Sutcliffe with a smirk.

"No, I couldn't do that, but I can give you some advice," said Vic. "There's only one surefire way to succeed in business: make something people want, make it well, and make it in one size."

"Henry Ford's formula, I believe," said Bob Busby. He wagged his beard from side to side, preening himself on this *aperçu*.

"Wasn't he the one who said 'History is bunk'?" said Rupert Sutcliffe. "It doesn't sound like a very promising model for an English Department."

"It's absurd," said Robyn. "If we followed it we would have just one standard course for all our students, with no options."

"Oh, well, there's a lot to be said for that, actually," said Rupert Sutcliffe. "That was the sort of syllabus we had under Masters. We seemed to have more time to think in those days, and time to talk to each other. The students knew where they were."

"It's no use hankering after the good old days, which were actually the boring old days," said Bob Busby impatiently. "The subject has expanded vastly since you started in it, Rupert. Now we have linguistics, media studies, American Literature, Commonwealth Literature, literary theory, women's studies, not to mention about a hundred new British writers worth taking seriously. We can't cover all of it in three years. We have to have a system of options."

"And you end up with a hundred and seventy-three separate Finals papers, and endless timetable clashes," said Rupert Sutcliffe.

"Better that than a syllabus which gives the students no choice," said Robyn. "Anyway, Mr. Wilcox is being disingenuous. He makes more than one thing at his factory. He makes lots of different things."

"True," said Vic. "But not as many as we made when I took over. The point is, a repeatable operation is always cheaper and more reliable than one which has to be set up differently each time."

"But repetition is death!" Robyn cried. "Difference is life. Difference is the condition of meaning. Language is a system of differences, as Saussure said."

"But a *system*," said Rupert Sutcliffe. "The question is whether we have a system any more, or just a muddle. A muddle this document"—he slapped the report of the Syllabus Review Committee with the palm of his hand—"will only exacerbate."

Philip Swallow, who had been listening to this debate with his head bowed and cradled in his hands, straightened up and spoke: "I think that, as usual, the truth lies between the two extremes. Of course I take Robyn's point that if we all taught the same thing over and over again we should all go mad or die of boredom, and so would our students. On the other hand, I think it's fair to say that we are trying to do too many things at the same time and not doing any of them particularly well."

Philip Swallow seemed to be in rather good form today, Robyn thought to herself. A small transparent plastic worm curling out of his right ear, and disappearing under a silver grey wing of hair, suggested that this might have something to do with his having adopted a hearing aid.

"It's partly a matter of history," he went on. "Once upon a time, as Rupert remembers, there was a single syllabus, essentially a survey course on Eng. Lit. from Beowulf to Virginia Woolf, which all the students followed in common, through lectures and a weekly tutorial, and life was very simple and comfortable, if a little dull. And then in the sixties and seventies we began to add all kinds of exciting new ingredients, like the ones Bob mentioned—but without subtracting anything from the original syllabus. So we ended up with an elaborate system of seminar options piled on top of a core curriculum of lectures and tutorials. Well, that was just about workable, if a little frantic, as long as there was plenty of cash to recruit more teachers, but now that the money is running out I think we have to face the fact that the present syllabus is top-heavy. It's like a three-masted ship with too many sails aloft and a diminishing crew. We're exhausting ourselves scrambling up and down the rigging, just trying to keep the damn thing from capsizing, never mind getting anywhere, or enjoying the voyage. With respect, Bob, I don't think your committee has addressed itself to the fundamental problem. Could I possibly ask you to have another look at it before we bring the matter before the Department Committee?"

"All right," Bob Busby sighed.

"Good," said Philip Swallow. "That should make room for another item on the agenda: DEVs."

"What in God's name are they?" said Rupert Sutcliffe.

"Department Enterprise Ventures. A new idea of the VC's."

"Not another!" Bob Busby groaned.

"He wants every Department to put forward projects for raising money from the private sector to support its activities. Any suggestions?"

"Do you mean something like a jumble sale?" said Rupert Sutcliffe. "Or a flag day?"

"No, no, Rupert! Consultancies, research services, that sort of thing," said Swallow. "Of course, it's much easier for the sciences to come up with ideas. But I understand Egyptology is planning to offer guided package tours down the Nile. What we need to ask ourselves is, what do we have as a Department that's marketable in the outside world?"

"We have a lot of pretty girls," said Bob Busby, with a hearty laugh that faded as he caught Robyn's eye.

"I don't understand," said Robyn. "We're already overstretched teaching our own students and doing our own research. Where are we supposed to find the time and energy to make money on the side as well?"

"The theory is that with the additional income we shall be able to hire more staff. The University will take its twenty per cent cut and the rest we can spend as we like."

"And supposing we make a loss," said Robyn. "What will happen then?"

Philip Swallow shrugged. "The University will underwrite any approved scheme. Of course, in that case, we shouldn't get any new staff."

"And we should have wasted a lot of valuable time."

"There is that risk," said Philip Swallow. "But it's the spirit of the times. Self-help. Venture capitalism. Isn't that right, Mr. Wilcox?"

"I agree with Robyn," said Vic, to her surprise. "It's not that I don't believe in the market, I do. But you people don't belong in it. You'd be playing at capitalism. Stick to what you're good at."

"How do you mean, playing at capitalism?" said Philip Swallow.

"You can't really lose because the University would underwrite any failures. You can't really win because, as I understand it, there are no individual incentives for success. Suppose, for the sake of argument, Robyn here was to come up with a commerical project for the English Department—say, a consultancy on the wording of safety notices in industrial plant."

"That's not a bad idea, actually," said Philip Swallow, making a note.

"And supposing it proved to be a terrific money-spinner. Would she get a bonus? Would she get a salary raise? Would she advance faster than Mr. Sutcliffe, who is clearly not going to have anything to do with it?"

"Well, no," said Philip Swallow. "But," he added, triumphantly, "in that case we should be able to keep her on here!"

"Terrific," said Vic. "She knocks herself out to earn the money to pay for her own lousy salary while the University takes all the profit and redistributes it to drones like Sutcliffe."

"I say, I resent that," said Rupert Sutcliffe.

"It would make more sense for her to set up as a consultant on her own," said Vic.

"But I don't want to be a consultant," said Robyn. "I just want to be a university teacher."

The telephone on Swallow's desk rang, and he tilted his chair backwards from the head of the table to reach the receiver. "I did say no phone calls, Pam," he said irritably; then his expression changed to one of expectant gravity. "Oh. All right. Put him through." He listened for what seemed a very long time, though it was probably only a couple of minutes, saying nothing except, "Oh," "I see," and "Oh, dear." As this one-sided conversation proceeded, he tilted his chair further and further back, as if he was being drawn away from the table by the magnetic force of his interlocutor. Robyn and the others watched helplessly as the chair approached an angle of no return. Sure enough, as Philip Swallow twisted to replace the receiver he crashed to the ground, and banged his head on the wastepaper bin. They hurried to assist him to his feet. "It's all right, it's all right," he said, rubbing his forehead. "The UGC letter has arrived. It's bad news, I'm afraid. Our grant is going to be cut by ten per cent in real terms. The VC thinks we shall have to lose another hundred academic posts." Philip Swallow did not meet Robyn's eye as he made his announcement.

. . .

"Well, that's that," said Robyn, when they were back in her room. "There goes my last chance of keeping my job."

"I'm sorry," said Vic. "You're really good at it."

Robyn smiled wanly. "Thank you, Vic. Can I use you as a referee?"

Raindrops trickled down the pane, distorting her vision like tears. The fine weather at the beginning of term had not lasted. There were no golden lads and girls disporting themselves on the sodden lawns today, only a few people hurrying along the footpaths under umbrellas.

"I mean it," he said. "You're a natural teacher. That stuff about metaphor and metonymy, for instance. I see them all over the shop now. TV commercials, colour supplements, the way people talk."

Robyn turned and beamed at him. "I'm very glad to hear you say that. If *you* understand it, anybody can."

"Thanks very much," he said.

"Sorry, I didn't mean to be rude. The point is, it means Charles was wrong to say that we shouldn't teach theory to students who haven't read anything. It's a false opposition. Nobody's read less than you, I imagine."

"I've read more in the last few weeks than in all the years since I left school," he said. "*Jane Eyre* and *Wuthering Heights* and *Daniel Deronda*. Well, half of *Daniel Deronda*. This bloke"—he took a paperback edition of Matthew Arnold's *Culture and Anarchy*, assigned for a tutorial that afternoon, from his pocket, and waved it in the air—"and Tennyson. Funnily enough, I like Tennyson best. I never thought I'd like reading poetry, but I do. I like to learn bits off by heart and recite them to myself in the car."

"Instead of Jennifer Rush?" she said, mischievously.

"I've got a bit tired of Jennifer Rush."

"Good!"

"Her words don't rhyme properly. Tennyson's a good rhymer."

"He is. What bits have you memorised, then?"

Looking into her eyes, he recited:

"In my life there was a picture, she that clasped my neck had flown.
I was left within the shadow, sitting on the wreck alone."

"That's rather beautiful," said Robyn, after a pause.

"I thought it was rather appropriate."

"Never mind that," said Robyn briskly. "Where's it from?"

"Don't you know? A poem called 'Locksley Hall Sixty Years After.'"

"I don't think I've ever read that one."

"You mean, I've read something you haven't read? Amazing." He looked childishly pleased with himself.

"Well," she said, "if you've acquired a taste for poetry, the Shadow Scheme hasn't been in vain."

"What about you?"

"I've learned to thank my lucky stars I don't have to work in a factory," she said. "The sooner they introduce those lightless factories of yours, the better. Nobody should have to earn their living by doing the same thing over and over again."

"How will they earn it, then?"

"They won't have to. They can be students instead. Robots will do all the work and produce all the wealth."

"Oh, so you admit somebody has to do that?"

"I recognise that universities don't grow on trees, if that's what you mean."

"Well, that's something, I suppose."

There was a knock on the door and Pamela, the Department Secretary, put her head round it. "Outside call for you, Robyn."

. . .

"Hi," said the voice of Morris Zapp when she picked up the phone in the Department Office. "How are you?"

"I'm all right," she said. "How are you? *Where* are you?"

"I'm fine and I'm at home in Euphoria. It's a warm starry night and I'm sitting out on my deck with a cordless phone enjoying the view of the Bay while I make some calls. Listen, I read your book. I think it's terrific."

Robyn felt her spirits lift like an untethered balloon. "Really?" she said. "Are you going to recommend it to your university press?"

"I already have. You'll be getting a letter from them. Ask for double the advance they're offering."

"Oh, I don't think I'd have the nerve to do that," said Robyn. "How much is it, anyway?"

"I've no idea, but whatever it is, insist they double it."

"They might say no, and back out."

"They won't," said Morris Zapp. "It will only make them more eager to sign you up. But I'm not calling you about the Press. I'm calling you about a job."

"A job?" Robyn covered her unengaged ear to shut out the noise of Pamela's typewriter.

"Yeah, we're making a tenure-track appointment in Women's Studies here, starting in the fall. You interested?"

"Well, yes," said Robyn.

"Great. Now what I need is your CV, fast as possible. Could you fax it to me?"

"Facts?"

"F-a-x, fax. Fax? OK, forget it. Send it airmail, special delivery. You'd have to come over here for a few days, meet the faculty, give a paper, the usual sort of thing—that all right? We'd pay your airfare, naturally."

"Fine," said Robyn. "When?"

"Next week?"

"Next *week*!"

"The week after then. The point is—I'll level with you, Robyn—there's another candidate some of my dumber colleagues are backing. I want to get you into the ball-game as fast as I can. I know they'll all be knocked out by your accent. We don't have another Brit in the Department at the moment. That's a plus for you, we have a lot of Anglophiles here, it must be because we're so far from England."

"Who's the other candidate?"

"Don't worry about her. She's not a serious scholar. Just a writer. Leave it to me. Do what I tell you, and the job's yours."

"Well . . . how can I thank you?" said Robyn.

"We'll work on it together," said Morris Zapp, but the innuendo seemed harmless, it was so obviously a conditioned reflex. "Don't you want to know what the salary is?"

"All right," said Robyn. "What is it?"

"I can't tell you exactly. You're young, of course. But I'd say, not less than forty thousand dollars."

Robyn was silent while she did some rapid mental arithmetic.

"I know that's not a lot—" said Morris Zapp.

"It seems very reasonable to me," said Robyn, who had worked out that it was exactly twice as much as she was earning at Rummidge.

"And it should go up very quickly. People like you are very hot right now."

"What do you mean, people like me?"

"Feminists who can do literary theory. Theory is all the rage here. Your life would be one long round of conferences and visiting lectures. And Euphoric State has just put in a bid to be the home of a new Institute of Advanced Research on the West Coast. If that works out, we'll have all the fat cats from Yale and Johns Hopkins and Duke lining up to spend semesters with us."

"Sounds exciting," said Robyn.

"Yeah, you'll love it," said Morris Zapp. "Don't forget the CV, and tell your referees to write immediately to our chairman, Morton Ziegfield. Speak to you soon. *Ciao!*"

Robyn put down the telephone receiver and laughed aloud.

Pamela looked up from her typing. "Your mother's all right, then?"

"My mother?"

"She was trying to get you earlier, when you were in the Agenda meeting."

"No, it wasn't my mother," said Robyn. "I wonder what's the matter with her."

"She said not to worry, she would phone you this evening."

"Why did you think it was her then?" Robyn said, irritated by the secretary's interest in her private life. Pamela looked hurt, and Robyn was immediately stricken with guilt. To make amends she shared her good news. "At last someone's offered me a job. In America!"

"Ooh, fancy that!"

"But keep it to yourself, Pamela. Is Professor Swallow free?"

. . .

"Désirée Zapp!" said Philip Swallow, when she told him her story. "The other candidate must be Désirée."

"You think so?" said Robyn.

"I'd take a bet on it. She wrote on the back of her Christmas card that she was looking for an academic post, preferably on the West Coast. Imagine Désirée in Morris's Department!" He guffawed at the scenario thus summoned up. "Morris would do anything to stop her."

"Even hiring me?"

"You should feel flattered," said Philip Swallow. "He wouldn't run you as a candidate if he didn't think you could win. He must have been really impressed by your book. Of course, that was why he wanted to read it in the first place. He must have been over in Europe scouting for talent. I expect Fulvia Morgana turned him down . . ." Philip Swallow stared abstractedly out of the window, as if trying to think himself through the labyrinthine ways of Morris Zapp's mind, and tenderly fingered a bump on his forehead caused by the wastepaper bin.

"How can I compete with Désirée Zapp? She's world-famous."

"But, as Morris said, she's not a serious scholar," said Philip Swallow. "I imagine that will be his pitch. Scholarly standards. Theoretical rigour."

"But there must be scores of good academic women candidates in America."

"They may not feel inclined to compete with Désirée. She's something of a hero to feminists over there. Or they may just be scared of her. She can fight dirty. You'd better know what you're letting yourself in for, Robyn. American academic life is red in tooth and claw. Suppose you get the job—the struggle only begins. You've got to keep publishing to justify your appointment. When the time comes for your tenure review, half your colleagues will be trying to stab you in the back, and not speaking to the other half. Do you really fancy that?"

"I have no choice," said Robyn. "There's no future for me in this country."

"Not at the moment, it seems," Swallow sighed. "And the devil of it is, once you go, you won't come back."

"How do you know?"

"People don't. Even if they can face returning to the English salary scale, we can't afford to fly them over here for interview. But I don't blame you for seizing the opportunity."

"You'll write me a reference, then?"

"I'll write you a glowing reference," said Philip Swallow. "Which is no more than you deserve."

. . .

Robyn went back to her room with a spring in her step and a confused swirl of thoughts, mostly agreeable, in her head. Philip Swallow had taken some of the shine off Morris Zapp's proposition, but it was a pleasant change to be courted by a potential employer under any conditions. She had forgotten all about Vic, and was, for an instant, surprised to find him hunched in a chair by the window, reading *Culture and Anarchy* by the grey rainy light. When she told him her news, he looked less than delighted.

"When did you say this job starts?" he said.

"The fall. I suppose that means September."

"I haven't got much time, then."

"Time for what?"

"Time to, you know, get you to change your mind . . ."

"Oh Vic," she said. "I thought you'd given up that foolishness."

"I can't give up loving you."

"Don't go soppy on me," she said. "This is my lucky day. Don't spoil it."

"Sorry," he said, looking at his shoes. He flicked a speck of dried mud from a toecap.

"Vic," she said, shaking her head sadly, "how many times do I have to tell you: I don't believe in that individualistic sort of love."

"So you say," he said.

She bridled a little at that. "Are you suggesting that I don't mean it?"

"I thought it was impossible to mean what we say or say what we mean," he said. "I thought there was always a slippage between the I that speaks and the I that is spoken of."

"Oh, ho!" said Robyn, planting her hands on her hips. "We *are* learning fast, aren't we?"

"The point is," he said. "If you don't believe in love, why do you take such care over your students? Why do you care about Danny Ram?"

Robyn blushed. "That's quite different."

"No, it's not. You care about them because they're individuals."

"I care about them because I care about knowledge and freedom."

"Words. Knowledge and freedom are just words."

"That's all there is in the last analysis. *Il n'y a pas de hors-texte.*"

"What?"

"'There is nothing outside the text.'"

"I don't accept that," he said, lifting his chin and locking his gaze on hers. "It would mean we have no free will."

"Not necessarily," said Robyn. "Once you realize there is nothing outside the text, you can begin to write it yourself."

There was a knock on the door and Pamela's head appeared round it again.

"My mother?" said Robyn.

"No, it's for Mr. Wilcox," said Pamela.

. . .

"Sit down, Vic. Thanks for coming in so quickly," said Stuart Baxter, from behind the sparsely covered expanse of his desk, which was elegantly veneered, like his wall units, in black ash, the latest executive fashion. The higher up the ladder people went in the conglomerate, Vic had observed, the bigger their desks became and the less paper and other impedimenta they had on them. The curved rosewood desk of the Chairman of the Board, Sir Richard Littlego, had been, on the one occasion when Vic met him in his penthouse suite, completely bare except for a leather-bound blotter and a silver-mounted quill pen. Stuart Baxter hadn't achieved that conspicuous simplicity yet, but his In-tray was virtuously empty and only a single sheet of paper reposed in his Out-tray. Baxter's office was on the eighteenth floor of Midland Amalgamated's twenty-storey tower block in the centre of Rummidge. The plateglass window behind his head faced south-east and overlooked a drab and treeless segment of the city. The grey, rain-wet roofs of factories, warehouses and terraces stretched to the horizon like the waves and troughs of a sullen, oily sea.

"I wasn't far away," said Vic. He sat down in an easy chair which was more of an uneasy chair, since it was low-slung and forced the occupant to look up at Stuart Baxter. Looking at Baxter was not something Vic particularly enjoyed doing from any angle. He was a handsome man, complacently aware of the fact. His shave was perfect, his haircut immaculate, his teeth white and even. He affected boldly coloured shirts with white collars, above which his plump, smooth face glowed healthily pink.

"The University, wasn't it?" he said. "I gather you've been spending a lot of time there lately."

"I'm following up that shadow scheme," said Vic. "In reverse. I sent you a memo about it."

"Yes, I passed it to the Chairman. Haven't had a reply yet. I thought it was just a suggestion."

"I mentioned it to Littlego myself, at the CRUM dinner dance. He seemed to think it was a good idea, so I went ahead."

"I wish you'd told me, Vic. I like to know what my MDs are up to."

"It's in my own time."

Baxter smiled. "I gather she's quite a dish, this shadow of yours."

"I'm the shadow now," said Vic.

"You seem to be inseparable. I hear you took her with you to Frankfurt."

Vic stood up. "If you've brought me in here to discuss office gossip—"

"No, I've brought you in for a much more important reason. Sit down, Vic. Coffee?"

"No thanks," said Vic, sitting down on the edge of the seat. "What is it?" He felt a cold qualm of fear in his guts.

"We're selling Pringle's."

"You can't," Vic said.

"The deed is done, Vic. The announcement will be made tomorrow. It's confidential till then, of course."

"But we made a profit last month!"

"A small profit. A very small profit, given the turnover."

"But it will improve! The foundry is coming on a treat. What about the new core blower?"

"Foundrax regard it as a good investment. You got a good price on it."

"Foundrax?" Vic said, hardly able to draw the breath into his lungs to speak.

"Yes, we're selling to the EFE Group, they own Foundrax, as you know."

"You mean, they're going to merge the two companies?"

"I gather that's the idea. There'll be some rationalisation, of course. Let's face it, Vic, there are too many companies in your field, all chasing the same business."

"Pringle's is rationalised already," said Vic. "*I* rationalised it. I was hired to turn the company round. I said it might take eighteen months. I've done it in under a year. Now you tell me you've sold out to a competitor that was on its fucking knees."

"We all think you've done a fantastic job, Vic," said Baxter. "But the Board just didn't see Pringle's fitting into our long-term strategy."

"What you mean," said Vic bitterly, "is that by selling off Pringle's now, you can show a profit on this year's accounts at the next AGM."

Stuart Baxter examined his nails, and said nothing.

"I won't work under Norman Cole," said Vic.

"Nobody is asking you to, Vic," said Baxter.

"So it's goodbye and thankyou and here's a year's salary and don't spend it all at once."

"We'll let you keep the car," said Baxter.

"Oh, that's all right then."

"I'm sorry, Vic, I really am. I said to the EFE people, if you had any sense you'd keep Vic Wilcox on to run the new company. But I understand it will be Cole."

"I wish them joy of the double-dealing bastard."

"To be honest with you, Vic, I think they were put off by some of the stories that have been flying around about you."

"What stories?"

"Like having all the pin-ups taken down at the factory."

"The unions backed it."

"I know they did, but it seems a bit . . . eccentric. And then spending one day a week at the University."

"In my own time."

"That's eccentric too. Somebody asked me the other day if you were a born-again Christian. You're not, are you?"

"No, not a Christian," Vic said, getting up to leave.

Baxter stood up too. "You might find it convenient to move your stuff out this afternoon. I don't suppose you want to be around when Cole takes over tomorrow." He extended his hand across the desk. Vic left it there, turned on his heel, and walked out.

. . .

Vic drove slowly back to Pringle's—or rather the car took him there, like a horse under slack reins, following the route it knew best. His mind was too choked with anger and anxiety to concentrate on driving. He didn't know what was worst—the thought of all that hard slog over the past year being wasted, or the irony that Norman Cole would profit by it, or the prospect of having to break the news to Marjorie. He settled for that one. A yellow Bedford van he was following along the inside lane of the motorway, with "RIV-IERA SUNBEDS" blazoned on it in orange lettering, evoked a poignant image of his wife vainly beautifying herself at home, unaware of the thunderbolt that had already struck her life. They would have to cancel the summer holi-day in Tenerife for starters. If he didn't get another job within the year, they might have to sell the house and move to something more modest, without an *en suite* bathroom.

Vic followed the yellow van off the motorway at the West Wallsbury inter-section and tailed it through the drab deserted streets that only filled when the shifts changed over, past silent factories with forlorn For Lease notices on their gates, past blind-walled workshops like oversized lock-up garages on the new industrial estate, past Susan's Sauna and down Coney Lane. The van seemed to be following a route that would take it past Pringle's, but to his surprise it turned into the firm's car park and stopped just outside the administration block. Brian Everthorpe climbed down from the passenger seat and waved a thankyou to the driver as the van moved away. He did a double-take on seeing Vic getting out of his car, and came over.

"Hallo, Vic. I thought this was one of your adult-education days."

"Something cropped up. What happened to your car, then?"

"Broke down on the other side of the city. Alternator, I think. I left it with a garage and hitched a lift over here. Serious, is it?"

"What?"

"The something that cropped up."

"You could say so."

"You look a bit shook up, Vic, if you don't mind my saying so. Like somebody that's just had a shunt."

Vic hesitated, tempted to confide in Brian Everthorpe—not because of any charitable impulse to forewarn him about the takeover, but simply to relieve his own feelings, to pass on his own sense of shock to another, and observe its impact. And if Everthorpe should leak the information to others—so what? Why should he worry about the possible embarrassment to Stuart Baxter and Midland Amalgamated? "Come into my office for a minute," he said recklessly.

The reception lobby was full of furniture and cardboard packing-cases. In the middle of the confusion, Shirley, Doreen and Lesley were tearing sheets of protective plastic off a long beige sofa, squealing with excitement. On catching sight of Vic, the two receptionists scuttled back to their posts. Shirley, who was on her knees, struggled to her feet and tugged down her skirt.

"Oh, hallo Vic. I didn't think you were coming in today."

"I changed my mind," he said, looking round. "The new furniture arrived, then?"

"We thought we'd unpack it. We wanted to give you a surprise sort of thing."

"It's ever so nice, Mr. Wilcox," said Doreen.

"Lovely material," said Lesley.

"Not bad," he said, prodding the upholstery, thinking: another little bonus for Norman Cole. "Get rid of the old stuff, will you, Shirley?" As he led the way to his office he wondered whether the three women would survive the merger. Probably they would—there always seemed to be a need for secretaries and telephonists. Brian Everthorpe, however, almost certainly wouldn't.

Vic closed the door of his office, swore Brian Everthorpe to secrecy, and told him the news.

Brian Everthorpe said, "Hmm," and stroked his sideboards.

"You don't seem very surprised."

"I saw this coming."

"I'm buggered if I did," said Vic. Already he regretted telling Everthorpe. "I shan't be staying on. I don't know about you, of course."

"Oh, they won't keep me on, I know that."

"You seem remarkably cheerful about it."

"I've been here a long time. I qualify for redundancy."

"Even so."

"And I've made contingency plans."

"What contingency plans?"

"Some time ago, I put some money in a little business," said Brian Everthorpe. "It's not so little any more." He took a card from his wallet and presented it.

Vic looked at the card. "Riviera Sunbeds? That was the van that dropped you just now."

"Yes, I was over there when the motor packed up."

"Doing all right, is it?"

"Marvellous. Especially at this time of year. There are all these women, see, all over Rummidge, getting ready for their annual fortnights on Majorca or Corfu. They don't want to go down to the beach on their first day looking white as lard, so they rent one of our sunbeds, to give themselves a pre-holiday tan at home. Then when they come back, they rent again to keep the tan. We're expanding all the time. Bought another fifty beds last week. Made in Taiwan, amazing value."

"You're involved in the day-to-day running, then?"

"I keep an eye on things. Give them the benefit of my experience, you know," said Brian Everthorpe, preening his whiskers. "And I use my contacts to drum up trade. A card here, a card there."

Vic struggled to control his anger, so as to coax a full confession out of Everthorpe. "What you mean is, you've been looking after the interests of

Riviera Sunbeds when you should be giving all your attention to Pringle's. Is that ethical?"

"Ethical?" Brian Everthorpe guffawed. "Do me a favour, Vic. Is it ethical, what Midland Amalgamated are doing to us?"

"It's cynical, it's shortsighted, in my opinion. But I don't see anything unethical about it. Whereas you've been working for yourself on the company's time. Jesus, no wonder we could never find you when we wanted you!" he burst out. "I suppose you were delivering sunbeds."

"Well, I have dropped off the odd bed at peak times—anything to make a sale, you know. It's different when it's your own money, Vic. But no, my role is a bit higher-level than that. In fact I wouldn't be surprised if I don't end up running the business. I'll be able to buy a bigger share with my golden handshake."

"You don't deserve a golden handshake," said Vic. "You deserve a golden kick up the arse. I've a good mind to report you to Stuart Baxter."

"I shouldn't bother," said Brian Everthorpe. "He's one of the chief shareholders in Riviera Sunbeds."

. . .

Vic found he had very few personal belongings to move from his office. A desk diary, a framed photograph of Marjorie and the kids taken ten years ago on the beach at Torquay, a table lighter given to him when he left Rumcol, a couple of reference books, an old sweater and a broken-winged folding umbrella in a cupboard—that was about it. It all fitted into a plastic supermarket bag. Nevertheless, Shirley stared curiously when he passed through her office on his way out. Perhaps Brian Everthorpe had already told her he was leaving.

"Going out again?" she said.

"I'm going home."

"I phoned an auctioneers, they're coming to collect the old furniture tomorrow."

"I hope the new stuff is just as strong," said Vic, looking her in the eye. "That sofa gets a lot of wear and tear."

Shirley went white, and then very red.

Vic felt slightly ashamed of himself. "'Bye Shirley, thanks for seeing to it," he said, and hurried out of the office.

. . .

He drove home fast, straight down the outside lane of the motorway, overtaking everything, wanting to get it over with. Marjorie sensed something was wrong as soon as she saw him in the kitchen doorway. She was standing at the sink, wearing an apron, scraping new potatoes. "You're early," she said, letting a potato fall into the water with a splash. "What's the matter?"

"Make us a cup of tea, and I'll tell you."

She stared at him, knitting her wet, podgy fingers together to stop herself from trembling. "Tell me now, Vic."

"All right. Pringle's has been sold to the EFE Group, and merged with Foundrax. I've got the push. As from tomorrow."

Marjorie came over and put her arms round him. "Oh Vic," she said, "I'm so sorry for you. All that work."

He had steeled himself for tears, perhaps hysterics. But Marjorie was strangely calm, and he himself felt strangely moved by the unselfishness of her response. He looked over her shoulder at the smooth surfaces of the fitted kitchen and all the shining gadgetry arrayed upon them. "I'll get another job," he said. "But it may take time."

"Of course you will, love." Marjorie sounded almost cheerful. "You knew, didn't you? You've known for some time this was going to happen. That's why you've been so strange."

Vic hesitated. He had been deceived so comprehensively himself, he was so sick with the sense of betrayal, that he was tempted to tell her the truth. But the least her loyalty deserved, he decided, was a merciful lie. "Yes," he said, "I knew it was on the cards."

"You should have told me," she said, drawing back her head and shaking him gently. "I've been that worried. I thought I'd lost you."

"Lost me?"

"I thought there might be another woman."

He laughed, and slapped her lightly on the bottom. "Make us that cup of tea," he said. He realized, with a slight shock, that till now he hadn't thought of Robyn Penrose once since Stuart Baxter had given him the news.

"I'll bring it into the lounge. Your Dad's in there."

"Dad? What's he doing here?"

"He just dropped in. He does occasionally, to keep me company. He knows my nerves've been bad."

"Don't tell him," said Vic.

"All right," said Marjorie. "But it'll be in the evening paper tomorrow, won't it?"

"You're right," said Vic.

So they woke up the old man, who was dozing in an armchair, and revived him with a cup of strong tea, and broke the news to him. He took it surprisingly well. He seemed to think that the year's salary Vic would get was a small fortune on which he could live indefinitely, and Vic did not disillusion him—not immediately. As the three children came in one by one, and were told, the gathering turned into a sort of family council, and Vic spelled out the implications. "I've got no assets except this house, and there's a big mortgage on that," he said. "We're going to have to tighten belts until I get a new job. I'm afraid we'll have to cancel the holiday."

"Oh, *no!*" Sandra whined.

"Don't be so selfish, Sandra," Marjorie snapped. "What's a holiday?"

"I'll go away on my own, then, with Cliff," said Sandra. "I'll work at Tweezers all summer and save up."

"Fine," said Vic, "as long as you contribute something to the housekeeping."

Sandra sniffed. "What about university? I suppose you don't want me to apply now."

"Of course I want you to apply. I thought you weren't interested."

"I changed my mind. But if you're going to make a fuss about money all the time—"

"We'll find the money for that, don't worry. It would help if you applied locally, mind . . ." He turned to his eldest son. "Raymond, I think it's time you gave your mother some of your dole money, too."

"I'm moving out," said Raymond. "I've been offered a job."

When the mild uproar that followed this announcement had died down, Raymond explained that the studio where his band had recorded their demonstration tape had offered him a job as assistant producer. "They hated our music, but I impressed the hell out of them with my electronic knowhow," he said. "I went for a drink with Sidney, the owner, afterwards, and he offered me a job. It's just a small outfit, Sidney's only just started it up, but it has possibilities. There are dozens of bands round here looking for somewhere to record without being ripped off in London."

"Hey, Dad, why don't *you* start up your own business?" said Gary.

"Yeah, what about that idea you had for a spectrometer?" said Raymond.

Vic looked at his sons suspiciously, but they weren't teasing him. "It's a thought," he said. "If Tom Rigby gets made redundant, he might invest his lump sum in a partnership. We'd still need a whacking great bank loan, but it's definitely a thought."

"Sidney got a loan," said Raymond.

"Trouble is, I've got no equity to speak of. The house is mortgaged up to the hilt. It would look risky to a bank. There's a lot of research to be done before we could even make a prototype."

"Ay, it's risky, going it alone," said Mr. Wilcox. "You'd do better to look for another job like the one you had. Rumcol'd probably be glad to have you back, or Vanguard."

"They've already got managing directors, Dad."

"Doesn't have to be a managing director's job, son. You needn't be proud."

"You mean like a storesman's job, Grandad?" said Gary.

"Don't be cheeky, Gary," said Vic. "Any road, I'm not sure I want to work for a company again. I'm fed up with flogging my guts out for companies and conglomerates that have about as much human feeling as a wagon-load of pig-iron."

"If you started up on your own, Vic," said Marjorie, "I could be your secretary. That would be a saving."

"And I'll do the accounts on my Atari," said Gary. "We'll make it a family business, like a Paki corner shop."

"You could do worse," said Mr. Wilcox. "They work 'ard, them buggers."

"I wouldn't mind having a job again," said Marjorie. "I'm bored at home here all day, now you lot are grown up. And if it was our own business . . ."

Vic looked at her in astonishment. Her eyes were bright. She was smiling. And there were dimples in her cheeks.

* * *

When Robyn let herself into her house that evening, the telephone was ringing as if it had been ringing for hours. It was her mother.

"Is anything wrong?" said Robyn.

"No, something rather nice, I hope. A registered letter came for you from a law firm in Melbourne. I signed for it and posted it on to you this afternoon."

"What on earth could it be about?"

"Your uncle Walter died recently," said Mrs. Penrose. "We heard just after you went back to Rummidge. I meant to tell you, but I forgot. We hadn't been in touch for years, of course. I don't think anybody in the family had. He became a bit of a recluse after he sold his sheep farm to that mining—"

"Mummy, what has all this to do with me?" Robyn interpolated.

"Well, I think he might have left you something in his will."

"Why? He wasn't a real uncle, was he?"

"A sort of uncle-in-law. He married your father's sister, Ethel, she died very young, of a bee-sting. She was allergic and didn't know it. They never had any children of their own, and he always had a soft spot for you, ever since you made him put all his money in the crippled children's box when you were three."

"Is that story really true?" Robyn remembered the painted plaster figure of the little boy, with short trousers and a peaked cap and one leg in irons, holding out a box with a slot in it for coins—it had been unique in Melbourne, brought there by an English immigrant shopkeeper—but she had never been quite sure about the incident with her uncle Walter.

"Of course it's true." Her mother sounded hurt, like a believer defending scripture. "Wouldn't it be nice if Walter had remembered you in his will?"

"It would certainly come in useful," said Robyn. "I've just received my rates bill. By the way, Mummy, I'm probably going to America." Robyn told her mother about Morris Zapp's proposition.

"Well, dear," said Mrs. Penrose, "I don't like to think of you being so far away, but I suppose it would only be for a year or two."

"That's the snag, actually," said Robyn. "If I go, it will be difficult to get back. But who knows if there'll be any more jobs to get back to in England?"

"Well, dear, you must do what you think best," said her mother. "Have you heard from Charles lately?" she added wistfully.

"No," said Robyn and brought the conversation to an end.

. . .

The next morning, when she came downstairs, there were two envelopes on her doormat. One was from her mother, enclosing the letter from Melbourne and the other was addressed in Charles' hand. To extend the rather pleasurable suspense about the putative will, she opened the letter from Charles first. It said that he was getting on well at the bank though the hours were long and he felt exhausted at the end of the day. But things hadn't worked out between him and Debbie, and he had moved out of her house.

> She was such a novel sort of person to me that I was rather taken in
> at first. I mistook quickwittedness for intelligence. Frankly, my dear,
> she's rather stupid. Most foreign exchange dealers are, in my experi-
> ence—they have to be to play that electronic roulette all day. And they
> think of nothing else. When you come home from a hard day's work
> at the bank, you need some civilised conversation, not more talk about

positions and percentages. After a while I took to watching television just to have an excuse not to listen. Then I decided I would have to get my own place. So I've bought a nice little maisonette in a new development on the Isle of Dogs—mortgaged to the hilt, of course, but the average London property is going up by £50 a *day* at the moment, so you can't really lose. I was wondering if you would like to come down and spend a weekend. We could do a show and some galleries.

I know what you will be thinking—"Oh, no, not all *that* again," and I agree, it is rather absurd the way we keep splitting up and coming back together, because it seems that nobody else will do, in the end. I wonder whether it isn't time we bowed to the inevitable, and got married. I don't mean to live together, necessarily—obviously as long as I'm working in London, and you're in Rummidge, that's impossible anyway—but just to put a sort of seal on things. And if you can't find another job when your contract at Rummidge runs out, you might find it pleasanter to be unemployed in London than in Rummidge. I'm fairly confident that I shall be earning enough by then to support you in the style to which you have become accustomed, if not rather better. There's no reason why you shouldn't go on doing research and publishing as a lady of leisure. Think about it. And do come down for a weekend, soon.

Love, Charles

"Humph!" said Robyn, and tucked the letter back into its envelope. She opened the second letter. It informed her in longwinded legal language that she was sole beneficiary of her uncle Walter's will, and that he had left an estate estimated at A$300,000 after tax. Robyn whooped and ran to consult the rates of exchange in the *Guardian*. Then she telephoned her mother. "You were right, Mummy, Uncle Walter has left me something in his will."

"How much, dear?"

"Well," said Robyn, "when I've paid the rates, I reckon I should have about one hundred and sixty-five thousand, eight hundred and fifty pounds left, give or take a few."

Mrs. Penrose screamed, and seemed to drop the phone. Robyn could hear her shouting the news to her father, who was apparently in the bathroom. Then she came back on the line. "Daddy says congratulations! I'm so pleased for you, dear. What a sum!"

"I'll share it with you, of course."

"Nonsense, Robyn, it's your money. Uncle Walter left it to you."

"But it's so eccentric. He hardly knew me. It should have gone to Daddy if he's next of kin. Or equally to me and Basil."

"Basil has more money than is good for him already. And your father and I are quite comfortable, though it's very generous of you to offer, dear. Now you won't have to go to America."

"Why not?" said Robyn, her elation subsiding a little.

"Well, you won't need to. You could live off the interest on a hundred and sixty-five thousand."

"Yes, I suppose you're right," said Robyn. "But I don't really want to give up work."

. . .

The rain cleared in the night. It is a calm, sunny morning, without a cloud in the sky—one of those rare days when the atmosphere of Rummidge seems to have been rinsed clean of all its pollution, and the objects of vision stand out with pristine clarity. Robyn, wearing a cotton button-through dress and sandals, steps out of her house into the warm, limpid air and pauses a moment, looking up and down the street, filling her lungs as joyfully as if it were a beach.

Her dusty, dented Renault creaks on its springs as she throws her Gladstone bag onto the passenger seat and gets behind the wheel. The engine wheezes asthmatically for several seconds before it coughs into life. It crosses her mind, with a little acquisitive thrill, that very soon she will be able to swap the Renault for a brand-new car, something swish and powerful. She could put Basil's nose out of joint by buying a Porsche. No, not a Porsche, she thinks, remembering Vic's homily about foreign cars. A Lotus, perhaps, except that you can hardly get into them in a skirt. Then she thinks, how absurd, the Renault is perfectly adequate for my purposes, all it needs is a new battery.

Robyn drives slowly and carefully to the University. She is so conscious of carrying a precious freight of good fortune that she has an almost superstitious fear that some maniac driver will come tearing out of a side turning and smash it all to smithereens. But she reaches the campus without incident. Passing the Wilcoxes' house in Avondale Road, glimpsing a hand, perhaps Marjorie's, shaking a duster from an upstairs window, she wonders idly why Vic was called away so suddenly from the University the day before, and why he did not return. She parks her car under a lime tree—the space is vacant because other drivers avoid the sticky gum that drops from its branches, but Robyn rather likes the patina it imparts to the Renault's faded paint-work— and carries her Gladstone bag to the Arts Faculty building. The sun shines warmly on the red brick and glints on the shiny new ivy leaves. A faint breath of steam rises from the drying lawns. Robyn walks with a blithe, springy gait, swinging her Gladstone bag (lighter than it was in January, for the examinations are about to begin, and her teaching load is tailing off), smiling and greeting the colleagues and students that she recognises in the lobby, on the stairs, on the landing of the English Department.

Bob Busby, pinning a notice to the AUT board, beckons to her. "There's an extraordinary General Meeting next Monday to discuss the implications of the UGC's letter," he says. "It doesn't look good."

He lowers his voice to a confidential murmur: "I hear you may be leaving us sooner than expected. I can't say I blame you."

"Who told you that?" says Robyn.

"It's just a rumour."

"Well, I'd be glad if you wouldn't spread it any further," says Robyn. She walks on, down the corridor, momentarily annoyed by Bob Busby's inquisitiveness and Pamela's indiscretion—for the secretary must have been the source of the rumour. Robyn makes a mental note, heavily underlined, not to tell anyone in the Department about her legacy.

As usual, there is somebody waiting to see her, standing by her door. When she gets closer she sees that it is Vic Wilcox: she didn't recognise him immediately because he is not wearing his usual dark business suit, but a short-sleeved knitted shirt and neatly pressed lightweight trousers. He is carrying two books in his hand.

"I wasn't expecting you," she says, unlocking the door of her office. "Are you making up for what you missed yesterday?"

"No," he says, following her into the room, and closing the door. "I've come to tell you that I won't be coming any more."

"Oh," she says. "Well, it doesn't matter. Teaching is nearly over now. You wouldn't find it much fun watching me mark exam scripts. Is there some crisis at Pringle's, then?"

"I'm finished with Pringle's," he says. "Pringle's has been sold to the group that owns Foundrax. That's what the phone call was about yesterday. I'm unemployed, as from today." He raises his hands and gestures at his casual clothes as if they are a sign of his fallen state.

When he has related all the details to her, she says, "But can they do that to you? Chuck you out, just like that, without notice?"

"Afraid so."

"But it's monstrous!"

"Once they've made up their minds, they don't mess around. They know I could screw up the entire company if I stayed another week, in revenge. Not that I would be bothered."

"I'm very sorry, Vic. You must feel devastated."

He shrugs. "Win some, lose some. In a funny sort of way it's had a good side. Misfortune draws a family together."

"Marjorie's not too upset?"

"Marjorie's been terrific," says Vic. "As a matter of fact"—he rakes back his forelock and looks nervously away from her—"we've had a sort of reconciliation. I thought I ought to tell you."

"I'm glad," says Robyn gently. "I'm really glad to hear that."

"I just wanted to get things straight," he says, glancing at her apprehensively. "I'm afraid I've been a bit foolish."

"Don't worry about it."

"I've been living in a dream. This business has woken me up. I must have been out of my mind, imagining you would see anything in a middle-aged dwarf engineer."

Robyn laughs.

"You're a very special person, Robyn," he says solemnly. "One day you'll meet a man who deserves to marry you."

"I don't need a man to complete me," she says, smiling.

"That's because you haven't met him yet."

"As a matter of fact, I had an offer this very morning," she says lightly.

His eyes widen. "Who from?"

"Charles."

"Are you going to accept?"

"No," she says. "And what are you going to do now? Look for another job, I suppose."

"No, I've had enough of the rat-race."

"You mean you're going to retire?"

"I can't afford to retire. Anyway, I'd be lost without work."

"You could do an English degree as a mature student." She smiles, not entirely serious, not entirely joking.

"I'm thinking of setting up on my own. You remember that idea I mentioned to you for a spectrometer? I talked to Tom Rigby last night, and he's game."

"That's a marvellous idea! It's just the right opportunity."

"It's a question of raising the necessary capital."

"I've got a lot of capital," says Robyn. "I'll invest it in your spectrometer. I'll be a—what do they call it? A sleeping partner."

He laughs. "I'm talking six figures here."

"So am I," says Robyn, and tells him about her legacy. "Take it," she says. "Use it. I don't want it. I don't want to retire, either. I'd rather go and work in America."

"I can't take all of it," he says. "It wouldn't be right."

"Take a hundred thousand," she says. "Is that enough?"

"It's more than enough."

"That's settled, then."

"You might lose it all, you know."

"I trust you, Vic. I've seen you in action. I've shadowed you." She smiles.

"On the other hand, you might end up a millionaire. How will you feel about that?"

"I'll risk it," she says.

He looks at her, holding his breath, then exhales. "What can I say?"

"'Thank you' will be fine."

"Thank you, then. I'll talk to Tom Rigby, and have my lawyer draw up a document."

"Right," says Robyn. "Aren't we supposed to shake hands at this point?"

"You should sleep on it," he says.

"I don't want to sleep on it," she says, seizing his hand and shaking it. There is a knock on the door and Marion Russell appears at the threshold, wearing an oversized tee-shirt with ONLY CONNECT printed on it in big letters. "Oh, sorry," she says, "I'll come back later."

"It's all right, I'm going," says Vic. He thrusts the books abruptly at Robyn. "I brought these back. Thanks for the loan."

"Oh, right, are you sure you've finished with them?"

"I haven't finished *Daniel Deronda*, but I don't think I ever will," he says. "I wouldn't mind keeping the Tennyson, if it's a spare copy. As a souvenir."

"Of course," says Robyn. She sits at her desk, writes in the flyleaf in her bold, flowing hand, "*To Vic, with love, from your shadow*," and gives it back to him.

He glances at the inscription. "'With love,'" he says. "*Now* you tell me."

He smiles wryly, shuts the book, nods goodbye, and goes out of the room, past the hovering Marion.

Marion pulls a chair up close to Robyn's desk, and sits on the edge of it, leaning forwards and peering anxiously at her. "It's not true, is it, that you're going to America?" she says.

Robyn throws down her pen. "Good God! Is there no privacy in this place? Where did you hear that?"

Marion is apologetic, but determined. "In the corridor. Some students were coming out of a tutorial with Mr. Sutcliffe . . . I heard them talking. Only I wanted to do your Women's Writing course next year."

"I can't discuss my plans with you, Marion. It's a private matter. I don't know myself what I'll be doing next year. You'll just have to wait and see."

"Sorry, it was a bit rude, I suppose, only . . . I hope you don't go, Robyn. You're the best teacher in the Department, everybody says so. And there'll be nobody left to teach Women's Studies."

"Is there anything else, Marion?"

The girl sighs and shakes her head. She prepares to leave.

"By the way," says Robyn. "Does your Kissogram firm deliver to London?"

"No, not usually. But they have the same sort of thing there."

"I want to send a Gorillagram to somebody in London," says Robyn.

"I could get you the name of an agency," says Marion.

"Could you? Thanks very much. I want the message delivered to a bank in the City, in the middle of the morning. How would a man in a gorilla suit get past the reception desk?"

"Oh, we always change in the loos," says Marion.

"Good," says Robyn. "As soon as you can, then, Marion."

When Marion has gone, Robyn gets out a pad of A4 and begins composing a little poem, smiling to herself as she does so. Soon there is another knock on her door, and Philip Swallow sidles into the room.

"Ah, good morning, Robyn. Can you spare a moment?" He sits down on the chair vacated by Marion Russell. "I've sent off that reference to America."

"That was quick! Thank you very much."

"It implies no eagerness to get rid of you, I assure you, Robyn. In fact, I don't know how we shall manage without you next year. A lot of students have signed up for your courses."

"You did say, back in January," says Robyn, "that if a job came up, I should apply for it."

"Yes, yes, you're quite right."

"I don't particularly want to emigrate. But I do want a job."

"Ah, well, that's what I wanted to talk to you about. You see, I've found out what 'virement' means."

"Virement?"

"Yes, you remember . . . I found it in the revised Collins. Apparently it means the freedom to use funds that have been designated for a particular purpose, in a budget, for something else. We haven't had virement in the Faculty before, but we're going to get it next year."

"What does that mean?"

"Well, it means that if we decide to curtail certain operations in the Faculty, we could redirect the resources. Since the English Department is bulging with students, and some of the smaller Departments in the Faculty are on the brink of disappearing altogether, there's a chance that we may be able to replace Rupert after all, in spite of the new round of cuts."

"I see," says Robyn.

"It's only a chance, mind you," says Philip Swallow. "I can't guarantee anything. But I was wondering whether, in the circumstances, you would consider staying on next year, and see what happens."

Robyn thinks. Philip Swallow watches her thinking. To avoid his anxious scrutiny, Robyn turns in her chair and looks out of the window, at the green quadrangle in the middle of the campus. Students, drawn out of doors by the sunshine, are already beginning to congregate in pairs and small groups, spreading their coats and plastic bags so that they can sit or lie on the damp grass. On one of the lawns a gardener, a young black in olive dungarees, is pushing a motor mower up and down, steering carefully around the margins of the flower beds, and between the reclining students. When they see that they will be in his way, the students get up and move themselves and their belongings, settling like a flock of birds on another patch of grass. The gardener is of about the same age as the students, but no communication takes place between them—no nods, or smiles, or spoken words, not even a glance. There is no overt arrogance on the students' part, or evident resentment on the young gardener's, just a kind of mutual, instinctive avoidance of contact. Physically contiguous, they inhabit separate worlds. It seems a very British way of handling differences of class and race. Remembering her Utopian vision of the campus invaded by the Pringle's workforce, Robyn smiles ruefully to herself. There is a long way to go.

"All right," she says, turning back to Philip Swallow. "I'll stay on."